Note To Our Amazing Readers

The authors in *Alpha Fever* wish to thank you for taking the time to read our *Alpha Fever* boxed set. We hope you will love every book we have brought in this boxed set just for you. Due to the length of this set, if you are looking for a print copy you will find Alpha Fever Volume One and Volume Two rather than a single book. This is the only way we could bring these tales to you in a print copy.

If you're of a mind, please consider leaving us a review on the distributor site you purchased this boxed set from. Reviews are our way of life, our bread and butter, and our driving force. Hearing your thoughts, knowing what you liked, and even what you may not have liked as much, encourages us to keep writing every single day. Knowing you're out there waiting for the next dreamy, steamy read means the world to us. Your reviews are the best advertising and motivation we could ever have, and we appreciate each and every moment, every reflection and feeling you put into your reviews. They don't have to be big, oh no, not at all; even one-liners will do. Every word from our readers is cherished and remains in the minds of our authors as they craft the next great book. So thank you, if you chose to review.

We adore you!

Sale of this book without a front cover may be unauthorized. If this book is coverless, it may have been reported to the publisher as "unsold or destroyed" and neither the author nor the publisher may have received payment for it.

Alpha Fever: A Boxed Set of Contemporary and Paranormal Romance is a work of fiction. Names, characters and incidents depicted in this book are products of the author's imagination or are used fictitiously. Any resemblance to actual events, locales, organizations, or persons, living or dead, is entirely coincidental.

This book is for ADULT audiences only, and may contain graphic language and/or sexually explicit situations offensive to some readers. If you are disturbed by multiple sexual interactions between characters of any gender, or vivid and clear descriptions of a multitude of consensual sexual acts, we ask that you refrain from reading this book.

2016 First Print Edition
2016 First eBook Edition
Copyright © 2016
All rights reserved.

Published in Canada by Naughty Nights Press LLC
www.naughtynightspress.com

Cover Design by ©Wilson Rowe
Credit to the individual editors of each author.

ISBN: 978-1-926514-37-6
eBook ISBN: 978-1-926514-30-7

Printed in the United States of America

The right of the individual authors to be identified as the authors of each separate written work this book has been asserted in accordance with sections 77 and 78 of the Copyright, Designs and Patents Act 1988.

Naughty Nights Press LLC First Print Edition: March 2016

Table Of Contents

Note To Our Amazing Readers

Fake It Till You Mate It by Jacqueline Sweet

Hold Me by A.C. Nixon

Hade's Playground (The Immortal Playground Series #1) by Isis Pierce

Shimmers in the Dark by Bethany Shaw

Club Stratosphere: Lexa and Tom by Danielle Gavan

Until We Meet Again by Paige Matthews

Always You by Tierney O'Malley

Watch the Skies by Tanith Davenport

Hidden Desires by Crystal Dawn

Dream Job by Abby Hayes

Sinister Outlaw: Outlaw Pleasure by Dawn White

About the Publisher

Fake It Till You Mate It by Jacqueline Sweet

Bear shifter Danny Morrissey is the total package. He's drop dead gorgeous, funny, wealthy and a god in the sack. He lives his life flitting from one pair of spread thighs to the next, leaving a trail of rumpled sheets and smiling faces in his wake. But a mysterious text message from his family is about to put an end to everything.

Sarah Honeywell is Danny's best friend and his only confidant. She has curves in all the right places and a bruised ego from a sudden breakup. So when Danny tells her he needs help with some bear business, she jumps at the chance to focus on someone else's problems.

There's a big pack meeting. Everyone will be there. And if Danny doesn't produce the mate he's been telling everyone he has, he'll be forced into an arranged marriage and shipped off to the country. Only Sarah can save him now, but what if pretending to be his mate feels too good? What if those glances he steals of her bare thighs are more than just an act?

FAKE IT TIL YOU MATE IT is a paranormal romance novella set in the sleepy and mysterious town of Bearfield. It's a standalone story with no cliffhangers.

Hold Me by A.C. Nixon

Fascination. Pleasure. Submission.

Depravity is my business, and trust me—it's lucrative. The penthouse on Lake Michigan, the women, the cars, the access, all of it—the embodiment of very boy's fantasy. Not bad for a kid voted most likely to wind up on death row.

Life is sweet and simple, or it was until a certain voluptuous waitress took residence in my fantasies. I'm a man used to getting what I want—and delectable Ryann is about to find herself on the menu.

If you enjoy dirty talking millionaires and a woman ready to take a walk on the wicked side, you'll love A.C. Nixon's chronicle of love, lust, and adventure.

Welcome to Club Surrender—embrace the pain.

Hade's Playground (The Immortal Playground Series #1) by Isis Pierce

Eva Zayas has finally come of age. As a witch, she's always had the gift of intuition, but nothing has prepared her for the full extent of her power. The dark man watching her from the shadows knows the truth, though. Hades has waited for her for decades–his chosen Queen, the woman fated to become his everything. He'll do anything to have her at his side and in his bed for all eternity, even if unlocking her true identity means risking both of their lives.

Shimmers in the Dark by Bethany Shaw

Eight years ago the world ended. The Wolf Flu stole everything Enid held dear. Pursued by witches and humans, Enid and her pack have taken to the underground tunnels inside Mount Rainier. She seeks out solitude inside her glacial home until a face from her past resurfaces.

After all she's lost can she love again?

Alex has kept his pack a secret from the humans and witches for eight years, but as the world rebuilds, their home is no longer safe. He joins the packs at Mount Rainier and is shocked to find his true mate, Enid, is alive and taking refuge there as well. She's changed over the years, broken and hurt from the devastating losses of the Wolf Flu. Can he mend her heart and keep everyone he holds dear safe from the attacking witches and humans? Or will the pack also succumb to this new, terrifying post apocalyptic world?

Club Stratosphere: Lexa and Tom by Danielle Gavan

Ever since Alexandra Porter told her husband, Barry, about the dark side of her sexual preferences—bondage, humiliation, pain—her house has been like the Cold War. A shared existence, not a life together.

Lexa needs a certain kind of man. A true Dominant to exert the control she craves, and administer the pain she needs. Until she finds Him, she scratches her itch by anonymously submitting to a gifted and sadistic Dom at Club Stratosphere. But with every searing slap of leather on flesh, she finds herself fantasizing about Thomas, her hunky neighbor, who's also her superior at work.

Thomas Daniels has been lusting after petite brunette Lexa since the day he met her. From countless backyard barbecues listening to her whiny husband's complaints, he understood Lexa's submissive nature...as only a true Dom can. Once he's certain the marriage is a sham, he makes his move, messaging her with a curt order to meet him in the back yard.

When they finally get together Tom realizes a truth which leaves him stunned, yet elated. But how will Lexa feel when all her worlds become entangled?

Until We Meet Again by Paige Matthews

The rules are simple: No names, no Identities, only one night...

It was supposed to be one night. One night to have her darkest desires sated. Overheard by a stranger one night, Anne Hart is given the chance of a lifetime: an Invitation to the most exclusive sex club in the city.

Secret and hidden is how Mason Montgomery runs his club. They come to him, not the other way around. Until he overhears Anne one night. On a whim he offers her the chance to have what she craves. She thinks it's random...but it's not...Nothing is what it seems until they meet again.

Always You by Tierney O'Malley

When always means forever...

He's been the one.

Rienne Cailler's only wish is to have a normal life and end her years of hiding from the reporters and Federal agents. But her world turns even more upside down when she lives with James, the man whom she has learned to love at a young age, who takes her virginity and shows her exquisite passion the two of them can share—in and out of bed.

She's always been his to keep.

James Huntington already knows Rienne is not his to claim, but something draws him to her like a moth to a flame. She crawls under his skin until James surrenders to the temptation that her nearness arouses in him, and the sweetness of his love for her.

And then Fate intervenes.

When Rienne's father, Roy, learns about her relationship with James, he tries to separate them. Afraid of what her father will do to James, she agrees to leave him, their dream together, and the cabin they share without getting the chance to tell him about her secret.

When two hearts refuse to bend.

James expects everything from meeting a special someone he hasn't seen in a long time, but nothing prepares him to hear from Rienne what he's been missing the whole time.

Will time, distance, and the unveiling of a secret keep James and Rienne, eternally apart or will they uphold their promises to each other... "Always you?"

Watch the Skies by Tanith Davenport

Alien hunter Aster is frustrated in more ways than one. Her team haven't had a proper encounter in months, and her cute teammate Wade is never going to see her that way - and no other man would let a woman like Aster take charge in a relationship anyway.

Until one night, out in the woods, when the team are engulfed in a white light - and overwhelmed with desire like they've never known. Suddenly Aster sees a new side to Wade, one that will let her give her alpha tendencies free rein...

But as the creatures they met return again and again, Aster begins to wonder what they really want - to see her and Wade together, or something more sinister?

Hidden Desires by Crystal Dawn

Six women and six men, the recipe for romance right? Not when the six women are white wolves and the six men are werewolves. Clinging to their humanity, they reject their would be mates refusing to have anything to do with them. Could it be that easy? Not when you are dealing with six alpha wolves. They band together plotting and planning their soon to be mates' downfalls one couple at a time. Two couples are mated and now it's Sharon and Ven's turn. Teaser: "Aren't you a sexy little morsel?" He asked as he moved all the way to the bed where he seemed to be considering what to do with her. Sharon decided the question didn't call for a reply and she just stared back letting her eyes roam over his hard well-muscled body. Especially the buttons he was undoing as he removed his shirt. His chest was hard, muscled, and tanned. The guy was mouthwatering and panty melting delicious. "Let's get things straight before we get started. I like to take charge." He explained in a low gruff voice. Even his voice reminded her of Ven but it was deeper. "I don't expect you to call me Sir, unless you want to. Just do what I say and we'll be fine. Any questions?"

Sharon felt excitement, anticipation, and a shiver of fear all run through her and she liked it. "What if I'm a bad girl?" Her voice trembled as she asked.

Dream Job by Abby Hayes

Kim was tired of still working non-field-related jobs three years after getting her B.A. in Film and Digital Media. After a bad break up, she talks herself into doing something about it and applies for a job in the adult film industry.

Thinking she's made a big mistake–looking at the cheesy posters on the walls while waiting for her interview–she comes close to leaving, taking another cashier job. However, when she catches a glimpse of her boss-to-be and his disheveled dusty blond hair, chocolate-brown eyes, and tight white t-shirt showing ripped abs above taut-fitting, torn-at-the-thigh jeans, she is more than intrigued.

Now, between her sexy-as-hell boss man, David, and filming a ménage shoot, Kim is having feelings and thoughts she never thought she would. She begins to realize this just might be her dream job after all.

Sinister Outlaw: Outlaw Pleasure by Dawn White

Before there was Becca and Gavin there was just Gavin and his brothers in arms. Gavin is the youngest Outlaw Biker Chapter president the Sinister Son's Syndicate have ever had. They are violent and don't play well with others. Gavin looks to make a name for himself, but will the parade of women, and the non stop violence stop his reign as chapter president?

Box Set Compiled and Organized by Gina Kincade

Alpha Fever

A Boxed Set of Contemporary and Paranormal Romance Volume Two

Naughty Nights Press • Canada

Fake It Till You Mate It
by Jacqueline Sweet

<u>Chapter One</u>

They were at after-work drinks at their favorite North Beach dive when Danny told Sarah his big news.

"Single again," he said with a wry grin as he slid a shot of bourbon over to his best friend.

Sarah whistled appreciatively and lifted the glass in two fingers. "That did not take very long, m'man. What was it this time? Weird toes? Snoring? Talked about having kids on the third date?"

Danny smiled and shrugged. "She wouldn't let me go down on her."

Sarah nodded sagely, clearly unsurprised that another girlfriend had fallen by the wayside. She held her glass high in a toast. "To the dear departed!" she yelled over the din of the bar and then tipped the amber liquid down her throat.

Danny followed suit and not for the first time marveled at how weird it was for him to be friends—*friends*—with a beautiful mortal woman. He wasn't the kind of guy who was friends with women. He had male friends. They did things together, like played rugby in Golden Gate park on muddy Saturdays. They hit the clubs and bars together, always on the prowl for something hot and tight dressed in something sleek and short. When he was with his mates, he could almost pretend he was with his pack. It wasn't the same, really. The bond wasn't there. But it was good enough to tide him over until he could see his pack in the flesh. He was a bear shifter. He didn't need anyone else. Most days he was a pack of one.

"I can't do shots tonight though," Sarah brushed a stray strand of her auburn hair back behind her ear. "I'm meeting Winston in like an hour. This is *just* work drinks. Okay? Not *let's see how drunk the mortal woman can get* drinks. Tell me you understand." She patted Danny's arm to emphasize the point and the coolness of her skin set off sparks within him. His bear took note and wondered why they'd never slept with her. It growled and stretched within him, already impatient for the next lay.

If you'd asked Danny, he wouldn't have known why he'd never slept with Sarah. They'd been in each other's orbits for years. First friends of friends, seeing each other at the same parties or at big dinners at Disco Pete's house. And then they both ended up working together at the same architecture firm. Danny was the junior partner and Sarah the marketing manager. She was head-turningly beautiful, even if some of her past boyfriends could never get past her curves. She was funnier than all his bro-friends put together. And she was—Danny admitted to no one but himself—much smarter than him.

But the timing had always been wrong. He was in a relationship when they met, with Jenny-Who-Hated-Movies and she was with Brian-The-First. By the time she and Brian split, he was with Natalie-Who-His-Bear-Thought-Smelled-Like-Old-Sandwiches. Every time Sarah got dumped, Danny was with someone. He was a shoulder to cry on. He bought the next round of drinks. He helped her move out of the apartments that she shared with increasingly douchey guys. But he never made a move.

Danny had rules. Rules are what separate man from beast, and gentleman from douchenozzle.

Rule number one: No cheating. Never. You stay true to the woman you're dating and you never seduce a woman away from her mate. His bear wouldn't even consider it. People who are together smell different. They have a mingled, muddled scent. A joined scent. Even when a hard-bodied hottie threw herself at him at the club, if she had the scent of a relationship on her, he had to leave. Danny would buy her a drink, give her The Look and tell her that she had someone special back home waiting for her. A boyfriend. A girlfriend. Sometimes both. It was San Francisco, everyone had more going on than you could see at first glance.

Rule number two: Relationships are like campsites. You need to leave them in a better state than you found them. He was always thoughtful and kind and mostly honest. But his bear could tell when it wouldn't work out. When that point came, it didn't do anyone any good to prolong things. He didn't always succeed in extricating himself without hard feelings, but he made damn sure he tried.

And most importantly, rule number three: Never, ever tell anyone about the bear thing. It was the lone exception to his honesty rule.

Sarah Honeywell was the one friend he had—the one mortal friend—who knew that he sometimes turned into a giant honey-brown bear. She found out by accident. Their friend group had rented a house in Tahoe for a long weekend. Get away from the city, they said. Get some fresh air. Go skiing. Drink hot cocoa and cognac by a roaring fire. Hike the mountains. Danny had known it was a risky idea. That close to real nature, his bear would demand to be let off the leash. Stuck in the city, the bear settled for a monthly full moon hike far from civilization. But in the country, surrounded by nature, it needed to explore. While twelve of their friends were crammed drunkenly into a hot tub meant for six, Danny had gone for a moonlit hike to "clear his head" and Sarah had sneaked off to make out with her then boyfriend, Brian-The-Second.

With the mountains cradling him and the moon singing her glorious song in his blood, Danny had forgotten to be careful. He went full bear. Cut loose. He'd romped and rolled and fished out of a stream. His great bear breath had burst from his lungs in clouds of steam. He'd felt alive and free. Maybe he was acting out a little. He'd just broken up with Cynthia-Who-Was-Perfect-But-Had-To-Move-To-Hong Kong-For-Business-Reasons and that one stung. Bearing out was a break from the heartache.

Sarah and Brian-The-Second had a spot picked out. A clearing ringed by evergreen trees. They had a picnic blanket and a bottle of Malbec and some chocolate-dipped raspberries, Sarah's favorite. What they didn't have were condoms, which Brian-The-Second discovered to his dismay he'd left back in the cabin. And all of the "I'll be really careful" and "I swear I'm clean" speeches wouldn't sway Sarah one inch. She was too smart for that. She'd dated too many hot guys with bad manners.

So there she was, wrapped in a blanket but otherwise naked in the moonlight, half drunk on wine, waiting for her newest hot, jerk boyfriend to return with protection, when Danny crashed into the clearing.

If you asked him, he wouldn't have been able to say exactly why he'd burst in. He was intoxicated by the moon maybe. The freedom of the mountains made him joyful and careless maybe. Or maybe, he'd admit that he smelled something wonderful and absent-mindedly chased after it, expecting to find some winter berries growing in the shade of a tree. But that something he smelled was Sarah and she was not prepared for the biggest damn bear she'd ever seen to leap into her sexy night time rendezvous.

She screamed and scrambled away from him, dropping her blanket and revealing the sweet roundness of her nakedness to Danny.

And then Danny, in a panic, *shifted*. He should have turned and ran. But his first instinct was to reassure her, to comfort her. Where there once had been a bear as large as a compact car, there was only Danny Morrissey, his big cock swinging in the wind. The spiced scent of the shift clinging to him like cinnamon cologne.

Before he could say or do anything, Brian-The-Second returned with condoms and a second bottle of wine, peeking into the clearing hesitantly, his handsome face a mask of worry.

"What was that sound?" he'd asked.

Sarah stared at Danny. His eyes. Not his cock. "Danny surprised me is all." She picked up her blanket and wrapped herself in it, more for warmth than decency.

Brian-The-Second blinked at Danny, definitely focusing on his cock and the sea of muscles surrounding it. At six foot four, Danny was the biggest of their friend group by half a foot and he had a good fifty pounds of muscle over Brian-The-Second. Even without heightened bear senses, Danny could sense the fear and capitulation in Brian-The-Second. The man was a natural-born beta.

"What the fuck, Daniel?" Brian-The-Second whined. He held up the wine and the condoms, as if crashing their outdoor sex party had been Danny's plan all along.

Danny winked at them. "Just out for a moonlit jog. It's quite bracing, isn't it?"

"But you're naked," Brian-The-Second said.

Sarah was pointedly not talking. But her eyes weren't scared. They weren't mad. She looked at Danny as if suddenly she understood him, as if he'd come into focus for the first time.

Brian-The-Second's scent changed, and before the douche could open his mouth and suggest a threesome, Danny nodded at Sarah. "My apologies for interrupting. Please, carry on."

"I won't *bear* a grudge," Sarah said with a twinkle in her eye. "You *barely* saw anything, right?"

"What if—," Brian-The-Second started to say, but Danny cut him off with a grin and a "goodnight" and ran out into the night. He didn't do threesomes. He didn't share. When he took a mate, he took her.

Danny beared out as soon as he thought he was clear of the couple. He ran up and down the mountains, hunting deer, fighting a cocky mountain lion, but mostly trying to get the sight of Sarah out of his head, and the lingering scent of her sex out of his mind.

When they got back to the city, Sarah texted him. "We've *bearly* spoken," she wrote.

"Coffee?" Danny typed.

"*Fur* sure."

They met at Mission Pie, the best pie shop in San Francisco. Danny ordered an entire strawberry rhubarb pie with a glazed honey crust. Sarah had coffee and a slice of chocolate silk.

"So," she said, her fork slipping through the buttery crust, "You're a bear."

A bearded man with arms of banded muscle overheard her and gave Danny the once over. "He's not hairy enough. Also, sister, that boy is *straight*."

Danny smiled at the man. "San Francisco is always a delight. So much more fun than the woods where I grew up."

"Are you a bear pretending to be a man or a man who is sometimes a bear?" Sarah asked, her voice conspiratorially low.

Danny tried not to think of that night, of the fullness of her hips, the strong lines of her thighs in the moonlight. He completely failed. Instead, he gave in and answered all of her questions, as truthfully as he could without breaking any rules or outing any of his friends.

He went into the conversation with concerns.

Would Sarah think he was a monster? Some shifters were. There was no denying that.

Would Sarah never want to speak to him again? The thought was like a sliver of ice in his chest though he didn't understand why. They were friends, but not particularly close.

Would she blackmail him? Expose him? Tell the rest of their friends? If she did, he'd have to run. Find a new city, a new name. Maybe even a new pack.

"Does it hurt?" she asked.

"Does food taste better as a bear?"

"Can you change into any animal, or just bears?"

"Is it weird wearing underwear after running around as a bear?"

"Are there more like you around?" And on and on.

They went into the conversation as acquaintances and came out as something more than friends. They ate pie and coffee and walked down Valencia Street. They stopped by her favorite bookstore, Borderlands Books. They went to a hole-in-the-wall Salvadoran joint and ate fresh pupusas. But mostly they talked.

Over the course of one afternoon, Sarah became his confidant and somehow his best friend. He hadn't realized how much he'd needed someone to talk to, someone who knew what he was. Being near her was like being home. If she hadn't been dating Brian-The-Second, Danny would have kissed her, and ruined everything. Silently, he was glad she was seeing someone. It gave him the freedom to be honest without worrying about what would come next. He could never tell the women he dated that he was a bear, because when the inevitable break-up came, what would they do with that knowledge?

Danny and Sarah first saw each other naked, and then became best friends. It worked for them.

In the bar, in North Beach, as Sarah told Danny about a particularly insane client she'd dealt with, Danny's phone rang out with a clanging alarm.

"What the hell is that?" Sarah asked. "That is the single most annoying ringtone I've ever heard."

Danny slid the smartphone from his jacket pocket and frowned at what he saw there. "Bear meeting," he said.

"Bear meeting?"

"It's a pack thing."

"Sounds fun?" Sarah offered hopefully.

"Imagine a family reunion crossed with—I don't know—a session of Congress. No, that's not bloody enough." He drummed his fingers on the table as he felt his world spinning away beneath him.

"Isn't that what all family reunions are like?" Sarah said. "At the last Honeywell reunion, one of my uncles literally punched out a car window to prove he was the strongest."

Danny looked down at the text and then lifted the phone, showing it to Sarah.

"Oh, it's from your mom," she said. "Bear Mute."

"Moot," Danny corrected.

"Bear Moot," Sarah read. "Bring your mate." She frowned at the phone, her forehead crinkling. "Mate? Since when do you have a mate?"

Danny signaled to the bartender to bring more drinks. All the drinks. "I am so screwed."

Chapter Two

Danny Morrissey was the total package, god damn him.

There were days when Sarah didn't know why she was friends with him. Not that he wasn't fun to be around because he was. Or because he wasn't thoughtful because of course he was. He was also handsome and brave and good at making things with his hands and he had bright eyes that were a thousand different shades of green at once so that when you stared into them you felt like you were at the edge of a great cliff and teetering at the edge.

No, it was that next to Danny, all the men in Sarah's life seemed so small in comparison.

Take Winston for example. They've been together for a few months and they both realize that they are getting to the *serious* point of deciding to stick with it and move in together and have the first of several important *talks* or that they needed to call it and break up and go their separate ways. He knew this. She could sense it in the way he elided certain topics or sweat when the names of their cohabitating friends came up.

If Danny were there, he'd tackle The Talk head on with grace and kindness. Somehow the man walked the razor's edge between being a gentleman and a giant whore with exquisite aplomb. He was friends with nearly all of his exes. Who does that? What kind of man sweeps a woman off her feet, spins her around, and puts her back down and then she thanks him for it?

Goddamn Danny Morrissey.

Winston had selected an oddball East German restaurant in the Mission for their date. Dour paintings of Karl Marx loomed over Sarah as she sipped her lager and waited for the surly waitress to return with her spaetzle. It was Sarah's least favorite of their usual haunts, which Winston knew, but ignored.

Danny wouldn't have picked this place, Sarah found herself thinking, as Winston launched into a long story about his day at work.

The real problem with Danny, Sarah knew, was that after she saw him she couldn't stop comparing other men to him. It wasn't healthy at all. It was the eating-an-entire-bag-of-Oreos of unhealthy relationship drama. But just like with the cookies, she couldn't help herself.

It wasn't that she was in love with Danny. She couldn't be. The entire idea was absurd. It would be like being in love with the moon, one-sided and cold and remote and doomed. He was a rich, handsome, supernatural creature. He was born on the finish line of the race of self-improvement. And he wasn't an ass about it, like every other handsome rich bro she'd met in the city. There were thousands of wealthy tech douchebags walking around San Francisco, desperate for a girlfriend. She should know, she dated like half of them.

Sarah made sure to make the appropriate noises while Winston spoke. She wasn't listening. She was barely pretending to listen, but Winston didn't care. At the end of every workday he had a monologue ready to deliver about shoddy coding or blind management or lazy outsourcers.

If she hadn't met Danny, would she have been happy with Winston? It was *the question* that once her mind had asked, plagued her. It was of course unanswerable but also had to be asked. Winston cared for her. He had nice teeth and clear skin. He was as tall as her in flats. He never pressured her to go to the gym or yoga, to lose the extra weight she knew she carried. He took her as she was, so why couldn't she do the same?

Winston's speech was interrupted when the frowning waitress—a thin blond in her forties who looked like she smoked instead of ate—brought their food. Winston's face lit up with delight at the sight of the giant sausage and mound of sauerkraut before him and for a moment Sarah knew that she could love him. There was a joy in Winston. An eagerness to please. He was a good guy at heart—that counted for a lot. With work and patience, she could make him into the man she needed.

But then again, Danny Morrissey.

Goddamn Danny Morrissey.

There was only one way a life with Winston could work, though she'd never told Winston or Danny. The only way it could work was if she never saw Danny again, socially. They could work together, sure. The man was very professional at work. Focused and on-task. But after work drinks? Dinner parties? Friend weekends at Tahoe or Napa with wine and hot tubs? No. Never. If she married Winston, moved in with him, had kids with him—then every time she saw Danny she'd compare the two of them. She wouldn't be able to help it and Winston would lose in the comparison. It wouldn't be fair to Winston. He was a good guy. He didn't deserve that. He couldn't be anyone's number two, their runner-up.

"...and that's why I think we should probably break up." Winston's words cut through her reverie like teeth through pasta.

"What?" Sarah said, her voice quiet as if waking from a dream.

"It's nothing personal. I think we both know this isn't quite working. And I'd hate to waste more of your time." Winston's voice was calm, but his big brown eyes held a deep panic.

If you asked her, she couldn't have said how she knew, but in Sarah's bones she sensed that this was a test—a loyalty test. He wanted to see if she cared enough about him—about them—to fight. Was she all the way in?

The thing about dating nerdy guys is that they don't start dating until their twenties, so all of the petty dramas and psychological bullshit that women get past in high school is still waiting for them. They need to go through the guilt and the fights and the bullshit things people do to each other so that they can learn and evolve and develop all of the thousand mental mechanisms other people have to deal with life.

Sarah opened her mental bag of resources and was surprised to find she had no fucks to give. Winston was a good guy, or at least, he would be one day. But Sarah didn't have to be the one to socialize him and teach him how to be a boyfriend.

"Yeah," she said. "Okay." And then Sarah pushed aside her spaetzle, untouched, grabbed her coat and left.

Past experience had taught her to expect a surprise cry to well forth. She'd get a pang of loneliness. Her mother's face would appear ghostly and incandescent and tell her that she'd never find a man and die poor and alone in a studio apartment one day. And maybe that would still happen, but for the moment Sarah felt buoyant. Like gravity had been turned down in her general vicinity. Untethered from the Earth, she could float away at any moment.

She immediately texted Danny.

"Winston dumped me. You hungry?"

Probably he was with some new girl already who looked like a fitness model and had a PR job and a name that ended in Y. Jenny or Ashley or Conny or something like that. Danny had a reputation after all and the man didn't stay single for long. He was the most eligible bachelor around. Among certain crowds, Sarah knew, he was the white whale. The big one. And not just because of his cock, either. Danny was like the glass slipper all the women wanted to try on, desperate to be the one that fit.

When he didn't respond, Sarah decided on nachos from her favorite dive.

The dive was such a dive, it didn't even have a name. Just an address posted on a piece of cardboard outside, hanging from the door on a string. Locals called it by the address or just said That Place and everyone knew what you meant. It was filthy inside, with trashcans overflowing and a floor that was always mysteriously sticky. The ceiling was low and not up to code. The servers spoke exclusively in Spanish and never made eye contact. But somehow it was the best Mexican food in the city. Whatever their secret was, Sarah didn't want to know. No one was ever allowed to tell her. She loved the mystery of it.

On their second date, Sarah had brought Winston to show him her secret favorite food place. He'd sniffed at the sign, opening the door with a napkin, and then immediately left when he saw the state of the inside. Sarah had to beg him back in. She ordered for both of them and he ate his burrito with the sour face of a man absolutely sure he'd get food poisoning later that night. He didn't and the food was amazing, but he was such a baby about it that Sarah had never taken him back.

She ordered the nachos with extra everything and found herself nearly drooling as the cook heaped olives and jalapeños and thick spoonfuls of refried beans on the chips. Had she really not been back since that time with Winston? How had she denied herself such pleasures?

Just as she was about to sit down at one of the teetering tables, the hairs on the back of her neck stood up. She turned and wasn't surprised at all to see goddamn Danny Morrissey walk in with a pint of ice cream in his hands.

He smiled and sat down across from her, the chair under him groaning in protest under his weight.

"Is that for me?" Sarah said, pointing a sharp chip at the unmarked pint. "Because after these glorious nachos of the gods, I don't think I'll be able to eat for like a week."

Danny held up the white cylinder of ice cream between two fingers. "This, my dear, is for me. I was picking up a pint of the good stuff when I saw your text. I knew you'd be here."

"You know me so well, don't you?" Sarah tried to keep her tone even, but something went wobbly inside her. Gravity suddenly reasserted itself. The absence of Winston in her life made itself profoundly felt. Hot burning tears ran down her face.

Danny scooted around the table and held her to his warm, hard chest. "You're my best friend. Of course I know you. And you can do so much better than Winston. He didn't appreciate you. You know that."

"He was a good guy though. What if I can't find a good guy again?" Sarah buried her face in Danny's flannel shirt and tried not to think about how great he smelled, like beeswax and rum and waking up late on a Sunday afternoon with your thighs exhausted from the night before.

"Of course you will. You're Sarah Fucking Honeywell and you're amazing. Any guy would be lucky to be with you and anyone who doesn't think so is a douchebag."

"Really?"

"Do you know why we call guys *douchebags*?" Danny said. "Because people say you need them but they're actually useless and you should never ever put them in your vagina."

Sarah snorted. "You are the worst at telling jokes. That is not even close to what the punchline is supposed to be."

Danny grinned and shrugged. "Your nachos are getting cold."

"Yeah? Well, your ice cream is melting."

Danny planted a kiss on the top of her head and scooted back to give Sarah room.

"I thought I was cool with this. I thought I wouldn't hurt with Winston." The nachos looked disgusting but tasted like heaven on Earth. Sarah would literally stab anyone who tried to tell her she shouldn't eat them.

"Rejection never feels good."

"Like you'd know."

"I *have* been dumped."

"Like once. Try twenty times and see how it feels."

"It can't be twenty," Danny said while popping the top off his pint. He fished a plastic spoon out of his jacket pocket and tasted the dessert.

"What flavor is that?" Sarah said, wondering if it was possible to eat trash nachos and ice cream and not hate herself at morning yoga.

"Secret Breakfast from Humphrey Slocum," Danny said and then clarified with, "It's corn flakes and bourbon ice cream. Scientifically the best food that mortals make."

"Sounds serious."

"Consider it my last meal as a free man." He said it lightly, but there was a weight to his words that didn't miss Sarah.

"Is this about that text you got? The Bear Meet?"

"Bear Moot," Danny said. "And yeah. It's this weekend, as in tomorrow, and so tonight might be the last you see of me. Ever."

The world dropped away from Sarah. All the restaurant sounds ceased. The world narrowed to just her and Danny and the crash of her heart in her ears.

"Explain, Danny Morrissey. Or I will fling nachos at you. And I love these nachos. The fact that I would waste good nachos by hurling them at you should serve to show you how serious I am." She hefted one experimentally, testing its aerodynamics. "I'm in a delicate place right now and have no patience for your tomfoolery."

"The Moot is like a meeting of all these different clans and packs. Treaties get hashed out. Feuds get settled or started. It's all very serious. It happens once in a generation and attendance is mandatory. If you don't show up, it's assumed that you're either dead or imprisoned and people come looking. Every bear west of the Rockies and north of Panama is coming."

"It's a big meeting. I got that. Why is it so dire?"

"Because my parents will be there," Danny said, stuffing more ice cream into his mouth. The man was lucky he'd been born with a shifter's metabolism. "And they gave me an ultimatum when I moved to the city years ago. I needed to find my mate by the next Moot, or they'd arrange a marriage for me to a nice shifter country girl."

Sarah dropped the chip she'd been about to eat and said, "Flabba wha?"

"Yeah. Arranged marriage. If I don't go through with it, I'm exiled. Disowned. Pack-less. Stripped of rank and privilege and protection."

"But aren't you the Alphabet of your pack?"

"Alpha, yeah. But it's complicated. The old timers have all these rules and can demote me if I don't adhere to them." Danny put down the pint. It was still half-full. He was saving the rest for her. Even on the edge of calamity, the man was thoughtful. "If I had more time, I could have faked something. I'm sure one of my exes would play the part well enough to fool my folks. It wouldn't even take long. The Moot lasts a while, but the meet and greet is over in a blink. But I have to leave in the morning to get to the meeting in time. There's no time to arrange anything. And it's not like I can meet someone new in the next five hours and throw her headfirst into bear country." Danny stared wistfully out the window.

"I'll do it," Sarah said.

"And even then they might be able to tell. Fooling their senses will be a challenge."

"I'll do it," Sarah said again, but Danny didn't hear her. He was too lost in figuring out how to save himself.

"They already have a girl picked out for me, I know it. Someone fertile and steeped in the old ways who can give them a dozen grandkids and spend Sunday afternoons at their place pretending like it's 1816 and not 2016. They probably timed the text just to catch me out, so I wouldn't have time to fool them."

Sarah jumped to her feet, tipping the rickety table over and spilling nachos across the floor. "I volunteer as tribute!" she yelled.

Chapter Three

Danny loved the drive north from the city. Once you got past the Golden Gate bridge and the initial snarl of tourists trying to find their way, the road opened up, civilization dropped away, and it was just you and the mountains. Driving through the country was the next best thing to being a bear, as far as he was concerned. His bear agreed. It was all he could do not to stick his head out the window and taste the scents of the world.

Driving was perfect, except maybe when you made a huge mistake and invited your inquisitive best friend to be your pretend girlfriend for the weekend.

Sarah had always been cool about his shifter blood. She made jokes. She sent him stuffed bears on holidays, but she'd never asked too many questions or made him feel weird. But being his fake mate for the weekend took down some wall he hadn't even realized was between them and the questions came flooding out.

She was wearing strappy heels and a bright red dress that showed off her thick, gorgeous thighs. Danny had to remind himself to keep his eyes on the road and that she was just pretending to be his mate. But his bear didn't seem to get it. She'd broken up with Winston. She was single now. He was single now. The bear wanted her. Hell, Danny wanted her. But he couldn't. He couldn't ruin their friendship. He knew what he was like better than anyone. If they got together now, they'd be split within the month.

Around her shoulders, Sarah wore one of Danny's flannel shirts. It was important to get his scent all over her, as much as possible, to complete the illusion of being mated.

"How many bears are there?" Sarah asked brightly, her eyes wide with delight as she saw a field full of fluffy sheep zoom past.

"Not as many as there used to be." Danny tried to keep his eyes on the road. Why did she have to wear that dress today? Even staring ahead, he could see her bared thighs in his mind. He could smell the raspberry scent of her skin, even now. His bear rumbled inside him and his cock twitched in his pants.

"Why is that? Didn't you say you couldn't be hurt?" Sarah was usually a low-makeup kind of girl, or at least used her makeup to that effect. But today she wore a slash of bright red lipstick perfectly matched to her dress. It was like she was trying to drive Danny insane.

"Yeah, the elders say *no weapon forged by man can hurt us* but it's trickier than that. If a bear shifter gets hurt, he sort of goes into a hibernating coma until his body and mind knit themselves back together. There's an old cave, up in Bearfield, where all the sleeping bears are held until they wake. It can take a week or a century. No one knows why. But the scarcity isn't from dying us off, it's just a low birth rate."

Danny focused on his words and tried to keep thoughts of Sarah's red lips wrapped around his cock out of his mind. He could see her, kneeling with her hands clasped behind her back, moaning as he fed her his hard cock. He shook his head and concentrated on the road, on the story.

"Shifter kids are rare amongst my kind. Very rare. The only way to be sure of a shifter offspring is to find your one true mate."

"Whoa, what?" Sarah's head snapped around. "Why haven't you mentioned this before?" Her anxiety burst from her in a scent like hot sauce and copper.

Danny shrugged. "It's why I was in the city, technically. The clans send us out when we're young to find our true mates and bring them home, but very few ever find them. It was easier in the old days, when the world was smaller."

"But what if your true mate is in China? Or is ninety-eight years old? Or not even born yet?" Sarah's heart raced, the ba-boom ba-boom of it ringing in Danny's sensitive ears.

"Yeah, that's kind of the problem," Danny said. "But also, what are the odds that the one hundred percent perfect person for you is a Chinese grandma? Not very likely, right? That's not who we fall in love with. It's not who would make us happy. It's not like some random stranger out there is holding your lottery number and you just need to find them. It's like anyone else falling in love. She's probably someone like me, but not too much like me. Of a similar age, from a similar place."

Sarah turned to regard him and her dress slid up even higher, revealing the spot where her thighs met and just above there was the scent of sweet raspberries. His bear growled low and hungry.

"When you meet your special mate, how do you know? Is it like fireworks go off inside you? Do you go all furry and freak out? Do you carry her back to your bear cave over your shoulder and make babies right there?"

So many questions. So much skin revealed. Danny wanted to stop the car, to kiss her, to slide his hand between her thighs and watch her eyes as he fingered her to her first big O of the day.

"It's never happened to me, so I don't know. But there are stories. So many stories. At the Bear Moot, the elders will gather around and tell stories to the younger generations. Some of these guys are over a century old. And besides stories of how easy life is now compared to the bad old days, and stories of great battles, and famous dudes they once met, they love to talk about how they met their mates. Every one of those guys found their fated mates. Some spent lifetimes looking for her." Danny maneuvered the car along the winding mountain roads, smiling when the Pacific came into view on his left. "My parents were fated. The way my dad tells the story, they knew each other for years before he realized she was his mate. They were neighbors up in Seattle. Lived across the street from each other. But he never knew. And then he went off to fight in World War 2."

"How is that possible?" Sarah asked. The shirt draped around her shoulders slipped off and revealed the low-cut top of her red dress. Her ample breasts were barely contained. Danny almost drove off the road.

"He's old. Really old. Anyway, he fought in the war and then came home. My mom was at the welcome home party for him and gave him a chaste little kiss on the lips. It wasn't the first time they'd kissed, but it awoke Dad's bear and right then, on the spot, he knew they were meant to be. Now maybe he changed in the war and couldn't be her mate until he'd gone through that horrible experience, or maybe *she* had changed and become someone who could love him? Maybe growing up so close to each other he never had the chance to realize she was the one. No one knows. It's poetry, not science."

"That's beautiful," Sarah said. "So will your parents think I'm your mated fate?"

"Fated mate," Danny said. "And no. I don't think so. Fated mates smell different. Very distinctive. They'll think you're my ordinary mate."

"Ordinary," Sarah said with a frown, and it was all Danny could do not to kiss the frown from her face.

"Well, not *ordinary*. Extraordinary. They'll think you're beautiful and charming and wonder how I could have been so lucky as to meet you, of course." Sarah's scent changed again, deepening into the flowery notes of embarrassment with some more primal underneath. It was a delicious scent and Danny made a note to tease her more.

The road curved around a mountain and then the world opened before them. The Pacific filled the horizon, dotted with sailboats and container ships. The blue majesty soothed Danny. Beside him, Sarah's breath caught in her throat.

"It's gorgeous, isn't it?" Danny said. His bear stopped grumbling for a moment, as a herd of elk came into view on a distant rise. The bear wanted to pull over. It wanted to shift and chase down the elk, not to eat, just to mess with them. His bear was kind of a bastard. "I wanted you to see this. I know you don't get out of the city much and this drive up Highway One is too spectacular to miss."

Sarah sighed and rested her chin in her hands. "A girl could get used to this." Then she flashed Danny a grin.

They stopped for lunch in Bodega Bay—fresh oysters right from the sea and cold beers from a local brewery. If Danny's scheme failed and he had to return to his dingy hometown, he'd miss all this desperately. He didn't say anything to Sarah, but he estimated his chances at fooling his parents at ten percent. Twenty at the best. The drive up the coast, hitting his favorite stops along the way—it was a last meal before execution for him. His last chance to taste the world, to see the sea, before family and duty and honor and an arranged marriage locked him down in Mercy Springs with the rest of his clan.

"What can I expect at this Big Bear Butt Meet and Greet?" Sarah asked, shaking hot sauce onto her oysters.

"It's a Bear Moot. And it's just for bear shifters and the bear-blooded. Mortal mates and friends attend like an opening ceremony. No, wait. That sounds too fancy. Ceremony is the wrong word. It's like a barbecue? Or a giant picnic."

"Now do you bring your own pic-a-nic baskets, or do you steal them from the ranger at Jellystone park?"

Danny frowned at her. "This isn't a joke. These are important rituals for my people."

"But you look so cute when you frown," Sarah said with a mischievous smile and then winced. She was getting into character, losing herself in the girlfriend role.

"That's good," Danny said. "You should say that kind of thing when we're around my folks. It'll really sell the relationship."

"Yeah, I'm just practicing now," Sarah said, and then after a moment, "You probably should, too. If we're going to make people think we're a couple, we'll need to look the part."

Danny looked out at the sea around Bodega Bay. It was calm and the sky was full of seabirds lazily circling. The sun danced on top the waters, dazzling him.

"You're right. I've been only thinking about getting the scent right. We need to do more. Are you cool with me putting my arm around you? Kissing the top of your head? All those little intimacies?"

Sarah sat back in her chair. "You're an alpha, right? Shouldn't you be all grabbing me and bossing me around telling me how it's going to be?"

Danny rolled his eyes. "An alpha is the master of himself and his pack. He has absolute confidence in his abilities. He is there when his pack needs him and in return knows they will back any play he makes without question. You don't get there by bullying people or shouting or treating women like meat. That isn't confidence, it's insecurity."

"So how does an alpha treat a woman?" Sarah cocked an eyebrow at him. Her mouth quirked up into a smirk. Was she testing him? Goading him on? The sun and sea were behind her, extending their dazzling glow like a halo on her skin. The scent of raspberries was strong now.

Danny Morrissey eased out of his chair and knelt in front of Sarah. He placed a hand on each of her knees and eased her thighs open. "An alpha," Danny said, sliding his hands up her hot trembling thighs, "is constantly seducing consent from his mate." His hands stopped when his fingers brushed the edge of her panties. She was biting her lip. Her brown eyes were huge with expectation. Danny's cock strained in his pants, hard and heavy with need. He leaned forward and brushed his lips against hers, a whisper of a touch.

She closed her eyes and her lips parted. If he kissed her now the way he wanted to, things would be weird at the Moot. He knew it. She was his best friend. He had no business seducing her. It wasn't fair to either of them.

Danny slid back into his chair, dragging his hands back down Sarah's thighs in the process. "That is what an alpha does."

Sarah kept her eyes closed, a half-smile on her red lips. "Mmm," she said. "That was nice. But maybe a little intense a performance to put on in front of your mom." She reached out for her beer and took a long pull from it.

"Oh that's nothing," Danny said. "At the end of the Moot we have to publicly mate in front of all the gathered clans."

Sarah spit her beer out in a shocked burst of foam. "We have to what?"

"Just kidding!" Danny laughed as he dabbed beer off his cheeks.

It wasn't just Danny's bear that was a bit of a bastard. He had his moments, too.

Chapter Four

Danny didn't speak highly of Mercy Springs. He used words like *dust hole* and *podunk* and *scrapheap*, so Sarah wasn't expecting much when they rolled into town.

Even "town" wasn't accurate. Downtown Mercy Springs could have fit inside Sarah's backyard growing up. It consisted of exactly one gas station, one bar, one grocery store and a diner all huddled together on one block, facing a field of sheep. Technically it wasn't a town or a village at all. It was *unincorporated land*, nearly lawless as far as California went. It existed at the intersection of four different counties and each of them thought it the responsibility of the others. The fact that the town even had electricity was a testament to the can-do spirit and general orneriness of the inhabitants.

The only attraction in Mercy Springs, aside from rolling hills and sleepy sheep, was a natural hot springs nestled in a valley about a mile from downtown. A tiny artists' community had developed around the springs a hundred years back and today it was an enclave of maybe a hundred people, operating a rustic spa for city folk.

"My people generally have nothing to do with the spa, though I hear it's pretty nice," Danny explained. "They're kind of snobs about it, actually."

The car ride after the almost-kiss had been quieter. A tension buzzed between them now. Sarah could still feel the ghost of his big strong hands on her thighs. She could feel his fingertips grazing the edge of her panties. Should she have leaned in? Slid closer to him? Encouraged him? She was achingly wet and distractingly horny. She kept crossing and uncrossing her legs. Why had she ordered the oysters? The last thing she needed was an aphrodisiac.

More importantly, Sarah realized they weren't going to fool anyone at the Big Bear Butt Bonanza.

One look at her and they'd know she was entirely wrong for Danny. She was all curves and plumpness, where his usual type really wasn't. Sarah did not have visible abs. She didn't climb mountains for fun. She ran only to catch the bus and her investment portfolio was a Sailor Moon lunchbox with an emergency $1,000 in it, hidden in her air vent. Sarah grew up in the suburbs. Her parents were decent people, if a bit closed off. And despite all the yoga classes and spinning and ellipticals at the gym, she did not have a bikini ready body.

She hoped at least the family would be gentle when they laughed at her. Danny didn't talk about them hardly ever. But the little bits he'd let slip made them sound like cruel, awful people. She hoped he was wrong.

All of her thoughts about helping him out, saving him from an arranged marriage, were gone now. She just wanted to keep her head above water and maybe have a little fun.

Because if she was going to lose Danny forever to some arranged marriage, why shouldn't she enjoy her last days with him?

They pulled off the main road and down a dusty farm trail. The car bounced and shook. If she didn't know better, she could have sworn Danny's eyes kept glancing at her girls, who were doing a little dance in her low-cut dress.

After a mile or two of dirt roads and farmland, they pulled up in front of an old Victorian-era farmhouse that had so many additions that the word *compound* sprung to mind. Strong oak trees encircled the house at a respective distance, casting shade but not near enough to touch. A fleet of beat-down cars and tractors covered in leaves and pollen hunkered nearby.

The house was eerily silent.

"I was expecting something more raucous," Sarah said, getting out of the car.

"Nobody's home." Danny's voice was tight, as if he was trying to avoid snarling.

"But what about the Furball Convention?"

"The Bear Moot isn't happening here. If my folks hosted it not a single shifter would come. No one likes them, not even their pack. And anyway, they don't have the clout. My dad is one of the elders, but he is pretty removed from the politics of it."

"If it isn't here, why did we come?"

"The Moot is nearby, in a little town called Bearfield." Danny sighed and adjusted his shoulders. "I just need to go in there to get something."

"Bearfield," Sarah said, biting her lip. "I've heard of that place. It's like a little resort area?"

But Danny didn't hear her. He stood, facing his childhood home, flexing his hands and forearms like he was preparing for a fight. His eyes were very far away but his face had the demeanor of someone psyching himself up to go face his demons.

Sarah walked around the car, all thoughts of sexy times and kissing behind her; her best friend was in pain and needed her. She took his hand in hers, marveling at how much bigger he was.

"Hey," she said. "Do you need me to go in with you?"

He shook his head, his eyes snapping back into focus. "If my parents came home and found your scent in their home, they'd go apoplectic. You stay here. But could you do me a favor?" Their eyes met and electricity moved between them, shooting through Sarah down into the earth. He'd never looked at her that way before, like he as truly seeing *her*.

"Anything," she breathed. And she meant it. Standing next to him, feeling the warmth radiating from his hot shifter body, it was like all of her reservations and inhibitions had been left behind. For a moment she felt like there was a second her, standing right behind herself like shed skin. She'd molted in the blink of an eye and left something cautious and frightened behind.

"Inside the house is a thing I need. A symbol of my office as Alpha. I don't know where it might be and going in there brings up lots of memories. Rough memories. The scents alone . . . " Danny trailed off but a squeeze from Sarah brought him back. "I need you to help ground me. Tie me to the present."

"I can do that," Sarah said. Then, "How do I do that?"

"Talk to me. Sing to me. Tell me stories. I'll be able to hear you just fine and as long as I can hear your voice, I'll be tethered to you."

What was even going on with her life? Yesterday she'd been comfortably dating Winston, prepared for a weekend of brunch and Netflix and maybe some chill and now she was on the remote compound of a family of bear shifters, singing to keep her best friend who she might actually be in love with from falling down a memory hole. Okay, sure.

Danny let go of her hand and stalked towards the home. His ass looked magnificent in his jeans. His white t-shirt hugged his shoulders and arms so tightly it was if it'd been painted on.

"I hate to see you leave," Sarah said with a smirk, "but I love to watch you go."

Danny turned back and smiled at her.

"Keep talking."

So Sarah did. She sang every song she could remember, messing up the lyrics more than she got them right.

But Danny didn't return.

She started telling jokes, any joke she could remember, which for some reason were all extremely filthy.

But Danny didn't return.

Sarah told stories about growing up near St. Louis, about her favorite Halloween memory—the time when she was eleven that she tried to see how far she could bike in one day and how she had to call her mom from a payphone when she found herself entirely lost after just two hours.

But still Danny didn't return.

It was hard to keep talking when she couldn't see him. Her mind kept wandering off, imagining all the horrible things that could happen to him. She checked the car and, sure enough, he'd left the keys in the ignition so at least she could flee if she needed to.

How well could he hear her?

Sarah closed her eyes and in a whisper said, "If you come back to me right now, I will fuck your brains out tonight. I've always been afraid of being just the next girl of yours, just another conquest, but if I'm going to lose you to some arranged bride, then I want our last night together to be memorable." Her voice grew quieter as she spoke, her whisper becoming something more solemn, like a prayer.

As if Danny would sleep with her.

When she opened her eyes, he was there.

He emerged from the house shirtless, his body glistening with sweat and streaked with dirt. Over his shoulder he carried a huge silver sword, longer than Sarah was tall. He met her eyes and smiled and Sarah's knees shook.

"What the hell is that?" she said as he neared.

"Every alpha has one of these. I have to present my glaive to the council. It's part of the ritual."

The sword had a two-foot-long wooden handle wrapped in white leather. The blade was gleaming silver, wider than a dinner plate but thin, with a mottled pattern glimmering just under the surface. Danny slung it off his shoulder and planted it tip down in the mud.

The sword didn't move or make any noise at all, but Sarah couldn't shake the feeling that it was alive and watching her with a cold intelligence.

"What happened to your shirt? Not that I'm complaining. I think you should always rock this look." Sarah's eyes traveled down the wide slabs of his chest, along his washboard abs, to the deep V of his hips. She wanted to lick the grooves of his muscles, to seize them in her hands and never let go.

"I had to shift to find the glaive. The shirt got dirty." Danny grinned. Now that he'd returned, a weight was gone from him. As if he'd carried some burden into the home and left it behind. He glanced up, through the oak branches at the dappled sun. "That took longer than I thought. We need to hurry."

Danny folded down the back seat of the car and wedged the glaive between them so that the blade was in the trunk while the handle hovered at shoulder height to Sarah.

Had he heard her confession? Could he hear a whisper across a field, from within a creaky old house? If he had, he didn't show it.

Sarah watched the world roll by as they drove out of Mercy Springs, across wine country, and up into the mountains of Bearfield.

"My family used to live here, in Bearfield, a generation ago," Danny said. "But I've never been."

"There's more bears there? Like, bears-like-you bears? Not just normal bears?" The closer they got to the Moot, the more anxious Sarah became. She rubbed Danny's sweat-smelling clothes over her neck and ankles and thighs. Would she smell like his mate? Would anyone buy their ruse?

"Yeah. It's like our homeland, at least on the west coast. But the family that rules there kicked all the rest of the bears out before I was born. The Alpha was this complete tyrant. He couldn't stand to share power or wealth, so he banished the rest of us. The guy was my uncle, I guess. But I never met him."

"I'm so sorry." The mountains were lushly forested with a thousand kinds of trees. It looked unlike any part of California Sarah had ever seen. It was as much the opposite of Mercy Springs as any place could be. What would it be like to have this taken from you? To find yourself condemned to a rundown farm in the scrublands?

The road wound between mountains, plunged into valleys, threaded narrowly between redwoods and sequoias competing to see who could be the most monstrously tall tree ever. Then the road turned abruptly and Sarah found herself staring at Bearfield.

It was a quaint little town, built into a large scoop of the mountain. A massive hotel loomed over a busy little downtown where a multitude of people were gathered. As they drove past, Sarah noticed a movie theater showing a Kurosawa marathon, a bakery with a line stretching around the block, and a dozen other little businesses that piqued her curiosity.

"The Moot is just outside downtown, in a campground," Danny said.

"How does it feel to see this?" Sarah asked. "This is where you could have grown up, yeah?"

Danny gritted his teeth and squeezed the steering wheel so hard it squeaked in his fingers. "Yeah" was all he said.

Past downtown, the road curved back around the mountain and Danny turned off into a campground that was stuffed with every sort of vehicle imaginable. RVs and campers stood next to a Tesla roadster, which was next to a fleet of motorcycles, which surrounded a hodgepodge collection of classic American autos. Hundreds of people stood around barbecuing and drinking and laughing and growling.

"There's so many people," Sarah said, suddenly wishing she was anywhere else.

"Are you ready to meet them all?" Danny said, his voice gentle.

"I don't know. Can I just hide here for like an hour?" Sarah knew they could hear her. They could all hear her. She'd imagined a dozen or two people, not this. Danny had warned her, but in her mind she hadn't painted the picture big enough.

With the big handle of the sword dividing them, Danny slid his hand onto her thigh. Electricity ran up and down her legs—mostly up.

"Sarah," Danny said, his eyes catching hers and holding them. "You can do this."

Anything she said now was being observed. "I know."

Danny's eyes sparked with golden fire from somewhere deep inside him, a spark of his shifter magic showing through. "I love you," he said.

Sarah's heart stopped in her chest. Her ears stopped hearing the world. Her skin felt two sizes too small and a thousand degrees too warm. "I love you, too," she said.

And *oh fuck*, she meant it.

Chapter Five

Sarah was really getting into character. Danny was impressed. The way she said "I love you" sounded so real it made his bear roar with excitement. If they could just keep it up and keep it together, maybe he wouldn't have to move back to dirt country with whatever fanatic his parents had chosen for him.

"You ready?" he said to Sarah. She was staring wide-eyed at everyone and they were starting to notice and stare back.

"Are they all like you? All shifters?"

Danny laughed, despite himself. But the shocked and hurt look on Sarah's face ended it quickly.

"There aren't this many bear shifters in all of the Americas, love." He didn't mean to call her *love*, it just slipped out. But he liked how it felt on his lips. "Mostly these are the bear-blooded. Relatives of shifters and the like."

"But they don't turn into bears?"

"You can think of it like they carry the genes for being a bear, if that helps. I'd say they're good people, because most of them are, but some of them are total bastards, too." Danny pointed out one group of particularly disreputable-looking men. They were bearded and tattooed, dressed like bikers, and glaring at Danny like they wanted to rip his face off.

"Who are they?"

"That, love, is my pack." Danny opened his door and then walked around to open hers. "Let's go introduce you."

Getting the glaive out of the car was more difficult than getting it in, but he managed to work it out without smashing any windows and only barely cutting the seats. The rental car place could bill him.

Holding the sword in his hand felt comforting to Danny. It was the privilege of the Alpha to wield the glaive. It was about the only damn thing in the world outside of a volcano or a nuclear explosion that could kill a bear shifter permanently. He'd never had to. His pack had always obeyed him and hadn't been stupid enough to break any laws. But his father—his father had killed plenty with the glaive and scarred even more. Danny had a scar that ran down his chest in a diagonal slash to remind him. His body hair mercifully obscured it now, but he remembered as a child looking in the mirror, seeing the angry pink line, and vowing to never be under his father's thumb again.

Around the gathering, other Alphas stood out like beacons with their glaives at hand. Danny counted nine total, including himself and Lady Nothing. He'd never met her before, but her rep preceded her. She was the only female alpha, leader of a pack of bear women noted for their ferocity. She was smaller than Danny expected, human-sized even. She had warm brown skin, hair cut close to her scalp, and eyes the color of fog. The female alpha wore shitkicking boots, skinny jeans that were more rip than fabric, and a white tank top that glowed against her skin. Her glaive was planted tip down in the dirt and Lady Nothing leaned against it, like a surfer watching the sea. She smiled and laughed with her pack clustered around her, but her eyes never stopped scanning the crowd.

Danny was impressed that she showed.

"Well, she looks badass," Sarah said, then clapped her hand over mouth. Clearly the idea that every shifter around could hear everything she had to say would take some getting used to.

"She is. She has to be. Any one of these bears here could challenge her at any minute to take her glaive and her pack."

"Just like that?"

"It doesn't happen much. It's a shitty thing to do, and trying to rule a pack you took by force rarely works out well for anyone involved."

The scents were layered and all swirled up on each other, mixed with the barbecue sauces and strong liquor, it was impossible to pick out any individuals. If his parents were near, he couldn't tell. But a casual glance told him none of the elders were present. Likely they were off having their own arguments and dramas that they'd pretend to clear up so as to put on a united front at the Moot.

The one scent that Danny couldn't shake was Sarah. She smelled like no one else on Earth. Raspberries, clear and strong. Now tinged with anxiety, sure, but still. She smelled so good he wanted to rub his face all over her. To dip his tongue inside her to see if she *tasted* of raspberries, too. Or maybe that was his bear talking. Raspberries had always been his favorite fruit.

He slung his silver sword over his shoulder with one hand and took her hand in his other. The crowd parted before him. Something in the glaive, some old magic, amplified his Alpha gifts. The bear-blooded couldn't meet his gaze. They recognized his strength and superiority. It was almost embarrassing. With Sarah in hand, they approached his pack.

"Sarah, I'd like you to meet Pretty Brandon, Rhett, and Good Boy. Guys, this is Sarah. My mate."

The three men dropped to their knees and then one by one pressed their foreheads to the ground in supplication. The glaive tingled in Danny's grip. Alpha magic was the oldest of all.

Then, supplication performed, they got to their feet. Brandon was the first up, popping onto his heels with a big smile on his perfectly handsome face. He pulled Sarah in for a bear hug and almost squealed with delight. "We are *so* happy to meet you," he gushed. "We've been telling Danny for years that he needed to get serious about finding someone. He won't be young forever." Sarah's gaze bounced from Brandon to Danny, back and forth, as if she couldn't reconcile the two of them.

"Is your mate here?" she asked.

"My Brandon couldn't make it. He had a work thing in San Jose that he just couldn't get out of. But everyone here has met him. He's old news. No longer shiny. Not like you." Brandon's eyes sparked as he regarded Sarah. Danny steered her away from him by the elbow, before Brandon could prod. They'd been friends forever, and pack almost as long, but Brandon had a way of talking things to pieces that he wanted to spare Sarah from.

"This is Rhett." Danny nodded at his packmate and wondered if the man's rough appearance would freak Sarah out. Rhett didn't wear shirts as a rule and all of the scars and tattoos that marked his flesh were fully visible. He looked far worse than Danny had ever seen him, with a haunted distance in his eyes.

"Hey," Rhett grunted, treating Sarah to an almost imperceptible nod, which for him was the height of respect. Any other alpha would have taken Rhett's attitude as a problem. They would have fought endlessly trying to break him down, to force him to respect them in public. But that would have been dumb.

Once, when they were teens, Rhett had challenged Danny for leadership. It'd been a brutal fight, lasting a night and a day. They'd destroyed two barns and a tractor in their fight, before Rhett cried uncle. He'd never challenged Danny since. His reticence had nothing to do with a lack of respect and more with a profound appreciation of silence.

Sarah nodded back at Rhett. She didn't try to hug him or shake his hand or even talk to him. And with her silent respect she probably earned his loyalty for a lifetime. Rhett was like that. Fiercely loyal to his friends and brutal to his enemies.

"And this is Good Boy."

"Good Boy?" Sarah asked. "That's your name?"

Good Boy stepped forward and took her hand, ducking his head in a repetitive bow. "That's my name. The only name I have." He smiled at her with a lopsided grin, not making eye contact. Good Boy never made eye contact. "It's really great to meet you. I've never heard of you before, so I can't say *I've heard so much about you* but I understand that's what human people say at times like this, so is it okay if I say it to you?"

"Yes?"

Good Boy's smile grew wider, his eyes crinkling with delight. "I've heard so much about you," he said, his voice syrupy with genuine pleasure. "Thank you. That felt good." Good Boy adjusted his clothes. He was wearing a hand-me-down suit, one of Pretty Brandon's, but it was two sizes too big for him, with rips at the seams and mud stains on the lapels.

"So you're Danny's pack? Just the four of you?" Sarah stepped back and regarded the ragtag bunch. "What do you all do together? He's never been keen on telling me."

Danny opened his mouth, hoping to deflect before Brandon could say anything.

"We rob banks together," Pretty Brandon said quickly, his voice giddy.

"You what?" Sarah's head snapped around to regard Danny.

"We haven't done that in years. I swear," he said. The scent of raspberries grew stronger. It was dizzying. Danny felt unsteady on his feet, like the scent was lifting him off the Earth.

"Your parents were asking for you," Good Boy said, hugging himself. "But you missed them. They went to the thing. The elder thing. Your mom was dragging around a girl, too. A woman girl. Pretty. A pretty woman girl."

"Apparently," Pretty Brandon drawled, "she's to be your bride. Did you not tell your mother about lovely, delectable Sarah here?"

"I don't think she believed me." Danny kept himself under control—his pack could smell fear, could hear a racing heart—but a coldness blossomed in his belly. If they didn't pull this off, he'd be married by the end of the weekend. A lull in the conversation opened between them. These men were like brothers to him. Closer than brothers. They didn't need to talk to be that. Well, maybe Brandon did.

"I missed the parents?" Sarah asked. Danny could smell her relief as clearly as if she'd written it on a sign and held it up for all to see.

"Until tomorrow, I'm afraid. In fact, all of the events have been postponed. *Something* is going on." Brandon waggled his eyebrows conspiratorially.

"Alpha," Rhett said, his voice the rasp of wind in dead leaves. "Can I talk to you?" He nodded at Sarah. "In private?"

"Of course." Danny planted a kiss on Sarah's head. They had to keep up appearances after all. "Stick with Brandon and Good Boy. But don't let them mix any drinks for you. Brandon's idea of a cocktail is a full bottle of vodka that someone whispered the word *tonic* to once."

"And that met a lemon at a party," Brandon added. He took Sarah's arm in his. "Can I show you around? There are so many fascinating people here to meet and with you on my arm I have perfect license to mingle and say terribly catty things to them all."

They walked off, with Good Boy trailing behind like the dutiful beta he was.

"What is it?" Danny said.

Rhett scanned the crowd around them. He had a nasty red wound on his back, as if he'd recently been gored by a bull. "Not here. Need privacy." Rhett nodded at the woods on the far side of the campground.

The two men walked in silence through the throng. It took longer than it should, as Danny politely acknowledged every shifter he knew and introduced himself to those he didn't. They didn't cross paths with any other alphas, thankfully. Those kinds of meetings were always tense. Too many alphas saw others as competition, and packs as a thing to be won. One alpha, a savage fighter named Dax, had a rep for ambushing others and killing them, stealing their glaives in the process and claiming their packs as his own.

Rhett and Danny walked deep into the woods. Into the land that should have been theirs.

"You ever wonder what it would have been like to grow up here? In this kind of wealth? These trees feel like home to me. The scents are like from a childhood memory." Danny could sense the power in the land. "The elders say that this mountain is where the Great Bear spirit first made a pact with people, where he shared his gifts with us. I can almost feel it. What would we be like now, if we'd grown up steeped in the tradition of this place? With a strong community to watch out for us, to keep our fathers in line?" A spark of rage ignited in his spine. "How dare they exile us? Exile everyone? A generation was ripped away from its roots, and for what?"

Rhett regarded him with his cold eyes. "That girl isn't your mate."

Danny stopped walking. "Of course she is."

"Maybe the others can't smell it. You've been working hard at masking it. But she isn't your mate. And if I can sense it, so will the elders."

Danny opened his mouth, denial ready to spring forth like a viper, but then he thought better of it. "I just don't want to get married, man. At least not to some shifter girl that I've never even met."

"You've had years to find a mate. You haven't. The law is the law." Rhett's voice was emotionless and tired.

"Fuck the law," Danny growled.

"Alphas don't get to say that," Rhett growled back. A fury suddenly raged within him. "You stand here and whine that you didn't grow up in tradition, but the second tradition prevents you from fucking your way across the city you abandon it," Rhett spat. "This is not the Danny I know, not the Alpha I swore allegiance to. The city has made you weak."

Did Rhett drag him out here to fight? To challenge him?

"No," Danny said. "Your way of life had made you hard, is all. You're in pain, Rhett. Let me help."

"I don't need your pity." Rhett turned from him. The angry red wound looked even worse now.

"I've never pitied you." Danny lay a hand on the wound. "Let me share your burden, brother. We are pack. Your pain is my pain. My life is yours."

The bond between them became a river as Danny's vitality flowed into Rhett. For a moment Danny glimpsed the pain inside his old friend. The scars that ran deep into his bones. Pain stabbed into Danny, running through his veins like poison. As Rhett's wounds healed and his body wove itself back together, Danny's body ached.

"What the hell happened to you? Did you fight a dragon or something?"

Rhett sighed. "You know what the elders will do when they find out you brought a mortal woman to the Moot, right? If she isn't your mate, she won't be allowed to leave here."

"They can't kill her. She's mine," Danny growled.

"They can. And they will. Or they'll mate her off to someone else. I think Dax wants more wives."

Danny's bear roared within him with such a fury that Rhett dropped to his knees in fear.

"I will kill anyone that touches her without her consent," Danny said. His bear had never been so ferocious. What was going on?

Chapter Six

Pretty Brandon and Good Boy were the perfect hosts to have at a shifter werebear conclave barbecue where you didn't know anyone and were terrified that everyone would realize you were a fraud the moment they laid eyes on you.

Pretty Brandon whispered catty things in her ear as he smiled and steered her towards the most interesting people, while Good Boy cadged drinks and food from every grill they passed. The man was broken in some profound way that his special magic powers couldn't heal. He reminded Sarah of a cousin of hers who grew up nearby her as a child. Joshua was a year younger but was on the autism spectrum, somewhere on the Asperger's end. He was very kind but couldn't make eye contact and was prone to saying things bluntly that made adults wince and children giggle.

Good Boy filled Sarah with a sense of protectiveness. She wanted to comb his hair or to wash his clothes and give him a good meal. Not that he needed any help in the food department. The Greater California Bear Hootenanny had a grill going every twenty paces, each heaped with more food than the last. Several of the clans were competing to see who could make the better grill up. There was a lot of beer and bourbon being passed around.

If you squinted and ignored the giant silver swords it almost seemed normal. It was like any other barbecue, except everyone present was possessed of a robust beauty, with so many sweaty biceps and washboard abs on display that Sarah's face flushed and her panties grew increasingly damp. She was surrounded by dozens of the hottest men she'd ever seen and none of them seemed to give a damn that she did not have visible abdominal muscles. In fact, they were all welcoming and polite, especially in the face of Brandon's sneering arrogance.

"And this one," Brandon said out the side of his mouth, "you would not *believe* what he got arrested for. Or what he was wearing."

"You smell nice," Good Boy said to her, bumping his head into her shoulder as if he wanted a scratch behind the ears.

"Thank you." Sarah patted his head and the big shifter sighed loudly.

"And now he's your friend for life," Brandon said in an exasperated tone. "I hope your couch is sturdy."

"I'm still sleeping on yours," Good Boy said.

"I know, sweetie. *Mi sofa es su sofa.*"

"Tell me about this robbing banks thing," Sarah said. A large hairy shifter wearing an apron that looked like a pirate flag sporting the phrase "Surrender Yer Buns!" handed her a plate of ribs and coleslaw with a nod and a gesture.

"I was just joking. We didn't really rob any banks." Brandon found a bottle of sauvignon blanc in a cooler and popped the cork out with one wickedly clawed finger.

"Yes we did. Robbing banks was fun," Good Boy said. "We were good at robbing banks."

Sarah shook her head. "I can't even imagine Danny doing that. He's such a rule-follower."

Brandon cackled. "Oh honey, it was his idea."

"It was a good idea," said Good Boy.

"Picture this," Brandon began gesturing theatrically. "Five poor shifters without a dime between them. They belong to different packs, but they talk. They meet. They have a rapport. They spend holidays together. Summers together. They're teens. Maybe tweens." Brandon took a long pull from the wine bottle. "I have to confess, I don't really know what *tween* means. But let's just assume it applies here. These five kids fall in together and a bond forms between them. It's a shifter thing. Before they know it, they've formed a new pack. It's the oldest of magics and while it binds them together it also frees them."

"Can't be in two packs at once," Good Boy added, nodding his head enthusiastically.

"Being free of the old pack bonds is explosive. Suddenly Danny's shitty father no longer has any sway over him. We were fourteen, I think—or at least Danny and I were—when we became pack. The adults laughed. They said he'd crumble at the first sign of adversity." Brandon's voice took on hushed, awed tones. "They didn't know him at all."

"Other packs came after us," Good Boy said. "But Danny was smarter than them. Jordan was tougher than them. Rhett could take a hit better than them. Brandon could talk them around in circles until they were biting their own tails." Good Boy's voice was full of wistful pride.

"And Good Boy was more loyal than any of them."

"And I punched them in their penises a lot."

Sarah laughed in surprise.

Brandon shrugged. "We were kids and these adults came for us, week after week. We were living in an old barn deep in Mercy Springs. We had a well for water and we hunted for food. It might not sound like much, but it was better than where any of us had come from. It was squalid and paradise."

"The good old days," Good Boy agreed.

"But the packs came. From all over the country they came."

"But why?" Sarah asked. "You were just kids."

"We were shifters. Your average year has one, maybe two bear shifters being born in the entire Western hemisphere. We aren't werewolves, we can't bite people and share our gift. The only way to make more of us is the old-fashioned way."

"He means sex," Good Boy said in solemn tones.

"But you survived? You're still pack."

"We don't all live in a big happy pile anymore, but yes, we are still pack. After spending a summer fighting an endless war against our own kind, Danny realized we needed help. We needed money if we wanted to stop being targets. So we robbed banks."

"That's where they keep the money," Good Boy added.

"Danny was the planner. Rhett was the muscle. I was the face and Good Boy here took care of alarms."

Sarah glanced at the ragged shifter. The idea of him using a phone, let alone mastering an alarm system was hard to picture. But a thought came to her, a sense of having been misled, like she'd just witnessed a magic act. "Who is Jordan?"

"Jordan was a good getaway driver," Good Boy said.

"Jordan was our fifth packmate. The one who got away," Brandon smiled and offered the wine bottle—now nearly empty—to Sarah, who shook her head at the drink. "She and Danny were rivals for Alpha. And then friends. And then lovers. You saw her earlier, I'm sure."

"I did?" Sarah said. "Danny didn't mention any exes here. Or any Jordans."

"She calls herself Lady Nothing now. And sister, she is *fierce*."

"She scares me," Good Boy said.

"The sexy supermodel with the shaved head and the giant sword? That's his ex?" Sarah remembered her. Of all the people she'd met, it was Lady Nothing who'd made the biggest impression.

"It was *not* a good breakup," Brandon drawled. "It was after our first real score. We did a bunch of practice jobs, knocking over banks in the boonies just to see if we could. And then we went to Sacramento. We knocked over five banks in one day. While the cops were all racing to the first, we were at the second. It was perfect. The FBI even gave us a nickname."

"The Five Furry Friends?" Sarah guessed. "The Bear Butt Bandits?"

"The Sex Walking Crew," Good Boy said.

"It's what one of the tellers described us as," Brandon smirked. "We made over five million that day. It set us up for years. Not that it stopped us from knocking over more banks. But the money got in the way. We lived in Mercy Springs, in that off-the-grid barn, because we had no choice. Money gives you a choice."

"And Jordan didn't want city life?" Sarah said. "I remember now, some stories Danny told about a high school sweetheart that he left behind. She hated the city and he wanted to see the world?"

"That's Jordan," Good Boy said.

"She's Peter Pan with breasts," Brandon drawled.

"Peter Pan is always played by a woman on stage," Sarah said. "Peter literally always has breasts."

"You know what I mean. She and her pack of Lost Girls roam all over Northern California, staying as far from civilization as they can. They like it up in Bigfoot country. I hear they even have a giant clubhouse."

"A clubhouse sounds good," said Good Boy.

"Do they rob banks, too?" Sarah asked.

"Danny may have given it up, but she never did."

Sarah's eyes narrowed. "Did you give it up, Brandon?"

He smiled wide enough to show her all his teeth. "Maybe not entirely."

"Robbing banks is a sometimes thing," Good Boy nodded.

"The last one was just over a year ago. Good Boy had the *best* idea."

"It was a good idea," he agreed.

"He sat outside the bank, with this bag full of french fries. This was down south, in a little coastal town."

"Don't those people *need* the money? How do you justify robbing people?"

Brandon cocked an eyebrow at her. "Oh honey, we're not robbing people. We're robbing *banks*. Multinational conglomerates. Fully insured. The amount we take from them is a rounding error. They make more than that by illegally foreclosing on one grandma in Florida."

"Banks are not good," Good Boy said. "Except to rob. And also for home loans." He paused and thought about it, screwing his face up with effort. "Also I like their suckers."

A tension grew in the gathering, as if a storm was about to roll in. Conversations became muted. Chefs ignored their grilling meats to stare up at the mountaintop. Good Boy looked too, though Brandon ignored it.

"So Good Boy was outside this bank, with this giant bag of fries. And he's throwing them one by one onto the ground. Slowly. And the seagulls take notice. They are such dumb little animals. They have brains the size of your fingertip. One by one G.B. tosses out a fry and the gulls get a little closer. He throws another, they get closer. Each fry draws them in and they fight, squabbling for it. It's a weekday morning—a Thursday—so there haven't been tourists around to feed the dumb beasts. They're starving and squawking loudly for G.B. to just hurry up and give them the whole bag. But he's patient, our Good Boy. He could win staring contests with statues. He throws out a fry, the birds fight and squawk. Other gulls hear the commotion and come over to see what's going on, and soon he has dozens and dozens of the silly little things gathered around him as he tosses one little fry after another into the air."

Nearby, a red-haired man who had been sitting atop a keg of beer got to his feet and started stripping off his clothes. Following his lead, others around the camp did the same.

"Then the door opens. A security guard pushes it open wide. He's about to tell Good Boy to get the hell out of there with his dirty birds. The guard is this real scrawny guy. He has a thin blond mustache and hair shaved high and tight. He looks like a broomstick doing an impression of a Marine. So without even looking at him, Good Boy takes his bag of fries and throws the entire thing into the bank. All of the gulls follow. All of them. Then it's total panic. It's not a big bank. They have low ceilings and these birds are just bouncing off everything trying to get the fries. The customers and the employees get all tangled up in it and run out of the building screaming. No one even noticed when Rhett and I slipped behind the counters and into the vault and made off with the cash." Brandon's eyes crinkled with the joy of remembrance.

Just then, a deep rough resounding note like a rasping foghorn sounded from higher up the mountain. Sarah's eyes slammed shut involuntarily. An immense pressure crashed down onto her, like an ocean wave. She stumbled backwards under the weight of it, and tripped over something warm and furry. The air smelled of burnt cinnamon, reminding her of that night years ago when she'd seen Danny shift for the first time. What had he called it? *Shift scent.*

Sarah opened one eye, then another. The rasping horn still blew. Her bones ached from it and her eyes watered at the effort of opening them. But that wasn't what worried her.

She was leaning against a bear. A bear with a lopsided grin that couldn't meet her gaze. She pat the bear on the head and whispered, "Good boy."

Another bear sat primly across from her, studying her with Pretty Brandon's lively eyes. All around, everywhere she looked, there were bears. Dozens of them stretched and shuffled and walked away as if hypnotized, heading up the mountain. Brandon the bear nodded at her, yelped at Good Boy, and then the two of them joined the rest of the procession up the mountain, into the woods, towards the source of that jarring tone.

Not everyone turned into bears, of course. Most of the people at the barbecue weren't actually shifters. They were shifter-kin, called the bear-blooded. Or they were mates. To a person they were flat on their asses, eyes squeezed shut against the summoning song. So apparently they weren't invited to the Moot. Bears only. No humans allowed. It hardly seemed fair.

Though once they all got up there, and shifted, wouldn't they all be stark naked? The mental image of all those ripped and taut bodies, clustered together, naked, made Sarah's thighs ache deliciously. Danny would be up there, with the rest of the alphas. She could see him clearly in her mind, his naked form limned in moonlight. She'd only seen him in the altogether once, but it'd made an impression.

Then she imagined the other alphas, especially Lady Nothing, also naked. They used to be lovers, her insecurity whispered to her. They haven't seen each other in a decade. It would only be natural if they got together. But Danny wouldn't do that to her, would he? It's not cheating because you aren't really together, her insecurity said, and Sarah knew it was right. It was always right.

If only she could have been like Lady Nothing. Strong and determined and resourceful. With a badass haircut and a magic sword. With a lean athletic bod and a kicking gang of bear ladies. Maybe then Danny would have been into her. But knowing Danny he would've been *into her* and then *out of her*. She would've been just another notch on his bedpost. Another conquest, like all the others.

But wouldn't it have been nice if she *had* been at the Mooting as his mate? If meeting his friends—his pack—had been real? If this wasn't some half-assed con meant to save Danny from assuming some responsibility, but instead the first steps towards her joining their community?

If the ragged *blarting* sound from the mountaintop hadn't been making her eyes water, she might have started crying. If she closed her eyes the tears might stop, but she was never one to do exactly what she was told. Her mother had called her sneaky. Her teachers had called her defiant. Sarah always preferred "strong-willed" as a description. So she kept her eyes open and watched the last of the bears disappear up the mountain. Surely the sounds would stop once they all arrived, right? They couldn't expect her to sit in the dirt all night with that horrible racket blaring.

One lone bear emerged from the woods. He was huge, with golden brown fur and shoulders wider than a car. The huge animal ignored the siren's call and locked eyes with Sarah. He tromped her way. A burst of panic surged through Sarah. Why was this bear ignoring the noise? What if it wasn't a shifter? What if this was just a *real* bear and he was going to eat her?

She tried to stand, to run away, but the weight of the sound tethered her to the earth. The bear didn't pay attention to any of the other humans around. It only had eyes for her.

Elbow by elbow, Sarah tried to crawl away, but the bear was unhindered by the sound and it reached her before she could crawl three feet.

"No," she said. "Don't eat me."

The bear looked at her with a familiar expression, an exasperated eye roll that she'd seen Danny deploy in the office a thousand times. It was him. The bear was Danny. Of course it was.

She didn't resist as he levered himself under her with his big bear head and rolled her onto his back. She clutched his fur and buried her face in his coat. The world rocked beneath her as the sound pummeled her even harder. Danny was running. His muscles bunched and shifted under her, reminding Sarah of nothing so much as one of those automated massage chairs they have at Sharper Image.

Down the mountain he ran, then on to the road. If any of the cars they passed thought it was odd to see a woman riding an enormous bear, they didn't show it. Knowing the Bay Area, they probably thought it was an elaborate Art Car made for Burning Man.

They swerved into the woods and cut across more roads, until they came to a cozy cottage.

At some point the noise had stopped.

At some point Sarah's fears and worries had been left behind.

At some point Sarah realized she was riding a freaking bear around like a goddess and laughed with joy at the wildness of it all.

At the front steps, Danny shifted, his bear body vanished and was replaced with his man form in the blink of an eye. He spun as he changed, catching Sarah before she could fall. He smelled of cinnamon. His arms were impossibly strong and his body blazed with heat. He looked at her with a hungry expression on his face, though his eyes were lost in the golden fire of the shift.

"Why aren't you up the mountain with your people?"

Danny nudged the door open and carried her over the threshold. The cabin inside was well appointed, if small. It had one of those open floor plans that meant the boundaries between bedroom and kitchen and dining room and living room were nonexistent.

"I'm right where I want to be," Danny said, his voice a low velvet rumble that did magical things to Sarah's skin. "I want you, Sarah."

Heat blossomed inside her, while a pinprick of icy reason stabbed her. "No you don't. I am totally not your type."

"Yes. You are," Danny said, his voice less rumbly now.

"I'm not and it's cool that I'm not. I've seen the girls you date. I'm not them." She climbed out of his arms. "I mean, don't misunderstand me. I definitely want to have sex with you. I just want to do it for the right reasons. *Because it'll be fun* is a great reason. So is *we'll never see each other again*. Just don't lie to me and tell me you love me when we both know it's not true. I'm a big girl—bigger than most—I can take the truth, but I can't take you sleeping with me out of pity."

The golden sparks faded from Danny's eyes. "Pity? You think I pity you? Why on earth would I pity you?"

"Because I'm going to die cold and alone. I'm single. Totally single."

"So am I."

"Then because I'm chubby. Not all muscly like you."

"You're beautiful, Sarah. You always have been."

The way he said the words, it was like he almost meant it.

"Then tell me why. Why now? I can tell there's something you're holding back."

Danny sighed. "We don't smell right."

"What?"

"Our scent isn't, like, *joined*. It isn't combined. We smell like people that shared a car together for a day. We smell like friends. Rhett picked up on it and warned me. And if he can scent it, you can believe my mother will, too." His eyes said there was something else, something he wasn't telling her, but she didn't care.

"How do we join our scents?" Sarah asked, her voice coming out in a hush.

"Like this." Danny tipped her chin up towards him and brought his mouth to hers, grazing her lips with his for just a moment. He made a satisfied sound, like he'd tasted something delicious.

Sarah felt herself hovering on one of those moments of decision. It lit up big and bright in her mind. Two paths, each starkly different from each other, stretched away before her into the future. Whatever she did, she would walk one of those paths. A decision had to be made.

The choice was simple. If she slept with Danny then maybe their scent could be altered enough to fool his pack. Maybe Danny could escape his arranged marriage and come back to the city. Things would be awkward after—how could they not be? But at least they'd still be friends and she would have gotten laid in the process.

If she didn't sleep with him, well, the consequences would be dire. Plus? No orgasms. That didn't sound like much fun at all. It might destroy their friendship, but when the alternative was losing him forever it wasn't much a choice.

Plus, orgasms.

Chapter Seven

Sarah's eyes glittered with expectation as she regarded him.

It wasn't exactly lying that he didn't mention the consequences of their ruse, that if they didn't sell their fake mating she'd be killed or mated off to someone else. If he had told her, she would have been too terrified to play the part. It wasn't lying, but it sure wasn't honest.

"You're looking at me weird," she said, narrowing her eyes. Her scent was excited but cautious.

"Are you ready for this?" he asked. He wanted to get it over with, to take her hard and fast so that if anyone came looking for them they'd find her dripping with scent. But that wouldn't be fair to either of them. They might only get one shot at this. They should make it a good one.

"You know I've had sex before, right?" Sarah said with a laugh. "Loads of sex. Good sex. Sometimes even great sex. You're not going to like blow me away with the power of your cock. We're just friends—good friends—who are going to have sex to preserve this illusion."

A challenge had been issued. "You think I won't blow your mind? Do you know how many of my exes say I'm the best they've ever had?"

"All of them."

"You're damn right all of them."

"That's what women always tell sexy exes they hope to get back with one day. What are they going to tell you, the sex was adequate?" Her voice transformed into a breathy high squeak, "You gave me so many adequate orgasms, baby. I can't wait for more of that merely satisfying sex." She twirled a finger in her hair and pouted her lips, leaning over to flash her cleavage at Danny.

A growl erupted from inside him. He could feel his eyes blaze with light. She was teasing him. Teasing an alpha. There was only one way this could end.

"Tomorrow morning, when you're lying in bed, trying to remember how many times I made you come—when every muscle in your body is spent and aching from our fucking—when your sweet pussy craves my cock like heroin—then you'll know just how *adequate* I am."

Sarah stepped closer to him and looked up into his eyes. His half-hard cock rubbed against her thighs. "What's my scent like? What can you tell about how I'm feeling right now?"

Danny closed his eyes and inhaled. "Fresh raspberries. You smell like ripe, dripping raspberries." He dipped his head and kissed her, but unlike before this kiss was not a tease. It was a promise. It was a kiss that went on and on. It began as a spark when their lips touched and then as he opened his mouth and ran his tongue along her lips it became a flame. When Sarah moaned into the kiss and darted her tongue forward to taste his, it became an inferno.

It was more than Danny expected. And judging by the wide-eyed shock plastered on Sarah's face, more than she expected, too. It was like kissing lighting. Like touching the infinite for just a second.

"Wow," Sarah said. "We should do more of that."

Danny took her face in his hands and kissed her again, deeper, letting the flame consume them. With every heartbeat his cock grew harder and heavier. It rose until it poked Sarah's dress between her thighs. An urgency took hold of him.

He could have thrown her on the bed, flipped her onto her belly and plunged inside her right then. They both would have been up for it, and his cock would have been happy. But he fought the urgency.

"Does it always feel like this? Kissing a shifter?" Sarah asked, her voice heavy with lust and wonder.

Danny's head swam with her scent. He couldn't think of anything else. "It's not usually like this for me. It's usually normal. But this feels—"

"Magical," Sarah said.

"Yes," Danny agreed. He kissed her again, seizing her hips with his hands and lifting her up off the floor. Her flesh was soft and yielding to his touch.

"Why does it feel this way?" Sarah asked, talking into his kiss.

His bear roared inside him, *Because she is your mate, you fool.*

But how could that be true? He'd known her for years. Wouldn't he have known?

You weren't ready to know.

"Because," Danny said, "I love you." He said it and knew it immediately to be true. The world was wrenched from beneath his feet, everything spinning around, until it reoriented itself around her, around Sarah. She was his north star. His guiding star.

"No one's listening to us now, Danny. You don't need to sell it so hard." Sarah reached down between them and took his cock in her hand. He murmured at the pleasure of it. "I'm going to fuck you, no matter what."

"You don't believe me?"

"You've said it to a lot of girls, I'm sure."

"You'll believe me. Because it's true. Because I've never felt this way before about anyone else."

"Show me," Sarah said.

He was naked, but she wasn't. That needed to be fixed. She was still wearing her delectable red dress, the one she'd been teasing him with all day. Part of him wanted to fuck her in it just as a matter of principle, but he held back, instead taking the zipper in his fingers and easing it down tooth by tooth, slowly, until the fabric fell from her shoulders like the last barrier between them crumbling. She was wearing black lacy underwear under it and the sight stole the breath from Danny's body. The light was low in the little cabin but it was like every ray of light clung to her, sparkling on the curve of her hips and the generous swell of her breasts.

Sarah bit her lip and looked everywhere but at him.

"What is it?" he asked.

"I'm just waiting for that inevitable sigh of disappointment. Guys always make it when they see me naked for the first time."

"What the hell are you talking about?"

"Winston only wanted to do it with the lights off, too."

A lifetime of dating fools could only be overcome in one way, as far as Danny knew. He took Sarah's chin in one hand and turned her face to look at him. "Your body is amazing," he said. "It's so fucking sexy that I can hardly control myself. You're a goddess and any man who tells you differently is a goddamn dope."

And before she could deny it he kissed her again while sliding one hand under her sexy lace panties. His fingers grazed her soft hair and then moved on to find her wetness. And she was so very wet.

"Goddamn," Danny whispered. "I've never felt a pussy this wet before." Sarah whimpered as he ran his finger slowly up and down her slit, teasing her with the penetration. He never went for the clit right away. That's a rookie mistake. She was so slippery that she almost sucks his finger in and he just can't believe how amazing she feels. The scent of raspberries was everywhere now. It's her cunt, he realized. It smells like goddamn raspberries.

He could see then, just for a second, sitting with the other mated bears at the Moot. All of them sharing their stories of finding their mates—the adventures and danger they went through. And when it came time for him to talk, they'd ask him "So how did you know Sarah was your mate?" and he would say "Because her pussy smells like fresh berries" and the other bears would just nod sagely, each of them suddenly remembering how sweet their mate's tasted.

Sarah clutched him close, kissing him hungrily as his finger slipped and slid around her opening. She made little mewling noises as his finger *almost* grazed her clit. Her noises were the sexiest thing he'd ever heard. He wanted to hear more of them. All of them. He needed to hear every little moan of pleasure her perfect plump lips could make, so he held her tightly against him, kissing her, and swirled one finger up into her hot wetness, curling it within the tight slick walls of her cunt.

She threw her head back and grunted, but somehow it wasn't ridiculous. It was *primal*.

"I could get used to this," Danny said. Her wetness dripped down his finger, his hand and his wrist. He could swear that it burned him, marking him as hers. *She's not just my mate,* he realized. *I'm hers.* He slid another finger into her and worked them in and out of her slowly, dragging them against the sweet spot inside her. Sarah's fingernails dug into his back. When Danny rubbed his big rough thumb against her clit her eyes flew open and locked on his.

An expression of absolute helplessness swam in her eyes. They focused on his and Danny's cock twitched appreciatively. Her orgasm was rising within her like a wave and she had no idea what to do. Sarah released her grip on Danny and bit down on one knuckle, then pushed him away, pulled him close. Her hands fluttered about like little birds as he stroked the walls of her pussy and rubbed her clit in firm little circles. Then her mouth fell open, her cunt spasmed around him, sucking him deeper in and her eyes unfocused as she fell apart in his arms.

Sarah held her breath for a moment, then another and then another.

"Breathe," Danny said in a gentle voice. "Breathe, my love."

Then in a great hungry gasp, Sarah screamed out, "Oh my fucking what was that god Jesus Christ yes!" then started laughing as she pushed Danny's hand away and fell onto the bed.

"You come amazing," he said. Was there a world outside the bedroom? If there was, Danny didn't care about it.

Sarah rolled over onto her belly and buried her face in a pillow. "Mmph muph ooo mmmph," she said.

"What was that? I don't speak pillow."

She lifted her head off the pillow. The wide greedy smile on her lips told Danny everything he needed to know. "I said it's all your fault. I am unable to stand or walk now. My legs have been replaced by bags full of honey and they no longer work. Send help. Get firemen. Sexy firemen."

Danny had never seen her so relaxed, so much *herself*. All of the layers of anxiety and caution that she usually wore had been stripped away, fingerbanged out of the room. The Sarah in front of him was the real Sarah. The true Sarah. And she would be his mate.

He climbed onto the bed behind her and kissed her toes until she squealed. Then he held her ankles tightly in his hands and kissed her ankles, her calves. The squeals grew hushed as she realized where he was going.

"Be gentle," she said. "Go slow. I need a moment to recover."

Danny kissed the back of her knee, nipping her with teeth. He slid his hands up her legs, spreading her open, so that her glistening cunt was on full display for him.

All he could smell were raspberries. His bear was very near the surface now, they were in harmony. They both wanted this woman to be their mate.

Danny's hands moved higher, his fingers stroking her vulva, opening her so he could lick every drop of her sweet juice. He stroked her opening with his tongue slowly, moving from her clit all the way up and then again. He preferred long drawn-out licks, like she was a popsicle made of sex, and judging by the noises she made, Sarah did too. She cried out in a warbling voice with every lick, starting low and ending high in a crescendo. Every lick brought forth louder cries until she was almost screaming.

She lifted her hips off the bed and pushed against the headboard, pressing herself back against his face. He worked his hands under her hips and lifted her higher so he could wrap his lips around her stiff little clit. The little hood had rolled back and her pink pearl was right there, begging for him. He took it between his lips and sucked at it, flicking his tongue softly then harder, following her moaned instructions.

"There, right there," Sarah groaned. "Not so hard." Then, "harder!" Her face was pressed into the bed where she moaned and panted. She gripped the sheets as if she was going to fall to the moon. In no time at all she was climaxing again, gasping and laughing as her orgasm overtook her. Her legs shook uncontrollably but Danny kept on working her clit until she wriggled away from him.

Sarah's juices dripped down his body, mixing with his sweat and steaming off his skin. Some old magic was at work in that room. He'd never seen anything like it, never heard of anything like it either. But he'd never met his one true mate before, so it was to be expected there'd be some surprises.

If you'd asked him before what he thought a fated mate was, Danny would have tossed off a flippant answer like "your one true love." Which would have been accurate, but shallow. What did *true love* mean anyway? How was a fated mate different from an ordinary mate?

If you asked him later, after he and Sarah left the cabin and took the next steps in figuring out life together, he would have said that a fated mate was a best friend that you had the most mind-blowing sex in the world with and then laughed about afterwards.

On the bed, in front of him, Sarah was a post-orgasmic puddle. "Okay," she said in a muffled sleepy voice. "You win. You blew my mind. You were totally right. You are sex heroin and I'm already craving more of you. But I think I need to take a break tonight. No more. If I come one more time like that I will forget my name. I'll change shape. I'll explode into a thousand pieces and never be able to be put back together."

Danny climbed onto the bed behind her, sitting just behind her ass. His cock was harder than steel. It ached with need. Precome dribbled down his shaft, coating the length of it in clear fluid. He'd never seen it like this before. He thought he knew his cock. It was predictable, in its own over-achieving sort of way. But this was different. There was a fire inside him that needed to come out. It needed to find its twin within Sarah, to meet and join with her.

"I'm going to claim you now," he growled. The room around him sparkled with golden light that he knew was pouring from his eyes. "You're mine. You know it."

Sarah half turned and regarded him through half-lidded eyes. "Yes. I'm yours."

"I'm going to fuck you now. To claim you as my mate."

She bit her lip, as if she was going to beg for a break so she could recover. But there was a fire in her eyes. She might have been a mortal, but she could sense the magic, too. "Please," she whispered. "Please fuck me. Claim me. Own me."

Danny had been holding himself back all day, but no more. The beast moved within him as he pressed the fat head of his cock against her wet sex. "Oh fuck you're big," Sarah grunted as Danny opened her with a thrust.

She squeezed him, hot and tight, with her slick pussy and Danny found himself moaning along with Sarah, in time with their thrusts. He seized her hips in his hands and buried himself deep inside her. The fire in him joined the fire in her and blazed within them both.

"This feels unreal," Sarah gasped. "I can feel something flooding me, flowing through me."

"You're mine," Danny growled.

"I'm yours."

"Forever," he thrust harder and faster, pistoning into her.

"Yes," she whimpered.

Something molten poured out of him. It wasn't come, but something more elemental. Some raw liquid magic pooled in his spine like lava and then shot into Sarah. He roared, shaking the house, at the pleasure of it. It was the claiming, the marking. Now and forever they were bound as mates. Sarah's cry joined his as she came again, her body forever marked as his and his as hers, their scents joining and merging and becoming something utterly new.

Afterward, they both collapsed onto the bed gasping, staring wide-eyed at the wooden ceiling.

Somewhere, not far away, the council of elders was busy being furious at him for ducking out of the Moot. But they could go screw. He'd found his mate.

Chapter Eight

"We missed you at the ceremony," was the first thing Sarah heard as she woke up. The voice was unfamiliar. A woman's voice, it dripped with harsh judgment. Dappled sunlight leaked in through the shaded windows. It was way past morning. Sarah's body was deliciously full of aches and decadent soreness, but sadly empty of coffee.

"We're a bit busy just now," Danny said, propping himself up in bed on his elbows. "Can you come back later? Maybe we can meet you in town? There's a delightful-smelling bakery that I'm dying to try out."

"When did you see a bakery?" Sarah asked. A cozy duvet that smelled exactly like sex was wrapped around her in a protective warm shield.

"When I was carrying you here, on my back, to claim you. It was literally the only thing I noticed. It really smelled quite divine."

"So you admit that she wasn't your mate yesterday?" The voice clearly belonged to Danny's mom, though Sarah enjoyed her cozy little cocoon too much to poke her head out to see the woman. If Danny was going to antagonize her, Sarah saw no reason not to join in. With her enhanced shifter senses, the little cabin must have smelled like a porn set. Sarah found the idea vastly comforting. No one could take their scent and not think they were together.

"Oh we were mates, I just didn't know it."

"That doesn't make any sense," snapped Danny's mother.

"*You* don't make any sense," Danny replied with a laugh.

A growl rolled out of the woman, deep and threatening. "You broke the laws. You brought a mortal woman to the pack Moot. Her life is forfeit."

Before the words had a chance to sink in, Danny was out of bed, standing naked before his mother. In his hand he held the glaive to his mother's throat—where had it come from? Sarah hadn't seen him carrying it at all. While leaping out of bed, he'd managed to tangle the covers around one ankle, yanking them clean off the mattress and off Sarah's very nude body.

This was not the kind of first impression she had wanted to make.

The blade gleamed in the reflected light. It nearly hummed with gathered power.

"I am an alpha. Sarah is my mate. You shall not threaten me."

"I'm your mother!" She spat her words like venom.

"Then act like it!" Sarah yelled from the bed. She crawled out of bed, woefully aware of how visible every inch of her was, but her dress and underwear were nowhere to be seen and anyway, she didn't want to celebrate her first day being mated by watching her lover behead his own mom. It just wasn't romantic.

"Danny, put the blade down. If we have broken pack law then killing her really won't solve anything. And if we haven't broken the law, then who cares?"

Danny's mother regarded her with icy eyes. The woman looked like a matchstick. Straight and narrow and thin, with a bob of ginger hair pinned close to her head. She wore black leather pants and a tank top. She may have been Danny's mom, but she hardly looked older than he did. Shifters aged slower than mortals, Sarah knew from Danny's stories, but it was still shocking to see.

"You smell like a whore." Her face contorted when she spoke, like she wanted to suck the marrow out of the words as she said them.

"Danny said I smell like raspberries."

"If you try to hurt her, I will kill you, Mother." Danny said in a quiet, matter-of-fact voice.

Danny's head jerked towards the door, and his mother's followed a half-second later. "Well, we can ask the justicar right now, can't we?" Her voice had a toxic glee in it. As if nothing could make her happier than delivering pain to her son.

Sarah couldn't believe the woman. How could Danny have grown up under her roof and turned out even halfway good? Let alone be the best man she'd ever known? What strength did it take to live with a viper and not become poisonous yourself? Maybe he had Pretty Brandon and Good Boy and Rhett and even Jordan to thank for that. Maybe taking care of them as an alpha let him be the better man.

Into the cabin walked the biggest, meanest man Sarah had ever seen. He was nearly seven feet tall and almost as wide. He had a shaved head and a face full of stubble and scowls. The man's muscles had muscles. His thighs were bigger than Sarah. He wore jeans and work boots and a t-shirt with the Bearfield city logo on it. At the sight of him, an animal fear gripped Sarah. She wanted to run, to hide, to play dead. She wanted to do anything but be in the same room as him.

"Who the hell are you?" Danny said, gripping his glaive but not raising the point.

The big man sighed. It was the sigh of a man tired of answering stupid questions all day. "I'm Marcus. Alpha of these parts, head of the council, and the law as far as you're concerned." His voice was tired, and not as scary as Sarah expected.

"He's the justicar," sneered Danny's mom. "He's here to take her life."

"He will not!" Danny yelled, lifting the blade in a defensive move.

Even witlh the sword, Sarah did not like his chances.

"Son, you are right. I will not take her life. Nor her freedom." He delivered the last words through gritted teeth, turning to lock eyes with Danny's mother. Her body trembled from the attention, then she collapsed and pressed her forehead to the ground.

"Please, Alpha. Please. Don't let her take my son from me."

"She arranged a marriage for you, you know that?"

"I do," Danny said.

"Damn fool thing to do, when you'd already found your mate." A hint of a smile played on the big Alpha's face. "When my father was alpha, he made a lot of mistakes. He killed a lot of people. A lot of humans, especially. He looked upon every challenge, like this sword you have drawn on me, as a threat that could only be extinguished with maximum force and trauma. He would have killed you. And her. And your mom as well. Then he would have burned down this cabin and pissed on the ashes. But I am not him. He banished all other bearfolk from this town and I'm changing that. You missed the meeting yesterday, but the doors are open again. To you especially, my cousin, the doors are open."

Danny lowered the glaive until the point sunk into the wooden floor.

"So you're not going to kill me?" Sarah asked.

Marcus picked up the blanket from the floor and tossed it to her. "You didn't know our laws, did you?"

"I knew I was pretending to be his mate, to fool everyone."

"Should that be punished with death? Of course not. But also, clemency isn't right. There must be some punishment." He stroked the stubble on his face. "Tell you what I'll do. One day soon, I'll come to you with a favor in mind. If you both do what I ask, then all is forgiven."

"And if we refuse?" Sarah said. "I mean, the favor *could* be anything. You could ask us to kill someone. You could demand our first born child." And as she said the words, she flushed with the heat of realization. They would have kids together. It was going to happen. Not soon, but one day. Danny was her mate and she was his and they'd make adorable chubby babies together.

Marcus spread his hands out in a calming gesture. "I'm not a monster. Well, I am. Actually, I am a monster. But I'm a monster who is on your side. Fated mates are rare. Too rare. And we can't afford to do anything to jeopardize them. We need more little bears running around this town. You two need to get busy."

"That's it?" croaked Danny's mom from the floor. "That's their punishment? He gets to fuck his whore human and make half-breed babies with her? Where's justice?"

The big Alpha knelt down next to her. "It's simple, Darlene. Love wins. How could justice demand anything else?"

Then with a curt nod, he picked up the woman from the floor and walked out of the house.

A silence hung between Sarah and Danny.

"They were going to kill me if they found out?" she said.

"I didn't know that was the punishment. I thought I'd just have to marry whoever my mom picked for me. I never imagined they'd try to hurt you."

"Promise me you won't lie to me ever again. Even lies of omission."

"Never again," he said. "I love you."

Sarah dropped the blanket to the floor. "Come here and show me."

And he did.

dangerous men close in on Mina, Matt has to prove he's got what it takes to defend the woman he loves from the mysterious forces pursuing her.

Heal Me
by A.C. Nixon

<u>Chapter One</u>
Dorian

I didn't do good girls.

Finding a partner or two and scratching that itch was easy enough—as long as they didn't expect pillow talk and breakfast.

It ain't that kind of party.

I'll fuck a woman until we're both so sated neither of us could walk—unless it's out the door.

I own a nightclub; that alone offers a smorgasbord of pussy—White, Black, Asian, Hispanic—you name it, I've tapped it. So why did I keep driving to Centerville, Wisconsin from Chicago for half-way decent food and second rate liquor?

Maybe I *was* losing my shit. This could be one of those midlife crises.

Nah, forty-two was too young for that. I have a life most men dream of—more money than I'll ever need, a business I love, and surrounded by the best fucking friends on the planet.

Yet here I stood, at Chuck's Chop House. How original.

"Welcome back." The perky and way too young for me hostess led me to my table. She tried to seat me in someone else's section last time—not happening. My table happened to be in whatever section Ryann worked. Jesus, I was a sick fuck. And if she knew just how twisted I was, she'd get a damned restraining order.

It wouldn't stop me, but it might make the chase that much more interesting.

The object of my current—and only—obsession walked toward my table with the sweetest smile I'd ever seen. She didn't fit my usual type, but everything about her worked.

She reminded me of a piece of sculpture in the making. As the sculptor chipped away at the marble it appears unimpressive, insignificant, and quite boring. Then with a flick of his wrist and a swipe with a rasp, *bam*, a masterpiece lay before you.

Even the drab uniform of a white shirt and black slacks failed to dim her radiance. I wanted to remove that offensive polyester uniform and cover her in nothing but the softest of wools and the most delicate of laces.

Of course that would be after I filled her with my cock. Her long, elegant neck begged for a collar. Maybe I could bring her down to Chicago and set her up in a place. It helps to own a building. And she'd have to live close, so she could satisfy my cravings whenever the fuck—

"Hello Dorian." Ryann placed a menu and a glass of water, no ice, in front of me and licked her lips. "How are you?"

"I'm good, sweetheart." I couldn't decide which part of her body I liked best. A lot of men liked tits, legs, or ass, but me, I loved the base of a woman's back, right where her ass begins its curve. Which was why the ass-less need not apply.

Don't get me wrong, I loved women—all women. But the only ones allowed in my bed needed curves—the more the better. This woman wasn't a just a soft place for my cock to slide into. No, not my Ryann, I wanted to fuck her unconscious, then wake her up with my mouth on her beautiful—

"You going to take a walk on the wild side and order something different today?" She pulled a pad and pencil out of the black half apron and waited.

"What would you recommend?" *Other than me bending you over this table and making you my dinner?*

"That you go to a better restaurant," she said with a smile that chased the sadness I sometimes saw in her eyes away. "Then again—" She shook her head, as if trying to dislodge the thought.

Too late. No need to fight it; at this point it was useless. We should just do this thing and get it out of our system. A couple of months, a couple of weeks, it didn't matter—we wouldn't last.

"I'll take the usual." I'd cut her some slack—for now. But this night would end with us in my bed. We didn't have to fuck tonight; I wasn't a damned animal. I could wait—until the morning.

I stopped hiding, stopped feigning mild interest. I put every bit of heat in my gaze. I put every dirty thing I wanted to do to her body and dared her to accept the challenge.

The widening of her eyes and the tiny whimper told me I wouldn't be waiting until the morning. As a matter of fact, if she kept looking at me like that, she wouldn't finish her shift unfucked.

"Okay." She spun and left so fast I felt a breeze behind her.

No way in hell should she be working here, and she sure as hell shouldn't be living in and that dump she called home. I'd never be a knight in shining armor rushing in offering happy ever after, but I sure as hell could and would help her out of a tight spot.

Something about being around her made me feel clean. Not my thoughts, because when it came to her they were downright filthy. She also eased me.

Centerville was a shit hole. I should know, I grew up here. Thank fuck for football and the scholarship that changed my life. Too bad it didn't stop me from being...well, me. No one in the neighborhood figured Dorian Zuba—the bad Polack—would amount to anything.

But Northwestern put me in the path of two men as fucked up as I was and we clicked. The rest, as they say, was making history, chasing woman, and making a shit-ton of money—most of it legal.

And that business put Ryann in my path.

The hostess sat an older couple, probably in their eighties, a couple of tables over. The sweet open smile Ryann gave them as she approached the table twisted something in my chest that I thought died a long time ago.

They didn't look like they had a lot of cake to throw around. Hell, coming here was probably a big deal, but you wouldn't know it by the way Ryann treated them. I liked that—she treated everyone the same until they pissed her off. Rich, or spending their last two nickels, I watched her treat everyone with courtesy and kindness—even those that didn't deserve it.

The last asshole I saw disrespecting her won't be coming back. It's kind of hard to dine out with two broken arms. What can I say? I hate assholes that take pleasure in treating someone like crap because of what they did for work. All those businessmen kissing my ass and wanting my money would cross the street and avoid eye contact if I were broke.

I was born with the opposite of the Midas touch, and with the exception of few things, I fucked up everything I came in contact with. With a clarity that damned near blinded me, I knew if she got involved with me, the trappings might be prettier, but sooner or later, I would ruin her. Maybe... No, no maybe about it. The best thing that could happen for her was me walking the fuck away.

Maybe I wasn't the world's biggest asshole after all.

I slid out of the booth and tossed all the cash I had on the table. One thousand dollars should be enough to cover my dinner and help her out of whatever jam she was in.

Of course, this being me, it happened as my fucking T-bone arrived.

"You're leaving?" Ryann looked down at the stack of fifties then back up at me. "I hope everything is okay." She sat the tray on the table and reached for my hand, and I jerked away.

"Pay for their meal too, and the rest is yours."

"It's too much." She shook her head.

"No." I wanted just one taste but I knew sure as shit one sip from her sweetness would never be enough. "You deserve more than that, and I wished I could be the man to give it to you. Goodbye, Ryann."

I didn't wait for a response, I couldn't.

I walked into the crisp April night, taking one last look at Ryann and the surprise and sadness on her face, and wished she knew that I was one apple she should never take a bite of.

Chapter Two
Ryann

What the hell was that? Maybe the mafia called and wanted their assassin back. Okay, that wasn't fair. From the way my big-hearted gangster looked, it very well could be. I cleaned the Goldstein's table smiling at the generosity of my bad boy. Not only did he make their night special, but I found myself one step closer to Seattle.

If my stupid pride would get out of the way, I'd already be enjoying the rain and kick ass sourdough bread with my girl Lisa. The nine hundred dollars in my pocket sure helped.

I finished my shift in a confused horny fog.

Once a week for the past five weeks Dorian came in, and all but the first visit made a point to sit in my section. He never said much, just watched me in a way I felt like he planned to make me his next meal.

I realize I'm out of practice as far as flirting goes, but I thought I made it clear enough that I was interested. How could I not? He had the whole Eastern European dispatcher of evil-doers' vibe.

Trust me, if I could afford a hit man, my scumbag of an ex-husband would be worm food. I sagged and made a face. Not really, but thinking about it made me feel better—a lot better.

I ended my shift concluding that Mr. Broody, Bad and Sexy would have to remain in my fantasies. Maybe I'd name my vibrator after him. I managed to make it to my locker and retrieve my purse and jacket before getting cornered. Great.

"You didn't really think you'd escape that easily?" Patricia, one of the other waitresses, caught me before I escaped. It would be so easy to hate her. Why the hell did she have to be tall, blonde, and nice?

"A girl can hope." I slipped my jacket on and slung my pleather purse over my shoulder. "I'll give you the abbreviated version. That man and me? Not going to happen. He won't be coming back." *I hope.*

"Sure didn't look that way to me."

"Did you spend your whole night up in my business?"

"Hell yeah. Did you see all the perverts I had to deal with?" She shivered and scrunched her face.

"Well, if he comes back I'll send him to your section." I was going to miss this restaurant and its people. Everyone had been nothing but kind, but I didn't get a nursing degree to wait tables again.

"Don't tease. If I had a chance, I'd shove you in front of the nearest bus."

"That's cold." I had to laugh. Some women were like that, but not Patricia.

"Just kidding, it would be something small, like a Mini Cooper." She stripped out of her uniform and shimmied into a little red dress that looked magnificent against her tanned skin. "You sure you don't want to hang out?"

"No, I'm good." I closed my locker and wondered what it felt like to be that young and carefree. Then again, maybe that was Patricia's disguise. I wore my own mask. I ignored the shame and embarrassment of my failed marriage and slapped on a smile. Fake it until you make it, or at least until the ache dulls.

No music, short dresses, and laughing for me. My night would consist of a water-safe battery operated boyfriend, a glass of wine, and a tub of bubbles.

First item on the menu when I reached Seattle—get a life—preferably one with orgasms that included a partner.

"Let me know when you guys plan another girls' night. I'd love to go." Eventually, I'd be gone, or they'd stop inviting me out, but I needed sex or stress-free fun.

And since the sex wasn't happening…

I'd spent three years trying to be the perfect girlfriend, then another ten trying, and repeatedly failing, to be the ideal neurosurgeon's wife. Time for me to take control of my life and rediscover Ryann. I used to like the person I saw in the mirror—time to get her back.

"No shit?"

"No shit." I hustled out of the restaurant to the parking lot that could use a few more lights. It sucked, but it was better lit than the stairwell to my apartment.

Three weeks, three more weeks, then I'd close the door on this part of my life and...

A sound, something like a groan, interrupted my pity party.

I stopped, my foot hovering over the dull asphalt and shook my head.

No.

Not just no, but hell no. This was how every cautionary tale began. The hapless heroine walking alone late at night, then making the unfortunate decision to be helpful. Next thing you know, she's shoved into the back of a van and an ugly tranny makes a suit out of her skin.

Screw that.

I slipped my keys between my fingers so they protruded beneath my knuckles. I might go down, but the cops would find some DNA.

The parking lot remained quiet and I unlocked the doors on my Mercedes SUV, the one decent thing I left the marriage with. Every morning when I found the car still in the garage I paid extra for, it was a pleasant surprise.

Just as I pulled the door open, another groan, then a curse in a familiar masculine voice made me stop.

"Dorian?" No answer. I tossed my purse on the seat and whispered again into the darkness, "Is that you?"

"Get the fuck out of here, Ree."

Well damn. I couldn't walk away from a man that already gave me a nickname. Not to mention a thousand bucks for a tough and overcooked steak.

I closed the door and walked between a variety of American vehicles to found him seated on the ground and leaning against a car as masculine and powerful looking as him. I stopped thinking about undressing him and feeling that powerful body pressed against mine, and rushed over. The dark stain on the formerly stark white shirt made me gasp even as I easily slipped back into medical mode.

"What the hell?" I asked as I ran my hands down his torso. This wasn't the way I'd planned to touch him. I had lousy taste in men, but I prided myself on being a damned good nurse. "You need an ambulance." I'm good, but this wasn't the movies where I could fix him with gunpowder and a match.

I slipped my hand into my new jean jacket pocket and remembered I'd left my cellphone in my purse. "Fuck."

"You eat with that mouth?"

"Seriously? I had you pegged for a man that liked dirty talk." I continued examining him, checking his pupils and his pulse, trying to keep my own heart from going crazy.

"Only in bed."

"Where's your phone?" Because we didn't need to be talking about me and him and any furniture we could get horizontal on.

"No. No hospitals." The rest of the sentence hung unsaid. No hospital and no cops.

Figures.

"I'm not going to watch you die."

"My boys are coming, It's cool."

"It's cool?" I squinted. "You have got to be—"

Tires screeched in the distance.

"Fuck, get out of here."

"It's probably your friends." He shook his head and reached up for the car handle. "No, I'm not leaving you here to get shot."

"Unless you plan to join me—"

"Come on, let me get you to my car." I squatted and somehow the both of us got him to his feet.

"No time." He handed me his keys. "I hope like fuck you can drive a stick."

Chapter Three
Dorian

"Don't speed."

"You have got to be kidding me?" Her head whipped in my direction then back to the almost empty streets. "How about, 'Hey Ree, thanks for saving my ass.'"

"I'm surprised you didn't let me bleed out." She hit a pothole, and I grunted. There seemed to be a lot of them. I should know, because it felt like she hit every one of them.

"Sorry."

"No, I'm sorry. About earlier."

"Let's not talk about that. It's done."

We were so not done, not by a long shot. "Thanks, but getting involved was stupid."

"I'm not stupid."

"Sweetheart, I didn't say you were stupid. But what you did tonight? Bad fucking choice." I had two wounds, one on my right side just below my ribs, and another in my shoulder. The latter worried me. I pressed the handkerchief tighter over the wound on my side. I must have made a noise other than the frequent f-bombs, because she turned my way.

"You okay?" I grunted and she made a chuffing sound. "I mean other than the bullet holes."

"Shouldn't you be saying sweet shit to me in my condition?" She made another noise. How the fuck was she so cute while pissed off and terrified? The blood loss must not be life threatening, because damned if my cock wasn't getting hard.

"It might be better if you didn't talk." She looked into the rear-view mirror and cursed.

The cell laying on my lap buzzed and I looked down. Not a good call; it felt like trying to read looking through frosted glass. "Turn left and go to Grant. My boy is almost here." And not a minute too soon. Keeping my eyes open didn't seem to be going too well.

"Dorian?"

"Yeah, beautiful?"

"Don't die on me okay?"

Fuck, I must be worse than I thought. I leaned against the headrest and looked at my cute little waitress. I was pretty sure with all the foul shit I'd done, I'd eventually glimpse a bright light, but the mother fucker wouldn't be white.

Well, at least if I had to go, it wouldn't be in a dark Centerville parking lot. I'd take my one-way ticket to hell with a glimpse at my own personal heaven. *Yeah, I must be dying; I've grown a vagina.*

"I'm trying not to get dead. I got shit to do."

Like you.

I found it kind of funny. She wasn't my usual type. She was a little older and a little more serious than the party girls. Plus, she had more morals than the socialites fucking around on their husbands.

Not that that set too high a bar.

I couldn't feel too bad about it, since those same husbands were fucking someone else. How did I know? Pleasure wasn't the only thing I dealt in. Information paid well. Almost as lucrative as other vices.

But then she happened—Ryann.

To tell the truth, the easy empty sex, the gold diggers—all of it—the shit was getting old. Still loved the work. I lived to make money. Other than fucking, fighting, and football, it was the only thing that ever came easily.

"Dorian?" Her voice came out soft and sweet, better than any narcotic, but it sounded like she'd run out of pissed off.

"The bullets haven't killed me, but your driving might." I chuckled, or rather I tried. My side hurt like a motherfucker, but I'll deal with all of my shit to keep her from being afraid.

Me, the world biggest bastard, giving a shit about someone other than my inner circle. Maybe my next home wouldn't be so hot after all.

"I hope your friends are more appreciative."

"You want me grateful, a blow job might do it." Pissing her off might not be one of my better ideas, but even in the dark, with Lucifer breathing down my neck, the shit made me laugh.

"I doubt you have enough blood left for an erection. Don't speak."

"Why? It's not like I need to save my energy."

"I might have to finish the job if you keep it up."

"Talk to me. That might keep me distracted, since you don't seem interested in—"

She cleared her throat.

"Fine. Why are you waiting tables? That doesn't seem like your gig."

"Want to hear the one about the bears and the blonde chick? That's about all you're going to get."

"Is there sex? I'd be down with that."

"Maybe I should just open the door and push your annoying ass out," she muttered under her breath.

At least that's what I thought she said.

Shit.

We were almost at the intersection, and I hoped we made it that far. Not for me, because I deserved whatever the hell I got, but she deserved none of it. I'd make sure she was taken care of. I couldn't undo all of this shit, but I could make it better—at least for her.

"After we pass the intersection, keep an eye out for a gray Suburban."

"You keep an eye out, I'm busy." She barked the words out like a drill Sargent. "If you die, I'm following you to hell to kick your ass."

"You always so bossy? I hadn't noticed that."

"I'm start to think you didn't notice anything."

I didn't have the fucking energy for this conversation. No way did she think I came there for the food. If she did, she wouldn't have looked at me like I'd drowned her kitten when I said goodbye.

When I slipped from this existence to the next I wouldn't have many regrets. Just two—disappointing my pops and not fucking Ryann.

Yeah, I'm definitely going to hell.

"I'm not one of good guys."

"I know that. I'm not blind—not anymore."

Interesting.

Then everything happened. She went through the light at Grant and Park. Then familiar a gray blur swerved from the opposite side of the solid double yellow lines, followed by the distinct sound of metal kissing and safety glass shattering behind us.

I fucking loved that Suburban.

I loved it even more now that our tail was out of commission.

The phone resting on my thighs buzzed, and my bloodied fingers slid against the glass as I put it on speaker. "Yeah."

"It's me." Antonio's deep rich voice filled the car. He remained one of my oldest friends from the block, and the best car thief I'd met,

"Sweetheart, go ahead and pull over." For the first time tonight she didn't argue.

The door flew open and Antoine's dark face frowned down at me before shit got fuzzier.

"I can't let you go anywhere." He looked across me at Ryann. "Who the hell is she?

"Take care of her." That was all I managed to get out before it went dark.

Chapter Four
Dorian

I must be dead.

If I wasn't, waking up with a soft ass pressed against me, a lot of questions, and no fucking answers wasn't the worst thing.

But who the hell left me bleeding and looking down at dirty asphalt? Despite my reputation, I've managed to keep my shit mostly legal once we earned enough capital to keep the clubs up and running. The rumors of us being mobbed up wouldn't die, but with Carmine's father as the boss of Chicago's largest crime family, that couldn't be helped.

Which is why we went out of our way to keep shit clean as possible, and avoid getting caught when it we couldn't. That's why tonight didn't make any sense. My initial visit to Centerville was for business, but nothing bad enough to get me killed.

I drifted off for a few minutes, or I thought I did, and swam back to consciousness grinding against an ass so perfect I damned near blew my load all over her back.

Wait a minute. I've been shot before, and I sure as hell didn't fuck my way to recovery. Of course, if Doc thought this might help...

My hand rested on a soft, slightly rounded stomach. I liked that. Women made me crazy worrying about every ounce of real or imagined fat. Did they not know all most men wanted was them naked and willing?

I'd rather be with a woman comfortable tossing back a few brews on the balcony as we ate our brats watching the Cubs.

Now, that was sexy.

My bedmate placed her hand over mine, guided it towards the sweet softness between her legs, and pressed my fingers against her clit. Baby girl was about to get a whole lot wetter. I raised her leg, and—

Holy fuck. That shit hurt—definitely not dead. My shoulder screamed. The battle between my cock and my wounds raged full force until she ground her heat against my fingers, and that ass against my raging erection.

My cock won. It convinced my mind and the rest of my abused body that once he got inside, the pain would go away.

Then my brain woke the fuck up.

How did I get here? Driving a stick with my right shoulder this banged up didn't happen. That seemed about as likely as a flying saucer.

First I needed to figure out where the fuck here was. Then I could see about getting laid.

No one could say I didn't have my priorities in order.

It took every muscle in my face to pry my eyes apart, but I managed, and I have to say I was happy as fuck when I did. Dim light illuminated a long graceful brown neck and a simple but familiar room—my room. I pulled my head back and groaned at the sight of the bun resting at the back of her head. If she had any idea how many times I imagined holding that fussy librarian bun while I fucked her face, she wouldn't be lying next to me.

Did she realize whose hand covered her pussy? Whose cock she prepared to ride?

Now, I had Ryann almost where I needed her. Screw the shoulder. Fuck the pain. The soft whimper as my finger grazed her clit hit me in the gut, then blasted lower.

Damn, her wetness soaked me. My finger slid into her tight cunt, and I wondered how long since she'd fucked someone else. I didn't like thinking about that shit. So, for the foreseeable future, she'd not be fucking anyone I didn't see in the mirror.

Too bad for her, I'd just decided that future might last awhile.

I'm a selfish prick, and don't have a problem admitting it. Tonight proved she put me off my game, and I needed her out of my life and my system. The only way I could think to make that happen was to fuck her the hell out of it.

Looked like I'd have a damned good time exorcising her from my mind. How could I not? Especially with her cunt threatening to snap my fingers in half. I needed to taste her. With my shoulder banged up, no way I could lift her and make her ride my mouth so I could fuck her with my tongue, but I'm nothing if not creative.

I slid my fingers out of her tight heat, and my lips curved at her grumpy protest. My little Ryann wanted what she wanted—and now.

"I'll give it to you, baby." I pinched her nipple, then sucked her nectar off my fingers. The sweet taste made my balls draw up so tight, they hurt almost as much as my side.

Almost.

"Ryann baby, I'm going to fuck you." There would be no finesse, no slow teasing seduction; we could do that later. This centered around celebrating the fact that I didn't wake up dead. Didn't wake up on one of the levels of Dante's inferno reflecting on my sins. This was a celebration of life on a level so primal I didn't even have the words. "If you're not interested, you need to move. I already told you I'm not a good man."

Her waking up and screaming rape equaled an instant soft on. The only screaming I want to hear involved my name as she came around my cock.

I'd pushed through pain before, and more than likely would again. However, I couldn't wait to push through—or should I say into—her.

I shifted more of my weight onto my side, hissing at the burn. Then I groaned again when the head of my cock nudged against her damp opening. I wasn't a small man, and causing her discomfort didn't appeal to me, but if I didn't get inside her soon I'd have another injury.

I wondered if blue balls could ever be fatal. My fingers gripped the hips I'd imagined holding and slowly invaded her body. Sweat dampened my temples and rolled into my eyes as I struggled to keep from hurting her. I wanted to drive my cock in so deep and so fast that she'd feel that shit in the back of her throat.

But this was one woman I'd try not to harm.

Too bad I already knew I'd fail.

Chapter Five

Ryann

When the hell did my vibrator get so big—and warm?

Or start working on its own?

My eyes snapped open, but not before calloused fingers flicked across my clit with the perfect amount of pressure.

"You finally with me?" Dorian's smoky voice rumbled against my ear as he sank his delicious cock a little deeper and stilled.

"What the hell are you doing?" My mind and that Baptist preacher's kid upbringing suggested I should be offended. Too bad my body was having none of that nonsense.

"Either it's been longer than I thought for you, or I'm doing something wrong." He moved his lips and closed his teeth on the back of my neck, chuckling at my responding shiver.

Oh, he did nothing wrong—nothing at all. I widened my legs, allowing him access, because I really didn't want him to re-injure himself.

Yeah right.

I squeaked and he pushed the rest of his cock inside me. At least I hoped that was all. If not, I was in trouble.

"You could hurt yourself. What the hell were you thinking?" I tried to use a voice as commanding and full of the wrath of God as the one my father used from the pulpit, but he chose that moment to move, and my eyes may have rolled back in my head for a minute or seven.

"I was thinking you were naked and in my bed."

I didn't want to even think about why I wore only his T-shirt, but the memories shoved the pleasure aside. The image of arterial blood soaking my white shirt and turning my plain white panties red filled me as surely as his cock.

I never wanted to see anyone hurt, especially him. Why I gave a damned about this criminally sexy man with the pale, not quite handsome face and expensive shoes was beyond me, but I couldn't stop it.

Nor could I stem the pleasure rolling through my body. He'd been correct on both accounts. It had been a while, and let's just say that old wives' tale about brother's—not true.

Ask my husband—ex-husband.

"You could always ride my cock if you're concerned." He thrust completely inside me again, and I couldn't think of a reason to decline his offer.

I tried to straddle him and almost dislocated my shoulder. "Ouch."

"Did I hurt you? Shit, Sorry." He stopped and tried to pull away, but I reached behind me and dug my short fingernails in his perfect ass. I've waited too long for this. No way in hell would he be taking that cock away from me.

"You have a handcuff key?"

"You into that?" he asked.

I looked over my shoulder in time to catch a smile somewhere between hopeful and wicked, and completely adorable.

"Because I have—"

"No jackass," I interrupted. Did I mention him being adorable ticked me off? "Because, I don't know, those troglodyte friends of yours handcuffed me to the bed."

"Why the fuck would they do that?" He frowned, but thank goodness he didn't try to take that cock anywhere. If he did, I might have to hurt him. Okay, not really, but it sounded good.

"Seriously? Are you telling me you don't recall telling them to take care of me?"

"I was busy bleeding to death."

This irritating and sexy man would be the death of me, in more ways than one. "Are we going to have this conversation now, or are you going to finish what you started?" He grinned again and I damned near came when he bit down on his lower lip. Why did this dangerous man have to be so fucking hot?

One dark-blond eyebrow rose in challenge—one I readily accepted. If I hadn't been so horny after my drought, I'd have found the do-you-think-you-can-handle-this-dick glare amusing. But I was a woman on a mission, and that mission centered on an orgasm—with him.

Dorian had bossy written all over his handsome face, and I didn't want any of it. Luckily they left some slack in the chain, so I reluctantly slid off of him, rotating my body as I threw my leg over his hip. I wrapped my fingers around his...holy guacamole. He put my battery operated boyfriend—B.O.B.—to shame. Maybe I need to handcuff Dorian to my bed instead.

"Babe, in case you didn't notice—"

"Shut up." I put the head of his cock at my entrance and eased down. In the books I read, they always slam themselves down on the guy. Obviously, they'd never met Dorian.

He might have been saying something, but I couldn't hear past the thudding heartbeat in my ears, or feel anything except how completely he filled me. Being a good girl appeared way over rated. I needed practice being bad.

And at the top of my Ryann-is-now-a-bad-bitch list was accepting my reward for his rescue—an orgasm.

"Fuck." He dug his fingers into my hips, and I realized two things. First, the lights were still on, and secondly he'd removed the sling I put on his arm. I didn't need complete darkness to have sex, or I didn't use to, until the husband-that-won't-be-named kept calling me fat.

And I believed him.

"Tell me I don't have to get shot for us to do this again," he said, thrusting his hips upward.

"You keep doing that and I'll tell you anything you want." Did I just say that out loud? I must have, because his chuckle sounded way too pleased. But I didn't have time to give him shit, because his finger found my clit again, and I forgot everything but pleasure.

"Good." I think that's what he said, because he chose that moment to pinch my clit.

I exploded.

This wasn't my first time at the rodeo, but if the ride was always like this, it sure as hell wouldn't be my last. My lashes fluttered as every muscle in my body pulsated along with my pussy.

I hoped they kept an AED in this joint, because my heart couldn't take much more.

"Eyes." His large hand connected with my ass, and I liked it.

A lot.

"I want you to know whose cock you're coming on."

"Oh, I know," I said, but I gave him what he wanted—barely. I watched him as the seemingly never-ending orgasm wracked my body.

That mouth. His filthy, sexy mouth needed exploring, but my fascination with the pulsating muscles on the side of his face as he clenched his jaws together held me as captive as his rather impressive attributes.

He thrust up into me again and his head arched as he emitted an animalistic howl. This man screamed porn material—and dangerous in ways far worse than bullets.

The sound of crashing wood made me jerk, but Dorian didn't give a shit, he didn't seem interested in letting me go.

"Holy crap. I got a boo-boo that needs fixing," an amused male voice said behind me.

Chapter Six
Dorian

"Somebody want to tell me why you handcuffed her to the bed?"

We sat in the living room of a farmhouse I bought for my pop. Yet another gift I purchased for him that he wanted no part of. Just like he wanted no part of me.

It didn't appear to be anything fancy, but it felt nice and homey—the opposite of my place on Lake Michigan. That was a showplace, this was a home. Comfortable oversized chairs and antiques, or shit that looked like antiques, filled the house. I couldn't bring myself to get rid of it, mainly because I'd hoped he'd change his mind.

He hadn't.

"What the fuck are you complaining about? She didn't seem to mind captivity a couple of minutes ago." Paul, a friend from the old neighborhood, shrugged and stretched the tree trunks he called legs out in front of him, resting his interlaced fingers across his stomach. "Plus, until I knew whether or not she'd put those holes in you, she wasn't going anywhere."

I wanted to knock that damned smirk off his mug. Hiring friends—something I'd have to reconsider in the future.

Who was I kidding? I had enough trust issues to pass around, and I'd trust the two men in this room with my life—and I had, more than once.

Having a woman handcuffed to my bed wasn't the problem. I wanted to be the one that put her there. Unfortunately, she'd been freed. Now she stood wet and naked in my shower—alone. I should be fucking her, watching her come around my cock to make sure the first time wasn't a fluke.

Paul kept the status of "muscle" for a reason.

"If she shot me, why would she drive me around?"

"Why do women do anything?" Antoine walked over with a glass of water and a couple of pills.

"Thanks." I tossed the pills back and said a silent thanks to the stubborn and sexy Ryann. My cock came back to life thinking about her tight, greedy cunt. If she'd been with anyone recently, not only did the poor sap have a pencil dick, he lacked a smarts to know you don't let a woman like Ryann escape.

"Don't have to ask what you're thinking about." Paul grabbed his cock. "If you're done—"

The fucker's words died in his throat.

The blue steel Colt .45 I clutched in my left hand probably had something to do with it. "What were you saying?"

"Damn, it's like that?"

"I would be dead if not for her." I didn't understand this thing with Ryann, but I knew no one spoke to or about her like that.

"Sorry, boss. Never saw you give a shit." He raised his hands in surrender, relaxing when I lowered the gun.

The pain pills started kicking in, but before I crawled back into bed I needed to tell them what went down. It wasn't much, but I gave them everything I had up until they found me and I passed the fuck out.

Not my proudest moment.

"She drug your big ass in the car?" Antione sat on the opposite end of the beige couch throwing his arm along the back.

"Yup. I tried to get her to leave, but she wasn't having it." I rubbed my thumb across the bandage on my shoulder. I must have really been out of it. "So, Doc Roager said everything seemed good?"

Antoine and Paul looked at each other before Antoine spoke. "He's coming this morning. We grabbed the woman and the Charger and brought the two of you back here."

I looked down at the neat row of stitches in my side and thought about last night. The memory of her yelling at me, and handing me a tampon. Me telling her I'd been shot, not started my period, and her begging me to stay awake and alive. Shit got fuzzy after that.

"Her nursing wasn't the only skill that came in handy," Paul said.

"If I didn't want to be cleaning carpets, I'd shoot your ass." I found myself grinning at the big guy, but that didn't mean I wanted him to ever see her bare ass again.

Looking back, she did manage to remain calm. The assholes with the guns freaked her out, but not the blood. What the hell was she doing working as a waitress?

"Doesn't matter." Antoine leaned forward, placing his forearms on his thighs. "Looks like she forgave the handcuffs and the...whole kidnapping thing."

"Don't make me ask." Not that I could do anything but shoot them, and they knew that wouldn't happen. Not for this.

"We had no idea how she was involved, and you were pretty bad off..."

"Can you hurry it up before I die of old fucking age?"

"We told her if you die, she dies." Antoine said the words as if he was ordering a pizza with extra sauce.

"Have I told you lately that the two of you are morons?"

"Yesterday." Paul grinned. "But I wouldn't worry about it. Last time I saw her, she didn't exactly look scared."

I knew my boys. They could be brutal and deadly, but they'd never harm a woman unless she had it coming. And Ryann absolutely didn't.

"Whatever. You're making my brain hurt." And I wasn't bullshitting. Not only was the room getting foggy, it was getting harder to form a full sentence. "Look, I need you to go to the restaurant and get her car, and grab some stuff from her apartment. She's going with us."

I looked over to table to grab a pen and scribbled her address.

"What time is Doc coming?" I stood, swiping my hand down my face. I didn't have time for this shit. I needed to get back to Chicago. Looked like now I'd do it with company.

Antoine looked down at his watch. "He should be here within the hour." He turned to Paul. "You want to babysit? Make sure she doesn't fuck him to death or go get the car?"

"I'd rather stay here. Maybe Dorian will let me see him get another treatment."

"Asshole." We've been friends for thirty years, so it wasn't like he was afraid of me or some shit. But he also knew if he fucked me over I'd put a bullet in his skull.

I'd feel bad about it afterward, but he'd be dead just the same. "I take it you called the boys?"

"Yeah. They know what's going on. At least knew what I did fifteen minutes ago." Paul clapped his hands together and stood. "We leaving if the doctor gives the all clear?"

"We're leaving, no matter what he says. If someone wants me dead, I'm not making it easy." I gave Antoine a chin left and turned towards the stairs, wondering if I'd make it.

I did.

Only when I paused at the top, sweating and gripping the white banister so hard it surprised me the wood didn't snap, did I hear the front door close. I stumbled to the master bedroom, remembering why I never did drugs. How the fuck did people function like this? I stepped inside to find Ryann staring at me. Damn she looked good wet, covered by only towel.

Keeping her naked once we reach Chicago sounds like a good idea right about now.

Back in the day, maybe when I was ten, I wanted to grow up and be a good man. By the time I was fifteen watching my father always doing the right thing, yet staying on the fast track to nowhere, I decided—no fucking thanks.

Now, standing here looking at my personal Florence Nightingale, I don't regret any of the foul shit I've done to get here. I didn't have a crystal ball, but I was pretty sure we wouldn't have met otherwise. I would have stayed in my own little circles with my boys and wouldn't have looked twice at a woman like her.

The woman was too good for the likes of me now, and sure as shit would have been if my life had stayed on that path. Hell, I'd probably be in prison by now.

"Are you planning to stand there and watch?"

"Don't mind if I do." I widened my stance, because I was too stubborn to sit down. Whatever the hell Antoine gave me threatened to knock me the fuck out.

She grabbed my arm and led me to the bed.

"You trying to take advantage of me again?"

"You're an ass."

Two feet from her intended destination, I flipped the script and stopped moving. I appreciated she wanted to care for me, but time for Ryann to learn—my game—my rules.

"You shouldn't be up."

"You care?" I couldn't help myself; I cupped the side of her neck, and trailed my finger across her soft skin.

"Like I have a choice." She was heated, and I couldn't tell if it stemmed from anger or my touch.

Did I give a fuck?

Not even.

"What the hell are you talking about?" One tug, and that damned towel would be history. Then, before she changed her mind or I grew a conscience, she'd be riding my cock.

Or my tongue.

Or my tongue then my cock.

She snorted, interrupting the image of her on her back, legs tossed over my shoulders, and begging for more.

"Are you telling me they lied?"

No.

"I can't tell you shit if I don't know what the hell you're talking about." The look she gave me almost made me laugh, and that caught my attention almost as much as the fat drop of water rolling down the side of her neck, pausing in the hollow created by her collar bone.

How long had it been since I'd truly laughed with a woman?

"Whatever." She tried to move, and I tightened my grip on her neck. Not enough to hurt, but enough to let her know she wasn't going anywhere until I gave her permission to. "Let me go."

"I don't think I can do that." Her eyes widened and if I wasn't staring into the most incredible brown eyes I'd ever seen, I would have missed it. "You scared of me?"

"No."

Thank fuck.

"You should be."

Her pulse thrummed beneath my fingers like a butterfly struggling to escape its cocoon. "Are you going to hurt me?" Her voice shook, but her lids were partially open and her body leaned closer as she waited for her answer.

"Probably." *But not in the way you think.*

"Well, I'm out of fucks to give, but if you plan to kill me I'd prefer to not do it naked."

I had plans for that sassy mouth. Shutting it permanently wasn't one of them, but she didn't need to know that.

Chapter Seven
Ryann

I thought my man-picker was damaged—no, that thing was broken, busted, kaput.

How else do I explain going from a neurosurgeon's wife and scrub nurse with plans to become a physician's assistant, to waitress? That was bad enough, especially since I did it to help pay my way through college, and swore never to repeat that particular experience.

Of course, being the overachiever that I am, I had to aim even lower. Now I found myself a hostage of some kind of oversexed criminal.

Although, my hostage status remained pending, considering I seemed a more than willing participant in a certain part of my captivity. Just the feel of his hand on my skin made me want to push him on the bed and do wicked things to his beautiful scarred body.

God, I am a horrible person.

He was drugged up and I had sex with him.

No, I rode him like a wild pony, and I hate to say it, but I would do it again. What did that say about me?

That I'm a desperate whack job that would have sex with a man that planned to kill me.

Talk about going out with a bang. Then to make matters even worse, I wanted a repeat performance.

Soon.

With multiple encores.

You know, just for science sake. No way in hell could he have been that good. Maybe they drugged me or something. Except I hadn't eaten or drank anything since I arrived.

I sucked on my lip, because him standing this close made my mouth dry and other parts of me wet—very wet.

Of course he noticed. He noticed every damned thing.

"I need you to lose the towel."

"And need you to kiss my ass." *And while you're down there...*

"Let me get this straight. You think I'm going to hurt you, and you're talk shit?" His dark eyes looked...amused. Asshole

"Well, if I'm going to meet my maker, it'll be on my feet." *If I'm going to be on my knees, it's going to be for a good cause.*

"Oh." He let go of my neck, but he didn't release me. No, he shifted his hold lower. Rested his hands on my hips and pulled me closer. "I could definitely make you beg."

If he didn't stop touching me, I might start begging sooner than he thought.

I looked up into his not quite traditionally handsome face, trying to discern what about him flipped every switch I had. I'd been married to a pretty boy. He represented everything women were taught to look for in a man—successful, tall, handsome, rich, and smart. Unfortunately, he was rotten to the core.

At least Dorian was upfront with his character flaws. Unless I read him wrong—which remained a possibility—he wanted me dead as much as I wanted to experience the condition. Maybe we could come up with a solution that worked for both of us. Preferably, something involving multiple orgasms.

A soft knock and the door opening stopped me from making a fool of myself.

The tall dark-skinned guy, the one that threatened me, poked his head in. "Doc is here."

He turned his gaze towards me and I wanted to find the nearest weapon and knock that smirk off his face.

"Oh, if you want to get dressed—" he sat my neatly folded clothes on the pine dresser "—your stuff is cleaned."

"Wow, full-service kidnapping. I'm impressed."

"I'll be out in a minute." Dorian pressed his body against mine, and I wondered if anything came between him and his soft slacks. "Sweetheart, get dressed. I'd hate to have to kill the doctor for seeing you naked."

"I'm sure he seen plenty of naked women. You didn't poke your friend's eyes out."

"Almost did." Then he lowered his mouth to mine like he'd been doing it every morning for the last twenty years, kissing me long and hard. That didn't taste like the kiss of a man about to kill a woman, but then again, what the hell did I know? And as good as Dorian's kiss felt—and it curled my toes—I couldn't trust or depend on a man. Any man.

When his lips finally pulled away from mine, I immediately felt bereft, empty, ravenous for more of him. That kiss…the word felt so insignificant for what just happened. He claimed me.

A nakedness that had nothing to do with clothes, and everything to do with the ferocity of his gaze. Those dark eyes peered into my very soul, examining every secret, caressing each flaw. I struggled to escape the quicksand of his gaze.

"Don't keep the man waiting. Time is money." Not the most artful deflection, but beggars couldn't be choosers.

"It's my time and my fucking money."

"Do you have to talk like that?"

He gave me another where-is-her-medication look and shook his head. Sliding his hands along the back of my thighs and raising the towel to cup my ass, Dorian reasserted my body existed for his pleasure.

"You need to learn to fear me."

"Is that what you want?"

"This—" he gave my ass a squeeze—"is what I need."

"The only thing you need right now is someone to attend those wounds."

He kissed me again, this time slow and sweet. So sweet I forgot the towel, the shooting, and even the kidnapping, and melted into him.

I managed to breathe and my sensitive nipples brushed against his warm chest. Dorian the inferno would consume me if I remained too close.

My mama didn't raise no fools.

This kiss would be our last.

He released me, but I had a feeling I'd never escape this man. How pathetic. After a month of waiting, watching, and dreaming, and one bout of incredible sex, I knew I'd never forget him.

Leaving would be easy. Erasing his touch, his taste, and the fire that heated my blood? Not so much.

I watched his scarred muscular back as he walked out of the room. If every scar told a story, his panther-like body revealed a veritable library. The library of which I would never read another tome.

And despite what he might think, it wasn't because I fear of him—I should—but because I had wounds of my own. When Dorian walked away I didn't want to be part of the wreckage left in his wake.

I needed to leave.

I scrambled into my clothes, and tore the room apart searching for my purse. What the hell did they do with—

"Oh my God. The parking lot." If it wasn't for bad luck, I'd have not at all.

My breaths came so fast; it took all my control not to pass out. I plopped down on the bed, wrapping my arms around my waist and leaned over, pressing my forearms against my thighs.

There are moments in life where we have to make a choice that will forever impact our future. Or, we could just allow life to make those choices for us.

Saving Dorian was the morally correct decision, so why did it feel like a mistake?

Screw it. I sucked in a breath and headed for the window. *All clear.*

Big girl panty time. I slid my feet into my sensible black work flats, and groaned thinking about the pain by the time I reached downtown.

Didn't matter, I'd be free. Free of Dorian and his goons, and free to create the life I chose, not the one I stumbled into.

I peeked through the curtain again and saw Dorian's Dodge Charger and a dark sedan that I didn't recognize.

Good sign.

My hands shook as I unlocked the window. "Please, please, please," I chanted as I raised the double-paned window.

"Crap." Looked like I'd have to Spiderman my way out of here. Okay so the guy in the red and black cat suit wouldn't have ripped his clothing and flesh on the roses covering the bottom of the trellis, but hey, we don't all have webs to shoot out of her hands.

When my feet finally reached the ground, I never thought I would be so damned happy. I brushed the leaves and bits of dirt off the front of my clean, but not quite pristine, white shirt, and took a cautious step away from the house and man holding my libido hostage.

"Going somewhere?"

Chapter Eight
Dorian

Watching Ryann's escape attempt from my laptop was funny as hell. What I didn't find amusing was watching her shimmy down the trellis to do it. I swear to fuck if I wasn't afraid to pop my damned stitches, I'd spank her ass. Of course the fact that the doctor praised her work may have spared her too.

Learning that both her car and home were trashed leeched the last bit of humor out of me. Looked like the shooters weren't as dumb as I thought—then again, they never are. Not when you need them to be.

Watching the anger and sorrow in her eyes when she saw the pictures of how the assholes violated her life made me want to kill. They'd already punched their card when they shot me, but doing this shit to an innocent woman?

Not cool.

And the way she looked at me, sitting in my penthouse, on my couch, made me want to fuck the sadness out of her eyes.

"Just let me leave. I'd planned on leaving the Midwest anyway, and after dealing with you for two days, I'm pretty much done."

"Do you have a fake identity I don't know about? Another social security card? Because that's what you're going to need."

She leaned back on the couch and pressed the heels of her hands against her eyes. I could get her those things by tomorrow. Help her start a new life—away from me and whatever the hell else she went to Wisconsin to escape.

Because she sure as hell was running.

I could do all that and more, but I wouldn't. Why? Because I'm a prick. And I wanted her—simple as that. Most women, I'd fuck them a few times, then one of us needed to bounce—preferably me.

I didn't bring them to my apartment. Nope, made that mistake once, and that was more than enough. Talk about level four clinger. The corporation owned the buildings that housed our businesses—kept shit simple and under our control. So I had an apartment above Club Surrender when I needed to satisfy certain urges.

Club Surrender was my baby. For most of the week, and to the majority of Chicago, Club Surrender represented one of the hottest spots to pack your personal baggage and check it—if only for a few hours. I ensured that from the moment a patron walked through my doors, all of their senses were assaulted. Acrobats performed high about the throngs, spinning and contorting, their hands and bodies the only thing preventing them from cascading to earth. I also employed go-go dancers, both male and female, who teased and tantalized to music spun by guest DJ's.

As profitable the dance side of the house was, the members only dungeon remained a source of not only revenue, but information.

"Are you listening?"

"You saying something I want to hear?" And that would be a no.

"What the hell would it take for you to let me out of here?"

"Language, Ryann." I didn't yell. I didn't raise my voice. But my tone informed her the time for games had passed.

I rubbed my hand over my buzz cut, watching the quickening pulse in her graceful neck. Hell, I could hear her small pants and imagine feeling the heat of her breath against my neck from across the room. "No games. You leave and they catch you, what do think will happen?"

"Can't be any worse than now."

"You're shitting me." I cursed under my breath.

In the short amount of time it took me to cross the room, she'd lost the fear. Good. That's what I wanted—needed, a fighter. Not all the time, but a woman that would put up with my shit in the bedroom or wherever I decide to fuck her, but my equal everywhere else.

I extended a hand and decided to burn that polyester the minute she fell asleep. "What?" She looked at me warily and sucked on her bottom lip. If she wanted something to suck on, I'd give it to her. I'd give her the fucking world.

"You trust me?"

"No."

Smart woman. "I do anything but give you the best orgasm of your life?"

"Conceited much?" She rolled her eyes, still being cute, but I didn't let her off the hook. I nudged her leg with my knee and bent over, trapping her with my hands on the back of the couch.

"What were you saying?"

Her soft lips parted, and all I could think about was how they'd feel wrapped around my cock. Yeah, I had a list of things little Ryann would experience before I sent her on her way. And she would leave.

My curiosity had an expiration date. Hers just happened to be longer than one night. I'd keep her a week, two tops. By then I should have fucked her out of my system.

"I need to take care of a couple of things, then you are going to cover these stitches, and we're taking a shower." I'd been so wrapped up in her, I'd neglected to call Sterling and Carmine. The last thing I needed was them banging on my door.

"I don't need another shower."

"After your efforts to ensure I didn't bleed to death, the last thing I'd want is to slip and crack my head open."

"That's the last thing I'd worry about," she mumbled.

I slipped my fingers into her hair and tugged her head back. "We're going to work on that attitude of yours."

"The life I had wasn't much, but I need to get back to it."

"You're mine until I say we're done, and we won't be done until I get the shit sorted with the dicks who broke into your place. Got it?"

She nodded.

"Not good enough." I ran my nose against the side of hers, and just the small puff of her warm breath against my cheek made me want to strip her and bury myself inside of her right here, right now. "I need the words." I gave her lip a quick bite followed by a gentle kiss. "Give them to me."

"Got it."

"Now be a good girl and go up to my room. I'll take care of my shit, then I'll join you. After? We'll talk." If she had any idea the last time I explained myself, she'd realize what a gift she'd just received.

But she didn't need to know. All she needed to do was obey, and I'd take care of the rest.

Why did I get the feeling that wasn't going to happen? And why did I like it so much?

Chapter Nine
Ryann

I walked into a bedroom larger than the one in my former Gold Coast home. And I hated to say, it was so amazing I think I had a mini orgasm. This suited my taste much more than the elegant but stuffy decor of my old house. The lines were modern, clean, and masculine—just like Dorian.

No way did an ordinary thug live someplace like this. I expected the typical man cave dwelling, not drug lord chic.

Two stories of windows overlooking Lake Michigan and a five thousand square foot penthouse purchased with dirty money—and it meant nothing. This may not be Guantanamo Bay, but a cage remained a cage, no matter how inviting.

If I were going to escape, this had to be the day. Because the odds of me overpowering him even injured sucked.

I invaded every personal nook and cranny for a weapon, a gun, hell anything to help. He didn't even have the decency to have a landline installed so I could call the cops.

I jerked a door open and discovered a closet that gave me a serious case of shoe envy.

OCD much?

Nah, not him.

Every piece of clothing was arranged by type and color. How many dark suits did one-man need? Each of his shirts, sweatpants, and basketball shorts in the center cabinets were folded and arranged by color, every corner at ninety degrees, and centered in each little cubby.

The precision escalated the desire to rearrange things so he couldn't find them.

I did, however, take a particular glee in disrupting his meticulous suits searching for the weapon to deliver his destruction.

Nothing.

Next stop—the bathroom. Crap. I had to ignore the marble and glass bathroom porn. Another thing to hate him for.

I searched it all.

Not even a Tylenol.

What kind of drug dealer was he?

That left violence as my only choice. My entire body rebelled at the thought of harming him. My stomach bubbling imagining adding another scar.

I stood in the middle of his bedroom looking for a weapon. A glass statue that reminded me of an abstract flame sat on the shelf nearest the window glittering as it caught the early afternoon light.

How could I do this?

"The same way he took me hostage," I said to the empty room.

I grabbed the statue, noticing the engraving on the base it was…it was…an award? *And the award for best garroting in a public space goes to…*

I shook my head. Maybe I do need meds.

Judging the weight, I decided it was heavy, almost too heavy, but I ran out of time. My body tensed at the steady thump of approaching footsteps. It was now or never.

Do or get done.

I scurried to the door, my palms so sweaty I almost dropped my weapon. Which side should I be on? I was a horrible criminal. Good thing I chose nursing.

I pressed my back against the wall, clutching the sturdy statue to my chest, closing my eyes.

No. Open your eyes, dumbass.

Maybe I should take Assault 101 as an elective.

He stepped into the room, his head moving back and forth, and I took a step forward raising my hands.

"I'm so sorry." I wasn't sure if I used my outside voice, but I closed my eyes and aimed two pounds of perfectly carved glass at his skull—and got nowhere except spun and pressed against the wall with his supersized hands circling my wrists.

"Get off me." I said, or tried to say, which proved difficult with my cheek pressed against the off-white wall. I struggled. Another of my bad ideas, because a certain part of him really liked that the friction. Jesus, did this man ever not have an erection?

"Babe, let me give you a tip. If you going to beat the shit out of someone, don't apologize first. "

I resumed my struggle for freedom, and the only thing that got me was his body pressed tighter against mine. "You might want to stop moving like that. Having a hard time not fucking you as it is."

"You just need to let me go."

He tugged at the statue, but no way in fuck did I intend on releasing it. "I thought you understood."

"No. The only thing I understand is that you're making me stay, and I don't want to." I've had it one too many men tell me what I needed to do with my life, and sex God or not, I was not staying in here with him.

"Oh, you think I'm a sex God?"

"What?"

He chuckled against my ear. How the hell did I go from pissed off to turned on with just a whisper of his breath against my skin? Then I thought of something else. What if he... What if he hurt me, like I attempted to hurt him? My body trembled, and this time it had nothing to do with sex.

No. I refused to be a victim to any other man. I struggled again, and he must've had enough of my shit, because he pressed his thumb against my wrist and pain shot down my fingers right before they sprung open.

"Ow." Yes, I would be definitely looking for an assassin class, and I was going to come back and beat his ass.

If I got out of this alive.

"You do realize it's useless to fight me, right?"

"Would you give up? Would you just let somebody do whatever the hell they wanted to you?"

"If it was you?" His tongue grazed the shell of my ear before he whispered. "Hell yeah."

"Well, I'm not you." At this point I didn't know why I continued tussling, especially when it seemed the more I fought, the more excited he got.

What kind of pervert was he?

What kind of pervert was I? Because dammit, I found myself exceptionally aroused. He kept his muscular body pressed against my back trapping me, exciting me.

"I'm tired, and I hurt. I want to take a shower, I want to eat, and I want to go to bed. Oh, and I want to slide into your warmth again. It doesn't have to be in that order, but I'm giving you a choice. In case you can't tell—" he moved his cock back and forth against my back "—I fucking like it when you struggle."

"You're sick."

He reached around me and cupped my breast. "So, are you going to take a shower with me now, or am I going to have to check off some of things I'd planned to do to you and with you? Your choice. Honestly, I'm hoping you want to go straight to the naughty list."

God, I was an idiot, because I thought, *I also had a list*. But that's not what came out of my mouth.

"I'd like to take a shower." *Then I'd like to make like Santa and check that list twice.*

"Good girl."

Chapter Ten

Dorian

Goddamn, this chick was hot.

"Here." I handed her a bar of soap.

"What the hell you expect me to do with that?"

I didn't even bother to respond—just waited.

"Asshole." She mumbled, but she knew I heard that shit. I allowed it for now.

I get it. She's in an unfamiliar place and not by her choosing. But she needed to come to terms with her circumstances—she's mine.

At least for little while.

She grabbed the loofah from the shelf, soaped it up, and ran it across my chest.

I grew fascinated by the soap trailing down arms the rich dark color of burnt umber. I recalled having her pressed between the door and my body and my cock thickened. I wanted to slide the knife out of my pocket and slice the clothes from her body and fuck her against my bedroom windows.

I loved watching her go through my shit planning her grand escape.

At least she felt bad about the concussion she planned to give me.

Now, here she stood wet, naked, and nipples erect and begging for my mouth.

"Use your hands."

She rolled her eyes, but she obeyed. Oh, I had all kinds of games I wanted to play with this woman. But I needed to ease her into them.

I grabbed the bar of special made soap—lemon verbena. Yeah, I'm kind of a pussy when it comes to the way shit smells. Sue me. But right now, I was happy that when she left this shower, she'd smell like me.

Before this day was over, not only would she be bathed in my scent, but she'd also be filled with my seed.

Starting at her neck, I massaged and caressed my way down her body to her heavy breasts. I'd seen my share tits. Small, large, fake, real, you name it. But the ones in my hands right now might be my favorite pair ever. Because they're hers.

I covered them with soap, flicking my thumbs across her nipples, then gave them a quick pinched. She gasped and her short fingernails dug into my sides.

"Like that?"

She shook her head.

Liar.

"Words. I need to hear from your lips what works for you." Not that I needed it. She was so responsive to my touch I could watch her pupils dilate. I felt her quickening breath against my wet skin. And even beneath the gentle scent of my soap, her arousal became the headiest perfume.

"No. I don't like it."

"If I glided my fingers into that tight hot cunt it wouldn't be wet?"

She glanced at the tile, as if the answer lay somewhere near the soap dish. Sweet Ryann had no idea she stood naked before the master of games, and I played to win. But I liked this shit. I loved the fact that she didn't fear me. I had too many people in my life kissing my ass. This chick, she didn't know shit about me and desired me anyway.

"Of course it's going to be wet. I'm in the damn shower." Her sass made my cock harder.

"Maybe I need to check and see." She moved to close her legs. "I don't think so." Even though she knew where my hands were headed, I took my time sliding my rough palms down her smooth, soft skin, then cupping her pussy.

I slid my finger over her clit, heading for my target. Her body tensed as if to move closer but I shook my head. I wanted her to watch me finger fuck her, and I needed to see her reaction to it. More than that, I wanted her to see my reaction to her.

Her chest rose and fell so fast, I thought she would pass out. But she didn't have to worry, because I would never let her get hurt. Not on my watch.

Even if she somehow managed to get away from me, I would hunt her ass down and bring her back. She was my responsibility; I would keep her safe.

She was mine.

We both groaned as my fingers slipped inside of her tight, hot cunt. Shit, I needed her—now.

My girl made a noise somewhere between a whimper and a growl, and arched her back as she widened her legs, giving me full access. Everything about this moment, touching her, and even more her acceptance of the pleasure I offered, exceeded every fantasy in which she starred. I withdrew my fingers and her short nails scored my bicep as she clung to me. The bite of pain helped me maintain control, keeping me in the present.

I licked her juices from one of my fingers, and the bouquet rivaled that of my favorite Rothschild's Bordeaux. This woman embodied one fountain I could sup from for eternity.

"Damn baby, if you had any idea..." I trailed a finger across her lower lip for a heartbeat before she opened her mouth and captured it, swirling her tongue around it until I went cross-eyed.

Reluctantly, I pulled my finger from her mouth. I wanted to watch her come again. That was one of the most beautiful things that I'd ever seen. A man could resist food, water, and a few other things if his soul was sufficiently fed with the pleasure of the right partner.

"Babe, if you don't want me fucking you this second—"

"Maybe that's the plan."

"Doesn't work that way. Open your legs."

She smirked, but she obeyed.

Yeah, we were going to have a good time. Before she left, she'd earn the privilege of seeing to my every need and trusting me to give her the pleasure or punishment she deserved. I reclaimed her cunt, preparing her for me as I pressed the heel of my hand against her clit.

Jesus, this woman was beautiful, and it wasn't just her looks, but the need—for me—shining through her eyes. When she looked at me I saw a kindred soul. She threw her head back as her pussy grew wetter as I plunged in and out, faster and harder, impatient to replace it with my cock. Her nipples must fucking hurt they look so hard, so lonely, so ready for my touch. I lowered my head and covered one of them with my mouth as I continued to finger fuck her.

"Dorian," she moaned. I curled my fingers inside of her as I withdrew, and her knees buckled.

Bingo.

"Yeah, baby, give it to me. Give me the orgasm."

"Please..."

"Oh, I plan to please you alright. First, you're going to come all over my fingers. Then, you're going to ride my tongue. After that I hope you're ready for my cock, because I'm planning to give it to you. I'm going to give you so much, for so long, you're going to wonder how you did without it."

I slipped my arm around her waist, and she surrendered her weight to me. Her mouth opened with a silent scream, and if I thought she came hard around my cock, this shit was about to break my fingers.

Before her orgasm became a memory, I rinsed her off, and had her ass against the wall. I lowered myself to my knees, placing one of her legs over my shoulder, and worshipped at the altar of Ryann.

"I can't take—" She tugged at my hair.

"You can, and you will." I didn't allow another argument, and returned my mouth to her engorged clit.

Fuck, she was so wet, and I swore to God if I touched myself, my cock would go off like a rocket. I wanted to come on her and in her. I wanted to fill her to the point that I would be in her DNA. Because God damn it, she already fused herself in mine.

It didn't take me long to get her ramped back up. Her lips kept saying that she wanted to leave, but her body told an entirely different story.

A story I liked.

Her tight sheath clenched around my fingers. I liked this. No way in hell this woman was walking out of my life. Not today, not tomorrow, not next month.

Shit.

I kissed the swell of her stomach and gave it a quick bite. I was going to have to keep this woman.

Chapter Eleven
Ryann

I don't have to worry about him killing me with bullets.

Dorian's diabolically planned to put my ass into some kind of sexual coma.

"I can't feel my legs."

He stood, looking at too cocky. Well, two could play that sexy game. "Baby, were just getting started. Think of what you would've missed if you would've knocked me out and left me lying on the floor."

"About that—"

He shook his head. "It's done."

He leaned closer and pressed his mouth to mine, swiping his tongue across my lower lip. Of course, I opened my mouth. I wanted all of him. Then he kissed me again, consuming me, making me forget every reason I shouldn't be here, and destroying every argument.

I couldn't believe it. After two mind-blowing orgasms, I needed him again.

I didn't understand his motives, and I sure as hell didn't understand my body's response to him. Dorian, my kidnapping bad boy—my drug of choice. Like crack; one hit and you were hooked, spending the rest of your life chasing that high.

Until I figured out how to get away from him, I sure needed to take advantage of every inch of that beautiful cock before I joined a Dorian twelve step program.

He brushed my wet hair out of my face. "Let's get out of here get some food."

He stepped back, and immediately I missed the feel of his corded muscles. I didn't let him go far. I wrapped my fingers around his cock, trailing my thumb across the swollen head.

"What happened to all that smack you were talking about me riding this." I gave him a little squeeze.

He thrusts his hips forward, giving me a I'm-just-pretending-to-let-you-be-in-charge look. "When's the last time you ate?"

"I *am* hungry, now that you mention it." I lowered myself to my knees without releasing my grip on my new favorite toy. The heat in those dark eyes was enough to re-light my fire—not that it ever extinguished. "Well before you give me food, may I have this?"

He smile looked so feral, if I had any sense, I'd run screaming. But I didn't. Instead, I swept the flat of my tongue across his tip as I watched him.

He shook his head, buried his hands in my hair, and pulled me away from him. "Why are you doing this?"

"Do you care?"

"Yes."

"We need to discuss your timing," I mumbled. He just stared at me, his face hungry but determined, and the leash controlling my temper unraveled. "What happens if you don't like my answer? You take your toys and leave?"

He captured both of my wrists with one of his large hands.

"I want you. Okay? You happy now?" No shame in wanting. I had from the moment I saw him. However, regardless of how hard I tried, that preacher's kid escaped at the worse times.

The grip on my wrists eased, and he gave me a little nod. A flush of adrenaline ran through my body at the realization and grudging acknowledgement of what just happened. The fact that he would easily forgo his own pleasure to ensure my comfort told me more about this man than anything that occurred prior to this point.

That, more than any type of tit for tat drove me, tempted me to trust him with more than my body. When I looked back on my time with Dorian, I'd pinpoint this moment as when I left a piece of me with him.

I slid my lips over his thick cock, knowing I would never be able to take all of him in. My mouth and hand worked in tandem up and down his shaft, I hummed and watched him enjoy the show.

Maybe he wasn't everybody's cup of tea, but he did it for me, and a big way. His gaze held mine as I worked him. I appreciated the fact that although now he had both of his hands in my hair, he never took control, or pushed me further than I could take him.

"Baby, if you don't want me coming in your mouth..."

That wasn't exactly what I had in mind. I sucked harder, adjusting the movements of my hand and mouth, watching him lose control. The muscles in his thigh flexed beneath my hand. His balls went from the low heavy to tight and drawn up against his body. His hips moved, thrusting, but still controlled. Still mindful. I took as much of him into my mouth as I could, and for the first time in my life, I wish I knew how to deep throat. That required a level of trust that I've never had with another man.

"Fuck!" Dorian's scream filled the steamy shower as he tensed, and shot a load of his sweet, salty cum in my mouth.

Once he was fully spent, he opened his eyes and looked down at me with a sleepy smile. "That was amazing."

I think this was the most relaxed I'd seen him, even at the restaurant. Astonishing what an orgasm can do for a fella.

"Come here." He helped me up and placed a large, callused hand on the side of my neck. "If you want me to let you go, that's not the way to do it."

I remained silent.

"You okay?" He looked down into my eyes and I gave him a nod. "Words, baby."

"Other than being a kidnap victim?" *I'm starting to think I'm the luckiest captive ever, but no need to share everything.*

"Yeah, other than that."

"I'm better than good." My stomach growled.

"And hungry. Let's grab something to eat."

"And then?" I hope I didn't sound as needy as I felt.

"And then we can do whatever you want—as long as it includes my cock."

The Stockholm struggle was real.

Chapter Twelve
Dorian

"You give good sandwich," she said as she crunched on a pickle.

Remembering that mouth and everything she did with it in the shower made my cock twitch. Shit, I don't even remember coming that quickly since I was a teenager.

Somebody should give me an award. I actually managed to make it out of my bedroom without a detour to my bed.

"We need to talk." I tossed a sheath of papers down on the counter.

"Is it about letting me go?" She ate a couple of strands of sauerkraut off of her sandwich, and did a shitty job of trying to look stern.

"Didn't seem like you wanted to leave when you had your lips wrapped around my cock."

She shrugged and took a bite of her Ruben, then daintily dabbed at the corners of her mouth with a napkin. "Well, it was there. It didn't seem fair to me that after two incredible orgasms that you should have to walk around like that. And I figure if I'm going to be hostage I may as well enjoy myself."

"Practical, I like that."

She wiped her hands and looked down at the papers. "What's this?"

"Test results." She didn't need to know how sexually active I was. But she wasn't a dummy. When I said I would look out for her, it meant even from myself. "I haven't been with anyone since the last test. But at the cabin we had unprotected sex."

"Thanks." She trailed a finger down the page and glanced back up and me. "But what's the point?"

"The point is tomorrow we're going to get tested again and when we receive the results nothing's coming between us."

"How do you know I haven't been with someone?"

"Because if you were, the poor fucker has the world's smallest dick." She coughed, and though I wanted to walk around the counter and pat her on the back, I stayed put. I knew, once I touched her, there'd be no speaking. "You been tested? You clean?"

"It's a little late now, don't you think? But, no I haven't been with anyone for a while, and I got tested because—" Her gaze darted to the counter. "Let's just say that I get tested six weeks ago, and I'm okay. Haven't been with anyone since then."

"Good. The doctor will be here tomorrow."

"That's nice, but I won't be."

"Are we going to keep going through this shit? Fine, tell me one reason you can't stay." I crossed my arm and leaned against the sink. She could say whatever the hell she wanted, but I wouldn't let her go.

As I watched her face, I could literally see her thinking her way through everything. Her internal debate danced across her expressive face. "But why don't you give me a reason, other than the fact because you said so."

Fuck it.

I pushed off the counter and walked to her, spun her around, and pried her legs apart, standing between them.

"You're running—"

"Of course I am—"

I touch her lips with my fingers and shook my head. "No. You were running from some shit before you met me." Thank fuck she didn't bother lying. "I don't know what it is, but I can make it go away. I've seen a lot of dark, shit. Sometimes my soul is so black, that I'd give Satan a run for his money. But that's not what I see in your eyes. I see pain. Somebody hurt you, and I want to fix it."

"You're good, I'll give you that, but sex can't fix everything."

"I can do a few other things."

"I don't... I don't want you killing anybody. What if I told you I just want someone to leave me alone? Could you make that happen?"

I'd promise her anything she wanted. I'd promise her the fucking moon—if she stayed. But this, I could do.

Maybe.

Unless what he did to her crossed one of the few remaining lines in my one-page personal code. I wasn't a good guy, but I never fucked anybody that didn't have it coming. And if the motherfucker crossed that line with her, I hoped like hell they've made their peace because they were going to meet their maker.

"I can do that." I pushed her thighs apart, and slid one finger inside of her moist heat. She wanted me as much as I wanted her.

"Take the condom out of my pocket." I extracted my fingers and added another one. Her pupils dilated as she slipped the package out of my pocket, then ripped it open with her teeth.

Maybe I should have her put it on with her mouth.

No, I needed to get inside of her, and now. My fingers and tongue were no longer enough. Especially after already being there, I needed to return.

"If you don't hurry I'm fucking you without it."

"How come you get to—" She moaned as I added another finger.

"I'm sorry, were you saying?"

She stopped talking, and covered me in record time, opening her legs in welcome. I grabbed the edges of the shirt she wore and pulled until buttons went flying.

I damn near laughed at her wide eyes. Instead, I hooked her knees over my elbows and pushed into her. I wanted to watch her face, but she felt so. Damn. Good.

"I'm sorry, baby, but you're so fucking tight. Your pussy feels like heaven. I never want to leave." I was going to tell her touch herself, but she reached up and started playing with her tits and she turned me on like a wet dream.

"Harder," she demanded.

"Your wish is my command."

She chuckled, and I joined her. How the hell could we both be laughing when the shit felt that good?

"Okay, well that's the case then how about you let me—"

It was time to shut her the hell up. I drove into her and she moaned again. She also slid a finger down to her clit and rubbed while I watched.

"Shit. Do you know how beautiful you are?"

She shook her head. "It doesn't count if you say it when you're balls deep in the me."

"I don't give a fuck if I'm in your greedy pussy or not. You will always be beautiful."

Her face grew relaxed and soft, not with passion, but with something else. I didn't know what the hell it was, but I would do anything to keep that look there.

"So, you gonna fuck me or what?" She opened her arms. "Kiss me Dorian," she whispered against my lips. "Please."

"Oh yeah."

And then I lost it.

This shit may have started with me stalking her, then her saving me, then me kidnapping her, but I had a feeling that no matter how this would have played out, we would've found ourselves together. I'd always heard assholes say crazy shit about when they met the one, they knew.

She was mine.

Plain and simple.

I might have to convince her of that, but she wasn't going any-fucking-where. I knew I said it was going to maybe last a couple of months, but who the hell was I kidding? If she left me, I would kill every man she even thought about fucking. So unless she wanted a trail of dead assholes behind her, she needed to get with the fucking program.

She moaned into my mouth just as the familiar tingle made me clench my ass. I wanted to watch and feel her come first, but her greedy pussy, the one made just for me, made the choice. And I went along for the ride.

I released her legs, and collapsed against her, burying my face in her neck.

"Wow." She laughed and kissed my cheek.

When I recovered enough that I wouldn't make an ass of myself, I gave her kiss and whispered against her lips, "I'll call the doctor tonight."

Chapter Thirteen

Ryann

Eventually there may come a time when I accepted this wasn't a dream. I'm the sensible one that always watches the movies wondering how did this woman fall for that psycho.

Until it happened to me.

Oh, not Dorian; my dirt bag ex-husband. And once I got out of that shit, and my broken ribs managed to heal, I decided I'd never surrender that much control to a man.

I was surprised last night when the doctor showed up. I learned that he was the same doctor that treated Dorian at the cabin. I learned that he complimented my sutures, which was incredibly flattering.

But today was off the chain.

I'd had money, I'd lived with the money—all of it wasn't mine. It was my husband's and his family's fortune. In all the years we were together, Keith never did anything like this. He never pampered me the way Dorian did today.

He woke me up a kiss and instructions to relax while he went to work. Okay, I had to admit that I giggled when he asked if I would be there when he got back. After the orgasms he gave me yesterday, I was a pretty sure thing—but he didn't assume that, and I liked it.

My day started with breakfast. I don't think he made it, as a matter of fact I know he didn't, but the woman he had to come and cook and clean for him. Grace was a nice older lady. Which was good, because I was pretty sure I might've been a jealous if some hot, young thing walked up in there in a sexy maid's outfit to get things cleaned up. *Maybe I should try that.*

And then the rest of the day just got increasingly amazing after my quiche, freshly squeezed orange juice, and flaky croissants, which I ate on the balcony. I was treated to a kick ass hour and a half Swedish massage, a facial, and waxing.

Dorian hired a personal shopper from Nordstrom's to come by with everything I needed. We're talking decadent lingerie, casual clothes—including jeans—flirty little springtime dresses, jackets, and even shoes. The strangest part was that he got my sizes right. I didn't even really want to think about how he knew so much about women's clothing.

It's obvious from the way he handled my body, he knew a whole lot about women's clothes, especially the removal process.

Cocktail dresses hung on the rack of clothes, and Mr. Dorian left instructions to select at least one for tonight, but he hoped I liked them all. From the sparkle in Catriona's eyes, I knew she hoped the same.

As I fingered through the little dresses, I wondered how the hell he knew so much about me? Because of the clothing he selected, many of them were geared towards my taste. I loved bold primary colors and a lot of the things he selected were just that—vibrant red's, blazing oranges, yellows as happy as a Caribbean sunshine.

Funny, but this roughneck man I'd known all of a month knew me better than my husband of ten years. Maybe it wasn't that he didn't know me, maybe he just never really liked me. Maybe saw me as some kind of project, someone to fix. But I couldn't think about that. I honestly didn't want to think about him again.

I chose a few dresses off the rack and sparkling strappy shoes that couldn't be sent back into the wilds.

He may be a criminal—I remained certain he was a criminal—but he treated me well. And that dirty talking, good fucking, bad boy was not someone that wanted to settle down.

Which was fine with me. We would have *mucho* sex and both walk away with a couple weeks of fond memories. Of course, he'd return to his harem, and I'd have masturbating material for the next fifty years.

I looked down at my functional watch, cursed, and left it on the dresser. I loved my black plastic watch, but it didn't exactly go with this red cocktail dress.

Oh, and did I mention he sent a hairdresser? One that knew black hair. So, I looked and felt like a million bucks right now. I threw my shoulders back, grabbed my little clutch, and sashayed my fabulous ass downstairs.

I only made it halfway down before I saw him. Mama had to pause, because damn, he looked good enough to eat. I would have to lick him first, then I would eat him. He stood holding a glass of some kind of brown liquor, probably scotch, and looking up at me in a way that made me feel like Cinderella.

Except this Cinderella's godfather probably had a pistol strapped to his ankle. Oh well, we wouldn't examine that too much. Those obsidian eyes damn near burned my dress off watching me descend the stairs. I hadn't seen him get dressed, I guess he came in while I was in the shower.

I was glad that we got see each other at this moment. I was happy that at the lowest point of my life, I met this charming, complicated, sexy as hell criminal. We wouldn't look at the whole kidnapping and shooting thing. That seemed a little inconsequential. But I thought about all the hot sex the two of us were going to have over the next couple of weeks.

He met me at the bottom of the stairs with an out stretched hand, and like a debutante at one of those stupid Jack and Jill balls, I set my fingers in his as he pulled me to him and kissed me. But he gave me a kiss that wasn't gentlemanly at all, and I fucking loved it.

"You look amazing." I set my hand against his lapel. "It's a good thing you never came in the restaurant looking quite this good, because I might've jumped you right there."

"Your tips would've been a hell of a lot bigger."

I laughed.

I did that a lot around him; another thing I liked. I needed to be careful. This guy was dangerous in ways far more harmful than a bullet.

"You look… good." The unsaid *but* hung between us like a shield.

I felt myself blinking a little too quickly, but I kept the smile plastered on my face. Wow. *That* fairytale didn't last long. My heart sank and resided somewhere down around my belly button.

He let go of my hand and reached inside of his jacket pocket and pulled out a long slender jeweler's case and sat it in my hands.

"What's this?"

"Open it."

I so totally felt like Julia Roberts in *Pretty Woman* right now. Except for the prostitute thing and I wasn't a six-foot-tall brunette. Call me shallow, but I liked a man handing me jewels.

I opened it, and gasped at the delicate filigree white gold masterpiece inlaid with bluish-purple stones that looked like tanzanite. Did I mention the center stone compared to the size of my thumbnail? I couldn't keep it forever, but this shit would be fun to wear.

"It's beautiful."

"Turn around."

"You're bossy, you know that right?" I gave him crap, but I turned around and let him place that beautiful piece of jewelry around my neck. The feel of his warm breath against my neck made me a little bit wetter. If he kept touching me, I would have to change my panties before we left. And I really liked these panties—the little bit of them that was there.

"You like?"

I turned and gazed into his bottomless dark eyes, noticing a tiny flinch. Could my devilish bad boy be nervous? Dorian, businessman of the year, completely sexy badass, looked nervous about my reaction. *He is so going to get lucky tonight.*

I brought my fingers up to the choker and nodded. "I love it. Thanks for everything."

He cleared his throat and grabbed my hand. "We better go."

"What's the hurry?" He put my hand on his perfect cock, and I gave a little squeeze. "Would it be so bad if we didn't go out?"

"Yeah, because I want to show you off."

"Okay, sweetie."

Cinderella never had at this good, because I knew this town car would never turn into a pumpkin. Not as long as I had my big bad wolf Dorian with me. When we pulled up to the front door of Club Surrender I squeaked. It wasn't an *oh my God he's really bringing me here* sound, it was more of a *shit, I know who you are and my throat is closing* noise.

"I guess you figured it out," Dorian said in the quiet darkness. "So if we go in there, am I going to have to worry about you trying escape?"

"Are you going to become a different person than you were five seconds ago?" The light reflected off his rugged face and he shook his head. I should be screaming no, no, no. But my lips had another freaking idea. "Well, why would I?"

As I said the words, I realized that I meant them. Completely.

"You know, Dorian, you never pretended to be anything but who you are. I don't know everything about you, and I'm not sure that I want to. But I do know this, other than the whole kidnapping thing—"

"Are you ever going to let me fucking forget that?" His brows drew together, but I thought I saw a little bit of a smile.

"Eventually. That's one thing you should know about me: I hold a mean grudge."

"Yeah, I noticed."

"Well anyway, I don't know what this is between us, but right now I need you. And for some reason you want me. That's good enough." We just sat there in silence for a few minutes, and he finally leaned over and kissed me. I had my problems, and he obviously had his—in addition to getting shot.

He ended the kiss and swiped his thumb along the bottom of my lip, and pulled the handkerchief out of his pocket to dab at his. As he sat watching me, I couldn't help but giggle as I dug my lip gloss out of my purse.

"What's so funny?"

"This." I waved my hand around the car and then back and forth between the two of us. "And us. But you know what?"

"What?" A slash of darkness concealed his eyes, but the swipe of nonexistent lint from his slacks left another sliver of my heart in his care.

"It is what it is." I grabbed his rough hand and rotated it, placing a kiss on his palm before wagging my eyebrows. "So, we gonna sit in the car all night, or are you going to show me a good time?"

"I may have to leave you to get some work done."

"I'm a big girl. You don't have to entertain me."

"You're with me, Antoine, or Paul. We're not out of danger yet."

"Then why didn't you just leave me at home? I'm not complaining, but it would have been okay."

Antoine opened the door and Dorian slid out, extending a hand. I felt like a celebrity as Dorian assisted me, and when he wrapped his large hand around the back of my neck, I became the luckiest woman in the Northern Hemisphere.

Leaning forward, he placed his lips against my ear and whispered,

"Because I've spent too much time away from you already."

Chapter Fourteen
Ryann

Finding myself the center of attention once we stepped through the doors of Club Surrender made me second guess everything—from my dress to the fact that maybe I would never be quite ready for prime time. Then again, standing next to Dorian, I had to doubt anyone paid attention to the cute but soft woman beside him. Despite his custom tailored suit, anyone with an ounce of sense recognized the predator beneath the polish.

And he was mine.

I wasn't quite sure what to expect of his club, but not this. The large space managed to simultaneously feel both intimate and spacious. Sex and sophistication reigned in Club Surrender, from the flattering lighting, to the strategically placed leather-clad dancers in cages around the space.

It seemed he hired beautiful people to populate and decorate the place. For a second, just a second, I wondered why I was in here.

Then, I noticed something else. There *were* stares and odd looks—all from women. Had he slept with all of them? I could see why, especially considering my behavior the past two days. I wouldn't even count the whole month of lust preceding us colliding.

My step faltered as I watched a woman suck in her hint of a stomach, arch her back to show off her impressive cleavage, and head our way. She appeared everything I wasn't—long, lean, and most of all young.

I was healthy. I worked out. Well, I used to swim every day, but I couldn't in Centerville. Without starving myself, there's no way in hell I would ever see a size 6 unless it hung on a rack. Getting below double digits would be as likely as getting struck by lightning—twice.

And you know what? I'd given up. My body leaned towards curvy. Even when Keith nagged me and I starved myself I remained curvy. When *that* wasn't thin enough, I said fuck it.

"Babe, I set you up in the VIP section."

"Are you going to be able to stay a while?" He pulled me in front of him, resting his hand on my stomach and pressing his hard body against my back. I forgot those women and turned to look up at him. "Was that too needy?"

"Do you really think I'm going to leave you out here with all these assholes without them knowing that you're mine? Not going to happen."

Okay, I had to admit that that made me feel really good. It made me feel even better when he kissed my temple. Not because how easily he showed public affection, but because Ms. Silicone damn near fell off her platform shoes.

Poor baby.

"That's sweet, but I already agreed to stay with you. You don't have to say that."

"Look at me."

"I am looking at you."

"No, turn around." This was scary Dorian, and I wasn't really sure I liked this guy. He tilted my chin up with his thumb. "I need you to hear what the fuck am telling you. You're mine. I came to that restaurant every week, and you know it wasn't for the food, right?"

He gave me a look that said he expected an answer, and I nodded. Before he could ask for them, I gave him the words. "I'd hoped it was me you were coming there for."

He stared down into my eyes with the ferocity of a pit bull. "I can get a steak in Chicago."

"Okay." I said, or least I think I said. I may have lost track when I licked my lips and his hungry gaze drifted down to my mouth. "Well, if it makes you feel any better, I lived for those Fridays too."

"Yeah?" His face relaxed. He looked less demonic, but every bit as hungry. "Don't want you taking any shit off of any these bitches, you got me?"

"I got you, babe."

"Good." He leaned his mouth down to mine and kissed me.

After those sweet words, all I wanted to do was rip his damn clothes off. Every little bit of insecurity, every bit of cellulite, none of that mattered. Because he looked at me like I was the most important thing in his world right now.

And I'd take it.

He ended the kiss and pulled away and I may have whimpered a little bit.

"My baby's greedy." He kissed my forehead, slipped his hand in mine, and moved through a crowd that parted like the Red Sea for Moses. "That's okay. I'll give you everything you need, and more."

The problem was that he already had.

The VIP section was sweet. The enclosed room with its own dance floor and bar sat higher than the rest of Surrender, allowing all to observe the minions below. The entire club sported all black and reds with silver accents. In a way, that seemed like it would be gaudy, but not here.

It was sexy, understated, and elegant.

As he settled me at the table, I looked out on the downstairs dance floor then up at the acrobats performing above the crowd. I'd worry about my boobs falling out of those little tops. *More power to you girls.*

He left to speak with Antoine and I watched the crowd. I completely understood why this place claimed to be one of the hottest nightclubs in the city. Despite the abundance of pretty people, something about Club Surrender made me want to shed my troubles and inhibitions and unchain the wild child struggling to escape the confines of civility.

I turned to catch Dorian studying me and smiled. For the second time tonight, he appeared uncertain, which surprised me just as much this time. He slid into the booth beside me, placing his arm around my shoulders, with the waitresses right behind him with our drinks.

"This place is amazing." The shrug he gave me appeared nonchalant, but the look in his eye told a different tale.

"I try."

I nudged him with my shoulder. "Come on, you have to be proud of yourself. Don't underplay it." Who'd hurt this man? If I possessed the means to time travel, I'd return to his past and kick the person who placed that shadow in his eyes in the junk.

The boyish grin he gifted me with at the complement had my heart performing handsprings. I couldn't help myself; I kissed him on the cheek and he just kind of chuckled. A surprising contentment filled me as I appreciated the music and the man beside me.

A hand gripped mine, startling me. "What are you doing?" I asked as I scooted out of the booth.

"What the hell do you think I'm doing? Dancing with my woman." Okay, he was so getting lucky tonight. At the rate he was going, I didn't think I would make it home.

Did I just say that? Did I just call his place home?

I needed to slow my roll.

He didn't give me any more time to stay in my head, because the man started moving. Whatever idiot spouting the white boys can't dance sure as heck didn't know Dorian Zuba.

The slow, sexy and sultry way he moved promised unrelenting

pleasure. I would have to say that he was the only truly decadent and selfish thing I'd ever done in my entire life. I knew he was bad, and I liked him that way. He didn't need to change one hair on his closely-cropped head.

I remembered the first time I saw him walking to the restaurant. Even then, I thought he looked like a panther, or some other dangerous animal.

My gaze drifted up his tailored suit, pausing at his mouth, and I recalled the feel of it against mine and craved another taste. When my gaze finally met his, relief flooded my body to see I wasn't the only one caught up in this crazy cyclone of lust and heat that always seemed to suck us in.

I turned my back to him and continued dancing. His big hands wrapped around my waist and skimmed my sides, stopping just beneath my breast, a thumb stroking the sensitive side. Yeah, he was absolutely getting lucky.

And so was I.

As lustful thoughts swirled around my brain I saw Paul approach and whisper something to Antoine, neither of them looking happy. Paul approached us with the precision and focus of a soldier, and Dorian's hands returned to my hip as he guided me to the table.

"Give me a second." He slid a hand down my bare arm and moved across the room like a general preparing for battle.

Normally, I would never place an unattended drink anywhere near my lips, but this was Dorian's club, and I knew that Antoine watched everything. As I nursed my Hendrick's and tonic, I glanced at Dorian's thunderous expression and prayed to never have that anger focused in my direction.

The jungle predator was back as he walked over to the table. This was his business, his work, so I refused to be that whiny girlfriend. You know, the one that can't handle a man being gone away from her for more than ten seconds. No, I refused to be that girl.

"Sweetheart, I have to take care some shit, and I don't know how long it's going to be. Do you want to hang? I can have someone take you home."

"It's okay, I'll be fine."

Dorian slipped his hand along the side of my neck, trailing his thumb across the choker. "I don't need this bullshit tonight. I want to take my lady out just..."

"This doesn't take away from the amazingness of my day. You made me feel like a princess. Thank you." I cupped his cheek and tilted my lips up for kiss. "Now go do your work then get back to me, so I can get my flirt on."

I thought he looked scary earlier. I was wrong. If looks really could kill, I'd be lying on the floor with a chalk outline around my body.

"Hey, that was a joke." That didn't seem to help so I cupped his cheeks. "You weren't the only one that waited for a month."

Antoine came up behind him and cleared his throat, and I wanted to knee him in his balls. I still owed them for threatening me. "Go. I promise to be good so you don't have to kill anyone in your place of business."

Chapter Fifteen
Ryann

Even if I hadn't been to his office, I knew the location, because he showed me earlier. I watched him walk out of the VIP section across the room and up another set of stairs. Wow, the view from the back tantalized almost as much as the front. Thank goodness he didn't have the pretty boy thing going on, because his sex appeal already leapt off the charts.

After he disappeared I noticed a group of men across the bar checking me out. Go me. A tall fine dark piece of chocolate moved in my direction. I had to stop myself from looking behind me, because his eyes were focused on my cleavage.

I had no reason why I didn't come this club before.

But I sure as hell liked it.

"Not going to happen man." Antoine stepped in front of the guy, and I kind of felt sorry for him. I turned away to save him from further embarrassment and a flash of pale skin climbing the steps to Dorian's office caught my eye.

It was one of those women—that one who started to approach Dorian earlier.

Whatever. He was busy, he didn't have time for her ass then, and he wouldn't now.

With the flip of gorgeous hair—bitch—she looked in my direction, and smiled. *Yeah, we'll see who's smiling in a few seconds.* She knocked on the office door, and my mouth parted in surprise when Dorian, not Paul opened it. He still didn't look happy, but he stepped aside and invited her in.

After, she trailed her hand down his chest, which he didn't move.

Okay.

Actually no, it wasn't okay. I had to remember he wasn't mine, and this was just fun.

Doctors appointment or no doctor's appointment, he would be wrapping his shit before he got anywhere near me. As a matter fact...

I shook my head. *No need for me to rush to judgment. She won't be in there long.*

At least that's what I thought. I danced by myself for at least three songs and had two more gin and tonic's, the last one very light on the tonic very heavy on the Hendrick's. I kept my eye on the room and she never left.

Antoine walked over to the table, cell phone in one hand, and extended the other to me. "The boss wants me to take you home."

Screw it. This was just one pit stop on the journey to the rest of my life. I mean come on, this was just great sex, not insta-love.

I grabbed my clutch off the seat and scooted over, taking his hand.

"You know what, that sounds like the best idea I've had all fucking night."

Chapter Sixteen
Dorian

I looked down at Ryann sprawled across my bed, and sat a bottle of Motrin and a liter of water on the nightstand. If she finished off that bottle of Hendrick's, her ass would be hurting when she woke up. She didn't strike me as a much of a drinker, which was cool. She was grown, she could do what she wanted, as long as she didn't get sloppy.

At home or with a select few do I choose to get drunk and loose, and that's what I expected from my woman. I drink, not much, and I sure as fuck don't use drugs. If I had a conscience, I would say that I was ashamed that I used to deal. But that would be a lie. If those junkies wouldn't have got it from me, they would've found it somewhere else. At least my shit stayed relatively clean.

Sounds fucked up. What could I say?

I didn't like seeing her passed out on the couch like that, empty bottle laying on its side and her clothes strewn all over the floor. By the time I got back at seven this morning, exhaustion tugged at me. Even after a shower and a few hours sleep with her wrapped around me, nothing much had changed.

I kissed her temple and brushed her crazy ass hair back. I preferred it like this—wild, curly, and aching for my fingers. I'd hoped she would wake up before I took off. I wanted to make it up to her for shit getting fucked up last night. Couldn't be helped.

I took one last look at the beautiful woman in my bed and closed the door before I changed my mind. I'd make it up to her, take her somewhere for a few days. Do some romantic shit.

Yeah, that sounded good.

I walked downstairs to find Antoine sitting his big ass at my kitchen counter eating up my damned food. "I'm out. Ryann's still sleep. If she needs to go anywhere, tell her I'll be back after my meeting."

"You get a chance to talk this morning?"

"What, she have a headache or some shit?"

"Not sure, but something was off."

"Well, I'm going to have to deal with that later." A vacation sounded better and better.

Other than working inside my apartment, I had what constituted the world's shortest commute. All I had to do was catch an elevator down a few floors. Living over the shop could be a pain in the ass, but the fact that I worked with my two best friends helped. Some would say we were workaholics, and that might be true to some extent. But we worked hard and partied even harder.

The top floors consisted of four apartments, one for each of us, and the other for our secretary, Amanda Morgan. We didn't make her work twenty-four hours a day. She needed a life too. Not that she had one. She'd been with us since the beginning, and I didn't know what we would do without her. She kept shit smooth and ran things we didn't even know needed running.

A whole five minutes later I walked into the conference room finding my business partners and friends hunched behind their laptops. The three of us were about his different as you could get. You had me, the Pollock from Centerville, Sterling Warner, the trust fund bad boy, and Carmine Errante, the former heir apparent to the largest Mafia family in the Midwest. I knew when I met those two, that they'd somehow become part of my future, and I was lucky enough to bring my past along with me for the ride.

"You look like shit." Carmine slid his reading glasses off and sat them on the coffee table.

"Thanks a lot, asshole." It only took half a glance to realize they didn't look much better. "That bad?"

"Worse." Sterling tossed a jewel case containing a CD identical to the one I received last night on the table. "We both got this bullshit last night."

"This makes the fifth victim. We have a choice. We go to the cops or they come to us." Sterling took a sip from his dainty espresso cup that I took great pleasure in teasing him about.

I walked over to the space-aged coffee maker and made myself one. Anything to unsee the video of a woman I recognized from my club getting gang raped and tortured. I just hoped like hell she still lived at the end—I couldn't watch that far.

Of the three of us, Sterling had the least tainted relationship with local law enforcement, but only because of old family money. "As long as you're the mouthpiece." I ran my hand over my scalp. What if someone did some foul shit like that to Ryann? There wouldn't be a place in this solar system those fuckers could hide. "We need to shut this down."

I nabbed a muffin and grabbed a seat at the conference table. When I raised my eyes, the two dumb fucks just sat staring.

"What? If you're waiting for me to pull a bunny out of my ass, I can't help you."

"Something you want to share?" Carmine leaned back in his chair.

"Not...shit, I almost forgot. Brittany told me one of her girls got roofed, but the guy played it off like he was helping her to the bathroom, and conveniently disappeared when she confronted him. We went over the surveillance tapes for hours, and have a halfway decent image."

"This might be the break we need." Sterling finally looked less like he wanted to beat someone to death. "Let's get one of the lawyers that work with your pop's to come in to advise us," Sterling watched Carmine, waiting for an answer.

"He might be a little busy, the family—"

"You'd think the mafia boys wouldn't get caught so much," I teased.

"Hey!" Carmine stuff half a croissant in his mouth. "Everybody's luck eventually runs out."

We kicked ideas back and forth for a few minutes, for coordinating events and ideas with the clubs. Our empire consisted of real estate and investments, but our pride and joy were the clubs, restaurants, and bars we owned.

"Speaking of getting lucky..." Sterling drummed his fingers on the table. I hated when he did that shit.

"What the fuck man, you move some chick in your crib and you don't tell us?" Carmine actually looked insulted.

"When did the two of you get a gash?" I tried to stare them down, but the identical slack jawed, wide-eyed expressions ruined the effect.

"She the one that saved your ugly ass?" asked Sterling

"Yeah."

"And she just decided to up and leave her life and run away with you?" Carmine asked.

Lying came easy for me with everyone except these two assholes. However, until I untangled the emotions surrounding Ryann, this remained personal. They didn't need to know everything.

"Not exactly." I took another sip of my double espresso. Did I mention I was tired as hell?

"What does that mean? Is she tied to your bed?" Now, Sterling looked really interested.

"That's your gig, not mine."

Sterling was truly into the scene, complete with personal playroom.

"I could help you out." Carmine smirked, grabbing his cup and heading back to the expresso machine. With his dark good looks and Sterling's icy Nordic perfection, I was the ugly duckling of the bunch. "You know, break her in for you"

"You do that, just make sure you prepay for your funeral. It's not coming out of business expenses."

The way they stared made me want to check to see if something slimy hung out of my nose. "What? She's not on the menu. Even if she asked, I wouldn't share this one. Not even with you." I stood, because I'd hate to have to punch one of my boys in the face. Especially since they'd return the favor. "We done?"

"No," Carmine shook his head, "but we can handle it."

I moved my empty cup to the side board. We might call Amanda our secretary, but I started to feel like we worked for her. She'd have my ass for leaving shit sitting around. Not that cleaning was part of her job description.

"You know how it is, something new and shiny." They both gave me the yeah, right look, since they knew I didn't bring women to my apartment. "Have you ever known me to ignore business for my personal life?" Thinking about it made me realize how empty that personal life was. I didn't mean it wasn't enjoyable, but I'd managed to avoid long term relationships of the romantic variety.

"Since it's like that, do you have time to check shit out in Centerville? I got a tip from my cousin Sal. I'd go, but they run with the crew you know up there."

"That'll work. Ryann can't return to her life until the threat is eliminated." And even then, she wasn't going anywhere until I'd finished, and that might take a while.

A long while.

I got the information and headed upstairs.

Centerville could wait until tomorrow. Some of what I said

downstairs was the truth; Ryann protected and safe remained a priority. Once that was taken care of, we'd deal with the rest.

When I reached the penthouse, Ryann was nowhere to be found and Antonio sat on the couch reading the newspaper. "She up?"

"Yeah, but I'm not sure what's—"

"I have to split," I interrupted, "so I need you to stay here with her. Should be back tonight. I'll have a word, but under no circumstances does she leave this building."

"Not my job to take care of your personal shit, bro."

"Your job is anything I say it is."

"What the hell you want me to do if she doesn't agree?"

"Whatever you need to." I scratched the back of my neck as I headed to the stairs. "Shit's escalating. I'll lay it out for her."

"Good, you can be the asshole this time," he mumbled.

I took the stairs two at a time. Being an asshole wasn't even a problem—not for me. Stepping through the door to my bedroom, I stopped and enjoyed the view. Ryann stood next to the bed wearing the scarlet lace bra and panty set I selected, and I had to congratulate myself on my exquisite taste.

"What are you doing?"

"How did I end up in your bed?" She grabbed a dress, holding it in front of her—pity.

"If you're here, when you sleep, it's in my bed." *Note to self, no more gin for her.* I think I preferred sweet Ryann. "What crawled up your ass?"

"Don't you have some *business* to attend to?"

"I'll be more than happy to—"

"You're an ass."

"Yeah, I am but—"

"Why did you send me home last night, Dorian?"

"Are you on the rag?" That seemed the only reason to explain this major personality shift. That or a brain tumor. Now I remembered why I remained single.

"Why do men immediately go there instead of accepting the fact that I'm angry? But if you have to know, PMS has nothing to do with how I'm feeling right now. It's all about you."

Centerville sounded good right now, unknown assailants and all. "I'm into you, Ryann, you know that. But you're not leading me around by my cock."

"Speaking of cocks, if that thing comes near me again, it won't be without a condom." She disappeared inside the closet. My closet, the one I made room for her to put her new wardrobe in.

"I got shit to do. I should be back tonight. If not, tomorrow morning. We can talk about it then, after you stop acting like a psycho bitch."

Her dark face paled and she looked at me like I slapped her. "Did you just call me a bitch?"

"Not another word. I'm done." I didn't think it possible, but her face grew paler. *Women.* I kissed her. Hard and fast. Even though she'd lost her mind and pissed me the fuck off, I needed her to remember who she belonged to.

Chapter Seventeen

Ryann

In two days, I moved out of his bedroom, which was quite a feat, considering I had to haul all of that crap to one of the downstairs guest bedrooms. After half a night of rolling around in an empty strange bed, I surrendered, ran back upstairs, crawled into Dorian's bed, and buried my face in his pillow.

Oh, but before I did that, I slipped into one of his shirts.

Oh my God, I'm pathetic.

Something about this man had driven me crazy. With all day to myself, Antoine gave me a tour of the building and office spaces, including an amazing swimming pool. A bathing suit was one of the few things Dorian didn't purchase, so I had to improvise.

Skinny dipping wasn't an option with Antoine and Paul refusing to let me out of their sight, so I wore the most conservative of my lingerie. Funny, a bikini miraculously appeared the second morning so I didn't have to do that again.

The mindless laps and the burn in my shoulders as my hands sliced through the water calmed me, forcing me to examine my response to Dorian this morning, and I didn't like my conclusions. He may be one step removed from a criminal, he may deal with the underside of the city—okay, there was a lot wrong with him—but he never lied to me.

I'm not going to morph into a man-eating bitter babe because of Keith, I refuse to give him that much power. This situation triggered a level three girlfriend emergency, and I didn't have my cell phone. Back in the olden days, in life before smart phones, I actually memorized phone numbers, now I did good remembering my own. Well, thank goodness for social media.

Along with all of the clothes, Dorian bought me a cell phone. Not just any cell phone, that thing could probably launch satellites it looked so complicated. I snagged it out of my clutch, and I realized that I hadn't actually even seen this on the market.

This sucked.

I sat on his bed, in his clothes, and all I wanted was his voice in my ear telling me we're good. I exhaled and pulled up the contact list. There were five numbers, and of course his number showed up first. Then Antoine and Paul, and his two friends that I had yet to meet.

I couldn't put this off anymore, so I just hit the number and hoped I found the words to say I'm sorry I acted like a bitch.

Unfortunately, he answered before I found them.

"Yeah?"

"Hi, it's me."

"Yeah, babe, I know that."

"Dorian..." This was really hard.

"Got shit to do." He'd never been short with me—just like that, he was done. I was glad we weren't Skyping, or he would have seen me wipe the lone tear trailing down my cheek.

When I didn't say anything he just sighed.

He spoke again, and this time his voice sounded gentler. "Sweetheart—" he started.

"I'm sorry I was a bitch," I blurted. He chuckled, and it made me feel a little bit better. "I was jealous. I saw that woman going your office. She stayed in there while. Then you sent me home."

"Who's in my house?"

"Me."

"Who shares my bed?"

"I guess that would be me again."

"And who couldn't sleep so they had to go back up to my bed and put on my shit to get there?"

I set up and peered around the room, I didn't see any cameras, but obviously they were there.

"Yes sweetheart, that's how I knew you are about to bean my ass with that statue."

"You are such a jerk."

He laughed again, and the sound was sexier than any Marvin Gaye song.

"And I'm sure the gin didn't help"

"Is that why you got faced?"

I didn't answer, but I did flip him off. And just to make sure he got the full view, I waved the middle finger around the room.

He chuckled, the sound rough and deep. I really liked this guy. "If you really want to make it up to me, you could lay back on the bed and show me that pretty pussy of yours."

"Not going to happen."

"We already established that. Anyway, I have to go but we're good yeah?"

"Yeah baby, were good." I felt my face and my entire body goes soft as my voice. "When will you—" Nope, not going there. "I'll see you when you get back.

"Can you call Grace and have her cook up some dinner for tonight? The boys are coming over to take care of business, but first I'd like you to meet them."

"Really?" My mouth went dry. Other than Antoine and Paul, his business partners were family.

"Tell her to make whatever and I'll be there around seven, no later than eight."

"You do know I can cook right?" I walked to the closet to grab an outfit, already planning a menu. He had no idea the culinary throw down taking place in his dining room tonight.

"I hadn't thought about it. As much as I appreciate it, it's not—"

"What if I *wanted* to do that for you? Consider it payback."

"For what, kidnapping you?" He chuckled again, and the sultry sound enveloped me like and embrace.

"Yes, and give me a plethora of orgasms, plus keeping me safe. I could easily continue."

"Knock yourself out. Nothing happened with Brittany, the woman from last night."

I tensed. I'd forgotten about why we were even fighting, and him bringing it up reopened the wound. "Okay…"

"There are some things going on at the club. Short version is a friend of hers was roofied and we went through surveillance tapes."

"That's horrible." I squeezed my eyes shut, remembering sexual assault victims coming through the emergency room. The physical trauma usually heals, but the emotional scars…

"Yeah. I'll fill you in on the rest tonight."

"Later baby." I whispered.

He didn't bother with goodbye; he just ended the call.

I grabbed a quick shower, making sure to give my baby a show if he decided to watch. After getting dressed and returning some of my crap to the master bedroom, I went about planning dinner. It felt good to have a purpose again. I wasn't well suited for a life of leisure.

Luckily, the kitchen was well stocked, but not enough to create a feast of chicken piccata, angel hair pasta, and roasted asparagus, so I convinced Antoine to take me to the store. Well, I didn't exactly convince him. He got permission from Dorian to take me out of the house. *No, we are going to have to talk about this. He is not—*

I caught myself mid-rant.

No need to be stupid just to assert my independence. I had my independence. And I could leave.

Eventually...

Antonio looked constipated walking around Giuseppe's, a small specialty market. I'd have to remember to never ask him to go to the mall, or shopping on Michigan Avenue, he'd stroke out. I'd given up trying to have a conversation with him a few aisles ago, since his responses were limited to grunts.

In this very high-end overpriced grocery store, everyone looked as though they were trying to figure out if I was someone special. Instead of pretending to be with me, he went out of his way to appear intimidating. It was rather amusing, and rather effective at keeping me occupied as I overloaded the shopping cart.

As I grabbed a jar capers from the shelf, I sensed something odd. I swore it seemed as though my body vibrated with a low-level electrical hum.

"You cunt," a familiar male voice yelled.

Shit, shit, shit, no. This is not happening. At this time of the day he would be in the—

Thank God for Antoine. He stepped in front of me as Keith charged forward.

"Yo, you need to back up." Antoine's posture didn't change, but that voice gave me the chills.

"So this is how it is? You leave me for this...thug?" Keith waved his hand dramatically, garnering more attention than his overly loud voice.

"I hate to have to embarrass you more than you're embarrassing yourself right now—" Antoine started, but Keith spoke over him.

"She's the one that's embarrassing herself, but she excels at that. Just in case you don't know, that woman you're protecting is my wife."

Antoine shrugged. "She shouldn't need protection from her husband, or is there something you'd like to share with these people you're putting a show on for?"

I so forgive Antoine for helping kidnap me.

People stared, and Keith probably assumed I'd retreat, do any and everything to avoid a confrontation.

"Keith? A sultry but simpering voice drew my attention. That and the long scarlet fingernails vibrant against his black jacket. "What's going on here?"

Seeing her, the latest of his many women, live and in person, hurt as much as one of the kicks to the ribs he gave me as a parting gift.

Screw him. "Oh, hello. I'm his wife."

"Excuse me?" She looked back and forth between Keith and I, and took a second to check Antoine out. Interesting.

"Honey, don't worry about it. He's all yours." I tried to move in front of Antoine, but he reached his arm out in front of me. "But word from wise, watch out for the left hook."

"I need to know where to reach you so my attorney can send you the papers," Keith said.

"I wouldn't worry about it, you'll definitely be hearing from her people," Antoine promised, his voice deep and menacing.

"Her people?" Keith snorted. "You mean the folks down at the legal aid office?"

"You done?" Antione slung an arm around my shoulder. "If I were you, I'd rethink how you spoke to Ryann."

"You may want to tell your homeboy who he's dealing with."

Antoine chuckled, and it was a terrifying I-can't-wait-to-see-the-skin-peeled-from-your-flesh sound. He dismissed Keith like an annoying gnat and looked down at me. "You get everything you need?"

"Yes, I think so."

Dorian wasn't the only one with secrets, but I would have to share mine so they didn't blow up in his face.

Chapter Eighteen
Dorian

I pulled up in front of the building in my Dodge charger to find Ryann leaning against the building with her arms wrapped around her waist. Glancing down at my reddened and scraped knuckles I struggled to reel in my fury. Luckily, a worthy target awaited our arrival.

Antoine led her to the car, opening the door. "The package is waiting." He gave me a nod and closed the door behind Ree and blended into the crowd.

Thank fuck I have strong teeth. Because they would have snapped in half by now.

I peeked over at her to find her staring at me. Her eyes were wide—too wide.

"Come here." I leaned over, sliding my hand behind her neck, giving her a gentle tug and meeting her halfway. I would always meet her halfway.

But not one step further.

I slid my fingers into her soft curly hair and covered her mouth with my own, sucking on her lower lip. Seducing her mouth the way I planned to do with the rest of her later. With my mouth and body, I attempted to convey my commitment—to her, to us.

The sexual attraction between us flared and burned so bright I knew it frightened her, but she still held tight. For the first time in my life, I'd met a woman who didn't give a shit about my money. Even as a regular Joe, she wanted me.

This little woman was my kryptonite, and before I took another step on our journey I had to ensure we were on the same page. I ended the kiss and pressed my forehead against hers.

"I take it you already know what happened?" she asked, her voice soft and wobbly.

I nodded. "You okay?"

Oh I knew, and I hoped like hell she'd known on some level, that her ex kicked his very last hornet's nest. She was about to see the pitiless man behind the wealth. She'd glimpsed shades of my ruthlessness, witnessed the darkness hiding beneath the mask, and she was still here.

I'd only cared about one other woman, and she waltzed out of my life and drove off into the sunset with a man my pops considered a brother. Maybe that fucked me up and left me distrustful. All I knew was I had yet to meet a woman with staying power. I'd find out if Ree was that woman tonight.

When she didn't answer, I merged into traffic. This was her shit; I'd give her time to deal, time to share. I glanced down at my watch and hoped for her sake she did it in the next thirty minutes. Otherwise, I planned to solve her problem for her—permanently.

"I'm sorry I didn't tell you. Does this change anything? For you I mean?"

When I glanced at her again, my baby looked... scared. Not of me, but what this meant for our relationship. I felt like an asshole filming and watching her at home, and I wasn't even going to lie, I was fucking glad her ass was miserable. But I saw something else, when she called. It looked like she'd come to some kind of decision, about us. Before this night ended, I needed to know.

It didn't mean I didn't plan to keep her, but it determined how far I allowed her in.

"What do you think?" The light turned red, and I shifted to look at her. "Ryann." She flinched. We didn't have time for soft and easy. I had to drag her to the right conclusion. "Just in case you haven't figured this out yet, when I want something I get it."

She didn't wearing much makeup. All she wore was mascara and some shiny shit on her lips. Still, she looked like a runway model. Like she always did when she was nervous or overwhelmed, Ree watched me, unconsciously rubbing her fingernails against each other.

"No, I don't give a fuck. He obviously wasn't taking care of what belonged to him, so he lost you. You're mine now. Everything I needed to know about your ex, I discovered in thirty minutes, and none of it impressed me. All of those letters behind his name didn't make him a better man." I won't bother to tell her I have enough dirt on his father, the not so honorable Judge Avery Hatcher, to ruin more than his career.

"You're right, he's my past." She exhaled and peered out of the passenger window. "Seeing him today made me remember how much of myself I gave away."

I glanced at her, to find her watching me with a sad smile.

"Thanks for helping me get back to myself." She gave my thigh a gentle squeeze and turned away again.

The rest of the ride remained silent. I drove down a deserted street in the warehouse district to a place we kept for special circumstances.

"What are we doing here?"

"Work." I entered the security code into my phone, disabling the alarms and raising the door high enough to drive a semi through.

We entered a darkness so complete, I couldn't see shit outside the beam of headlights in front of me. That was just how I wanted it.

"You trust me?" That was a stupid fucking question. She'd known me for how long? Most of that wasn't really a relationship but just her bringing me food. The rest—a car chase, a convalescence, a kidnapping. Great basis for relationship.

But it was what it was.

"Strangely enough, I do."

"Good." I open car door, walked around her side, and took her hand. "I hope you still feel that way in a few minutes." The motion-activated lights came on, and I guided her up the dimly lit stairs to a sparsely decorated office. After closing the door behind us, I wrapped my arms around her and pulled her to my chest.

"You still love him?"

She stiffened in my arms and I looked down into a sea of pain this should never be seen on a woman's face, especially this one. "No, not at all."

"Good. I don't know what happened, but I can imagine. Did that prick of a father touch you?" Getting rid of him might prove more of a challenge. It wouldn't be impossible, but an official in appellate court would be missed.

"What? How do you know the judge?"

"Did you miss the part about me digging into Keith's past? When I found out a man yelled at a woman—my woman—like he'd lost his damned mind, I made it my business to find out." Plus, judge or not, his father played a little too rough with his subs, and had been banned from our dungeons.

"I don't want you to—"

Too late. "Keith put his hands on you?" She didn't speak, not that I gave her a chance. "A man, any man that lets his woman walk out of his house, no matter how angry he is with no money, no nothing, isn't a man at all. I don't give a shit how mad I got at you, I would make sure you're safe."

She tried to wiggle out of my arms but I held tight. She wasn't going anywhere until I said she could move.

"You're scaring me."

"Good." I let go of her and stared at my boots. "No, it's not good. I don't want you scared of me. What I want is for you to be safe. What I want..." I looked at her trembling lips then up to her eyes.

If she wanted me, she needed to want all of me. The real me. I wasn't just money and penthouses. I was just as much bareknuckle brawls and back alley shankings. If the shit was going to work—and I hoped like hell it did—I wasn't hiding anything. I didn't want her hiding shit from me. For a minute, I rationalized keeping her, at arm's length, but in the end, both of us would finish the relationship more damaged than when we started.

I moved close enough that if she took a deep breath her breasts would brush against my T-shirt. "What I want, no what I need, is for every asshole in Illinois to know they mess with you, they die."

I hit the button to turn the lights on in the warehouse and jerked the blinds open.

"Oh my God."

What was in her voice?

Disgust?

Shock?

Fear?

"It's up to you." I stared down at the battered and bleeding male tied to the chair and none of it made me feel better. The swollen eye, the busted lip, the seeping wound on his forehead; none of it lessened the rage. Each time my fist slammed into his too pretty face I wondered if he'd done the same to Ryann.

"No. Dorian, no." She slapped her hand over her mouth and lurched closer to the glass.

I wanted to wipe that fat tear rolling down her cheek away. That fucker didn't deserve her tears. He didn't deserve anything—not even her hate.

"His life is in your hands." She gasped and I shook my head. "No, not that simple. When I said I needed it, I wasn't bullshitting. His life. That prick no longer walking this Earth; that's what I need. But you have to give it to me. So what's it going to be?"

"If you were asking me to choose any man on the planet, it would be you. I knew when I first set eyes on you I'd never be the same. I'll give you me—all that I am." She jabbed her index finger at the dusty window. "That man out there means less than nothing, and as much as I despise him, his life is not mine to give. I'm not God, and neither are you."

I knew. One look into those eyes and I knew she would choose the dirt bag. Was my ultimatum fair? Probably not. But I need her to give this to me and she couldn't—simple as that.

I closed the physical distance, cupping her cheeks, pressing my lips against hers. Damn she had the best lips. I'd never see or feel them again.

Because we were done.

"You don't want this on your soul."

"I'm good, sweetheart." My soul was so black this one thing would make little difference. "I'll make sure you're safe."

"I don't want to go."

"Is his life mine to do with what I choose?"

"No."

"Then I guess that's it." It was fun while it lasted. Looked like I was right; she was too much of a good girl for me. "Until I get your shit sorted, you sleep downstairs."

"Dorian, no—"

"No, we're fucking done." A soft knock sounded at the door and Antoine poked his head in. "Good, you're here. Take her back to the penthouse."

I turned my back on her and the last bit of goodness in my life.

Chapter Nineteen
Ryann

The last four days were like a merry-go-round that sped up each time I wanted to step off. I didn't know whether I was right or wrong to ask Dorian not to kill Keith. Keith was an asshole, and he hurt me. Not just physically—which sucked big time—but emotionally and worse financially.

Dorian assumed I still loved my ex. To tell the truth, I hoped he got run over by a bus. His life meant nothing to me at all. Less than nothing.

Despite that, I still didn't want his blood on Dorian's hands. When time came to atone for our sins, that's when Keith would pay the price—not before.

I've observed Dorian with Antoine and Paul. Allegedly, they work for him, but they're more family than employees. No one could be all bad and treat someone the way he treated me. I just refused to accept that.

It hit me, standing in that warehouse, even with all the fancy lake view penthouse, the money, and the real estate, Dorian felt undeserving on some level. I'm no psychologist, but from our initial meeting until the fiasco in the warehouse he never trusted that I would choose him. Much of the time he did everything to remove the power to make a decision by either kidnapping or coercion.

If I would have chosen to gift Dorian a life which didn't belong to me, I may as well have murdered Keith myself. Were it in the defense of myself or anyone I cared about, I don't believe I'd have a problem defending myself. However, participating in cold-blooded murder?

My fall from grace wasn't so steep that I'd grab that branch. Those thoughts and the threat of eternal damnation almost lost out to the plea in Dorian's eyes to covet a life with him over my moral imperatives. That line I refuse to cross—not even for him.

Someone in his past took his love and abandoned him. I knew disappointment personally, so I felt his pain. I'd never seen anybody as deserving of affection and loyalty than Dorian. Now, when it's too late, I realized I would have loved to be the person to spoil him.

Even if it wasn't me, I prayed he found love.

I placed my items in a grocery bag, because I didn't want to take anymore from him than I already had. I wouldn't even take what I did, but walking the streets of Chicago naked? No, I wouldn't want to scar the public like that. My lips twisted into a half smile, knowing he'd give me shit for that depreciating comment.

Another little piece of my heart flaked off thinking about not just how he looked at me, but how I felt when he did it.

Whatever.

I grabbed my cell phone and glanced over my shoulder at the guest room before closing yet another door.

Seattle was on hold temporarily. I learned my best friend Lisa's mother was diagnosed with cancer when I called her three days ago. Hearing her awful news put my problems in perspective. The wounds of my heart paled in comparison with Lisa losing her rock.

After twenty years of friendship she recognized the sound of sorrow in my tone and cajoled it out of me. I told her everything, except the murder solicitation. She then proclaimed she would handle it.

The last few days gave me time and space for reflection. Right now, if the police were to stop me, I could say with all honesty I had no idea the whereabouts of my former husband. His life and family were no concern of mine. Time to rebuild my life.

I'd finally pulled my head out of my tush and accepted help from Lisa's father, an attorney who hated Keith's father. Maybe it was time to accept help from the people who love me. I didn't have to do everything on my own.

I walked into the empty living room. I guess since he decided that he was done with the relationship, that meant he was done guarding me. I snagged a beer and plopped down on the couch, raising it in a silent toast. "To good times and heartbreak." The melodious tones of the doorbell rang out in the empty apartment. Even the doorbell sounded classy.

I grabbed my things which consisted of underwear, slacks, and blouses, leaving the cocktail dresses and jewelry behind. My fingers fluttered to my neck and trailed across my choker.

Except for this. I couldn't bear to let this go, I needed something to remind me of the ten days of crazy. *Well, time to get on with my life.* I sucked in a breath, and pulled the door open to crazy Lisa Chen.

"Holy shit. Are you sure you want to move out of this place?" She gave me a hug, and stormed into the room like a category five hurricane.

"Yes, I'm sure." *I'm sure I wasn't even close to ready for this to end.*

"Where's your stuff?"

I picked up my grocery bag and gave her a little shrug, mostly because I really didn't want to talk.

"You shitting me?" I shook my head. "Sister girl, you need to go back and grab your hostage stash."

"I don't want it."

"You wouldn't be in this situation if it wasn't for him. So, the way I see it he owes you."

"I'm not having this discussion with you. I'm ready to go."

"It's probably better anyway, because my dad is a kick ass divorce attorney, but if you hang out with this guy too much you might need a different kind a lawyer, if you know what I mean. By the way, did you know that Google is your friend?"

"I'm starting to regret calling you. I should have caught a taxi."

"Okay, there's rumors that he's connected with the mob and—"

"Stop." I raise my hand in her face. "I really don't want to hear you talk shit about him. I know what he is, and who he is and I'm fine with it."

"Then why are you leaving?"

The words broke something inside of me, and my eyes filled with tears again. Shit. I didn't think there was any water left in my body.

"Oh honey, I'm so sorry." Then she did what I needed most; she wrapped me in her arms and held me tight.

If I told her the real reason things ended, she might slap me upside the head, because she thought Keith needed killing, even offered to do it herself. Even though she was my sister from another mister, I didn't see this little Chinese chick doing well in Cook County jail, so I had to talk her down when she learned why I finally left.

"Let's go." She slipped her arm through mine, hooking them at the elbows. "This calls for wine and chocolate—a lot of it."

The door opened and for a minute hope bloomed so bright my chest I thought it wouldblind me—until I saw Antoine.

"Damn. Some chocolate I could overdose on," Lisa said in a stage whisper.

Antoine stopped moving when he saw her, his eyes sliding down her slender body.

"I was just leaving, but since you're here I can just leave my key." He looked like he wanted to say something and I shook my head. I didn't want to hear it. "Thanks for everything Antoine, it was lovely meeting you."

"Do you need a ride anywhere?"

"I need a ride," Lisa said, her voice bright.

"Lisa *really*?"

"Sorry." The grin on her face said she was everything but. "Let's go catch charge."

Antoine's *what the fuck* face had me chuckling for the first time in four days. I gave him a finger wave and moved to get the hell out of there.

"Hold up." He handed me an envelope. "Dorian wanted me to give you that. And for what it's worth, I think you two will find your way back to each other."

"I doubt it." I set the keys and my cell phone on the glass and chrome side table and said goodbye.

"Not even going to look?"

"No." *The sooner I left this building the better.*

"I will." She snatched the envelope.

For the life of me, at that moment I couldn't remember why we were friends. She ripped it open like it was hers and she didn't care. Oh, I know why—because she didn't.

"Holy shit," she said as she read the piece of paper. She waved it back and forth, holding it with two fingers. "Girl you must have a gold lined vajayjay. I can't believe this shit."

I snatched the piece of paper out of her hand and my jaw fell open.

"That son of a bitch."

Chapter Twenty

Dorian

She defended me.

But then she left her key and cellphone, the only method I had to contact her, and walked out of the penthouse and my life.

They did once; birth control pills weren't a hundred percent. Maybe she'd leave with a gift other than the collar I gave her. She had no fucking idea what it meant, other than a pretty piece of jewelry. I got a wild hair and gave it to her knowing it meant something entirely different to me.

And maybe I'd sprout wings and fly.

I pulled my desk drawer open and withdrew my phone, tapping the power button on the side. Ree had no idea I'd taken a picture of her one morning while she lay sprawled on my bed. She was both a fucking cover hog and a bed hog. Even though it felt like someone ripped my chest open to extract my heart, I had to smile at how every damned morning I woke up on the edge of the bed because no matter where I moved, she needed to be pressed up against me.

Not even Ambien would help me sleep now.

Thank fuck for work.

Speaking of work, I fired up my desktop, pulled up my notes about everything that happened, and Amanda's report with Brittany's account of the night her friend was roofied. That shit would stop.

To make the entire situation worse, we'd received more discs.

Of all the victims, either Sterling, Carmine, or myself, had fucked them. There was never a relationship, and not even animosity after—just orgasms. This smelled personal.

My office door opened, and Sterling and Carmine walked in.

"Please, come in and have a seat."

"You can't let her go man." Carmine, ever the romantic, sat on the couch across the room.

"I can, and I will." I sent the file on my desktop to the printer in the conference room. "Doesn't matter, she left a few minutes ago."

Then it struck me, I never even brought her to my office. I would have fucked her bending over my desk. That was one of the things on my list. Of the three of us, I was probably the only one that hadn't done a woman in the office.

"You left the software on her phone right? You can always go get her after you get shit sorted." Sterling leaned against the side of my desk with his arms crossed.

"Look, I appreciate your—"

"*Ma'am*, don't make me have to take your ass down." Amanda didn't yell, never raised her voice in the five years she worked with us, but she did it now.

"Call security." I looked at Sterling, who already had the phone in his hand when the door flew open.

"You fucking asshole." Ryann marched in, looking cute as hell, and a lot younger than thirty-six. She walked up to me and flung a handful of shredded paper in my face. "You can't pay me off like some whore."

A hot Asian chick, looked Chinese, followed her as far as the door. Instead of watching the show that was my woman, she stared at Sterling.

"Dorian, I'm so sorry." Amanda walked as fast as she could in her pencil skirt, followed by Chicago Police Department's finest.

"Looks like we're going to jail, so you might want to hurry this up." The chick at the door stepped in, slammed it shut, and locked it. Then she slipped an iPhone out of her pocket and pressed a button. "Dad? I'm good. Yeah, I'm with her right now." She listened for a few seconds nodding her head. "We'll get there as soon as we can, but I think I'm going to need bail money."

Sterling and Carmine looked back and forth between the two women, but all I could see was Ryann.

"Sweetheart, did you destroy a hundred-thousand-dollar check?" It took every fucking thing I had not to laugh. She was meant to be in my life and in my bed.

"Hell yeah, she did. I don't know what kind of magic you have in your pants, because I think she's lost her damned mind."

"Do you need some help? I could call the people with the little white jackets?" Carmine didn't look too concerned, seeing that he'd leaned back on the couch with his hands behind his head.

Lisa reached in her jacket and pulled out a cute little .380 and aimed it at Carmine.

"What the..." Sterling said.

Ryann spun around and stared at her friend. "Are you kidding me? I swear to God; I am telling your mother when we get to the house."

"I'm assuming this is Ryann? Hello," Sterling moved and froze when the barrel of the crazy woman pointed in his direction.

"Open up." Something pounded against the door. "CPD."

"You're too hot to shoot, but I will. Ryann, these guys are criminals. I told you I had your back."

"Annie Oakley," Carmine said. "Your friend is fine."

This was some crazy shit, but I didn't care. Ryann stood in my office furious and hot as hell in that little dress that made her tits look awesome. "Why are you pissed?"

"Because...because..."

"Everybody out." Ryann jerked and I wrapped my hand around the back of her neck. No one moved. I swear if I didn't know better, I'd look around for hidden cameras. But seeing that I'm a paranoid fuck, either my boys or myself swept the office for bugs daily. So the only cameras in here belonged to me.

That crazy woman wasn't the only one packing, and my gun was way bigger than hers. She found that out when I whipped it out and pointed it at her.

"Show off." And as if nothing happened, she slipped her gun back into her holster and smiled.

"Amanda, we're good," Sterling yelled.

"Except that we're trapped in a telenovela," Carmine said.

"No hard feelings, right?" The crazy woman walked up to me and extended her hand. "Lisa Chen, best friend."

"Sir, we're going to need you to open the door," a frustrated male voice said as the pounding at the door grew more frantic.

Lisa's phone rang and she pulled it out. "It's my dad Ree-Ree. Is he going to have to get us out of jail? I have a consultation with a patient tomorrow."

"Please tell me she's not a psychiatrist?" Carmine muttered.

"No, I'm a proctologist, that's why I know an ass when I see one." She looked at Carmine then back at me. "Is this the point where you two have hot and dirty make up sex?"

Ryann fell into me, burying her face against my chest. That's when I decided I liked her whack job of a friend. "Tell me this is a nightmare and I'm going to wake up any second now."

"Sorry Ree," I wrapped my arms around her and swore I'd never let her go again. "This is the good part of the dream, where we have dirty make up sex."

"I'm going to throw up." Carmine opened the door and let swarm of people in. "It's just a personal matter. Although her friend may need a psych eval."

"Hey, have you fixed your erectile dysfunction problem yet?" Lisa asked with a straight face.

Chapter Twenty-One
Ryann

The office finally emptied without Lisa and I getting arrested. Amanda, the too pretty secretary, accepted my apology and an invitation to lunch, but only under the condition that I told her the entire story. I liked her. And Dorian's friends? Well, I'm sure they thought I was out of my mind and understood why he dumped me.

Overall, not a bad afternoon after getting evicted and breaking up with your millionaire boyfriend.

Now I just needed to get the heck out of here.

"I'm sorry about all of that. I'll get out of your hair. I'm sure you have a ton of work to do." I sat in a chair in front of his desk like I attended a job interview or something.

"That doesn't work for me." He sat behind a dark wood desk that was an interesting blend of modern and traditional. "I'm glad you stopped by."

"I don't want to play your games." He confused the hell out of me. Earlier he was all touchy feely, now it felt like he didn't even want to get close. "Thanks for not pressing charges."

He moved from left to right in his swivel chair, studying me like a bug under a microscope. Screw that, and screw him. I stood and wondered what I ever saw in this handsome, complicated man.

Just as my fingers wrapped around the doorknob, the click of remote controlled door locks that sounded like jail bars clanging shut made me jump. "You wouldn't dare?" I tugged at the door knowing I wouldn't be going anywhere until he decided it was acceptable.

I was so focused on my escape I didn't know he was behind me until his body pressed me against the door. This brought back memories of another time a million years ago when I really wanted to escape. If I knew how much it would hurt when it finally did end, I might have tried harder to get away.

"Don't go," he whispered against my hair as he eased my dress up. "I'm sorry I gave you that fucked up ultimatum."

The brush of his pants against the back of my thighs, and the evidence of his want pressing into my lower back, made me want to make love to him one last time, but that would make the walking away so much more difficult.

"I forgive you, but I need to leave."

"No." He pulled away, sighed, and tugged me over to the couch.

If he seduced me, I probably wouldn't be able to say no, but sex couldn't fix what was broken between us.

He sat and pulled me onto his lap, straddling him. "Look, I don't know how else to say this, but I'm an asshole. Other than my friends you are the only person I've let in, and I've known them for over twenty years."

"You've never been married?"

"Fuck no." He leaned back and rested his hands on my thighs. "You really didn't do a simple internet search?"

"No, I figured you'd tell me more about yourself either when I asked, or when you felt ready."

"No shit?"

"What was the point; I was already hooked," I confessed.

"You want to push play and start this shit over?" He cleared his throat, slipped his hands under my dress, and gave my thighs a squeeze. "Maybe we can date. You know like normal people."

"Sounds good." That wasn't what I'd hoped for, but it was a start.

"I'll give you Lisa's number, and you can call me."

"What the fuck are you talking about? You're moving back in."

I wasn't even going to lie; my heart did a summersault. "I thought you wanted to date."

"I do, but I can't sleep if you're not there pushing me off the bed."

"Me either. I mean, sleep without you there."

"So you'll stay?" He made that face again. That face that said he was prepared for everything to go to shit. But I was tired of running, tired of not grabbing what I really wanted. It was time I became ruthless.

"I'll stay."

"Thank fuck." His hands were in my hair and pulling me in for the kiss of a lifetime.

I'm not sure how long it lasted, but by the time he finished, I lay on my back beneath him, and my ripped panties were flung across the room.

"So is this where I get the dirty sex?"

"I could do that." Someone knocked at the door and he let out a foul curse. "What?"

"Sorry to interrupt," It sounded like the dark haired crazy handsome one, I think his name was Carmine or something, and he didn't sound sorry at all. "The meeting's..."

"Shit, I really need to—"

I touched my fingers to lips I didn't think I'd ever tire of and smiled. "Go to your meeting."

"Wait here?"

"For you? As long as it takes." He kissed the tip of my nose and got himself together while I watched. There were no declarations of love, but at least no felonies were committed in this reunion. One thing I knew for sure, being with Dorian would never be boring.

Hade's Playground
by Isis Pierce

"Damn, I'm hot," Jamie said, plopping herself down in the booth next to Eva.

Jamie's bright red hair was plastered to the top of her head, tendrils sneaking out of the tight bun she had started the night out with. Her teal eyes sparkled, and her ivory complexion appeared to be quite rosy after her tryst on the dance floor. She had spent the last hour out on the dance floor, sandwiched between two of the most delectable alpha males Eva had ever seen. Eva had watched in amusement as her succubus friend had teased both males with her undulating hips. She'd been stuck in a smoldering tornado of lust and Eva had also felt a twinge of envy watching what appeared to be a private show between the three.

This was the first time the two friends had ventured into this bar and, after Jamie's little dance, Eva doubted it would be the last. Diablo was the only supernatural bar in Nevada, accurately located in Sin City, a.k.a. Las Vegas to the rest of the world. The bar itself was owned by none other than Dionysus. Rumor was that he delighted in the carnal sin that saturated the mortal realm.

He opened up this business with Hades, who took care of the running of the club, because all Dionysus wanted was to drink and seduce the women. Hades tolerated this outrageous behavior so he'd have an excuse to leave his depressing realm. After all, the God of the Underworld dealt with whiny, restless, twisted perversions of spirits on a regular basis. It was a full time job but he had an assistant he could call upon if he needed to leave. He made sure he had to leave on a regular basis.

Eva had just turned twenty-five and was finally old enough to visit. That was the only rule to the bar. Jamie had met the age requirement three months ago, but like a real trooper she'd waited for Eva so their first time could be together.

The two hunks Jamie had been dancing with were eying her, like a delicious sexual steak, juicy and just begging to be eaten. The sexual pheromones those men were throwing off had Eva fanning her face. The men sat at a corner in the bar, diagonal from where they sat, nursing a couple of beers, if the sweat on the bottles were any indication.

What captured Eva's attention the most had to be because the men were complete polar opposites of each other. They reminded her of the Yin-Yang symbol. One Light. One Dark.

The first man had blonde hair, icy-blue eyes, and perfect snow white teeth. He even had dimples when he smiled. He wasn't smiling now, but Eva had spotted him flashing that heart-breaking grin almost the entire time on the dance floor with Jamie.

The second man sported ebony black hair that brushed his broad shoulders, dark smoldering bedroom eyes, and full lips that just begged to be kissed and nibbled on. Unlike his friend, he wore a full blown scowl that twisted his face into menacing lines and seemed to be directed solely at Eva. She almost snorted her fruity beverage up her nose at the fierce gaze directed her way.

"What's so funny?" Jamie's growl of annoyance had Eva laughing out loud.

"Nothing."

"Nothing, my plump ass." Jamie scrutinized her, arms folded beneath her breasts, lifting them up for a tantalizing view to the room.

She raised her eyebrows at Eva, who was still watching the men, and then turned to look with suspicion at them. Both men adopted wide-eyed innocent expressions. Her eyes connected first with the blonde man. Her intense stare held his for a moment before she turned her attention to the dark haired one.

When the men started to squirm from her succubus stare, Eva coughed to break the tension and asked, "So, which one are you taking home for dinner?"

"Who says I'm taking only one home? I missed a feed last night, and I'm really hungry." Jamie pulled the black V-neck of her shirt, trying to air out her still flushed breasts. Now that she wasn't staring at the men, they both watched her with ravenous looks. Eva shivered from the charged sexual air they were throwing off.

It reminded her of the episode she had recently seen on the Discovery channel. It had showcased lions taking down their prey, working together to herd the clueless gazelle away from the pack before they had cornered it and taken it down with one vicious bite to the gazelle's neck.

That's not to say she thought the men wanted to tear into Jamie's neck and rip her to shreds. No, it was in the predatory way their slowing eyes tracked each of her small movements, big bodies tense like they were about to pounce and fight over a new toy.

Eva felt like a voyeur in this group, glancing back and forth between the three, all who were throwing off sex-me-up pheromones.

Normally, she would place her bet on Jamie, her being a sexual energy succubus, but in this instant she would have placed her bets on the two men.

"I wonder what they are?" Eva mused out loud to herself.

A twinkle lit Jamie's teal eyes.

"Shapeshifters," she said in a matter-of-fact tone.

Jamie could sense energies and auras, and Eva didn't doubt her claim of species.

"Yes, but what kind?"

Jamie shrugged her shoulders, "Who cares? They're hot." She gulped down the rest of her Long Island Iced Tea and stood. "I'm going back out to dance, you coming?" She started to walk away, but Eva snatched her arm, preventing her from taking another step.

Jamie glanced down at Eva, who was still sitting, her eyes glowing brightly in the dim club, a sure sign she was hungry.

"Just be careful with them," Eva said.

Her eyes dimmed for a moment. "Did you sense something?" Jamie knew Eva's powers as well as she knew her own. Eva's witch intuition wasn't perfect, but it was rarely wrong.

Eva pushed the blonde bangs out of her eyes. "Yes," she said simply.

Jamie folded her arms across her chest. Her boot started to tap with impatience on the sticky bar floor. "Eva Zayas, are you going to tell me exactly what you sensed or sit here all night looking mysterious and shit?" She had the patience of a saint so the sight of her boot and defensive stance had Eva letting out a small, hysterical laugh.

"Eva! Focus!" The glare shot her way could have melted asphalt.

"Sorry," Eva snorted.

She thought back to the feeling, her eyes darting over to the shapeshifters, who were still patiently stalking their meal. Her voice dropped lower to account for their supernatural hearing, and Jamie leaned down to hear her better.

"It's not a negative or a positive feeling," Eva said. Jamie looked relieved until she continued, "But if you continue down the path you're going on, it will be life-changing in many ways."

Jamie's looked stunned for a moment before she masked her expression into a more neutral one.

She peeked over her shoulder, and then looked back at Eva and mouthed, "They're still staring at me." She straightened up, her hands fussing with the hem of her skirt, smoothing out non-existent wrinkles. She took a deep breath and said, "You only live once, and I'm not going to die with any regrets."

Eva nodded. She had already known how this was going to play out. At Jamie's words, she bit her cheek to keep the smile off her lips, as she knew her friend wouldn't appreciate the humor of the situation.

With those parting last words, Jamie sashayed back over to the gorgeous two hunks, who stood up at her approach. They took her offered hands to lead her back to the dance floor.

Eva gave a sigh before calling out, "Bartender, another Sex on the Beach, please." Under her breath she muttered, "Because Hades knows, this is the only sex you're going to be getting tonight."

***

Hade's shifted in the corner booth to get a better look at the blonde, violet-eyed witchling beauty, who was currently chugging down fruity drinks at his bar like someone had announced it was the end of the world and she was trying to fill some unseen drinking quota in the next five minutes.

This had to be her first time in the bar, Hades knew everyone who came here. She had probably just turned twenty-five, since all supernatural creatures visited at least once after they turned the magical age, to see what all the fuss was about. After that they became regulars, hence how Hades knew who everyone was.

Diablo was a strictly paranormal-only hang out that was a mix of a bar, a nightclub, and a dorm. Admittance was enforced, not only by protective wards placed around the perimeter of the building to keep humans out, but Hades also had two shapeshifters positioned at the front and back entrances of the club. He paid them astronomical amounts to do their jobs, and they earned every penny.

Humans were naturally curious about the supernatural world: immortals, vampires, shapeshifters of all walks of life, gods & goddesses, demi-gods, angels, and demons. Basically anything they'd ever read about existed, but they'd only been made aware of it in the last twenty years or so. To humans, they were exotic. Sexy. Mysterious. They were like moths to their flame, tempting to fly towards, but burned to a crisp if they wandered too close. Hence the exclusion of humans from entering his club.

Diablo gave all paranormal folks the chance to be themselves and not have to worry about any of their powers or instincts creeping in. He made a lot of money, because who wouldn't want the ability to be themselves in a world they had to hide in everyday at mortal jobs? A world that could reject them or shun them or kill them, all because they were different.

Hade's recalled a time when a human female had actually made it into his club before the doormen had realized something was wrong. The female had been average. Mousy brown hair. Brown eyes. Nothing spectacular about her face. If spotted in a crowd of humans, she wouldn't catch or keep anyone's attention. But, this creative genius female was determined to get into the club. She was determined that she was some shifter's destined mate. Most would classify her as a book nerd, reading paranormal romance and dreaming of a love that she knew she'd never find in the human world. After all, how could a regular mortal man ever compare to a paranormal man?

It had been a Saturday night. Diablo had been packed beyond compare. Bodies literally touched bodies, so it had taken some time to notice the woman. He later found out her name was Sassy, and he knew from personal experience her name had been fitting. Sassy had somehow convinced a witch she worked with to cloak her in a shapeshifter essence. Her human side had been completely hidden and the only thing his employees could smell on her was a female wolf in heat. They'd let her in because no one had known what witches could do and, at the time, Hade's hadn't had the perimeter wards installed.

After she'd entered the club, chaos had ensued. The club housed a number of shifter customers at any time and shifters weren't particular about what species a woman was; if she was in heat, their animal side would feel the call. Fights broke out between the shifters wanting to claim the girl. The club floor was painted bright red before Hade's and his men could separate everyone. At least twenty shapeshifter men had felt the woman's pull that night. Right before Hade's put Sassy in isolation, she had been about to be bitten and claimed as a mate by a lone werewolf Jaxon. As his razor sharp teeth had inched towards her neck, Sassy blurted out, "Stop, I'm human! You'll kill me with a bite like that."

Jaxon's fangs had retracted, and he'd stumbled back in disbelief. He leaned down and sniffed her. "No, you smell like wolf. You smell like home. You can't possibly be human."

"I am," she had replied quickly. "I swear to God I am. I came in here to find someone to be with. I'm not beautiful, and I figured if I was a shifters mate, his instincts would want me and I could be happy with him."

Jaxon had shaken his head, "You are beautiful. Your hazel eyes spark with warmth when you are dancing. Your hair reminds me of the forest, the earth that houses the trees. Your smile, filled with mischief and laughter. Your body and the way it moves against mine makes my wolf howl with satisfaction. The man in me who finds all of you exquisite. How can you think you're not beautiful?"

Shiny tears had filled Sassy's eyes, "That's not me. It's because of the shapeshifter essence I ingested. You wouldn't be saying any of that if it weren't for some dumb spell I had my friend Samantha cast."

A big smile had illuminated Jaxon's face before he replied, "The spell is wearing off, and I can smell the human side of you. I stand by what I said before. You are beautiful. You are lovely. And my wolf and I agree that you are still our mate, human or not."

Sassy's face lit up and took on a hopeful expression. "You aren't just saying that because you're a man and want to get into my panties? I'm not saying I'd object to that, but I'd rather know the truth going in, rather than having my heart broken later down the line."

Jaxon let out a snort of laughter, "First, I'm not a man. I'm a wolf shifter. Second, I have no reason to lie darling. You're in heat and I know your body wants to connect with mine, just as my wolf and I want to share that connection with you. Third, the only way you could possibly smell like home to me, is if you were irrevocably my mate."

Hades had snapped his fingers and Toby, one of his panther bouncers, had scurried over. "Somewhere in this crowd is a powerful witch. I've felt her power pulsing through the club all night. Find her. Grab her and bring her to my office. Let her know she'll be well compensated for her time and skill at breaking a spell for me."

Toby nodded and hurried off to do his master's bidding. Everyone who worked for Hades knew the raging, inferno temper he had. He was, after all, the God of the Underworld. He lived underground in a dark, damp playground. The only real fun he had was traveling from his domain to the mortal realm, via the Styx river. It was fun because he was able to get the hell out of the pathetic excuse they called a domain.

Zeus got the beautiful stormy skies, his famous lightning bolt, and Olympus. He was the king of gods. Poseidon got all of the bodies of water and any sea lives that entailed. He got a trident with immense power that made all the creatures under the sea quiver in fear. Hades? He got the Underworld, which had to be the most depressing place in all the realms. Most people would rather cut out their own heart than live there. Made it really hard to gain followers.

Both Zeus and Poseidon acquired weapons that looked like they were made for them, and Hades got landed with a pitchfork. Granted the pitchfork caused some hellacious earthquakes, but why did he feel like he was a farmer and he should have a straw hat on and a piece of straw in his mouth? Maybe ride around on a stallion.

He just wasn't known for love and patience. Most gods weren't, but there were a rare few capable of love.

Not one of his staff wanted to be on the receiving end of Hade's rage if things didn't go as he demanded. Toby would be quick in bringing the witch to his office. He was a hard ass to his staff, but he expected the best and he gave back what he could to his team so they'd be willing to do anything he asked of them.

Hades pointed to Jaxon and his supposed mate, "You two follow me. We'll meet with the witch to confirm or deny these mate suspicions immediately."

Jaxon didn't know Hades and started to protest, but as soon as he'd caught the literal flames jumping in Hades eyes, he shut the fuck up and grabbed Sassy's hand to follow.

Hade's gave an exhausted sigh and ran a hand over his face, "Look, I'm not trying to be a bastard but when humans are involved, certain protocol has to be followed or this club gets shut down by the Paranormal Government. Believe me, if this club ever shut down, I'd never hear the end of it from Dionysus, and I have enough shit to deal with, without adding family drama to the mix."

Jaxon muttered, "I heard you liked being called a bastard."

At any other time, Hades might have cast a fireball at the shifter or sent his favorite hellhound to give this wolf a run for his money, but he was tired tonight. The shifter would live to see another day.

A small smile crossed Hade's face that couldn't be seen by the couple behind him. "You're right, I do like being called that. The only reason I don't mind, is because people don't want to cause trouble when you're a dick. It's a technique to keep people in line and if they don't follow the rules, they pay the consequences."

He gave a dark laugh. "Bloody shows of power are the best possible lesson I could teach anyone. Throw in a few of those, and people will behave like they are in church. Especially if you show your power in front of a crowd, say on a busy Saturday night. There is not one person in this club who wants to fall prey to my evil clutches." He paused for a moment and added, "Or fall prey to my hellhounds. It's like a horror movie when the hellhounds get added to the mix. You can literally hear the screams of pain and terror for weeks after, haunting your nightmares. Or so I've been told. I have no trouble sleeping at night."

He turned around to face Jaxon directly because the next words were important for the young shifter to grasp.

"However, while I like being the asshole that everyone pees their pants in fear to tick off, I don't want to stand in the way of mates." He chewed on his bottom lip for a moment before speaking again. "Mates are hard to come by and should be cherished above and beyond anything else. A woman's love is the most precious gift any of us could ever be blessed with. That love should be held above anything, and a man should have the opportunity to prove to his woman that true love really exists. It's not just a fairy tale. A man can be faithful and true to one woman. One woman he can be honest and truthful with. One woman he'll do anything to protect and keep safe. Not just physically, but emotionally, too. One woman who he honors and cherishes above anything else. One woman that he'd rather cut out his own heart and die before he caused a single unhappy tear to spill from her eye. One woman he'd move across galaxies to find if she ever vanished. That kind of woman is worth any sacrifice."

Hades grew quiet, lost in his own thoughts. His dark eyes flashed with emotion. "A mate is worth more than anything. So, yes, I'm a complete bastard, but I'm not completely insensitive. I understand the gift you've been given, if she truly is your mate."

Sassy stared at him, her soft pink lips opened and a look of utter astonishment across her features. The only thing she could mutter was a breathless, "Wow."

Hades glanced over at her and gave her a small smile.

Jaxon looked between them, then shot Hades a resentful glare. Hades gave a small shrug. He couldn't give a flying fuck if Jaxon had to work twice as hard to woo her now. He knew the shiny jewels that mates were. How incredibly rare they were to find. How difficult it was to discover the missing piece to a puzzle. How improbable it was to find a mate to connect with, on every facet of a person's soul. Mind, heart, body, energy. After all, he was thousands of years old and he still hadn't found his. This thirty-year old pup had no idea how lucky he was to have found her this young in his life.

Hades had watched thousands of others find their mates over the years. He'd watched the all-consuming love those individuals had for each other. He'd watched the good and the bad times, and how each couple dealt with the same situation differently. He'd tried to put himself in their shoes when they faced numerous problems, and wondered how he and his future mate would react to a similar state of affairs. Some couples couldn't handle the pain that certain incidents brought. Infidelity, dishonesty, and lies, to name a few. Some of those situations were excruciating. Some had brought those problems to the marriage when there hadn't been any problems. Sometimes, watching those couples, he had felt that one party was not as equally dedicated to the relationship as the other.

Those were the relationships that made Hade's romantic side scream inside his mind. *You idiot, why would you do that? Can't you see she loves you? Why would you ruin the beautiful love you've been given? How could you claim to love them, and then cheat on them?*

Those were the relationships he watched fall apart. Sometimes, very rarely, he'd see a couple pull back from all the pain and suffering and take a path of healing. He watched the tears, the hurt, the regret, the anger. Then, somehow, those rare duos would burst from the ashes of agony like a phoenix, tougher than ever, feathers glistening with a shine that hadn't been there before.

He'd offer advice to those rare twosomes who clamped down on their love and wouldn't let it go for anything. If one of them brought a problem to the relationship, he'd point it out and ask them why they carried that issue, when there'd been no trouble to begin with. He watched the couples from afar, and they gave him hope of finding his own love.

His staff would get a kick out of the hopeless romantic he really was, if he'd let them live with that secret. If Jaxon loved Sassy, he would make any sacrifice. Do anything to secure her affection. Make choices to ensure that he'd never lose her.

Hades said softly, "Don't glare at me like that, Jaxon. Mates are precious. Listen to my words. I know your wolf is ruffled up, but if you repeat the words in your head, you'll see I'm right. You and your wolf should be willing to do whatever it takes, if she truly is your mate. From this point on, her wants and needs trump any desires you have for yourself.

Jaxon's jealous glare faded and he gave a small, grudging nod of acknowledgment.

He turned an admiring gaze to his new mate. "You're right. They are worth more than anything, and I will honor her every single day till the air leaves my lungs and my heart can no longer sustain its beat."

Hades watched him, making Jaxon fidget, before he said, "Remember, not every day of your relationship will be perfect or easy. Going in thinking that is unrealistic. There are going to be days where everything is fucked up. Everything that could possibly go wrong in your lives, will. Shit will rain down from the skies, and it will try to drown you in its overpowering, disgusting stench. The difference between success and failure in your relationship will be on how you handle what's thrown your way. How you chose to deal with each problem. How you both chose to deal with each problem.

"You can face the problems together or you can try to fix them on your own. But remember, if you chose to try and fix the problems on your own, you can create problems that don't even exist. You can choose to fight it together. You can fight tooth and claw for the love you've been given. You just have to remember in the end, even with all the bad, is it still worth all the good?

"In most cases with true love, even with bad, the good still outweighs any negative. Basically, you'd rather be with this one person the rest of your life, even when shit's not flawless, than be with someone else who might be a perfect life partner, but she'll never make you feel the way your mate will."

Jaxon looked thoughtful, absently scratching his blonde beard before replying, "It's kind of like human marriage. Humans marry and they promise to love one another till they die. Through sickness and health. Through good times and bad times. It's making a promise to love one another, not just when life is picture-perfect. The true test of that love is when you stay with someone, even through all the bad times. You aren't promising to love just the good parts of a person or just the good parts of the marriage. You are promising to love all of them. You're promising to love that person even with all of the negative that comes with it.

Things that even that person might hate or loathe about themselves, you stand by them and you show them that you still love them. You couldn't be more naked or vulnerable until you've had that with someone. There is nothing more intimate than baring all the parts of your soul to a person. You can bare yourself, be completely naked, with someone skin to skin and you're vulnerable physically."

He paused. "But sharing the personal demons that all individuals carry? Sharing that emotional side of yourself, with the one you love is an intimacy that some people can't handle. Because you are sharing the deepest, darkest recess of your soul that you find ugly. If you share that with someone you love, you fear they'll reject your or they won't accept all of it. They'll only accept the good side.

"That's why those marriages fail. People go in with unrealistic expectations. They expect their life and love is like a storybook. It's all happily ever after with no problems ever. People want to believe that they can have that, that there doesn't have to be work involved and that perfection is just handed to them on a silver platter. When reality hits home and they realize there is a boatload of shit that goes with all the good, they actually have to bust their ass and fight for that happy ever after, they give up. Most people are lazy. If it's not easy, they feel like it's not worth the effort."

He glanced over at Sassy and his expression lightened up. She just stared at him, and Hades knew she was thinking about what kind of demons her future mate had hidden and if she would ever get to discover them or if he would hide them like many other men did.

Jaxon spoke softly to her. "I have demons. Everyone does. I have never shared them all with one person before. People have expectations on who you are supposed to be. If you expose your shortcomings, you always wonder if the people who love you will really stand behind you. The shame can keep that side of yourself hidden from the world forever.

That doesn't mean I won't share with you, but I might need time to share everything. I don't want you to see me as a monster. I don't want you to decide I'm not worth the effort because of my past and things that I'm ashamed of. I don't want you to leave me because I have insecurities that are hard for me to share."

His big hands reached for her smaller ones. He held them for a moment, looking down at their intertwined fingers. His thumbs absently rubbed circular motions across the backs of her hands.

He glanced up, and his steel blue eyes locked onto Sassy's. The connected gaze between those two held a thousand unspoken words and promises.

Hades smiled inwardly. He felt that whatever crap life threw their way, they'd be more than willing to fight for what was important. At the end of the day, the most vital thing was having each other. Everything else came second. If they could remember that, they'd do fine.

He still had to have the witch take off the spell that originally was put on Sassy so Jaxon could confirm one hundred percent that she was indeed his mate. There was a protocol to follow, and the humans were real sticklers about certain rules being monitored. In this case, if he didn't document and confirm this situation, it could come back later and bite him on the ass. This kind of circumstance could cause them to shut down Diablo.

Since Diablo was the only supernatural club in Nevada, he didn't want to take the risk of shutting down what some of the patrons considered to be a sanctuary. There was no other public place in the state that a paranormal being could completely be themselves, because the rest of the world and places of business were human only. No paranormal being wanted the undue attention or to be targeted and hunted down later on because someone knew they weren't human. In a way, the club was like being home. But, it included everyone else's home, so people could visit and mingle with other supernatural beings. Not only was it a sanctuary of sorts for his patrons, but it was also a refuge for Hades himself. He could handle the Underworld on a regular basis, but sometimes the darkness and screams of tortured souls became too much. Sometimes he needed to be in a place surrounded by life. He couldn't exactly find that in abundance in his shack below the earth.

He opened the door to his office and ushered Sassy and Jaxon to the loveseat. He strolled over and leaned against the edge of his wooden oak desk. Before he could speak, a quick knock on the door announced Toby's presence. He shifted some papers on his desk before calling out, "Come in."

Toby opened the door and stuck his head in. "Sir, I've got the witch you've asked for. She doesn't want any monetary compensation. She wants something else."

"Something else? Like what?" Hades didn't know what this witch could want, but if it was in his power to do so, he would. He refused to let his club get shut down.

The witch came around the corner of the doorway. She was middle-aged. Long black hair and vivid blue eyes accented her doll-like face. A snug black dress hugged her slim frame. Pale skin that had not been kissed by the sun made her look like a vampire.

She spoke, and there was a husky quality to her timbre. "I require a favor in return, at a time of my choosing. Since this will be for a future time, I can't tell you what that favor will be. Only that is what I need in order to help you with your situation here." She gave a nod to the couple wrapped in each other's arms on the couch.

Great. A future favor never worked out too well. Normally a favor promised was more than what a god got from a person in return. Well, he could promise her the favor she asked for and then decide when the time came if it was a favor that he could honor. Otherwise, he could just blow her off, if she asked for too much.

"Okay. You help me with this situation and I'll give you a favor in return, at the time of your choosing." Hades thoughtfully scratched the black stubble on his chin.

The witch with no name offered a small smile, like she could hear his thoughts. "I need you to swear your promise on the River Styx." She presented him with an expectant, challenging stare, her blue eyes sparkling.

Fuck. She wanted a promise. Not just any promise, but an unbreakable promise. If Hades or any of the other gods swore on the River Styx, they *had* to honor that promise or the consequences would be severe. This is why he hated his brothers sometimes. They were vain and wanted to be worshipped. Back in the day, humans knew if a god promised on the River Styx, they couldn't break their vow. It was a way to build trust with followers because they knew a god wouldn't screw them over or they'd have to face the consequences of their actions. If they weren't so vain, the humans wouldn't even know about the unbreakable promise. But no, the other gods wanted myths and tales speaking of their greatness. Which in turn, announced to the humans any weaknesses they had.

Motherfucker. He needed to get this taken care of tonight. He had nowhere else to go. He hadn't sensed any other witches in the club tonight. He wanted to tell the witch to go screw herself, but judging from the look on her face, she already knew what he did. He needed to get this taken care of. He was backed into a corner, and the god part of him rebelled on the thought of being caught, like a wild animal. He didn't lash out at her, though he wanted to.

"I can make the promise to you, but there are some rules. I can't give you god-like powers. I can't grant you or anyone else immortality. I can't bring back the dead if their body has been destroyed beyond repair." Hades felt like he was missing something else that he couldn't provide, or at least not without great cost, but it had been a long night and he was frazzled. He just wanted to get this taken care of.

The witch gave a small, respectful nod in his direction, her long black hair briefly obscuring her face. "Those are acceptable exclusions to your promise."

Hades gave her the promise she was asking for by repeating the words but this time, he swore by the River Styx. What was it that the humans always said? Dot all your I's and cross all your T's? Something like that. He still felt like he was missing something, but he'd worry about it when and if it became a problem.

"Okay, what do you need from me specifically?" The witch strode over to the couple. "Something to do with removing a spell from this human female? What spell was on her in the first place?" She gave a questioning look directed at Sassy.

Sassy said, "I work with a witch friend. I really wanted to come here, but I knew that unless I was supernatural, I'd never be able to get into this club. My witch friend put a spell on me, so that I'd smell like a werewolf shifter."

The witch nodded, her right hand outstretched. Her left hand seemed to be following the contours of Sassy's body. "Ah, I see it. Wonderfully detailed work. Your witch friend is very talented, indeed. It's a good thing I've had a few years on her or I might have trouble taking this off."

She ran her hand over Sassy's body again, but this time she pulled her right hand back. It looked like she was playing tug-o-war with the air. Hades couldn't see anything, but he could feel the magical energy in the air as she dragged the spell from Sassy. The witch's hand fell back down to her side when she was done. A damp sheen of sweat covered her brow, and she reached into her purse for a napkin to blot her face.

The raven-haired witch nodded. "It is done. There is nothing magical left on this one's body."

Hades looked over at Jaxon. "It's up to you now, buddy. Pull your wolf to the surface and confirm or deny if you believe she's still indeed your mate."

Jaxon nodded and gave a quick dog-like shake of his head. His blue eyes shone before the green eyes of his wolf took over and peeked over at everyone in the room, assessing the situation. Sassy caught the wolf's attention because a low growl rumbled out of Jaxon's still human throat. The growl didn't sound friendly, but it didn't sound like it was threatening yet either. What was that about? Hade's hoped he wasn't mistaken about the situation. If Jaxon lost it and ripped her up, he'd have a hard time cleaning up that mess.

"Control yourself, pup," Hades spoke to the wolf, who was clearly in charge.

The wolf turned and half of his face came up in a small snarl.

"Don't growl at me," Hades snarled. "We don't have time for this shit. You are still Jaxon in there. You need to sniff Sassy or whatever it is that you do to confirm your destined mates. After that, you need to let Jaxon back to the surface. That is, if you ever want to take your assumed mate home."

The wolf began the most detailed sniff search Hades had ever seen. He started from her feet and climbed all the way to the top of her head. As he investigated, he let out growling snarls.

Hades tensed up. There was no way he was going to let this pup get his club shut down if his wolf decided Sassy was not his mate but an enemy to be ripped to shreds and devoured. He'd love to throw them both out but he had a soft spot for mates finding one another. Damn wolves were such savage creatures.

Sassy sat on the couch, motionless except for her shaking hands folded on her lap and the shallow heaving of her chest. Hades knew she was on the brink of hyperventilating. He couldn't blame her. If he was a fragile human female and this big hulk of a wolf shifter was sniffing him and making not so friendly sounds, he'd be a little nervous too. Her gazed remained downcast. Smart girl. Meeting Jaxon's eyes could be seen as a challenge.

After a few minutes, Jaxon's nose went to the hair resting on her neck and he buried his nose in there and gave what sounded like a happy chuff. Sassy must have sensed he wasn't going to tear her up, because her tightly wound body sagged onto the seat cushion in apparent relief.

"Jaxon?" Sassy spoke softly and tentatively reached her hands to stroke his back. "Come back to me, love. Your wolf and I can play later, but I need you now."

Jaxon shook his head, and his muffled voice came out scratchy, "I'm here, Sassy. And I stand by my original statement. You smell like heaven. You smell like freedom. You smell like home. I know you are my mate. If you will give me the chance, I promise I'll prove to be a worthy mate to you."

Sassy burst into happy tears and wrapped her small body around Jaxon's large frame.

"Can we go somewhere private and get to know each other better?" Jaxon glanced over at Hades for permission.

Hades gave a small smile. "I'm happy for you both. Yes, you can take her, as long as you are one hundred percent sure she's your mate. Just remember, she's human, so once you leave this club she is completely your responsibility. If she breaks any rules or exposes us in any way, you'll have to face those consequences. Do you agree to these terms with the people in this room as witness?"

Jaxon said, "Yes, I understand. Sassy is without a doubt my mate. My wolf is chomping at the bit to get her home, so he can get to know her better. I take full responsibility for her and any actions that might reflect back on the paranormal community."

Hades glanced up to find his panther bouncer waiting for further instructions by the door. "Toby, can you escort our guests to their vehicle and make sure they exit the property safely?"

Toby's slim frame leaned up from the door by using his elbows to push up in a standing position. His forest green eyes sparked with something Hades couldn't identify. He gave a mental shrug. He'd ask later if there seemed to be a problem.

"Yes, sir, I can do that." Toby gestured towards the door. "If you two would follow me, I'll make sure you make it to your motor vehicles."

After the three had left, the witch still stood near the door, watching Hades.

"Can I help you with something else?" Hades inquired with a politeness he didn't feel.

"Actually, I can help *you* with something," she said. Her eyes sparkled with a mischievousness that made Hades nervous.

"Oh, really?" He tugged on his beard, squeezing his chin and debating if he wanted to know what she had to say. Yes, he didn't like secrets and the way the witch was poised screamed of secrets. "What can you help me with?"

He hated dealing with witches. They were always so cryptic.

"I'm going to tell you about your future queen."

He perked up. He had been lonely and waiting for his mate for more years than he could count. Some witches had psychic ability or visions and generally what they foretold would come to pass.

She pulled her long black hair into a tight bun on the top of her head and continued. "She'll come into this club, a few years from now. She'll show up on her twenty-fifth birthday. She'll be fair of hair, and her eyes will sparkle with not just one eye color, but two. She'll be mortal, but after she's been with you, she'll come into her immortality. She'll be resistant to your many charms. When you touch her for the first time, your souls will connect and you'll both be able to feel that electrical charge up and down your bodies."

Hades heart started to pound. Hard enough that he could feel a pulse in the side of his neck start to twitch. He struggled to keep his emotions in check. He was a god and he'd be damned if he showed any kind of emotion to anyone who could use it against him. "Anything else?"

"Yes, the advice you just gave that young couple is advice you'll need to swallow yourself when the time comes. You'll want to clam up in fear that you'll make your future queen run. What the young pup said about demons? You'll need to be willing to share those with this woman, if you want to keep her that is. Oh, and don't try to get rid of the cat. You'll only piss her off, and she'll make your life a living hell for the next thousand years."

"What cat?" Hades felt bewildered.

The witch shook her head. "You'll know when the time comes what I'm talking about. You'll recall our exact conversation right now, and then you'll just *know*."

The witch turned to leave the room. "I'll be in touch about that favor when the time is ripe to collect a debt from the God of the Underworld."

***

Hades shook his head to clear the memory of the human Sassy and her mate Jaxon from a few years ago. Since then, Sassy had been turned into a wolf shifter by her husband and occasionally they'd stop by the club to say hello.

He turned his attention back to the most scrumptious woman he'd had the pleasure of viewing. All he wanted to do was take off her clothes. Nibble her from head to toe. Ravish kisses up and down her smooth skin. Spend hours making love to her, like only an immortal could do. If this was her first time at Diablo, she'd probably never had an immortal lover before. She was the kind of woman a man kept.

Now the real question was how to get her into his office and show her what immortal sex was all about. The other question was how he could get her to repeat that experience over and over again. He hadn't had a lover in a few years, not since that witch had told him about his future mate.

He appraised the woman, assessing if she could be the one the witch had spoken of. She was light of hair and had violet eyes. Only one color, not the two the witch had spoken of, but maybe that came out with power.

This woman was also a witch, which meant she wasn't immortal. There was a possibility this woman could be his future lover. Now how to convince her to join him for a romp in the sheets, or on his desk, or on the floor. He wasn't picky. She also met a few of the criteria he was looking for in his future queen so why not test that theory out? Especially the touching.

Most especially the touching.

Hades smiled to himself when he watched her friend walk away and heard her mumble, "Because Hades knows, this is the only sex you're going to be getting tonight."

From across the room, Hades dark and deep chuckle vibrated his chest, "Well, let's see what we can do about that witchling."

***

"Can I buy you a drink?" a husky voice asked.

Eva glanced up and sucked in a sharp breath. Woah. This guy looked like every female's fantasy come true. Dark brown hair, a little long but styled. Dark brown sideburns with a sexy one-day stubble sprinkled across his dominant chin. His eyes were dark, his nose a little big and crooked like it had been broken more than a few times. Sensual full lips that made a girl think all kinds of naughty things. How was it fair for a man to have lips like that?

He was the kind of guy Eva would love to take to her bed. She wouldn't expect anything else from a playboy. Guys that looked that good were afraid of commitment. They liked to use woman just for sex. As long as Eva expected just a one-night stand, she wouldn't be let down if it didn't turn into anything more.

"A drink would be lovely. How about a coke?" She undressed him with her eyes, conveying she was perfect with a sexy romp on the sheets, if he was willing. Hopefully his looks matched his skill in the bedroom. It would be a shame for a man that sexy to be a dud in the sack.

"Can I get you anything stronger?" he asked. "By the way, I didn't catch your name?"

She offered him her palm, "It's Eva. Eva Zayas."

He took her offered hand and placed a gentle kiss on it, his eyes rolling up to watch her face.

"It's a pleasure to meet you, Eva. I'm Hades, part owner of this lovely establishment."

Eva felt a blush sweep her cheeks. Good thing he hadn't heard her comment a few minutes ago.

Maybe he should have. Sometimes the courtesies people had to exchange in order to get straight to the sex was frustrating as hell.

"Hades, let's cut through the red tape. We know how this is going to end. You'll buy me a few drinks, and then you'll try to get into my panties. Instead of wasting that time drinking and making small talk, we could be having mind-blowing sex, instead. I don't know about you, but I'd prefer the pleasure of a few orgasms versus. sitting here wondering when we are going to get to it."

Hades looked surprised at her bluntness. Oh, well. He'd just have to get used to it. Life was too short to spend on pleasantries. If he wasn't interested in sex, then he could leave the same way he came and she could possibly find someone else to scratch her itch tonight.

"That can be arranged, Eva. I've never meet someone as forward as you are. But I do agree with your sentiments. The time wasted on drinks could be better spent bringing pleasure to both of us." His hand reached down to help her from her seat. "I could give you a tour of my lovely office."

She reached up and grabbed on the offered hand. A charge of static electricity raced through her entire body. She could feel the tips of her hair standing on end. She tried to snatch her hand back, but Hades' hand had tightened on hers so she couldn't let go. His dark eyes widened, and he regarded her looking just as surprised as she felt. An odd expression she couldn't decipher flashed across his features. The charge stopped.

"What the hell was that?" she asked.

Hades raised his eyebrows. "No idea. Might just be the static electricity in the air from the club and all of these people dancing. It's not unheard of." He pulled her to her feet. "Let's start with a tour of my office."

***

Hades dragged Eva through the club and down a short hallway, and then pushed her into his office before slamming the door closed. He dropped to his knees before her, hands reaching up to stroke her silky black thigh highs. His callused fingers brushed against the top of the stockings and he felt her creamy, soft thighs with delicate, reverent strokes. He reached up to push her short skirt out of his way and stared in fascination at her bright pink silky panties. Flamingos had nothing on the color scale compared to these. His cock pulsed when he spotted her arousal clinging to the soft fabric, and he gave a groan of appreciation before grabbing her plump ass and burying his face into her mound and breathing deep.

"Hades, please," her beseeching voice cried out.

He gave her a quick, teasing lick through the barrier of her panties, and her hands fisted his hair, crying out in frustration.

"Please what?" he asked in a deceptively unattached tone.

Inside, his heart pounded, and his shaft ached. All he wanted to do was pull her down to the floor on her hands and knees in front of him and tug those sexy platinum locks in his fist while slowly feeding his cock into her wet scorching sex.

But this was Eva's first time in the club, and her first time with him. She didn't understand how the rules worked. His rules. When he took her, it wouldn't be the only time. He'd known when he'd watched her from that booth that she was his. His little witchling was just coming into the full extent of her powers, so she didn't understand the significance of their mating yet. By the time she realized, it would be too late.

"Hades." The growl that tore from Eva's throat rivaled that of any shifter.

Hades chuckled darkly.

"I said, please *what?*" he repeated the question, his voice low and mocking.

He was ready to put her over his knee and spank the correct answer out of her. The jasmine scent of her arousal filled the room, and he took in a deep breath of air, tasting it on his tongue. His fingers trailed upward and lightly stroke her damp panties. He wanted to bury his face in her ambrosia in the worst way, but he waited patiently for her response. This part was important to his plans.

Eva sighed, the sound echoing in the small room. "Please don't tease me."

"I want you to tell me what you want," he ground out through clenched teeth. Hades had a difficult time controlling the lust surging through his body, like sand in an hourglass. Taking his mate during their first time together needed permission. Without that it probably wasn't the best way to start eternity with her. Women could hold resentments for eons, and he knew this one would certainly not let him live after something like that went down.

"I want you to fuck me. Fuck me with your mouth. Fuck me with your tongue. Fuck me with your hands." She panted anxiously on his desk, hips fidgeting up and down, expectation making the rest of her body tight and taut. "After that, I want you to fuck me with your cock. I want your dick buried so deep inside me and you fucking me till neither of us can walk."

"I thought you'd never ask." He savagely ripped her panties from her trembling body, and he relished her gasp of surprise before burying his face between her smooth thighs.

He didn't bother to start out slow. Instead, he ravenously suckled her little clit, pausing to lightly nibble the bud and then giving it a quick flick of his tongue. At her gasp, he paused to thrust two of his fingers into her glossy heat. Wanton moans filled the room, and he had to forcibly keep her legs down on the desk or she'd have squished his head with her strong legs wrapped tight around his neck. Less than a minute passed before her convulsing sheath clamped down his on digits and she cried out, clasping his head tighter to her mound, undulating against his face.

"Fuck," he growled, standing up and pinning her to the ornate wooden door in one quick move.

His lips crushed down on hers, his hard body thrusting against her soft one. He swallowed her little meows of pleasure. He inched across her cheek and down her neck, and he gave sharp love bites as he went.

"You taste like ambrosia," he whispered in her ear. "I could eat you all night."

She shivered at his words, clinging to him as one of her satin thighs snaked up his leg, nestling his body up against her damp heat. His cock welcomed it, even with his slacks on. He lifted her other leg up until both were wrapped tight around his waist.

He used one hand to reach down and free himself, enjoying the cool breeze that circulated up to caress his hotter than hell shaft. He chuckled darkly at his musings, convinced his cock was indeed hotter than the underworld at the moment. Eva braced her tiny hands against his shoulders and used them as leverage to slide on the outside of his aching shaft. She leaned down and gave a sharp nip to his bottom lip.

"Are you going to fuck me, or are we going to stand here all night?"

Her saucy rebuke had him fisting her blonde locks and guiding himself to her entrance, where he paused.

"You are mine, little witchling," he said darkly.

She nibbled on her bottom lip and gave him a tiny nod of confirmation.

"Say it," he growled.

"I'm yours, Hades."

Before the words had finished leaving her lips, his shaft was buried to the hilt and they both groaned at the tight fit. His hands reached down to grasp her hips while he helped her ride his long, hard cock. He stretched her almost to the point of pain but when his hips swiveled, a cry of pure pleasure was torn from her lips. At the sound, he pounded into her with a ferocity of a man on death row, execution at dawn, and her as his last meal. His dark eyes started to spit fire and she stared transfixed at the flames swirling there, while he effortlessly played her body to a tune only he could hear or control.

"Come for me. I want to feel that pretty pink pussy gripping my cock." His big hand reached down to flick her little clit. Once. Twice. She exploded right before he released his seed into her with a roar of pleasure that could probably be heard throughout the entire club. Even after his seed filled her, he slowly rocked her onto him, causing ripples of sensation to explode and mini orgasms to rack her body, making her cry out from the sensitivity.

"Oh, god." Her voice came out on a shaky moan and her head titled back, resting against the door, her eyes closed.

"Not quite the god you're imagining, but it will do," he rumbled.

After a few moments, her bleary eyes popped open and she squeaked in surprise, "But you're still hard."

His laugh held sensual, erotic promise, and she shivered at the sound.

"Oh, little witchling, you've only had inadequate mortal boys, I see. Fortunately for you, I'm more than willing to teach you the joys and positions of immortal sex." He lowered his voice. "And, baby, we haven't even scratched the surface yet."

***

Shit.

That was all Eva could think as Hades carried her over to the beautiful hand carved desk. His dark eyes stared into hers, and she bit her lip nervously at the raw carnal hunger she saw in him. His gaze tracked the movement before his mouth came down hungrily on hers. His soft lips dominated her own, and his tongue flicked the outside of her lips, demanding entrance.

She opened her mouth and Hades swept right in, a triumphant rumble vibrating through his chest. The kiss wasn't just an invasion. It was a conquering. Winner takes all.

Eva felt the edge of the desk brush against her ass, and Hades rested her on the top to support her weight. His hands left her ass, and he reached up to tangle one hand in her nape, pulling her deeper into the kiss, needing all of her energy and everything else she had to give. His other hand trailed to the front of her body. His callused palms swept across her shoulders, leaving little charges of electricity in their wake.

She felt overwhelmed by all the sensations flooding her body. His sandalwood scent. The cool desk on her bare bottom. His rough palms grasping and stroking her. The taste of his kiss. Sweet. Addicting. Scorching.

The heat. Oh, gods, the heat. From his hot body to his hot tongue dueling for dominance with hers. The heat on her arms.

Wait. The heat on her arms?

Her eyes cracked into little slits and the trance was broken. Hades eyes were still closed, and he let out a growl of displeasure when she didn't respond to his kiss. His eyes snapped open, and he looked down to see her staring transfixed at something over his shoulder. He turned around. Flames covered the walls of the entire office. These weren't regular flames, either. They weren't orange and smoking. No, these flames were blue, a cheery hue that danced and leaped and appeared to have scenes playing out in them.

***

Shock held Hades paralyzed for a moment before he snapped out of his daze. That was not a witch power. This was a goddess or god power.

"Eva." He kept his voice quiet but firm.

He feared losing her to the god flames that covered the office. She appeared oblivious to everything but her gaze was transfixed on the fire.

He reached down and tilted her face until her bright eyes met his own. The color in those depths startled him. Instead of the dark amethyst before, now they were blue. Not just any blue but a deep hue that matched the sky on a dark, cloudy day. Only, unlike a cloudy day, they glowed with a fervent fire and she stared at him, her expression blank. She had entered into the transition trance.

What. The. Fuck.

He snapped his fingers in front of her face. Nothing. He eyed the bright flames surrounding them and wondered if he could get her out of here, before the fire closed in on them.

Before he could come to a decision, the door to his office opened and Dionysus hurried in, a sheet of paper in one hand and a flask of wine in the other.

Dionysus was tall, even by god standards. He topped a bit over seven feet. Like Hades, he preferred the snug leather pants on Earth over the long, white flowing robes on Olympus. Both men had agreed it was not right for a man to wear a dress, no matter how great a breeze felt on the balls on a hot summer day.

His piercing grey eyes took in the scene and whatever he'd been about to say cut off as a streak of foul ancient Greek curses filled the room.

He reverted back to English, "What the hell, Hades? Why aren't you controlling your powers? Walking through god-power really fucking burns, you know? Hurts worse than even piercing my cock."

"That's enough. I don't need to hear about any piercings." Hades' gaze flicked down to the man's leather pants. "Anywhere." He gave a significant pause. "I'm not the one creating the fire."

Dionysus's head whipped around to stare incredulously at the petite blonde perched on this desk. His eyebrows shot up at her raised skirt, and he provided Hades with a look of approval.

He gave a small cough. "Her lips are showing."

"Of course her lips are showing, you idiot." He glanced over at her full pink lips that sported an adorable Cupid's bow he wanted to nibble on, even now.

Down boy, he mentally commanded his erection. Now is not the time to stand up.

Dionysus gave him an insolent smirk. "Those aren't the lips I was referring to."

A leer towards Eva's southern region caused Hades to see red.

"Stop looking at her like that," he snapped.

Family or not, if Dionysus' didn't keep his eyes to himself, Hades was going to rip them out and feed them to his hellhounds—after he let the puppies chase him down, of course. Good training exercise.

The other god's eyes widened like he could hear Hades' plans, and he threw his hands up in surrender. "No offense meant, Uncle. I'm the God of Wine and that kind of goes hand-in-hand with lust. She's an exquisite little specimen, and you expect me not to notice her?"

The room started to crackle with another kind of heat, and Dionysus abbreviated his last statement.

"Okay, I get it. Eyes to myself. You know you're going to have to bring her to Olympus." Dionysus said.

The room lost its heat, and both men turned as one to stare at Eva. Hades hands became clammy at what he would have to do.

Hades didn't say anything and just stared at him.

Dionysus asked, "Well, when are you going to take her? She doesn't have forever, you know."

Hades took a deep breath. "Now."

"Need some help?" Dionysus asked in a hopeful tone.

Hades shook his head. "No, I'm good." He turned to look at Eva. She was still lost in the transition trance. She would remember some things about it later on, but for the moment she wasn't completely here.

He had no plans to bring her to Olympus. If he voiced that thought out loud, Dionysus would fight with him for hours and he wasn't in the mood to deal with that shit and then wind up forced to take her to the last place on earth she needed to be. Besides that, she might burn the club down by then.

The gods were a cruel and vicious lot and if he took her there, the other goddesses would be jealous and petty because of her beauty and try to kill her. The gods wouldn't care because, after all, she was just a witch and a halfling and had no real place in their world.

Not going to happen. No matter what, she was his and he'd kill anyone—god or otherwise—that tried to take her from him.

"Can you stop your whoring ways for a few nights to take care of the club?" Hades voice expressed worry and doubt.

Dionysus chest puffed out with indignation. "Of course I can. This club was my idea, remember?"

"Yes, I remember. I also recall that I'm the one who's ran everything for the last twenty-years." Hades tone was dry.

"I'm not a complete moron. I can handle it," Dionysus said, then mumbled, "Or find someone else to do it."

Shaking his head, Hades walked over to wrap Eva in his arms.

Before Dionysus vanished in a puff of teleportation smoke, he said, "Be careful with her. Those goddesses are vicious bitches, and they'd eat a pretty little thing like her up."

Hades nodded and wrapped her in a cloaking spell before teleporting them to his home.

***

Hades managed to teleport them directly into his spacious bedroom in the Underworld. He set his precious bundle down on the god-sized bed, before stepping back to look at her.

He gave a satisfied growl. He hadn't expected to bring her to his home this soon, but he liked seeing her there. She looked like she belonged. He knew if he could bring her out of her trance she'd look gorgeous sprawled naked on his black silk sheets. Her long blonde hair would be fanned out over the pillows, her violet eyes beseeching him. She was made to be his queen. Her light to his dark. Her innocence to his guilt. Yin and Yang, to be precise. The bright blue dancing flames had followed them, and they started to hungrily lick their way up the walls. He scrubbed his face, feeling the edges of a beard starting to form, and sighed.

The task ahead of him was a long and grueling one. A task so momentous he couldn't recall a time in all of his eons of existence that any god before him accomplished it alone, much less successfully. In the past, it had taken at least six gods at full strength and it was better to have eight for the transition to be successful. Of course, the high number also ensured none of the other gods weakened, because it could take days to complete.

He walked over to his treasure, who still sat on the bed. Her pink lips were still swollen from his earlier kisses, puffed up with a slight redness around her chin and neck from his scruffy beard. He cupped her face with gentle, shaking hands. His eyes stared into her vacant gaze and he whispered, "Please forgive me, love, but I might have killed us both."

Four Days Later

Dionysus took a deep breath and let out a tired sigh. It had been four days since Hades had taken his little witch to Olympus, and he was exhausted. Even with the help of one of his trusted vampire employees, the club was still not operating as smoothly as it should.

He ran a hand through his mussed hair and glared at the paperwork on his desk. Unfortunately, all the glaring in the world did nothing but give him a pounding headache. His eyes closed and he rested his head on his hand, his fingers massaged his scalp, desperate to relieve some of the ache.

"Dio?" Onyx practically whispered. Almost like he knew his immortal vampire life was hanging in the balance and one wrong move would snuff him out quicker than basking in the sun.

He opened his eyes. Onyx stood a safe distance from the desk. His ash blonde hair was spiked tonight, and his aqua gaze connected with Dionysus's direct grey stare.

"Yes, Onyx?" Dionysus's voice held a note of impatience. "What can I do for you?"

"No, Dio, it's what I can do for you." Onyx swept up the paperwork from the desk with blurring speed. "I can take care of this for you. I've been helping Hades with this type of stuff for the last six years. Not every day, of course, but I step in so he can have a few days off each week."

Dionysus put his hands together like he was offering a prayer, "Thank you, thank you." He stood up and headed for the door. "I'm not sure how much I could have handled." His hand paused on the knob. "I'm also concerned about Hades. It normally doesn't take this long for a transition."

Onyx nodded. "It's been four days. Doesn't it only take forty-eight hours with all the gods helping?"

"Yes." Dionysus's voice was soft. "I'm going to head to Olympus and find out what the hell is going on."

"Do you need me to manage the club for a few days?"

"That would be great, Onyx. Remind me to give you a raise when I return."

Onyx let out a loud chuckle. "Don't worry, I will."

***

Dionysus thought of home and instantly his body drew him to his pad in Olympus. A few sexual nymphs lay sprawled out on his leather couch. Lusty moans echoed throughout his household and once again he was grateful that his nearest neighbor was miles away. The two nymphs were wrapped so thoroughly in each other that they didn't sense his presence.

He leaned his big frame against the doorway, crossed his arms, and put one big boot against the wall to watch. These two particular nymphs were a favorite of his among his hundreds of potential sexual partners. His followers were large in number, both male and female and across all parts of the globe. He might not be one of the three big gods---Zeus, Poseidon, or Hades—but his followers surpassed each god's individual followers and in another hundreds years or so, he'd surpass their combined followers with his own.

There was just something about drinking wine and being uninhibited that folks could relate to. When they worshipped Dionysus, they got to do something none of the other gods allowed. They got to be free, and they got to be themselves. In an earthly world where everything was a prison—jobs, family, children, and friends—being a Dio follow meant one didn't have those concerns.

Okay, they still had those concerns, but by worshipping him, they got to take a break from all of that. A chance to forget about mortal worries.

Zeus followed the old ways. He wanted sacrifices, and he didn't just want someone giving up their phone for a week as a sacrifice. No, he was all about the blood sacrifices. He wasn't too particular about who died, but the bloodier, the better. And if a mortal sacrificed family or their child, he held them in the highest favor. Because the world was different nowadays, those special demented mortals who were willing to pay the ultimate price were rewarded beyond measure. He'd give those followers anything they desired that he could provide. He wouldn't make anyone a god, but any material items a blood sacrifice person made was rewarded in leaps and bounds. That is, if they could get over the fact they had mutilated someone they were supposed to love.

Most mortals on Earth today wouldn't make such a sacrifice because they preferred love over wealth, but Zeus still had about seventy-five devoted favored members. He'd made those followers immortal, because the of the blood sacrifices they made in his name. As long as they continued to worship him and make blood sacrifices every few years or so, he'd let them keep their immortality.

Dio knew that Hades didn't agree with Zeus's practices. He might be the god of the Most Depressing Place on the Earthly Realm, but he valued love above anything else. Reap what you sow and all of that. Of course, he was smart not to tell Zeus his thoughts, as he wouldn't approve.

Poseidon also held to the old ways of sacrifice. Controlling the ocean could make for some very unpleasant waters if one pissed off the god of the sea. Not only did he control the ocean and earthquakes, he also controlled every existing being in the water. If mortals really knew what lived under the ocean, they'd never set foot on a boat again.

Poseidon mainly favored sailors. There were still sailors out there who worshipped him because of myths passed on from their forefathers. And when their boats didn't sink, they took note that it was the god Poseidon who protected them because of their continued sacrifice to him.

What did one sacrifice to Poseidon to hold favor? Horses were a particular favorite. Sailors took them out onto their boats and threw them alive into the water. A big wave would come up and swallow the horses, and then the sea would be calm. He wasn't as bad as Zeus, though. When mortals made sacrifices to Poseidon, he actually kept the horses alive. He turned them into sea horses, and not the little ones. No, these were honored horses that carried Poseidon and those he favored around on his underwater chariot. If he used a horse one had sacrificed, that individual could expect great favor for at least a few years to come.

Stallions and beautiful mares with unusual markings were a favorite. Those horses were favored more than some worshippers, especially sailors who were cheap and sacrificed the bare minimum when Poseidon knew they could afford better. He took care of his followers so they wouldn't starve, but most people didn't know that. He just wanted the willingness of the sacrifice, that one would be willing to starve to please him. That's where he got his sea rocks off, so to speak.

Then there was Hades. He was probably the least worshiped out of all the three big gods. Most related him to death and the underworld, and he held no particular favor for any worshippers. He didn't give a crap about any sacrifices made to him. The only sacrifices he cared about were those that increased his population in the underworld. Those factions had a slight sway with him. But any other sacrifices one could make to him wouldn't matter. He'd just roll his eyes and move on. It didn't matter what one surrendered. There was nothing he wanted that he couldn't get on his own and, unlike his two brothers, he didn't need to be worshipped to feel satisfied in his life.

Zeus and Poseidon needed the reassurance of having followers, where Hades just didn't give a fuck. Most mortals wouldn't even mention his name, in fear that he'd hear them and come after them and their families. He might have been a bit scarier, back in the day, but only because he didn't like to be bothered by followers who needed reassurance constantly. Who had the time for that? Hades didn't care if a mortal worshipped any of the gods, or if they worshipped goats. He just wanted to be left the fuck alone. Mortal prayers bothered him. That's when he became testy and flames started to dance in his eyes. That's when a human had to worry, because that was usually the last thing they saw before being incinerated.

Dionysus liked to be worshipped, too, but unlike the other gods, he preferred worship of the flesh. His followers enjoyed the sensual devotion, as well, and that's why Dio was always seen depicted in drunken orgies.

It wasn't always like that. Maybe in the old days, but presently, more people were reserved about getting naked and having sex with multiple partners. Especially now that technology could pinpoint exactly who the father was, even if a woman had sex with twenty men. Most mortal men lived in fear of being the one who'd get a girl pregnant. They assumed a pregnancy would end their lifestyle, so most wouldn't participate unless they were sterile. That's not to say those men wouldn't enjoy pleasures of the flesh. No, they definitely enjoyed that, they'd just make sure to wrap up, so to speak. Mortal men had to worry about STDs, even with oral sex, so that kind of took the pleasure out of bare flesh on flesh. He'd been told it was not quite the same.

He wouldn't know. He'd never had to use a condom. He was never more grateful for his god status. Imagine if sex was diminished even slightly because one had to cover his pecker with a rubber? He might prefer to be a monk if that was his only choice. Hell, he did have a hand, so if he had been susceptible to condom sex, he imagined he'd prefer the use of his hand. There was nothing quite like a woman's warm, slick heat. The contours of their walls that gently stroked the tip of his cock. Feeling the cool air on his wet shaft as he pulled in and out. No, he would rather go without than put a barrier between him and the joy he got out of a bare pussy.

Thinking of the pleasures of pure, animalistic sex, Dio's gaze tracked the two nymphs. Callie was currently grabbing the back of Lili's blonde hair to pull her in for a deep, sensual kiss. Callie's pink tongue darted out to lick along Lili's red bottom lip. She pulled back a bit before Lili could lean into the kiss. She licked her ruby lips and reached for Callie. Callie teased her a bit by leaning back and staying slightly out of her reach, before darting back in for a nibble on Lili's bottom lip. There was something sensual and arousing about watching two people who were so into each other that the rest of the world faded away. There was only them. Their hands. Their lips. Their bodies. Dio could practically see the electricity of their sexual energy spark in the air.

Dionysus could feel his shaft begin to pulse in his leather pants. He gave a gentle rub over his pants and told himself, *soon*. There was a reason these two were his favorites out of hundreds of followers. Callie and Lili had been part of his life since the very beginning. They were a couple who had been together for at least a few hundred years before they had met him. The chemistry he got to watch between them made sex all the better when he got to join them.

Dio was the only one they'd ever let into their couple bed. They'd both been with men before they had found each other. They found all males lacking and didn't feel that there were any magical cocks out there. Until they'd found Dio, and he offered them whatever they wanted. The only thing was they had to give him a chance to change their minds. Dio had pulled every trick out of his sexual hat and had used every bit of his charm in and out of the bedroom to completely satisfy these erotic creatures.

At the end of the two weeks, the women agreed that they would allow Dio into their bed whenever he wanted. In return, he let them stay at his pad on Olympus. They didn't like socializing with the other nymphs, who wanted them in their beds, too. Callie and Lili were so much in love they abhorred the idea of getting into the sack with anyone else. Living at his warded place gave them the space they both wanted and needed. Both also had a jealous streak about a mile wide. That became apparent when they tried to be with others at the beginning of their relationship. Needless to say, the nymph that was originally involved in the sharing was never the same again. The cuts on her face healed eventually but that kind of turmoil leaves a mark on a person's soul. Both emotional and physical. Because of that one incident the other nymphs wouldn't want to be in their beds, but they saw what Dio saw and even at the risk of being cut into little ribbons, they wanted to be a part of the magical sexual connection those two shared. Ironically enough, the nymph Kelly who got sliced and diced now preferred the company of mortal men in her bed. There were plenty of other nymphs who'd have been suitable, gentle bed partners but she wouldn't have anything to do with any of them anymore.

He turned his attention back to the women.

Clothes had come off, and Lili had noticed him. "Hey sexy, do you want to come play with us?"

Dionysus got ready to shuck his clothes and then realized he couldn't right now, even though he really wanted to. Damn. He had come here on a mission, and he had to fulfill that. Damn family obligations.

"Oh, pet, I really wish I could engage today. But, there's some other business I have to take care of on Olympus first. Rain check in a few days?"

Both Callie and Lili gave him big smiles and together said, "You bet."

Within seconds, they were wrapped up in each other again, Dionysus forgotten in their heated passion. He gave a sigh. His uncle owed him big time.

He walked outside and started to transport to each of the gods' homes to inquire about Hades. After he visited five of the gods, he realized his uncle hadn't been up to Olympus in at least a few months. None of them seemed too concerned. Hades didn't like to visit Olympus, so his lack of visitation didn't come as a shock to any of them. A few of them had started to ask questions about Hades and if he was missing. Dio had been evasive in his answers, claiming he was only looking for him to speak with him about Diablo and nothing more.

He shook his head. If his uncle was attempting what he thought, he was an idiot. Transitions needed at least four gods helping the female in question before her goddess powers would come through. The gods didn't mind the servicing of any sexy female. There was always more than one, because otherwise the power and strength needed to transition could drain a god and actually kill him.

What. A. Fucking. Idiot.

Not only was Hades risking his own life, he was risking the life of the violet-eyed beauty. It was one thing to be willing to risk his own life, but he didn't want to risk other people's lives in the process. Great. He'd have to go confront his crazy uncle. Shit was going to hit the fan. Just going to confront him would be suicidal.

Guess insanity ran in the family.

***

Hades was exhausted. The transitioning of a goddess took an enormous amount of power and energy. Normally, with the other gods helping, it took less than forty-eight hours for the woman to blossom into her new role of immortality. It had been four days, and Hades had never felt this tired in his very long immortal life.

How the hell did humans live with this kind of exhaustion? Especially new parents. He'd watched over the years and new moms had an abundance of patience for their tiny little human offspring. He watched them go countless hours of sleepless nights and then watch them repeat the same process the next day, over and over again, for years at a time. Honestly, he couldn't have done it. He'd have killed the little bastards and been done with it.

He had no sentimental value for anything that caused anything other than pleasure. If he wasn't one hundred percent convinced this was his mate, he'd just let Eva die. But he was convinced she was his future queen. That's why he couldn't share her with any of his family. Imagine spending the rest of eternity with the love of your life and then going to any family function where your brother had helped your future wife transition? This would put any human gathering to shame for awkwardness.

No, thank you. He was the God of the Underworld. This was *his* mate. If he died in the process, so be it, but he wasn't going to share her, not now, not ever. Call him what you would, but he was a possessive jealous god and he didn't really want to kill someone because the other gods would retaliate and it would just be a bloody war for the next decade.

He glanced over at Eva. She was sleeping on his god-sized bed. Her skin still had a sheen of perspiration dotting her delicate, white skin. After four days of non-stop sex, she had passed out from sheer exhaustion. She was mortal, so who knows how she survived that long. He was a god and this was taking a toll on him. He hoped and prayed that this was the last of it and that he had successfully helped her transition. It would be interesting to see what she was now the goddess of.

He strode naked to the door and called out, "Jeffrey, can you bring me and my lovely companion some wine and food? On second thought, a lot of substance."

Silence greeted him. That was weird. Jeffrey was the most attentive servant he'd ever had and Hades adored the demon butler.

He stuck his head out in the hallway and saw Dionysus standing at the end of the hall with his arms crossed and a scowl on his normally handsome face. Great. Dio knew what he'd done and he thought to come here and lecture him. There was something about young gods that never respected their elders.

He raised his eyebrow at Dio, "Something I can help you with, nephew?"

"You're a fucking idiot! I'm surprised you're still alive and breathing at this point. Is the girl alive?" He started to walk down the hallway, but Hades growled and halted his steps. "Well, is the girl alive or did your stupid plan get her killed? We don't have that many female goddesses and it would be really shitty if you had killed her before we got to add her to the Parthenon."

Hades shrugged. "She's my future queen. Do you really think I'd have let my family fuck her? She's going to spend eternity with me. Imagine how she'd feel knowing she fucked them all and she can't even recall that? The shame and embarrassment mortals feel would be tenfold for her, especially with her new immortal life. Besides that, she's *mine*. I wasn't willing to share her. I'm not ever going to be willing to share her."

"Oh, that's just perfect. Because you're a possessive bastard and you didn't want to hurt her feelings, you risked both of your lives? You shouldn't be the God of the Underworld. God of the Morons is more appropriate."

Before the words even finished leaving his lips, his legs were covered in flames. "Really, Uncle? You know I can't feel pain."

Hades snapped his fingers and the flames dissipated. "She's perfectly fine. I'd let you go see for yourself, but she's finally sleeping. I'm sure when she wakes up she's going to want a long bath and some food. But, as you can see, we are both in good health. Well, you can see me and take my word on her."

Dionysus shook his head. "I don't know why I bothered. Heaven forbid one of your family members gives a fuck on whether you live or die."

"I'm sorry if I worried you. I'm glad you care, but one day you'll meet the one you're destined to be with forever. Believe me, you won't be willing to share her with your family, either." Hades tapped his chin thoughtfully, "There is something you can do for me, though."

"What's that?" Dio asked with suspicion.

"I need you to go back to the club. Grab Eva's purse from my desk. Find her address and bring her stuff to me. When she wakes up, I want her to have familiar things surrounding her. I'd go and do it myself, but I don't know when she's going to rouse and I don't want to leave her here unguarded."

Dionysus's eyebrows raised up. "But you have hellhounds. How would she be unguarded?"

"The hellhounds don't know her yet, and I don't want to risk one of them biting her." He glanced over at Jasmine, his head hound. I don't want to leave her with Jasmine's new pups as they aren't trained like my older hounds. A bite won't kill her but it can cause grueling pain. I want a real person watching her, and I'm not willing for that to be anyone but me."

"Makes sense," Dionysus replied. "Though, I still think you're a fucking idiot for risking both of your lives." Flames flew out of Hade's eyes to climb Dio's legs and he amended, "I can swing by there to get her address and have you some of her things within the hour."

"If I don't answer the door, we might be in the shower. Just leave her things outside the bedroom. By the way, where the hell is my butler?"

"Why are you asking me?" At Hades' hostile glare, Dio admitted, "I might have stuffed him in a closet."

"Why in hell did you stick my butler in a closet? Hades looked outraged at the notion. His butler wasn't as innocent or docile as he appeared—after all, he was a demon—but he still loved the bastard.

"Because he tried to stop me from entering your hallway to see how you were doing." Dionysus shrugged. "Something about the master must not be disturbed, yada yada. I didn't have time to go through the hired help, so I might have used my powers to duct tape his mouth shut and tie his hands and feet. I'm not even sure which closet I stuck him in…but I'm sure he's around here…someplace."

Hades shook his head, "Never mind. Can you please go get Eva's belongings?"

Dio saluted him with a mocking smile and disappeared. Hades waved away the puff of smoke that followed. Gods didn't need to use smoke when teleporting, but Dio liked to show off. He also liked to annoy family who hated it.

Hades turned back to the bedroom. His mate was awake and she was leaning against the wall, a sheet draped across her bare breasts. It was obvious she'd been listening to his conversation.

"Hey." He kept his words to a minimum. He knew she'd have questions, and he was bound and determined to start her immortality with him on good footing.

"Hello." She coughed, trying to clear her scratchy throat. Hades didn't bother telling her that the only thing that would help that would be time off from screaming in ecstasy. She looked around the bed and then down at his naked body. A sweet pink raced across her cheeks as she must have realized the implications of their naked bodies.

"What is going on? I recall us going into your office. We started to get hot and heavy, and that's when things get a little blurry. I'm remembering bits and pieces as time progresses, but I still don't have the full picture yet." She slouched down a bit when she asked the question, like she was afraid of his response.

"Well, you, my little witchling, are more than you appear. You aren't just a witch. Apparently your father or mother was a god. Half gods come into their power with their first sexual experience after they've turned twenty-five, which kicks in your immortality. Goddesses transition into their power with the help of other gods. It's all sexual in nature. I'm your first lover after you had turned twenty-five. I brought you to my home so that I could take care of you."

Her face turned beet red and she looked outraged at his response. "That seems a bit presumptuous, that I'd want to come to your home and have sex with you. Wow, how long did we have sex for?" Her hand reached under the sheet and felt around with a slight wince. "I feel like my pussy is broken. What the hell, Hades?"

He chuckled. "I'm sorry you feel your pussy is broken. I assure you that it's not. Normally, when a halfling transitions, at least four gods are on hand to help with the sexual needs of that individual so they can claim their goddess power and of course their immortality. But you are my destined mate, Eva. I knew it from the first moment I touched your skin at the club."

She looked doubtful at his response. "You knew it from touching my skin?"

"Yes. Don't you remember the charge that flowed through our bodies the first time you took my hand?"

Recognition dawned on her features, and she simply said, "Yes, I do remember that. But how did you know it meant anything? You said it was just static electricity from the dancers."

"I know because a few years ago I had a run in with a witch who was frequenting my establishment at the time. I needed her help with a situation that popped up, and she was the only available witch. Before she left, she gave me clues about my future queen. She said you'd be fair of hair and your eyes would change to two different colors. She also said the first time we touched, we'd feel that charge in the air. And since in my thousands of years of existence I have never felt that before, I just knew."

"Why is it that I can't remember everything? Isn't that like taking advantage of someone who's helpless?" Her icy glare could have cut daggers.

Good thing he was immortal. Ouch.

"I'm sorry, darling. Your memory will start to come back, and you'll remember everything we did together. Believe me, you'll want a repeat performance."

She snorted before he could continue and muttered, "Cocky bastard."

His smile held razor sharp teeth when he replied, "Not cocky. Confident. There is a difference. And I'm sorry about how it all happened. But the thing is, your power was eating up the walls of my office and would have burned down the club. Not only that, if I had left you and taken you elsewhere, you'd have died. Once the transition starts, there is no putting Pandora back in the box, so to speak. You're my mate, my destined queen. Do you really think I'd let anything stop me from saving you?"

"Wow." Her blonde hair was covering her face as she muttered into her palms. "I would have died?"

The thought seemed to shake her up. Her breaths started to come in shallow and she struggled to breath. She didn't want to die, but no one had warned her this could happen as a result. Gods 101 or something would have been helpful.

"Yes. Actually, you might have died with just me servicing you. We both could have died. Luckily for me, the place is well guarded with hellhounds. I was weaker than I have ever been in my entire existence, a vulnerability I didn't care for. But I was willing to risk our lives if that meant I didn't have to share you with anyone. I do not share." Smoldering, sensual flames danced through his eyes and she stared, mesmerized. She had no idea her eyes would do the same thing…her flames were blue, though. Like ice to his fire.

"Anyway, I have Dionysus stopping by your place for a few things. I wanted you to be comfortable living here with me. I know it's not the most cheerful home, but you are welcome to decorate it however you'd like."

Eva glanced doubtfully around his dark shack. "I love decorating, but I'm not sure even I could fix something like this."

At her spoken words, Hades watched a blue glow surround her. After a moment, flowers started to burst out of the rock walls. Gorgeous, colorful flowers of every kind. Hades watched it spread across the cave in fascination. He blinked his eyes a little because suddenly the cave seemed brighter than usual. Interesting.

"I think that's caused by your new goddess powers. I'm curious now to know which goddess you are." He glanced around in contemplation. "My realm is always so dark and dreary, and I deal with the dead on a regular basis." He swept his hand around to showcase her new flowers. "If my guess is correct, your gift has something to do with either Life or Happiness. I'm not sure which but judging by the brightness in the room now and your blossoming buds, I'm gain to vote for the Goddess of Life."

"What happens now?" Eva looked around at his place with uncertainty stamped across her pale features.

"We get to know each other. We have wild, crazy sex on a regular basis. Every time we do, you'll feel a surge to your powers. Not just your new goddess powers, but your witch powers, too. Now that you're a goddess, with a bit of practice you'll be able to transport, too. You'll still be able go to the mortal plane to visit with family and friends. We'll take it one day at a time."

Hades strode over to the bed and sat down next to her. He grasped her hands and when her little ones wrapped willingly around his, he gave a sigh of contentment.

"I know this is new. I know you're going to have questions. All I ask is for the chance to prove worthy as your mate. For the chance to make you my beautiful queen. I can't promise you that we'll never fight, but I can promise I will battle to keep us together. I will do anything I can, every single day to make you happy. Will you give me a chance, Eva? The chance to be your king? To be the other half to your soul?"

Eva stared at Hades intense bedroom eyes. Had she ever had a man stare at her that way before? Had any man promised to do whatever he could to make her happy? Promised to be the king to his queen? How could a girl say no to that?

She leaned over to place a hand on his tense arm. "I'll give you a chance. I just have one rule that must be followed at all times."

Hades leaned forward so quickly he almost fell over. His dark eyes met hers and with all the sincerity he could muster, he replied, "Anything."

"We have amazing sex. Every. Single. Day. I want at least two orgasms, or I get to kick you to the curb. Think you can handle the heat?"

Hades tackled her and positioned himself so he was leaning on his forearms to stare down at her.

"I can make that promise. We'll have scrumptious, delicious, tantalizing sex. Every. Single. Day. And I'll make you come at least four times every day." With those words, he swooped down to give his new queen the loving she deserved. As he fell into the passion of his mate, he wordlessly said thank you in his head, to whatever deity had granted him his deepest wish. Someone to love. Someone to spend eternity with. He'd be forever in their debt.

Shimmers in the Dark
by Bethany Shaw

Eight years ago the world ended. The Wolf Flu stole everything Enid held dear. Pursued by witches and humans, Enid and her pack have taken to the underground tunnels inside Mount Rainier. She seeks out solitude inside her glacial home until a face from her past resurfaces. After all she's lost can she love again?

Alex has kept his pack a secret from the humans and witches for eight years, but as the world rebuilds, their home is no longer safe. He joins the packs at Mount Rainier and is shocked to find his true mate, Enid, is alive and taking refuge there as well. She's changed over the years, broken and hurt from the devastating losses of the Wolf Flu. Can he mend her heart and keep everyone he holds dear safe from the attacking witches and humans? Or will the pack also succumb to this new, terrifying post apocalyptic world?

Chapter One

Enid slid across the wet ground, sloshing watery mud as she made her way. Her hazel eyes narrowed as she overlooked the forest beneath her. Wisps of curly, auburn hair blew in her face and she huffed, blowing them out of her eyes. She needed to see. The icy ground numbed her thighs and belly, but she ignored it.

Her gaze darted to the full moon as she pressed her assault rifle against her shoulder. She blinked, shifting her eyes to those of her wolf, allowing her to see further and sharper than any human eyes ever could.

"Enid, are you in position?" Darren's voice boomed over her COM.

"I am. All clear so far," she commented, never taking her eyes off of the trees.

Enid listened as Darren questioned Parker and Martin, the other shooters, before giving the changing youngsters below the all-clear signal. She drew in a deep breath and surveyed the area. A child wasn't going to die on her watch. Losing a kid was a pain no parent should ever have to endure.

She cleared her throat and blinked, forcing the tears that pricked her eyes away. Now was not the time to let her thoughts stray. The past sixteen full moons humans and witches had been hunting and attempting to kill the newly turned wolves. Six babies had died due to their insolence. Tonight, there would be no casualties.

Howls erupted in the air and she smiled softly. The kids had completed their first transition and were now roaming the woods close to the caves they called home. She couldn't see the wolf pups from her vantage point, but she had a perfect view of the road; their enemy didn't have the skill to come up the side of the mountain any other way.

So far, the frigid night was quiet. Her breath misted and she swallowed as she surveyed the slopes below while listening to the youngsters yip and bark at each other. The first full moon after a child born with werewolf blood turned twelve was an opportunity to transition into their alternate form for the first time. Tonight there were six youngsters, but they would be the last group making the change into adulthood for years.

Enid sighed as she swallowed a thick lump that had lodged its way into her throat.

"Do you hear that?" Parker's voice inquired in her ear, drawing her out of her thoughts.

Enid tipped her head to the side. Seconds ticked by and she held her breath. She opened her mouth to tell Parker he was crazy when a whirling sound came toward her. *What is that?*

The steady thwacking grew louder. It was a sound familiar to her, yet from another time. Her mind spun trying to place the sound.

"Helicopter," she screeched as realization dawned on her. "Parker do you see it?"

"No. You?"

"No. Martin?" she questioned as she drew in a deep breath.

"I don't see anything," Martin responded.

"Darren we need to get the wolf pups inside," Enid hissed as more howls and barks flitted through the air. They'd be sitting ducks out in the open if a helicopter were being used. The trees would provide some cover, but not enough for skilled shooters.

"Already on it," Darren replied.

Enid swallowed and said a silent prayer for the kids to make it into the safety of the mountain before whoever was flying that chopper got close enough to see them.

Leaves rustled beneath her and Enid slid closer to the edge, aiming her gun. She licked her lips as she curled her finger around the trigger. Before the world turned upside down, she'd been on the police force, one of the finest sharp shooters the state of Washington had ever seen.

Her eyes searched for the source of the noise as she drew in an even breath.

A gray and white wolf, an alpha, *I didn't realize there were any alpha kids here,* stepped into a clearing and Enid sighed, closing her eyes. *The kid must have come with the new group that just arrived. I guess I should've paid attention to the new arrivals.* Lights flickered in the trees and she scooted forward, using her heightened sight to see. The orange—not so conspicuous—biohazard suit gave away the location of her enemies.

Crap. There are humans on foot.

"I've got movement over here. One of ours, a pup by the looks of it, and at least six men on foot," she radioed as she pressed the gun into her shoulder.

"Shoot to kill, Enid," Darren ordered.

She didn't need to be told twice. There was a time when humans and wolves lived in harmony. Until the Wolf Flu, humans hadn't realized werewolves, or witches, existed. Once the flu spread from wolves to humans and witches, the werewolves had been hunted mercilessly. They were blamed for the deaths of millions of innocent people that perished due to the nasty illness. But not everyone knew the entire story.

Enid squeezed the trigger as she found her first target. The gun popped. Men hollered as her victim collapsed lifelessly to the ground. She bit her lip, locking on to her next target and firing.

The whirling of the chopper grew louder and Parker's voice bellowed in her ear, "Enid, find cover, the helicopter's coming your way."

"They'll get the wolf pup," she argued as she took another shot. *Three down, three more to go.*

"Enid!" Parker hollered into her COM.

Enid ripped the device from her ear and focused on the remaining three men. The child wasn't dying on her watch.

The blinding, white of a chopper light loomed overhead. Its searching light scanned the trees beneath Enid.

Shit. They're going to find the kid.

She rolled to her back, staring up at the darkened sky. The dark green army chopper was hard to pinpoint with the glaring spotlight, but she managed.

Men hung out both sides with their guns poised and ready to fire. Enid curled her finger around the trigger and took out the men on the right in rapid succession. Their bodies dropped out the side and plummeted to the ground below, crunching against the rocks.

The spotlight jumped, landing directly overtop of her. Enid grunted, rolling to the side as she squeezed her eyes shut against the offensive light.

Bullets sprayed down around her and she hopped to her feet, dashing behind a boulder.

The bullets clinked against the rock and she ducked down, waiting for the rain of metal to stop.

Voices called over her radio, but she couldn't make them out over the gunfire. *In retrospect, it probably wasn't a good idea to take that out.* Surely with a wolf's excellent hearing the pack would know she and the pup were in danger. She just hoped they'd come for the kid.

The bullets stopped and she jumped up, spun, and unloaded most of her artillery at the chopper. Pings filled the air as sparks flew. The small aircraft pulled up and jolted to the right as black smoke billowed out of the lower panels.

Good. I hit them.

A wolf howled from the woods below and Enid swore under her breath. The child was in trouble. She fired at the helicopter again before darting to the edge of the cliff and skidding down the side of it. Dirt and debris fluttered down around her as she hurried to the wolf pup.

The three men were still out there and had been close to the kid's location.

Her eyes whipped over the terrain wildly until she found the wolf hunkering down in the bushes. A man tiptoed toward her, his gun raised and ready to fire. To the child's credit, she'd attempted to hide, but it appeared the approaching human hit her with a tranquilizer dart.

Since when did they start taking prisoners?

Enid pushed herself faster, determined to save the child in time. Her heart thumped in her chest and her pulse roared in her ears as sweat trickled down her forehead. The gun banged against her side as she continued her hurried descent.

Her lungs burned as she leapt off a ravine and landed in a squatting position. She pushed up, drew her gun to her shoulder and shot the human point blank. Blood splattered on the inside of his biohazard suit as the bullet found its mark and the man toppled face-first onto the ground.

"It's okay," she whisper-yelled as she searched the brush for the wolf pup.

The leaves swayed and the timid wolf stepped out, bowing its head as it blinked rapidly at her.

"We need to get home," she instructed as she peered up at the sky before kneeling down to scratch the wolf behind the ears. Two men and a helicopter were still out there, though, she didn't see either at the moment. "Can you run?" Her fingers found the tip of the dart and she plucked it from the wolf's skin. "That should help a little." With a wolf's accelerated metabolism, the drug wouldn't knock the girl out, but she would become progressively sluggish as more time passed.

The wolf whimpered and crouched down as if she were going to transition into her human form.

"Wait," Enid spoke up. "That will take a lot of energy and you've already been drugged. We need to get home as quickly as possible." The sooner they got there, the better. She pointed in the direction of the caves and nodded. The drug was already taking effect. Sure, she could carry the girl if needed, but at five-foot-three and one-hundred-and-ten pounds it would slow her down.

The pup bobbed her head up and down and yipped as it took off ahead of Enid. Enid sprinted after the girl while keeping a vigilant eye on the trees. The humans didn't just disappear. Though they may keep their distance, the idiots wore the biohazard suits in case the wolves were still carrying the disease.

As the first species hit by the devastating illness, and after three quarters of their population on the West Coast had succumbed to it, the survivors had learned they were immune. The humans and witches hadn't gotten the memo. For the past eight years, the surviving wolf community had been hunted to near extinction.

"Stop!" Enid gasped as lights danced across the trees.

The wolf halted. Enid motioned with her hands to the side of the cliff. It didn't provide much cover, but it might give them the edge they needed.

Together they darted to the ridge and pressed their bodies against the icy rocks. The wolf panted as her eyes darted around.

Enid clasped the gun tighter as she focused on the light drawing near. Just one man. She could take him in combat without her gun. She didn't want to draw the other guy or the chopper to their position until the female pup was safely inside the caverns.

The man crept forward, his movements clumsy in his large suit. Enid waited until he was close enough for her to strike him. She swung the gun out, using it like a baseball bat and hitting him in the gut. The guy grunted as he doubled over. He gurgled inside his suit, sputtering as he tried to breathe.

She didn't give him time to recover. Lifting the gun over her shoulder, she whipped it around again, connecting with his head. Her enemy slumped to the ground, flopping like a fish out of water as he tried to right himself. Part of her wanted to give him the chance to fight back, but that wasn't the world they lived in anymore. It was kill or be killed.

Enid bent down and tore the mask off the man's face. She lifted the rifle and struck him with the butt just above his temple. The guy's eyes rolled to the back of his head and she sighed as she knelt down and placed her fingers on his pulse point. Nothing.

Death. It was the one thing she craved, but never managed to achieve.

The wolf yipped and stumbled over her feet as she approached Enid. "Let's get back to the caves," she said, patting the girl's head.

The wolf zigzagged as it hobbled over the uneven ground. Enid darted her eyes over the terrain, ensuring the remaining man and copter were nowhere near them. Hushed voices and pawed feet padding over the earth met her ears and she narrowed her eyes. She couldn't see her companions, but knew they were near, escorting them the rest of the way home. The group would likely go out and hunt down the human she hadn't gotten before returning home.

Home. Almost there. They just had to climb up the icy sheet that led into the caves.

Enid's feet slid under the sheet of ice covering the trek up to the cave entrance. She leaned forward, using her gloved hands to grip the slippery ground as she pulled herself up. The wolf ambled along, slipping and sliding back down to the bottom.

"Come on," Enid encouraged the girl.

The wolf tried again, whimpering as it darted up. It reached the top, but her hind legs slipped out from under her. Enid reached out, clasping the girl around her front legs and hauling her the rest of the way up.

"Enid," Darren's voice called as he jogged up to them and offered her a hand. "Are you two okay?"

"She's been hit with a tranquilizer, but I think she'll be fine," Enid commented ignoring her comrades hand as she stood on her own.

Darren motioned over his shoulder and two more people hurried out of the caves, wrapping the pup in a wool blanket and lifting her off the ground.

"You're bleeding," Darren commented.

Enid frowned and glanced down at herself. Mud caked her jacket and pants, but she didn't see any indications of an injury nor did she feel one.

"You hit your head," he said, wiping his thumb across her forehead.

Enid shrugged as she pulled back. Her gaze darted to the blood smear on Darren's finger before she pushed past him. "I'll be fine."

A warm bath, book, and her bed were all the medicine she needed. She trudged forward slipping inside the caves, or at least that's what everyone called them. It was easier to think of home as a set of long tunnels inside Mount Rainier instead of the lava tubes that they truly were. Despite the ice, the temperature inside the tunnels was remarkably warm due to the volcano lurking inside. Once she got out of her sopping clothes she'd be fine.

"Cori, thank God," a familiar voice cried out as a tall man pushed his way through the crowd gathering at the entrance.

Enid's head snapped up, her eyes narrowing as the man rushed to the girl Enid had rescued. She'd returned to her human self and was bundled in several wool blankets now. The girl couldn't stand, but that didn't stop the man from rushing to her and enveloping her in a tight hug.

A twinge of jealousy raced through her and she swallowed, fighting back tears. Her eyes misted and she swiped at them with the backs of her muddy hands. The father and daughter spoke as they embraced, but she couldn't make out their words. She didn't even realize she was staring until the girl lifted her finger, pointing it at Enid.

"Enid?" the familiar voice called out.

Enid paused, her gaze snapping up to meet amber eyes. She gnashed her teeth together to keep from crying out. *Alex!* Her hand flew to her mouth as her eyes darted to the girl next to him. She had the same amber eyes and chocolate-colored hair as Alex. The girl she'd saved was his daughter.

Questions tumbled through her head. *When did he come to Mount Rainier? Is Melissa here too? Why did he come?* She knew the answer to the first question. He'd come with the pack that had just arrived.

Damn it, I really do need to pay more attention, she berated herself. *Alex is here. He's alive!*

"Enid," Darren's voice cut through her train of thought. "Get yourself cleaned up and out of those clothes before you get frostbite." He placed a hand on her shoulder as he glanced at her.

Enid shrugged away from him, meeting Alex's eyes one last time before she bolted to her cavern.

She made her way through the icy, narrow tunnels until she came to the fork that broke off from the main chambers. No one came down this way; flooding occurred occasionally when the weather got too warm. Enid didn't mind; she liked the solitude. Everything that mattered was gone. What she had was material possessions and they could be replaced.

Her fingers shook as she pushed back the sparse, yellow sheet that acted as a door to her cavern and then drew it shut again. She let out a long breath and shook her head, willing her racing heart to calm. Alex Andrews was the last person she'd thought to see here. There had been rumors of his death. Her heart pattered faster at the realization that he was alive and he was here.

Melissa might be too, she reminded herself. Not everyone had succumbed to the Wolf Flu. The survivors were the *lucky ones*, according to Darren. She preferred to think of it as a curse.

Enid closed her eyes and shook her head. She walked to the stack of clothes that rested on a rock. Shuffling through the cotton garments, she tugged out her well-worn sweats and hoodie.

She slipped off her shoes and tiptoed to the hot springs that were in the corner of her cavern. One of the perks to exploring was finding this little gem. It was a cozy bath and a place to wash her drab linens. Much to Darren's chagrin, her interaction with the pack was as little as possible. The idea of being banished from the pack had terrified her into submission fourteen years ago. Now, she relished the idea of solitude.

Stripping off the rest of her soiled clothes, she sunk into the steaming water and closed her eyes, praying her troubles would leave. But it would be hard to relax knowing that Alex was here and under the same rock as her.

He's alive.

***

Enid is here and alive, Alex thought as he wrapped an arm around his daughter.

She looked the same as he remembered. Her hazel eyes enchanted him and wisps of her long auburn curls had fallen out of her ponytail, begging to be twirled around his fingers.

Alex's lip curled as Darren stepped in front of Enid and touched her. He had no respect for the acting alpha of the aligned packs. The man wasn't fit to lead the wolves and if Darren knew what was best for him, he'd get his hands off Enid. Alex had no right to claim the beautiful wolf, but he couldn't help his feelings.

"Dad," Cori sighed as Darren marched toward them. "I think I'm in trouble...I wandered off," she mumbled.

"It's okay," he assured.

Great! I can only imagine what he's going to say. If he thinks he's going to berate my little girl he's going to have another thing coming. I wonder if Enid is coming to. She saved my girl's life.

His attention darted back to Enid, but the auburn-haired beauty was nowhere to be found.

"I know your pack is new here, Alex, but we have rules in place for a reason. Your daughter and Enid could have been killed tonight," Darren reprimanded.

Alex ground his teeth as he inhaled through his nose. Darren's putrid pine scent infiltrated his senses and he huffed. "It was her first transition into a wolf. She deserves the right to explore. I'm sure you can remember what an exhilarating experience your first change was," he reminded the man.

Darren opened his mouth to argue, but Alex spoke up first, "Where is Enid?" he questioned, forcing his mind to focus on what was important. He had to see her again, speak to her, to make sure she was really here and alive.

"Why? I am an original member of the Rainier pack," he reminded. "I know about the feud between your alpha and Enid's father," Darren replied as he laced his fingers behind his back. "All packs live peacefully here. I don't want any trouble."

"She saved my daughter's life. I'd like to thank her and, like you said, that feud was between our parents. It has nothing to do with us," Alex quipped, casting a glance down to Cori for emphasis. That wasn't the only reason he wanted to see the she-wolf, but he wasn't going to tell Darren that.

"Enid keeps to herself. I'm sure she wouldn't want any visitors. You can thank her at breakfast tomorrow," Darren dismissed as he twirled on his heel and returned to the wolves guarding the entrance to the caves.

Since when did Enid keep to herself? The woman he remembered was vibrant, full of life, and loved being social.

"What feud?" Cori wondered, drawing him back to the present.

"It doesn't matter anymore," he answered as he led Cori down the main corridor toward their cavern. The caves were imbedded deep within Mount Rainier. Enid's pack had called this place home for generations. Now what was left of the werewolves on the West Coast took refuge here, too. His pack had been the last to join the alliance and it wasn't because he'd wanted to. They'd literally just arrived. If there had been any other option he would've seized it.

But Enid was here. Maybe it wouldn't be so bad after all.

Chapter Two

Enid tossed her wet hair up into a messy bun and blew out a few of the candles that hung from lanterns on the walls before making her way over to the stuffed blanket she called a bed. The nightstand next to the bed held a few dozen books she'd read at least five times each. She shifted through the piles, finally settling on Stephen King.

In the beginning, the wolves had raided the abandoned towns nearby. Most of their supplies had come from early runs. It was too dangerous for that now. Humans and witches were taking back the streets, returning power to areas, and moving back in. The werewolves were public enemy number one. As long as there were wolves, the humans and witches feared another outbreak.

She couldn't blame the humans; the witches on the other hand were responsible for the outbreak to begin with. Chase was ill *before* the incident involving her brother and the witch, Chloe. Enid didn't know how they'd cursed the wolves with the devastating sickness, but the witches had.

"Enid?" Alex's voice whispered.

Enid froze, holding her breath. *Alex? Is he here?*

"I know you're in there, Enid. Can I come in?" Alex questioned.

"Okay," she croaked as her knees wobbled. She cleared her throat. "Come in."

The curtains swished as he opened them and his footsteps thudded against the concrete earth.

Enid drew in a breath before she turned and met Alex's amber eyes. Alex's mouth opened as if he was going to say something, yet nothing came out. She swallowed meeting his gaze and holding it. Heat surged through her, awakening emotions she'd buried years ago.

It had been fourteen long years of separation. Time had been kind to him. His muscles were sculpted and rippled beneath the form-fitting red sweater he wore. Sexy stubble covered his upper lip and chin and she wondered how it would feel as it scratched her face.

"Hi," Alex whispered.

"Hi," she breathed. Her tongue darted out to wet her lips as her feet shuffled forward.

"I didn't realize you were here. If I'd known I'd have sought you out sooner," he admitted.

She took another few steps forward. "I keep to myself. I heard that your pack had come, but..." she trailed off as she twiddled with her fingers. "I thought you were dead."

"Not yet," he chuckled. Alex looked around the cavern before meeting her gaze again. "You are here...alone?" he gulped.

Enid swallowed. "It's just me...and you...are you here with your...daughter?" There was no mistaking the girl she'd rescued was his blood. They shared the same eye and hair color as well as a similar sea salt and apple aroma. She'd just been too caught up in the rescue to recognize the similarity sooner.

Alex's face fell. "It's just Cori and I. When my father quarantined our pack it protected us from the Wolf Flu for a while, but it made its way into our family. Melissa and my youngest, Tate, passed. We lost over three quarters of the pack, including my father."

"I'm sorry, Alex," she told him, reaching out to touch his hand. Electricity surged up her arm from the simple touch and she inhaled, surprised by the reaction after all these years.

"Me too. You had two boys?" Alex asked as he entwined his fingers with hers, his gaze searching deep within her eyes.

"Chase and James," she answered as a sad smile slipped over her face. Tears pricked her eyes and she blinked them away. "Chase caught it first, James a few weeks later. Nik…" she trailed off and shook her head as a rogue tear trickled down her cheek. She hadn't spoken about her boys or her brother, Nik for ages. It was too painful.

"For what it's worth, I never believed Nik had anything to do with that witch's disappearance," Alex told her as he swiped the tear off her cheek.

"You hated my brother," she laughed as more tears fled from her eyes.

"I did. He was reckless and had a temper, but I never thought him capable of murdering an innocent and defenseless woman," Alex replied as he caressed her cheek with his thumb.

"He wouldn't have done it." She closed her eyes as her bottom lip trembled. It had been years since she'd seen Alex, yet it felt like only hours. He'd always made her feel complete and she knew she could tell him anything, even after all this time. "Besides, he went to the shop hoping to find a cure. Chase was already sick with the virus."

"Already sick?" Alex questioned. "But…I thought the Wolf Flu was the witches' curse for Nik murdering Chloe Sullivan?"

Enid huffed and folded into Alex's arms. No one had believed her when she'd tried to defend her younger brother. Nik's disappearance after the matter didn't help the rumors. "That's what they say," she muttered. "But it's not true. Chase was already sick. Nik went to the witches for help after the doctors tried everything they could. He loved his nephew; he wouldn't have done anything to cause him harm."

"I know." Alex wrapped his arms around her, burying his face in her hair. "I've missed you, Enid."

"Me too." She wound her arms around his neck, resting her cheek against his chest. The steady thump of his heart met her ears and she let herself get lost in the rhythm of it. "I've missed this...you."

For a moment, everything was perfect. The years and tragedy that had separated them didn't exist. It was just the two of them. Her heart lurched in her chest as desire and warmth flooded her.

No!

Enid reeled back and shook her head, using the edges of her hoodie to wipe the salty tears from her face.

"Enid?"

"It's been a long time, Alex," she reminded him.

"I know. Not a day has gone by the past fourteen years that I haven't thought about you," he said, taking a step toward her. "Our parents aren't here to separate us this time. You're my mate, Enid. You always have been. Finding you here and alive...I thought you were dead, too. I'd heard of the pack at Mount Rainier, but when I learned Darren was in control I assumed you had passed during the outbreak. If I'd known you were alive I'd have come here much sooner," he admitted. "I don't want to lose you again. Give us a chance to get to know each other again."

"Alex," she whispered as she licked her lips. "I can't. I've lost everything. I can't open my heart up again. I can't lose anyone else."

Alex took a step forward and cupped her chin with his palm. "You were always so stubborn," he murmured placing a kiss to her forehead.

Enid quirked her brow at him. "Me?" She should pull away.

Alex smirked. "Both of us." He looked up at the glacial ceiling and then back to her. "Cori wants to thank you for saving her life. Join us for dinner tomorrow night."

Enid sighed and shook her head as she crossed her arms over her chest and took a step back, needing some distance from Alex and his intoxicating smell. Her body screamed at her. It begged her to get close to him. To let Alex take her, make her his. Her heart refused to budge. It was broken—destroyed—and she wouldn't let herself be hurt again.

"I'm not taking no for an answer," Alex challenged. "If you don't come, we'll come to you." He grinned and motioned with his hands to her home. "I know where you live," he paused, pointing to his nose. "And I can follow your scent anywhere."

"Fine," she caved. He would hunt her down until he got his way.

"Don't make it sound like such a chore," he teased. "I'll see you tomorrow night at seven."

"All right," she agreed.

"Good night, Enid," Alex said as he took a step back.

Enid clasped her biceps, determined to keep her hands from reaching out and stopping Alex. "Night."

***

Alex eyed the table, ensuring everything was just right. Cori was fetching food from the cafeteria, if you could even call it that, and Enid would be here any minute for supper.

The little cavern wasn't anything he'd ever consider home, but it was safe and he had Cori *and* Enid here.

The gorgeous wolf had slipped through his fingers once. He wasn't going to let it happen twice. Enid was his mate and it was time to claim her. There was nothing to stand in their way this time—except Enid it appeared.

Footsteps scuffed over the rock outside the curtain separating his room from the main tunnel. They stopped outside, hesitating for a long moment. He drew in a breath and inhaled Enid's crisp vanilla and sandalwood perfume.

Alex breathed her in and smiled. "I know you are out there," he commented.

Enid huffed and tossed the curtain open as she strode in. Her jeans had holes in the knees and the black zip-up sweater she wore was so worn you could see through the fabric at her elbows.

The packs in the mountain had it worse than his had. They were cut off from the world and it had been that way for some time. His pack had stayed in the shadows, lost to the world until a few weeks ago.

"Hey," she greeted.

"Hi," he smiled as he motioned to an old, wicker rocking chair. Everything in the caves was old. Raiding parties hadn't left the comforts of home for years from what he gathered or Darren had given him the crappiest furniture because of whom he was, it was hard to tell. "Have a seat." He struck a match on the card table that was their dining table and lit a few candles.

"Where is...Cori?" she questioned, glancing around the dreary cavern as she took a seat and began to rock.

"Getting our dinner," he commented.

"Darren can be a real stickler at times. Hopefully, he doesn't delay her for taking three portions. I'm hungry," she told him.

"How did Darren get to be the alpha here anyway?" Alex asked, lifting a brow. "I would have assumed you would be. You are the daughter of an alpha."

Enid scoffed and shook her head, sending tendrils of auburn hair gliding around her head. "No. I'm not interested in leading the pack. Besides, most people blame me for the Wolf Flu. Nik isn't around to be held responsible, so I'm found guilty by association." She forced a smile and looked away. "Darren's a good guy. These are our caves, it's only fitting that someone from the Rainier pack would lead the group."

"No one's challenged him?" Alex persisted. *How did a guy like Darren, a man with no alpha blood, become the leader of the remaining wolf packs on the entire West Coast?*

"Alex," Enid spoke, tossing her hands up in the air. "My father died,

Nik went missing, I was devastated after losing Chase and James. Darren picked up the pieces and rallied what was left of our pack together. He brought other wolves here and has probably saved their lives in the process. The old way of living is gone. We've gone from a network of twenty thousand strong to a few hundred. Our numbers are much too low for a few dozen men to be fighting to the death over who gets to be alpha. Have you met everyone here? You and I are the only alpha bloodlines in the mountain. Everyone else is a beta or omega. With the way the witches and humans keep coming after us, our species will be extinct within the century—maybe even sooner. Werewolves are a dying breed."

Someone cleared their throat and both Alex and Enid spun around. Cori stood at the opening of their cavern with a platter of food in her hands. "Hi. I hope I'm not interrupting anything," she said as she shifted her gaze between them.

Alex cursed under his breath for not paying better attention. Cori was growing up fast, but that didn't mean she needed to know the burdens of adulthood yet. "Of course not. What did you get?"

"It's deer stew," Enid answered as she stood up and walked to the card table, taking a seat.

"She's right," Cori replied as she turned to Enid. "How did you know?"

Enid chuckled. "It's always deer stew. It makes the meat go further that way. There are a lot of mouths to feed and the deer population isn't what it used to be." Her face sobered and she met Alex's eyes.

Things were even more dire here than he'd realized. His pack had come here because they had no other place to go. But if he was reading Enid's unsaid words correctly, the pack in the mountains was in just as much trouble.

"You seem well," Enid said, smiling at Cori. "How are you feeling?"

"I slept sixteen hours," Cori laughed. "I don't think I've ever slept that long in my life. Thanks for last night, Enid. Can I call you Enid?"

"Of course and it's no problem at all," Enid answered with a laugh.

Her laugh was music to Alex's ears. It was the first genuine smile he'd seen from her since he'd arrived. Enid used to always smile.

"Where'd you learn how to shoot? I've never seen a werewolf with a gun before?" Cori questioned as she set the meal on the table.

Alex opened his mouth to answer as he began to set out the bowls and food, but Enid answered first, "Well, before the world turned upside down, I was a police officer. I trained in Tacoma before returning home and joining the force here. As far as I know, I hold the record for the best long distance shot at the academy."

"Really?" Cori asked as her eyes widened. She plucked a piece of bread from the table as she sat down and stared at Enid. "Tacoma? That's close to our home, right, Dad?"

"It is...was," he sighed as he sunk into his chair. It was going to be hard not to think of Tacoma as home. The human population was coming back and after the attack on his pack a few weeks ago, it simply wasn't safe for werewolves there anymore.

Cori frowned before turning her attention back to Enid. "That's a bit far from here."

"Yes. I had to get permission from your grandfather to come onto your pack's territory. My time in Tacoma was only temporary. Most of my work was done in the small towns around Mount Rainier. A pack's territory is sacred and not a place any wolf is allowed to be on for any length of time unless they are a member of the pack."

"I've heard people talking that Dad's pack and the Rainier pack don't get along," Cori said as she took a bite of her stew. "Is that true?"

Alex cleared his throat. This was a chance to start anew. Cori didn't need to know about the past and the feud between the packs. Plus, the more she meddled the more she stood to discover. He wasn't sure how his daughter would take the news that he and Enid had been lovers once. Cori didn't remember much of her mother, but he didn't want her to think he didn't care for her either. Melissa would always hold a special place in his heart. She'd given him Cori and Tate. But Enid...she was something so much more. She was his mate—his reason for being. He just needed to make her believe that again, too. They'd separated because of fear and their parents. The less Cori knew about the past, the better—at least for now. "That's all water under the bridge, sweetie. Don't you think you should eat?"

Cori nodded as she dug into her soup. "Do you know these caves well, Enid?" Cori continued between bites.

Alex chuckled at his daughter's persistence. She was always so curious. It was an endearing quality. One that hopefully wouldn't get her into too much trouble like it had last night.

"I do. I grew up here. Most of the tunnels are safe this time of year, but when it warms, the ice melts and can cause flooding. A few of the tunnels...have gases in them that can be overwhelming as well. I wouldn't go exploring on your own. You could find yourself in a bad spot if you do," she cautioned.

"Maybe you could show me around," Cori invited herself.

Alex raised his brow in warning. Enid was a good person and he knew her, but he didn't want Cori trusting everyone. Not until he had his chance to get a feel for things here first.

Enid smiled, but it didn't quite meet her eyes. "Sure."

"When can I expect Darren to give me my chores? It's been three days since our arrival. Everyone else from my pack has them," he pointed out, sensing the need to change the subject.

"He's probably not sure what to do with you," Enid said answering Alex's question. Her eyes darted to Cori then back to Alex.

"Or, he's worried about me outranking him and trying to take control," Alex pointed out.

Enid shrugged.

"I think he likes you," Alex grunted as he stirred his soup.

"Darren?" Enid shook her head. "No." She cast a glance to Cori who looked between the two of them with a smile.

"I saw the way he looked at you last night," Alex commented. A growl bubbled up his throat at the memory of Darren touching her.

Enid quirked her brow up. "And?" she wondered.

"I get the sense you don't care for him." Alex crossed his arms over his chest as he scooted back from the table and stared at her.

"I don't like or dislike anyone. I prefer to keep to myself," she told him honestly.

"Then I'm honored you joined Cori and me tonight," he smirked.

She cocked her brow up and licked her lips. "You? I came for Cori." Enid took another bite, but he could see a small smile on her lips. "How many came with you?"

"Eighteen. Our pack was raided. We lost twenty-one men and women in the attack. After that, I knew I couldn't keep them safe where we were." Alex grimaced and tapped the table with his fingers. "I had hoped when supply trucks started running through the area eight months ago we could continue living as we had, but I should have known better."

"We've all made mistakes, Alex. You did what you thought was best for your pack," Enid comforted him. "Nobody wants to be uprooted from their home. These caves run through our territory and I frequented them often, but I miss my house."

Enid went back to sipping her soup for a moment as silence lingered between them.

"Did you at least get to enjoy the luxury of electricity again once people moved back into the area?" Enid mused, lightening the mood.

"No. We ran generators for the first year after the blackout, but no, we never got it back once we ran out of fuel. Poor Cori doesn't even remember what TV is," Alex chuckled.

"I remember watching cartoons from when I was younger, but Alice, my friend talks about some of the other shows and I'd love to have the chance to see them," Cori blurted.

"Everybody needs TV," Enid agreed. "It is a shame that we don't have that anymore."

"You've got some modern conveniences here," Alex pointed out.

"Most of it is old tech. We have a small group of people who spend the better part of their days keeping it working. One of the first groups that came to live with us lived near the National Guard building. During the mass evacuations and chaos they were able to get weapons, radios, and a few other things that have been really helpful to us. No one has left the safety of the mountains for the past three years. That's when they started rebuilding Seattle, putting it back together and moving people into the walled city. That's when the raids started here."

"I wish we could go back to a time when things were simpler and all we had to worry about was keeping the existence of magic and werewolves from the humans," Alex sighed.

Cori grunted as she finished chewing. "That reminds me, Dad; everyone is supposed to meet after dinner tonight. Darren wants to have a town hall meeting or something."

"Where?" Enid questioned.

"The main cavern by the entrance," Cori answered around a mouthful of food.

Enid nodded, accepting the answer.

Alex shook his head. This wasn't how it should be. It'd be one thing if Enid were running the show. This land belonged to her pack and she had alpha blood. The beast inside him could take orders from her. Darren on the other hand was a wannabe alpha and he'd never quite fill the shoes.

"I'd like to go on ahead if you don't mind?"

Alex nodded his consent.

Cori stood up, leaned in, giving him a chaste kiss on the cheek before smiling down at him. "I'll see you later, Dad."

"Stay out of trouble, Cori," he warned.

"I will," she promised before skipping out of the room.

Alex met Enid's eyes as she took a sip of her broth. She set her spoon in the empty bowl and set back.

"What do you suppose the meeting is about?" he questioned.

Enid sighed and ran a hand through her snarled locks. "Whatever it's about, I doubt it is good."

Alex sighed; that didn't sound good at all. With Darren at the helm of the pack, nothing sounded promising. It looked like he would have to wait and see. At least it wasn't a long wait.

Chapter Three

Enid leaned against the cool rock wall, crossing her arms over her chest as everyone filed into the large cavern. Alex had excused himself to look for Cori and she hadn't seen him since. She needed a break from him anyway.

Alex's scent intoxicated her and being with him reminded her of her carefree days in Tacoma. Her heart thrummed in her chest, kicking up a notch as a tremor of desire coursed through her. They'd been good together and had fun while their affair lasted. Their fathers had discovered their relationship and forced them to separate or face banishment. Two wolves couldn't make it alone—wolves needed a pack to survive. As banished outcasts, no other pack would've taken them in. There hadn't been another option.

She licked her lips and blinked, sending the memories of her past where they belonged. The hushed whispers silenced her thoughts and though she couldn't see Darren, she could sense he was in the middle of the crowd.

"Thanks for coming tonight," Darren began.

Enid inhaled sharply and closed her eyes. Knots twisted in her belly and she squirmed as an uneasy feeling filled her. Whatever he was going to say wasn't going to be good.

"As most of you are aware, humans came close to the caves last night. Their intentions are to kill us and they won't stop until every last one of us has perished," Darrin began.

Enid tucked her bottom lip between her teeth and shook her head.

Here we go again, great way to start a pep talk, Darren. To think, I just told Alex you were competent.

"Our situation is becoming dire. There is no way for us to know if more werewolves live throughout the territories in the United States or anywhere in the world. For all we know, we could be the last of our species." Darren stopped and cleared his throat. "Our numbers are dwindling, and our young are few. Over the past few years, I have encouraged mating within our group. However, my suggestion seems to be falling on deaf ears. At this time we only have four children under the age of twelve. If we are to survive as a species we must mate. Effective immediately, all women over the age of twenty must mate with one of the males of age in our community. The only way to ensure our survival is to reproduce."

Enid's eyes flew open as heat crept over her cheeks. *What the hell is he thinking? You can't force that type of thing.*

"I ask that all women choose a mate by the end of the week. For some of you, this is asking a lot, but I assure you this is something we must do to survive. Only one man and woman will be allowed to mate so please choose your partner carefully. This will ensure we keep our bloodlines pure and untainted."

Enid drew in a deep breath and let it out as she stomped forward, shoving her way through the crowd. The rest of Darren's words were deaf in her ringing ears. By the time she reached the center, Darren had finished his speech and was making his way through the crowd.

The people around her spoke loudly, but she didn't care about what they were saying; Darren was making a huge error in judgment.

She followed him as she clenched her fists at her sides. Darren made his way into the tunnels that led to his private quarters. Enid blew air out her nostrils as she marched after him. He was going to get a piece of her mind before he retired for the night.

"Darren!" she bellowed as she marched up to him.

Darren slowed and turned to face her. He gritted his teeth, but he didn't give her a chance to respond before he grasped her arm and tugged her into an abandoned tunnel.

"What do you think you're doing?" she hissed.

"I'm looking out for our pack, Enid," he replied as she snatched her arm out of his grasp.

"You can't force us to choose a mate," she snarled. "This isn't the stone ages."

"It may as well be. We don't have electricity, food is scarce, and we are being killed—"

"Exactly," she cut him off. "Listen to yourself! Does this sound like an environment helpless children should be brought into?"

"Enid," he sighed.

"Don't," she snapped, jabbing him with her finger. Angry tears pricked her eyes. "I told you I would never have children again. You don't know what it's like to hold your baby in your arms as they struggle to breathe and not be able to do a damn thing for them. I'll never do that again. You can't make me. Nor can you force anyone else to do the same."

"Enid, please. I want our pack to survive. To do that we have to procreate. How many couples are here? How many children? Somewhere inside that thick skull of yours you know I'm right," Darren argued as he crossed his arms over his chest.

"It shouldn't be mandatory," she stated. He did have a point—a very small one. Children were needed if the pack were to survive. "But why now, Darren? Why is this so important right now?" What brought on this sudden need to force mating?"

"If I make exceptions for one person, I'd have to do it for everyone," Darren argued. "If you're worried about finding a suitable mate I'd be happy to—"

"No!" she barked as she crinkled her nose not wanting to know what his offer was going to be.

"Why not? We would be good together, Enid. Is it because of him?" Darren ground out.

"Who?" Enid scoffed as her heart skipped a beat. Did Darren know about Alex? How could he? No one knew except for the spy her father had sent to follow her. He wouldn't have told anyone else. Her relationship with Alex was a disgrace to the pack.

"You know who, Enid. I shouldn't have even let them in this place. It's a dishonor to your father and our pack to even have them on our land. If we weren't shorthanded, I would have sent them away," Darren admitted with a growl. "It's a disgrace that you ever let that mutt touch you."

Enid gasped. Her hand whipped up and connected with his face. "You're the one that told my father," she accused as the realization dawned on her. Her father had never said who had been sent to spy on her and told him about the affair.

She flexed her hand, willing the burn out of it. Red blossomed on Darren's cheek as his upper lip curled.

"Of course I did," he admitted with arrogance. "Is that why you won't have me now? Because of him?" Darren gripped her elbow and yanked her closer to him. "I should have done this before that piece of shit showed up. I might have stood a chance then."

Enid shoved him back, pinning him to the wall. She might be tiny, but she was strong. "Don't touch me. Don't you dare ever touch me." The compulsion rolled off her tongue with ease. All werewolves born to an alpha had the ability to force their will on their subordinates. She'd never done it until now.

Darren's hand dropped away from her and she stared into his eyes, daring him to make another move. "Do you feel that?" she whispered with a smile. Judging by the wide-eyed look he was giving her he was just as shocked as she. "I'm an alpha, Darren. Don't you ever forget that."

She shoved him against the wall and backed away.

"Enid," he sighed. "The Wolf Flu is over and we need more wolves or our pack will become extinct. At least consider my offer."

Like hell!

Enid swallowed as she took a few more steps back. She spun on her heel and darted away. Darren was right. If no more children were born, the pack was doomed. Damn him for being right.

***

Alex trudged down the long tunnel toward Enid's room. Cori and the rest of his pack were preparing to leave. He wasn't leaving without her. She'd been outraged by Darren's decree, the anger on her face was evident, but he hadn't been able to catch up to her. With the chaos after the announcement, he'd needed to make sure Cori was taken care of too.

Her scent grew stronger as he approached her room and he breathed it in, allowing the aromatic essence to calm him.

"Enid," he called as he stopped in front of the curtain hanging from the opening.

Footsteps smacked the rock as she stomped to the door. "What?" she growled as she shoved the curtain aside and glared at him.

A thick black robe covered her body and he let his eyes roll over her, wondering if there was anything underneath the bulky garment. *Focus*, he chastised himself.

"I'm taking my pack and leaving." He reached out, touching her elbow. "Come with us, Enid."

"Leaving?" she whispered. "Where will you go, Alex?"

"Anywhere. I don't know yet," he admitted, gripping her elbow harder as he drew her closer.

"How many of your pack are there? Do you really think a small, handful of wolves can survive?" she questioned with a shake of her head.

Alex licked his lips. Their numbers were small, dangerously so. "It doesn't matter." They couldn't stay there under those pretenses. He wouldn't subject his pack to this way of living and there were too many wolves to forcefully take control. His pack would undoubtedly win, but not without casualties on both sides.

Enid closed her eyes. "It's not safe out there. Think about Cori...about any other children in your pack. The only way we are going to make it is by banding together. Darren has that part right at least."

"Yeah, well, when he starts preaching about forcing us to mate that's where I draw the line," he snarled. "That is not our way."

"It isn't," she agreed. "I'll never have another child. But I think it is important that people who maybe do want those things get the nudge to do so. There aren't many kids here. Only two babies have been born since the flu. If we don't procreate our species dies."

"But he's forcing this on people. If you won't leave then help me take this place. We are alphas, Enid. We shouldn't be taking orders from anyone," he argued. "We can enforce our will and take the mountain without any fighting. The other wolves won't have a choice but to follow our orders."

Enid inhaled a sharp breath and let it out. "The people here respect Darren. If we take him out by force we'll accomplish nothing and they will resent us. Respect is earned, not forced. Even if they have to follow our orders there will be unrest and that is dangerous."

"So, what are you saying, Enid?" Alex grunted as he met her gaze.

"We can't leave...nor can we take this place over," she muttered.

"Then what are we doing? Mating?" he hissed. Personally, he wouldn't mind a passionate encounter with Enid, but he wasn't sure he wanted to have children again.

"No." Enid closed her eyes as she wrenched her arm free and covered her face. "Everything's exactly how it was fourteen years ago. We're trapped. Forced to make decisions we hate."

"This isn't the same thing," he insisted as he placed his hands on her shoulders. "We are older now, wiser. We have other options this time."

"It is the same thing. The circumstances are a little different, but either way we are screwed," she mumbled as she turned on her heel and slumped down into an old recliner. The seat creaked under her weight, wobbling slightly.

How old is that thing?

"The only difference is nobody is telling us *we* can't be together," she pointed out. "In fact, Darren practically gave us permission to be intimate."

"I thought you didn't want to get close to me?" Alex questioned as he strode toward her and knelt down in front of her. *Women can be so confusing at times.*

"I was merely referencing the difference," she huffed, rolling her eyes.

"Enid." He placed his hands on her knees. Darren might have suggested the appalling need to mate, but it was something entirely different if Enid still had feelings for him. Pregnancy could always be avoided. Werewolves could only conceive when the female wolf was in heat or close to it. Enid wasn't in heat. He could smell it. "There is still something between us. Tell me you don't feel it," he challenged.

Enid ground her teeth together and looked away.

"I know you were hurt, but you can't shut everyone out forever," he insisted, lifting his hand and tucking it under her chin.

She met his eyes with a glare.

"Let me in, Enid," he pleaded, stroking his thumb over her chin.

Enid licked her lips and leaned forward, capturing his lips with hers. Alex sucked in a breath as his brain caught up to what was happening. Her tongue trailed over his upper lip and he moaned at the contact.

She tasted better than he remembered. Her fingers blazed over his chest as they skimmed up his shirt. Alex grunted as she pulled back and lifted his shirt up, and over his head. Enid bit her lip as she met his eyes.

He opened his mouth, but her lips found his again, sucking and nipping at his mouth.

The palm of his hand slid inside the cotton robe and he growled, finding her naked, plump breast. His fingers kneaded her tender flesh, eliciting a gasp from Enid.

Alex's other hand roamed over her smooth, soft thigh towards her core. He grinned against her kisses. She wasn't wearing any panties either. His fingers skimmed the outside of her pussy before he sunk one digit into her wet folds. Enid whispered something he couldn't understand against his mouth as she spread her legs wider for him.

Alex pumped his finger in and out of her, loving the way her hips rolled in time to his thrusts. He pulled back and sunk down so he was sitting on the cool floor that did little to simmer the fire burning inside him.

Enid drew in a deep breath, leaned her head against the back of her chair and spread her legs further, already anticipating his actions. He blew a warm breath against her pussy, beaming when she squirmed in her chair.

Her fingers threaded through his hair, drawing him closer. Alex flicked his tongue over her core and tasted her sweet juices.

It had been too long since he'd tasted a woman, but no one had ever tasted as wonderful as his Enid. She was his and always would be.

Her fingers grasped his hair, tighter, pulling lightly at the strands as her hips began to thrust against his mouth. Alex ran his thumb down her belly and placed it on her clit. He rubbed her sensitive nub as he lapped the juices up from her center.

Enid's cries grew louder and her thighs trembled against his arm. She was close. He wanted to taste everything that she had to offer. Flicking his tongue one last time as he gripped the inside of her thigh with his free hand, he held her to him as she came.

Her sweetness flooded his mouth and he sucked harder, not wanting any of what she had to offer to go to waste. She mumbled his name over and over again as her fingers pulled him impossibly closer to her.

She might not be willing to admit her feelings—yet—but he knew they were there. Love like theirs never went away. He'd stay here for her. The first time he'd walked away from Enid it had nearly killed him. It was a regret that haunted him for years. There was no way he'd be doing it again, especially now that he knew she was alive. Enid was his and he was nowhere close to done with her yet.

He placed tender kisses to the inside of her thigh as his fingers fumbled with the knot binding her robe together. Once undone, he shoved the fabric aside and looked up at her glorious body. She had more curves than he remembered, but they suited her well. Her breasts were plump, fuller and he couldn't wait to nuzzle them.

His cock strained against the confines of his jeans and he stood up. Enid peered at him through hooded eyes as she shrugged the cotton robe off of her shoulders. She stood up and strode bare across the room to her bed, laying herself out on it. Her finger curled as she motioned him forward.

Alex strutted forward as he worked at his belt. "I don't have any protection," he warned even though he could already tell she wasn't fertile. She'd been specific about not wanting any kids and he wouldn't hurt her like that.

"I know. I take a supplement using the plants in the area. It keeps my heat cycle at bay," she explained patting the bed next to her.

He didn't need any further encouragement. Without a heat cycle, the chances of her getting pregnant were unlikely.

Alex slipped onto the bed as Enid rolled to her back, blinking up at him. He nestled between her thighs and rubbed the tip of his length over her glistening folds.

Enid moaned and wiggled her hips. One of her hands went to her breast as she squeezed the nipple, turning it into a tight bud.

"I love it when you touch yourself," he admonished as he nipped at her other breast.

He stared down at her as he picked up a strand of her silky hair and wrapped it around his finger before letting it spring away.

"So you like it when I do this?" she questioned as she slipped her other hand down her body. She slid two fingers inside her core and closed her eyes as she bit her lip.

"You drive me crazy," he told her as he licked her bud.

"Show me," she breathed.

Alex grasped her wrist and moved her hand away from her center. He pressed the tip of his cock against her entrance, watching Enid as he pushed inside.

Enid arched her back and drew in a breath as he stretched her. She was so tight, sheathing him like a snug glove. "You feel fantastic," he told her as he dipped down to capture her lips.

Alex rocked against Enid as his mouth explored her jaw, neck, and collarbone. He licked her earlobe, loving the way she hissed and moaned as he stroked her.

Her nails scratched up and down his back as she wrapped her legs around his waist, pulling him deeper.

"I've missed you," he whispered into her ear between nibbles on her lobe.

She sighed as her nails dug deeper into his back. He'd have marks later, but he didn't care. Enid was his and he belonged to her. Any marks she left on him he would wear proudly.

"Alex," she panted as her hips ground against his harder.

Alex put his hands on Enid's hips and flipped them over. Enid gasped, her eyes widening as she sat up. She splayed her hands over his chest as she rotated her hips. Her head tilted back and her eyes fluttered shut as she moved up and down his shaft.

Her body trembled and her cries grew louder. Alex grasped her sides tighter, pushing up into her as she crashed down on his cock. Her breasts bounced as she moved urgently against him.

"Come for me, Enid," he coaxed with a growl. His muscles tensed as his length began to pulse. He was going to come, but not before her.

Enid screamed as her juices gushed from her center and her inner walls milked his cock. Alex growled as he pumped into her two more times before following her into bliss. She collapsed on top of him, panting as she pressed her sweat-slicked forehead against his.

"I've missed this," he told her again.

She smiled and closed her eyes as she rolled off of him. "Good night, Alex."

He pushed her matted hair back from her face to place a kiss to her temple. "I'm staying the night," he informed.

"What about Cori?" she mumbled.

Alex paused. He'd never left her alone before. She was safe, tucked away in their cavern. Cori had been sleeping when he'd left. Even though she was curious, she'd never leave the room in the middle of the night.

"I'll leave first thing in the morning," he told Enid.

"Okay," she whispered as he wrapped an arm around her.

She stiffened and then nuzzled closer, throwing her arm around his waist and one of her legs over his.

Alex closed his eyes and inhaled Enid's scent. He could spend every night like this for the rest of his life. Fourteen years had changed his lover, but deep down, she was still the same girl he'd fallen for. Once he helped her through the pain of the past, taught her how to let go, but not forget, she could begin to heal.

"I've missed you too," Enid whispered as she snuggled closer.

Alex smiled, but didn't move in case she thought he was sleeping. It was a baby step. The first of many he hoped.

Chapter Four

Alex rolled over and reached out for Enid, but all he felt was the chill of the bedding beside him. He peeked one eye open and then the other. *Alone.* Enid was gone. He sat up, letting the blankets pool around his waist. His eyes darted around the room. *Empty.*

The thick cave walls made it impossible for him to tell what time it was. If he had to guess, he'd put it at early morning—real early. He yawned and sighed as he ran a hand through his hair.

Where was Enid at this hour? Who in their right mind would be up if they didn't have to be?

He kicked the blankets off his feet and gathered his clothes from the ground. Tossing them on, he jogged out into the tunnel and towards the main cavern.

He inhaled and picked up traces of her scent as he walked. Why had she left? He already knew the answer. She'd shut off her emotions to keep from getting hurt. He couldn't blame her he supposed.

The packs talked amongst each other and he'd heard through the grapevine that her mate, Carter, had passed due to a hunting accident. Then the Wolf Flu had come along almost a year later. If he'd lost his entire family he'd probably feel the same way.

"You're up early," Darren's voice grunted from behind him.

Alex grumbled under his breath annoyed with himself that he'd let the other man sneak up behind him.

"Have you seen Enid?" Alex asked as he turned around.

Darren inhaled and let it out through gritted teeth. His eyes narrowed into tiny slits as his lip curled up.

Alex hadn't bathed since yesterday and there was no doubt he was covered in Enid's scent. The corners of Alex's mouth tugged up and he swallowed, biting his lip to keep from grinning. The other wolf had a thing for Enid. She was Alex's and always would be. "You're the one who wanted people to mate," he reminded as he lifted his brow in challenge.

Darren's hands fisted at his sides. If the wolf thought he could best Alex in a fight, he was sadly mistaken.

Alex took a step forward, pinning Darren with a lethal glare. "I know it was you who told my father about Enid all those years ago. That's the only time our fathers worked together to make sure their two children didn't bond any further than they already had."

Darren's eyes glistened as he growled. "My only regret is when she came home to the pack she didn't choose me. I should've imposed my rule about mating sooner. I never anticipated that you'd show up."

Alex chuckled at the irony of it. "Enid's always been a good judge of character. Whether I showed up or not, I doubt she'd have chosen you. She's extremely stubborn and she doesn't do anything unless she wants to."

Darren opened his mouth like he wanted to argue, but closed it. If Darren knew anything about Enid, then he would know Alex was right.

"I've called a meeting with a few other people. Join us," Darren ground out as he brushed past Alex, jamming his shoulder into Alex's as he passed.

Alex huffed and flexed his hands as he reigned in his anger. He turned on his heel and marched after Darren. His pack would always have his back. The rest of the residents here he wasn't sure about. If it came down to a fight for control, his pack would be greatly outnumbered. He would have to win over the residences of Mount Rainier before he could claim the title of alpha. It looked like he would have to play nice for now.

He stood several feet away from Darren as he followed him down the winding corridors of the caverns. The hushed voices of people waking for the day faded and were replaced by the drip, drip, drip of melting ice.

Where are we going?

Alex wiggled his fingers, allowing his hands and nails to partially shift. He wasn't paranoid, but the deeper they went into the caverns the more he wondered if Darren was somehow leading him into a trap. If he was, Alex wanted to be prepared.

Voices echoed in the distance, one of them sounding like Enid's. Alex retracted his claws and picked up his pace. They rounded another bend before entering a wing of the tunnels he hadn't been in yet. The ceiling was raised well over one hundred feet tall, and long, thick icicles dangled down from it.

Rays of light flitted in through the ice, casting the room in a dark blue. It was eerily beautiful and he could see why Enid loved these caves so much. He let his eyes roam over the rest of the occupants, three men and one woman, but he only recognized Enid.

Enid met his eyes for a moment before they darted away to meet Darren's. The acting alpha leaned against the rock wall and Alex mimicked his movements, tossing his arms over his chest as he quirked his brow in question.

"As I'm sure you're aware, we listen to radio transmissions whenever possible," Darren began to address the room. "We picked up an incoming call late last night. A few witches are coming back to Eatonville. They are going to the Apothecary."

"Why?" Enid interrupted.

"I don't know," Darren admitted. "But that store is where everything started. If they are going there I want to beat them to it and see if we can find what they're looking for."

"I'll do it," Enid volunteered.

"Enid, no," Alex objected, pushing off the wall and glaring at her. *Is she crazy?*

"I know this town better than anyone else in this room," Enid argued.

"She's right. Enid knows the most about the witch, Chloe Sullivan. If anyone has a chance at finding whatever it is that she had, it's Enid. I don't want her to go alone either," Darren interjected, causing all eyes to dart back to him. "It's dangerous. I do want you to take your gun, Enid. This could be an opportunity to take out some key members of our opposition."

"You want her to assassinate the witches," Alex realized with a growl. Killing in combat was one thing, but assassinating…that was something completely different.

"We've never had an opportunity like this before," Darren replied. "Enid never misses her shot."

"I'll do it," Enid said again.

"Just like that?" Alex questioned.

"These witches have been hunting us for eight years, Alex. They are responsible for both of my sons' deaths. Yes. I'll do it," she exploded.

"I was hoping you'd accompany her, Alex," Darren said, turning to him.

Ah, so that's why I was invited here today and why he hasn't given me a job yet. If I didn't know any better I'd think he's trying to get rid of me.

"I can't just leave my daughter," he argued. "She's a twelve-year old girl and I'm the only family she has." At the same time, he didn't want Enid going out alone. He didn't trust anyone but himself to keep either of the women he loved safe.

"Surely someone from your pack will look after her," one of the other guy's spoke up.

Of course there were people who would look after Cori, but that was beside the point. If he didn't come back...he couldn't think like that.

"Your daughter will be safe here. In fact, if we complete this mission successfully, she'll be that much safer. Enid is the best shot and you by far have the most training in combat," Darren pointed out.

He's using my alpha training against me. Not to mention, my love for Enid. Bastard!

"Parker and Martin, I'd like the two of you to go as backup. Enid knows the town and will go to the store; the two of you will provide cover fire if needed," Darren ordered.

The two men nodded their obedience.

"Are you in?" Darren turned to him.

Alex stared at Darren. "I'll need time to think about it," he admitted. *I can't leave Cori, but I can't leave Enid in the hands of two men I don't know. I thought she was dead once. Now that I know she is alive, I won't lose her again.*

"The team leaves tonight. I'll need an answer by lunch in order for us to be prepared," Darren instructed as he shoved off the wall. "Meeting is dismissed." He didn't wait for any replies before he left the room.

The remaining occupants filed out after him without a word, leaving Alex and Enid alone.

Enid combed her hair with her fingers as she stared at the rocky, muddy floor.

"Isn't it customary for the person who stays over to do the skipping out super early in the morning?" he teased in an effort to break the tension.

Enid smiled as she met his eyes. For a second, the woman he'd loved fourteen years ago was back. *Good. I'm making progress.* "I couldn't sleep and I didn't want to wake you. You looked peaceful. I didn't realize Darren planned on inviting you to this meeting."

Darren probably didn't think of asking me here either until he saw me, he told himself. *That's not important right now.* Alex took a step forward, brushing long strands of hair away from her face. "Who says I would've minded if you woke me?" He twirled one of her curls around his finger as he stared at her.

Enid bit her lip as her hands came up to rest on his chest, gripping his shirt and tugging him closer. "We're both awake now."

Alex cocked his head to the side as he grinned at her while listening to make sure everyone was gone. He'd take that as a challenge and from the sounds of things they shouldn't be interrupted.

He captured Enid's lips with his as he backed her against the wall. His hands roamed down her sides, stopping at her sweats. One of his palms slid inside, reaching around to cup her core.

No panties again, he mused.

"You're already so wet," he mumbled as he slipped two fingers inside her folds.

She hissed, silencing him with a kiss. Her tongue darted into his mouth, gliding along his as her fingers worked at the button on his jeans. The fabric loosened at his waist and her hands shoved at the garment, pushing the jeans and his boxers down.

His cock sprang free, alert and ready. Enid wrapped her hand around his shaft, pumping it slowly as she rolled her thumb over the tip of his cock. She always knew how to touch him and if she kept that rhythm up, this interlude would be over too quickly.

He withdrew his fingers causing Enid to pout as he stepped back. Lifting his fingers to his mouth, he sucked her juices off of them and grinned. "I love the way you taste, Enid," he breathed.

She batted her eyes at him as she rolled her sweats down her petite, toned legs, exposing her creamy flesh. Then, she went to her hoodie, unzipping it and sliding it off her arms, leaving her in her white tank top and a lacy, red bra.

Alex reached behind her, smacking her ass and grinning as she gasped at the contact. He grabbed her bottom and lifted her into the air as he pressed her back against the wall. Enid squealed in surprise and gripped his shoulders to support some of her weight.

He positioned his cock at her entrance and thrust into her tight, wet heat. They groaned together as she pulled him closer. He pressed her against the wall, only allowing her to move as he thrust in and out of her.

Enid clasped his waist tighter with her legs, gripping him like a vice as her nails dug into his shoulder blades. Alex groaned as she left her mark on him, moving his tongue against hers in time to his thrusts.

"Harder," Enid rasped against his mouth.

Alex grunted as he pushed into her harder, faster. Enid clung to him as she nipped at his lower lip, catching it between her teeth and sucking it into her mouth. She released his lip and peppered him with open-mouthed kisses along his jaw, down his neck, and then to his ears.

He'd forgotten how much of a biter she was. *God, do I love it.* Her teeth grazed over his lobe and he grunted, tilting his head to give her better access.

He shuddered as her warm breath ghosted over his ear. She gripped him tighter, pulling him closer as her body trembled.

"Alex," she mumbled over and over again as her orgasm flooded over his cock.

Alex lifted her hips higher, finding a new angle. He thrust a few more times before he followed her over the edge.

Enid tipped her head back, resting it against the rock wall as she panted. Alex kissed her shoulders as he set her back on her feet.

He could spend every day of the rest of his life in these caves if Enid were here. "I don't suppose I can convince you to stay, can I?" he questioned.

Enid pulled away and slid her pants back on along with her hoodie. She fluffed her hair, dragging her fingers through the locks as she attempted to comb it. "No."

"You're being reckless," he cautioned.

She shook her head. "They're coming back for something. I want to know what it is," she countered.

"How do you find something when you don't even know what you're looking for?" he questioned as he yanked his jeans up and buttoned them.

Enid huffed as she twirled her hair up on the top of her head. She pulled an elastic band off her wrist and tied it at the nape of her neck, allowing wisps to fall out around her face. "I don't know, but we have to try." She looked away and then back to him. "That's the last place Nik was before he disappeared," she lowered her voice to a whisper. "I might find answers about what happened to him there."

"You haven't been there since he disappeared," he guessed.

She shook her head.

"It's been eight years, Enid. The chances of finding something useful are highly unlikely," he pointed out as he rested his hands on her shoulders. "Once the illness became widespread, people panicked. Stores were looted and thrashed."

"He's the only family I have left...I don't know what happened to him. What if he's still out there somewhere? This could be my only chance to get a lead. After everything went down, the witches were all over the store. We never got to investigate it and then the Flu got worse and..." she trailed off as her eyes darted back to the floor. "I just want some answers and if I can get something to help us against the witches in the process then that's just icing on the cake."

"If it was just me I'd go with you in a heartbeat," he told her.

"I'm not asking you to leave Cori," she assured. "Stay with her. Cherish your little girl. But I'm going and you're not going to talk me out of it. Speaking of, there are a few things I should do before tonight. If I don't see you again before I leave, good bye."

She reached up on her tiptoes and placed a kiss to his lips before brushing past him.

Alex closed his eyes and let out a breath. *What if this goodbye is her final goodbye? Now what am I going to do?*

Chapter Five

Enid stuffed a few bran muffins onto her plate, shoving her deer jerky to the side to make room for them.

"Hey, Enid, have you seen my dad this morning?" Cori asked as she joined her at the buffet.

"We had an early morning meeting with Darren. I haven't seen him since," she admitted as she looked up and scanned the room. Even though she'd bathed, Alex's scent lingered all over her from their personal "morning meeting." It wouldn't be hard for anyone to guess what her and the other alpha had been up to. *I don't know how much Cori knows about wolves and mating, but I sure don't want to be the one to tell her. Where is Alex?*

Alex wasn't here.

"Oh. Was it about the trip into town?" Cori whispered.

Enid frowned and turned to the girl.

Cori smiled with a shrug. "Parker told his girls he was leaving. They told me."

Enid nodded. *Kids will be kids.*

"Is my dad going?" Cori questioned.

"I don't think so," Enid told her honestly. It would be nice to have Alex watching her back, but she understood his need to stay with Cori. If her boys were here she'd have second thoughts, too.

"Are you going?" Cori wondered as she grabbed a handful of jerky and dropped it onto her plate.

Enid stared at the girl for a minute before grabbing another piece of jerky. "Yeah, I am."

"Oh." Her lips turned down into a pout.

"It will be fine," Enid assured. "I grew up here. I know the ins and outs of this land like the back of my hand."

"You'll be careful out there, right?" Cori worried as she squeezed a pair of tongs repeatedly in her hand before finally grasping a muffin with them. "Our journey to Mount Rainier was dangerous. There are humans everywhere, setting things up so they can move more people back into the abandoned cities."

"We'll stay off the roads. It will be perfectly safe and I'll be back before you know it," she chuckled. It had been a long time since someone had worried about her wellbeing. "Sit with me?" she offered, inclining her head to an open table.

Cori bobbed her head up and down as she plucked a few more items from the buffet and set them on her plate. The girl followed Enid to the table and they both took a seat.

"So, are there any other kids in your pack?" Enid wondered as she took a bite of her muffin.

"Yeah. Eric and Dale. They're three years older than me. I'm glad there are some girls my age here," Cori confided.

"It's always nice to have other girls to talk to. Especially ones that are your own age," Enid agreed. *Like you're one to talk. When is the last time you spoke to anyone for any length of time?*

Enid pursed her lips, realizing she'd invited Cori to have breakfast with her. It was easy to push Alex away—sort of, but Cori was the same age Chase would have been this year—twelve. Her heart skipped a beat at the reminder and she forced the food in her mouth down her throat and guzzled down her water.

"Katie even has some makeup," Cori went on as she beamed. "I can't wait to try it out. I hope my dad doesn't freak out over it though."

Enid crinkled her nose. Whatever makeup the girl had must be really old. She'd never been big on it when she'd had access to it. Give her lip balm over lipstick any day.

"I'm sure he won't mind," she replied.

"You know my dad well?" Cori asked tipping her head to the side.

Enid nodded. It had been years since their romance, but if the past few days were any indicator, he hadn't changed much. "We were good friends during my brief stay in Tacoma."

"Even though your parents didn't like each other?" Cori questioned around another mouthful of food.

"Our fathers had a dispute that turned very ugly. To be honest, I'm not even really sure what it was about. Anyway, they weren't too happy when they found out Alex and I were friends with each other." That was putting it mildly. They'd been threatened with banishment from their packs.

What would have happened if she and Alex had run off together? Cori wouldn't be here. Chase and James would've never been born. She could've spared herself a lot of heartaches. Tears pricked at her eyes and she cleared her throat. Even though she'd lost both of her boys, she wouldn't trade the time she'd had with them for anything in the world.

"There you are," Alex's voice boomed over Enid's shoulder.

A plate dropped down beside her as the chair next to her was tugged out.

"Sorry," Cori smiled. "You were gone and I was starving."

Alex turned to Enid. "Hi."

Enid shivered under his stare, her insides trembling as she recalled their encounter this morning. Heat pooled in her belly and she clenched her thighs together hoping her arousal wouldn't permeate the air.

"I heard about the trip, Dad," Cori began, tearing off a piece of jerky.

"You told her?" Alex lifted his brow as he met Enid's eyes.

"No!" Cori rolled her eyes.

"I should've known you would find out before I could tell you," he sighed. "Sometimes you're too nosy for your own good."

"That's part of being a good alpha," she reminded as her eyes lit up.

Alex chuckled as he set his napkin in his lap.

"Enid says you're not going," Cori replied. "Is it because of me?"

"We're new here, Cori. I can't leave you and...if something were to happen to me..." he trailed off as he picked up his fork.

"It sounds important, Dad. Besides, Alice is always happy to have me over," she pointed out.

Alex blew out a breath. "Why do you want me to go?"

"You went out all the time at home," she pointed out.

"I did," he agreed. "But I knew you'd be safe there."

"You don't trust Darren?" Enid questioned.

"Enforcing a mating rule isn't ideal. What if he lowers the age?" he questioned.

"Darren is a sensible guy," she told him, following his gaze to Cori.

"Is he?" Alex probed.

Enid took a bite of her jerky and set it down on her plate. If she had a little girl would she feel any differently? She eyed Cori as the girl tore into her food. "She's only twelve, Alex." Cori was too young to mate. The girl wouldn't have a heat cycle until at least sixteen or seventeen.

"Well, she won't always be twelve," he quipped.

Enid nodded. He had a point.

"And you won't be gone but a few days," Cori piped up.

Enid took another bite. Even though Cori didn't appear to be listening, clearly she was.

"You're being a little pushy, aren't you?" Alex replied as he lifted his brow.

Cori rolled her eyes. "Dad, we lost our home. This place is our last resort—it's everyone's. If we lose Mount Rainier we're goners."

Enid narrowed her eyes as she stared at the girl. "Are you sure you're only twelve?"

Cori giggled and gave her a big grin. "Yep. But everyone tells me I spend too much time with my dad."

"It probably is my fault. I haven't given her a proper childhood. There aren't any other kids in our pack. That probably didn't help," Alex admitted. "Are you sure you will be okay here?"

"Alice is like a big sister. I'll be fine," Cori assured. "Besides, Katie, Parker's daughter, is quickly becoming my best friend." Her eyes snapped to the entryway as the girl in question strode in with her older sister. "Can I be excused?"

Alex nodded at his daughter around a bite of food. Cori didn't need to be told twice. She popped up from her seat and bolted to Katie.

"It's good to see her making friends." Alex turned to Enid. "I guess I'm in."

Enid squirmed in her chair as her heart skipped a beat. He was coming with her. "Are you sure?" she questioned, flicking her gaze to Cori who was speaking animatedly with Katie.

"Yeah. If we lose the mountain, Cori won't have a place to call home. She's not losing two homes," he insisted. "It's bad enough she's lost her home and half of her family. I won't let her lose anything else."

"I'm sorry about Melissa and Tate," Enid told him in a whisper.

Alex cleared his throat. "Carter… was he good to you?"

Enid smiled as she chewed what was in her mouth. "Carter was a great guy. He was a good friend and an even better father to our boys," she spoke honestly. Her love for him hadn't been the same as it had for Alex, but she had cared for her mate.

"Your dad forced you into that relationship as soon as you got back home, huh?" he sighed as he looked over her shoulder.

Enid picked at her muffin. "I fought with him about it, but I couldn't shame the pack. He'd already promised me to Carter and if I'd fled back to you it would have hurt my entire pack. I couldn't do that to them."

"Don't apologize for being loyal to your pack—your family," he assured.

"Carter was kind enough to allow me to stay here. Not many men grant their mate's wish to stay with their pack family." Enid smiled as she plucked a piece of muffin off and popped it in her mouth.

"I'm glad the two of you were happy," he told her.

"What about you and Melissa?" she wondered. Had he been happy with his mate?

Alex met her gaze. "She was a good mother to our kids, but honestly, I could never love her. She wasn't you."

Her heart skipped a beat at his admission and she swallowed hard as she held his gaze. Warmth flooded her chest and the pesky emotions she was trying to keep at bay crept back in. *I don't want to fall for him. I don't want to get hurt again.*

Enid nodded as she stood up. "I'm sorry you weren't happier. If you'll excuse me I have a few things to attend to before we go. We leave at dusk. I'll see you then." She didn't give him a chance to respond before she strode out of the common area and into the comfort of the tunnels she knew so well.

***

"Are you sure you're okay?" Alex asked as he tossed a small duffel bag over his shoulder.

Cori nodded as she wrapped her tiny arms around his middle. "I'll do everything Alice asks," she assured.

"I can stay if you want me to," he reminded as he squeezed her tighter. Part of him didn't want to leave, the other part wanted to ensure

Enid was safe.

Cori pulled back and tucked a lock of hair behind her ear. "You like her, Dad."

"What?" he smiled as he shook his head.

"Enid. I've never seen you look at someone like that. She needs you more than I do right now," she whispered as she shifted on her feet.

"You're too grown," he sighed.

"I've had to grow up fast," she murmured. "It's the world we live in now."

"Maybe I've been too hard on you," Alex grunted as he placed his hands on her shoulders.

"You trained me to be a leader, but you're also a caring father," Cori told him with a smile. "I love you, Dad."

"I love you, too," he said, pulling her into another hug. "Be good while I'm gone, promise?"

Cori nodded against his shoulder.

"Do you like Enid?" he questioned as he pulled back and stared at his daughter.

Cori beamed and bobbed her head up and down. "I do. She's nice, but seems really sad."

"She lost everyone to the Wolf Flu," he told Cori with a sigh.

"That sucks," Cori said as she looked at the floor.

"It does," he agreed. "Take care of yourself. I'll be back in a few days," he said bending down and kissing her forehead.

"See you soon," Cori said as she wrapped her arms around herself.

Alex met her eyes one last time before he made his way back into the main tunnel. Leaving Cori was never easy. There were no guarantees in the world they lived in, but she was safe, and his daughter was right—Enid needed him.

He nodded at a few men and women as he pressed through the

cavern and into the cafeteria. Enid, Parker, and Martin were already sitting at a table with Darren. He had a map rolled out and Enid was pointing to it as she spoke.

Alex tugged his bag up higher and made his way over to the meeting.

"You're late," Darren commented as he looked up.

"I was saying goodbye to my daughter," he growled as he leveled Darren with a glare.

"It's always rough," Parker commented as he clapped him on the shoulder. "Leaving my two girls behind is the hardest thing."

Alex offered the other guy a smile. Parker seemed like a decent enough guy.

"All right, to recap," Enid spoke up, meeting his gaze before darting her eyes back to the map. "Parker is going to set up here." She tapped a spot on the map. "Martin will go here." She pointed to another spot. "The shop we are going to is right here. If we find what we need and have a chance to set up. This will be the best spot to take a shot. We'll only have one chance at this. If we blow it, the witches could use magic to deflect our bullets. Nobody fires without my order." Enid glanced up meeting everyone's eyes.

Parker and Martin both nodded and she turned to Alex. "Got it. Any idea what we are looking for?" he questioned, hating that they were going on a wild goose chase.

Darren cleared his throat. "There has been more chatter as they iron out the details of the trip. You and Enid should have a full twelve hours before the witches arrive to conduct your search. What they are looking for..." he trailed off and shook his head with a sigh.

"Chloe Sullivan's family owned Apothecary. They were big on spells and potions. If I had to guess, we are looking for a book," Enid answered as she folded her arms over her chest.

"A spell book?" Alex asked.

She nodded. "Yeah. If I'm right and that is what they are seeking, then it's important we find it first."

"Why?" Alex wondered.

Enid licked her lips. "What do you think started the Wolf Flu?"

Alex gaped, swallowing hard. "A potion or a spell."

"Maybe that's why Nik attacked the witch," Darren guessed. "He knew what she and the coven were up to."

But Enid doesn't think Nik had anything to do with the witch's disappearance? Has she not told him her theory? He glanced to Enid as she twirled her hair up at the base of her neck.

"We should gather our weapons and get going. Does anyone have any questions?" she asked, glancing around.

Alex shook his head. He cast one more glance around the caves and vowed he'd be back soon to see Cori. The sooner they got this over with, the better.

Chapter Six

Enid breathed in the icy night air and let it out, watching as her breath misted. "I'm going over here," she commented, pointing to the trees to the right.

Alex, Parker, and Martin nodded at her as they veered to the left. It was a twelve-mile trip to the city. As humans, it would take them hours to hike across the terrain, but as wolves they could run the distance in about an hour if they pushed themselves. Considering their time constraints, the sooner they reached their checkpoint for the night, the better.

She skidded down the slope and set her pack on the ground. Her fingers shook as she unzipped her jacket and stepped out of her clothing. Shivering, she folded her clothes and stuffed them into her bag before settling on all fours.

The cold snow bit into her bare skin and she gritted her teeth, willing the change. Her back lurched up, snapping as her joints realigned. The bones crackled in her legs and arms as hair sprouted all over her body. Her eyes narrowed and blinked, shifting into those of a wolf.

Enid drew in a deep breath as the transition completed and let it out. Her thick coat shielded her against the wintry conditions and she leaned forward, stretching. She shook out her coat and bowed her head down, lifting her pack with her muzzle so it fell over her shoulder blades and lay securely around her middle.

She trotted back to the clearing, emerging from the trees at the same time as her partners. Parker and Martin bowed their heads as she trotted toward them. Their inner beasts recognized both she and Alex for the true alphas they were.

Her and Alex's coats were white and gray—alpha colors. All other wolves had browns and blacks mixed in with white.

Alex yipped at her and she chuffed in response. If it were just the two of them, she'd nuzzle his neck and inhale his scent, but their two companions didn't need to see that. Besides, wasn't she supposed to be avoiding her feelings for him? The more time she spent with him the harder it was getting to keep her heart locked away. *I'm falling for you.* She eyed him for a moment longer before barking and zipping down through the snow.

White spray kicked up around her and she narrowed her eyes as she darted through the darkened woods. The frozen ground thumped beneath her paws and she relished in the way the frozen snow crunched and broke with each step.

It had been too long since she'd been able to stretch her legs. The icy air cooled her burning lungs as she pushed her legs to move faster.

Home. They were going to her home for the night. It was much too cold to stay outside in the elements. She hadn't been to the homestead in years. Her heart raced faster, eager to see the large two-story house again.

The aroma of apple blossoms flitted through her mind. It was her imagination, there was no way they were in bloom now, but she inhaled it anyway. She pressed herself faster, hopping over logs and zigzagging around the trees that littered their path.

Enid slowed her stride, panting as she came to a slope that overlooked the homestead. The house was still there, but no smoke billowed from the chimney as it usually did this time of year. No one was there to start a fire. Siding hung from the house and the porch swing hung by one rung on the large front deck.

Her heart sank at the sight. The home was in shambles. Alex joined her steady trot as his gaze flicked over the home.

She blew out a breath and increased her pace. It would always be home no matter what. The three other wolves' paws crunched against the ground as they fought to keep up with her. She leapt over the pasture fence and sprinted for the door.

The front door was closed and all the windows appeared to be intact with the large drapes drawn shut. She strode to the bushes to the right of the house and flexed her body as she shifted back. The crackle of bones nearby told her the others were doing the same.

Once shifted, she dressed and jogged to the front door. She twisted the knob, but it was locked.

Enid chuckled at the irony. In their rapid departure someone had actually taken the time to lock the front door. Maybe the action had kept looters out. It wasn't likely. Desperate people would've broken the door down or busted out the windows. The house was far enough out of the city that no one would stumble upon it. That was the only explanation she could think of for the lack of vandalism.

She twisted the frigid knob, breaking the lock. The door creaked as it opened and she led the way inside. Someone shut the door behind her.

Her eyes darted over the beige walls. A thick layer of dust coated the furniture, but everything was where it belonged.

"We should see if we can salvage anything while we are here," Parker said from behind her.

Enid turned and shot him a lethal glare. It was silly to want to leave everything as it was. They needed things inside the mountain and could bring back quite a bit. Darren must have told the scavengers they'd sent out in the beginning to steer clear of the homestead. It was the only explanation for why it was untouched.

"There are some guest quarters down that way." Enid pointed straight ahead to the long hallway.

Parker and Martin mumbled a good night and made their way down the corridor, slipping into two of the guestrooms on the right side of the hall.

"I don't suppose you mind sneaking me up to your room," Alex flirted with a grin.

"What makes you think you're welcome in my room?" she questioned with a straight face.

Alex pouted and met her eyes as he took a step forward. "I don't know why I'd have that idea."

"Do you want to take a walk?" Enid suggested instead.

Alex frowned, but nodded. She beamed and motioned for him to follow her with her pointer finger.

She strutted ahead, leading him back out the front door and into the solitude of the trees. Alex's footsteps padded behind her and she swayed her hips, feeling his eyes on her.

"So, where are you taking me? You know I'm not big on surprises."

"It's not much further," she commented as she looked at him from over her shoulder. Their destination was just ahead she could already see it.

Steam billowed out of the hot springs and she unzipped her jacket, glad that the pool was still here. She slipped her coat off as she continued to walk and dropped it on a boulder.

"Is that what I think it is?" Alex questioned.

Enid bit her lip as Alex's clothes rustled and landed with a thwack against the rock she'd left her coat.

"I assume you're talking about the hot spring?" she inquired as she lifted her shirt up and over her head.

"I noticed you had one in your room. I was meaning to ask you about it," he replied.

Enid unzipped her pants and slid them down her legs as she stepped out of her sneakers. She set the garments on the rock and peeled off her panties. Naked, she sauntered to the hot springs and dunked her toe into the steamy water.

Perfect!

"I find them relaxing," she told him as she sank into the clear water and found a rock to sit on.

Alex followed her, taking a seat opposite from her. "You always did like to rent the hotel rooms with the hot tubs."

Enid giggled as she ran her hands through the water. "Why didn't we get those rooms more often?"

"We were both broke and we didn't want to charge those rooms to one of our father's credit cards. They were a lot pricier than the cheap-o motels we stayed in," Alex supplied. "Do you think they ever wondered why there were always so many charges from different pizza companies?"

Enid shook her head with a laugh. "Probably not. My dad knew I loved pizza." She groaned and licked her lips as her belly rumbled. "I haven't had a slice of pizza in forever."

"Me either. Do you remember Benito's Pizzeria? They had the best wings," Alex said as he leaned his head back.

"Do you think they still have pizza and wings in the cities they've rebuilt?" Enid wondered.

Alex let out a breath. "Maybe. They have power in some areas."

"It must be nice," Enid snapped.

"Things will get better," he promised.

"How can you be so optimistic?" Enid questioned as she arched her brow at him. "Things have only gotten worse for the werewolves."

"The moment we stop believing and hoping for a better future we lose everything. It's bad enough the Wolf Flu took so much from us, I'm not going to lose anything else," he commented as he stood and waded through the waist-deep water toward her.

Alex clasped her hand beneath the water. "You used to see the glass half full," he reminded her.

"How am I supposed to do that when I've lost everything?" Enid whispered as she bit her trembling lip.

Alex grasped her chin and turned her toward him. "We still have each other and nothing on this Earth is going to separate us again. I'm not going anywhere, Enid," Alex promised as he pressed his lips against hers.

Enid inhaled his scent, closing her eyes as his lips moved against hers. "What about Cori?" she questioned between kisses.

Alex pulled back, narrowing his eyes. "What about her?"

"She's your daughter," she pointed out.

"Cori is quite taken with you," Alex grinned as he pushed loose strands of her hair behind her ear. "I don't think she'd mind at all. She has my good sense of character," he teased with a chuckle before turning sober. "Let me in, Enid."

Enid blinked as tears pricked her eyes. If she didn't feel anything she couldn't be hurt again, but Alex was already wiggling his way into her heart again. The past eight years she'd been shrouded in darkness, consumed with the pain of losing her boys, father, husband, and brother.

Alex's reemergence in her life had brought specks of light—shimmers in the dark, giving her a reason to hope again. All she had to do was reach out and grab onto one.

Enid cupped his face with her fingers as she met his eyes. "I can't lose anyone else," she told him.

"You won't." He didn't give her a chance to say anything else as his lips found hers again.

Enid pushed him back, meeting his eyes as she beamed. She stood up and straddled him as she combed her fingers through his matted hair.

His pert member pushed against her belly. Her fingers tiptoed down his body, grabbing his shaft as she began to pump it. Alex growled and she nipped at his bottom lip as she rolled her thumb over the tip of his cock.

Alex thrust up and she continued her movements, loving how his length grew harder in her hands.

"Enid," he breathed.

She lifted up onto her knees and guided him to her entrance. "Look at me," she demanded.

Alex's eyes met hers and she sank down on his shaft, crying out as his cock stretched her. He fit inside her perfectly like he was made for her and she him. They were mates—true mates. Most alphas were forced into a relationship with a neighboring pack's son or daughter. Fourteen years ago she'd have given anything to mate with Alex.

It hadn't been in the cards for them then, but now, now they could be together.

Enid rocked back and forth, setting a slow and steady motion, pulling out to the tip and then sliding back down.

Alex's hands went to her breasts, squeezing them as he leaned in and captured her lips. His thumbs rolled over her nipples and she cried out against his mouth. The man always knew how to touch her.

She increased her rhythm, loving the way his engorged cock slid in and out of her, hitting just the right spots.

"I want you to make yourself come," Alex instructed as his tongue dipped into her mouth.

Enid grunted against his mouth as she moved her hips faster, enjoying the friction building in her core. Her muscles tensed and she gripped Alex's shoulders harder, giving herself more leverage.

"That's it, Enid, keep going," Alex encouraged with a growl as he thrust his hips up.

Enid cried out as he went deeper. She was on the verge of falling over the edge. Alex pumped into her one last time and she called out his name as sweet release cascaded over her. Dots blurred her vision. Alex gripped her hips and continued their frenzied pace.

She rode out the waves of pleasure as another orgasm coiled inside her. "Alex," she panted.

He caught her lips with his own, delving his tongue into her mouth and flicking it across her teeth. Enid gasped for breath between kisses.

She clung to Alex as she began circling her hips, eager to come again. The water sloshed around them, doing little to cool her overheated and exposed skin.

Alex growled and she screamed as he buried himself deep inside her silky folds. His cock spasmed as his seed spilled inside of her. Her release swept over her again and she shuddered from the sheer joy of it.

She collapsed against him, burying her face into his neck as she fought to regain control of her breathing.

"I love you, Enid," Alex whispered into her ear. "I've always loved you and I'm never leaving your side again."

Enid smiled, placing a tender kiss to his neck. She opened her mouth, but the words got stuck in her throat. He might not intend to leave her, but that didn't mean it couldn't happen. Her heart clenched in her chest at the thought.

I want to love you, but I don't know if I can.

Chapter Seven

Alex reached across the bed, fumbling for Enid. The sheets were cool to the touch. He peeked one eye open, then the other. Empty—again. He was going to have to remind her that he didn't like waking up alone.

He tossed back the covers and grimaced as the cold air assaulted him. The almost too-hot climate of the caves was growing on him. It was freezing in the room, probably only a dozen degrees warmer than the arctic temperatures outside.

Alex opened the door and peered into the hallway. Enid's scent was fresh on the air and he followed it. Her perfume led further down the hall of bedrooms.

At the end of the hall, a door stood ajar and a slight creaking came from it.

He tiptoed across the chilly hardwood and ducked his head in the opening. Enid sat in a rocking chair, swaying back and forth. Her back was to him and her gaze was focused out the window at the snowy tundra.

"You can come in," she invited as she twisted in the chair.

Alex stepped into the room and swallowed. It was a nursery. A crib was in the left corner and a changing table to the right. Sheets covered the mattress though it was obvious from the thick layer of dust that no one had slept in it for some time. He took a step forward, looking over Enid's shoulder and staring down at the photo she had in her hand.

The family smiled back at him; he recognized Enid instantly and Carter next. He licked his lips, placing a hand on her shoulder as he stared at the two boys. One was an infant; the other would've been about Cori's age by now.

"Once the flu started spreading to humans and the witches told them it started here, they marched toward us with guns and weapons. We fled so fast I never got to grab anything." She trailed her fingers over the edges of the photo. "I guess they left this place alone when they realized no one was here. They probably didn't want to risk infection by coming inside. By that point, the sickness had run its course through the pack and every one that was alive was also immune. I suppose we could've been carriers."

"How old were your boys?" Alex asked, though he wasn't entirely sure he wanted to know the answer.

"This is the last photo of all four of us. It was taken a week after I had James." She trailed her fingers over the infant. "Carter died eight days after this photo was taken. Then not even a year later, Chase got sick and then James too. James never saw his first birthday, and Chase was barely four."

Alex squeezed her shoulder. "I'm sorry, Enid."

She swallowed and turned to him as she swiped tears out of her eyes. "We have to stop the witches. No one is safe until we do," she told him as she cleared her throat.

Alex knelt down next to Enid and clasped her hand. "We will," he promised. He had no idea what they were looking for but he wouldn't stop until they found it.

***

Enid stopped a few feet away from Apothecary as she adjusted the pack on her back. The windows were shattered and the door hung open, attached by a single hinge. Shelves were dumped over and their contents strewn all over the floor.

She gulped and pushed her feet forward. The wooden steps creaked beneath her weight as she slipped inside. Shards of glass littered the floor, crunching under her feet as she walked to the counter.

"There's a lot of damage here," Alex commented from behind her.

She nodded in agreement. The other stores down the street had been looted, but this place was trashed as if it'd been deliberately torn apart. A woman allegedly died in this store and Enid's brother was the murderer. It looked like a crime scene, especially with the spray of dried blood across the counter. The spatter was faded from time, but she'd seen enough blood to know what it was.

Enid inched closer to the stain, knelt down and inhaled. The coppery scent was faint, but strong enough to tell her it wasn't Nik's. *It must belong to the witch.*

Nik wouldn't have hurt an unarmed woman, she reminded herself.

"I don't see how we are going to find anything in here," Alex replied as he shoved a shelf, pushing it upright. A few glass bottles rolled off the shelves and crashed to the floor. Broken glass sprinkled all over the floor as liquid oozed out of the bottles.

Chamomile and lavender filled the air and Enid wrinkled her nose at the strong odor.

"For all we know, some random person could've picked up what we're looking for," he continued as he heaved another shelf out of his way.

Alex did have a point. "Maybe."

He went to the wall and trailed his fingers across the panels.

"What are you doing?" she questioned as she followed the trail of blood droplets to the back of the counter.

"Looking for a secret compartment. If the book was important they might have hidden it somewhere," he suggested.

Enid nodded in agreement as she crouched down on the floor and ran her fingers over another patch of dried blood. She gasped and sniffed again.

"Did you find something?" Alex asked, peering over the counter at her.

"Nik's blood." She touched the spot on the floor as she met his eyes. "I assume the witch's blood is on the front of the counter. Its also here, too." She tapped a smear that was close to Nik's. "For a murder scene, I would've thought there'd be more blood."

Alex turned around and looked at the shop then back to where she was. "Look at the way these shelves are parted."

Enid stood up and glanced at the shelves. They were knocked over either to the right or left, creating an aisle straight to the counter.

"They are pushed out of the way," she told him.

"Too perfectly for Nik to do in a fit of rage," he supplied. "But a witch who has active powers..." he trailed off as he pointed to the blood.

"What do you think it means?" she questioned as she stood up.

Alex shook his head and let out a breath. "I don't know, but I think something definitely went down here. Unfortunately, without Nik or the witch it's impossible to know what."

Enid sighed as she ran a hand over her hair. "Let's check out upstairs. Chloe lived here. If she were keeping something important like a spell book I imagine it would be there."

"Lead the way." Alex motioned toward the stairs behind her.

Enid turned on her heel and marched up the steps. The staircase creaked beneath their stomping. At the top, the room opened to a loft. A bed and dresser stood on one end and a couch, TV, and bookcase on the other.

"Quaint," Alex said as he brushed past her and went to the bookcase.

"You think it will be there?" she asked as she strode to the bed and sank to her knees before lifting up the quilt and peering underneath it.

"The best hiding spots are in plain sight," he replied.

Finding nothing under the bed, she lifted the mattress and next ran her hands under the pillows.

She stood up and flipped the blanket down. "Nothing but dust bunnies under here."

Enid went to the dresser and flitted through the clothing. There were a few pairs of comfy sweats that she thought about nabbing, but there was something odd about wearing the clothes of the woman your brother maybe murdered. She set the garments back in the drawer and closed it.

"Anything?" she called over her shoulder.

"No. You?"

"Nope."

The radio in her backpack crackled and Parker's muffled voice broke through the static. Enid shrugged the bag off her shoulders and unzipped it, removing the long-range walkie-talkie.

"You're breaking up," she said as she mashed her finger over the button.

"Company's coming early. Get out of there!" Parker's voice boomed.

"Shit," Alex muttered as he darted to the window and drew the curtains back.

"How long?" Enid questioned over the radio static.

"Ten minutes. Tops," Parker answered. "You've got two covered convoy trucks heading your way. I can't tell if anyone is inside them or not, but I wouldn't wait to find out."

"We got to go, Enid," Alex said as he marched toward her and grabbed her elbow.

"We didn't find it. What if they do?" she protested.

"We can't risk getting caught here and we still don't even know what it is we're looking for," Alex reasoned. "Witches and the army are coming. They most likely have weapons. I don't care how good a shot you are or how well you fight as a wolf, we are outnumbered and outgunned. We can't stay."

"I can't leave without it," Enid hissed, snatching her arm out of his grasp. "What if they do it again? What if they create another Wolf Flu?"

Alex sighed and looked away.

"What if next time there are no survivors?" she whispered.

"After they leave we can try to come back," he argued. "Let's get out of here while we can."

Enid opened her mouth to argue but paused. White light poured out of a seam in the paneling on the wall. "What's that?" she questioned, brushing past Alex to the light. She cocked her head to the side and ran her fingers over the shimmering flecks.

"I don't know," Alex said as he joined her. His hands skimmed over the paneling. "I thought the stairwell was on the other side."

"Maybe it's some sort of secret...lair," she guessed, shrugging when he looked at her. "What? It's possible. The light is coming from somewhere. Weren't you looking for a compartment downstairs?"

"You're not wrong about that," he commented. He crouched down and grazed his fingers along the floorboards. "I've got something. Stand back."

Enid took a step back and gasped as the paneling shifted away from the wall with a hiss. Alex turned to look at her. She shrugged in response.

"Might as well check it out, but do it quickly," he said, motioning for her to go in first.

Enid stepped through the opening and stared at the mountains of books that littered the tables and chairs. Cobwebs hung from the ceiling and dust at least an inch thick lay over everything. The door clicked shut behind her and she turned.

"This isn't going to be a quick look and it's safer in here than out there. Hopefully they won't find us in here," he said as his eyes darted around the room.

"They won't," a voice spoke.

Enid whirled around, but she didn't see anyone. "Who's there?" she and Alex demanded at the same time. The room was empty. It was just the two of them.

Her heart hammered against her ribs as she whipped up her gun. *Oh crap, we walked into some sort of witchy trap.*

Chapter Eight

Alex stepped in front of Enid as his eyes darted around the empty room. "Show yourself, witch!"

Lights glistened in front of them and a translucent form materialized. Alex took a step forward, placing his arm in front of Enid.

"I mean you no harm," the woman assured with a smile.

"Why should we believe you?" he inquired, glancing at Enid as she moved to stand beside him.

"Her brother saved my daughter's life. I am returning the favor," she replied as she clasped her hands together. "I am Theresa Sullivan."

A car engine grumbled in front of the building and Alex whipped his head around to the door, ensuring it was secure.

Parker's voice called over the COM and he reached out and took the walkie-talkie from Enid and switched it off, praying no one heard the commotion.

"You need not worry about them. This room is protected by magic. They will not find it, and they cannot see us," the witch replied as she met Enid's gaze.

"Do you know where my brother is?" Enid questioned without a care to whether the witch before them was being honest.

Alex pressed his ear against the paneling as footsteps pounded across the hardwood downstairs.

"I've already told you they cannot hear us," the woman said again before addressing Enid. "I do not know where my daughter and your brother are. They were attacked and a spell was used, but I do not know where it took them. I wish I could tell you more."

"But he's alive?" Enid whispered.

"Yes. They both are," the woman replied.

Footsteps thumped up the stairs and Alex gritted his teeth as the furniture in the loft crashed to the floor. Voices echoed through the thin wall and he held his breath waiting for someone to discover them.

"They don't know you are here," the woman said for the millionth time.

Alex would like to believe her, but giving their history with witches he was finding it a little difficult.

Seconds ticked by and one glance at Enid and he could tell she was holding her breath, too. The voices continued to shout in the other room and more furniture was turned over.

Theresa moved across the room and Enid jumped back from her. Alex flexed his hands at his side as he eyed her. She stopped at one of the stacks of books and pointed. "The book you need is right here," she said.

Alex turned to the door, but the voices outside continued to speak unaware of the conversation in the other room. He let out a breath and met Enid's eyes.

"Why are you doing this?" Enid questioned as she crossed her arms over her chest. "Why help us?"

The woman sighed as she glanced between the two of them. "It seemed only fair to save the sister of the man who saved my daughter," she repeated her earlier explanation.

"What happened?" Enid pressed. "Everyone thinks that Nik *killed* your daughter."

"I know. The witches made it look that way on purpose. I'm afraid your brother happened to be at the wrong place at the wrong time and he took the fall for something that wasn't his fault," she began to explain.

"So, why did the witches try to kill your daughter?" Alex asked as

Enid sunk into a chair. He reached out and touched her shoulder, giving it a small squeeze. She'd been right about Nik all along and he was alive—somewhere.

Theresa turned around and walked away from them. "There are two types of witches. Those with active power and those who can do spells and potions. The two factions have silently been battling each other for years. My family has been writing in these spell books for centuries." She motioned to the overwhelming piles of books. "The witches with active powers have been attempting to overrun the witches council. They stole one of our most powerful spell books." She pointed to the book again. "This one. With it they created the Wolf Flu."

Enid gasped and covered her mouth as she leaned forward in her chair. Alex gripped her shoulder tighter already sensing where this was going.

"Why attack us? We did nothing to them?" Alex asked through gritted teeth. "Whatever fight there was between our species ended long ago," he growled. It was true there had been a great war between the two mythical creatures, but that had ended over a century ago. The truce still stood—or it had. Witches remained on their land and wolves on their own. The only time they crossed paths was in public areas.

"No, the wolves did nothing. The witches wanted to ensure their spell worked and that they'd targeted the correct genes. The werewolves seemed a safe bet to experiment on without it getting out of control or being noticed by the witching council. I suppose they assumed no wolf would come to a witch for help and their experiment would go unnoticed by my group. Only, I did notice that one of our sacred books was missing. I took it and tried to leave, but was caught. I managed to send the book here, to this room, before they killed me," Theresa told them. "I didn't realize they'd already polluted the water supply to target the wolves until after my ascension. If I'd known I would've warned someone."

"We were just guinea pigs." Enid breathed as she buried her face in her hands. "Thousands of wolves lost their lives—their families for an experiment!"

"I'm so sorry," Theresa apologized. "I wish I'd have seen the deception sooner. They killed millions of people with one bad strain of potion. The witches didn't take into account there were humans who had mated with werewolves. The sickness passed to them and then mutated, affecting the humans and then other witches as well."

Alex let go of Enid's shoulder and picked up the thick, leather-bound book Theresa had been pointing to. "So many deaths over a stupid book," he growled as he stared at the weapon. He'd burn the damn thing the first chance he got.

"Take the book home with you. I will point out a few others. Chloe will need them when she returns," Theresa said as she moved to another stack of books.

"Returns?" Enid asked.

"She did a spell, whether she knows it or not she did. I'm just not sure where she and your brother went, but they'll be back," she assured. "It is important that Chloe get these books when she comes back."

"I'm sorry, but I still don't see how my brother fits into all of this," Enid mumbled as she sat back up. Her face was ashen and tears sparkled in her eyes.

"He was in the wrong place at the wrong time. They'd come to kill Chloe the night he came to seek a cure for your son. When the two disappeared, they simply made it appear he had killed her and used his deceit and breach of the truce as a reason to unleash the virus. At that time, only your boy was sick; no one could've known the spell had already been done," Theresa told them.

"I did," Enid muttered.

Theresa flinched as glass shattered on the other side of the wall. Shouts filled the air and she shook her head. "I fear if they don't find what they're looking for they will burn this building down to keep someone else from finding it."

"Burn it down?" Alex asked, his voice rising. "Today? We're in it."

Theresa's eyes widened as she looked between them. "I have some magic still. Our faction of witches believes in ascension and the afterlife. That is how I am able to appear before you. I can get the both of you out of here safely if you promise to take care of the spell books and not destroy them."

"We will," Enid replied.

Alex shot her a glare as the witch smiled. "Thank you." She took a step toward Enid. "Would you tell my daughter I love her when you see her? I never got to say goodbye."

Enid swallowed and nodded.

"I appreciate that."

Glass shattered on the opposite side of the wall causing Alex to turn back. Their hideaway hadn't been located—yet. More voices yelled and items collided to the floor. Things were getting bad on the other side of the wall.

"I fear we better get moving," the witch commented.

She flitted around the room showing them which books to grab before finally announcing they had everything they needed. Books were stuffed into their bags and they each had a stack in their hands.

"All right then. Where shall I send you?" Theresa inquired looking at both of them.

"To my homestead," Enid spoke up.

Alex nodded in agreement. It would get them out of the town and close to Parker and Martin without letting the other two wolves know what had happened.

"Very well then. The spell can be a bit disorienting; you may wish to close your eyes."

Alex swallowed as he took Enid's free hand with his. The witch mumbled something in a language he couldn't understand. His belly flip-flopped as dizziness passed through him. He opened one eye and then the other.

"Wow," he whispered as he looked around Enid's bedroom. "She did it."

Enid's eyes popped open and she gaped as she took in the room. She let out a heavy sigh, walking to her bed to sit down as she placed the books in her hand beside her.

"I think we should find a safe place to hide these books. All of these books. If we need them we can always come back for them later," he suggested.

"You don't want to mention what just happened?" Enid questioned.

Alex shook his head. "I don't trust Darren."

Enid licked her lips and opened her mouth to protest, but he spoke up first. "Trust me, Enid. I don't think it's a good idea to tell everyone what happened. These books contain the key to creating an illness that killed millions. I don't think we should give them to just anyone."

"What about Parker and Martin? They'll wonder how we got out," she reminded him with a raised brow.

"There was a back exit into an alley. We took that and stayed low. They just didn't see us," Alex told her as he held her gaze. He needed her to play along with his story.

"I can clear Nik's name. Everyone thinks he killed that witch. He saved her life," Enid pressed.

"Which is more important? Clearing Nik's name or keeping these books safe?" Alex asked her as he grasped her hands.

"We're taking them back to Mount Rainier. Why wouldn't they be safe there? There are no witches living in the mountain."

"I don't trust Darren. Besides, the fewer people who know we have them, the better. Please, Enid," he pleaded with her. Maybe she was right and Darren could be trusted, but he couldn't take that chance. It was better that no one knew what they'd found.

"Okay," she sighed.

"Thank you," he leaned up and placed a kiss on her lips. "Is there a safe place to hide them here?"

"No one has been here in years. I imagine we could put them on my bookcase until we can return." She pointed to the mahogany shelving in the corner of her room.

"All right," he agreed as he stood and set his stack on the shelves before returning for hers.

Enid sat on the bed staring absently and he sunk down next to her again. "What's wrong?"

"My family died because of an experiment. Thousands of wolves died because of an experiment. Millions of humans died because an experiment went wrong." Her eyes misted and she swiped at them with the pads of her fingers. "They're going to try to do it again. We can't let that happen, Alex."

Alex swallowed as the realization hit him. "We probably still have time to get into position if you want to take that shot." He hadn't thought he'd be okay with assassinating a witch, but things had changed in the past few hours.

Enid met his gaze with her red-rimmed eyes as she nodded.

"I'll radio Parker and Martin while you get ready," he stood up and opened her bag. Violence wasn't his go-to for situations, but after what they'd learned there was no other option but to end the witches responsible for so many deaths. If they didn't take the opportunity now, there was no telling how many more casualties there would be.

***

"We are in position," Alex spoke into the walkie-talkie as he stared down at the city. He shoved the device into his pocket and glanced at Enid as she positioned herself on the ground and placed the butt of the rifle onto her shoulder. "Can I do anything?"

"Don't take this the wrong way, but I'd like it if you were quiet, please."

"No problem," he chuckled as he stared at the town below.

He blinked, shifting his eyes into those of a wolf, giving him the opportunity to see what everyone else saw. Two large army trucks sat in front of Apothecary. Their backs were covered with canvas, making it impossible to see if there was anyone or anything back there.

There were three men dressed in military gear standing outside of the trucks, guarding the vehicles with rifles. There was movement, shadows from inside the store, but he couldn't make out how many and doubted Enid could either. All they had to do was sit and wait, but that was easier said than done.

"Do you think they found the room we were in?" Enid questioned. She continued to stare through the scope of her rifle and he pondered if she'd shifted her eyes while gazing into it. *How does she work that thing anyway?*

"I'm not sure. Theresa seemed pretty adamant they wouldn't," he replied as he crouched next to her. "They do want those books."

"Do you still think leaving them behind at the house was a good idea?" she questioned.

"Yes. I thought you didn't want to talk?" he inquired with a smirk.

"What is it about Darren you don't like?" she wondered, ignoring his question.

"I can't explain it. Maybe it's simply the fact that he's acting as an alpha when he shouldn't be," he told her.

"I guess I never really thought about it. I've been too busy wallowing in self-pity," she murmured as she scooted across the ground.

"You lost your entire family," he reminded her. "Most people I've met didn't lose everyone they cared for."

Enid shrugged as she squared her shoulders.

"Do you see something?" he questioned.

"There aren't as many shadows in the upstairs loft," she commented.

"How do you know which ones to shoot?" he wondered as he watched the door to the shop.

"I'm assuming anyone in civilian clothing is a witch," she replied.

"See anyone yet?" he asked.

I wonder if she can see something I can't? I don't see anyone yet.

"No. But I imagine they are going to come soon," she said as one of the guards started one truck, then the other. "Radio Parker and Martin, tell them to be ready, but to let me take the first shot."

Alex pulled out the radio and followed her instructions. The two other wolves mumbled their consent and he shoved the walkie-talkie back into his pocket as he continued to wait.

Feet appeared at the edge of the awning, the black boots looked to be military grade. Hopefully there were witches here. After the revelations this afternoon he'd feel better knowing a few of the responsible parties were six feet under.

His mind wandered to Tate. His son had been two. The boy hadn't stood a chance against the flu. He was too young. After Melissa and Tate's deaths, he'd waited for Cori or himself to get sick. Those were the worst few weeks of his life.

A pop cut through the crisp air, drawing him from his thoughts. Alex snapped his head back in the direction of the shop. A woman crumpled to the ground unmoving. Another bang echoed through the mountains followed by several pops further away. Two more bodies dropped to the ground.

"We've got trouble," Martin's voice hollered through the radio.

Loud crackles vibrated through the radio.

That sounded like gunfire.

"Martin," Alex called. "Martin!"

He was met with static.

"Shit," he muttered as his eyes darted around the landscape. Someone else was out there with them.

The steady thrum of a helicopter ricocheted off the rock walls as it rose over a ridge and approached them.

"There's a chopper out here," he bellowed into the walkie, hoping Parker would get the message.

Alex darted to Enid as she fired rounds from her gun. "We have to go. Now!"

He didn't wait for her to respond; instead, he hauled her up by the elbow as she was firing. Probably not the best or safest idea, but it got her attention.

"I almost had her," she argued, wrenching her arm free.

"We're about to be killed," he shouted at her. "I want them dead as much as you do, Enid, but right now we have to move."

Enid swallowed as she cast her glance back to the shop.

"Now!" he bellowed as he shook her.

Enid jumped and took a step back from the ridge. She slung the gun over her shoulder and Alex gripped her hand, pulling her into a sprint. If there was more time he'd transition, but the sound of the helicopter engine loomed over their heads. It would be on top of them soon.

Together they zipped into the trees, but without foliage, they provided little cover.

"There's an entrance into the lava tubes this way," Enid panted as she leapt over a log. "We'll have to go down a steep slope to get inside."

"Lead the way." The less time they were exposed the better.

"It's just over this ridge," she called over her shoulder.

Enid's eyes widened and she dove to the ground pulling him with her. A spray of bullets rained down around them and he curled himself around Enid, doing his best to protect her.

"Are you hit?" he cried out when the gunfire stopped. He peered down at her as he inhaled. The coppery scent of blood was overpowering to their sensitive noses, but thankfully, he didn't smell it.

"No. You?" she gasped.

"No." He tugged her back to her feet and they shot over the terrain.

The edge of the slope was only a few feet away. Enid slid down the rocky ground first, skidding down in controlled movements. Alex tried to keep up with her, but she was faster and more fluid than he was.

The chopper hovered over them and he pushed himself to move faster as gunfire erupted. His eyes darted over the rocks, but there was nowhere to take cover.

Enid screamed as a spray of blood splattered through the air. She pitched forward, face first and tumbled down the ravine.

"Enid!" he cried out as he rushed after her.

Her body bumped, colliding with the rocks as she plummeted down the steep hill. She rolled, landing on her belly, face first on the rocky earth below.

The chopper opened fire on him. Bullets pinged against the rocks and he prayed that none of them hit their mark. He had to get to Enid. Her form lay below on a slab unmoving.

"Enid!"

Dear God, please let her be okay.

Chapter Nine

Enid coughed as the taste of metal flooded her mouth. Her body pulsed like it'd been jabbed with hundreds of needles simultaneously. She groaned as she rolled over and sucked in a burning breath. Alex's voice floated on the breeze as she stared up at the blurry sky.

Was this it? Was this how it ended?

"Enid!" Alex called as his face loomed over hers.

She blinked up at him, opening her mouth to speak, but croaking instead.

"It's okay. I got you." He covered her like a second skin as something clanged around them.

She gasped in a deep breath as she forced her mind to think. *The caves. We have to get inside.*

Her heavy, trembling hand wavered as she pointed to her right. Alex followed her gesture and nodded.

Enid groaned as he jostled her while lifting her into his arms and sprinted towards the tunnel opening. She blinked up at the offensive sunlight as the trees bounced above her. The light disappeared and darkness enveloped her.

She closed her eyes and opened them as heat encompassed her like a blanket. Her body screamed as Alex jostled her, laying her on the cavern floor. His fingers shook, or maybe it was her body, she couldn't be sure as he unzipped her jacket.

"Shit," he muttered as his hands pressed against her side.

Enid cried out, sputtering as she forced air into her screaming lungs.

"I'm sorry. It's okay," Alex said as if trying to assure them both. "I have to get the bullet out," he told her as he rolled her shirt up.

"How bad is it?" she grunted as she closed her eyes. It'd be so easy to shut her eyes and drift off to sleep. Would she wake up if she did?

"Enid! Stay with me," Alex barked as he tapped her cheek.

Her eyes fluttered open and she met his wide-eyed gaze. He shoved off his bag and pulled out the small first aid kit they had.

She exhaled and gritted her teeth as he pulled out a pair of tweezers.

"This is going to hurt," he warned.

His warm fingers probed her skin and she closed her eyes. The tweezers dug into her flesh and she howled as Alex fished for the bullet. Stars dotted her vision and she tensed, willing her body not to thrash.

"Got it," he exclaimed.

Enid panted as nausea coiled in her belly. Alex's hands pressed something to her side.

"Open your eyes, Enid," Alex insisted. "Were you shot anywhere else?"

"I don't...think...so," she slurred.

"Stay awake," he ordered as he tapped her cheek again.

"Trying," she whispered as darkness tugged at her.

"You're losing a lot of blood," Alex said as his fingers ran up and down her body. She assumed he was checking for injuries.

"There are no more bullet wounds," he told her as he grasped her chin. "Are you still with me?"

"Mmmhmm," she mumbled as dizziness clouded over her. *Sleep. I want to sleep.*

"You have to transition," he explained as he removed her shoes.

Her body jostled as he undressed her, but her leaden eyes refused to open.

"Enid! Fight this. Stay with me. I love you, Enid. You have to fight. Do you hear me?" Alex's voice floated over her.

Shimmering light called to her and she moved toward it. She'd wished to join her family a thousand times the past eight years.

"Stay with me, Enid. I need you. Open your eyes. Please!" Alex's frenzied voice called to her.

Enid took a step back from the light. *I'm not ready to die*, she realized.

Her fingers trembled as she lifted them. Alex's hand found hers and she snapped her eyes open.

"Enid," Alex breathed as he bent down to kiss her forehead. "You got to transition. It will heal the wounds."

Enid grunted as he rolled her over. Alex had removed the clothes from her body and she trembled as she rose to her hands and knees.

"You can do this," he encouraged as he brushed wisps of hair out of her face.

Enid pictured her wolf as she drew in a burning breath. Her lungs were on fire and her side pulsed in time to her frantic heart rate.

The bones in her back snapped and realigned. She screamed as her already gnarled flesh tore.

"You're doing good. Keep going," Alex told her as he scooted back.

Her vision darkened and she forced air into her lungs as her legs broke. She fell onto her belly, whimpering as her arms crackled. Hair sprouted over her body and she became a wolf.

Alex moved forward again, ruffling her head with his palm. "Rest a minute before you change back," he whispered as he kissed her snout.

Enid closed her eyes and fought to control her labored breathing. The second shift wouldn't be as difficult, but she was ready to get it over with now. She focused on her human form as she began the change.

Shifting sped up the healing process. Instead of a gunshot that was minutes old she'd have one that was days old by the time she was done.

The flesh would be healed and scarred, but she'd be exhausted from the injury and forced shifts.

"How do you feel?" Alex asked as he smoothed his hand over her face.

She opened her eyes and met Alex's. "Better," she whispered as she struggled to sit.

"Take your time," Alex warned as he wrapped an arm around her and helped her into a sitting position.

"We should get back," Enid replied.

"Are you sure you're ready?" he questioned.

She wasn't, but she wasn't going to tell him that; afraid her words would betray her, she nodded.

Alex held her as she wobbled into a standing position. Her knees jiggled, ready to give out on her, but she pressed forward. The further she went, the easier it became.

"It's getting hot in here," Alex commented breaking the silence between them.

"Some tunnels are hotter than others," she told him as they made their way down a narrow corridor. It probably didn't help cool him that he was helping to drag her along.

"This is a volcano. Are you sure it's not going to erupt?" Alex questioned.

"It is overdue according to scientists." She shrugged.

"What?" he asked as he gaped at her.

"The last eruption was in 1894. Before the flu, scientists said it was a matter of if, not when," she replied.

"We are living in a mountain—a volcano that is a ticking time bomb?" Alex's voice rose to a shout as he spoke.

"Technically. But it gives us everything we need," she argued. It was true. They had water, warm baths, adequate food sources nearby, and the tunnels had natural heat from the lava.

"Until we are all incinerated," he mumbled.

Enid bit her lip. She wanted to tell him that she was sure they'd have a warning before an eruption, but she wasn't sure if that was true or not.

"We should go left at this fork up here," she told him as she limped alongside him.

"How'd you get to know these tunnels so well?" Alex wondered.

"I liked spending time by myself. Darren tasked me with finding alternate ways through the caves in case of an emergency," she explained.

"Like an eruption?"

"Or an attack," she teased, though she'd prefer that neither happened.

"It's sweltering down here," Alex said as he swiped his arm over his forehead.

"We're almost there," she told him, though she was sure he could probably hear the frenzied chatter from the main cavern.

I wonder what is going on?

The voices grew louder into shouts and screams.

Alex didn't comment while the two of them hobbled along the corridor faster. The voices grew to hushed whispers as they emerged into the main chamber.

"Dad!" Cori cried as she hurled herself through the crowd.

Alex opened one arm to his daughter as he held onto Enid with the other, still supporting her weight.

Cori crashed into them and wrapped her arms around the both of them. "Parker just got back. Martin's dead and he said you guys took on heavy fire."

"The two of you are okay?" Darren questioned as he approached with Parker on his heels.

"I wasn't sure what happened to you two," Parker told them as he offered his hand to Alex. "I couldn't make it to you without coming under fire myself. Then I saw the trucks on the move. I just got back a few minutes ago."

Alex shook his hand. "Enid knows these tunnels really well. We found an alternate route home."

"You got five hits in," Parker said placing a hand on Enid's shoulder. "Good shooting, but I'm afraid the convoy is headed our way. We don't have much time before they are at the mountain."

"I've already sent out a few strike teams, but we are preparing for an attack and the possibility of retreat," Darren stated.

"Leave?" Alex growled. "Where will we go?" *There was nowhere else.* Enid had told him as much the other day when he'd wanted to flee.

"Avalanche," Enid whispered.

"What?" Alex and Darren asked at the same time.

"Avalanche," she repeated. "We start an avalanche."

"How?" Darren questioned.

"We have all those grenades. Why not use them?" she pointed out.

"Is that safe?" Alex argued.

"We can't let them get to the mountain," Enid replied.

"Is this something you can do?" Darren questioned as he looked her over.

"No. She's hurt," Alex snapped as he tugged her closer into his side.

"Yes," she quipped. If it meant saving the pack and Alex and Cori she would find the strength.

"You can barely walk," Alex fumed.

"I'll do it," Parker volunteered. "Get her someplace where she can rest. I'm sure I can figure out what I'm doing."

"At least let me draw him a map and give him an idea of where to pinpoint the explosions," Enid insisted.

"Can you do that?" Parker asked tilting his head.

"Our pack tried to integrate into the human world as much as possible. My father worked as a ranger here. Occasionally he was tasked with setting off controlled avalanches," Enid explained. "I watched him work. The tunnels and the mountain have always fascinated me."

"Let's find you someplace to sit down while you work that out," Alex suggested as they hobbled forward.

Enid nodded as she held him tightly, limping to the cafeteria. She inhaled a deep breath and let it out as her insides screamed. It had been a long time since she'd helped her father and she'd never done it herself. She prayed that she did this right. If she was wrong, it could be deadly for more than just the humans.

***

Alex winched as an explosion echoed through the caverns. The walls shook and he held his breath, praying the icy walls didn't collapse on them. He wrapped Cori in a hug and held her close as the seconds ticked by.

Enid lay in bed, sleeping soundly through the ordeal. It was good she was resting; her body had been through quite the calamity.

Another boom ricocheted off the walls and Cori gripped him tighter.

"It's going to be okay," he assured even though he had no way of knowing if that was true.

"Do you think they'll send more humans here?" she questioned.

"I think they'll come sooner or later," he admitted with a sigh, though he'd wager a successful attack might ward them off a little longer, especially if they thought the wolves would keep to the mountain. No one had seen them in town.

Cori remained silent for several long minutes before asking, "Do you think it's over?"

"Probably." He didn't know much about avalanches, but he'd guess that the blasts were most effective when done together.

A throat cleared on the opposite side of the curtain that draped over the opening to their room.

Cori pulled back and arched her brow at him.

"Come in," Alex called.

The curtain rustled as Darren stepped in. His eyes went to Enid who was still resting in the bed before darting back to Alex. "How is she?" he asked.

"I think she'll be fine after she gets some decent sleep," he said honestly.

"Good. The avalanche appears to be successful," he commented. "One truck was inundated and the other vehicle fled. There is no sign of the helicopter."

"I would assume you have posted lookouts to be sure?" Alex questioned. Darren might not be an alpha, but surely he had common sense—at least he hoped he did.

"Of course," he answered smugly.

"Was there something else we could do for you then?" Alex dismissed him.

Darren opened his mouth, his gaze drifting to Enid again. "No." He turned and strode out of the room, leaving the three of them alone again.

"I don't like him," Cori whispered.

"You're not the only one," he told her. "But he has the loyalty of all the other wolf packs. Until we earn their trust, we can't afford to do anything rash," he admitted.

If anything, the other wolves looked up to him being a lower ranking wolf that had risen into a role of power. It was going to be hard to win them over, but he was always up for a challenge.

Chapter Ten

Enid groaned as she blinked her eyes open. The aroma of deer stew called to her, which was laughable because she'd had enough of that crap to last her a lifetime.

"You're awake," Cori's voice floated through the room.

Enid rolled over and met the girl's eyes. "How long have I been out?"

Her body didn't ache anymore, but her eyes were heavy like she'd been sleeping for years.

"Two days," Cori replied.

Oh?

"Dad says it's a side effect of being shot and forcing yourself to shift twice so close together after a serious injury, but I think he's going to be really glad to see you awake," she said as she made her way over and sat down on the bed. "How do you feel?"

"Like I've slept for two days," she sighed with a smile. It had been a long time since she'd gotten a good night's rest. Most of her nights were filled with nightmares of the events that led up to the death of her boys. She couldn't recall dreaming of anything. That's probably why she'd slept so soundly.

"Dad will be back in a bit. Darren has him on guard duty," Cori told her as she fiddled with her fingers. "He insisted you stay with us while you healed. I think he wants you to stay indefinitely."

"And what do you want?" Enid inquired. Did Cori want her to stay too?

Red bloomed over the girl's cheeks. "You saved my life and you make my dad happy. I'd be happy if you stayed with us. Do you want to?"

Enid shifted beneath the covers. "I think I'd like that," she smiled.

Alex had awoken her spirit and now that she had a glimpse of what could be she didn't want to lose it again. Opening her heart was a risk, but she couldn't ignore what she felt for Alex and Cori was quickly worming her way into Enid's heart as well.

Cori reached out and hugged Enid. "I'm so glad."

Enid clasped the girl to her, smoothing her hands up and down her back.

"I'm sorry. I'm not hurting you am I?" Cori pulled back as her eyes widened.

Enid chuckled. "I'm fine."

"I hope I'm not interrupting anything," Alex's voice spoke from the entryway.

Cori grinned and shook her head. "Enid's going to stay with us, Dad," Cori blurted with a giggle.

"Is that so?" Alex asked meeting Enid's eyes.

"It's a little lonely in my cavern," she told him. "Do you mind?" She bit her lip and swallowed. Cori could have extended the invite on a guess as to what Alex wanted. *What if he didn't want her to stay? Sure the sex was amazing, but it had been a long time since they'd been a couple.*

"We're glad to have you with us," Alex beamed as he strode to the bed and sat down on the mattress beside Cori. "Have you eaten?"

"I was just about to offer her a bowl of stew," Cori said as she stood.

Enid's stomach rumbled before she could speak and she placed a hand over her abdomen and laughed. "I'd like that. Thanks."

Cori hurried over to the table and snatched a steaming bowl from the table. "Here you go."

"Thank you," Enid told her as she accepted the food.

"You're staying at Parker's tonight, right?" Alex asked.

"Yes." Cori said bobbing her head up and down. "Is it okay for me to go now that you're back?"

"Go ahead and have fun," he told her as he pressed a kiss to her temple.

"See you in the morning," Cori called as she skipped to the door.

"Sleep over?" Enid questioned.

"Just because we survived the apocalypse doesn't mean she shouldn't get to be a kid," Alex teased. "I'm just glad there are kids close to her age here. She's really taken a liking to Parker's girl Katie."

"It must've been hard being the only girl," Enid agreed.

"You know, you don't have to stay with us, Enid," Alex told her as he met her eyes.

"I know. I want to. I've been in love with you since the first time we met. I can't walk away from this," she whispered as she set her bowl down on an end table and pulled him in for a kiss by the collar of his shirt.

"Good," he mumbled against her lips.

Enid sighed as he cupped her face and flicked his tongue into her mouth. Everything in this moment was right. She wiggled her fingers up his shirt and ran the pads of them down his back as she pulled him closer.

"Are you sure you're up for this?" Alex questioned between kisses.

"Hmmm, I'm not sure. Maybe you should check my wound and be sure," she flirted with a grin.

"That'd be my pleasure." Alex lifted her tank top up and over her head, exposing her breasts.

His fingers trailed over her nipples as they tickled their way down to her side. The tips of his digits skimmed over the puckered, pink scar. He leaned forward and placed a kiss to it.

"Looks good," he said as he kissed it again.

Enid ran her fingers through his thick hair, loving the way his mouth felt on her bare skin. It wasn't enough. She wanted to feel more of him.

Her hands dipped down his body and tugged at the hem of his shirt, rolling it up his sculpted body and tossing it to the floor. She smoothed her fingers over the plains of his chest and smiled up at him.

Alex grinned as his hands went to the buckle on his jeans and he unfastened it. He stood up and shoved the fabric down his long legs. His pert cock sprung out to greet her and she bit her lip, shuddering as she imagined what it would be like to have him inside her again.

Her body hummed with excitement as she reached under the covers and slipped her pants and panties off, depositing them on the floor next to her tank top.

Alex climbed back on the bed as he shoved the blankets back. He nestled between her thighs and tugged the covers up over his shoulders as he leaned forward, placing his hands on both sides of her.

One of his palms kneaded her breasts, rolling his thumb over her nipple, drawing the bud into a tight peak. Enid leaned up and nibbled on his lower lip. She traced his lips and teeth, exploring his mouth.

Alex grunted as he pushed her down onto the pillows. The tip of his cock probed her entrance and she wiggled her hips, encouraging him to enter.

She stared into his eyes as she lifted her leg and fit it around his waist. Alex groaned and tilted his hips forward, sinking into her tight, wet, heat. Enid arched off the bed as her eyes fluttered closed. His cock stretched her wonderfully and she slid her other leg around him, drawing him in as deep as she could.

Alex pulled out and then thrust back in. He set a slow and steady rhythm. Enid bucked her hips, meeting him thrust for thrust, eager for more friction.

He chuckled at her eagerness as he took her nipples between his thumb and forefinger, rolling them into tight buds. She reached down and grasped his firm ass with her palms as she gripped him tighter with her thighs. He was in so deep and she loved every second of it.

"Don't stop," she panted as her eyes rolled into the back of her head. Her hands jutted out and she fisted the sheets in her hands as Alex pumped harder. Her inner walls clenched around his cock. Unable to hold back any longer she teetered over the edge, burying her face in his shoulder to help muffle out her cries of pleasure.

Alex picked up his pace, driving deeper and harder, spurring her orgasm to intensify. Enid dug her heels into the small of his back as her nails dug at the sheets. He cried out as his body stiffened above hers and his seed spilled inside of her.

Enid panted, releasing her vice grip on the sheets and wrapping her arms around Alex. She held him close as he rested his forehead against hers and stared into her eyes.

"I love you," she told him as she brushed her fingers through his hair.

"I love you, too," he sealed it with a kiss as his cock began to harden inside her again.

It was going to be a long, wonderful night.

***

Alex walked hand-in-hand with Enid down the corridor to the meeting room. He grumbled under his breath wondering what Darren wanted this time. Maybe he was finally going to relinquish control to him or Enid.

In the three weeks since their trip into town, all had been quiet. However, Parker had made sure to let everyone know that the avalanche that had saved the wolves had been Enid's plan, not Darren's. There had been unrest and whispers questioning his command, especially with the imposed mating. Not so surprisingly, no one was a fan of the idea; like he and Enid, most people that lived in the tunnels had lost a child or children and few were willing to travel down that path again. Losing a child was too painful and not something he ever wanted to experience again.

"You're late," Darren informed as they entered the cavern.

Alex rolled his eyes as Enid shrugged. They'd been a little caught up and he was certain everyone could smell their lingering arousals. He didn't mind if others knew what they'd been up to. Enid was his mate and he loved that they smelled like each other all the time.

"What's going on?" Enid questioned as she folded her arms on her chest and leaned against the wall. "Is everything okay?" she jumped right into business.

"I wanted to discuss a few things with you before I address the pack," Darren said as he flitted his gaze from Alex to Enid, then to Parker.

"I was going to lift the requirement of finding a mate and I thought we could introduce a council consisting of the four of us to the pack. All major decisions go through us before being passed down to the pack," he replied.

"Or you could just make Enid and I leaders. We do have alpha blood. It's in your instinct, in everyone's instinct to follow our lead," Alex pointed out as he stared Darren in the eyes.

Darren looked down to the ground in submission. "Maybe so, but for now, the majority of the pack still looks to me for guidance."

A fight for dominance might not go over well—yet—but it was only a matter of time before Alex and Enid could take the helm. Keeping things peaceful was the right thing to do for the moment. Enough wolves had lost their lives in the past decade. There was no reason to add to it.

Enid shook her head and Alex sighed as he held her gaze. He trusted her decision when it came to Darren. She knew him best.

"If we join this council, then can I deem it a safe assumption our opinions will actually matter when it comes to important decisions?" Alex questioned.

"Of course," Darren grunted.

"Fine." Alex nodded. "I'm in."

"Me too," Enid piped up.

"Me three," Parker added.

"Good. I've called a town hall meeting after lunch. I'll announce it then," Darren said as he walked to the exit and made his way out without another word.

"There has been a lot of unrest lately. There are some who think the two of you could lead us better than Darren," Parker admitted as he met their eyes.

"I know you made sure everyone knew the avalanche was Enid's idea," Alex said, nodding his thanks.

"We need people who can think on their toes and protect this pack. There is a reason alphas are leaders," he told them.

"Thank you," Enid whispered.

"I'll see you two later," Parker excused himself.

Alex waited until he was certain both men were out of hearing distance. "We're making progress," he commented.

Enid nodded her agreement. "If we keep things amicable, it will make it easier when we get the chance to transition power to us."

"Do you think that will happen?" Alex questioned. He hoped so, taking orders from Darren was grating on his last nerve.

"The bigger presence we are, and the more people that view us as leaders, the sooner it will happen. I don't want anyone to get hurt," she told him.

"Me either," he agreed.

"So...we have until after lunch with nothing to do..." Enid trailed off as she batted her lashes at him.

"Cori's in the cafeteria preparing lunch," he added with a grin

Enid bit her lip as she smiled. "Sounds like we can go back to bed."

"I can't think of a better way to spend my morning." And he couldn't think of anything he'd rather be doing. Enid was the love of his life. Though they'd missed years, there was always time to make up for it and there was no time like the present.

Chapter Eleven

Three years later...

"She's late," Alex growled as he paced back and forth across the grass.

Enid nibbled on her lower lip as she scanned the streets. They were abandoned. Debris littered the streets of the deserted town. No one was there.

"I'm sure she's fine," she whispered as she met Alex's gaze. "She's nearly as good a shot as me and she's with Marc."

Alex's lip curled up at the mention of the male. "I shouldn't have let them go together. I've seen the way she's been looking at him."

Enid giggled. "She's fifteen. It's only going to get worse."

"I know," he admitted. "But he's nineteen and—"

"Marc idolizes you," Enid cut him off. "He's not going to do anything to jeopardize your relationship."

"He better not. Cori's still a kid," he grumbled. "I remember what it was like when I was his age." His eyes darted to her. "I couldn't keep my hands off the beautiful wolf I was seeing."

"I remember," she whispered with a grin. "You still seem to have a problem keeping your hands to yourself," she teased as he stopped pacing and wrapped his arms around her, hugging her from behind.

"I can't help myself," he admitted, peppering kisses down her neck.

Enid brushed away from him and held her hands over her belly where the precious life was growing inside her.

"You're still upset with me?" he questioned with a sigh.

"I'm not upset with you," she told him as she turned to face him.

"I'm upset with the situation. I never wanted this."

She'd realized her precarious situation three days ago, but still had no idea how it happened. Well, that wasn't true, she *knew* how it happened, her and Alex shared their love for each other multiple times each day. But she'd never had a heat cycle. It didn't make sense.

"We'll be home in two days. Once we get into the protection of the mountain I'll feel a lot better, and I hope you will too," Alex comforted as he pulled her to him.

This time she nestled into his embrace, burying her face into the crook of his neck. "Part of me can't wait to meet this life we've created," she whispered as she clutched his shirt tighter. "But the other part remembers what it was like to hold Chase and James as they gasped for a breath they couldn't have. I can't do that again. I can't bury another child." Tears pricked her eyes and her bottom lip trembled.

"You won't." Alex pushed her back as he cupped her cheeks. "We are immune to the Wolf Flu. Our child will be, too. The books the witches used are still tucked away safely. There hasn't been any humans or witches near the mountain for three years," he assured her. "Besides, you're already a mother. I see the way you dote on Cori. You love her like she is your own."

It was true. Cori wasn't her daughter by birth, but she was her daughter in every way that mattered.

Enid nodded. The witches hadn't returned since the avalanche. But the pack had other problems. "What about food?" she questioned as she met his gaze.

That was the reason they were out—food was scarce at the mountain. She, Alex, Cori, and Marc had come out to raid some of the nearby towns. They'd been gone for nearly three weeks, collecting all the supplies they could.

"We did pretty well," Alex encouraged. He nodded his head to the beat-up pick-up truck and trailer that was stuffed to capacity with items.

"Yeah," she agreed with a sigh. "But our pack is growing." In the past three years four babies were born. It wasn't much by any means, but it was something.

"And we'll figure it out like we always do," Alex promised. "Everything is going to be fine. Trust me."

Enid drew in a breath and let it out as she closed her eyes. "I do."

Alex placed a kiss to her forehead and pulled her back into an embrace. Enid knew she was safe when she was curled in his embrace. They lived in a world of darkness, but occasionally shimmers of light emanate. When that happened she grasped onto them and hung on for dear life. The shimmers had brought her happiness so far and she wasn't going to question it.

"Cori and Marc are here," Alex told her as he pulled away.

Enid spun around and watched as the pair hiked toward them both holding onto a rope that pulled a large sled behind them.

"It looks like they did well," she commented.

"Yeah. We'll have to come back out and hit up the ocean towns again. If I'd have known we'd get so much, we'd have figured out how to bring another truck," Alex told her.

"When will you go back out again?" She wouldn't be going on any raids again for quite sometime. Alex and Cori would be leaving her behind. *What if something happened to them?* Her belly churned at the thought.

"We've got enough here to last us for a while. I doubt this stuff is going anywhere if its been sitting for eleven years," he told her. "I don't want to let the power of running the pack go to Darren's head," he grinned.

Darren was the acting alpha when Enid and Alex were gone on raids. Once the pack realized Alex and Enid were responsible for the raids that had been bringing them food, clothing, and other essential items, it hadn't taken much for the shift of power to take place.

"You're late," Alex boomed as he marched toward the pair.

Enid suppressed the urge to laugh at the scene. Cori was growing up beautifully. Sure she was concerned about her daughter being in the presence of an older guy for fourteen days unsupervised, but she knew Cori—and Marc. They were good kids and they knew how important their job was for the survival of the pack. Cori was too young to have a true romantic relationship and Marc, who wasn't an alpha, was too terrified of Alex to act on any feelings, if he had any to begin with.

"It took us longer to haul this back than we expected," Cori apologized. "We got a bunch of stuff." She waved her hand over the giant sled they'd been dragging behind them.

"You did well," Alex agreed. "Did you run into any trouble?"

"No, none. You?" Cori answered.

"It's been quite a trip. Let's get home and pray our luck continues," he said as he took the rope from Cori's hand and he and Marc tugged the haul the rest of the way to the truck and trailer.

Enid beamed and spread her arms wide as Cori raced toward her and embraced her. She placed a kiss to the girl's head and smiled into her hair.

"Dad wasn't too worried was he, Mom?" Cori wondered.

"A little," she admitted as she wrapped an arm around her shoulder and pulled her to the truck.

"Everything okay? You seem..." Cori trailed off as she frowned.

Enid licked her lips as a smile tugged at the corners of her mouth. "Everything is great," she replied. Everything was going to be just fine. "Your father and I have something we want to tell you when we get back to the mountain."

"A surprise?" Cori giggled as her voice rose.

"Yeah." Enid let out a long breath. It was a surprise that was for sure. But it was good and she believed Alex when he told her everything was going to be okay. Somehow it would be.

***

"I'm going to be a big sister!" Cori squealed. She banged her fists on the table as a large, goofy grin spread across her face.

Alex chuckled at his daughter's enthusiasm as he swallowed the bite of food in his mouth. "Yes," he told her with a grin.

"Oh my gosh. I can't wait," she whooped. "When do you think you are due?"

Alex looked to Enid.

"It's difficult to say without an ultrasound," Enid began. Cori tilted her head and frowned. "You don't know what that is, right. Um, I'd guess sometime at the end or beginning of the new year," she said.

"Do you think we could find an ultrasound?" Cori wondered as she took a bite of her bread.

"We would need a doctor who knew how to read it and electricity. Even if we found one, we don't have the means to use it," Alex replied.

"Darn. I don't suppose you'll be leaving the mountain anytime soon either," Cori guessed. "We could always look for one out on a raid and see if we could get some juice to it from a generator."

"No. I'll be here for the foreseeable future," Enid admitted.

"Actually, I've asked Parker if he minds taking over runs for a while. I'd like to stay here with Enid," Alex spoke up as he took Enid's hand in his.

"Oh?"

"Parker plans to take his two girls out with him. Things have been calm in our region for a while. I'm not fond of the idea of you going without me, but I won't stop you either," Alex told Cori.

"I'll think about it. The next run isn't for another two months," she replied as she took a bite of her deer roast. "So, I don't suppose you've thought of any names yet have you?"

"Not yet," Enid replied as she dabbed at her mouth with her napkin.

"We have plenty of time to think about it. Maybe you can help us come up with a few," he offered.

"Really?" Cori asked as her eyes widened.

"I think it would be great," Enid agreed.

Alex sighed as he stared at his family. Their world had been flipped upside down, but they'd made it. They'd survived, but it was more than that. This was their second chance and he was going to hold onto it and enjoy every moment of it for the rest of his life.

Club Stratosphere:
Lexa and Tom
By Danielle Gavan

Prologue

Slut. Dirty whore. Disgusting. Freak. Deviant.

Lexa flinched with every word her husband threw at her. Words she'd heard before. They were all endearments used frequently within the circles she traveled. Terms usually uttered with the utmost affection, not the venom with which Barry uttered them. There wasn't a hint of warmth in his tone of voice, rigid posture, or the words he spat at her.

Huddled on their couch, a throw cushion clutched to her abdomen, she listened as he paced beside her and railed a veritable litany of obscenities. Bile churned in the pit of her stomach, burning a hole through her focus. He kicked the back of the couch. Lexa jumped, a shudder rushing through her small frame. His blue eyes flashed, red mottled his fair skin from the collar of his shirt to his strawberry blond hair. She turned her face away from him, unable to continue seeing the rage contorting Barry's handsome features.

"Please," she whispered, wiping a tear from her cheek. The skin beneath the back of her hand was warm to the touch. "Stop, Barry. It's not as bad as you think."

Her husband rounded the couch, bending to bring his six-foot frame down to her level. Warm, beer scented breath fanned her face. Lexa fought not to wrinkle her nose and gag as the yeasty odor washed over her. "Not as bad as I think?" he shouted, spittle flecking her cheeks.

"My wife just told me she's a fucking dirty whore. Not bad? Jesus, Alexandra."

Barry straightened, his arms flung out to the side as he stared her down. "The woman I've known for the last two years—the one I married six months ago—suddenly tells me that she likes to be choked, beaten and humiliated because it gets her off. How is that not as bad as I think, Lexa?"

"But," she sputtered, lifting her eyes to meet his. Barry's face contorted, wrinkling his nose as he turned away. "You had no problem with tying me down before. You've spanked me in the past, and enjoyed it when we had rough sex. I... I don't understand." Lexa wiped her face on the sleeve of her light pink hoodie. "Our sex life until now hasn't exactly been what you'd call 'vanilla'. How is what I've asked so different?"

She sniffled, watching as he paced. Barry pinched the bridge of his nose between a thumb and forefinger, his eyes squeezed shut. His broad chest heaved beneath the thin cotton of the dark blue dress shirt.

He rounded on her, quickly moving to crowd Lexa's space, and bent to point a thick finger in her face. "A little slap and tickle is not the same thing," he growled. She hunched her shoulders, shrinking from the violence of his gestures. "Not even close to the same. What you want," he hesitated, eyes searching her face. "It's sick. Twisted. I won't have any part of it, Alexandra."

Barry straightened, peering down his nose at her. Lexa's eyes widened as she recognized the resolute look on his face—hard eyes, mouth set in a firm line. "I'm moving into the guest room. I can't sleep in the same room as you, let alone touch you. God!" He shuddered. "You... Get some help."

Pivoting on his heel, Barry walked down the hall where the bedrooms were located. She watched him yank open the door to their guest room and slam it shut behind him, the loud reverberation putting a punctuation mark on what, to her, symbolized the end of their marriage as she knew it.

Lexa laid her head on her knees, heat suffusing her face as fresh tears cascaded from her eyes. What had she done?

Chapter One

Lexa sat on the couch, laptop across her knees while she scrutinized the half dozen marketing images on the monitor. The television droned softly in the background and lit the room with a faint blue glow. A quick glance at the forty-two-inch screen showed her an infomercial for some newfangled hair removal product. She rolled her eyes, returning her focus to the laptop screen and the project she'd been working on.

A soft thump made Lexa turn her head to the right and peer down the hallway. She narrowed her eyes, staring at the guest room door. Barry, her husband, must have fallen asleep with the remote in his hand, again. She waited to determine if the noise had woken him up. Two minutes ticked by on the big wooden clock above their dining table and no sign of Barry. *Thank goodness,* she breathed a mental sigh of relief. Explaining why she was still up equated to an argument she didn't feel like having, again.

Taking a deep breath, Lexa turned back to her computer. She closed her eyes for a moment, rubbing the fatigue from them and nearly jumped out of her skin when her cell phone pinged and a subsequent ping announced the arrival of an instant message on her laptop.

"What the hell?" she muttered to the empty room, and clicked on the chat box blinking at the bottom of her screen.

The chat box read: *Why are you still up?*

She read the name displayed in the upper left corner of the window and blinked. Thomas Daniels. A small avatar beside his message revealed Tom's familiar smile, patrician nose and green eyes. His dark blond hair was unkempt and his shoulders were bare in the photo. *Must be his personal chat account,* she wondered. And how had he found hers?

Why was the hunky Account Manager messaging her at...? What time was it anyway? Lexa glanced at the clock again and jerked, her eyes widening as she noted the time. Two thirty-one in the morning. Shit. She was going to be craptastically tired for work in the morning.

Her cursor flashed in the reply box, daring her to answer him. She sighed and typed: *Tweaking the images. Colors aren't right. Why aren't you sleeping? At least one of us should be bright eyed and bushy tailed for the presentation.*

Ping. His response came almost immediately.

I couldn't sleep, his message read. She nodded in understanding and then smirked at her silliness; he couldn't see her nonverbal response. They were due to present the firm's biggest client with a new ad proposal at ten that morning. At this rate, they'd both be sleep deprived and liable to bomb the pitch. Perfect. Just what her life needed.

Another line of text popped up on the screen and her eyes widened, breath caught in her throat as she scanned the lines. It read: *Can't get you off my mind. I know that I'm taking an epic risk by doing this, but... I keep thinking of how you were bent over the worktable on Monday when I walked into your office. You have the most amazing ass I've ever laid eyes on, Lex.*

What? She typed and hit enter. Thinking over the day in question, Alexandra recalled the moment where she bent over the table in her office to stretch her achy back. The Saturday night before that she had paid a visit to Stratosphere, the local dungeon, and engaged in a scene with one of the house Doms, Sir Daniel. A master with floggers, whips and paddles, he'd lain it on thick that night and left Lexa spent by the time he was done with her.

Lexa shook off the memory and frowned at the screen. Tom knew she was married, everyone in the office did. None of them were aware of the state of her marriage; it wasn't any of their business.

She and Barry hadn't been happy together for quite some time. She had tried to make it work for the first six months, to give a traditional 'vanilla' marriage a try. Then Lexa confessed some of her long suppressed needs, and realized the true nature of the cruel man she'd married. They'd moved into separate bedrooms and agreed to put a good face on it for the time being. Barry expected her to seek help for what he called her deviance; but, Lexa knew there was nothing wrong with her. The desires she had were completely normal, natural even. That had been two and a half years ago.

Look at the message on your phone, the chat box flashed with Tom's reply.

Lexa picked up her cell phone, flipped to her text inbox and opened the message. Her eyes widened, staring at the picture he'd sent her. She blinked, swallowing the sudden rush of moisture filling her mouth as she let her eyes wander over the details. Heavily muscled pectorals, a lickable six-pack and—holy hell, that had to be a good eight inches of thick, hard cock.

Her mind flicked back to another hard body, a physique very similar to the one in the picture on her phone. Memories of thick biceps and rippling abs flashed back to her. Memories of Sir Daniel as he brandished a single tail whip, the end of it flying through the air to land on her thighs. Lexa shook her head to dispel the imagery and refocused on the present. Mild mannered Tom, he of the quick wit and devastating smiles, was not the brutally sadistic Sir Daniel.

Quickly deleting the image, she put the device down and stared at the chat box for the space of several long, deep, thought clearing breaths. Her pulse thudded hard and fast. No way. That wasn't him in the photo. He'd found it online and was just playing with her. No matter how she tried to explain the reasoning behind it, the image stuck in her mind, burned into her retinas.

Ping. The chat box flashed on the screen, demanding her attention.

Lex? It prompted. The cursor blinked, silently imploring she respond.

She chewed her right thumbnail for a moment, the fingers of her left hand twitching against the keyboard. *You know I'm married, right?* She typed quickly, hit enter and closed her eyes as she dropped her head back against the large cushion behind her. Was this really happening? The man she fantasized about every night wanted her. She'd achieved some of the best orgasms of her life picturing Tom while she masturbated. Yeah, right. He wanted her, and she would wake up a lotto winner tomorrow morning. Pigs might even begin to fly.

The soft ping came back almost instantly. *Technically, yes. You haven't been husband and wife for a very long time though. The two of you don't even share a bedroom.*

She straightened, pulling away from the cushions at her back and shuddered as she took in her surroundings—the dim living room, the sheer curtains covering the open windows and the patio doors just beyond the dining room. A chill ping-ponged its way down her back, and it had nothing to do with the warm breeze filtering in through the curtains.

How do you know? Have you been spying on me? She typed quickly and hit Enter as she continued to scan the room.

No. The word stared at her, short and sweet.

The breeze through her living room windows carried in the sound of a door opening and closing outside. *One of the neighbors must be letting a pet out*, she thought.

Come outside, Lex. Leave the laptop on the couch and go out the patio doors.

Lexa cocked her head at the odd request. She set the laptop aside and padded quietly across the carpet to the set of sliding doors leading to her backyard. She slid the screen door open, flinching as the motion detectors lit up the patio when she stepped out onto the wooden planks.

Barely discernible beyond the bright light in which she stood, Lexa noticed a figure on the deck across the expanse of lawn separating the two houses. The general proportions of the shadow matched those belonging to a male. Tall with broad shoulders, her neighbor waved casually. She returned the gesture and scanned the yard. Why had Tom sent her outside?

"Lexa," the man across the way spoke. "It's me."

"Tom?" she gasped, squinting at the figure across the way. "How long have you lived there?"

His soft laugh floated across their shared yard. A shiver skated down her spine and goose bumps bloomed on her skin courtesy of the deep, melodious sound. She blamed the reaction on the coolness of the wooden planks beneath her feet but, deep down, she knew Tom was the cause. The deep tenor of his chuckle had soaked more pairs of her panties than Lexa cared to admit, even to herself.

"I moved in two years ago," he replied. "You'd know that if you spent time out here."

A blush heated her cheeks at his teasing. She rested her hands on the railing, her left shoulder rising in a half shrug. The backyard was Barry's domain. Beer, barbecue and boisterous behavior. She avoided him, and it, as much as possible. "I prefer the front yard. There's more shade." *And silence*, she thought, but left that part out.

"I know," he admitted. Tom stepped back from the railing, opened the gate and started down the stairs. He glanced at the hedges lining either side of the yard and turned back to her. "More privacy back here though. The neighbors can't spy through those."

Lexa stared as he moved closer and the motion detector lights revealed more of him with each step. She couldn't help but gawk at the squares of his chest, the six-pack of abs and the deep grooves curving into the waistband of his dark boxers. Every part of him bulged with muscles. The pic had certainly been of him and her mind instantly recalled the other detail, the one barely concealed by his shorts as he drew closer.

"Tom?" she squeaked when he reached the bottom of her steps. He smiled and held out a hand for her.

"Come on," he urged. "Barry's room is at the front of the house. He'll never know you left."

***

She glanced over her shoulder at the patio doors and Tom thought for a moment Lexa might say no to his request. Her small, white teeth worried at the full sweep of her lower lip when she looked back at him. He smiled encouragingly and waited to see what she would do.

It had come as a surprise when he'd started working at Page and Butler, Inc. and found out the luscious Junior Account Manager was his backyard neighbor. The biggest shock had come when Tom discovered her husband barbecuing one Sunday afternoon. They'd gotten to talking. After a few beers, Barry had been all too happy to spill the beans about the state of his marriage, and his wife's deviant preferences, over medium rare steaks and potato salad. The man really was a jackass, and an even bigger fool for not seeing the treasure a woman like Lexa was, the rarity of a woman like her.

Tom glanced up at Alexandra. Long, straight hair hung down her back in a gorgeous curtain of chestnut brown. A light blue camisole covered high, perky breasts and a trim, flat stomach. His cock twitched against the soft silk of his boxers; she wasn't wearing a bra and the pebbled tips of her nipples pressed against the thin cotton of her top. He could almost make out the dark circles of her areolas through the fabric.

"I can't," she finally replied. "We can't. We've got a huge presentation in less than eight hours, Tom. Not to mention," Lexa glanced over her shoulder at the house and Tom cursed the man sleeping inside of it.

He laughed softly and climbed the first step up to her. "The presentation is perfect and we'll do fine. You're obsessing when there's no need to. Come to me," he pled. "Let me kiss you? If you don't feel it, or don't want to come with me after that, I'll leave you alone. We'll be work buddies, and nothing more."

Suddenly, the light turned off and plunged them into inky darkness. Tom climbed another step to kick it back on and then decided if he was going that far, he might as well go all the way up.

Standing on the ledge of the deck, the gate separating them, he smiled down at Lexa. Her wide eyes, filled with uncertainty in their chocolate brown depths, stared up at him. She was such a petite thing, so delicately built. He lifted a hand to cup her left cheek. She pressed into the caress and he took it as her agreement to the terms he'd offered.

Heart pounding in his chest, Tom lifted his other hand to her right cheek, bent and gently pressed his lips to hers. The kiss started out as a hesitant, shy caress. A chaste brushing together of mouths. Her lips, soft and supple, moulded to his. Testing, Tom slid his tongue over the seam of Lexa's lips. She opened on the second pass and he swept inside, a soft groan escaping from him.

Soft and cautious, her fingers brushed his skin, tracing the contours of his ribs. He fought the urge to shudder, her touch inflaming his already hyperaware senses, and continued kissing her, waiting for her next move. She didn't disappoint. Lexa gently dug her nails into his lower back, the slight sting urging him closer.

Exultant, Tom moaned, wrapped his arms around her small frame, and crushed Lexa to him. The soft rounds of her breasts pressed firmly into his chest, her upper body shaped perfectly to his above the separation of the patio gate. God, had anything ever felt so damn good?

Lexa pulled back, her lips swollen and glistening in the moonlight. She glanced down at the barrier between them, a frown creasing her brow. Her teeth made another appearance, worrying at Lexa's lower lip.

"What's wrong?" he asked, lifting a hand to caress her cheek. He traced the soft sweep of her lip with his thumb, putting a stop to the adorable nervous tick. "Why'd you stop?"

She lifted her gaze to meet his, the moon reflected in the deep pools of her eyes. "The gate," she replied with a rueful smile. "It was pressing into my hips."

"Oh," he said simply. "So, am I leaving alone?"

Her face gave nothing away. They were inches apart and yet he felt like they stood on opposite ends of a chasm while she debated the possibility of a future relationship between them. He wanted desperately to be a fly on the wall inside her mind. Would the one kiss they shared be it and they would continue on as work associates? Or, would she take a leap and trust him? He'd been doing everything, anything, he could to show her that he was a decent guy. The kind a woman like her needed.

Since coming to the realization that what he felt for her was more than just a passing fancy between co-workers, Tom had set out to prove himself to Lexa in the hopes that when he made his move, she'd see him—the man, the Dominant—and not just her co-worker.

Finally, she took a deep breath as if she were about to speak. He froze, anticipating the worst.

"Yes," she began. Tom closed his eyes, deflated, and let his shoulders droop. "I'm all yours. But, after the presentation. We'll do dinner and see how things go from there. Okay?"

Opening his eyes, he grinned at her. His heart beat a mile a minute as elation coursed through him. He leaned in, kissing her hard and fast. It took everything he had not to launch into a victory dance, complete with fist pump, and ruin the moment.

"Really?" he asked, his eyes jumping from one feature to the other, trying to discern her sincerity. She nodded, a small smile playing at the corners of her luscious mouth. Tom couldn't resist and kissed her again. He pulled back, chuckling softly as he met her gaze. "You realize, this is totally going to screw with my concentration, right? I won't be able to think of anything else but you through the entire presentation."

Lexa looked up at him and bit her lip. She traced a slim finger down his chest and winked at him. Damn, but she was sexy as hell and he couldn't wait to finally have her under him.

"Good," she smirked. "Make sure you think of me without panties on, because I won't be wearing any."

His erection jerked behind the waist band of his shorts and Tom recalled the image he'd texted her. He smiled, reaching out to flip a strap off her shoulder with the tip of his index finger. She shivered and his lips spread into a wide grin.

"That's fine, as long as you're thinking of the pic I sent you earlier."

"Trust me," she chuckled, her eyes twinkling as she looked up at him. "I will be; haven't stopped since I first saw it. I have to admit, though—the real thing is much, much better."

Tom reached out to flick the other strap from her shoulders but she caught him by the wrist and shook her head. She pulled the strap back up, a small smile stretching across her lips.

"Damn," he laughed. "Can't blame me for trying. I've been waiting forever for this—for you."

She lifted his arm, turning his palm up and pressed her lips to the center of his hand. "Later. For now, I think we should both get some sleep."

He nodded, hiding his disappointment when she released his hand and stepped back. Lexa was right, they'd been working on the presentation for weeks and it needed to be stellar. If they didn't knock the socks off their client, the chances of winning the account went down the drain along with all of their hard work.

"Okay. After work. Dinner at my place to celebrate."

"Deal."

Lexa gave him a smile and Tom watched her walk back into the house. Her hips swayed with each step, the firm rounds of her backside tempting him. He stood in the moonlit darkness for a moment more before slowly making his way home. There was no way in hell he'd sleep with images of her swimming through his lust addled brain. He doubted she'd be getting much sleep either. The sexual tension flowing between them as they stood out on the patio edge had been off the charts, undeniable and potent.

It was going to be a long day, but so worth it. His only hope was that she didn't rethink things and back out. Tom had lusted after her since going to work for Page and Butler, Inc. four months ago. Now that he'd gotten up the nerve to approach Lexa, there was no way he was backing down. She would be his, no matter what it took to make that happen.

Shutting the patio door behind him, Tom made his way down the hall and flopped down on his bed to wait for his alarm clock to go off at 7:00 AM. It was going to be the longest five hours of his life.

Chapter Two

Wrapping a thick cotton towel around herself, Lexa left the steamy confines of her bathroom and ventured out into the carpeted hallway. She took two halting steps toward her bedroom, paused and glanced at Barry's door, listening for any sign that he was up and prowling around his room.

How the man managed to sleep through his own snoring continually amazed her. Akin to the ripping of phone books or a diesel train roaring by, her so-called-husband's loud snores reverberated throughout the house.

Lexa gave a brief snort and continued on to her room. Closing the door, she dropped her towel in the hamper and padded naked to the closet. She reached in and pulled out the new dress purchased a few days earlier for the presentation today. Black, with a fitted blouse bodice and full, knee length skirt—the dress was simple, elegant and perfect.

Laying the garment across the end of her bed, Lexa turned to her dresser. She pulled open the top drawer, the one containing her lingerie, and stopped short of reaching for a pair of panties as she recalled the words she'd uttered to Tom. Heat crept up her face as she looked over the bits of silk and lace in front of her. Could she really go through such an important and possibly life changing presentation without panties? Maybe, if she managed to keep the insane urge to blush under control. The teasing comment was so unlike her usual reserved self, she wondered what had possessed her to act so rashly. There was something about Tom, the raw sex appeal he exuded as they stood in the semi darkness that short circuited her brain. Shy, reserved Alexandra had turned into bold, sex kitten Lexa in his presence.

She reached into the drawer, pulling out her favorite hot pink lace bra, the matching garters and sheer black stockings with pink ribbon detailing along the top. In another drawer, she found a slim, red leather belt and tossed it onto the bed while she put her undergarments on. Her nipples pebbled as she thought of Tom and the surprise she expected to see on his face later when he realized she'd followed through on her promise to go commando. She had no doubt they would end up in bed together. The way she lusted after him, and the clear desire shining from his eyes when they'd talked earlier made it pretty clear that was the agenda for the evening.

A soft tap on the window drew her from the daydream. Lexa fastened the second stay on her left garter and put her right foot down onto the plush carpeting. She crossed over to the window and pulled the curtain aside to peer out over the patio. Tom stood a few feet from her window, his briefcase beside him in the grass.

The early morning sun shone down on him giving his golden hair the appearance of a halo. He caught sight of her, smiled widely and wiggled his fingers in a brief wave. Feeling brave, Lexa smiled back and pulled the curtain further aside to allow him a view of her from the waist up.

Tom's eyes widened momentarily and then narrowed. Undisguised lust burned in the green depths of his eyes. His heated gaze tracked her movements as she reached out and pulled the window pane up to allow them to speak. The glass provided her with a pale reflection as it rose, and showed that the action lifted her breasts, pushing them together in a tempting display for him.

"Good morning," she said cheerfully through the open window.

He adjusted his tie and smirked. "It was. That little display just made it a whole lot better."

Lexa smiled, resting her hands palms down on the wide window sill.

"What brings you by? Hoping to discuss a few last minute details before the presentation?"

"No," he said. Tom dangled keys from between his right index and thumb, jangling them lightly. "I wanted to see if you'd like to ride in to work together. We can discuss a few things about the presentation on the way in. Plus, it will save you having to ride the bus with no panties on."

She looked him over while contemplating his offer, smothering a chuckle at his no so subtle reminder. He wore a tailored black jacket, a crisp white shirt and a red silk tie. From what she could see of his pants above the gate, they were his usual black slacks. Their outfits matched. Cute.

"Too funny," she chuckled softly.

Tom eyed her quizzically. "What is?"

Lexa shook her head and smiled at him. "Nothing. Give me twenty minutes to finish dressing. I'll meet you out front."

"I think you're perfect just the way you are," he quipped and turned to exit the backyard. "See you in twenty."

Laughing, Lexa let the drapes fall back into place and turned to slip into her dress. She slid her feet into her favorite pair of black leather pumps, wrapped the thin belt around her waist and went to fix her hair. Nothing fancy today, a quick blow dry of her bangs—half of the wavy mass tied back with a clip, and she was done.

Lexa applied chocolate brown liner to her eyes, brushed a dusting of bronzer over her cheeks and skimmed her lips with a clear gloss. Giving herself one final look over, she turned off the light and walked down to the kitchen.

Her leather portfolio bag sat on a chair at the small breakfast table. Reaching inside, she pulled out a slim packet of paper from the inner pocket. For three weeks the pages had been sitting in her portfolio, taunting her every time she reached in for something, but she hadn't built up the courage to hand them to Barry. Now, with her career about to take a jump for the better and Tom's obvious mutual interest, the time had come to put the dead horse of her marriage to rest.

She set the bundle where she knew Barry would find it—in front of his beloved coffee machine. The man was disgustingly predictable in his routines, and was a bear to deal with until he'd had at least two cups of coffee. Lexa knew, without a doubt, Barry would find the paperwork and life as she knew it would take a drastic change. The question was, for better or worse?

Butterflies took up residence in her stomach as she looked at the pale blue exterior page. She'd done it. Now all she needed was Barry's signature on the divorce papers. Then she could file them and move on with her life.

The sound of a key turning in the front door lock drew Lexa's attention. She turned, surprised to see her housekeeper arriving on a Friday morning.

"Oh," the pretty redhead exclaimed and stopped in her tracks. "Mrs. Porter. I didn't expect you to be here."

Lexa cocked her head to the right. "I could say the same, Carissa. You're supposed to come on Tuesdays and Saturdays. Is there a reason you're a day early?"

"Barry, um, Mr. Porter asked me to come by today instead." She bit her lip and quickly glanced down the hallway. Lexa didn't miss the direction of her maid's look. She shook her head and let out a slow breath. "I can come tomorrow if you want but, I'm already here."

"No, it's fine," Lexa said. She picked up her bag, keys and purse. "You go ahead. I've got to get going. Make sure he..." The maid tilted her head, eyes wide as she waited for Lexa to finish. "Forget it. I'm sure he'll pay you well enough."

The maid has the decency to blush as she nodded and Lexa exited without her morning cup of tea, or breakfast. *Great*, she thought. *I let the little hussy chase me out of my own house.*

Making her way down the front steps, Lexa shook her head and laughed softly. What did she care about her soon to be ex-husband and the maid getting it on while she worked? It wasn't like they'd be having sex in her bed anyway. As soon as Barry autographed the divorce papers she would be a free woman and the hunt for a cozy little apartment of her own would begin.

A sleek, silver Lexus pulled up to the curb and Tom smiled at her from the driver's seat. He climbed out and came around to her side, taking her bag to place it in the backseat.

Tom held the passenger side door open for her, sweeping his arm out in a grand gesture. "Your chariot, milady."

"Thank you, kind sir." She laughed at his silliness and climbed inside.

***

Lexa smiled and shook hands with Philip Watts, the middle aged CEO of Watts & Associates. She studied his moderately handsome face, trying to keep the elation bubbling inside of her firmly under wraps. Tom stood to her left, his hand firmly in their boss' grip, and accepted the hearty congratulations being offered. Their presentation had gone off without a hitch and met with a rousing round of approval from everyone present. The account, Mr. Watts had announced almost immediately after she and Tom completed their pitch, was theirs. Lexa and Tom had looked at each other, wide eyed and slack jawed until the reality sunk in. They'd been prepared to wait days, possibly weeks, before hearing whether they'd successfully landed the project or not.

Messrs.' Page and Butler took Lexa and Tom out for a celebratory lunch at one of the most expensive and exclusive restaurants in town, Scotia's. As anticipated, they announced her promotion to senior account manager, effective immediately. Tom smiled proudly at her from across the table. Their coup with winning the Watts project was nothing short of brilliant and their bosses firmly believed in giving reward where it was due.

So far, the day had been a banner one for her, but Lexa couldn't ignore the little twinge deep in her belly. Four o'clock rolled around and she had yet to hear a word from Barry or his lawyer about the divorce papers. Nothing from her attorney either, for that matter. It was all going too easily for her, and the skeptic in Lexa waited for the axe to fall. Barry had become a vindictive jerk since the breakdown of their marriage. Any chance he could do something to slight her was met with much relish. Expecting him to sign the paperwork without putting up a fight wasn't something she counted on happening.

She gave the artwork on her desk one final look over and decided to call it a day. The photographs for this new project wouldn't get any better no matter how long she stared at them. The art department would have to do a reshoot. There was no alternative. That conversation, however, would wait for Monday.

Shutting down her laptop, Lexa gathered everything she'd need to get some work done on the weekend and placed them in her bag. Knowing her soon-to-be ex-husband, that plan was likely to go off the rails faster than an out-of-control freight train. A soft knock at the door made her look up. She smiled at Tom as he leaned against the frame, his arms crossed over the breadth of his powerful chest.

"Looks like you're ready to go," he said.

She nodded and zipped the bag shut. "Yep. I was hoping I could entice you into playing hooky with me for the rest of the day. We deserve it."

Tom grinned, leaned down and showed her the briefcase he'd stashed out of sight. "No enticing needed. I was planning the same thing."

"Well then," she laughed, picked up her bag and slung it over her shoulder. "Let's go. No point in hanging around here when there are much better things to do."

He stepped aside to allow Lexa to close her office door. When she turned, Tom leaned in and whispered in her ear. "Each other?"

"Yes, exactly." Lexa shuddered, a zing of desire skidding down her spine like a pebble across water. She nodded and smiled up at him as she turned to leave the office.

***

Lexa stood with her back to him, arms folded across her chest, while Tom prepared a light supper for them. He noted the way her fingers clutched her biceps, the skin around each fingertip white from the pressure. Something in the back yard had caught her attention and he glanced out the kitchen window to see what might be out there.

Across the yard, on the steps leading down from her patio, several suitcases and boxes sat waiting. He shook his head, rubbed his eyes and looked again. The view hadn't changed. *What the hell?*

"Am I seeing right, Lexa?" he asked.

She nodded slowly, releasing the grip on her arms. Lexa shrugged and let out a soft breath. "Can't say I'm totally shocked. I did serve him with divorce papers this morning. Wonder which box or bag they're in?"

Tom stopped his chopping and gaped at her. "You what?"

"I served him with divorce papers. This morning." She turned to face him without meeting his eyes. A sheepish smile curved her lips as she studied something on the floor just off to his right. "I've been holding on to them for a while now. This morning just, I don't know, felt right. Guess this means I need to speed up my search for somewhere to stay."

Putting down the knife he'd been using to chop mushrooms, Tom crossed the room and wrapped his arms around her. He hugged her gently and brushed a loose curl from her cheek.

"You can stay with me," he offered, leaning back to look her in the eyes. "I have plenty of room in the garage to store your stuff, and a guest bedroom, if you want it."

Uncertainty flashed through her eyes. She frowned and looked away from his steady gaze. "I don't know."

He gave her an encouraging smile. "Come on. Let's get the boxes in the garage and your bags in the house. You can think about my offer while we're moving stuff."

She nodded and he gave her a gentle kiss. Mother Nature, ever the opportunist, chose that moment to punctuate the caress with a thundering boom and flash of lightning.

"Oh, shit." Releasing Lexa, Tom moved to the patio doors and yanked the sliding glass panel open. The first thick drop of rain hit the decking with a splat as he gestured for her to precede him. "Let's get that stuff inside before it really starts to pour."

Lexa dashed outside and Tom hit the garage door opener button beside the door on his way through. He quickly followed her across the yard and joined Lexa in moving boxes and bags.

**

They were down to the final two boxes and one of her suitcases when the skies fully opened on them. Tom looked up at the steel gray clouds above and cursed the torrential rain falling from the sky. He picked up two boxes and ran for cover. Lexa passed him on her way out of the garage as she ran for the last suitcase.

Several minutes later, soaked to the skin and laughing at the ridiculousness of the situation, Tom deposited the largest of Lexa's suitcases on the dining room floor. Despite their mad dash to get everything in the house, the water dripping off the bag formed a large puddle on the tiles.

"Oh well," Lexa sighed. "The stuff inside will dry. They should only contain clothes."

Tom nodded, "We can throw them in the dryer or hang them to dry later." He let his gaze travel over her waterlogged dress. The thin material moulded to the curves of her breasts, showing off nipples pebbled by the cold rain. He swallowed the lump blocking his throat and stepped closer.

Lexa met him halfway and reached out, bringing her hands to rest on his chest. One by one she undid the buttons on his wet dress shirt, parting the material to run her fingers over his chest. He groaned, and she smiled, a mischievous glint in her eyes.

"Lex?" he asked, his voice wavering. She looked up at him from beneath her thick lashes and winked.

"Shush," she replied, putting her right index finger over his lips to silence him. "I've been waiting all day to get my hands on you and I'm not going to let being kicked out of my house keep me from getting what I want. And right now? I want you."

He chuckled softly and her nimble fingers continued their path down his stomach. She pulled the bottom of his shirt out of his pants, making short work of the last few buttons. Chilled by the rain, her fingertips brushed his skin and set off a cascade of goose bumps that ended with his nipples pebbled beneath the thin layer of his shirt.

Tom lifted a hand to caress the full sweep of her lower lip and noted the way she trembled. He caught one of her hands in his free one and took a step back.

"Come on," he urged. "We're both freezing and I have the perfect solution to meet both our needs."

Tugging gently on her hand, Tom led Lexa down the hall to the bathroom. He stepped inside the glass walled shower and, careful not to stand directly in the trajectory of the spray, turned the water on to warm up. Steam began to billow in the bottom of the enclosure after a minute or two, and he swivelled back to face Lexa.

She smirked and spread wide the already unbuttoned sides of her dress. Dark pink lace encased the creamy swells of her breasts. The puckered, brownish tips stood erect and visible through the thin material. Small silver barbells decorated each nipple. The piercings were a delectable surprise and his cock bucked in response to the visual stimuli.

"God," he said in a low voice as he stepped closer. "You're beautiful."

Her cheeks and the tops of her breasts colored with a soft blush. She turned her face away, giving him a view of her profile as she demurely cast her gaze toward the floor. Tom reached out and slid the dress from her shoulders. He bent to press a kiss to the curve of her neck as she reached up to slide his shirt off. The material, tailored to fit him perfectly, bunched around his elbows and trapped his arms to his side.

Tom chuckled low, kissed the curve of her neck and stepped back to shuck the garment. He tossed it in the general direction of the hamper, the slither of wet material on plastic confirming he'd nailed the shot.

"Don't move," he ordered and began stripping. "Eyes up, Lex. Watch."

She did as he instructed, hands clasped in front of her as she stood still and focused her attention on his actions. Hunger and desire darkened her eyes with each piece of clothing he removed. He couldn't wait to see how she looked when they were naked, and he was inside of her. The thought of her delicate pink flesh parting, taking him in, pulled a deep groan from Tom's throat.

"Good girl," he praised, voice modulated just loud enough for her to hear over the rush of the shower. She flicked him a glance, eyes narrowed, and he winked. Yes, the gesture communicated to her. He knew her little secret.

Taking his time, Tom undid his belt buckle. Lexa's eyes tracked every movement as he slid leather through metal, pulled the clasp free of the hole, and let the sides hang loose from the belt loops. He moved to the button on his pants and popped it open. He undid the zipper, one slow torturous inch at a time, and revealed his naked erection. Tom palmed his cock, running his hand up the shaft and back down again. The tip of her pink tongue swept out over Lexa's lip and Tom knew he'd won her full attention.

"You went commando?" she asked breathlessly, her eyes making a quick trip up to meet his before diving back down to the show he was putting on for her.

"Yep," he replied, a cocky grin curving his lips. "Figured you shouldn't be the only one walking around bare assed in front of the bosses."

Lexa laughed huskily and his shaft bucked in response. It was long past time to get naked. He dropped his pants, toed off his socks and stepped out of the pile of clothes. Any pretense of taking his time gone the moment she let out that sexy little laugh.

"Come here," he beckoned with a crook of his finger. "You're overdressed."

The room had been relatively quiet while he stripped. Behind him, thick glass muted the shower's spatter against the tiles, dulling the noise to a soft shush. His clothing had rustled during its removal and exile to the hamper. All of the sounds were quiet compared to the suddenly loud beating of his heart as she stepped into his space.

He skimmed his hands over her ribs, sliding them around to caress the curve of her lower back. Tom marveled at the way her body fit his, so petite he could almost span her waist with both hands. Encountering the damp material of her dress, he pushed it down over her rear and it dropped to the tiles with a soggy plop.

Bending to lay a series of kisses along Lexa's shoulder, Tom glanced down the line of her back. Dark curls tumbled down over her smooth, creamy skin and pooled in the narrow dip of her waist. The hot pink garter belt she had on barely covered the rounded swell of her rear. Hands down, it was the best ass he'd ever seen, naked or otherwise. He noted a few faint bruises, crop marks from the shape of them. The pattern in which they were laid out struck him as familiar, and he resolved to ask her about them later.

"Tom?" she whispered hesitantly against his ear. She tried to pull away, but he tightened his grip and held her to him.

He shuddered, closing his eyes for a moment as he gathered her close. Her warm breath against his chest zinged lust straight to his groin.

Lexa flicked her tongue over one of his nipples and he pulled back to look at her. Mischief glittered in the dark depths of her eyes and it made him wonder for a minute what kind of submissive he had on his hands.

"Sorry," he said. "You've got me feeling like a teenager with his first girl. A bad girl. One who likes to lick things without permission."

She chuckled and nipped at his chest. "You're definitely not a teenager and, that I can make you feel this way… it's a huge compliment." Lexa smiled at him. "What I wanted to say though, was that I accept your offer. I'll stay here until—."

He cut her off, a wide grin spreading over his lips. "You can stay as long as you want." Tom cupped her face between his hands and leaned in close. "Now, shush. We're both freezing from the rain. Let's warm up in the shower, and we can discuss it later. Okay?"

Lexa nodded, her eyes downcast. Tom grinned and swatted her backside. "Good girl. Let's get you warmed up. I want to fuck you, but I want something more than shower sex for our first time together, Lex."

Chapter Three

Tom laid her out on the bed. Standing between Alexandra's parted thighs, he bent and kissed the midway point between her navel and the cleft of her pussy. Moisture from their shared shower dotted her pale skin, and he darted his tongue out to taste her. His head swam as the intoxicating blend of sensory input overtook him. The slightly salty taste of her skin and his favorite shower gel combined with her natural scent to form an powerful mix, and Tom knew he would never get enough.

She moaned, draping a supple thigh over his arm where he'd rested a hand on the bed to steady himself. Her hips rocked up, backside lifting from the bed, demanding more than the light touches on offer. Tom smirked against Lexa's warm skin and nipped at her labia as a subtle warning. He'd overlook the bold move, for now. Soon enough she'd learn to trust him to take her where they needed to go.

"Patience, kitten," he murmured against her mound. "We'll get there. All in good time."

He inhaled deeply, breathing in the scent of her arousal. *Damn. She's sexy as sin*, he mused and licked a trail from the smooth skin of her mons up to her belly button. Lexa shifted and Tom looked up to find her raised up on her elbows, watching him.

"Please," she pouted and reached down to sweep a finger over his bottom lip. "I need you, Tom. Now. Please?"

Tom pushed down the surge of lust raging through him. He nipped at her finger tip, smirking when she pulled her hand back, her mouth forming a little 'o' as she cradled the offended digit. The heat blazing in her eyes nearly undid his will to hold out as long as he could.

"Kitten," he groaned and slid up to kiss her pouty lips. Placing a hand between Lexa's breasts, he firmly pushed her back down. "As tempting as that offer is, I want to make this good for you. I need to." He pushed the fingers of his free hand through her damp locks, gripping a thick fistful of them at the back of her head, and held Lexa's gaze with his own. "Can you relax, and trust me to do that? Let me take control. I'll make it better than you could imagine, Babygirl. Promise."

He gave Lexa's hair a gentle tug, urging an answer from her. The Dominant in him knew this situation required patience, but the man— the one who'd waited months to get her exactly where she was—he wanted an answer right now.

Determined to wait her out, Tom gave her hair another tug to remind her of his request. He watched her breath catch, noting the rapid rise and fall of Lexa's chest against his own as she resumed breathing. Her pupils dilated, turning the chocolate brown irises almost black as they expanded. Every other part of Lexa's body stilled, her submissive nature finally asserting itself.

"Well, kitten?" He prodded once more. Lexa managed a faint nod, but that wasn't enough for Tom. He wanted, needed, the verbalization of her consent. "Say it. Out loud. Look me in the eyes, Lexa. Do you consent?"

The bubble gum pink tip of her tongue darted out, moistening her lips. She looked him straight in the eyes, unwavering, and smiled. "Yes, Sir."

Tom groaned, a shudder running through him as she gave the appropriate response. "Good girl," he bent to kiss her once more. He looked her in the eyes and smiled wickedly. "Now relax, and no cumming until I say so. Understood?"

Lexa nodded, and rested her hands on his biceps. "Yes, Sir. Understood."

He smirked, the slight pout on her lips not unnoticed when she responded to his command. She was definitely submissive. He'd known as much from conversations with Barry in the backyard. Get a few beers into him and no secret was safe with the bitter, angry man. He'd been all too happy to divulge Lexa's sexual proclivities with Tom one Sunday afternoon.

Giving himself a mental shake, Tom refocused on the woman laying open and willing beneath him. He nipped at the swell of her right breast, sinking his teeth into the soft underside. Lexa's breath caught and she rewarded him with a small moan, her back arching to press the flesh up in supplication. He flicked his tongue over the tiny bite to soothe away any pain, loving the small shudder that worked its way through her body.

Tom moved lower, flicking his tongue over the barbell piercing the tight bud of Lexa's nipple. He closed his lips over the areola, drawing the tip into his mouth. The metal clicked against his teeth as he flicked his tongue over the turgid flesh. Releasing her nipple, Tom slipped his arms beneath Lexa and scooted her higher onto the bed. She squeaked as he lifted her from the mattress and he fought a chuckle at the adorable sound. What other sounds, he wondered, could he elicit from his bold little submissive?

Settled on the bed, Tom stretched himself out against her. He closed his eyes and bit back a pained groan. His hard cock pressing into the mattress reminded Tom of how much he wanted the delectable woman spread out for him. His mouth practically watered, the need to taste her driving him mad. He fought the desire to lose himself in her. There would be plenty of time for that if he had his way, and it would be so easy. Of that, he held no doubts.

"Tom?" The hesitation in Lexa's voice pulled Tom from his thoughts and he opened his eyes. Her brow was furrowed, concern wavering in the dark depths of her eyes as she reached to caress his cheek with her fingertips. "Are you okay?"

He nodded as he shifted to ease the pressure on his erection. "I'm great."

Lexa glanced down the length of him, her lips curving up in a small smirk as she surmised the source of his discomfort. His cock jumped, the intensity of her gaze almost a physical touch. "Yes, you are."

"Smartass," Tom grinned. Submissive, with a touch of brat. Fuck. Yeah. "I'll have to think up a suitable punishment for that one, little girl." He cocked his head at her, one eyebrow lifted in question. She bit her lip, eyes widening as realization sank in. Tom's lips lifted in a knowing smile. "Maybe a nice, firm spanking. One meant to put smart mouthed little subs in their places. But first…"

Before she could form a response, Tom slid down Lexa's body. He licked and kissed a trail down the center of her abdomen, circling the shallow dip of her belly button. She shuddered, goosebumps scattering across her pale skin. He smirked, licking from the top of her cleft and over the smooth expanse of Lexa's mound. The rasp of fingernails on material caught his attention, and Tom glanced over to see her fingers flexing against the heavy cotton coverlet.

Tom refocused, nipping down the crease of Lexa's left leg. Her muscles twitched and trembled beneath the smooth skin of her thigh, but she kept still without a direction to do so. Tom switched sides, repeating the motion down the crease of her other leg. He delighted in the small moans Lexa emitted, the light tremble increasing with each flick of his tongue.

Turning his face slightly, Tom flattened his tongue and slowly dragged it up the length of Lexa's vulva from the tight pucker of her ass to the tiny bundle of her clit. As he reached the very top of the crease he pointed his tongue, dipping between her labia to tease at the tiny nub hidden beneath.

Lexa gasped his name, her hips bucking as he pushed deeper and sucked her clit into his mouth. Cream gushed from her hole and he dipped his tongue out, licking up every drop. Tom groaned, the sweet and tangy taste of Lexa's fluids coating his tongue and filling his senses. Sliding his hands up, he rested them on her upper thighs and used his thumbs to hold Lexa's labia wide open. Nestled near the top of her glistening pink sex, Lexa's clit peeped out from it's hood, beckoning him in for more, like a siren to his Odysseus. It was the sexiest, most erotic thing he'd ever seen.

Looking up at Lexa, Tom nipped at her clit. She jerked and mewled, her back arching as he blew over the sensitive little nub. His cock kicked in response, the erotic sight she presented as she struggled to keep control driving him to the brink with lust. He needed to be inside of her, soon. "No cumming, Lexa." He licked her, slowly circling the flesh surrounding Lexa's clit but not touching the swollen bundle of nerves. "Not until I say."

She licked her lips, her head rocking against the coverlet. "Yes," she panted. Lexa lifted her head, meeting his gaze, and gave him a slight nod. "When you say. I want... Can I, please?" she hesitated, and Tom cocked a brow as he dipped down for another taste of her.

"You want what, Lexa?" He lazily circled her clit, daring her to answer him through the haze of lust clouding her eyes, and undoubtedly, her head. "You want to cum?" He lapped at the cream oozing from her opening, tucking his tongue inside to gather more of the savory treat.

***

Lexa moaned, her hips twitching each time he pushed his tongue inside of her. Her body was on fire, nerve endings firing frantic messages throughout her system. Every muscle tensed, her heart pounding like a bass drum with every flick of Tom's skillful tongue and soft gust of breath against her sensitive flesh. Oh, how she craved this man, desired and needed what he offered. Control, release... freedom. "No," she whimpered, hands hovering over the heavy, swollen rounds of her breasts. "I want to touch. Please, Sir?"

She lifted her head, finding the flash of his green eyes as they studied her above the dip of her belly. A lock of blond hair curled across his forehead, the tousled mass so different from the usual polished and professional look she was used to from Tom. Lexa's eyes widened as he dragged another slow, teasing lick over her sex. She silently implored him to answer the request, her fingers flexing over the mounds of her breasts. The need to cum was quickly overwhelming her, and Lexa knew well enough how to keep that from happening. She needed a little pain to keep her off the edge until Tom gave her permission to jump off and into the pool of pleasure at the bottom. The pain would only stop her for so long. Soon enough it would simply be another layer of pleasure and when that happened... She could only hope that Tom understood what he was dealing with when he'd taken her to bed. Somehow he'd known she was submissive, but had he guessed at the masochistic part of her as well?

"Yes, kitten." He kissed her clit, the subtle suction causing her pulse to jump and her nerves to skitter. She bit her lip, stifling a groan as she clamped down hard on the need to cum. He'd given the order not to, and she would obey. "Give them a good twist. Show me what you like."

Lowering her hands, Lexa curved each one around the firmness of a breast as Tom resumed his feast between her thighs. She pinched her nipples between a thumb and index finger, twisting the swollen nubs viciously. Pain and pleasure lanced through her in tandem, bowing Alexandra's back off the bed. A heavy moan slipped from deep within her throat, a plea for more. More pain. More pleasure. More him. Her focus narrowed, all external stimuli ignored as her brain tried to make sense of the warring sensations within her body. She managed a faint whisper of thanks as the tide of pain washed over and eased her back from the edge of orgasm.

Alexandra released the vice grip on her nipples, a fresh wave of agony hitting as blood rushed backed in to fill the sensitive tips. She whimpered, the probing of Tom's fingers at the entrance to her pussy drawing her attention away from her throbbing tits. He pushed in, fingertips pressing and turning the pain into pleasure with each slow, torturous drag through her sensitive flesh.

With her eyes squeezed shut, Lexa panted hard as she tried to stave off the orgasm looming just out of reach. She rocked her head back and forth, her fingers grasping frantically at the coverlet on either side of her hips. "Please," she moaned. "I'm going to cum. Please, Sir, let me." Lex begged. She groaned, locking down her muscled, desperate to keep her hips from jackknifing off the bed and riding his hand like the shameless slut she was.

"Not yet, little girl." Tom growled, pinching the top of her right thigh and driving back the orgasm. She bucked, the sharp pain doing very little to stop the wave of heat rushing through Lexa's body. Hyperaware of her body, Lexa groaned as she felt a heavy surge of wetness gush from her opening. His tongue was there instantly, catching it as he sealed his mouth over her pussy and sucked. Lexa screamed, limbs trembling as she fought against the current and struggled to keep herself from drowning in it. Tom released her, his breath labored when he spoke. "You'll wait until I say that you can, and not a moment sooner. Understood? Open your eyes and tell me you understand."

He pinched her harder and drove the point home. Lexa nodded, biting her lip to stop herself from crying out. Tears spilled from the corners of her eyes, running in warm trails down her temples to vanish into her hair.

"Yes," she whimpered. Wicked pain exploded from her clit and Lexa's eyes flew open. She gasped for air, her mouth working like that of a fish as she struggled to overcome the sudden torment.

Tom rose above her, roughly shoving her thighs apart. Her eyes met his, brown clashing with green. "Answer me properly." He punctuated the request with another pinch to her clit, the second no less agonizing than the first. "Be a good little slut, and I'll let you cum while I fuck you, kitten."

Lexa swallowed, her tongue thick in a mouth dry from panting hard and fast. She drew in a shuddering breath, her body still despite the storm raging inside, and answered him. "Yes, Sir. I understand, Sir."

"Good girl." Tom smiled, kissing the tip of Lexa's nose as he slipped his arms beneath the crook of her knees and opened her up to fit between them. Her hips, no longer used to being spread so brutally wide, protested the position, an ache settling in the joints.

She looked down, inexplicably drawn to watch as Tom positioned his cock at her seeping entrance. He pushed in with one thrust, the condom sheathed length sinking balls deep into the pink depths of her pussy. Lexa gasped, her back arching as her body fought to accommodate the sudden, forceful invasion. He stretched her, the girth borderline painful as he forced her body to accept it.

Lexa met Tom's gaze as he pulled out, and then pushed in torturously slow. Lust blazed from the darkened depths of his green eyes, his breath rushing out in short, staccato bursts. She moaned, bowing her back into the mattress and lifting her hips to meet his on the down thrust. Warmth rippled through her, curling Lexa's toes as Tom built a slow rhythm of deep, penetrating thrusts. She lost track of time, her world narrowed down to the slide of their bodies together and the pressure building low in her belly.

Tom ground against her clit each time their pelvises met, the friction turning her into a writhing, whimpering creature beneath him. He dipped down, releasing Lexa's legs, and kissed her between breaths. "Cum, Babygirl. I'm not going to last much longer. Let it go, and cum for me, kitten."

His command broke through the fog and Lexa let go, shattering into a million pieces. Pleasure exploded through her body, a cascade of bliss that lit up her soul and obliterated the darkness within. Legs locked around Tom's waist, Alexandra lifted her hips from the bed as she held on tight. Her toes curled, flexing with each pulse of the orgasm rippling through her pussy.

She heard Tom curse beneath his breath, his pace becoming quick and erratic as his own release drew closer. Her nails dug into his biceps, a crime Lexa knew she'd pay for later, and she arched her back as a fresh bloom of pressure built, lightning quick and just as intense as the last. "I need..." she panted. "Please. Again."

Tom nodded, sweat trickling down his forehead. He opened his eyes, looking into hers. "With me," he grunted. "Now." He shuddered, his hips flexing hard against hers. "Fuck, kitten. Cum. Now!"

His cock kicked inside of her, pulsing with Tom's release and Lexa's body tightened, cumming once more as commanded. Head tilted back, belly to belly with Tom, she let loose the scream built up in her throat as a series of warm gushes streamed from her pussy.

"Fuck," he half growled, half panted above her. "Jesus, kitten."

Lowering himself down on top of her, Tom rolled them so that Lexa lay on top of him. She closed her eyes, settling against his chest for a moment to regain her senses. Strong arms wrapped around her, his fingertips tracing the line of Lexa's right shoulder as he cuddled her close. Loose limbed with a small smile curving her lips, Lexa let out a sigh and let herself do something she hadn't thought would ever happen again. She drifted off to sleep in the arms of someone who made her feel safe, and accepted.

Chapter Four

Tom listened as Lexa's breathing settled into the steady, even pace of sleep. His left hand smoothed down the length of her back, gently tracing the bumps of her spine on the return trip up. He brought his nose to her hair, breathing in Lexa's scent, and let his mind wander back over the last couple of hours. The marks on her body and the familiarity of their distinct pattern continued to puzzle him.

Gently easing her down onto the bed, Tom brushed the tangle of Lexa's hair aside to reveal the smooth skin beneath. Faint bruises peppered her shoulders, their light yellowish color indicating they were almost healed. He leaned in closer to get a better look at the pattern of what he suspected were riding crop marks. Each mark connected at the bottom with its neighbor to form what resembled a butterfly shape.

He sat back, heart racing. A cold shiver ran down his spine. His eyes remained glued to the telltale proof that confirmed what he'd suspected since seeing the marks in the bathroom earlier. A butterfly shaped bruise decorated the curve where her left thigh met her buttock. A bruise that matched one he'd given to a submissive at the club on the Saturday prior. He knew now for certain, Lexa was the woman he had sessions with in the dungeon at Stratosphere. She was known at the club as Angel, an incredibly sexy, confident and masochistic submissive. Tom had never seen her full face due to the half mask she wore to conceal her identity. But those marks. There was no denying he was the one to put them there. None of the other Doms at Stratosphere patterned their crop marks the way he did.

"Fuck," he muttered and ran a hand over his face, recalling the session that had left the marks in question. Angel had been fastened to the St Andrew's cross, petite wrists bound high above her head and her ankles spread wide. She faced the wooden form, thick hair in its usual twist at the crown of her head, and her body naked with the exception of the heavy leather cuffs at wrists and ankles. Angel was a thing of beauty when she climbed up on the platform and submitted to Sir Daniel's sadistic penchants. There was yet to be anything he dished out that she couldn't take. She was a sadist's dream come true, and there she was laying naked in his bed.

Lexa's back, buttocks and legs knew no mercy from Sir Daniel's riding crop that night. Tom's alter ego had laid a heavy pattern of welts into her skin, already forming angry red and purple marks when he was through with her. Tom had released her from the restraints when they reached the line of what he knew Angel could take. He'd kept an eye out for the signs, her head bowed forward and a loosening of the firm grip she kept on the clips keeping her bound to the wooden structure. Releasing her, he'd cradled the delicate woman to his chest, and carried Angel to a private room reserved for the house Dominants to provide aftercare. She never spoke, the only sounds she made were the occasional soft grunts when whichever implement Tom was using touched upon a sensitive spot. In accordance with Angel's aftercare guidelines, he'd curled up on the large bed with her, cuddling the trembling woman as he gently applied ointment to her back and allowed her to come down from wherever she went while he wailed on her dainty little frame.

He knew she was far from delicate considering the strength Angel showed each time they came together at Stratosphere. Her pain threshold, and the level of punishment she could take, had left him stunned on more than one occasion. Over the nearly three years since they'd been paired together at the club, Tom had developed a deep respect and affection for the little submissive under his protection. No words had ever been exchanged between the two of them. She carried out all communication via a series of hand signals, never once speaking a word to him; yet Tom felt a deep kinship with her—as if they were good friends and had a relationship that extended beyond the end of his whip or flogger.

Laying a gentle kiss in the small of her back, Tom crawled out of bed and covered Lexa with the blanket. He slipped on a fresh pair of boxers, his mind racing with the possible reactions she might have if he brought their previous association as Angel and Sir Daniel to light. It would come out eventually. There was no way he could continue to service her as Angel and not see Lexa at the end of his favorite single tail.

He set one of his t-shirts on the bedside table for Lexa to slip on when she woke up and padded quietly from the bedroom. All of her clothes were in the suitcases currently soaking his garage and kitchen floors. She would have to make due with something of his until they could dry off some of her stuff. The thought of her in his clothes brought a smile to his lips.

The discussion surrounding the topic of Sir Daniel and Angel played itself out in his imagination as he made his way to the kitchen. He was starving, their earlier dinner preparations interrupted by the discovery of Lexa's belongings outside, and the incredible lovemaking afterward. Tom smiled, mentally thanking Barry for being such a massive prude and epic asshole.

He surveyed the chopped mushrooms and julienned peppers on the counter, deciding on a quick stir-fry instead of the more elaborate dinner he'd originally planned. Opening the fridge, Tom gathered ingredients—celery, sprouts, carrots and ginger. He straightened, a devilish grin spreading over his lips as he eyed the ginger root in his left hand.

Placing the rest of the items on the counter, Tom retrieved a small paring knife from the block and began whittling down a piece of the spice into a long cylindrical shape. Satisfied with his handiwork, he set the ginger on a small plate and put it on the end of the island counter where Lexa would undoubtedly see it when she came into the kitchen.

Tom resumed his prep work, careful not to make much noise and wake Lexa from her slumber. Were it not for his inability to stop thinking about the origins of the marks on her skin, and his stomach's incessant demands for food, Tom would be right there napping with her. The last couple of days had been brutal for both of them as they worked toward that day's presentation. Their success at winning the account putting paid to all of their hard work. When he added in the emotional turmoil of what Lexa had dealt with since her decision to serve Barry with divorce papers that morning, Tom couldn't fault her for being exhausted.

He looked out the kitchen windows as he stripped celery stalks from the bundle. His eyes peered through the rain to the house across the way. The place was dark, except for the dim flicker of the television in the living room. A shadow crossed in front of the window, one with curves and much smaller than what Barry would cast with his linebacker build. Tom shook his head, returning his attention to the vegetable in his hand. He wanted to be surprised that Barry had moved on so quickly, but couldn't bring himself to muster the energy to feel anything beyond contempt for the man.

Shaking his head, Tom resolved to ensure the beautiful woman sleeping down the hall in his bed never regretted her decision to pursue things with him. She deserved the best, and he planned to give it to her.

***

Lexa yawned and stretched, luxuriating in the warm blankets wrapped around her. She rolled to her back, the silky smoothness of unfamiliar sheets sliding over her bare breasts and hips.

"What the...?" She sat up, eyes flying open as her brain fought to catch up with reality. A small lamp shone from its perch on the tallboy dresser across the room, highlighting the café-au-lait walls surrounding her. Dark wooden furniture dotted the space and she sat in the middle of what appeared to be a California King bed piled high with lush sheets and a thick coverlet.

Tom's bed, his room. She frowned. But where was Tom?

Glancing around the spacious room, Lexa located an alarm clock on the left bedside table. What appeared to be a folded gray shirt lay next to it. The clock's LED display read 7:35 PM. Lexa let out a long breath, her shoulders relaxing as she scooted to the edge of the bed and swung her legs over. She picked up the shirt, slipping it on as she slid off the mattress. The thin material covered her to mid-thigh, highlighting the pebbled tips of Lexa's nipples where it draped over her chest. Her toes curled, digging into the heavy pile as they touched down on a plush, cream colored area rug extending from beneath the bedframe. The man was definitely a creature of comfort. Everything she had seen of his house so far attested to the fact.

"Tom?" she called out as she walked to the doorway and glanced down the hall. Dim light shone from somewhere off to the right, and she stepped into the hallway to follow it.

The delicious smell of what appeared to be chicken cooking intensified the further she progressed down the hall. Her mouth watered. Dinner. Lexa had completely forgotten her hunger as they'd rushed to bring her things in from the rain, and the events following their mad dash. They'd satisfied a different appetite then, but the rumble of her stomach reminded Lexa that she hadn't eaten anything since their celebratory lunch.

"I'm in the kitchen, kitten." Tom called to her from down the hall and Lexa followed the sound of his voice. She rounded the corner, smiling widely when he came into view. Bare chested, boxer briefs hugging his hips, Tom stood in front of the stove and stirred something in the wok on top of it. "Good timing. Dinner is almost ready. I made us a quick stir-fry." He winked and popped a piece of what looked like green pepper into his mouth.

Stepping into the kitchen, Lexa drew up short as a red pie plate on the end of the counter drew her attention. A small, plug-like item rested in the middle of the dish. She smirked and moved to stand at the end of the island, nudging the edge of the place with a fingertip.

"Interested in trying out figging, hm?" Lexa picked up the piece of ginger root and brought it to her mouth. She winked at Tom, enjoying how fixated he was as she flicked her tongue over the tip of the plug. The ginger's fragrance tickled her nose, its warm spice tingling on her taste buds. "It's been a while but, sure. There's nothing like a little ginger in your bum to spice things up."

Tom snorted. Lexa grinned, mentally patting herself on the back for the pun, and put the spice back on the plate. She rounded the cupboard, putting herself between the counter and his body, and tilted her face up to his. Lifting her arms, she placed her hands on his bare chest. Heat radiated off Tom's skin, warming the front of Lexa's body where it pressed against his.

"Dinner's almost ready," he murmured against her mouth. "I just need to plate everything up and we can eat." Tom nipped at her bottom lip and a frisson skipped its way down her spine. "Are you hungry?"

Lexa threaded her fingers through his hair and tugged him closer. "Mhmm. Stir-fry sounds good. Smells good, too. Is there dessert?"

He chuckled and kissed her once more. Lexa smiled as he nudged her, and scooted aside to let him put their plates together. She raked her hands through her hair, leaning a hip against the countertop as she watched him go through the motions of putting a steaming mound of fluffy white rice on each bright red plate.

"Dessert is you, kitten." Tom grinned, a devilish glint twinkling in his eyes, and nodded toward the table on the other side of the kitchen island. "Go on. Be a good girl. Face down with your elbows on the table, ass in the air, and wait for me."

Butterflies fluttered in her stomach as his words registered. She nodded, pushing off the counter and making her way around it to do as requested. Her heart pounded, each beat echoing through Lexa's body with every step closer to the glossy black table dominating Tom's dining room. She wiped her palms against the soft cotton of her t-shirt and then placed them on the table, bending at the waist with her feet braced slightly apart for balance.

"Right cheek on the table." Tom's voice came from right beside her and Lexa jumped, her pulse skipping a beat. His pelvis pushed against her backside as he leaned over her to put a plate on each place setting. Lexa complied, the right side of her face pressed to the cold wood beneath her. "Good girl. Don't move, kitten. I'll be right back."

Lexa bit her lip, suppressing a groan. Her stomach growled, the amazing aromas coming off the plates set on either side of her head spiking her hunger to a new level. She listened to the soft pad of his feet on the hardwood as they retreated and then returned. Wherever Tom had gone, it wasn't very far. Her ears pricked at the sound of a cap popping open, and the soft squish of something being squeezed.

"This is going to be a little cold," he warned mere seconds before something cool pressed against the tight bud of her rear entrance. Lexa jerked despite the warning, her fingers flexing against the tabletop. *Lube*, she told herself. The corners of her mouth lifted in a small smile as she realized what he was up to.

Drawing in a breath, Lexa closed her eyes as she felt Tom probe her entrance. She relaxed, slowly exhaling, and the nubbin of ginger slid inside with a gentle push. Tom rested a hand on her lower back, the other smoothing over the rounded contour of her backside.

"I promised you a punishment, little girl." He bent over her, hips pushing into Lexa's as he whispered in her ear. "Wait until I'm seated before you move. You'll eat dinner with the ginger plug in that delicious little ass of yours." His weight lifted off her body, Lexa's entire being super focused at the mention of punishment. She listened to the faint rustling as Tom took his seat and shook out his napkin, the material snapping sharply in the air beside her. Gooseflesh pebbled her skin, the tiny hairs on her arms standing at attention.

Rising, Lexa flexed her backside as she adjusted to the feel of the ginger in her anal passage. She sat, glancing at Tom as she attempted to balance on the chair without putting weight on her bottom. A faint warmth had already begun to radiate through the delicate flesh in the few moments since insertion.

"Sit properly, Lexa. Butt flat on the chair." Tom smiled, a glimmer in his eyes as he watched her.

Lexa stifled a mutinous glare and lowered herself fully. Her lips parted, a soft gasp slipping free as the ginger pushed in a fraction further, the flange Tom had carved nestled tightly against the outer rim of her ass. She closed her eyes, giving herself a moment to settle before opening them again.

Picking up her fork, she scooped food from the plate without looking at what the dish contained and took a bite. The sharp tang of ginger burst inside of her mouth and Lexa narrowed her eyes at Tom. He burst out laughing, clearly enjoying her discomfiture. She finished chewing and shook her head, a small smile tugging at her own lips.

"Sadist," she muttered.

Tom grinned and winked at her. "You have no idea, kitten. No idea whatsoever."

Chapter Five

Lexa fought the urge to squirm in her seat as a bead of sweat crawled its way down her spine. Shuddering, she swallowed the last bite of her dinner, and studiously ignored the intense scrutiny from across the table. It had taken every ounce of her self-control to get through her plate of food while keeping her backside planted firmly on the chair.

Tom set his fork down beside his empty plate and sat back, a small smirk tugging at the lush sweep of his lips. His long fingers curled around the base of his glass, nonchalantly tracing patterns through the condensation. "How's your bum?" he asked, brows raised as he met her eyes with his pale green ones.

"Fine." Lexa tilted her head, arms crossed over her chest as she leaned back and mirrored his posture. She forced herself to ignore the ginger root as it shifted with the movement and ping ponged a wave of lust up her spine. Warmth radiated out from her backside and caused fresh droplets of sweat to bead on her brow. She swallowed, staring back unflinchingly. "Why do you ask?"

Rising from his seat, Tom picked up their plates. He stacked them together in his left hand and bent to her level. "Because," he whispered in her ear, his soft breath rustling her hair. She closed her eyes, goosebumps spreading from the top of her spine straight down to the base. Her nipples tightened, the peaks rubbing against the soft cotton covering them. "You're sweating, kitten."

Lexa groaned, and opened her eyes as Tom straightened. He turned toward the kitchen and glanced over his bare shoulder, naked heat blazing from his eyes. "Go wait for me in the bedroom. Straighten the sheets and assume the same position as earlier. Remove the t-shirt. Fold it properly and set it on the nightstand, kitten. I'll be in shortly to discuss what you've learned from this little punishment."

Careful not to relax and drop the object lodged in her rear, Lexa rose to her feet. Her backside clenched, fresh beads of moisture popping out on her skin with each step. The thirty feet she traversed from table to bedside felt like an eternity. Her mind whirled as she trekked down the hall. How had she missed this side of Tom? They worked together hours upon hours daily, weekly. If asked to describe Tom, Lexa would have used the words self-possessed, considerate and easy-going. Quick to laugh and make others feel comfortable, Tom had easily fit in with the team at Page and Butler, Inc. His model handsome looks, and charming smile hadn't hurt either.

Reaching the edge of the bed, Lexa bent and straightened the sheets, smoothing out any perceived wrinkles. Her nipples tightened as she pulled the t-shirt off, this time from the cool temperature of the room instead of the lust Tom created within her. She folded the shirt neatly and set it in the same place she'd found it earlier. Legs drawn up close to the side of the bed and bent at the waist, she pressed her right cheek to the cool navy blue duvet cover. Hands clasped at the small of her back, Lexa widened her stance and settled in to wait for Tom.

Lexa focused on her breathing and heart rate, allowing them to slow and settle into an even rhythm. Eyes closed, she began her relaxation technique of visualizing the things that brought her to a state of peace. Soft, fluffy teddy bears. Suede flogger tips brushing over her skin. Pastel pink balloons. Thick leather cuffs encircling her wrists, ankles and throat. Warm fleece blankets wrapped around her.

Fingertips feathered along her backside, moving slowly from right to left, and broke her concentration. A fresh wave of gooseflesh rippled down the length of her legs, curling her toes into the carpet. She fought back a shiver, fingers digging into her palms as she held herself immobile.

"Very nice, kitten." Tom nudged the plug in her rear and the moan she'd been fighting back slipped free. Lexa clenched, sending another wave of low intensity heat through the delicate flesh of her anal passage. She was desperate for the punishment to end, but the masochist in her wanted the discomfort to continue. She wanted more. She needed more.

Tom's hand connected with the bare flesh of her right butt cheek, the sharp crack of the slap followed by a bloom of heat. "Good girl. You didn't drop it." His hand smoothed over the area, soothing away the sting and leaving the heat of the impact behind. "Tell me, kitten. What have you learned from this little exercise?"

Lexa let out a slow breath, turning her mind from the pulsing imprint of Tom's hand on her ass to the question he'd posed. What, indeed, had she learned? "To not be sassy," she replied in a clear voice. "Or bold, Sir."

"Very good." His hand connected with the other cheek, the crack from the impact of his hand on her skin loud in the quiet surrounding them. "And, do you think you've learned that lesson, or is further instruction required?"

He repeated the soothing rub over her abraded backside, the soft shush of skin on skin the only sound as he waited for her answer. Lexa closed her eyes, the coverlet beneath her cheek offering little to help cool the flush of heat enveloping her. "I'm good, Sir."

She tensed as soon as the words left her lips, waiting for the next smack to land. The response was not appropriately worded, and incredibly informal. The lesson, apparently, not learned.

"Hmm..." Tom tapped her bottom, the hint of a chuckle in his voice. "Widen your stance a smidge, and we'll take this out."

Lexa complied, standing still as she listened to his faint rustling behind her. Tom's fingertips brushed against her and she let out a slow breath, relaxing as the plug slid free into his grasp. He stroked her bottom, rubbing wide circles over each globe. A short burst of air blew over her rosette and Lexa bucked, her belly pressing hard into the edge of the mattress. "Such a fuckable ass." Tom probed her entrance, the tip of a finger slipping into the relaxed opening. "What do you think, kitten? Should I bury my dick in your tight little asshole and fuck you like the dirty little slut you are?"

Her breath caught, cutting off the whimper building in Lexa's throat. She slid her arms beneath her body, moving to rise up on her elbows and peer at him over her shoulder. Tom moved behind her, flattening his palm to the middle of Lexa's spine and forcing her back down. "Did I say you could move?" he growled, administering a sharp crack to her right butt cheek. Lexa bit her lip and shook her head, a light tremble making her body quake in the aftermath of the impact. "That's right. I didn't, but I did ask you a question that I'm still wanting an answer to, kitten. Shall I fuck that delectable ass of yours while it's still sensitive from the punishment?"

"Yes," she whispered. Lexa cleared her throat and, with a clear voice, gave him the consent Tom required to proceed. "Please fuck my ass, Sir."

He hummed softly behind her. His finger continued to tease her ass. The muscles flexed beneath his touch, greedily begging to be filled and fucked. Curling her fingers into the heavy duvet cover, Lexa closed her eyes and waited for his next move. Her ears pricked with every minute sound. The rustle of fabric. The shuffle of Tom's feet on the thick carpet. The soft snick of a drawer closing.

Unwilling to risk losing what Tom had planned for her by wiggling around, Lexa struggled to keep still. Her muscles twitched, desperate to feel the bite of pain and the rush of pleasure she knew would come when

Tom took her ass. He wasn't small, endowed more than the average man, and there would be pain. Sweet, exquisite pain. She craved it almost as much as she did her next breath.

Lexa couldn't remember the last time she'd engaged in anal play of any sort, with a partner or when pleasuring herself. Her body would adjust, she knew. It didn't ease the twinge of apprehension, however, and she curled her toes into the pile of the carpet beneath her feet.

Something cold touched her tight rosette and Lexa jumped, gasping as the chill caused her to clench against the impending invasion. She relaxed, recognizing the slick slide of a lubed finger over her flesh as it pushed and probed, seeking access to her hole.

Little by little, Tom pushed his finger inside until his knuckles brushed her skin. Lexa flexed, testing against the invasion as he withdrew and pushed in once more. She heard his gentle inquiry regarding her comfort and nodded to indicate she was good. His single finger was no bigger than the ginger root that had occupied the passage a few short minutes ago.

Tom pulled out slowly, teasing a shiver from her. Lexa moaned. The sound cut off, strangled by a cry brought on by his swift re-entry. Two of his fingers filled her, scissoring against each other and stretching her ass. Lexa rocked her hips, the bite of pain from the thrust fading as Tom found her clit with his thumb and rubbed the tiny nub. He sank deeper with each push, grinding his knuckles against her backside and forcing her hips into the edge of the bed.

"Such a good little slut," Tom crooned in her ear. He withdrew his fingers and Lexa whimpered, protesting the loss of his touch. The faint scent of latex and lubricant accompanied his soft chuckle. "I'm going to have so much fun with you, kitten. I just know it." He gently tapped the backs of her legs. "Knees up on the edge. I want you in presentation pose."

Scrambling up on the bed, Lexa folded her legs beneath her and pressed her chest to the mattress. She stretched her arms out, face down, and presented her backside to him. Her sex clenched and released, wetness oozing from between her labia to coat her thighs. Moisture flooded Lexa's mouth. She swallowed, saliva and desire going down her throat in a hard lump, to keep herself from drowning in either.

Warmth draped across her back as Tom settled above her. He rested a forearm alongside her left shoulder, the light sprinkling of hair on his belly tickling the curve of her ass. The broad tip of his cock nudged at her rosette. He tested, pushed, gauging the resistance of her body. The head slipped inside, a slight burn shooting through her tissues as they stretched to accommodate him. Lexa closed her eyes and drew a breath in through her nose, letting it out slowly through her mouth as she absorbed the pain. Soft, feather-light kisses dusted her shoulders, encouraging her to relax further. The wild beat of her heart gradually slowed and Lexa wiggled her bottom, enticing Tom to keep going, to push in deeper.

He was an all-in kind of guy and when he thrust again, his balls swinging forward against her pussy as he sank deep inside of her, Lexa knew it didn't just apply to Tom's work ethic. She clutched the duvet, rising off her knees as pain seared her senses.

"Fuuuuuuck," she moaned as she struggled to adjust. Her fingers flexed, gripping the heavy cotton. Her thighs trembled. Her heart skipped a beat, the heavy thunder when it resumed echoing through each and every part of her body.

A sharp crack across her right ass cheek added another layer of discomfort to the level of distress Lexa was experiencing. She grunted, her back bowed as she fought to relax and absorb the pain.

"Watch your mouth, little girl." Tom twitched his hips, his pubic bone grinding into her backside. He reached beneath her, pinching the bundle of nerves at the top of her vulva, and sent a spasm of pleasure through Lexa's body. She cried out, short breaths sawing in and out of her mouth as her system attempted to blend the two sensations into something it could understand. Tom tweaked her clit again, his warm breath tickling her ear as pleasure speared through her. "Do not cum. I forbid it. Little girls with dirty mouths don't get to cum. Understood?"

He continued to strum her nub, sending a tingling heat through her body and out to her extremities. His touch robbed her of coherent thought, and Lexa gave him the only response she could formulate at that moment. She nodded.

Firm hands grasped her waist, holding Lexa still as Tom eased himself out. He paused, the head of his cock wedged just inside. Lexa exhaled, waiting for the punishing thrust that would take her into the next level of ecstasy. Her body hummed, muscles vibrating. She waited. Her heartbeat pounded in her ears, drowning out all sound but the heavy *boom-boom, boom-boom*. She waited. Her ass flexed, enticing him to continue. She waited.

"I know what you want," he growled softly from behind her. His fingertips traced large whorls across the globes of her ass. Shudders ran through her, the fine hairs on her skin standing on end with each sweep. "Take it, kitten. Make me want to let you cum. Fuck my cock with that sweet little ass of yours."

Lexa groaned. The man knew just how to work her, which buttons to press to achieve the desired effect. *I'm in so much trouble with this one*, she thought. She wiggled her hips, easing herself down the full length of Tom's cock. Her bottom impacted his belly and she rocked forward, launching back in one swift motion to take him all the way in again. The sharp gasp Tom emitted as she worked herself up and down his shaft sent a rush of warmth flooding through her. She smiled, curved her back until he was nearly unsheathed and stopped, flexing the ring of muscle around the thick head of his cock.

"Fuck, kitten." He ground out, his fingers kneading the globes of Lexa's ass. "That's so fucking it. Good girl."

Straightening her spine, Lexa thrust her hips back. Skin slapped against skin, her breath rushing out on a heavy moan to mingle with Tom's shout as she took him down to the root. Her toes curled, pleasure overriding her system as she bucked and rocked beneath Tom. Every sense narrowed, focused on the push and pull through her tissues, the warm tingle sweeping her body. Tom felt so good inside of her, so right.

"Please," she begged, faltering in her rhythm as she teetered on the edge. "Please let me cum. I can't… I can't hold it back, Sir."

A hand curled in her hair, tugging a thick swatch of it until her back bowed and her head fell back against her shoulders. She met Tom's eyes, the green dark with lust as he continued to thrust forcefully into her ass. "You can cum when I have, and not a second sooner. Clear?"

Lexa jerked against the pull of her hair, unable to give a full nod his grip was so tight. "Yes," she panted, licking her lips. "Clear, Sir."

Tom released her hair and smacked her ass hard enough to send her reeling back down onto her chest. She braced herself on her forearms, belly flat on the bed, and bit down on the coverlet to muffle the cries punctuating each powerful thrust. He placed a large hand in the middle of her back, holding Lexa down as he rode her. Deep growls rolled over her, his rhythm growing more erratic with each passing minute.

"Now," he ground out, hips tight against her ass as he bucked wildly. "Cum, kitten. I need to feel you squeezing my cock."

Lexa released the mouthful of duvet cover she'd been using to stifle her cries and let fly, a scream tearing from her lips as her body shattered into a million pieces. Her toes curled, calves rising to meet her thighs as she fought the tide of the most violent climax she'd ever experienced. Lights danced behind her eyelids, her mind blanked of everything but the feel of Tom as his cock bucked inside of her ass with his own release.

Tom dropped down to his elbows, his sweat soaked belly pressing into her back. Her muscles twitched beneath his weight, the final twinges of her orgasm chasing each other out of Lexa's body.

"That was," he panted against her ear. "Holy fuck."

Lexa smiled, her eyes drifting closed. "Mmmm… You're welcome."

He rolled off, pulling her to his chest and Lexa settled into Tom's embrace. His soft chuckle the last thing she heard as she fell asleep.

Chapter Six

Lexa clicked off the browser window she'd been staring at for the last ten minutes and sat back in her chair. She sighed, looking out the floor to ceiling windows of her office. It had been a month since she and Tom found her belongings on the back steps of her house. Four weeks of fruitless searching for a place of her own.

Finding something that fell within her criteria was proving to be impossible. Anything within her budget usually turned out to be the size of a shoebox, and in less than favorable areas of town. The apartments that boasted enough room to take a deep breath without feeling claustrophobic, and within walking distance to work, were so far out of her price range as to be laughable.

She pushed the subject aside. Nothing was changing on that front any time soon. For the time being she would stay at Tom's and deal with things one day at a time. Tom had gone with her this morning to fill out paperwork with Human Resources advising them of the changes in her life. Her divorce. Her name reversal from Porter to Rodenberg. Her relocation to Tom's, and their relationship status as far as that was concerned.

Turning back to her laptop, Lexa brought up a new tab on her browser and entered the website address for Stratosphere's 'Members Only' section. Username and password entered, she logged in and immediately went to her inbox. No new messages waited for her as she scanned the history of emails between herself and Sir Daniel. Short communications, usually confirming times and dates for play sessions. They'd never corresponded beyond those short bits of "be here at this time, on this date".

With the edge of her thumbnail between her teeth, Lexa worried at it as she pondered the last few weeks. She heard the murmur of Tom's voice, the deep tenor carrying over from the office he occupied beside hers, and smiled. He'd turned out to be everything she could imagine wanting in a Dominant. Kind, attentive, always seeing to her needs before his own. He requested nothing of her, trusting that she would submit when she was ready; and she did, without reservation. What they discovered that first night together had felt natural—the dynamic of Dom and sub falling into place with ease.

Lexa knew one thing for sure. Whatever it was between her and Tom, she wanted to see where it led. The journey, she knew, would be amazing. The destination didn't matter, as long as they were together.

Decision made, Lexa opened a new message and addressed it to Sir Daniel, asking if they could meet that evening at their usual time and location–eight thirty by the St Andrews Cross in the left corner of the playroom. She pressed 'Send' and waited. Sir Daniel would reply promptly. He always did. True to form, a handful of heartbeats later, his reply hit her inbox. *Of course. See you then.*

Logging out and shutting down the browser, Lexa rose from her seat. She took a slow, deep breath and stepped out from behind her desk. Shoulders straightened, Lexa left her office. Butterflies churned in her stomach, and she vowed with each step toward Tom's office that this would be the one and only time she would allow herself to lie to him.

Paused in the door, Lexa observed him for a moment. He studied the screen of his laptop, green eyes intent on whatever he was reading. Tom scratched at his jaw and then ran his left hand through is hair. She frowned, recognizing the gestures for what they were.

"Hey," she called out, breaking his concentration. Tom looked up at her and she gave him a small wave. "I've got something that just came up. An old friend wants to meet for drinks later, and I said I could make time for dinner rather than drinks. I don't expect to be too late. Around nine thirty-ish, maybe?"

He cocked an eyebrow, gaze flicking from her, to the screen, and back again. "Uh, sure. Something just came up on my end, too. I forgot about a dentist appointment that was scheduled months ago." Tom gave her a small smile, leaning his elbows on the edge of his desk. "Do you need a ride?"

The hairs on the back of her neck stood on end and she fought off the associated shiver. She felt like such a rat for lying to him, but what other option did she have? Lexa knew that she'd have to tell Tom about Sir Daniel at some point. This, however, was not that time. She shook her head, waving off the unspoken offer. "Nah, I'm good. We picked a place within walking distance from here, and I'll grab a cab home afterward."

His smile widened at her mention of home, and her heart plummeted. She was doing the right thing, Lexa reminded herself. This had to be done so they could be together, move forward. Still, she couldn't shake the nagging feeling in the pit of her stomach. The one that said no matter her good intentions, things were about to take a turn—one she might not be prepared for when it happened.

"Okay," he smiled. "Text me when you're on the way home. Oh, and save room for dessert. I've got something special in mind for us later."

Lexa narrowed her eyes at him, a small smile tugging at her lips. She shook her head and turned slightly to go back to her office. "It's probably a good thing I did laundry last night. I have a feeling we'll be needing that load of towels I washed."

His laughter followed Lexa to her office, wrapping around her as she sank down into the leather office chair. She mentally crossed her fingers and hoped it was a sound she would enjoy again.

***

Tom stood in the shadows, scanning the crowd. For a Thursday evening, Stratosphere's dungeon was surprisingly busy. He sipped at the bottled water a waitress had brought for him earlier. The staff knew him by sight, the single tail he wore wrapped diagonally around his chest was his signature accessory. House Doms wore masks to conceal their identities, and each chose something singular to identify themselves. Sir Daniel's weapon of choice was the single tail whip, and he wore it as his badge.

Sconces lined the walls, giving off a soft light that left most of the room in some degree of shadowy privacy for its occupants. A red spotlight shone down on the stage and cast a sensual glow over the naked man bound to a frame in its center. The submissive's wrists and ankles were bound with simple jute, the heavy rope cuffs securing him suspended from the sturdy metal.

Mistress lifted her flogger, a heavy fall of long, thick leather straps, and flicked her wrist. The tails whooshed through the air, landing with a solid thwack across her submissive's broad back. Tom flinched, familiar with the feel of Mistress' powerful swing and the brutal sting of her flogger. He would have felt bad for the sub, except he knew just how much Jonas, Mistress' boy-toy, loved the pain she meted out to him.

The opening notes of Nick Jonas' *Levels* boomed out from the sound system and Tom straightened. He took the few short steps to where the Saint Andrews Cross stood and scanned the crowd for Angel. The song was her cue that she was on the floor, and on her way to him. He grinned, spotting the familiar shape of her face beneath the mask she wore. His eyes roamed from the top of her head, and the tight bun at the crown, to the sweep of her forehead and the curve of her cheek beneath the leather strip covering her eyes.

Her eyes met his and her lips curved into a small smile of acknowledgement as she made her way through the crowd. Tom noticed the short robe Angel wore, the article of clothing out of place with her usual appearance. His beautiful little sub wasn't one to hide her body. Clad in nothing but her custom made cuffs, she strode through the club from the locker-room to the play area confident and comfortable in all of her naked glory. Tonight, she wore her nerves like an uncomfortable sweater. Her shoulders rounded, head bent forward as if avoiding the gazes of the other subs and Doms in the room.

This is it, he thought as he watched her approach. *She's going to break it off with Sir Daniel tonight.*

Handing his water to a passing waitress, Tom unwrapped his whip and set it in the deep v of the cross' notch. He stood, legs braced wide and arms crossed over his chest as she finally stopped in front of him. She was close enough he could discern the lemony vanilla of her perfume; a scent he associated solely with Angel. Lexa preferred the scent of strawberries and cream in her everyday life. He'd been immersed in it every morning for the last month whenever he got in the shower after her. The soft, sweet scent floated through the office behind her, teasing his senses and inciting his lust.

Angel stood in front of him, her eyes cast downward, as expected. He waited. This was her meeting and she would speak when she was ready. He wouldn't interfere with whatever plan she had for how this was going down. When she was done saying her piece, then and only then, would he step in and set the record straight for her.

"Permission to speak freely?" she asked, her familiar voice soft but loud enough to be heard above the music. He flicked his wrist, giving her the signal to speak and bring her eyes up to his. The mask and lighting kept the color of her irises hidden, but he didn't need to seem them to recognize the familiar shape of Lexa's eyes as she looked up at him. He smiled, head tilted to the side encouraging her to continue.

She bit her lip, fingers fussing with the sash of her robe. Signs of the shy and reserved Lexa breaking through Angel's calm and confident façade. It tore at his insides to see her go through this, but he knew it was something she needed to do so they could move forward together as a couple.

"I've met someone," she began. "Outside of the club. He's..." she hesitated, as though searching for the right word to describe him. "He's amazing. Everything I've dreamed of but never thought I'd have. He gets me, you know?" Angel looked up at him again and he nodded. "So, anyway. I wanted to tell you face-to-face, and explain why I won't be back for another session. I want to see where things go. With him. I should have done this sooner, but couldn't bring myself to work up the nerve and actually do it. But, he deserves my full attention and I'm going to give him that. I hope you can understand."

Tom nodded to signal that he did understand her request. He held up a leather glove clad finger and signed for her to close her eyes. She hesitated a moment and then did as requested. *She's such a good girl*, he thought as he reached behind his head and undid the mask covering his head and half of his face. He shook out his hair, running his fingers through the tangles.

Dropping the mask at her feet, Tom touched a fingertip to her chin. She turned her face up, eyes meeting his.

"I do understand, kitten." He grinned as her eyes widened and her mouth formed a small 'o' of surprise. "I've understood since that day when you came to me after work. The butterfly marks on your back were all my doing, and I recognized them instantly." He cupped her cheek, bending to flutter a kiss against her lips. "It's always been me. Since the very first time you stepped onto the floor here. I've always been the one giving you exactly what you needed. I want to continue being that for you, if you'll let me, kitten. Let's see where this goes. Together?"

She stared silently at him for long minutes and his heart beat wildly in his chest as Tom waited for her to say something, anything, in response to his revelation. He'd known it would come as a shock to her when he unmasked their long standing relationship but, as the minutes ticked by, his certainty of her reaction became less and less firm.

Finally, after what felt like eternity and a day, Lexa brought her hands up and undid the sash on her black silk robe. She pulled the right side, the length slithering free into her hand. Lifting her eyes to meet his, Lexa held out the sash.

"Together," she said with a wide, beaming smile. "I didn't bring my cuffs." She let out a short, rueful laugh and shrugged. "I wasn't planning on things going this way. I never would have guessed it was you behind the mask, but I'm so happy it is. I can't even begin to tell you…" Lexa lifted the length of silk and offered it to him. "It's not much but, like my heart, it's all I have to offer. Take it, please? Use it. Bind me. Make me yours."

Tom took the sash, wrapping it around his fist as he stepped close and pulled her to his chest. He lowered his lips to her ear and whispered, "I already have. You've been mine since the first time I clipped you to that cross, kitten. We just didn't know it until now."

Pressing a kiss to the soft spot beneath Lexa's ear, Tom guided her to the Saint Andrews Cross where his single tail waited for them. He bound her right wrist with the length of silk, tying it to the thick slab of highly polished wood. She placed her left hand, palm down, on the other side of the large x and adjusted her stance, mimicking the shape of the apparatus to which she was bound.

Tom kissed her hair, breathing in the sweet scent of her. He traced the tip of the whip handle down her spine, his cock twitching inside his leather pants when she shivered from the touch. Leaning in, Tom murmured against her ear. "Be a good little slut now, kitten."

Lexa nodded and Tom moved to his preferred striking distance. He drew his arm back, flicked his wrist and let fly. The whip snaked through the air, cracking as it kissed Lexa's back and branded her with his declaration of love.

Epilogue

Sirens screamed in the distance. Hushed voices tinged with concern tried to push through the fog of her consciousness. Pain ripped through her abdomen but she was too tired to scream. So, so tired. A baby's sharp cry broke through the miasma and she frowned. Something was missing.

Lexa woke with a start, sitting up in bed suddenly as the dream dissipated. She glanced at the baby monitor on the bedside as another cry echoed from across the hall. Tom rolled toward Lexa, mumbling a sleepy offer to go get the infant and bring her to their bed.

"It's okay. I've got it." Slipping from the bed, Lexa made her way to the nursery across from their bedroom. The baby let out another wail and Lexa's breasts began to tingle, signaling her milk was about to let down. If she didn't get to the baby soon there would be a milky mess to clean up down her front. "Crap. Crap. I'm coming. Shush, Angel. Mommy's coming, sweetheart."

Reaching the crib, Lexa picked her daughter up and pivoted to sink into the rocking chair beside it. She adjusted her tank top and settled the newborn to nurse. With the baby latched on, Lexa quickly setup the breast pump on the other side, and leaned back to rock slowly. She looked down at her daughter, smiling as she watched her tiny hand flex against the curve of Lexa's breast. "Good girl," she cooed as she patted the baby's onesie covered bottom.

Lexa let her gaze wander to the other crib. It sat empty, the baby that should have occupied it absent. She recalled the dream that had woken her up and shuddered, the trauma from the birth still fresh.

The pregnancy had been a breeze. From the moment she and Tom had decided to try conceiving on their wedding night, to when the first contraction hit, everything had gone without a hitch. Angelica Rose Daniels came screaming into the world six hours after the onset of labor, and was a healthy six pounds, five ounces. She had a set of lungs on her to rival an opera singer, the sound filling the birthing suite when she let out her first cry. Tom had beamed, tears streaming down his handsome face as the nurse presented them with their daughter. Her tiny little face had been red and scrunched up. Tiny fists waved in the air as though she were mad at the world and letting it know, in no uncertain terms, that she was unhappy with having been evicted from her comfy little spot.

What came next was unclear to Lexa. She had to rely on Tom's account of the events and the brief flashes of memory that came to her in dreams and nightmares such as the one that had woken her up moments earlier. From what Tom had recounted, while the medical team were busy helping deliver the first baby, the placenta had partially detached for the second. Lexa was hemorrhaging, and the twin she had yet to deliver was quickly losing its oxygen and blood supply.

The obstetrician and nurses moved quickly. An emergency C-section was setup and the second twin was delivered within minutes. The room was silent during the delivery; Tom had told her. Everyone held their breath while they waited for the baby to take his first breath and cry when the doctor gave the bottom of his feet a tap. Nothing. The baby lay limp and bluish in the doctor's arms, his chest unmoving.

Chaos erupted as nurses sprang into action, whisking the unresponsive baby away while the obstetrician put Lexa back together and dealt with the complications from the ruptured placenta. Tom had stuck by Lexa's side, dumbstruck and grief-stricken by the turn of events. The nurses encouraged him to stay with her while they tended to the second baby, assuring there was nothing he could do until his son was stabilized. Right then, they advised, his wife and daughter needed his support.

Lexa had woken up in recovery a few hours later, confused and in pain. She recalled none of the harrowing events after passing out from the blood loss. Tom had been there, sitting in a chair beside her bed, with their daughter sleeping peacefully cradled in his arms. He'd looked up when she whispered his name, smiling softly as he reached out to squeeze her hand. His beautiful green eyes had been filled with sadness, the smile not quite reaching them as he told her about their son's birth, and subsequent close call.

Shaking her head to clear it of the memories, Lexa refocused on her daughter. She smiled, tracing the light blond fuzz on top of her head. "Your brother comes home tomorrow, my little angel." The baby snuffled against Lexa's breast and she smiled. "I know. It's been a long two weeks without Luke to keep you company, but our Lucky will be home with us and you'll have your partner-in-crime back."

"Yes, she will." Tom chuckled. Lexa looked up to see him leaning against the doorframe of the nursery, his arms crossed over his chest.

Lexa grinned at the love of her life. She thanked her lucky stars that she'd decided to fill out that application five years before and taken on the persona of Angel. Had it not been for that, and the excellent pairing skills of the staff at Club Stratosphere, her life might have taken a very different turn than it did. She would forever be grateful that Angel had been matched with Sir Daniel, and that things had turned out the way the did when Tom revealed himself to be her sadistic dominant. He made her dreams come true that day, and continued to do so every day since then.

Until We Meet Again
by Paige Matthews

"I swear to Christ if I don't get laid soon, I'm going to dry hump the mailman!" Anne said as she looked around the bar and then back at her drink, an oversized margarita that Gillian had bought her just seconds ago.

"And I know you'd do it too." Gillian raised her glass and toasted her friend. Anne and Gillian had known each other for a few years now, and knew everything about each other that friends could possibly know. They had been through two rigorous years of nursing school, the bond forged between them was unlike any other. Each of them dealing with their own divorce, raising children and becoming nurses had taken its toll on their sex lives, social lives and anything else that seemed to pop up.

"You realize next weekend is Valentine's Day, and I loathe the holiday?" Anne asked taking a gulp of her fruited margarita.

"It's a stupid holiday bent on promoting the repeated failures of men to remember the darn thing! It's another way to stimulate the economic spending of Americans." Gillian burst out laughing as the words escaped her mouth. "That sounded better in my head. I think I've had one too many."

"Seriously, why must there be a holiday for couples to show each other love? Shouldn't they show their passion, desire, lust, love to one another every day? No we have to have a holiday centered on flowers, cards, chocolates to make us fat, and dinner reservations you have to book weeks in advance. Fuck that, I'm glad I'm single now." Anne rattled on as Gillian looked around the bar.

She noticed some of the regulars she'd come to know from the weekly trios here during nursing school. She saw the newer crowd, but what caught her eye was the mysterious man sitting in a booth just behind Anne and her. Dressed in all black, wearing a fedora, the man eluded an air of confidence, a way of being that filled the bar with electricity, and excitement. Gillian watched as the man drank his beer, the way the sculpted angles of his face led down his long neck to the collar of the black button down, with its top two buttons undone. Gillian allowed her eyes to continue wandering south, imaging what actually lied under the clothing as she reached the band of his pants. Checking him out again, Gillian raised her eyes back up the length of his body. Complete horror filled her when she made eye contact with the mystery man.

"Were you listening to a word I was saying?" Anne asked as Gillian's body turned back around, her back now facing the man.

"Um, of course I was. Valentines day...corporate scheme...chocolate....fatness..."

"Screw you! That wasn't anything I just said!" Anne wasn't angry. She knew her friend had a way of slipping into a sporadic daydream.

"I know what you were saying. I told you that all ready." Gillian stared at her friend.

"I heard what you said." A deep, baritone voice said from behind them. Both women turned and were face-to-chest with the tall, well-dressed man Gillian was admiring prior.

"I'm sorry...and you are?" Gillian asked as Anne's mouth was being lifted from the ground.

"I am the one person that can help your friend succeed in what she just said while you were drooling over me." His tone was authoritative, deep, and rich.

"Excuse me? I'm not sure I heard correctly nor do I understand?" Anne asked running her eyes up and down the man standing in front of her.

Gillian took another look as well; at least 6'4, black hair that was shaped to his head but longer in front hitting his eyes. The black shirt was now covered by a leather boomer jacket, and he had on black dress pants. He looked like he had stepped out of GQ magazine.

Mystery man casually handed each woman a card, the size of a business card. "Show up at the address on the back next Saturday-Valentine's Day. Make sure you are dressed in something sultry and have a mask. This type of party is a little different." He winked and smiled, then walked away without another word. The women watched him slip out into the darkness of the bar.

"Who was that?" Anne asked as she flipped the card back and forth in her hand.

"Who the fuck knows?" Gillian flipped the card as Anne did, attempting to gain any clues as to the identity of the man. The card was black with white and red writing. On one side, it simply stated "Desires and Pleasures" and the other side boosted the address the man mentioned.

"What the hell is Desires and Pleasures?" Anne looked at Gillian and they both shrugged their shoulders.

"I don't know." Gillian pulled her phone out and typed it into Google along with the city. Nothing returned in the search. "Interesting. Nothing at all shows up."

"Google the address." Anne offered still staring at the card.

"Good idea." Gillian paused. "Hmm. Lists a factory, but that address is in the Merryall section-there aren't factories there."

"Interesting. I think we might have to check it out," Anne said sliding the card back into her bra.

"Are you serious? We don't know who he is, what the heck will be there next week or what we are getting ourselves into." Gillian was going on and on as Anne ordered another drink.

"Don't you think you need to live a little? Maybe we can get some." Anne responded drinking her drink.

"And… and maybe we'll get raped or molested and killed too! Did you think of that?"

"He didn't seem like a mass murderer." Anne perched her lips.

"You are ridiculous."

"You need a little more fun in your life." Anne ordered a round of shots and the girls took them quickly.

"You just need to get laid." Gillian quipped back.

"Fuck yeah."

***

The week went by quickly. Anne had persuaded Gillian to live a little, and take a chance with the mysterious man. Gillian arrived at Anne's roughly ten minutes to nine.

Gillian wore a short black dress, with a V plunge in the front showcasing her enormous cleavage. A red costume mask added to her outfit. It covered her eyes and had a rose attached over the right eye. Gillian placed her hair in an up-do, with a curl cascading down the left side of her face.

Anne chose a strapless, red colored dress that hit her knee. The dress swept across her waist in the front and had a simple sequin design in the bust area; subtle and alluring. She chose a black mask that had a lace patterned look with feathers attached to the sides. Anne kept half her hair down, opting to place the front of it up in a semi-bun.

"Wow, hot mama. Damn you look good. I am sure our mysterious man will be happy to see you," Gillian said as Anne opening the door.

"You don't look too bad yourself. Are we ready to go?" Anne asked looking at her watch.

"Yup. We have to be there around nine thirty. According to the small print under the address."

"Let's go." Anne grabbed her long dress coat. February in Massachusetts was brutal. The women walked to Gillian's car and began the ten-minute drive to the Merryall section of town. Gillian's nerves were on edge and her stomach was churning as they pulled up the long driveway of the now recognizable mansion- Evan Smith's mansion. But the man they met was not Evan Smith.

"Are you kidding me?" Anne said as Gillian paused at the gate. A burly security man stepped out of his little hut and knocked on the window.

"Can you state your business here?" He asked arms crossed over his shoulder.

"Um, we were told to come." Gillian fumbled with words when Anne handed her one of the cards the mystery man gave them. "Here, see?"

The security guard took the card and looked at it, flipping it over and handed it back to the women. "Mr. Smith and his associates are waiting. Have a pleasure filled evening." He stepped back into his hut and the gates to the residence opened.

Anne looked at Gillian as they drove up the remaining driveway, "associates?" Gillian shrugged and drove her car up to the front door where a valet was waiting. Gillian handed her keys off and the women entered the massive mansion through the double front door and were immediately acknowledged by a man whom they assumed was a butler.

Anne looked around, hoping to see if anyone else was there. The extensive foyer, graced on both side with staircases that wrapped and met in the middle, held only themselves and the butler. "Please place your masks on and follow me this way ladies," he motioned to the right with his arm and walked to another set of double doors. Anne and Gillian exchanged glances as they placed their masks on and followed behind.

The butler opened the door and led the women in. Anne surveyed the room; multiple women were dressed as they were with their own masks, seated in the middle of the room. Men in business suits, also wearing basic costume masks, lined the walls of the great room. The room was situated with oversized couches and chairs in the middle of the room. The outside walls were decorated with artwork. The back wall hosted a make shift bar, the corner to the right-a grand piano. "Please make yourselves comfortable on the couches. Your hosts will be with you shortly."

Anne and Gillian placed themselves together on a black settee. Anne observed the room. Champagne was being passed my waiters, a detail she hadn't seen before. The women were chatting amongst themselves as the men congregated into pairs or groups along the walls, sipping their drinks. Anne surprisingly was at ease although she had occasional bouts of anxiety. She didn't know what to expect, who any of these people are-she knew nothing. But it was that nothingness that made the whole night exciting. Was this a dinner party? A masked get-together? Or was it the exact thing Anne was hoping it would be; one of the events she read about in her books.

Anne felt Gillian squeeze her hand and followed Gillian's gaze toward the door. Two men, roughly six foot four, walked in side by side. Anne recognized one of the men from the bar. A chill ran down her spine. He was still her mystery man; dressed in a black, pinstriped, three-piece suit, his brown hair cut tight to his scalp, his green eyes penetrating the stares from the other guests. His presence demanded attention, exuded authority. A simple black mask covered some of his face, but Anne knew it was him. The other man was as tall, not as authoritative- mystery man was the alpha in the room. The second man wore a basic black suit, like many of the men in the room. He had longer blonde colored hair and blue eyes to match. He was good looking, but not what was getting Anne wet between her legs. No, that honor belonged to the man she met a week ago.

"Welcome ladies and gentlemen. We are glad that you could join us for tonight's affair." the deep baritone voice echoed throughout the room, hitting Anne's ears and sending tiny sensations through her body as she imagined that voice inches from her ears.

"Tonight is a special night," Mystery Man continued. "A night of desire, a night of fantasy all under the mask of invincibility. Tonight, we hope all of your deepest desires, darkest wants, and repressed fantasies are met."

The blonde man stepped forward and addressed the women, "You will all be given a number in a few moments, that number will correspond to both a room and a person of the opposite sex. Each of you have been paired with a member of the opposite sex that fits your needs, your wants, your desires. We have carefully screened and matched the couples up based upon your questionnaires."

Gillian's hands tightened around Anne's. They hadn't filled out any questionnaires.

The blond man continued, "The men will leave shortly to their assigned rooms. Ladies, once you receive your number, you are expected to go upstairs and find your appropriate room. We have taken all liberties in stocking the rooms with everything that you will need for this evening's pleasures. Be safe, be consensual and most of all…do not remove your masks."

Anne glanced at Gillian, and then back to her hosts. Anxiety was building in her stomach, her hands began to shake and sweat at the same time. She had known this was a bad decision. Anne took another glass of champagne from a waiter that was walking by; downing the liquid in one sip hoping to calm her nerves. Anne watched as the men were motioned to leave, taking a piece of black paper from the butler as they exited the doors. Another butler made his rounds through the women, handing them each a matching black paper. Anne watched until no other numbers were handed out. She and Gillian sat on the settee, eyes at the ground when two sets of feet filled Anne's line of sight.

"Ms. Hart, a pleasure to meet you." A hand extended toward her, the familiar baritone voice filled the air around her.

"I…I…I thought you didn't know us? Wait, how did you know us?" Anne responded, her voice shaky.

"You think I wouldn't know who I've invited into my home? Do you find me ignorant?" The mystery man questioned, as he held his hand out in front of her. Meanwhile, Gillian was already leaving the room with the blonde man.

"No. I'm sorry, I didn't mean to imply that." Anne was stumbling on her words, something she rarely did.

"Very well. I am glad that you came tonight. I had my doubts." Mystery man pulled Anne from the ottoman and into a standing position a mere few inches from his body.

"You did? I don't understand why?" Anne answered, feeling dizzy as she inhaled his cologne.

"You strike me differently; I can read you. It's my job to read people, to understand them. It is how I am so good at what I do." He took Anne's right hand and brought it to his mouth, curling her fingers before placing a chaste kiss on her knuckles.

"And what is it that you do?" Anne asked not prying her eyes away from his.

"I'm a very successful business man in one realm, and the master of your fantasies in another." A slick smile formed from his lips. "Now, I have personally chosen you tonight. Are you ready for some fun?"

"One question first."

"Go on." Mystery Man placed another kiss on her hand.

"How did you know who I was?" Anne pulled her hand from his waiting for an answer.

"Because I've watched you, Anne. I know who you are, and surprisingly you know who I am as well-you just haven't figured it out yet."

Anne looked at him. "I beg your pardon?"

"Shh, ma Cherie. The only thing you will be begging for tonight is me. Now let's get on with the night. Time is wasting." Before Anne could say another word, Mystery Man was leading her back into the foyer and up the right side of the foyer stairs.

The second level hallway was laid with a velvet red carpet and extended to Anne's left and right. Mystery man led Anne to her right, to the very last room on the left. Anne could hear a mix of noises filter out into the hallway as she strolled through; moans, screams, the smacking sound of a hand hitting someone's flesh. Another chill ran down her spine, as Anne tried to imagine what fantasy, which of her hidden desires would be fulfilled on this Valentine's Day.

Anne's host opened the door and ushered her into the room, shutting and locking the door behind them. Anne surveyed the room. A king sized bed sat on the left hand wall, flanked my two night tables on either side. Directly in front of the bed, on the opposite wall, was a leather wrapped X, and a wooden armoire. In the corner was what Anne believed to be a spanking bench of some sort, also padded and wrapped in leather.

"Undress and stand at the end of the bed." The directions were clear and precise. Anne watched as the man made his way to the armoire and retrieved a couple of toys and bottle of lube.

"I'm sorry. I'm not sure I understand what is going on here." Anne stood in place and watched as the man placed the items he was holding on the bed.

"What do you think is going on? We are at a costume party held by moi, in my home. You said you needed to get laid. I am here to service your needs. Now strip."

The request was stern, unyielding. Anne watched as the man stared at her, waiting for any type of movement from Anne. Anne took a deep breath and began to unzip her dress, the material flowing over her hips and falling to the floor. The man watched as Anne now stood in a pair of black high-heeled shoes, a black lace panty set, and the mask.

"It's not fair that you know my name and I don't know yours?" Anne's voice was low, almost a whisper.

"My name isn't needed, although you can call me Mace." The man moved in front of Anne, his fingers gliding over both collar bones; a shiver ran down her body.

"As in danger…I'll get you with my mace?" Anne paused. "Are you dangerous, Mace?"

"That depends on your definition of danger."

Another shiver ran through Anne's body as Mace's hands ran down her arms and back up her abdomen. Mace moved slowly in until his lips were inches from Anne's. She could feel the heat from his breath, as she involuntarily wet the identical pink flesh. Mace lightly brushed a kiss across her lips as he ran his finger down the side of her face.

"What are your deepest fantasies, Anne? Your deepest desires." He took a step to the side, his fingers still exploring the silkiness of her skin.

"I…I…don't know. Be loved. Be cherished, not be in control." Anne's voice was strained as she attempted to make coherent sentences, words even as Mace ran his hands up and down her body, eliciting sensations and feelings she had long forgotten she could feel.

"I can help you not be in control, but you need to trust me. Do you trust me?" Mace said as he removed Anne's mask and replaced it with a blindfold.

"Do I have a choice?" Her breath caught in her throat.

"You always have a choice. You are in control, even though you don't want to be. You will have the ultimate control. I can help free you. Give you want you want. Give you the best night of your life, but you have to let me." Mace secured the blindfold, running his fingers down the back of Anne's neck. The tease was the best part, watching a submissive or a partner get excited by the simplest touch, the gentlest graze.

"Yes. Please give me what I need." Anne's breath was now ragged, deep and short. Her arousal at the prospect of the night was evident in the way she moved uncomfortably in her stance.

"Good. Then we shall proceed. Turn around, bend over the edge of the bed and put your arms out to the side." Anne did as instructed, her ass now on display for Mace's inspection. Mace stepped closer, his groin resting against Anne's cheeks as he traced a path down the length of Anne's spine. Mace stepped to the side to secure Anne's right arm into a leather cuff attached to the bed, rubbing her wrist before sliding the leather strap throughout the latch. Mace repeated the procedure with the other wrist.

"What are you doing?" Anne's voice shook as she responded.

"Shh...you said you trusted me, now trust me. I am going to give you a night to remember." Mace moved his hands to Anne's hips, grinding his cock into her ass again. He was aroused, how wouldn't he be? Linking his fingers around the edges of the lace thong, Mace pulled them to the ground, smelling her musky arousal as he bent down.

Mace's nose grazed the area behind Anne's right knee causing her body to shift at the contact. Anne couldn't see a thing, but heard Mace step away from where she was. His footsteps returned as he again ran his hands up and over her back, unlatching the bra in a single motion. "You are beautiful. Do you know that?"

"No."

"You are. I knew in the bar that you'd show up, and I am glad you did."

"You are? You did?" Coherent thoughts were not happening in Anne's mind as she was focused on the sensations running through her core. Her moistness increased between her thighs as Mace moved his hands over her body.

"I did and yes, I am. How about a little more fun?" Mace said as his fingers danced across her labia, splitting her lips with one finger, dipping into her wet, moist core.

"Ohh...ahhh..."

"Like that huh?"

"God, yes...been so long."

Mace's finger moved in and out at a slow pace, prolonging the buildup. Anne was stirring at the anticipation, her hips bucking for more.

"Be a good girl and I will give you what you need, but first..." Mace pulled his fingers from her, leaving her with a hollow feeling.

"Mace..." her voice full of need. She heard him moving and felt the bed dip in front of her.

"What Valentine's Day isn't complete without strawberries, champagne and chocolate?"

Anne felt the coolness of a glass on her lips, and she parted them without hesitation to sip the bubbly liquid. The smell of strawberries assaulted her nose as Mace ran the plump fruit across her mouth. A little nudge and Anne was opening again, this time biting into the juicy goodness. A truffle followed and the mixture of cocoa, strawberry, and champagne mixed and tantalized Anne's taste buds. Mace alternated between the three, allowing Anne to indulge.

Anne felt a little tipsy, adding to her already aroused state. Mace removed himself from the bed and walked back behind Anne, rubbing his palms over the curves of her ass, slightly smacking the roundness.

"Your ass is magnificent. I can't wait to redden it." Mace said as he pulled back his hand connecting with the flesh. Anne gasped but settled into the sting. Mace repeated the action on the other cheek, establishing a rhythm as he continued to spank Anne. Anne found herself involuntarily pushing her ass out for more, the sting turned quickly into pleasure as each smack sent vibrations to her pussy. Mace landed a quick swat on Anne's core, more vibrations hitting the sensitive nub.

Mace ran his fingers over the length of Anne's labia, focusing in on the tiny bud, now aroused and prominent between the lips. A quick flick of his fingers and Anne was moaning. Mace continued to circle the clit, spreading the moisture around her pussy.

"Like that?"

"Oh god, yeah, I like that." Anne's response came through bated breaths. Her body moved in sync with Mace's movements, her pussy clenching involuntarily as her orgasm built. Mace, sensing her need, picked up his speed, inserting two fingers back inside as his thumb ran over her clit.

"That's it. Give it to me, Anne. Give me your orgasm, then I'm going fuck the shit out of your pussy." The desire laced his voice as Anne gave over to the pleasures and feelings coursing through her body. She felt her body tighten as Mace continued to work her over. A few more strokes of her pussy and Anne's body convulsed against the bed, tightened around his fingers. Anne rode out the waves of her orgasm as

Mace undid the leather cuffs.

In one quick movement, he had Anne flipped over and repositioned on the bed. The familiar sound of a zipper opening and Mace removed his pants. He enjoyed the commando feeling under the suit he donned most days. Anne squirmed under him as he positioned his knees between her thighs. Anne heard the tear of the foil. Placing his hands on either side of Anne's knees, Mace spread her wider taking in the view that awaited his throbbing cock. Anne felt him lining the head of his cock to her opening. Mace teased her slowly pushing the tip slightly into her and quickly pulling out, repeating the motion as Anne arched under him.

"You're so responsive, Anne. Your pussy wants my cock. I can see how excited you are."

Anne moaned as he pushed back in, this time fully sheathing himself in the tight orifice.

"That's it, take me. Your body aches for this. Your cunt is dripping wet. So fucking warm and tight." Mace started to move in and out, varying his pace as he teased Anne's clit with his fingers. Grunts and half words escaped her mouth. Mace circled her bud with his finger, changing the intensity of his flicks. Anne felt her body tightening; her muscles contracting as they rushed blood to her core. Mace continued to play with her bundle of nerves igniting a fire within her as her orgasm took hold. Letting out a slew of incoherent words, Anne let her body fall into the rhythm of the aftershocks. The tightening around his cock urged Mace to increase his thrusts as he finally emptied himself into her. Mace pulled out and Anne groaned at the loss of his heat. She heard him cleaning up in the room and was surprised when he returned with a warm cloth and cleaned her as well.

Removing the blindfold, Mace slid next to Anne. "I hope you enjoyed your night at the mansion." He placed a chaste kiss on the top of her head.

"I did. Thank you." Anne looked up at him, afraid of what she might see and what she hoped she'd see. There was only adoration and fulfillment in Mace's eyes. What she had hoped for she didn't see.

"Get dressed. I'll have a car bring you home." Mace stood and walked toward the door. "And Anne?"

"Yes?" she responded as she gathered her dress from the floor.

"This isn't the last you'll see of me." And with that Mace left the room and left Anne to dress. A knock on the door a few moments later alerted Anne to the fact her time was up. She opened the bedroom door, taking one last look at the room, locking memories into her mind.

The car ride home gave Anne time to gather her thoughts, and think about the cryptic message Mace left her with. Did she want to see him again? What did he mean by that? What the hell was the night anyway? Who was this mystery Mace?

When the driver pulled up to Anne's home, he quickly opened the door and extended a hand to help Anne out. "Mr. M wanted you to have this." The driver handed Anne a letter. Anne opened the letter and read the handwritten letter.

Dearest Anne,

I hope that some of your fantasies have come true on this holiday for lovers. It was my greatest pleasure assisting you with yours. We will speak soon.

Sincerely,

Mace

Anne watched as the driver drove off. She turned and unlocked her door. Entering her home, Anne quickly ascended to her room. She undressed quickly and curled herself into her duvet, and closed her eyes to dream about her mystery man.

Mardi Gras

"I wonder if we'll get an invite again this month," Gillian said as we sat side by side at the computers.

"I don't know. Mace suggested enough in his letter." Anne put her pen down on the desk. "Did yours mention anything?"

"You mean the other 'host?' Nope, not really," Gillian replied shrugging her shoulders.

"I wonder. Guess we'll see huh?"

"Guess so. Let's go round before Hitler comes around screaming again." Gillian stood and grabbed a COW, or computer on wheels, and headed toward her patients.

Anne nodded and went in the opposite direction. Her usual motto was "if they ain't complaining, leave them be." A quick glance at her watch and Anne's shift was over in an hour and half. Thank God, she thought to herself. She knocked on the door to patient number one.

"How you doing, Ms. Adams?"

"Fine." The woman responded with a short curt tone.

"Do you need anything? Pain meds?"

"Nope."

"Okay, well ring your bell if you need something." Anne offered back as she cleansed her hands with the Purell again. Repeating the process with the next four patients, Anne sat back in the chart room and entered her notes while she waited for her replacement to come in and get report.

Anne arrived home shortly after five. The kids were with her ex-husband again and she reveled in the solitude afforded to her by the quietness. Throwing some leftovers in the microwave, Anne picked up her Kindle to catch up on some book boyfriends. Just as she settled into the couch, her food on her lap, a blanket over her legs, a knock on the door interrupted her. Anne sighed, stood and walked to the door.

"Ms. Hart?"

"Yes, that's me."

"Then this is for you. Good night." The courier handed her the box, turned and walked away. Anne took the box inside and shut the door. Walking back over to the couch, she sat down and opened the tape that secured it. Inside it was a letter and another mask.

Dearest Anne,

I told you that we'd meet again. Next weekend is our annual Mardi Gras party. I've included the mask you need to wear and the only other requirement is a cocktail dress. My number is included on the card in the box. Text me to let me know you'll attend. Don't worry, Gillian has caught the attention of my partner and will accompany you as well. A car will pick the two of you up at seven sharp.

Until we meet again,

Mace

Anne picked up her phone and immediately texted Gillian.

Anne: Did you get a package?

Gillian: Yes. You?

Anne: Yes. I guess we need to go shopping?

Gillian: Hell yeah. Tomorrow after work.

Anne: Ok.

Anne searched the box for the business card and handwritten on the back of it was Mace's number. Anne punched it into her cell and sent off a response.

Anne: I got the invite and the beautiful mask. I'm shocked you want me there again.

A response was almost instant.

Mr. M: Dearest Anne, why wouldn't I want you there? I have much to show you. You have much to discover. Until we meet again...

Anne toyed with the idea of responding back, but thought better of it. His last words seemed to finalize any other communication. Anne fingered the mask in her hand. The typical masquerade mask had a black base with purple and gold details in a filigree pattern. The cat eye cutouts and the diamond like gems accented the mask's detail. Gold swirls extended up and off of the mask itself. I definitely need a new dress for this, Anne thought again to herself.

The next day's shift flew by. Two new admits to the floor and a few discharges, made for an eventful day. Gillian grabbed her purse from the staff locker room as Anne shut down the charting program.

"Ready?" Gillian asked.

"Yup. Give me five minutes to grab my stuff."

"Okay."

Anne headed to her own locker and left her stethoscope and watch in it, and grabbed her purse. Off to find a dress for another night of secret kink.

"Where do you want to head?" Gillian asked as we headed for the parking garage.

"Meet at the mall?" Anne offered up unlocking her car.

"Guess so," Gillian responded back.

The ride to the mall was short- fifteen minutes or so. Anne pulled into a spot outside of Macy's as Gillian pulled in beside her.

"Let's go shopping!" Gillian exclaimed as they headed into the store.

Anne mewled around the dresses not finding one that would accent the beautiful mask Mace sent for the event. Feelings ran through Anne. Feelings she wasn't used to feeling.

"What about this?" Gillian held up a black tea length dress. The neckline plunged below what would be the breast line, the spaghetti straps held close to the material.

"No. Absolutely not."

"Why what's wrong with it?"

"For one, I'm not showing that much of my breast to anyone and secondly, it doesn't do the mask justice." Anne continued to skim through the racks. Nothing drew her attention: nothing that she would feel comfortable in, comfortable with Mace seeing her in.

Why were these feelings here? She hadn't cared about what people thought about her in years, and all of sudden one freaking night of torrid sex and she was now worried?

"Anne Hart, snap out of whatever funk you are in! This dress would be amazing. You need to get it!"

Anne held the dress up again and looked it over a few more times. What the hell? She headed to the dressing room to try on the low cut fabric. The dress hugged every single curve of her body. The low neckline showed off the curves of her full bosom leaving not much to the imagination.

"Walk your ass out here, so I can see," Gillian yelled from the opposite side of the dressing room door. Anne rolled her eyes and unlocked the door that separated them.

"Holy shit," Gillian exclaimed as Anne stepped out from the room.

"Yeah, I guess."

"You guess? You look fucking hot in this dress."

"I'm aware, and before you say anything else, I've already decided to buy it." Anne replied as she turned in the three-way mirror.

"Good. I'm pleased. Get changed, we need a drink."

"Hell, yeah!"

***

The week went by slowly as Anne hoped she'd receive another text or anything from Mace. As six o'clock approached, Anne looked at herself in the mirror again. She looked damn good. There was no denying that. Gillian strolled into the bedroom wearing a red strapless, knee-length dress. Her hair was whipped up into a bun. Anne had left her shoulder length hair down and flowing across her back.

The knock on the door drew the girls' attention away from clothing and towards the night ahead.

"Ready?" Gillian questioned as she grabbed her mask from the table.

"Yeah. You?" Anne responded grabbing her own mask.

"Fuck yeah."

***

The car drove up the windy driveway of Mason's mansion. Anne was still not sure how it didn't leak out or that it wasn't known that this was Mace's house. Well, it could be the fact it was listed under his associates name and the corporation he owned.

Anne's nervousness didn't go away like she thought it would have. The driveway was lined with black sedans and guests were stepping out of each of them. The car that Mace had sent pulled to a stop.

"Your night awaits, ladies," the southern drawl of the driver was a welcomed distraction. Not an accent one usually heard this north.

"Thank you, sir." Anne replied as the door opened, and was helped out of the sedan by a white-gloved man.

"Follow the path to the main waiting room. Your hosts shall be with you soon."

Anne and Gillian nodded as they added their masks to their faces and secured them in place. They followed the rest of the guests up the stairs and through the grand foyer to the waiting room off to the right. It was just as Anne remembered. The waiters were walking around with trays of champagne. Anne grabbed one and downed it in a gulp before reaching for a second. She needed to calm her nerves and quickly.

"Calm down," Gillian said as she sipped her glass.

"What do you think I'm trying to do?"

Gillian chuckled and the two found a seat on the black settee from last month. The guests mingled as they waited for the hosts to grace them with their presence.

"I wonder what they have planned for the night?" Gillian whispered as she took another sip of the bubbly alcohol.

"No clue. I wish I did, but this set up is as crazy as us being here."

"But you know you love the thrill of it. The mysteriousness of the whole club, the monthly nights of kinky sex."

"Yeah, who would have thought that you and I would be in this situation after meeting a man in a bar?" Anne mewled back.

"For some reason I get the feeling that he knew us before he offered us a card."

"How is that even possible?" Anne questioned her friend.

"Doesn't make sense otherwise? He hands us a card to a random secret sex club? One that could ruin his reputation or those that attend?"

"Then he already knew our names?" Anne added.

"Yup."

"I guess. The whole thing is weird, yet surprisingly arousing."

Gillian laughed, "that it is."

The ringing of the bell quieted the guests to a whisper as Mace and his associate appeared at the top of the stairs.

"Good evening, everyone. We wanted to thank you again for coming. As per the ritual every month, everyone is assigned a number that coordinates with a partner and a room. Please find your name on the table in the foyer and proceed to your assigned room. Women first of course." Mace's voice bolstered through the room.

"Let's go," Gillian offered, her body standing from the settee.

"If we must." Anne offered back taking Gillian's outstretched hand. The girls found their names, the names they were given as a protection to their identity.

"Room seven," Gillian said.

"Room twelve. Like last time," Anne replied back. The girls ascended the grand staircase and Gillian headed left as Anne followed the velvet carpet to the right. The room was the last one on the left and Anne hesitated as her hand touched the knob. She could still walk away, but her body was already aroused at the thought of what could happen tonight.

She turned the knob and entered the room. It was as she remembered. The King size bed still dominated the left side of the room, the St. Andrew's cross opposite that, the spanking bench in the back right hand corner. On the bed was a note.

My Dearest Anne,

Please strip and kneel at the foot of the bed facing the back wall of the room. I will be with you shortly.

Sincerely,

Mace

Anne did as she was instructed and removed the material from her body, a little upset that Mace wouldn't see her in it. She placed her dress and heels over the chair next to the door. Anne knelt on the plush carpet and faced the wall opposite of the door. She shut her eyes and took a few deep breaths to calm her nerves.

The quiet click of the door handle turning and the padded footsteps of her mystery man stepping into the room brought all of the butterflies back. She heard the familiar lock engage as she held her breathe for Mace's commanding voice.

"Anne, you look amazing," the smooth voice of Mace filled the air.

"Thank you, Sir." Anne responded as she focused on Mace's steps.

His body was up to her back in no time flat, his knees level with the top of her shoulders, his fingers deftly playing with the strands of hair that hung low on her shoulders. She felt his touch leave, and heard the noise of him undoing his jacket and shirt before resuming his light caresses on her shoulders.

"I am glad you came tonight. Mardi Gras is a special event – one where we give way to all of our glutton desires, before reforming ourselves for forty days. Well, something like that," his voice comforted Anne as his hands continued to lazily sweep across her skin.

"Yes, sir, something like that." Anne mumbled back as Mace's hands began to knead at her breasts.

"So, tonight let's give way to your desires and let me make you feel, deal?"

"Yes, Sir."

"Good, I love hearing that name roll off your tongue. Now, pick a number between one and five."

"Three, sir." Anne drew a breath in as Mace rolled her nipple through his fingers.

"Three, it is my dear." The other nipple rolled and pinched. "Now stand so I can appreciate your body before I strap you to the St. Andrew's cross."

Anne stood and watched as Mace's eyes trailed over every inch of flesh on her body. She was completely naked in front of him. His hands caressed her abdomen, and fell over the curves of her hips. Anne took a sharp breath in before Mace led her to the St. Andrew's Cross.

Mace stepped to the armoire and pulled out the four leather restraints needed for the cross. Anne's body trembled at the unknown. He was quickly at her side pulling her wrist to his body. He placed a small kiss on her wrist before securing the leather around it. Mace repeated the process with Anne's other wrist and secured them to the O rings at the top of the X. He ran is fingers over the length of her body as he knelt to secure her ankles to the bottom of the contraption. Anne instinctively pulled against the restraints, knowing she was locked in and not able to move. Her arms were above her head and to the side. Her legs were opened enough to allow access to her most intimate spot.

"You chose the number three, Anne. Therefore, you will have three orgasms before I fuck you." Mace murmured into her ear as his hand grasped her core. "So, wet already and we haven't even begun."

"You have a way of doing that, Sir." Anne answered in a hushed voice.

Mace's fingers began to travel along Anne's labia gently rubbing back and forth. His other hand cupped her breast as he pulled it into his mouth teasing her taut nipple between his teeth. Mace released the one breast and brought the other one to his mouth as his fingers split Anne's lower lips. His fingers found her clit as his mouth closed around the peaked bud of her nipple.

"Oh my god…" Anne moaned as Mace's fingers entered her wanting core.

"That's it Anne, focus on my fingers fucking your pussy. Focus on the feeling of them inside you, pulling you closer and closer to the edge."

Anne couldn't focus on anything else if she tried. It'd been a month since she had any action, let alone the fingers of her mystery man in her.

"You're so tight, my dearest Anne, have you not been getting what you need?" Mace said as if he could read Anne's thoughts.

"No, Sir, not since last time."

"That's a shame, a beautiful pussy like yours going to waste." Mace increased his finger fucking and added a thumb to her clit circling the bundle of nerves.

"Jesus...." Anne mumbled pulling on the restraints that held her up.

"That's it, give me number one," Mace purred into her ear, his speed increasing yet again. Anne couldn't help but tumble over the edge as her first orgasm hit her. Her body convulsed against the leather bound X, her legs twitched as much as they could, her breath ragged and short. Not being touched in over a month, the sensations over took Anne's body quicker than she'd like, but as Mace removed his fingers, Anne slumped.

"Now for some fun."

Anne heard the distinct vibration sound coming from the toy. She opened her eyes to see Mace holding an orange wand vibrator. He moved the object to the inside of her thighs. The sensations travelled up her legs and hit her already over stimulated core. Mace teased her, switching from one leg to the other, higher than lower until he grazed her clit with the tip of the vibrator. The constant vibration changed to a pulse; a quick couple pulses followed by a pause followed by one pulse. The pattern kept up, teasing Anne as Mace moved the vibrator along the length of her labia, the opening of her pussy and back to her clit.

"You do that on purpose," Anne mumbled as the pulse of the machine made her body flinch.

"Do I, now?" Mace questioned back changing the intensity of the vibrator again.

"Ahhh..." Anne moaned as Mace now set the device directly on her clit. "Need more..."

"Oh, you'll get more when I determine the time. Now, come again, Anne." Mace commanded and Anne's body obeyed, her second orgasm hitting her like a tidal wave. Mace kept the orange vibrator directly on

Anne's clit as her body pulled against the restraints as it tightened and convulsed. She rode out her orgasm and found Mace pulled back quickly discarding the machine in exchange for a crop.

Mace stepped up and ran the leather patch of the implement against Anne's flesh. A slight flick of his wrist landed the leather right under her right breast. Another flick landed under her left. Every nerve ending in Anne's body was firing at this point. The smallest touch had her shuddering against the X, fighting against the leather that held her up. Mace ran the crop down over Anne's abdomen and her pelvic bone stopping shy of her pubis.

Another light swat hit the inner flesh of Anne's thighs as she growled out in frustration. Her body was humming, needing to feel the touch of his hands, his tongue, his cock.

"Patience, Anne, everything will come in due time." Mace knelt in front of her. His hands gripped her thighs and pulled her legs as far apart as her confines allowed. He feathered kissed over the welts from the crop before he settled his mouth on her pussy.

"Fuck…" Anne mumbled as Mace pulled her clit into his mouth, his fingers probing her core again.

"So fucking good," he moaned as he pulled her pussy back into his mouth sucking and flicking her clit with his tongue. His fingers thrust in and out of her body, his mouth sucked her nub as she felt her body tighten again. Her stomach pulled in tight, her breaths quickened and became short bursts of moans and grunts. The restraints strained against their O rings as Mace continued his assault on her pussy.

"Fuck…FUCK FUCK…" Anne screamed as her third orgasm washed over her. Mace gripped her ass and stilled her as he continued to suck her clit as she rode out the aftershocks on his mouth. Anne's body went limp against the X, her body spent from the pleasures given in rapid succession.

Mace removed the restraints from the X, picked Anne up, and carried her to the bed. He undid the leather that surrounded her wrists and ankles, massaging blood flow back into them. Anne was laid out on the bed, her skin flushed from her orgasms.

"Mace, please…"

"Please what, Anne?"

"I need you in me, now," Anne said in a hushed mumble.

"Your wish is my command," Mace said as he pulled down his pants and positioned himself between her creamy thighs.

The familiar sound of the wrapper tearing had Anne focusing on Mace's cock. Erect and ready, he sheathed himself in the latex and positioned himself at her opening.

"It's going to be fast and hard, Anne. No sweet stuff tonight."

"Please…just fuck me. Use me," she responded as he gripped her thighs and impaled himself into her. "FUCK!" Anne screamed as Mace began thrusting into her core. An unrelenting pace, hard thrusts, his hands digging into the skin of her hips.

In and out, Mace pulsated his hips, dragged his cock out, and thrust it back in hitting the depths of Anne's pussy. Over and over, Mace never lessened his movements. Anne felt his body still over her as he paused to let the full effect of his own orgasm over take him.

"So fucking tight. So fucking good…" Mace growled as he finished pumping into her. Breathless, Anne laid on the bed as Mace pulled out and discarded the condom before pulling her to him.

Anne nuzzled into him, as he made sure she was okay. The soft purr of his voice left Anne sleepy and tired, her eyes succumbed to sleep as she heard him say, "until we meet again."

Garden Pleasures

Another month passed, two actually. Anne was in fact pissed that she hadn't heard from Mace in over a month and half. What the fuck? Guess I read too much into it, she thought as she sat on the couch curled up in a blanket. The weather was warmer, but there was still a chill in the air at night. Anne tried to push the thoughts of Mace out of her mind and concentrate on her glass of wine and book in her hand, well Kindle. Anne had been trying to finish the same book for over a month and half. Not that the storyline wasn't intriguing, life just seemed to get in the way.

Pouring herself another glass of wine, Anne heard her phone buzz from the other room. It could only be one of two people; her asshole ex or Gillian. It was neither.

Mr. M: My dearest Anne, I am sorry about last month.

Anne: It's fine. We're not a thing or anything.

Mr. M: We most definitely are a thing; a very kinky thing, but in all honesty you deserve an explanation.

Anne: No explanation needed. You don't report to me, I'm not your girlfriend or anything.

Mr. M: I was out of the country on business, I am sorry that I did not make you aware of that prior to now. We had cancelled the event last month.

Anne's heart skipped a beat. There was a reason for the lack of the event and it didn't have anything to do with him not wanting her.

Mr. M: I've been thinking about you.

Anne: You have? That surprises me.

Mr. M: Why would that surprise you?

Anne: Well, you are who you are and I am a relative nobody in comparison.

Mr. M: You most definitely are a somebody.

Anne: Nice to hear that. I'm surprised the texts are more than instructions.

Mr. M: You intrigue me, Anne.

Anne: That's a new one, me intriguing someone.

Mr. M: Indeed. I'll show you how intriguing you are…This Saturday I wait to see you.

Anne: Another party?

Mr. M: Indeed.

That was the end of the texting; a sideways invite to the month's party and a half-hearted apology. Well, he did at least try to apologize. Anne wondered what this month would include. No mask this month, no mention of any instructions. Anne tried to turn her attention back to her book and glass of wine, but the frustration building in her veins deterred her attention. FUCK! Instead of reading, Anne ended up heading to bed to sleep the rest of the evening off. A twelve-hour shift was up for the morning.

***

"Did you ever find out what he does?" Gillian asked as the girls entered the med room.

"No. I never really asked," Anne responded back as she pulled the meds she needed.

"It's weird that in the months since this started you never asked, did you Google him?"

"Nope."

"Seriously?"

"Yes, seriously. Why do I care who he is outside of what we do? It's not like we will have a future family or anything." Anne retorted back as she walked out the door.

Gillian followed quickly behind, "no but isn't it worth knowing?"

"No, it's not. I'm not going to sit around all day and dream about someone that I can't have, nor wants to have a relationship outside of the monthly get-togethers. End of discussion."

"Fine," Gillian offered back and walked away. Anne continued on with her med passes and making sure her patients were stable, questions answered and everything else. The shift dragged on, which was both a blessing and a punishment. A blessing that nothing major happened, but a punishment because it made the day go by so slow.

It was shortly before seven, and Anne's replacement came in. Anne gave report quickly and grabbed her shit before Gillian could assault her with anymore questions. Once home, Anne was greeted by her sixteen-year-old daughter. Anne had been young when she gave birth to her, just out of high school. It was a miracle that she passed nursing school having an infant at home, but Anne was determined beyond anything.

"Hey, mom, you received a package today," Arielle said as she looked up from her homework.

"You didn't open it, did you?" Anne asked as she picked up the package off the table.

"Of course not, you think I'm Tyler?" Arielle said mentioning her younger brother.

"Nope. Speaking of Tyler, where is he?"

"Dad was picking him up from practice."

Anne nodded at the thought and remembered that her ex had agreed to pick him up due to Anne's schedule.

"Right. Okay, I'm going to take a shower, I feel gross." Anne said walking up the stairs.

"Okay, I'm going to finish my homework. There's pizza in the fridge from earlier." Arielle yelled up.

"Thanks," Anne answered back placing the package on her bed. Sitting, Anne quickly undid the package interested in what was inside. As Anne opened the box, she was surprised by the delicate tissue paper and the note that laid on top.

My Dearest Anne,

This month we'll be outside. Enclosed is your mask and outfit. I look forward to Saturday.

Sincerely,

Mace

Outside?!?! Is he insane? Anne thought as she opened the tissue paper to reveal another mask, this one of greens and blues with a vine pattern. Under the mask, Anne found a green colored, short maxi dress that matched the coloring of the mask. Anne grabbed her phone and shot a text off to Mace.

Anne: The mask is beautiful, as was the last one. Do you have a closet full of them?

Mr. M: Wouldn't you want to know?

Anne: There's a lot about you I want to know.

Mr. M: I'm sure there is.

Anne: That's all I get?

Mr. M: What do you want to know?

Anne: What you do for work? How old you are? How did you know who I was? Why me?

Mr. M: Answers in due time, my dearest Anne. As for why you…because you intrigue me.

Anne: What does that mean?!?!

Mr. M: Due time, Anne. Due time.

Frustrated, Anne threw her phone on the bed and headed for a shower. Maybe a few minutes under scalding hot water would help relieve some of the tension in her body. No, nothing could relieve that until Mace has his way with her. As her thoughts trailed back to Mace, Anne stepped under the hot water and inched her hand lower until her fingers grazed her clit. She rubbed a circular motion over the bud until she was panting at the closeness she was to her own orgasm. A few more strokes, and Anne's body bucked against the wall she was leaning up against. She stifled her moans holding her breath as the pleasure washed over her body. It wasn't like anything she felt when Mace brought her to orgasm, but it was a slight release to the built up tension.

Anne finished her shower and dressed in a pair of sweatpants and a tee shirt. Anne padded back down to the kitchen to grab and reheat a piece of pizza from the fridge.

Arielle was still sitting at the table finishing her homework.

"Thanks for grabbing a pizza," Anne said as she sat down next to her daughter.

"Thanks for leaving money." They laughed as Tyler and her ex barreled through the back door.

"Mom, you're home," Tyler exclaimed as he hugged her.

"I am as are you." Anne turned to her ex, "Thank you for grabbing him."

"No problem. Lise was working anyway." The mention of the other woman shot through Anne like a bullet. Even though they've been separated for over a year, the sting was still there.

"Nice to know that if she wasn't, you wouldn't have picked him up."

"That's not what I meant, Anne and you know it."

"I don't know what I know anymore," Anne quipped back and stood up. She walked to the counter and retrieved a glass and the unfinished bottle of wine from the previous night. She poured a glass and toasted him, "congrats on the engagement, by the way."

"Um, thank you," he replied as Tyler returned to the kitchen. "Well, I should get going. I'll see you guys Friday night." Anne watched as her ex hugged her children and said their goodbyes.

After he left, Anne got the kids settled for bed and listened to the stories of their day. She was always happy for them, happy that she had them. Life wouldn't be the same without them. Another glass of wine was in order as Anne settled into her bed as her phone buzzed again.

Mr. M: You went quiet

Anne: Didn't think you were the chatty type. Had stuff to do anyway.

Mr. M: you can Google me to see what I do.

Anne: If I wanted to know that bad, I would have. I rather you tell me.

Mr. M: One day, maybe.

Anne: So that's how this is- one night a month and that's all.

Mr. M: It's all I can offer to you- to anyone.

Anne: How many of these other ones are there?

Mr. M: I'm a one-woman man, Ms. Hart. At least when I'm with someone.

Anne: Are we "with" each other?

Mr. M: When my cock is buried deep in your pussy, we are. So, yes, there's that.

Oh, shit, Anne thought to herself.

Mr. M: Good Night, Anne. I'll see you Saturday.

Anne: Goodnight, Mace.

***

Saturday came and Anne was thankful for not having to work.

Gillian made her way over as she usually did on society nights, as they called them. Each of them dolled themselves up and waited for the time to leave. Again, this month, Mace sent a car.

The girls arrived at the mansion on time, and like the last time, they were ushered out of the car and into the waiting room off the grand foyer. Champagne was served by waiters, and the girls found their spot on the settee again and waited. Shortly after eight, Mace and his associate appeared at the top of the stairs.

"Good evening, everyone and welcome to another night at the mansion. We apologize for last month's cancellation as we were taken out of the country on business. This month, we've moved the play to the back gardens. Don't worry, we've tented the gardens for privacy and have added low lighting throughout. You are welcome to use any of the stations. At the very back is an area for whip and bondage play. Please enjoy yourselves." Mace descended the stairs and made his way toward Anne.

"You look amazing as always."

"Thank you, Sir." Anne took his hand, which was extended out for her and stood up.

"Let's have some fun, shall we?"

Anne nodded and let Mace lead her to the gardens. She threw a glance back at Gillian and saw that her suitor had retrieved her as well.

"What is on tap for tonight?" Anne asked as she was lead in and out of bushes of flowers, statutes, and stations. Anne took in the scene. It looked like a huge play dungeon in the garden. Numbers of St. Andrew's Crosses, impalement shackles, spanking benches, rigs, and implements of all sorts were carefully placed around the garden. Not to mention random massage tables placed in corners. One had wax play going, one fire play and one even had knife play.

"Don't feel awkward, Anne, I've got a corner reserved for us," Mace said as he continued to lead her through the maze of kink. Once they reached their destination, Mace sits on a couch that has placed within the area.

"Where are the implements? Play toys? Tables? Anything," Anne asks as she looks around.

"I figured you wanted to get to know me a little better, that we could sit here and watch the scenes unfold and talk."

The idea stunned Anne, "I thought we were here for unrequited passion?"

Mace let out a laugh, "unrequited passion, huh? No, we're here to help you fulfill all of your deepest desires, but I don't think you'll let me in as deep as I need to be to do that unless you get some answers to the questions twirling around that beautiful head of yours."

Mace pulled Anne to sit next to him, her legs swung over his, his hands settled on her thighs.

"So what do you want to know first?" Mace asked as they watched a woman get strapped to a spanking bench. Her feet bound to the metal legs, her body bent at a ninety-degree angle, and her arms secured to the front legs of the bench.

"Your name?" Anne asked. "You already know mine."

"Mason Montgomery, you should have known that from the first letter I sent you."

"How could I? You signed it Mace."

"Did I?" he questioned. "I guess I did. Next question?"

"What do you do?" Anne watched the couple in front of them. The man has now begun a rhythm of running his hands up and down the back of the thighs of the woman and around her ass, slightly slapping her flesh as he moved his hands around it.

"I run a very successful corporation, on top of overseeing a few charities. Once a month, I invite men and women to my home for a night of unbridled passion." Mace's fingers ran up and down Anne's thighs, fueling her want, her need more than usually. "You can Google my accomplishments now that you have my name, Anne." His hand inched closer to her core.

"I suppose I can," she answered as she continued to watch the couple. The man now possessed a thin rod-like piece of wood in his hands.

"A cane," Mace offered up as the Dominant swatted the female's skin, just below her tailbone on the flesh of her ass. A yelp escaped from the female's mouth as another swat landed lower on her ass. Anne jumped at the impact; a shiver ran through her body as Mace tightened the grip on her leg. "Relax, Anne."

"Doesn't that hurt?" She asked unable to tear her eyes away.

"It does, but she likes it. You can tell by her breathing the way she's actually pushing her ass toward him for more. Subtle changes in her body that contradicts her yelps." Mace moved his hand further up under Anne's skirt until he felt the warmth of her core. "Seems to be you're actually turned on by this."

"Intrigued might be the word," Anne replied still watching the way the man struck the submissive, where the red lines formed on her skin. He maintained the lashes across the meat of her ass and her upper thighs, nowhere higher, nowhere lower.

Mace moved Anne so that she was straddling his lap and hiked her skirt up to her hips giving him full access to her pussy. "You are soaking wet, does the thought of the cane arouse you, Anne?"

"The thought of your fingers on me, arouses me, Sir," Anne answered back.

"I think the thought of the cane arouses you as well." Mace moved the barely there lace from Anne's core and ran his fingers up and down the length of her lips, teasing her clit in the process; squeezing and flicking it as he inserted two fingers into her tight hole. Anne's hands gripped Mace's shoulders as the penetration of his fingers, his free hand wrapped around her back and his erection against her inner thigh over took her senses.

"Sir..." she panted as he moved his fingers in and out of her wet pussy, trailing them roughly across the inside of her hitting that rough patch at the top. Thumbing her clit in a circular motion, Mace curved his fingers and inserted them again into her tight cunt.

"That's it, Anne, ride my hand, fuck my fingers till you come."

Something in the tone of his voice fueled Anne on. There was an abandonment of fear, for in this moment, Anne didn't care who saw her, or who watched, she took what she needed and that included Mace's fingers and the orgasm he was handing out. Mace continued to thrust his fingers into her pussy as Anne gripped his shoulders and moved with the pace that he set. Before she knew it, her body tensed, her legs squeezed against Mace's, her hands clenched the fabric that covered his shoulders. Her body convulsed as she bowed her head to his shoulder to stifle her moan.

Mace continued to fuck her pussy with his fingers as the subsequent tremors ripped through her body. "So beautiful when you come, Anne."

Mace pulled his fingers from her and sucked them clean, another act that fueled Anne's desire more. He pulled her skirt down and pulled her into his lap to finish watching the scenes in front of them unfold.

"I thought tonight would be more centered on us," Anne said as she stood up.

"It was Anne, more than you know. Not everything in this lifestyle is about pain and pleasure. Sometimes it's the closeness that is needed. I gained a lot of information about you tonight, just watching you watch the things around you."

"How?"

"Don't worry about that. My driver will take you home." Mace led her to the car and placed a kiss on her hand, "until we meet again."

The Yacht

"This has been the shift from hell!" Anne said as she threw herself into a chair next to Gillian.

"Tell me about it. What was up with that code? It was the worst one I've seen in a while." Gillian responded, turning her attention away from the computer she was currently charting notes in.

"Yeah, I don't know, but the team didn't seem happy." Anne turned away from Gillian and began inputting her own shift notes when her cell phone chirped. Reaching into the pocket of her navy blue scrubs, Anne pulled out the device. There was a text from Mace.

Mr. M: Are you free next weekend? Saturday night specifically? Monthly event- I want you there.

A shiver ran down Anne's spine. Of course she was free, she'd requested every event weekend off, as did Gillian. They had attended a couple of events since Valentine's Day, and were on the way to being full members of the monthly, secretive sex club.

Anne: Of course. I'm surprised that you want me there?

Mr. M: This month is special. I will send you an outfit to where and directions to the location. Make sure your friend grabs an invite as well.

Anne: I'm intrigued. I will tell her.

Mr. M: Until we talk again...

Anne jostled the phone in her hand as she stared at the screen. The last event that Mace had played at was the Mardi Gras event. April's event had Anne sitting in the corner observing; it was different without Mace, but she knew that his time with her was not a monogamous thing. Even though part of her wanted it to be.

"Why the sour puss?" Gillian said closing out of the charting program.

"I was just thinking about something." Anne replied placing her phone on the desk.

"And that would be what?"

"Next weekend's event. Mr. M said it's supposed to be special."

"Interesting." Gillian replied. "Okay. I am going to give Shelby report. Meet you here in ten?"

"Sounds good. I'm almost done with notes."

Anne finished charting and made her way to the locker room to grab her stuff. She was looking forward to a relaxing night at home. The divorce had been the right thing to do. The animosity between her and her ex was unhealthy for anyone. He however, had already moved on to the next dumbass blonde, ten years his junior. A twenty-five-year-old with the fakest set of tits imaginable. Where did that leave Anne? Alone, pining for a millionaire she only saw under the veil of secrecy.

"You ready?" Gillian's voice broke Anne from her daydream.

"Yeah, let's go."

***

Anne found herself sitting in a tub a couple hours later; after coming home and ordering take out. Anne had poured a glass of wine, lit a few candles around the Jacuzzi tub and slid her tired body into the warm and bubble filled liquid. The heat of the water started to soak into her sore muscles as Anne closed her eyes to relax. Having her phone on the side next to her, she heard the familiar tone go off. Mace.

Mr. M: What are you doing?

This was odd. Mace never contacted her usually unless it was about an event.

Anne: Soaking naked in my tub, why?

Mr. M: Naked, huh? Sounds tempting…

Anne: Tempting? I'm naked in a tub, but you are not here.

A moment later instead of a text, the phone rang. Mace's name populating the caller ID.

"Hello?" Anne answered.

"My dearest Anne, don't tempt me to spank that round ass of yours when we meet next weekend." Mace's voice was deep, rough, and downright sexy. Besides being surrounded by water, Anne felt her excitement pooling in her legs. A single word from his mouth could just about make any woman come.

"Maybe I want you to spank me." Anne was teasing him, hoping to tease him into some playing. Maybe.

"All you have to do is ask, Anne. You know that." The voice hit her core again…

"I don't know that. Where are you now? Maybe you could come and personally spank me before next weekend." Anne shocked herself at her boldness. Immediately regretting the words as they left her mouth.

Anne heard a groan escape Mace's mouth. "As much as I would enjoy that, I am currently preoccupied."

A wave of jealousy washed over Anne. "Another lucky lady?"

"No, Anne. A dinner with highly influential businessmen. No women…" He let his voice trail off.

"Then I shall let you get back to that."

"Touch yourself." Mace's command was stern and took a moment to register with Anne.

"Excuse me?"

"What part of touch yourself did you not understand?" Mace replied. "I am currently in the bathroom away from an important meeting, my dick rock hard at the thought of your naked body. Now touch yourself. I want to hear you come before I go back for dessert."

WOW! Anne felt her nipples harden under the water, the water felt cool against the heat radiating from her body. Anne moved her fingers to her pussy, slipping them on either side of her clit.

"Are you touching yourself?" Mace growled into the phone.

"Yes, sir."

"Good, run your fingers up and down over your clit. That's it. Keep going, Anne. I am imagining those fingers dancing through that pink pussy of yours."

Anne moaned.

"Now insert them into yourself. That's it Anne fuck yourself with your fingers. Pretend I am fucking you with mine right now."

Anne's breath quickened as she started to pant into the phone. She could hear Mace's own moans as she pumped her fingers into her own pussy.

"Come on, Anne. Let me hear you come. I know you are close. I need to hear you cry my name as I bust my load."

Mace was touching himself? Anne sped up her thrusts, circling her thumb on her own clit. She felt her body tighten and the familiar feeling of ecstasy washed over her body. Her mouth opened as she screamed Mace's name into the phone. As Anne's orgasm calmed down, she could hear Mace grunt as he came.

"You're amazing Anne. Simply amazing. Enjoy your night. I know I already have." And without a further word, the phone went dead.

Anne placed her phone on the floor and shut her eyes again unable to wrap her head around what just happened. Mace never called. Mace barely texted. The three times they've had sex was only at events and he left her high and dry at the last one. She needed to regain her composure- he was too easy of a person to fall for.

***

"Did he mention anything else?" Gillian asked as we made rounds.

"No, he didn't. It was the strangest of phone conversations and yet that was all there was. I got off as he touched himself, and now I haven't heard from him in a week." Anne grabbed a computer and wheeled it to the med room, verifying the patient's medication as she withdrew them from the automated computer.

Gillian came up behind her. "Well, what do you think this weekend's event might be like?"

"I really don't know, Gil. He didn't say anything and you know that he really doesn't say much generally." Anne turned and handed her a syringe. "Here, while you are standing there be my double and sign off on the morphine."

"Yes, captain." Gillian took the syringe and verified the dosage, adding her credentials into the computer.

"Hell, I still haven't received the outfit he promised."

"You're the only one who gets delivered outfits." Gillian stuck her tongue out and moved out of the way, pulling her own computer behind her. Gillian had attended the events with Anne and has also become attached to a certain partner that she was paired up with during the Valentine's Day event. The two other events that they had attended together, the mysterious man requested Gillian on both accounts.

"Yeah, well at least you have more conversations with yours than I have with mine." Anne responded as she disappeared into the patient's room.

Coming out a few minutes later, Anne sat down next to Gillian at the front desk. "His whole behavior has confused me lately."

"What do you mean?" Gillian asked.

"I don't know. I just don't know. The past few months it's been a text the week before, a package with a mask and then a night of, well you know. But this was out of the blue, different, like there was an underlying need to it."

"Maybe he sees what we all see."

"Not him. Not me. Come on Gil, what would a man of that stature see in me?"

"A lot of passion, love and you. Now I've got to go check patients. I'll see you Saturday night."

Anne nodded and watched as Gillian walked off. They usually worked the same shifts, but this was Anne's alternating twelve-hour shift week and the following three days she was off.

Anne finished her work and headed home a few hours later. The kids were with their father again, which was part of the arrangement when she had to work. Finding the house dark, Anne turned on some of the lower lights, projecting a sensual feel.

Grabbing a glass of wine, Anne curled into the corner of the couch, her hair up in a bun, a ratty tank shirt and pair of pajama pants on, IPad in her hand. Pulling up the browser, Anne typed in Mace's name. His real name. The normal stuff came up. Biography of a millionaire, information about his businesses, the charities that he oversaw, the ones his corporation funded, yet nothing about the flip side of his life; the dark desire that fueled their trysts. All that she found was everything that she already knew from similar searches over the past two months.

Anne thought back to the night at the bar those months ago. She and Gillian had gone out, the need to get laid was fueled by a need to forget about the stresses of her asshole ex and her job. Anne didn't know that that night was going to open her life up to desires and wants that she didn't realize she had. One of those being with Mace. A situation she knew would never happen. They were too different. He a rich bachelor; she a divorced woman. So she settled for the monthly meetings, the monthly passion. Again the reasons he chose her still filtered around her mind. Anne wasn't naïve enough to think that Mace hadn't run a background check or information on her. The society requested information during their first visit, and having the resources that he had, she was sure there were other resources.

Anne grabbed her phone, finished her wine, and started to head upstairs to bed when a knock on the door stopped her. Checking the clock, she realized it was only nine. She double-checked the peephole before opening the door to find a small package. On the envelope was Mace's handwriting: Anne. Until we meet again... Her package arrived. She grabbed it quickly, the excitement building inside of her.

Ripping the wrapping off, Anne tore off the top cover revealing first an intricate white and pink mask. She ran her fingers over the cut outs and held it to her face, immediately relaxing, feeling the veil of protection it offered and the promise of what was to come. Unfolding the cream colored tissue, the outfit was not what she suspected. A white bikini lay in the box. Around the edges, a deep pink color outlined the material. She pulled out the top and held it up examining the almost nothing-there material. Anne noticed that the bottoms were actually crotch-less. Interesting. Below the bikini and still wrapped in a pearl colored tissue was a magenta cover up dress.

Anne removed the dress from the box and stood to put the material against her body. The material was a solid color, not see-through like most cover ups. The neckline plunged to reveal an area where her breasts would be. She packed the outfit and mask back into the box and headed toward her bedroom. Reaching her bed, her cell phone went off, the familiar text tone.

Mace: Did you like your gift?

Anne: Of course. They are always so beautiful.

Mace: Just like you. See you Saturday.

Anne: You said it was special? Where are we going?

Mace: Surprise, but I'll have a car pick you up again this time.

Anne: Okay.

Mace: Okay? I can't wait to see you in the outfit.

Anne: Can't wait to wear it.

Mace: Sweet Dreams, Beautiful.

The texts brought a smile to Anne's face. Although there could not be much more between them, the monthly meetings were by far becoming her favorite times. Anne placed her gift on the chair in the corner of her room and made her way to bed. Her king sized bed set on the back wall, flanked by two night stands on either side of it. The bed was filled with pillows and an oversized down comforter, although it wasn't cold enough to use. Crawling into the middle, Anne pulled the sheet over her body and fell asleep.

***

Saturday finally arrived. Anne had spent the morning prepping. A quick trip to the nail salon had a new pink colored manicure and pedicure applied, a little waxing as well. Anne was sitting in her bedroom wrapped in a silk robe. Her unsteady hands opened the box that Mace had sent. Anne didn't know why opening the box had her nerves standing on edge; it was just filled with clothes. But it was so much more. It was the promise of the unknown, the promise of his desire for her and hers for him.

As Anne pulled out the mask she laid it next to her on the bed and turned her attention to the bikini. She pulled out the top and the bottoms pausing to look at them one more time before placing them on her body. Anne let the silk robe drift off her shoulders and secured the bikini top. Removing the magenta dress from the box, Anne stood from the bed as she slid the material over her body. The cover up was strapless and zipped up the side. The material clung to her curves and flowed away from her body at her hips. The length was short, roughly four inches past her crotch.

Anne reached into her closet and grabbed a pair of black heels. As she secured them to her feet, a knock on her door indicated that her ride was here. Quickly grabbing her mask and clutch, Anne made her way to the door. Opening it up, she noticed a white limousine waiting. Oh My God!

A chauffeur dressed in a black suit escorted her to the waiting vehicle, opening the door to allow Anne to slide on to the leather bench seat. Anne settled into a seat and noticed a bottle of champagne uncorked and a small note beside it.

My Dearest Anne,

Enjoy a glass of champagne and relax. Tonight will be amazing.

~M

Anne wasn't able to relax. She was never able to relax on these nights until Mace touched her. The drive was longer and Anne noticed the limo did not turn off toward Mace's residence.

"Where are we going?" Anne asked the driver.

"To the harbor," he replied dryly.

The harbor? What could he possibly have in mind?

The car pulled up to the docks about fifteen minutes later. Anne stepped out of the limo and turned to face a yacht docked at the end of a lit pathway. Holy Jesus!

"Your adventure begins." The driver motioned toward the path and Anne walked toward the monstrosity. Arriving at the gate for the dock, a gentleman that Anne recognized was checking in the guests.

"Your mask, Miss?" Anne handed him her mask, he scanned the inside corner and handed it back to her. "Please place the mask on your face now."

Anne nodded and did as she was told. As soon as her mask was in place, another gentleman ushered her to a main room aboard the yacht. Anne was amazed at what she saw around her. The yacht was not your typical yacht. Instead of a grandiose layout, that one would see on those Yachts of the Millionaires shows, this one had been redone. The main room was redesigned to house a small bar and oversized couches. The perimeter of the room was dressed with St. Andrew's Crosses, spanking benches, and various attachment options. A waiter circled the room with a tray of champagne flutes. Anne immediately grabbed one hoping to calm her nerves.

She scanned the floor for Gillian, but without knowing what her mask looked like she was unable to place her among the crowd. Anne waited impatiently until she heard the familiar ringing of the bell that signaled the beginning of the night's festivities.

"Ladies and Gentlemen, this evening is a bit different from those previous. We, your gracious hosts, wanted to unveil the new addition to our monthly parties." The man speaking was not Mace. Anne looked around and did not see him within the room.

"Please enjoy yourselves. This main room is similar to one you'd find in the club. There are private rooms on the decks below all outfitted the same. Please be courteous tonight and keep to a one-hour limit. In the future we will be offering advance reservations on the rooms. But for now, enjoy your kinky selves."

The crowd started to disperse to various areas of the room, and some even to the staircase leading downstairs. A masked man approached Anne. "Miss, please follow me."

"I'm waiting for someone."

"Mr. M has asked me to escort you to a different area of the boat. Now please follow me."

Anne nodded and followed the man to a private staircase that led to the bow of the boat. Anne looked at him, "this says not to enter?"

"Please miss, go up and wait by the railing."

"Okay?" To be thrown off??? Anne climbed the stairs and made her way to the railing. Off to the left she saw two O rings attached to part of the bow. A small table held a candle, a rose and a set of white leather cuffs. Another note placed in the middle of the table.

My Dearest,

Please enjoy the view. I will be with you shortly.

M

Anne did just that bringing herself to the railing to look out into the water. The faintest of steps came up behind her as Mace's arm circled her waist. He brought his mouth to her ear and whispered. "You look amazing."

"This whole thing is amazing. The yacht, this…us."

Mace turned Anne around and placed a gentle kiss on her lips. His mask was in place as it always was. The difference this time was his attire. Instead of his normal black suit, a pair of black board shorts and a black button down shirt graced his body.

"You're looking a little under dressed, Sir."

"Doesn't matter in a little while when you will be undressed." The declaration stirred Anne's core.

"I can't wait." Anne responded as Mace's hands gently removed the bikini straps from her shoulders. Lowering the magenta dress from her breasts, Mace unzipped the side zipper and let the material fall to the floor. Gripping the small of Anne's back, Mace pulled her tight to him.

"I have a surprise for you tonight."

"You do?"

"Yes, I do. First it starts with me removing this top, turning you around and spanking you."

A shiver ran through Anne as her response came out lighter than a whisper. "What did I do?"

"You made me jerk off in a public bathroom during an important meeting." He responded unlatching the bikini top and pulling it away from her body. Anne's nipples tightened from the soft breeze of the ocean air. Her body was hot with desire, flushed with arousal and he had barely touched her.

"As I remember you texted me."

"Yes, but you telling me you were naked in a bath didn't help my case." Mace turned Anne around and bent her chest over the railing slightly allowing him access to her round ass. "So beautiful."

His hands caressed the mounds as he prepared for the first swat. Landing it on her right cheek, Anne hissed through clenched teeth. Another swat landed on the left side. The process continued until her ass was a nice glowing red. Shifting her legs, Mace positioned his knee between them, snaking his hand around to her abdomen he continued south over her bottoms. The crotchless set had its advantages. Running his fingers over her slit, Mace could feel the wetness escaping her labia. Anne arched into his chest as Mace drove his fingers into her core. Mace pumped his fingers in and out of Anne's pussy as the breath escaped from her lungs. As Anne's muscles tightened around Mace's fingers, he pulled them out denying Anne of her orgasm.

"You sadist." Anne said as Mace picked her up and moved her to the table.

"You know I'm not sadist, but if you do insist I am, I might have to hold off your orgasms tonight." Mace grabbed the leather cuffs and secured them around Anne's wrists. Positioning her on her back, Mace secured the cuffs to the silver O rings on the angled floor of the bow.

Anne squirmed attempting to test the range on the cuffs-no go. Anne looked at Mace through the slits in her mask, a flogger in his hand.

"What's that?"

"Your surprise."

"You've flogged me before."

"Not strapped to a boat, my belle." With that the first strike landed against Anne's thigh; another strike on the other leg. Mace trailed the leather fingers over Anne's abdomen. Mace pulled the implement back and landed a softer strike against her right hip. He repeated the motion this time landing it on her left side.

A moan escaped from Anne's mouth as Mace continued to work the flogger over various parts of her body.

"You are so gorgeous spread out for me." Mace said as he ran his fingertips up the length of Anne's thigh reaching her wet core. Trailing his fingers over the closed lips, Mace teased her clit, gently flicking it with his finger.

"Oh…" Anne moaned as Mace picked up his assault on her sensitive bud. Being on the edge of an orgasm earlier, it wasn't taking much to build her back up. Anne could feel the familiar tensing radiate throughout her body as Mace continued to circle with his thumb. Anne's body moved in rhythm with Mace's. Just as her body became rigid and ready to explode, Mace pulled away.

"I hate you." Anne cried out.

"No, you don't. You enjoy what I do to your body."

Anne heard Mace move away from her and the familiar sound of the condom wrapper ripping. Her body arched toward the noise, anticipating Mace's cock.

"As much as I want to tease you all night on the bow, we do need to get back to the party. I am going to fuck you senseless and then we grab something to eat. Understand?"

"Yes, Sir."

"Good. Now spread those legs and let me see that beautiful pussy of yours."

Anne did as she was told and Mace slid quickly into her. Mace began a rhythm, slowly pulling out of her and thrusting back in. The contradictory movements had Anne's body on fire again.

"Come on, my belle, give me that orgasm." Mace barked as his speed increased.

The muscles in Anne's body contracted and her body released. Anne barely heard Mace as he emptied himself into her cunt. Pulling out, Mace cleaned himself up and removed the cuffs from her wrists. He handed her the magenta dress, and Anne covered herself back up.

"I hope you enjoyed yourself?" Mace asked as he ushered her back to the main room.

"Although a little short, I always enjoy myself." Anne winked at him as he swatted her ass.

"Just wait until we meet again.

Always You
Tierney O'Malley

When always means forever...

He's been the one.

Rienne Cailler's only wish is to have a normal life and end her years of hiding from the reporters and Federal agents. But her world turns even more upside down when she lives with James, the man whom she has learned to love at a young age, who takes her virginity and shows her exquisite passion the two of them can share—in and out of bed.

always been his to keep.

Huntington already knows Rienne is not his to claim, but something draws him to her like a moth to a flame. She crawls under his skin until James surrenders to the temptation that her nearness arouses in him, and the sweetness of his love for her.

And then Fate intervenes.

When Rienne's father, Roy, learns about her relationship with James, he tries to separate them. Afraid of what her father will do to James, she agrees to leave him, their dream together, and the cabin they share without getting the chance to tell him about her secret.

When two hearts refuse to bend.

James expects everything from meeting a special someone he hasn't seen in a long time, but nothing prepares him to hear from Rienne what he's been missing the whole time.

Will time, distance, and the unveiling of a secret keep James and Rienne, eternally apart or will they uphold their promises to each other... "Always you?"

Tom,

The best thing I have done in my life

is share my life and heart with you.

I love being yours.

You and me. Always. Forever.

G.

Prologue

Our Cabin. James read the old sign carved out of wood that still hung above the front porch. As he stared at the small cottage, memories that flooded his senses quickly broke his resolve not to cry. He remained rooted where he stood. It was here where he and Rienne had held their hands, deliriously happy, although they had nothing but few clothes in their bags.

James closed his eyes. Many years had gone by already, but he could still hear Rienne's voice, her laughter. He could see her scowl, the one that never failed to make him laugh. Oh, yeah. She would give him her sour face simply to earn a kiss and a hug.

He had never missed a day without taking her into his arms, to whisper, "I love you."

"You found us our little heaven, James," Rienne had said, laughing and crying at the same time when she'd seen the cabin for the first time.

Indeed, a secret cove was their little heaven where they had built their dreams and future. It was the witness to their six months life together.

He would never forget how Rienne had wrapped her arms around his neck, kissing him while he'd carried her inside the one-bedroom cabin. He particularly loved the way she ran her fingers through his hair. That habit of hers would forever stay in his mind...one that he had been missing for years.

James took a deep breath as memories of Rienne swirled around him. God. They loved each other so deeply that they'd defied their parents' rules, ignored the consequences, and had lived happily in this cabin.

That was, until the Fates intervened and made them pay for their wrongs.

Wrong. Mistakes. Those were the words that his father and Rienne's dad had called their relationship. An affair of two stupid hearts that let their foolish love sweep them away. Their parents *were* wrong, though. He and Rienne hadn't just fallen in love. No. They loved each other. Deeply, passionately.

Too bad they had both realized that even a strong love could be defeated.

With an ache in his heart, James admired the cabin. It had been six years since he'd had Rienne in his arms. Six years of searching, wondering what had happened to her. Where her dad, Roy, had taken her. Whether she thought about him constantly. Now, he knew. His heart jumped at the thought of seeing her again. Sweet tart. After all these years, it had always been her.

Drawing in a deep breath, James took the front steps toward the past that he had never forgotten. As if it had happened only yesterday, he began to hear and see the woman he'd learned to love when he was a young man, the woman he still loved with all of his soul and heart...*Rienne Tori Cailler.*

Chapter One

"Where does one begin when telling a story so beautiful it hurts you? I suppose I should start with the beginning, when an unexpected love struck me blind. When a simple soul who loved simple things entered my life. However, what can I say about a beautiful young woman who unselfishly gave her body and heart to me? That she is perfect, intelligent, loved green apples, and playing the guitar? That she loved me? It is not easy. I doubt my words can do my Maldita justice."

—James Huntington

James could not believe he was looking at the same girl he had a big fat crush on when he was just a teenager. *Good fucking shit.* She changed. His annoying brat turned into a golden young goddess. He knew she'd be one, but not this stunning.

How many times had he stayed awake at night thinking about Rienne? She was barely eighteen, then. Now, soon, she would be twenty-one and the word *beautiful* couldn't even give Rienne's beauty justice. She had grown taller with the right shape in all the right places, with long straight black hair, lips still full, and her dark brown eyes still the same—sleepy looking. She had a face that any man could fall for. Wow. What a beauty. If he weren't careful, he might just fall in love with her in a hurry. That would be disastrous. His dad and Rienne's dad, Roy, had been best friends for years. It goes without saying that she was off limits.

Too damn bad.

The first time they'd met, Rienne was thirteen and he was sixteen. He told her that her eyes reminded him of a drunk he once saw living under the bridge—sleepy. She retaliated by narrowing her eyes, scrunching her nose, followed by a punch in his stomach. It had been the beginning of their never ending bantering. Then, she left and came back at the age of eighteen to stay with them while Roy was gone to some unknown place.

During the short time that Rienne had spent with them, he enjoyed having intellectual conversation with her. Not only that she was highly informed about the politics, but in economics as well. Oh, yeah. Rienne had the brain for numbers. She was eerily good in finance. Just like her father.

Her choice of television shows was admirable, too. *The Simpsons, South Park, History Channel, Animal Planet, and Inventions.* Those were just a few. He loved her sense of humor the best of all.

James also quickly found out that if Rienne was mad, you'd better run. She would simmer first until she couldn't hold her anger anymore, then would erupt like a dormant volcano and destroy everything on her path. However, once she calmed down, *sorry* would come flowing out of her mouth. Rienne always knew when she was out of line and when to back down. He loved that part of her personality, too. She was never pretentious.

When she said goodbye, he missed her so fucking bad, he believed to be in love with her. It took a while before he finally was able to wake up in the morning and not look in the room that she had occupied. He didn't even want his dad to cook bacon and pancakes because they only reminded him of Rienne.

While she was gone, he tried finding her through social media, but failed. Not only had her dad tucked her in some weird place, but Roy had also cut off their communication. It was as if she never really existed. *Until a few days ago.* Roy called and asked if Rienne could stay with them again because the club where she had been staying had been compromised and he hadn't found a new place for her yet. Roy knew that reporters and Feds had their eyes on James' house. Still...the man felt comfortable leaving Rienne with them. Roy trusted them that much.

So now, once again, the beautiful teenager who had kept him awake at night was back. With her, she brought something that stirred his blood. Almost at a legal age to drink, she stood in front of him as composed as an intelligent woman. James could sense strength in her, but showed her femininity as well. With confidence, she met James' father's stare and offered James an enchanting smile. Rienne definitely reminded him that he was a man.

Wow. My little Rienne is now a young woman.

"James, you remember Rienne, I'm sure? Roy Cailler's daughter and my only

Goddaughter."

"Of course." To Rienne, he said, "Good to see you again, Rienne."

Rienne stared at him openly. "Is that right? I don't remember you enjoying my stay here last time. Let me see..." She tapped an index finger on her lips. "I heard you talking to a friend. You compared me to a shoe lying on the floor where everyone could trip on."

James grinned. "As I recall, you were never good in remembering things. That's why you'll never be a good witness. You're forgetful."

"Maybe, but I *do* remember *certain* things. I'll never forget when you called me Maldita, which means a bitch in Spanish."

"Naughty in Tagalog word. It's actually an endearment."

"Oh yeah. And you know that because...what did you say? Ah, yes. Your girlfriend that resembled a fire hydrant was a Filipino."

"She was just a friend who has big thighs, real short, but...damn. Why am I even defending her."

Rienne laughed.

"You're a brat, you know. A brat who *Googled* the word Maldita right away and took the first answer you found. Now, do you remember why I called you Maldita? Because you compared me to a Punjabi.

"Nothing wrong with being a Punjabi."

"Yes, but coming from you, you made the word sound like an insult. And, oh, yeah. You thought it funny to compare me to a black olive left under the sun. Not to mention the other *endearment* like *silly boy, silly duck, goof*. Just to name a few."

Rienne grinned while looking him up and down. "Still a Punjabi and an olive. I'm sure a goof, too."

"Maldita."

Rienne shrugged. "You grew. I remember being taller than you."

"Baby, you were never taller than me. What are you now? Four feet and two inches?"

"Ha. Ha. Five feet and five inches, just so you know. What about you? Two inches? I mean…something two inches, right?"

"Very funny."

"So how tall are you now?"

Still naughty, eh. "Six-three."

Rienne's brows arched prettily. "Not bad. For a thirty-five-year-old."

"You're almost twenty-one. Can read and write, I assume?"

"I know more. You'll be surprised, *baby*." Rienne put emphasis on the word baby while giving him a sly smile.

James raised a brow. So, Roy raised a sensual brat. He wondered what else she knew. Before his mind began to wander, his father spoke again, reminding them both that they were not alone.

"Rienne is staying with us indefinitely, James."

"Is that right?" James said, but kept his gaze on Rienne. Man, she was a sight to see. He wanted to touch her face just to see if she were real.

"Do I hear objections?"

"Well, with you staying here would mean less popcorn and ice cream for me."

"Ah, that explains the middle age sign." Rienne pointed her gaze on James' stomach.

"I know, right?" James said sarcastically. He wasn't offended by Rienne's joke. The way she stared at his abs, he could tell she was actually impressed with his six-pack.

"Don't' worry, James. I won't touch anything that gives you pleasure."

What the fuck. This girl changed!

Rienne grinned like a cat full of milk, then turned to Hal. "Thank you, Hal. Dad shouldn't have asked you. I could've gone with him, but he said maybe next time. Just like before."

Just like that, James saw the sparkle in Rienne's eyes dim.

Due to lack of evidence, Roy had been one of the few CEOs of Pacific Northwest Rock who had not landed in jail after the company's fraudulent activities had been exposed, but his name was already buried in shit. He couldn't go anywhere without being followed or harassed by reporters. Companies who had lost their investments wanted their hands on Roy. More cases mounted and filed against him. Oh, yeah. They wanted to hang him, But Roy had made a difficult decision. He disappeared. He went off the radar. His plan had been to provide evidence that he wasn't involved in siphoning people's money and robbing them of their life's savings. He wanted to clear his name for Rienne's sake without going behind bars, even if it meant leaving his daughter alone months at a time.

The FBI focused on Rienne because Roy was slick, and great in covering his tracks, and skilled in burrowing himself in hard to find places. They thought if they followed Rienne, she'd drop crumbs everywhere. They were wrong.

Although father and daughter were separated for months, they had their ways of communicating with one another. Also, James' dad was suspected that Roy hired someone to watch Rienne twenty-four-seven without her ever seeing him. James would bet his toe that Roy knew everything that went on with Rienne's life.

Money was never a topic in James' home as far as Rienne was concerned. She never asked for it, but he knew Rienne would never want for anything in her life. Roy had made sure of that.

"I'm sure he would have taken you with him if it was a good idea, Rienne," Hal explained. "Besides, knowing that you're in good hands would help him focus on more important things."

"It had been years, Hal."

"I know it hadn't been easy for both of you, but I believe in Roy."

"Me, too."

"Roy is my good friend. He asked me to keep you safe. That's what we'll do," Hal said.

Rienne shook her head. "But me staying here would mean losing your privacy."

"Who cares," James replied.

"I know what we're up against, Rienne. We've done this before, right? We know how to dance to those agents' tunes. Don't worry about anything."

Last time Rienne stayed with them, FBI agents parked their cars outside their house for hours. They were pretty stupid and predictable—always driving a black *Crown Victoria* with tinted windows. Repairmen and house inspectors would be knocking on their door, all pretending to check the house for termites or leaky sewer. What they all wanted to do, though, was to plant bugs all over their house. Yeah. They'd been there, done that. So it wouldn't be a big deal for them if those agents started paying them a visit—again.

"Yeah, don't worry. If we see those agents outside, we'll give them marijuana- laced brownies."

James winked at Rienne, hoping to raise her spirit again. *It worked.*

Rienne smiled. "Like last time."

When his dad's eyes grew big and his jaw slacked, Rienne laughed. Man, he missed that sound. Like an angel singing, melting his heart a little.

"Oh, dear. I remember seeing agents laughing their heads off outside, wondering what happened to them. So it was you two who did that? But you were just, what, eighteen last time you stayed with us."

"Yes. James was twenty-one. An adult. Hal, did you know that he'd smoked pot when he was fourteen, bought his own pipe on his fifteenth birthday with the money that you gave him. And yeah, he knew all about marijuana." Rienne placed a hand against her chest. "Oh…sorry. You didn't know, Hal."

James wanted to wrap his fingers around her beautiful neck. *Sorry his ass.* Who would say *sorry* while smiling like a Cheshire cat?

"I knew you walked on the wild side, son."

"Not really that wild, Dad. Just the usual teenager thing." James looked at Rienne. She looked to be having a hard time trying not to laugh.

"I didn't know it's a usual thing for a teenager to lose his virginity at—"

"Rienne!" James was mortified. He didn't know whether to laugh or kiss Rienne hard. How in the world did she find out about when he had lost his virginity? Hot damn!

"What? Was I wrong? I swear I heard you talking on the phone. You were saying that losing your virginity when you were fourteen was as good as—"

"Stop. Christ! We're not talking about this, especially not in front of my dad. Wanna see your room now? Take a bath or a nap?"

"A nap?" She laughed infectiously. "I don't nap. Life is too precious to spend in bed napping." Rienne looked at Hal. "Sorry, Hal. It's just I've been carrying that information about your son for years now. And it's kind of like a heavy load, you know. Well, I can breathe better now that it's no longer a secret."

Hal adjusted his collar, obviously feeling uneasy. "Er, well. Glad you're relieved."

James, on the other hand, was so embarrassed he wanted to turn into a rock so he wouldn't have to meet his dad's gaze. Dad didn't need to know about personal information like that, but he was glad to see the spark back in Rienne's eyes. As far as he could remember, Rienne had been around adults all her life, which explained her wit and smart mouth.

"You need help with your bags?"

Rienne nodded. To Hal, she said, "Thank you. For letting me stay with you again. This is the third time now."

"I don't care how many times you stay here, Rienne. I'm sure Roy would do the same for us if we reverse our situation. What are friends for if we didn't help each other?"

"Thank you, Hal."

"No problem at all. By the way, how was your stay at that place where Roy hid you?"

"*Sugar's*? It's great. I've made good friends there."

"I was actually surprised that Roy put you there. I mean, Sugar's isn't a place for a…decent…young lady, you know. But from what Roy told me, the employees there protected you. Your privacy. Also, the owner didn't let you go in certain areas of the club. So, you didn't really see a lot of things that's going on in that place, right? I mean, the inappropriate stuff, but—"

Rienne smiled. "Nobody exploited me, Hal. I have respect for them and they for me. Sad that a lot of people treat dancers and prostitutes the same even outside their work place. Those Sugar's employees are just like every woman we know. Once they stepped out of that building, they were students, mothers, and women who love to shop and enjoy wonton soup once in a while."

"And Roy trusts them."

"Yes. The owner, Jimmy Caceres, has been friends with Dad since they were in middle school. I would've stayed there longer if it weren't for the harassment from the Feds and private detectives looking for a bit of information about Dad."

"How did they find out you were staying there?"

"One of the employees slipped and mentioned my name."

"That's too bad. Well, I'm glad Roy chose us as an alternative."

"He trusts you, too, Hal."

"I know. Well, we can talk later. Let us know what you've been up to. Now, I have to prepare dinner. James will show you to your room. We'll eat in two hours." Hal gave Rienne another hug then left the room.

As soon as his dad was out of earshot, he tugged Rienne's stray lock. "You brat. You eavesdropped on my conversations."

"I didn't. You were just too busy to notice whenever I was in the same room with you."

Of course, he would know whenever Rienne walked in the room. Like a beacon, a beautiful full moon, and a mist on a still water of the Puget Sound, she would command anyone's attention even at a young age. "Impossible. You followed me like a shadow and your noxious shampoo always told me you were around."

"Noxious shampoo? What the heck! You're mean. For your information, James, I know not to follow you around. Do you remember how many times you snubbed me? You didn't like it when I stayed here last time. You couldn't even stand being in the same room with me. Always. *Always* you would come up with an excuse to leave."

It's because I had a crush on you, which quickly turned into an obsession, and made me feel like a creepo. "Hmm. It must be your cooties that made me stay away."

Rienne scrunched her nose at him. "I hate you."

"You love me, admit it."

"Ha! Never."

James grinned. He wondered what it would be like hearing Rienne say that she loved him. *Fuck.* Why was he even thinking about that? So damn weird. It seemed he would have to stay away from her again. Just like last time. Good fuck. He was still attracted to this woman, whose lips begged for someone to kiss them, with eyes that he couldn't stop staring at, and a body that he wanted to feel against him. He wondered if she tasted as good as she looked. James glanced at Rienne's lips again. Oh, baby. After all these years he still wanted a taste of her.

Keep it cool, James. The fuck is wrong with me?

"Anyway, bedrooms are upstairs. You already know that. Just thought to remind you since you're forgetful." James picked up the brown gym bag that sat beside Rienne's feet then slung the strap across his shoulder. Next, he grabbed the two matching luggage bags, then started walking upstairs. "You'll have the same yellow room. You like watching the sunset, I remember."

"I do? I don't remember telling you that."

"And you probably don't remember telling me that you will marry me someday, right?"

"What? I...I did...Did I? I would've..."

James laughed. "No, you didn't. But I'm sure you were thinking it."

"Boy, you haven't changed. You're ego is as big as your—"

"What?" James stopped walking then turned to look at Rienne.

"Shoes."

"My shoes? Uh-huh. You know, I'm curious to find out what you've learned in the past few years. There is something crawling in that brain of yours that seems to want to come out. I could almost hear it scraping your skull."

"Eew!"

"Seriously."

"It's called teenage angst."

"You sure? Cause I sensed innuendos earlier."

"You're a boy. You hear innuendos all the time. Even if there is no innuendo."

James grinned. Damn, how he loved to banter with her. It had been the one thing that he missed when she left.

He walked ahead of Rienne, trying to create a distance between them, otherwise, he might end up kissing her. Jesus, those sexy lips would drive him nuts! This girl possessed a sex appeal that older women wished they had.

In silence, they took the winding hallway. He was glad actually, because looking at Rienne's mocha brown eyes did something to his insides. Damn.

Reaching the last bedroom at the end of the hallway, he used the toe of his boot to open the door. "Here we go." He walked in then stood at the foot of the bed where he placed the luggage. "If you need anything, just let me know. We have a housecleaner that comes in every Friday. No cook. That's Dad's job."

"Thank you."

James turned to look at Rienne when he heard sadness lace her tone. He stood in front of her then tugged a lock of her hair. "Hey. You'll see your dad soon."

"James, I'm no longer a child. You don't have to tell me there's no monster under the bed." Rienne sighed. "I know it might take months, worse, years before I see Dad again. Or never. Since he started hiding, I'd seen him only three times. We stayed together not even a whole week. Once, I got to see him for one whole day, and then he was gone. This isn't the first time that he had to move me, remember?"

Of course. How could he forget? Rienne was a girl so broken inside she stayed inside her shell for weeks after Roy had left her. He slowly coaxed her into coming out, and when she did, she'd brought sunshine with her wherever she went. Her wit, sharp mind, and innocence had brought laughter in their home. James and his dad were actually sad when Roy showed up one night to take Rienne away.

Now, she was back in their lives. Not a scared girl anymore, but one with a face that he'd find so sexually attractive. Her body alone could make a man imagine erotic images in the middle of the day. Damn, she looked amazing. And not even twenty-one yet.

James let out a sigh. He should stop this nonsense before his growing infatuation turned into something else. Rienne had been a family friend and for fuck sakes, barely legal.

"What are you staring at?"

"You changed big time. You used to have long tangled hair and buck teeth."

"What?" Laughing, Rienne punched him in the stomach.

James pretended to stagger. "Still know how to punch, huh?"

"Of course. I have a good teacher."

"Because you were a good student."

"Guess what?"

"What?"

"I'm a good shot, too. So be careful."

He didn't doubt her. Roy wanted his daughter prepared for anything.

"Really now. What kind?"

"Handguns like Glock Three Four, Kel-Tec PF-Nine, Sig-Sauer, Taurus PT Ninety-Two, etc. I can shoot Heckler & Koch MP Seven A One. Those are sub-machine guns. Shotguns are not my favorite, but I trained in shooting Winchester Thirteen Hundred Defender, Serbu Super Shorty. Now, rifles. Those are sweet weapons to use. Like AK-One Oh Four, Heckler & Koch G Three 6 C, M-Sixteen. Just to name a few. Have you tried firing a sniper rifle? If you are interested, try Accuracy International AX Three Thirty-Eight, Remington Seven Hundred AICS. Should I keep going?"

James raised his hands in mock surrender. "I'm warned. Do you carry a gun with you?"

Rienne just smiled.

"My, God. How old are you again?"

"Old enough. Thanks for letting me stay here. I'm totally invading your privacy."

You invaded my brain, that's all. "No problem. This room okay with you?"

Rienne looked around the room. "I liked it before. Still like it now. Thank you."

James watched Rienne move like a dancer—graceful, gentle. Even at a young age, she had good physical qualities, but now...beautiful, delicate, and ethereal. No one would know what she'd been through just by looking at her. Like a woman who knew what she wanted, she spoke with confidence, and he found that so arousing. *Fuck me. Stop, James.* "Need help unpacking?" Jesus. He should leave the bedroom. Pronto, before he lost his mind and start attacking Rienne. James, however couldn't seem to move his feet. He just wanted to stand there and take his fill.

"You're staring again. Is that a newly acquired trait?"

"Sorry. Just thinking."

"About what?"

Whether you have a boyfriend. "Nothing. By the way, your bunny rabbit still has a hole."

Chapter Two

Our hearts were young when we fell in love
Love that cannot be, forbidden and not right.
But distance and years failed to erase what we felt for one another.
Because love is stubborn and blind.
Oh, love is blind.
Now that I found you once again. I know. It's always been you.
—Rienne T. Cailler

She knew exactly what James was talking about. Rienne's heart doubled its beat as she walked toward the bed, then moved the pillows leaning against the headboard that was made out of wooden planks. Smiling, she tapped the bottom plank. It fell forward to reveal a hollow spot where she used to hide her satellite phone. A rabbit hole.

She looked at James. He was watching her with his hands on his hips. Then, he nodded. Quickly, Rienne grabbed her handbag and took out the phone. It was her only connection with her dad and she was to use it only for emergencies. A reminder that she wasn't alone. Without it, she wouldn't know what to do.

Rienne placed the phone inside the secret compartment, then closed it again. It helped to know that she could call her dad right away. *Anytime.* Even in the middle of the night.

Like that one night when she woke up on this same bed years ago, feeling wet and sticky. Wondering what had happened, she turned on the lights. She'd been shocked to find blood on her hand. Getting off the bed, she looked down at her white cotton underwear. It, too, had been covered in blood. At first, she didn't know what just happened. When she finally gathered her wits, she realized then that she just had her first period. Not knowing what to do, the first thing that had come to mind had been to call her dad.

While holding the phone, she could feel blood coming out from her and it quickly ran down her thighs. Panic began to set in. She dialed the ten-digit numbers. As soon as her father answered in two rings, she told him that she was bleeding really badly. He replied with a loud curse then hung up. She was still staring at the phone, dumb-founded that her dad hung up on her without saying anything when Hal barged into her room, screaming her name. The man wore only his nightshirt and boxers. Without preamble, Hal grabbed her shoulder asking if she was okay. It had been the most embarrassing time in her life—especially when she noticed James standing inside her room, staring.

He saw.

What happened next was a blur. Hal, who breathed a sigh of relief that she wasn't injured at all, had sent James to the store to buy tampons. While waiting, Rienne stayed in the bathroom and washed. When she came out, Hal had already stripped the bed and replaced the sheets with the clean ones.

He assured her that there was nothing to worry about and that she was finally a woman. A flower that bloomed. A girl turning into a beautiful butterfly. Hal went on and on comparing her into an insect, fruit or animal. She took pity on him and said that she had her first period. Hal slumped on her bed, nodding.

That night, James ended up going back to the store three times because she refused to use the tampons, and the thin panty liners didn't work. When everything was settled, different brands of napkin were stored in her bathroom closet.

It took a few days before she finally overcame her embarrassment. No one mentioned what happened that night. Ever. But whenever they talked about the *rabbit*, she could see a tiny smile on James' lips.

Just like right now. Rienne glanced at James again. *Oh, yeah. He's remembering.* She could tell that he was thinking what she was thinking.

She fluffed the pillows back in place. There, she thought. Later, she would put her gun in there, too.

For the past years, she had lived in different places. She understood why and never complained. She'd been fine with wherever Dad placed her. This time, though, when he explained that he needed to move again and that she must stay with the Huntingtons, excitement bubbled in her chest. It was horrible, really, because moving meant that wherever she'd been staying wasn't safe anymore or her dad's location had been compromised and had to find a different safe place to burrow himself, which also meant not seeing him for months and months. However, finding out that she'd be living with the Huntingtons again, overshadowed the fear and sadness of leaving her friends at the club by her excitement at the prospect of seeing James again.

For years now, James hovered at the back of her head. She dreamed of seeing him again, of hearing his voice. She even wished they lived during the regency period so she could trap him into marriage. If that wasn't nutty, she didn't know what was.

Now, giddiness whirled around her. She feared that she might fall. Goodness, what's wrong with her?

She shouldn't entertain this feeling. James saw her as an annoying brat. A friend in need of help. Nothing more. Then again, how could she bend this feeling of wanting to touch him, to kiss him? Rienne ran her tongue on her lips. Lord, she just wanted to plant a big smooch on his kindly and humorous mouth. It wasn't helping that he'd been staring at her as if she was some kind of a delicacy.

Well, he looked yummy himself. Dark-skinned like his Italian mother, over six feet tall, with ingenuously appealing face and beautifully proportioned. She loved his dark-chocolate eyes and lips that curled as if always on the edge of laughter. Whenever he looked at her, those gorgeous eyes made her forget even her name.

James raised a brow. "Done staring?"

"Just doing what you're doing."

"You're sassy. Like always."

"You're a flirt. Like always," she bantered back.

"Come here."

Rienne sighed when James pulled her gently toward him. Like seeing an old friend after missing him for years, she practically dove into his arms. "This may sound corny, but I've missed you."

"I've missed you, too. Why didn't you send me a message? I didn't know how to reach you."

She leaned her cheek on his shoulder, closed her eyes, and savored the feel of him kissing the top of her head. He smelled wonderful. Like rain, soap…fresh. "My cell phone was disconnected. The club has a rotary phone, but you gotta have a good reason to use it and everyone knew not to lend me their cell."

"Social media?"

"No computers. "

"Damn. That's what everyone craves for now. Especially the teenagers. Some of them are like vegetables—useless, because all they want to do is use their cell phones and take *Selfies*. You know what Selfies are, right?"

"Yeah. *Facebook, Instagram,* and *Twitter* littered the Internet with those."

"Oh, hey! You're not that isolated, then."

"When I get lucky and someone lends me their computers, I could look at websites, but not sign-up on any social medias. Watching television is also not forbidden."

"Too bad cell phones are."

"It's all right. You probably wouldn't answer me anyway. You're always busy with friends and girlfriends."

"Love, that's not true. I would've called you if I knew where to call."

"Yeah, right. You'll call your girlfriends before you call me."

"I've had a few. But you're number one on my list."

"Ha. Ha." Before she started drooling on his shirt, Rienne pulled away from James' embrace. She missed his warmth instantly. "Thank you for letting me stay. Promise I won't cramp on your style."

"Cramp on my style?" He laughed. "Hey, tomorrow is a Saturday. If you're up for it, we could go down to Edmonds Marina, and drive to downtown Seattle or something. Unless a date to go to."

Rienne tapped her chin. "Yeah, I forgot. I already said *yes* to Daniel Craig's invitation to have lunch with him. So, sorry. Can't go."

"Ha. Ha. I bet you don't even have a boyfriend."

Darn it. Why did he have to mention boyfriend? No way she'd tell him her love life had been dry. Never even been on a date. Not even a guy name on her really short list of friends.

Rienne met a few boys who were homeschooled like her, but they were all as awkward as a newborn baby. None got her attention as James. So, yeah. She'd never been kissed. For some reason, she felt embarrassed about that.

"I take that frown as a *no*," James said with a grin.

"What? Don't give me that look. I'm not that ugly."

"I know that. So, how's school?"

Rienne was so glad James changed the topic. "I finished last year."

"Yeah?"

"Took advantage of homeschooling and online classes. Besides, I got nothing to do with my life than study anyway."

"And you didn't get any problems with your online schooling? I mean no one figured that you're connected with Roy Cailler?"

"No. Thankfully. So now, I have a degree in linguistics. I can use it to springboard to another field."

"Like what?" James asked.

"Law."

"Wow. Aside from trained in using high-powered guns, you also have beauty and brains. You're scary."

Rienne shrugged. He was right except maybe on the beauty part. She didn't think she had a face and body that anyone could call beautiful. "I'm just an ordinary and boring young woman who has been missing a lot in life."

"You've been square since I've known you."

***

Not exactly true. She changed. Staying at Sugar's and being friends with dancers, bartenders, bouncers had its perks. They got rid of her inhibitions. She could now say *cock, pussy, dick,* and *fuck* without feeling so embarrassed. Through gaps on the curtains, the thin bedroom wall, and partly opened doors, she'd heard and seen enough to know what goes on the real world. Her body had not been touched by anyone, but her eyes and ears weren't *virgins* anymore. She'd been educated in the art of sexual pleasure—unintentionally.

The image of one of the dancers with her customer formed in her head. Rienne had stumbled on them when she got up one night to find food in the kitchen. Both had been on the couch naked and their bodies glistened with sweat. Chikka sat on the man's lap, making sounds that had affected Rienne's mind and body in ways that had made her stay awake most nights staring at the ceiling wondering what it was like to have a man touch her.

Anyone in his right mind should have walked away, but Rienne had remained rooted on the floor. She watched Chikka move her hips while the man licked and sucked her nipples. From where she hid behind the curtain, she saw the man's wet cock go in and out of Chikka's pussy, and each time, Chikka would moan.

While Rienne watched, her breasts had begun to feel heavy. Her own pussy had become wet. As if her hand had a mind of its own, she touched her breasts. While her body reacted to her own touch, the man whispered something to Chikka. He shifted from his position so both of them could lie on the couch with him on top. He spread Chikka's legs so wide, it was a wonder she hadn't break. Then, the man did something that Rienne had not expected to see. *Cunnilingus*. Otherwise known at the club as muff diving. Right there where Rienne stood, she witnessed the man give Chikka pleasure by licking her.

He sucked her clit repeatedly, but Chikka begged for more and asked him to finger-fuck her. Chikka gripped the man's hair while she aimed her pussy on his mouth. She urged him to flick her clit with his tongue and to suck her hard. He obeyed. Rienne wanted what the man had been doing with Chikka. She wanted to feel the pleasure of having someone's mouth lick and eat her pussy. She continued to listen to the sound of two bodies joining and their pleas to satisfy each other. The sound had been pure pleasure—elemental, and passionate. The scene had been something that she would never forget. Oh, how could she forget? Her body was on fire, her skin sensitive, and when she touched her pussy through her shorts, a jolt of something sweet mixed with ache grew deep inside her. She throbbed.

Chikka's slim body writhed on the couch, her face flushed from exertion and began chanting, *I'm coming*. She squeezed her breasts while the man jerked off. Chikka let out an erotic sound that Rienne would never forget.

Chikka came.

As soon as her legs became limp, the man positioned himself between Chikka's legs and then he fucked her. *Hard.* He'd been wild with his thrusts and Chikka loved it.

Somehow, Rienne had managed to walk back in her room where she laid in bed, not hungry for food anymore but for something she knew only a man could give.

Regaining her senses back to the present, she stared at James and wondered what it would be like applying everything that she'd learned at the club with James. He believed her to be innocent. Well, physically, yes. But mentally... "You're wrong if you think that I am square, James."

"Learned a lot from your friends at the club, eh?" James said smiling.

You have no idea. "Some."

"All right. So, since Daniel Craig, I'm sure, would cancel your lunch date tomorrow, we could go out instead."

"Fine."

"That means you're all mine tomorrow then."

The way James said the word *mine* served as hot chocolate in her belly on a cold night. Rienne returned his smile. "Guess so."

Chapter Three

It took fifteen minutes of driving around before they finally found a spot to park, but it was worth the wait. A car parked on a prime spot facing the water, pulled out.

Sitting in James' truck enjoying her *Slurpee* from *7-Eleven*, Rienne took in the beautiful view of Edmonds Marina.

The whole place was packed with Seattleites deprived of sunshine. Kids were playing on the beach, along with bodies on the sand, and groups of people playing instruments. Even the fishing pier was elbow to elbow with people casting their fishing poles. And Rienne loved it.

This, she thought, was what she'd been missing all her life. *Freedom.*

With Rienne being a daughter of Roy Cailler, the infamous CEO of an insurance company accused of stealing millions from people, life hadn't been easy. She couldn't go anywhere without being followed. The Feds, reporters, and private investigators, for some reason, believed that trailing her would lead them to her father. She wouldn't be surprised right now if a bug had been attached to James' truck. Luckily, no live-on-paycheck-to-paycheck reporter sniffed her trail yet. Otherwise, she'd end up on a tabloid tonight with the reporters talking about her clothes, nails, and shoes. And they'd probably speculate that she bought the truck for James. When that happens? Lunatics and serious victims of fraud whether connected to her father's case or not, would chase her as if she had anything to do with the ruination of their lives. Yeah, it already happened a long time ago, and it could happen again.

For the past years, Sugar's had been littered with listening devices where the dancers were practically tripping on them. They all expected that to happen, but when gung-ho reporters started harassing them, Rienne's dad had decided keeping her longer in the club wasn't fair to everyone at all. Especially to his best friend Jimmy.

So, here she was now, living with the Huntingtons again.

"So, what have you been up to? Aside from shopping and hanging out at Starbucks."

Biting the tip of her straw, Rienne shifted from her seat so she could stare at James. "First of all, I don't hang out at Starbucks or anywhere. Coffee there sucks and I don't drink anything caffeinated. And shopping is not my thing."

"You don't like to shop? Isn't that a woman thing?"

"Not this woman." Sighing, she looked at the sun's reflection on the calm water of Puget Sound. "My life is different than most, you know. I had no senior prom, homecoming, sleepovers, bonfire at the beach, and making out with boys. Do you know anyone who spent time living with the hookers, dancers, and bouncers? I mean, it was fun. I have met all kinds of people there. Still, it's not a kind of home I dreamed of."

"I'm sorry, love. I know it's been tough."

"It's all right. My situation will get easier once I turn twenty-one."

"What makes you think that?"

"Well, I mentioned it to my dad before. I told him that when I'm twenty-one, I'll try to live on my own. Then, I wouldn't have to impose on anyone and Dad wouldn't have to worry about finding a place where to hide me."

"What did Roy say about that?"

"He didn't want to discuss it at the time."

"All right. So what about the people following you hoping that you'll lead them to your dad."

"I have nothing to do with my dad's case. I'll travel. Get a job. Maybe disappear, too, like Dad. Get a different identity. Anything. As long as I don't have to impose on anyone anymore."

"So you're thinking about establishing a life."

"Exactly."

"You'll be twenty-one soon."

"Yes. I want a home. It doesn't have to be big, but something that I can call mine."

James nodded. "Sounds good, but how about we enjoy our *Slurpee* for now. Enjoy youth while you can. It's not really that grand when you get old, you know."

"Right." Rienne drawled the word. "You should know because you're old. What, you're taking meds now for blood pressure and constipation? Mental faculties malfunctioning? Oh, no! You've had colonoscopy and failed it?"

"Very funny. You are such a brat. I'm thinking more like, *you have to pay full price on everything and you can say goodbye to the kids' menu.* Something like that."

Rienne grinned. "We abused the kids' menu at McDonald's, didn't we?"

"Yes, we did."

"So, you've been dating girlfriends left and right? Engaged? Divorced already?"

"Nope. Just enjoying my work right now. Like you, I want to establish myself first."

Rienne let out a long sigh. "Nobody can take knowledge and experience away from you."

"You sound so skeptical," James said with his brows arched high.

"I'm not even sure what I'm going to do with my education, right now. I know I said I want to be on my own, but can you imagine me going to work? Holy cow! The Feds and ambulance chasers would have a party outside my office."

"Not good if you work for a university."

"Right. I'd be distracted. What do you think if I become a masseuse?"

James threw his head back and let out a laugh. "God help us if you become a masseuse."

"What? What's wrong with becoming a massage therapist?"

"I'm sorry. A massage therapist with a degree in linguistics. I can't imagine you rubbing or massaging people. You'll probably end up breaking their bones and then fixing them for free."

"What made you say that?"

"You're beautiful, love. Guys, especially, would make a pass on you. Knowing how protective you are, you're not going to let that happen."

"Maybe you're right. Well, I could open my own green cross. It's legal in Washington now." Rienne shrugged.

"Just what you need, eh? A weed store so you'd suffer from migraine twenty four seven." James chuckled. "You still get migraines, right?"

"Yeah. Well, you're right. Weed stinks. How something so nasty tastes wonderful to some, baffles me."

"Weeds are like a tryst. You know you shouldn't use it, but the call of excitement, rush, makes you want to still do it," James explained with a grin.

"Oh, dear. I wouldn't know. Never had a tryst before."

"Me, either."

"But you've tried weed. So it's the same?"

"Same orgasm, I suppose."

"Eww!" Rienne punched James on the arm.

"Stop. You're so violent. Seriously, I think you should just stick to your plan of taking Law."

Rienne stuck her tongue out at James. "What about you? What do you do now?"

"I'm a co-pilot right now, but I want to travel, so I'm torn between working as a pilot and take more training so I could fly the Seven-Forty-Sevens or become a maritime captain. We'll see."

"Take me with you. I want to go places."

"I'd love to. We'll visit exotic places, eat funny looking food, and sleep under the stars."

"But?"

James laughed. "You're too smart, you know."

"We'll, there's got to be a *but* with the way you ended your sentence."

"All right. I think the only way to enjoy life or anything in this world is to have your freedom first. With love, freedom is what makes it the sweetest. When you're free, you can love anyone without hurting another."

"Or I could go anywhere without worrying about anyone following me or recognizing who I am."

James nodded. "Find your freedom, love."

Sighing, Rienne put her drink on the holder. "So what you're saying is, *accept the cage where my wonderful father has put me in?* And wait and hope that I'd be able to fly away someday. In the mean time, I should just watch life pass me by. Watch everything around me grow and die, shine and lose its sparkle, and tell my heart to stop beating for anyone and not fall in love. Oh yeah, you mentioned love. Do you think a heart knows if and when I should or should not love? Do you think that I could tell my heart not to fall in love yet because I'm still not free? What if I indeed fell in love? What then? Should I just ignore it?

"You fell in love before? Or still in love?"

Rienne stared at James. "Isn't it love when you think of someone all the time? Especially when you're alone in your room staring at the ceiling, and while thinking about that special person, your heart beats so fast, you feel dizzy. You play the guitar and sing love songs, write love quotes on your notebook and wished the two of you were together. Even his name alone could make you sigh and forget the day."

"Could be just an infatuation."

"That lasted for years?"

James frowned. "Who is he?"

Rienne shook her head. No way she'd tell James that it was him who made her mind wander all the time. "Never mind that, James. I've spent the majority of my years in hiding. I am afraid, you know. Afraid that I'll grow old without experiencing life. But I'm also afraid to be on my own."

James cupped Rienne's face. "Baby, baby. I'm merely stating that life is better lived if you are free. Look at me. Don't be afraid. I don't think your fear has its merit. Your fate is not to shrivel and waste away in a cage. I doubt it." He kissed Rienne's cheeks. "Please don't cry."

Rienne tried to look away. God, she didn't even realize she was crying. "I'm sorry."

"It's all right. I'm here to help make things easy for you. Just tell me what you need. What you want. You know, I like your idea of trying it on your own."

"Really?"

"Yeah. See what happens when you're out there doing what any person would do."

"Like shop or go to the salon and get my hair done."

"Yes. Don't change your hair, though. I like that way it is."

The simple compliment from James served as a melting butter on her toast. Really yummy good. "Okay."

"I have a suggestion."

"What?"

"Forget who you are while you're here. Live the way you wanted to live. Fuck it if you're recognized. If those rabid dogs want to follow you, let them. Show them that they're just wasting their time. They'll get tired eventually."

"Easy for you to say."

"I know, love. But listen. Did it ever occur to you that maybe those mother shit-heads are bent on finding you because you're hard to find?"

"You mean, like I'm a mystery to them, so they want to find out what I'm hiding."

"Precisely. Now, if you're out like you want to do, where they can see you, the thrill of finding or getting a glimpse of you will disappear."

"That's your theory?"

James shrugged. "Why not try it. Now, if you started getting harassed, or cameras and microphones start appearing in front of you, then we'll do something. For now, though, have some fun. It is summer after all." He kissed Rienne again then leaned back down on his seat.

If he kept on doing that, she might just kiss him back, Rienne thought. "Forget who I am. Is that what you're saying?"

"Yes."

"Ignore everything that I've been running from for years."

"Yes. Starting today."

"With you."

"Uh-huh. Lucky you."

Rienne laughed. She wasn't surprised at all that James wanted to help her. In the past, he had shown that he truly cared for her. Because she had stayed indoors most of the time when she was younger, James served as her eyes outside. He had brought her a wild baby Blue Jay that had fallen off the tree. He took pictures of anything he thought she'd be interested in. Once, when she had a flu, he even surprised her with, what he called, a jar of sunshine. She would never forget that day. James had walked in her room with a big smile on his face, holding a clear-lidded jar. He said he found a cure to her flu. He stayed in her room talking, telling her stories about what he and his friends had done all day until both of them had fallen asleep.

He cared. She knew that. Maybe like a friend would to another friend—but the fact was—he cared.

"I like the idea."

"Good. So, Miss Cailler. Now that you are on your own, tell me what you want to do. At the top of your head," he added, pretending to be a reporter using his straw as microphone.

Rienne grinned, then looked at the water. "Swim. I want to go swimming. Haven't done any swimming in a long time."

"What? That's too bad. Do you think you still know how? You might sink like a rock," he said in jesting quips.

"Forget it, then. You're annoying."

James stared at her, then burst out laughing. "No one ever called me annoying."

"Well, you are. I don't like you."

"Lie. You know what? You're good at hiding what's really going on inside that beautiful mind of yours."

"Got years of training."

"But you can't lie."

Rienne shrugged. "Maybe that's why Dad chose to give me little information about where he was going, where he was at, and what he'd been doing."

"Don't know about that. He trusts you."

"I know. Too bad he can't just step out of the shadow where he'd been hiding in all these years."

"It'll happen. For now, though, enough with the pouting."

Maybe James was right. It was time to show the world that she had nothing to hide. She had enough moving of from one place to the next, and enough depriving herself with simple things in life like using *Facebook* or cell phones. It was time to live. "So you're going to hang out with me. You sure you want to do that?"

"It's a privilege. My friends will probably get jealous 'cause I get to hang out with an angel."

"Yeah, right. And you? With that package of yours, I'm sure a lot of women would die from happiness if you just call them. I don't want you to miss out on some fun on the account of me."

"A package, eh? Well, if you must know, this body has been busy chartering passengers back and forth, which is my priority. Not women or having fun. As you already know, I'm still living with Dad. But I'm helping with the bills even when he refused to take my checks."

"Because he doesn't want to live alone in your beautiful house. It's just the two of you anyway."

"I know. It would be tough for both of us, I think, if I move out. Not to mention senseless. He doesn't hover, keeps to himself most of the time. So in a way, I feel I'm on my own."

"Except he cooks and cleans for you."

"Yup." James grinned.

"So, where do you work as a co-pilot?"

"I work part-time at Kenmore Air. I have a license to fly. Co-pilot for now. If you're interested, we could go on a trip to the San Juans. We'll even go to Canada. Whichever way you want to go."

"Sounds awesome. So you make tons of money, eh?"

"Being a pilot sounds glamorous, but that's about it. Unless you're a captain with years and years of flying hours under your belt, then maybe you'll make over a hundred grand. It still depends on the airline company you work for, though. But if you're just a pilot for small chartering company...pittance."

"But you can't put a price on the experience and fun of flying."

"Exactly. However, if you're married to a small-time pilot, you'll probably say *the hell with the experience and fun. Get a job that can feed a family*."

"Well, being a pilot is cool. Chick-magnet."

James laughed. "Yeah, they're stuck all over me."

"You sure no girlfriend would pull my hair or throw acid on my face if she sees me with you?"

"No girlfriend."

She basked in the knowledge that James was single. "That's hard to believe. What? Girls in Washington all blind? Sheez, look at you. Your skin color alone would make anyone fall in love with you. They'd kill to have a taste of your...uhm..."

"Of my what?"

Rienne met James' stare. In a span of a heartbeat, something changed. She saw something different with the way he was looking at her now. Sweet apple. He unnerved her.

"My what, Rienne?" James repeated.

"Your...lips. You have kissable lips. I'm sure you already know that." She paused. "Sorry. I shouldn't have said that. It's just...it's true."

Oh, God.

"Have you been kissed before, Rienne?"

"Me? Of course. Many times. I'm square, but not *that* square." She punctuated her statement with a nod.

James, though, didn't look convinced. Well, what did she expect? That he would believe her? No boy had ever even touched her.

"You're very beautiful. You would've been a homecoming queen if you—"

"Don't patronize me."

"I'm not."

"No one would come near me. Almost everyone knows my face. Roy Cailler's daughter. Remember. Many people believe that Dad stole their money. Whatever I am wearing now, everything I own belongs to one of the people Dad sent early to their grave. I'm a pariah, a leper, a disgusting daughter of—"

Her last word she found smothered and forgotten when James mouth captured her lips. The moment they touched, a shock wave travelled through her entire body, her heart beating so fast, making her feel heady. She'd never been kissed, but it must have been a natural inclination to part her lips when being kissed, because that was exactly what she did. She welcomed him, his taste, and his tongue. For a long time, she'd wondered about this—what would it be like to have another person's lips pressed against hers? What had Chikka felt when the man kissed her. Now she knew. It was indescribable. Her body came alive as if James' mouth was fire and she a dying ember.

Rienne returned James' kisses with hunger that contradicted her outward calm. She drank the sweetness of his kiss, loving the delicious feeling deep down in her belly. She moaned when James gently wrapped his hand at the back of her neck while his other hand travelled from her shoulder down to the rise of her breasts. His touch, his kisses slowly transported her back to her vivid dreams—of James' lips all over her skin.

Rienne felt her breasts tingle and that familiar need to be touched formed in between her legs.

"James…" Parting her lips, she returned his kiss without care. All she knew was that she loved having her mouth glued to his.

James' tongue plunged deep inside her mouth. *Seeking, exploring.*

Rienne quivered at the sweet feeling. An aching need to press her body against him was overwhelming. She wrapped her arms around his neck and pulled herself.

"Love..." He planted kisses on her shoulders, neck, and the rise of her breasts.

Rienne could hardly breathe, unable to believe that this was really happening. My word, it would be impossible to describe what she was feeling right now. She felt like melting and floating at the same time. She was so into the moment that she nearly jumped when a quick tapping sound came from the windshield of the truck.

James chuckled. "Baby, we have an audience. Look."

A fat seagull sat on the hood of the truck, eyeing them. More decided to join. A few even marked the hood. Laughing, she tapped her knuckles on the window. When she looked at James again, she found him staring at her. Embarrassment quickly enveloped her. Without looking in the mirror, she knew her cheeks were red. "I don't know what came over me. It's just—"

"What...you regret kissing me?" James raised a brow.

"Regret? No. Embarrassed maybe. You?"

"I feel many things right now, baby, but not regret. You sure you've never been kissed before? Because you did fantastic for your first time."

"You're just saying that." She paused. "Why did you kiss me?"

"To stop you from belittling yourself. Love, you shouldn't carry Roy's shame. You have nothing to do with it. Besides, Roy didn't participate in the scheme. No shame there. Let others think the worst about your dad. Fuck them. And you...you should enjoy life."

"And you'll help me do that. Live?"

"The best I can."

"What about your girlfriend. She might get jealous."

"I told you, silly. No girlfriend."

"Since when?"

"Four months now."

"What happened?"

James shrugged. "She wanted more than just holding hands. I told her, *sorry but I can't give up my virginity yet.*"

"Yeah, right." Rienne smiled. Always, James knew how to make the situation comfortable. She loved bantering with him. He'd always been so relaxed around her, making her feel like she could tell him everything. "If I were to give up my virginity, it would be to the man whom I've been in love with and would marry someday."

James leaned his elbow on the stirring wheel, then stared at Rienne. He'd never looked at her that way. As if he just saw her for the first time. Not as a girl, but as a woman.

"How would you know that he's the right one? I mean, a lot of people believed they'd met the right one until they spotted another on a subway or train or classroom that made their hearts beat so fast."

"There is no way to know that the man I'd marry is the one. All I am saying is that I'm not just going to have sex for the fun of it. I will have sex for the first time because we are both in love and know that we're going to marry."

"So you'll tell your boyfriend, *baby, we'll have sex only if you promise to marry me right after.*"

Rienne laughed at James' poor attempt to copy her voice. "Something like that. Bottom line, I'm not going to sleep around. My first time would be special, memorable, and something that I would never regret."

"You're a romantic."

Rienne shrugged. "Call me what you will, but that's how I feel about it."

"Rienne, sometimes making love happens when you least expect it.

When you fall in love…on occasion, you just get swept away. You stop thinking and not care about anything, but give the person you love everything."

"Is that why you had sex with that girl? She's a senior and you were only fourteen?"

"Ugggghh!" James pretended to choke Rienne. "You little eavesdropper!"

"You were talking aloud. Did she really have inverted nipples?"

They laughed until they couldn't laugh anymore. It was a fine day for Rienne. For a moment there, she was just a girl hanging out with a guy who stole her heart in his truck, having drinks and burgers. It was marvelous.

Chapter Four

Rienne lowered the car's window, loving the cool breeze and enjoying the view of the downtown Seattle when James reached for her hand, then squeezed.

"We're being followed," he mouthed.

"Damn. And so it started. *Again*." Rienne looked behind them. "Black. Tinted. With antennas. And of course, a Crown Victoria."

"It's all right. We'll shake them off."

James took the freeway, exited, stopped at the gas station to fill up the tank, then entered the freeway again. As expected, the *Crown Victoria* did the same except for getting gas.

"They're so thick in the head. Can't they tell that we know they're following us?" Rienne laughed when James took the same exit and freeway entrance twice.

"They're idiots, aren't they?" James managed to drive beside the Crown Victoria. He lowered his window and motioned for the driver to lower his. He laughed when the driver showed his resigned look. "Need gas?" he asked, then drove away.

Rienne lowered her window, too, hooted loud, and stuck her arm outside to flip off the Feds next. "That was brilliant."

"Did you just flip them off?"

"Told you. Not that square."

James grinned. "They were paid to follow you. That's what they did. I'm sure they are tired of doing it, too."

"But they make good enough money to complain," Rienne added.

"Exactly. You know, being followed like that is just an example of what's going to happen if you *live*. Are you ready for this big change?"

"If change means I'm going to have this much fun all the time, yes. I'm ready."

James grinned. "All right. I think that was too much excitement. I'm hungry."

"Me, too."

"How do you feel like fish and chips?"

Rienne clapped. "You kidding? Oh, wait. What about your dad? He's cooking dinner, yeah?"

"Before we left, I told him not to wait."

"All right. Fish and chips, then."

They stopped at Spuds to order fish and chips, and chowder to go. The restaurant was across the street from Alki Beach Park and it was a perfect summer day to eat out anyway. Once they got their food, they walked along the beach strip looking for an available picnic table. Rienne admired the water and the busy environment—joggers, roller bladers, beachcombers, and sunbathers out to enjoy the sun-littered the area. She stopped in front of the monument to read about the first settlers on 1851, but James grabbed her arm.

"We'll read that later. Our mission is to find a picnic table."

"All right!" Rienne laughed.

A family of five was putting away their food, so Rienne and James waited until they finished. As soon as the table was clear, James told her to sit down while he split their food.

"This place is beautiful."

"Yeah. All year you'll see people here. Not just tourists, but locals as well. They couldn't get enough of the Puget Sound, Olympic Mountains, and all kinds of crafts that float on the sound. Later, I'll show you the old anchor that the Nor'West Divers—"

"Northwest?" Rienne asked, thinking that he mispronounced the word.

"Nope. There is a group called Nor'West Divers Club. They secured the site. We'll check it out later. For now, eat. You're so skinny. What did you eat at Sugar's? Grass?"

"Practically. Dancers are not supposed to eat a lot. If they gain weight, Jimmy will give them hell. Therefore, their diet becomes mine, but we have potatoes every Friday and bacon on Saturdays. By the way, I'm not skinny."

"No? You probably weigh like ninety pounds."

"I only look smaller to you because you're fat."

"Ha!"

She watched James shove food into his mouth. He ate like a starving man. "You always eat as if this is the last time you'll see food."

James shrugged. "Why eat slow?"

"Never mind." Rienne savored her food while enjoying the view.

"Are you going to finish your chowder?"

"No."

James didn't wait. He took Rienne's bowl and finished what was remaining. "What about your fries?"

"You can have them. Want half of my fish?"

"You bet."

She handed him her leftovers. "You eat a lot. It's a good thing you don't weigh three hundred pounds."

It took only a few minutes for him to finish everything. Rienne watched James with fascination.

"What?" he asked while chewing.

"I'm expecting you to lick the bowl and wrapper."

"Can I?"

Rienne laughed. "I should have brought a collar."

James threw a small, burnt fry at her. "Ready for a walk?"

"Sure."

James jogged towards the garbage can, then walked back beside her. "Aren't you too hot?"

"No. Feels good, actually."

They began walking toward the seawall. She was watching the little girls fill their buckets with sand when James laced their fingers together. Rienne didn't say anything. Not that she couldn't. She just didn't want to fear that she might break the spell. Maybe James holding her hand was just that. Simply holding a friend's hand. To her, it was a dream come true. She imagined this moment many times and wondered if it would ever happen. Finally, it did, but not for the reason that she had in mind, but she'd take this and the kiss they had shared. Something to remember when she moved out again.

Sighing, Rienne savored the feel of her palm against James. So, this was what it was like, to walk at the beach with a boy. Really nice and made her proud, especially when she saw women looking at them.

They passed a Latino-looking man wearing dark sunglasses and holding a newspaper. He glanced at her briefly, then looked away.

"What are you thinking, love?"

"Nothing. Just enjoying the view." She looked at the man again, but he was already reading his newspaper. Did her dad pay him to follow her? Or was he one of those investigators bent on finding her dad. Had he been following them since they left Edmonds? Did he take pictures? Rienne could have sworn she'd seen him before. But where?

"Hey, you're tripping on your own feet. What is it?"

"I just thought I've seen that man sitting on the bench before." Maybe she was just paranoid. Always suspicious that someone was watching her.

James smiled. "Seen him before."

"Really?"

"Yeah. The movie *Machete*. Danny Trejo. Pocked mark face."

"What?" She looked up at James. He was grinning down at her. "Ha. Ha."

"Hey, remember what we talked about earlier? You're going to live. So *live*. The hell with that guy. Like the Feds, let him follow us."

Rienne looked back at the man. "Yeah. Fuck him."

"Yes." Suddenly, James stopped walking. With his other hand, he pulled her close to him. "You look so lovely with the lowering sun reflecting on your skin."

"Thank you."

"Do you have any idea how beautiful you are?"

"Beautiful enough for a boy to want to kiss me?"

Without answering, James lowered his head. Rienne met him halfway.

Just like in the truck, their kiss had made her whole body react. James' hands gently cupping her face wasn't enough. She wanted more, more of his touch, of his heat. As if James heard her thoughts, he pulled her against him. Instantly, she found herself transported to a place where only the sound of water lapping on the shore existed. Rienne gave in to the sensation so foreign it scared her. She clung to James' shoulders as the sexual excitement took her to a higher level where she felt she could fall any moment. His tongue stroked hers, fanning whatever heat that was currently swirling deep inside her belly. She loved his taste, the way he gently suckled her lower lip, and the sound that he made as if he, too, wanted more. Desire, foreign and new nearly consumed Rienne. All too sudden, though, James ended the kiss. He wrapped his arms around her just tight enough that she could feel his heartbeat pounding hard against his chest.

"You're a temptation, Rienne."

"But?"

James chuckled. He ran the pad of his thumb on Rienne's lower lip. "This can't go on, you know. You're barely legal. More to the point, Roy entrusted you to us, to keep you safe and provide you haven. I'm not supposed to be kissing you like this."

"But you kissed me twice now. So why did you do it?"

"The same reason why you kissed me back."

"So, what are we going to do now?"

James began walking again. "Nothing. Just don't make me kiss you again."

"What? I didn't make you kiss me!" She would have melted from embarrassment if James hadn't smiled at her.

"Yes, you did. You just didn't know it."

James didn't say it, but he might as well have admitted that he was attracted to her. Rienne walked beside James with her heart singing. He took her hand again and together they admired the beauty around them. If James looked at Rienne again, he would have had seen her wide grin.

Please, God. If you really exist. Make this last.

***

A few feet away from them, Santiago, the man Roy hired to follow Rienne, lowered the newspaper that he'd been holding. He had just sent Roy the picture of Rienne while she was having fish and chips with James. Roy would love it. Rienne was actually laughing as if the sun belonged to her.

Whew. He stretched his legs in front of him. Rienne had seen him a couple times before. And for a minute there, he thought she recognized him. If she saw him again after today, she'd really know he was following her. Most likely, she'd call her dad. He must be careful from now on.

Santiago stood up then looked at James and Rienne walking hand in hand. Shock hit him when the two kissed.

Damn shit. What was that about?

He didn't like what he saw and would surely make Roy's head hurt when he heard about it. He needed to tell him, though.

Oh, hell. This is new.

Roy had been paying him good amounts of money to follow his daughter's shadow and tell him everything, including tidbits like Rienne's clothes, hair, and facial expressions. *Anything.* The man loved Rienne so much that he would do anything for her, including spending time miles and miles away from her just to keep her safe, which Santiago wanted for the girl also. He'd been following Rienne for years now and he'd kind of gotten attached to the girl. Heck, he would probably make sure Rienne was doing okay on his own even without Roy's money.

He wouldn't wish on anyone the kind of life that Rienne had been living in. The poor girl spent years avoiding them seeing him. Like a leper—away and hiding from everyone. Which begged the question... *What's up with her strolling along the beach—and kissing?* Santiago looked around. There were so many people at the beach. He'd bet his bunion one of them was an agent hoping to catch her with her father.

Man, she'd never been this careless before. What the fuck! Well, he was paid to report to Roy and report he would do.

Santiago folded his paper then took out a cell phone from his shirt's pocket. Taking a deep breath, he dialed Roy's number.

Here we go.

"Hi Roy. She's with Hal's boy."

"James is a good kid, but you wouldn't be calling me with that tone if everything were okay. Tell me. What's going on?"

"I think they kissed."

"You think? They kissed or they didn't."

"They kissed."

"What the fuck do you mean?" Roy's voice turned hard.

"They kissed. James and Rienne. You know, like...like boyfriend and girlfriend. If they're related, I would say it was an innocent kiss. But—"

"They are not. Damn it. You saw them kiss? Why?"

"Yes, I saw them. And I don't know why. Maybe—"

"You've been watching Rienne for years, Santiago, and you said you've seen them together. They were buddies. Not lovers."

"That's when they were younger, Roy. Maybe this time they had gotten even closer."

"How the fuck is that even possible? Rienne stayed away from the Huntingtons for a long time. Her contact with them was cut off. And why the fuck would that boy kiss Rienne anyway?"

Anyone would want to kiss Rienne, Santiago wanted to say. "She's beautiful, Roy."

Roy sighed. "I know. I'm looking at the picture that you took while they were eating earlier. So beautiful, it's hard not to look at her. Her mother was beautiful, too. Could be an innocent kiss that you saw, Santiago."

No, it isn't. It's a lover's kiss. "I don't want to jump to conclusion here, but I think you're daughter is not safe with him. Emotionally."

"Fuck. Just what I fucking need."

"Roy, Rienne is not a little girl anymore. She's more than beautiful and anyone who goes near her, even a blind man, would see that. She's irresistible and looks like James couldn't resist her."

Santiago winced as he heard the sound of a glass crashing.

"She doesn't know what she's doing, Santiago. She's my girl. *My* girl. And—"

"I know. Growing up fast."

"Don't I fucking know that? We spent so many years apart. I missed so many things already. And she...a normal life. Maybe this hiding and trying to prove myself innocent is not worth a fucking shit."

"Roy, don't go that route. Don't give up now. Rienne sacrificed her time, too. So don't go waste those times."

"Yes! She sacrificed her years living from one place to the next. So why is she out on the beach and fucking kissing a boy? What does she think she's doing? Damn it. "

Santiago felt sorry for the man. He had millions, but couldn't buy his freedom right now. "Why not call her?"

Roy sighed so loud that Santiago had to hold the phone away from his ear. "Call and ask her about the kiss? I've never talked to her about boys or a boy. I heard it's a sensitive topic. What if Rienne..."

Santiago just listened. He didn't have to see Roy to feel the man's fear. Fear admitting that his daughter was no longer a baby.

"I trusted James and Hal. That boy is the last kid on earth that I would suspect of doing anything like kissing my daughter. Fuck!"

Santiago almost snorted aloud. He wanted to tell Roy that placing his daughter in a house with a hormonal young man living in the house wasn't a good idea, but thought better of it. Roy and Hal had been friends for years. Both trusted each other, but Santiago had a bad feeling about this.

"I'll clear my name. Once done, I'll punish those who took my name down the sewer. My daughter is in the situation she's in right now because of those mother fuckers."

Santiago rolled his eyes. The problem with the rich is their ego is as big as their bank account. Even if Roy proved his innocence, his name would never be clean. He'd been marked already.

"What do you want me to do? Find a place for Rienne?" Santiago could almost hear the man's brain crank. He felt for him. It must be horrible living away from his only daughter.

"Rienne is smart. She could protect herself from anyone who would try to take advantage of her."

Santiago agreed, but could Rienne protect herself from getting her heart broken? "So what should I do?"

"It's too soon to take actions. I don't want Rienne to think that I don't trust her. Keep watching them closely. There must be a reason why James kissed her. They'd been friends for a long time. Maybe…I don't know. Just keep an eye on them. I'll get in touch with Hal."

"I will do my job, Roy, but once they're inside the house, I won't know what they're—"

"Damn it. Santiago. I hired you to keep an eye on my daughter. You do everything for me. If you have to live in their ceiling so you could follow her, do that. Oh, and you will give me updates every fucking single day. Don't give me any excuses."

What, should I plant cameras inside the Huntington's house now? "I'll do my best."

"Good. Call me if you have other news than my daughter getting mauled by a boy I trusted."

"I didn't say she was being mauled, Roy. Rienne kissed him back and—"

The line went dead.

Fuck. Santiago pocketed his phone again. He looked at Rienne and James again. Both were bare footed and picking up rocks. They were laughing. Even from a distance, he could tell that there was something going on between the two. Maybe he was reading too much on James' action, but he could tell the young man was infatuated. And Rienne. The way she smiled at James…hell. He'd bet his life on it. James and Rienne would lose their friendships soon. Oh, yeah. They'd be lovers before the week was over. And how was he going to stop that?

Chapter Five

Except for the porch light, James' house was in total darkness. He parked the car beside his dad's Subaru station wagon then turned off the engine. After unbuckling his seatbelt, he shifted from his position so he could face Rienne. The moment he looked at her, his breath was caught in his throat as if someone had punched him in the gut. Rienne looked so lovely with her head resting on the headrest and her eyes closed. A hint of a smile still held her lovely mouth. The moon gave her an ethereal glow. So beautiful, enchanting, and peaceful.

Earlier, they'd drove around Seattle, walked on the cobbled streets, which Rienne enjoyed a lot, had ice cream and crepes, then watched the sunset until they both got chilled. He loved every part of it. Having his arms around Rienne felt so natural. Like puzzle pieces, they fit together as though he belonged beside her. The best part of the day, though was watching Rienne relax and just be herself with not a care on who would recognize her or if there were Feds following them. She stopped and smelled the flowers, laughed at the vendors, throwing fish at each other at a fast speed without dropping them, danced with an elderly man while listening to the street violinist play a sweet song, and talked to a husband and wife selling handmade jewelry. She even bought leather and woven bracelets. James had to drag her away from the tattoo parlor, though. Man, if he'd let her, they'd go home with Rienne covered in tattoos and riddled with piercings. If Roy saw that, he would probably pepper him with bullets.

Rienne had acted like someone finally given permission to step out the door and breathe fresh air. She was fascinating to watch. Her laughter so infectious, everyone around her couldn't help but smile with her. James felt sadness, too. Rienne should have been living life like everyone else long time ago.

After seeing her run around the beach, kicking water with little kids, he promised himself to help Rienne experience what it was like to see the world around her, what it was like to be a young woman, to feel the rush of bungee jumping, swimming in the cold lake, and watching squirrels climb from one tree to the next. Those, at least, he could try giving her while they were living together. He would protect her, too, from all the nastiness of the world, if he could. Something nagged at him, though. Could he protect her from him?

Damn. He must keep his feelings tucked deep in the bowels of his soul. Rienne wasn't his to touch, to dream of, to fantasize. As it is, he was already betraying their friendship. Having Rienne this close could be dangerous. She was a forbidden fruit—a delicious one.

James touched Rienne's cheek. It was warm, smooth, and felt good on his skin. God, he wanted to kiss her and not just where the pad of his thumb ran back and forth. He wanted to kiss her all over.

Rienne opened her eyes then looked at him. Instantly, his cock thickened. She had just given him an idea of what it would be like to have her beside him, to wake up in the morning and see her sleepy eyes. She was unbelievably enchanting.

"Hey, love. Tired?"

"Yes, but happy," she replied sleepily. "I had a great time today. Thank you."

"You're welcome." James opened his door then quickly went to the passenger's side. Rienne had already unbuckled herself. Leaning down, he planted a kiss on her forehead, just because he couldn't control himself. "Hang on to me."

"What? Are you going to carry me inside?" Rienne smiled.

James had to look away at those beautiful lips. Damn. "Uh-huh. Looks like you're dead on your feet." As soon as Rienne wrapped her slender arms around his neck, he knew right away that carrying her was a bad idea. She smelled of shampoo, sunshine, summer, and a woman.

He scooped her up and held her tight. "What am I going to do with you?" He didn't expect an answer and he didn't get it. Rienne just sighed. Her breath tickled his neck. That simple action sent a delicious feeling down to his cock. Fuck. If he kept this up, they'd end up in bed—naked. Moreover, the way Rienne returned his kiss earlier, he had a feeling she wouldn't mind if they shared a bed tonight.

Damn, damn, damn.

"Am I really that heavy?"

"What?"

"You've been grunting."

"Sorry, love. I just thought of something."

"Not about dropping me, I hope."

Rienne said the words with her mouth almost touching his neck's skin, her breath warm and arousing. "Never crossed my mind." With a little bit of maneuvering, he managed to open the door. His dad never locked it whenever he was out at night.

Inside, a lamp left on gave him enough visibility to find the stairs. He pretended to drop Rienne. She screamed like an angel. "Shh! Brat, you'll wake Dad."

Rienne giggled. "You're fault." She wrapped her arms around his neck tighter.

Sighing, James tried to ignore her breasts pressed against him. *Fuck, this is big time lunacy.* He quickened his pace. The sooner he put her to bed, the better. In his arms, he held an innocent young woman. Inexperienced. And he had a huge hard on for her.

Fuck!

As soon as he reached Rienne's bedroom, he used the toe of his shoe to kick the door open. Two vanity lights on each side of the headboard glowed softly in the room.

"We're home."

"Home," Rienne replied with a soft voice that was very very sexy.

Damn. Why did she have to be a friend? Why couldn't she just be someone he'd met, became infatuated, and fallen in love with? *Fuck*, he thought. He was just temporarily in love with Rienne the last time he saw her—*if* there was such a thing as temporary love. Now, seeing her again had brought out all the feelings and fantasies he'd had about her. A feeling that had been scratching his chest had started as a friendly affection, admiration and strong physical attraction. Now, he wanted more. His heart yearned for more.

As gentle as he could, he placed Rienne in the middle of her bed. He expected her to let go, but she didn't.

"Thank you again for the wonderful time," she said while her fingers played with his hair at the back of his neck.

"My pleasure, love." He stared at her for a full minute while his thoughts ran amuck. He wanted so badly to kiss her again. Instead, he ran his hands through her hair. "Do you need anything?"

"No, thank you."

"I had fun hanging out with you."

"I'm not boring?"

Far from that. "Not at all. I'll think of something to do tomorrow."

Rienne smiled. "Do that."

He kissed Rienne's forehead with the intention of saying goodnight and leaving after, but he couldn't.

"James..."

That was it. Rienne's sensual way of saying his name snapped the thin thread he was hanging on to. Every sane reason why he shouldn't be in her bed flew. What he wanted, won—to kiss Rienne again.

He took Rienne's face in his hands. For a brief moment, he stared at her, admiring her face. "You're beautiful." James' mouth came down on top of Rienne's. The contact shot an instant sweet pleasure deep down his belly. *Damn fuck!* His already thickening cock hardened in an instant. He deepened his kiss, taking possession, thrusting his tongue inside to meet hers.

Rienne's taste, her lusty moan, the way her hands snaked inside his shirt added fuel to his want to know all of her, to kiss every part of her, to make her his. James kissed Rienne the way he imagined it until it turned carnal. His tongue moved in and out of her mouth. Shit, she tasted so good.

At the beach, when he kissed her, he really forgot where they were. All he thought about was that she was in his arms. He was hard, throbbing, and fucking in pain that he wanted to bury himself deep inside her.

Few more kisses and I'd stop. I must.

Rienne's hands felt so warm against his skin. She clung to him while returning his kiss. James could feel her tremble. "Baby…" He kissed her jaw, the side of her neck and her smooth shoulder.

"James…"

"Hmm…" He bit the soft skin lightly before kissing the very same spot.

Rienne shivered. "You're driving me crazy."

"I missed you. So much, you know."

"Me, too." Rienne panted.

He nibbled her earlobe before sucking her neck hard, which left a red spot right away. James smiled proudly that he'd done that to her. Because he liked marking her, he did it again. Tomorrow, she'd be shocked to see her neck. He continued torturing her with more kisses.

Rienne became more restless beneath him. "You feel so good, love," he whispered.

"I love what you're doing."

James chuckled. He slipped his hand inside her top, loving the smooth skin beneath his palm. Rienne wore a soft bra with a clasp on the front. He could feel her nipple against the material. James rubbed it with his thumb.

"James."

"Good?"

"Yes..."

It was good for him, too. But not enough. A little more and he'd really stop.

He pulled Rienne's top to expose her body. His cock throbbed at the sight. Slim, flat stomach, almost flawless skin if it weren't for the small birthmark just below her left breast. James inhaled the skin above the rise of her breast while he spanned her body with his hands. "Perfect," he whispered. He unclasped her bra then sucked one hard nipple. "Hmm..."

Rienne's erotic moan urged him to do the same with the other one.

"James. Oh, my."

He knew what she wanted and he wanted it, too. Nothing wrong with giving her a little taste of what it was like to make out. Still, he wouldn't take advantage of her naïveté.

Quickly, James sat up to take off his shirt and then tossed it on the floor. From the very back of his mind, something told him to keep his fly buttoned. *Fuck it.* He needed to feel her skin against him, rub his dick on her warm pussy. Kiss and lick her until she begged him to stop. He wouldn't take her virginity. No. Just a taste. His dick hurt from its confinement. James couldn't take it anymore. With a little maneuvering, he shucked his pants, but kept his boxers.

Wearing only her panties, Rienne remained still, watching him through her heavy lidded eyes.

"You're beautiful, love." Desire knifed through him, but James held on to his control. He gathered her into his arms then held her snugly. The moment he felt her breasts against him, the sensation was so inexplicable, it had him gritting his teeth.

Once again, he explored Rienne's body with his hand and mouth. It was like nibbling on a tasty piece of bread when all he wanted to do was eat her whole. He reclaimed her lips while massaging her breast gently. He gave her slow thoughtful kisses, but he could feel himself shattering with hunger for more.

Fuck. So good.

James fucked Rienne's mouth with his tongue before licking each of her nipples. When he sucked one deep into his mouth, Rienne's reaction boldly told him that no one had done this to her before. She tried to cover her breasts, but for only a scant second. Her gasps of surprise turned into begging for more. Damn, she had great breasts. Firm and perfect for his hands.

Rienne's willingness to give herself freely to his kisses and soft exploration on his body wasn't helping James' thin hold on his senses. Gritting his teeth, he moved so he could lie on top of Rienne without putting his weight on her. When he felt her warm pussy through his boxers, he thought he'd ejaculate in them. Damn, she felt heavenly.

He couldn't remain still. James nudged Rienne's legs apart. She didn't resist. The position gave him room to move his hips. They weren't totally naked yet, but might as well. The thin barrier of their underwear melted the moment their bodies touched. Slowly, he thrust his hips in synch with the way he sucked her nipple. He pulled as much flesh as he could inside his mouth, then used his tongue to caress her.

"Damn good, love," he said in between sucking.

"James..." Rienne held James' head while her body arched giving James more of her flesh.

James gave her other nipple equal attention before slowly moving down to kiss her stomach and lower belly. He was so fucking hard, he wanted to pull down his boxers and fuck her hard. Instead, he continued thrusting. When he looked down, though, he saw that the tip of his cock was already out of his boxers. Thin sheen of pre-cum covered the head of his cock.

He wanted to tell her to push him away, to stop now while he could, but the words remained at the tip of his tongue. "Are you good?" he asked instead.

"Yes," Rienne replied breathily.

He dipped his tongue on her belly button. She squirmed. "You're magnificent."

"James...what are you—"

"Just relax your legs, love." He ran his tongue on her smooth thigh savoring the taste of her.

"Please, James..."

"Please what?"

"I don't know." Rienne replied. Her voice laced with frustration.

James smiled. Oh, he knew. Rienne was definitely fucking horny as he was. He pressed his mouth on her pussy mound then inhaled deep. She smelled so good, of a woman in heat. "Rienne?"

"Yes?"

"I will taste you." He didn't wait for her to say something. Using his fingers, he spread her pussy. Rienne tried to clamp her legs, but the moment he licked her clit, she let her thighs fall apart. She was so wet and fucking beautiful. Heart hammering, he stared at Rienne's pinkish pussy, and then helped himself to her wonderful taste.

James gave her a long lick. He almost came at the taste of her.

Rienne let out a little scream. "James, ohh. What…"

He trapped her clit between his lips then sucked it gently. In between sucking, he murmured, "Hmm, it's all right, love." Using the tip of his tongue, he teased her clit the way he knew that would drive her crazy. "Fuck, yeah. So good." He clamped his mouth on her pussy then sucked. James used his thumb to penetrate Rienne's untried pussy. She was tight, hot, and fucking slippery. Slowly, he thumb-fucked her while he savored her taste.

Rienne's fingers dug into his scalp, her moans in synch with his sucking.

"James, is this…oh Lord. It feels so wonderful."

"I know, love. Just let me and let your body take in the pleasure. Fuck. I love your taste." He held on to her waist to keep her in place then pleasured Rienne with his tongue and mouth.

He loved hearing Rienne catch her breath and feel her body tighten. Somehow, his heart soared knowing that he was the first to see her naked body, the first to taste her pussy and put his thumb where no one had been in before. He'd help her come using his mouth. Oh fuck. He'd swallow her come. Damn, good. He pressed his thumb deeper. Rienne tried to close her legs again, but he urged her to spread her thighs with the heel of his hand.

"It's all right. Just my thumb." He pumped his finger slowly. "Baby, you're hot."

"James. I can't…I need."

While James' mouth remained on Rienne's pussy, he looked at her. She was practically sitting up, watching. "Come in my mouth, love. Come for me."

Rienne's lips were wet from her constant licking. She was breathing hard, too.

"Fuck my mouth, love."

"Oh!" Rienne began to move her hips. Slowly at first, then her tempo quickened. "Don't stop, James."

James thought he'd go nuts from ecstasy. He didn't let go of Rienne's clit even when she screamed his name. When her body began to relax, James ran his tongue up and down her pussy before he tongue-fucked her. His hand shook, his body wound tight and his mind screamed. He wanted to make love with her. As if it had a mind of its own, his hand reached down to squeeze his cock.

Damn fuck. He needed to come. "Baby?"

"Yes?"

James kneeled. "I have to do this. Fuck, I have to."

Rienne sat up in front of him. "Let me."

"Rienne..."

"I've never done this before, but I've seen enough, James. I lived with dancers and had seen them make-out with their one-night lovers. But you, you have to tell me what to do."

James was beyond thinking now. All he wanted to do was to reach his orgasm. "Hold me." He took Rienne's hand. "Like this." As soon as Rienne wrapped her long slender fingers around his cock, he began to pump. Rienne, however, surprised him when she lowered herself.

"This is better," she whispered, then wrapped her wet lips around the head of his cock.

"Yes! Fuck."

James moved his hips as he watched his cock go in and out of Rienne's mouth. She knew enough to make a man become delirious with pleasure. Her other hand cupped his balls gently. With her eyes closed, she stroked. His hips replied by thrusting his cock in her mouth. James watched as pure pleasure registered on Rienne's face.

Even with James' hazy mind, he saw Rienne cup her breast. Right then, he decided to show her another way to pleasure each other. With all the strength that he could muster, he slowly moved back.

Rienne looked at him questioningly. Instead of giving her an explanation, he laid down on his back. "Do you want to continue?"

"Yes."

"Come sit on my chest."

Rienne eyed him for few seconds, but did what was told. James cupped her ass, then urged her to move higher until her pussy was directly above his mouth.

"This is naughty," she said.

"And delicious."

"I thought I'm supposed to continue."

"You will. Turn around." He didn't have to say more. Rienne knew what he wanted her to do. She bent down to suck his cock again while her pussy was wide open for him to own.

James labored for breath. The head of his orgasm reared, but he wanted to make her come again. She was already dripping juice in his mouth. While cupping his balls with one hand, Rienne's sweet mouth moved up and down his cock.

"Hmm…baby. I won't last," he said, then continued to make love to her pussy. The way she held him, he knew he'd have to let go.

As soon as Rienne's second orgasm wracked her body, she stopped sucking on James' cock. It was then that his cock finally erupted, spraying on her neck and boobs.

It took all of James' strength to help Rienne settle back on the bed before wrapping both of them with a blanket.

"Did I hurt you?"

Rienne shook her head, her eyes closed. "Wow!"

"Wow, indeed. How did you learn to do that?"

"You're really asking me that?"

"Yes."

Sighing, Rienne opened her eyes and looked at James. "By accident."

"What?"

"Saw a couple making love at the club."

"And you watched?"

"Couldn't help it."

"How many times?"

Rienne shrugged.

"You little brat. The first time maybe an accident, but you kept watching whenever you can, didn't you?"

"Wouldn't you?"

Laughing, James buried his face on Rienne's neck.

"James, I know what we did was just a preamble to something more heavenly."

Oh, God. There is *more. This is just a taste.* "Never heard anyone referred to a foreplay as preamble."

"There's more, yeah?"

James met Rienne's gaze. She may have had seen things, but her question showed how naïve and innocent she was. He wanted to laugh at Rienne's question, but decided not to. She looked embarrassed already. "Right." He rested his forehead on her chin. "Rienne, my love. We...we're not supposed to be doing this."

"Isn't it a little too late for second thoughts?"

James sighed. "You're a temptation."

"And you're beautiful."

"Rienne..."

"I know what you're doing, James. You're being a gentleman."

James couldn't help it. He laughed. Every part of her he wanted to kiss again and stake his claim, but Rienne had been a friend for years. A young woman who'd never had fun in her life. So pure and innocent despite what she claimed herself to be. She was new to this and only responding to what her body had been seeking for or what she'd seen at the club. She wasn't thinking right, but tomorrow when all of this was over, she'd wake up and regret everything.

"If I'm a gentleman, I wouldn't be in your bed right now." With remorse, James rolled off Rienne. He stared at the ceiling, trying not to look at the beautiful young woman beside him.

"You don't want me?"

Rienne's voice was so small that James couldn't help but turn to pull her for a hug. "You felt me, love. That means I want you. Too much. However, this shouldn't go any further. Remember what you said about giving up your virginity?" Rienne remained quiet so James continued with his explanations. "You said you'll give it to someone you want to marry someday. Right now, it's your body that's dictating your actions—not your heart."

"How'd you know that? Never mind. You're right. Thank you." Rienne then tried to turn her back on him.

James tightened her hold on her. "I don't want our friendship to end because of this."

"I think our friendship would even get stronger because we have each other. You're all I've got."

And I took advantage of your vulnerability. James felt so small. *Fuck.* "Rienne..." He wanted to tell her that his feelings for her went deeper than just a romp in bed, but he didn't think right now was the good idea to tell her that.

"Stay with me until I fall asleep?" Rienne whispered.

It would be hell for him because he wanted her still, but he nodded anyway. "Sure. Goodnight, love. We'll go swimming tomorrow."

"Okay."

James stayed in Rienne's bed, his arms around her, until the sign of the new day appeared through the blinds. He looked at Rienne. Damn, she was a live fish even when asleep. She tossed and turned, kicking the blanket all night. James had to cover them both repeatedly. It was only when he wrapped his legs and arms around her that she finally stopped moving, but had kept James awake all night. After planting a kiss on Rienne's shoulder, he left the bed. He promised that this would be the first and last time he'd be in Rienne's bed.

God help me.

Chapter Six

Rienne stared at the ceiling. Jiminy Cricket! What was she thinking last night? She practically seduced James into making love with her. Wait, they made love, right? Without the actual union?

Ugh! She couldn't imagine what he must be thinking about her right now. Crazy? Sluttish? Heck, he's probably not going to hang out with her again.

She asked him to kiss her. Whatever followed after was based on that. It was her fault. How could she face him now?

Jesus. I'm such a nincompoop?

What to do now? Well, she could stay in her room until her dad comes to get her or she could pack her bag now and escape through the window. She would leave a note of course. Yeah, she should do that...but where would she go? Back to the club? What would she tell her friends? *Oh, I seduced my friend into making love with me and we did the wicked sixty-nine, but we didn't really have sex. Just extreme foreplay.* No. Not cool. Okay, there were hotels around. She could use her cards. Maybe she should do that, but that wouldn't solve anything.

Shit, shit, shit!

James offered friendship. She offered him her body and then sat on his face. Oh, God! She sucked his cock, too.

Then, her stomach grumbled. Rienne looked at the clock. Nine thirty. Father and son must have had their breakfast already. Maybe James stayed in bed late or gone somewhere and Hal's cocooned in his office. Okay, she'd go out there, eat fast and then come back here in her room. On the other hand, she could just face James and tell him that he was right last night. It wasn't really her that acted like a slut, but the evil that had been hiding deep inside her, which, by the way, he released. She would also make it a point that it wasn't all her fault. He kissed her, which insinuated that he more than liked her. Yup. She'd tell him that. Her stomach made a sound so loud that she instinctively put her hand on top of it.

My, I'm hungry.

Surely, after what happened, things would be different from now on between her and James. He'd probably avoid her and never want to hang out anymore. Well, fine by her. *Shit happens, yeah.*

Deep inside, though, a part of her rejoiced. James touched her as a lover would, kissed her as if he'd wanted to do it for so long. He was burning hot and very hard. She felt his body quiver, and when he came, she felt marvelous. She'd heard from her friends that sometimes men couldn't reach their peak because women failed to please them. Rienne was sure James was pleased last night.

Both of them enjoyed what happened. So yeah. She shouldn't feel *that* bad about last night. But holy crap! His hands were everywhere. Touched her in places where no man ever touched her before. James also made sure that she was satisfied before stopping.

Ahhh!

All right. She'd be a big girl about this. Good heavens. Girls younger than her had been finger-fucked and lost their virginities in middle school. Making-out was no big deal anymore. Modern world, yeah?

Rienne got up and went to the bathroom to take a quick shower.

When finished she decided to wear her new *Victoria's Secret* underwear, faded jean skirt and a tank top that her friends from Sugar's gave her as an early birthday present. They teased her that she should show off more of her skin, especially her long legs whenever she could. They went on to say that wearing sexy clothes wasn't all about attracting men, but to make you feel good, confident, sexy, and beautiful—and they were right. She wished wearing different clothes could solve every problem in the world. Life would've been easier that way.

She thought about what James had said yesterday about stopping from hiding. He was right. Why punish herself from spending life indoors and missing life when she'd never done anything to those people who wanted to hang her dad. She felt bad for them, yes, but it was time to destroy the wall her dad had built around her for her protection. Dad would understand her decision. As long as they communicate using her rabbit, his location would stay unknown.

After tying her hair in a bun, Rienne checked herself in the mirror. Faint dark colors under her eyes made her look tired. Her pronounced cheekbones made her nose seem even thinner. Well, she couldn't do anything about her physical appearance. She could, however change her tank top. She pulled it up to hide her upper chest, but it didn't work. Times like this, she wished her breasts weren't so big. She couldn't wear tops with buttons because the gap would open to show her bra. At least her butt wasn't so big. Running her fingers on the waistband of her shorts, she thought the Huntingtons wouldn't care about what she wore and what she looked like. They never did in the past, so why would they mind now.

Fifteen minutes later, she stood in the middle of a neat kitchen. No one was around, which was good. She stared at the cupboards. The one on the left held all kinds of cereals. From what she recalled, the Huntingtons liked to eat those in the morning. Except on weekends. Hal would cook bacon and pancakes or waffles. Oh, yeah. She loved Hal's pancakes loaded with chocolate chips and bananas. His bacon was always perfect—not too crispy and not too soft.

Thinking about food made her stomach grumble again.

"Are you just going to stand there and stare at the cupboards?"

Rienne jumped. She turned around and found herself facing James. "Why in the world would you do that?"

"What?"

"Scare me like that."

"I didn't. I've been standing here watching you, but you didn't move so I thought to say something."

He stood with hands on his hips and legs apart. If she were to make a guess, she'd say James just showered and skipped combing his hair. Oh, and where in the world did he find those jeans that hung on his hips so low she could almost see his pubic bone. That pair must be illegal in the state of Washington. Wow, he was sexy. Thoughts of what happened last night came back in a hurry. Rienne tried to block them before she turned into a ball of fire. "Well, you should make your presence known right away."

"Noted. So, you hungry? I hope so 'cause I am."

Like a cat stalking its prey, James walked toward her. Rienne swallowed. Lord, his swagger alone was enough to make her want to take off her clothes and feel his body all over again. "You haven't eaten?"

James replied with a grin.

Oh, sweet apples. She had a feeling he was thinking about a different kind of eating right now. One that involves their body parts. "Knowing you, you must be starving to death."

"Been waiting for you to come down. What do you want for breakfast?"

"You're cooking?"

"Sure. Let me guess. Pancakes with chocolate chips and bananas?"

Well, this is a good way to start our morning. It seemed both of them didn't want to talk about what happened last night. Boy, she was glad. She would probably melt on the floor from shame. Maybe he realized he'd acted like a horny monkey at the zoo and now wished he could take everything back. If that were the case, she would safely tuck their sweet memories of yesterday away in the deepest pocket of her heart. She wouldn't mention it ever unless he started talking about it. Then, she'd explain why she acted the way she did. Rienne sighed.

"Is that sigh, a yes?" He stood in front of Rienne. Using his forefinger, he traced her nose.

Their bodies were so close, Rienne could smell his shampoo. "Yes," she replied.

"How about we add bacon."

"Sounds lovely."

"I think you can afford to gain more weight."

For what seemed to be forever, they just stood there staring at one another. They didn't have to say a word. Rienne wondered if he was remembering her sitting on him or his cock in her mouth. How could anyone forget something like that anyway?

James gave her a smile that she interpreted as *I know what you're thinking* before moving away from her to open the freezer. Rienne's shoulders sagged. Blimey, she didn't realize she was so tense. If her heart would bounce around her chest like this all the time, she'd be dead from a heart attack within a week.

She literally had just arrived here, but friction started flying around the moment they saw each other. Judging by the way James had looked at her, they'd be kissing again before the day was over. What in the world was she going to do about that? James' laughter yanked Rienne out of her deep thoughts.

"What's funny?"

"You. What's up with the frown? Thinking about how to solve the world's problems?"

No. Just my heart problem. "Don't we all think about world peace from time to time?"

"Uh-huh. While contemplating food, you're also thinking about the world. I get that."

"Oh, stop it, James Hungtington."

"What?" James laughed. "All right. I'll make breakfast. You have to help, though."

"That I can do. At the club, I helped in the kitchen."

"Really?"

"Uh-huh. I liked it. Made the days go by faster when you're busy."

"True. I'll tell Dad. I'm sure he'll welcome all help that he can get around here. So, I'll start with the bacon. It takes longer to cook these babies than the pancakes."

James had the bacon thawed out in the microwave. While preheating the griddle, he set the bowls, whisk, and pancake mix on the counter. "You can work on the pancake when the bacon is almost done."

"Okie dokie, Chef." Rienne saluted James. Instead of using the bar stool, she moved the bowl to make room for her, then sat on the counter.

With a smile, James shook his head. "I suppose kitchen counters make good chairs."

Rienne shrugged. "Dad said the first day he brought me home from the hospital, he placed my baby carrier on the kitchen counter so he could watch me. Since then, he would put me on the same spot everyday. It became a habit."

"Some habits are just hard to die, huh."

"I believe so. Where is your dad?"

James stood in front of Rienne, then reached for the bananas behind her. "Meeting in Olympia." He placed the bananas on the cutting board.

"The Capitol?"

"Yeah. He's still advocating for a free housing for homeless people. He'll be home late tonight. So, it's just going to be you and me today."

Maybe James was just stating a fact, but to Rienne, his words had a totally different meaning. Thoughts of being alone with James again stoked the growing fire inside her. Heat flamed Rienne's cheeks, betraying her emotions. Instead of moving away from him though, she succumbed to the overwhelming need to be close to him. She combed back his hair with her fingers. James, to her surprise turned his head to kiss her arm. The simple touch flared something deep inside her. It was so intense that she could hardly breathe. She knew what would happen next if he kissed her again. And it made her wanton.

"You smell nice." With James' eyes on Rienne, he placed his hands at the back of her knees, and spread them wide real slow.

"James…what are you doing?"

James smiled. "Making room."

"For what?"

"What do you think?"

Her cheeks grew warm at the thought that maybe he wanted a repeat of last night. "I…I don't know. You…want to open…uhm…oh, man."

James laughed. "Yes, I want to open the drawer here so I could get the spatula. Why do you think I moved your legs?"

"So you could open the drawer," she lied, but laughed with him anyway.

"You look so beautiful in the morning." James traced the shape of her eyebrows. "Did you sleep well?"

"I did. You?"

"No. Do you know why?" James stepped in between Rienne's legs, bringing them even closer together, then placed his hands on her hips.

"I don't." She didn't want to guess, but she was dying to hear what he had to say.

"I couldn't stop thinking about you, sleeping next door to me. *You kept me awake all night wondering if I should go back to your room or* tie myself to bed. I don't know. It's crazy."

The tenderness of James' gaze made it difficult for Rienne to think, and their closeness created feelings that had nothing to do with reason. James said the right thing. This was crazy, but why did it feel so blissfully right?

"I don't know what came over me last night. I lost my good sense."

"It's not your fault. I should have taken control of the situation. Rienne, love. You're here because Roy trusted us—and he is right. We *can* be trusted. But what happened last night—"

"I wanted for it to happen, James."

"Me, too."

Rienne sighed, glad to hear his admission.

"But, love. I don't think I can trust myself to stay away from you. You're just too irresistible for me and I've been…" James raked his hair with his fingers.

Cupping his face with her hands, Rienne stared at James "Neither can I."

As if given a reprieve, James sighed, then pulled her against him. "Roy will kill me for this."

"What he doesn't know won't hurt him."

"Still."

"I'm not a child."

James tightened his hold on her. "Believe me, I know, and I love the woman in you."

Rienne wrapped her arms around James. As soon as their bodies touched, her whole being began to sing. "You have no idea what your words do to me."

James nibbled on her jaw. "Baby, I'm even hotter now than last night. If I put my mouth on you, I might not be able to stop. Not this time. I want you that badly."

Oh, Rienne knew he wanted her badly. His hard-on pressing against his jeans proved it. She wanted to touch him again. This time though, the need between her legs was stronger. When James made love with her with his mouth last night, the world of temptation and sensuality opened for Rienne. A sweet ache that quickly became familiar with her curled inside her. *Lust.*

This had been what lovers couldn't resist—temptation, fire, thrill, and pleasure so addictive you look for it once you've had the taste. She wanted another to feed her feelings so strong and primal, it was clawing its way out.

She'd never done the actual intercourse, but after last night, she didn't consider herself a virgin anymore. In fact, she'd seen enough at the club to know what gives a woman pleasure and how to pleasure a man.

Rienne closed her eyes as sensations of James' teeth scraping the surface of her skin travelled from her neck down to her pussy.

"Soft…smelled wonderful. I could kiss you all night, baby. Would you like that?"

"Yes."

James lifted Rienne's top over her head leaving her in her bra and skirt. However, it took only a few seconds before he had her totally naked. James pushed up her breast then clamped his mouth on her nipple. Yum! She loved it when he sucked her like that. It filled her with inner excitement that built up like a bonfire. Rienne cupped James' face as she watched him take pleasure on licking and sucking her nipples. He took his time kissing her breasts, rousing, melting sweetness that dripped down her pussy. Then, James wrapped his arms around her. Slowly, he lowered her down on the counter.

"Fucking beautiful." James lifted her skirt then pulled her panties off her. "Spread your legs, love. Let me see you."

Like last night, Rienne felt ashamed being so open for James, but as soon as he ran his fingers on her lips, her inhibitions deserted her. God, she loved this man. "James, I love this. I love you." Too late. She already blurted the words. She waited for James to stop, but he just looked at her with his passion-coated eyes.

"I love you, too," he replied.

James kissed her. This time it was as tender and cool as the summer breeze. He lingered on each lip as if savoring each moment. Unlike their first kisses, this time there was a dreamy feel to their kissing. Rienne felt like crying.

"Say it again."

"I love you, Rienne."

"Since when?"

"Since I've met you. I am just now recognizing that what I felt before was love and not just infatuation."

Rienne felt her tears roll down the side of her face. "I've loved you forever."

"Ah, baby." James peppered her face with wet and loud kisses. He moved down slowly and stopped to pay homage to her breasts before continuing down to inhale her pussy mound. "Mine," he whispered.

Breathing hard, she looked down at James. "Yours," Rienne replied.

"What do you want, love?"

"You. I want *you*."

James smiled. "I'm yours." He reached to flatten his hand on her chest. "You're breathing hard, your nipples like pebbles. I'm sure if I touch your pussy, you're hot and wet. You want me that much, right?"

"Yes."

"I love hearing you say that."

James planted a kiss on her thigh before giving Rienne what she'd been waiting for. He licked her pussy repeatedly, moaning as he did.

"Ahh. So good. Can't get enough of you, love." Using his two fingers, he spread Rienne open, then clamped his mouth on her clit.

"James!"

"Hmm. Yeah, move your ass like that. Fuck my mouth."

The erotic sound that James made heated Rienne's already hot body. She loved hearing him moan as if she was the best tasting morsel he'd ever tasted. Rienne cupped her breast and closed her eyes. She took in all the pleasure James' mouth was giving her—until she felt her orgasm peaking. She opened her eyes, then and looked at James. She licked her lips at the sight of him eating her pussy.

"James, I'm coming. Don't stop. Don't. Please, baby. Ohh!" Then, it happened. Her orgasm took her so high, she thought she'd float forever.

Rienne was still breathing hard and her thighs quivering when a loud ear-piercing sound startled them. It was the smoke detector going off.

James and Rienne stopped moving, both frozen, unsure what was happening. When it finally dawned on them what exactly was happening, James looked at Rienne.

"Ceiling is covered in smoke, James!" She pushed his shoulders.

"Shit. The griddle!" James bodily lifted Rienne off the counter, then helped her find her footing. "Open the slider," he instructed while unplugging the cord off the wall. He picked up the toast griddle then placed it into the sink. When he turned on the water, more smoke formed.

Rienne picked up her top, quickly put it on, then adjusted her skirt. She didn't know where her panties went. Later, she'd look. With the smell of burnt grease heavy in the air, she opened the slider. Man, how in the world did they not notice something burning? What if the house caught on fire? What would they tell Hal and the firefighters? *Oh, sorry. We were making out on the kitchen counter and we forgot about the griddle!* The thought was so hilarious, she began laughing.

"You think this is funny, eh?"

"Don't you?"

James gave her his heart-melting smile. "Kinda."

Rienne watched James. He stood on a chair fanning the smoke alarm with a dishtowel. Lordy, he looked so delicious without his shirt on and wearing only his unbuttoned jeans. Rienne took her fill. Oh, yeah. She wanted to crawl on top of his body, glide over her palm on his skin, feel his flat stomach contract, and lick his nipple. Her gaze went lower where the beginning of his pubic hair showed. What if she walked over to where he stood, pulled his pants down, then put him in her mouth? She bet he would love it, especially when she cupped his balls, and ran her tongue along the length of his cock before putting the tip inside her mouth to suck him. Yeah, he'd pump his hips slowly to fuck her mouth.

I love you, Rienne. Rienne repeated the words in her mind. This man whom she dreamt of for years loved her back. *Holy smokes*, she wanted to squeal.

"I don't like that grin."

Rienne looked at James. "What?"

"You're grinning and I want to know why."

"Nothing. Just thinking about something."

As soon as the alarm stopped making noise, James stepped off the stool he was standing on. "And that's why I'm worried. You were looking at my—" James looked down. "My pants." He walked toward Rienne like a predator zooming in on his prey. "Tell me."

"Tell you what?"

"What made you grin."

Rienne looked behind her. "If I don't?"

"You'll be punished."

"Yeah, but only if you catch me." She ran. Screaming.

Chapter Seven

James laughed while he tried to lunge for Rienne when she ran past the kitchen counter. Man, she was fast. He followed her, but she was gone. The soft click of the door upstairs, however, gave away her location. Instead of following her right away, he made coffee and toasts. Just to make sure, he also poured orange juice in a glass, then placed everything onto the tray.

When he saw Rienne standing in the kitchen, wearing a short skirt and a tank top, he thought about wrapping his arms around her and kissing her hard. He'd been thinking about doing it all night and even went as far as fucking her from behind. He wanted an absolute possession of her. Twice now, he'd nearly taken her virginity. If he touched her for the third time, he would fucking explode if he didn't claim her.

Unlike any other women he'd dated, Rienne stayed in his mind since the beginning. He never stopped wondering about her when she was gone. Now, he found out that she loved him. That revelation pumped his heart like an air balloon.

Love. Just a four letter word, but could create havoc, bring nations together, and make the weak stronger. When it blooms, it lasts and wouldn't easily die. His love for Rienne seeded long time ago. Now, it had sprouted, making him feel like a teenager again.

James grinned. Since there weren't any flowers in the house, he plucked a few leaves from the green houseplant in the kitchen, then scattered it on the tray. Satisfied, he picked up the tray and headed for the upstairs.

He knew exactly which room Rienne was hiding....his father's study. It had been Rienne's favorite room in this house.

When he reached the study, he opened the door, making sure he wouldn't hit Rienne if she were hiding behind it. Inside, he placed the tray on the table.

"All right, Maldita. Come out, come out, wherever you are. Breakfast is ready. Not bacon or pancakes, but mouth-watering toasts loaded with melting peanut butter, jam and jelly, butter, and marmalade. You take your pick." He leaned against the table and waited. He almost laughed when he heard a soft sigh. After a few seconds, he took a toast with peanut butter and started eating. "Hmm...delicious. I suppose I could eat all these and drink the coffee, too."

Rienne came out from behind the couch. "You're no fun."

He laughed, then. She was so adorable with her deep frown and pursed lips. Also, he knew that she wasn't wearing panties because he tucked them in his pocket. *Oh, boy.* "Come have breakfast and we'll have fun later."

Rienne shrugged. "I'm hungry anyway." She walked toward James with her eyes on the plate. "Glad we didn't burn the house down."

"Nah." He handed her the cup of coffee and a toast with marmalade. Last time Rienne had stayed with them, he caught her snacking on crackers and marmalade in this same room.

"Thank you." She sat on the table, then started eating her toast. "I've always liked this room. Cozy. Especially when it's raining. I used to read here, remember?"

"I do. That's why I knew where to find you. So, did you read Dad's *Playboy* magazine hidden in his drawer?"

"You bet. I even saw *Hustler, Heavy Metal, Girls Gone Wild, Penthouse, American Curves* and something else."

"What the hell." James stood in front of Rienne, then placed his hands on her sides, trapping her. "Should I even ask where you found those dirty mags? From the club, I bet."

A mischievous look came into her eyes. "They were just lying around."

"My God. You really are not square."

Rienne narrowed her eyes then leaned so close to him that James could almost see the beautiful brown chips on his eyes. "Punjabi, you are the only one that thinks that."

James stared. He knew she had beautiful eyes, but this close and in a bright room, he could see they showed intelligence and independence of spirit. They made James want to dive into their depths and feel her soul. Holy hell. This young woman would be the death of him. If not, he'd walk with a fucking hard-on morning, noon and night. *And what am I going to do about that?*

"What was that frown about?" Rienne smoothed his brow.

"You."

"What did I do?"

"Crawled under my skin." He then kissed her. She tasted of marmalade and toast. "I don't think I can face another day without you." He snaked his arms inside her top, then hugged her tight.

"Me, too. I dream of you, you know. All the time."

"Love, I dream of you, too, but I don't think mine is the same as yours." James grinned.

"I think I have an idea."

"I love you, Rienne."

"Love you more."

"Wrap your legs around me." As soon as Rienne obliged, he lifted her up, then walked toward the big couch. Even before her back hit the soft material of the brown furniture, his cock was already fully erect. This time, he didn't think he could stop himself from staking his claim.

It didn't take long before both of them were naked. James had to fight the overwhelming need to shove his dick deep inside her. Instead, he took his time, stimulating and exploring her body with his touch and kisses. With her legs spread apart, he rubbed the length of his cock on Rienne's wet folds. Her pussy was hot and soft. She felt delicious beneath him, but not enough. James suckled Rienne's taut nipples, loving the feel of them at the roof his mouth. He could do this all day. Except he'd be a eunuch if he didn't release his orgasm. On fire, he made his way down Rienne's body. She squired and gripped his hair.

"James…"

James inhaled the sweet scent of her skin. "Baby, you're beautiful."

"You, too."

He licked both her crotch, then looked at her glistening pussy. "Ah, love. You're fucking sweet." James watched his middle finger go inside her tight passage. Slowly, he finger-fucked her, purposely avoiding her clit.

"James, please. I can't wait."

"Neither can I," he replied, then sucked her clit hard. He didn't stop until Rienne's thighs tightened and chanted his name. Quickly, he crawled up again. "Look at me, Rienne."

Rienne met his gaze. She looked thoroughly kissed and breathing hard. "Yes."

"You're mine." He aimed his dick on her juice-covered entry then slowly penetrated her. "Oh, fuck."

"Ohhh…"

He felt her hymen, but he surged and broke it in a hurry. Rienne's nails dug on his back. "Am I hurting you?"

"No."

That was all he needed to hear. He made love with Rienne like a man who'd never seen a woman in years. Right there on the couch, he pumped his hips slow and hard. He wrapped his arms on Rienne's narrow hips, keeping her in position, then buried his cock in her, repeatedly. He watched Rienne. Her breasts bounced with each thrust that he gave her. Feeling like a wild man, he couldn't control himself now even if he wanted to.

"Rienne, I love you. I love you." He then released his seed.

Spent, James lay beside Rienne and waited for their hearts turn its beat to normal.

"So that's how you lose your virginity. Nothing to it, yeah?"

James laughed.

Chapter Eight

As soon as Rienne got off the truck, she felt transported to an untouched land. It had a secret feel to it and made her want to walk barefoot like a fairy in the forest. The narrow footpath lent access to the lake and the four-car parking lot told her very few people knew about the place. She bet they could swim on the lake naked and no one would even see them. It was early in the afternoon and the sun was high, but the whole atmosphere made one think it was early in the morning. The trees and foliage around looked wet with dew, but the weather was cool.

According to the information board, the Duwamish tribe once called the lake, Calmed *Down A Little*, because it had been a refuge during the slave raids. Rienne liked that. The name suited her situation. After all the moving and hiding, she needed a place like this. A refuge.

James took their small red cooler, blanket, and a bag with their suits in it from the back of his truck. "Ready to see the lake?"

"Yeah. This place is beautiful."

"Glad you like it."

"Do you come here a lot?"

"Been here many times."

"Alone?"

"Most of the time."

Rienne took the bag from James then they started walking on the footpath. Away from manmade noises, the surrounding trees and critters provided the sound around them. She loved it.

When they reached the end of the path, James pointed at a grassy spot where the sun was shining. It was perfect for a picnic. They could actually sit anywhere because no one was around. It was amazing.

Sheltered from the wind, the lake was still giving it a glassy quality that one might think it was solid. She saw on the sign that there was a park nearby. They allowed dogs that were off-leash, which was neat since more and more parks started banning pets. Someday, she'd get a dog—a golden retriever maybe. She'd call him *Brandy* or *Spice*. Sighing, Rienne felt glad James had picked Haller Lake.

James spread the blanket then placed their bag and cooler on top. "Are you hungry?"

"We just ate half hour ago."

"I know, but I thought to ask." James took her hand in his then pulled her close to him. "How are you?"

"I'm good." Damn, she hoped he wasn't inquiring about her sore legs and other parts that she didn't want to think about right now. "You?"

"Happy. I feel like calling all of my friends and tell them about you. I wanted to shout and say *Rienne is back and she's mine. My heart is smiling.* There. That's how I feel."

"Dear oh dear. When was the last time you got laid?"

James laughed. "You're such a brat. I'm happy, okay?"

"Me, too."

They'd talked about silly things like they'd buy the whole lake and turn it into Garden of Eden. One of the many things she loved about James was his sense of humor. He could make up stories in a hurry. A quality that women often found so attractive. Rienne remembered something that James had said. *No girlfriend.*

"James, I don't want to get in a way of your plans."

"What do you mean?"

"You told me about your dreams. Of travelling around the world, becoming a maritime or airline captain and no girlfriend. I don't want you to change anything on the account of me." If this was just a summer love and short lived, that was fine with her. She would take everything with her when she leaves. Yes, James loved her, but they were both young and he might find another, but he would occupy a spot in her heart for the rest of her life.

"Rienne, you are a part of my dream that now came true. The rest will come later. If it doesn't happen, that's fine. As long as I have you."

"You're not just saying that."

"No. I love you, Maldita."

"You sure you're not just swept away?"

"No, baby. I know what I feel and it's not fleeting. It's been many years, Maldita, since I fell for you. This is forever."

"Forever is a long time, Punjabi."

"I know. We are forever as long as we make it to be."

"I love you."

James stared while cupping her cheek with his hand. He gave Rienne a wet kiss that promised of something more. "Now, we should try the water while the sun is high. There is a shallow part and then a drop."

"Okay."

"Let's go swim."

Since she wore her two-piece underneath her shirt and skirt, she didn't have to go to the bathroom to change. James was already ankle deep in water when she joined him. He gave her an appreciative look then held out his hand. She took it. Together they slowly walked toward the deeper part of the water.

"It's freezing!" She let go of James' hand and tried to run back to the shore, but James caught her.

"Didn't I warn you?"

"Let go!"

"Don't be a chicken. You know, if you don't do this, you'll regret it."

"But the water is too cold, James."

"You'll feel better once you're wet."

"Yeah, right. Just put me down."

"No."

Rienne wrapped her legs around James' waist, trying her might not to touch the water, but James kept on walking until her butt submerged into the cold water. "James!" She couldn't help it. She laughed. "I hate you, Punjabi."

"You like me, Maldita. Your blood on the sheets proved it." He kissed her lips, then both of them went underneath the water.

James released Rienne. Both of them swam and then took a breath.

"You had to mention the sheets, huh?" Rienne's embarrassment helped ward off the chill. Besides, the sting of cold water went away after a few minutes. Rienne splashed water on James who retaliated by squirting water using his hands. He did it repeatedly and fast where Rienne decided to dive under water.

She swam fast towards James, then tried to pull his swim trunks down. Unfortunately, the string was tied, so it wouldn't go down past his pubic bone. Disappointed, Rienne took a breath.

"Two can play pull the *pants down* game." James swam closer to Rienne.

She prided herself for being a good swimmer and tried to show it. Laughing, Rienne did a backstroke in a hurry, getting away from James, but James was even faster. He pulled her feet.

She spattered. "I give up."

James didn't let go of her. Instead, he swung her back and forth above water. "Oh, really?"

"I was just kidding!"

Finally, James pulled her close so she could straddle him. "Maldita, what am I going to do with you."

"You can start by kissing me."

***

Santiago lowered his binoculars then leaned his forehead on the tree where he was hiding. He knew this would happen. And in such a short time, too. God damn it. What would he tell Roy now? He learned to like Rienne and he wanted her to be happy, but if Roy hears about this, he would definitely take Rienne away from the Huntingtons.

He'd never seen Rienne like this. Playful, laughing, free. This had been what he wanted to see. Maybe not what Roy wanted for his daughter, but fucking tough luck, eh? The girl was not a girl anymore. She needed to spread her wings, experience life, and feel what it was like to fall in love.

Santiago listened to the sound of Rienne shrieking and James' booming laughter. He smiled. Roy had been right to trust James—and he trusted the boy, too. Over the years, he got to know the young man. James was every mother's dream boy for her daughter. However, to a father like Roy...*Fuck!* The man would probably cut James' balls, then feed it to him. Scary thought. Unfortunately, a father wouldn't want to hear that someone had been touching his daughter. Didn't matter if said daughter would be twenty-one soon.

Santiago didn't have a choice here. Right around this time, Roy was probably pacing already, waiting for his phone to ring. One more glance at Rienne and James, he fished his phone from his front pocket, then dialed Roy's number.

"Santiago. You were supposed to call three minutes ago," Roy snarled.

Santiago rolled his eyes. Since he started working for Roy, he'd never miss a day without reporting about Rienne. You'd think the man would trust him not to fail now, but he understood Roy's situation. Rienne was all he'd had left in the world. He wanted to protect her. At all cost.

"Sorry," he began.

"So? How's my girl? Did you see anything unusual again? Come on, man. Don't make me ask questions."

Well, you didn't give me a chance, dude. "She's doing good." He looked toward where Rienne and James lay on the shore. He couldn't really see them without the binoculars, but he could tell they were still intimate. Then, he heard Rienne laugh again. Right then, he'd made a decision. "She's doing good," he repeated. "James and Rienne went to the store and bought ice cream. She picked *Ben and Jerry's*. She also bought a lot of green apples."

Roy sighed. "Just like her mother."

Even through the phone, Santiago could sense a smile from Roy's voice. Damn. Too bad Rienne's mother died during childbirth. Raising a child alone was one hell of a job for a father who had to watch his daughter through the eyes of a hired investigator.

He felt so fucking badly about lying, but on the other hand, he'd made the man happy. He'd let Roy bask on the thought that Rienne was having fun. Later, he'd tell him. Jesus, he just hoped that no other reporter would snap their pictures and beat him to the task of telling Roy, otherwise he wouldn't live to see the sun again.

Chapter Nine

Dinner consisted of broiled steaks, mashed potatoes, green peas, and sautéed green beans. Dad loved to cook even before Mom had passed away. It was just one of the many things he enjoyed doing. James was glad for that because he preferred to do the clean up, not the preparation. They sat at the kitchen nook, being lazy from hours of swimming and basking in the sun enjoying the marvelous food, but James' mind kept going back to the events of the day. What happened between him and Rienne was inevitable. Just being near each other was enough to start a fire. On top of that, they both loved each other. He couldn't believe it. So it was true what they say that love would appear in front of you when you least expect it. She'd never been kissed, and no man had ever touched her before, but she responded to his touch without inhibitions. They shared each other's bodies wholeheartedly, passionately. He hoped that when the time came to tell Roy everything that he would understand.

James watched Rienne. Her eyes were half-mast, but still pretending to be listening to his dad talk away about his meeting in Olympia, oblivious to what was going on between James and Rienne.

His dad trusted James to make Rienne's stay an easy one, but little that Hal know that James had been infatuated with Rienne since they were younger. An infatuation that James couldn't control and now turned into a full-blown obsession. He loved Rienne, and he would move mountains to keep her.

What if she woke up one morning and said she would have to leave for some parts of the world where he couldn't find her, not hear her laughter, or meet her gaze? Ever? Would he be able to move on and just forget? A sharp pain that made James wince, answered his question. He couldn't imagine waking up the next day and finding Rienne gone. He loved his Maldita. Yes, he loved her. So fucking what if they'd only been intimate for a few days. Who said that love only happened when long courtship was involved. Love blooms in a heartbeat with just a glance, or first meeting. There had been no rule when a person should fall in love. He didn't want to wake up again, not knowing where she was. If Roy got whiff of their relationship, he would take responsibilities.

James winked at Rienne who caught him staring. Her nose, cheeks, and shoulders were red due to the sun. They had fun. More so, *he* had fun seeing Rienne shed her cloak. Tomorrow, he'd take her to work. Show her around, introduce her to his friends, and if she was up to it, they'd fly over the San Juan Islands.

"...I think the bill might pass." Hal was saying, referring to the draft of his proposed law on free housing for the homeless that he had presented to the House of Representatives. "Anyway, how are you two doing? How did you spend your day?"

James met Rienne's gaze. As they stared at each other, her cheeks turned a darker shade of red. Asking questions and sharing the highlight of their day had been a part of their dinner together. He forgot to tell Rienne that. "We took the truck for a spin, then went out to Haller Lake."

"Ah, that explained the sunburn. You should've brought sunscreen with you. The sun may not be too hot, but it could damage your skin. A lot of people don't understand that concept."

"Next time we'll go to the lake prepared, Dad."

"Good. I don't want Roy to come back here and find Rienne looking like a dried up prune from sun exposure."

James laughed when Rienne made a face.

"Did you enjoy the lake, Rienne?"

"Yes. Cold, but the sun was high enough to…keep us warm," Rienne replied.

"Oh good. Just make sure you have your wrap with you when you go out again. It gets really cold in the afternoon."

"Wrap?" Rienne asked.

"Dad, I don't think anyone uses the word wrap anymore. Sweater or jacket or a coat is a common term now."

"Well, something to keep you warm. Seattleites are out and about today, wearing their sunglasses like vampires who hadn't seen the sun in ages. Were there lots of people swimming?"

James grinned at Rienne. She kicked him from under the table. He caught her foot and didn't let go. Ignoring Rienne's scowl, he put her foot on his lap, then rubbed her heel. "A few," he lied.

"That's good. You don't want it to be too crowded. There are a lot of good places to swim. Try Dashpoint Beach in Federal Way, Fremont Rope Swing in Phinney, and Greenlake."

"Greenlake is not clean anymore, Dad. Too many ducks."

"Oh, right. Still, it's a good place to go for a walk."

"Rienne likes to swim. I would like to take her back to Haller Lake?"

Rienne raised a brow at James. "I'd love to do that, provided that we're going to swim and not just stare at the water."

He knew what she was talking about. After they made love at the grassy bank of Haller Lake earlier, James joked that he liked swimming on the shore better than swimming in the water. Thinking about what they did made his blood quickly rush down to his cock. He shifted from his position to ease his discomfort. "There's more to swimming than just waving your arms and kicking your legs, Rienne."

"I believe I learned that already, James."

"And you don't mind doing it again?"

Rienne stared at James. "It depends."

"On what?"

"Whom I'm doing it with," Rienne replied with a straight face.

"Ah, because you love him, is that it?" James grinned.

"Yes. Even though he's a knucklehead sometimes."

James' heart constricted. He had thought about what Rienne said about giving up her virginity. It would be with the man whom she loved and wanted to marry. He'd been the one she said who had kept her awake, his name she wrote on her notebook? Wish he could just get up from his chair and kiss her.

James was aware that his dad was watching them, most likely wondering what the hell they we're talking about, but right that moment, he didn't care. He kept his eyes on Rienne. Above the rim of her glass, she raised a brow in a challenge. *What a brat.*

Hal cleared his throat. "So, James. What happened to the griddle?"

Rienne sputtered the water she was drinking.

"You okay, Rienne?" Hal asked.

"I'm okay."

Hal nodded. "James, I saw the griddle in the sink and there was a smell of something burnt in the kitchen. You didn't try to burn the house, did you?"

"No, Dad. Just tried to cook pancakes and bacon."

"And you forgot?"

"Got distracted, Dad."

"By what?"

"The spatula," Rienne answered for James—but that was all she said.

Hal leaned toward Rienne as if trying to listen to what she would say next, but she just went back to eating her food. Hal looked at James, then at Rienne again. He looked confused, but his eyes told James that his brain was whirring past and without a doubt beginning to suspect something was afoot. Hal lowered his fork, then placed his elbows on the table while he steepled his hands. An action that James had seen many times whenever his dad wasn't satisfied with an answer.

"How did that spatula distract you, James?"

"I couldn't find it, Dad."

"You searched for the spatula while the griddle was burning."

"The smoke alarm went off," Rienne said, laughing.

"What were you doing the whole time James was looking for the spatula, Rienne?"

"Watching James."

"It took so long to find the spatula that the griddle started to burn until the smoke alarm went off. Both of you didn't even notice it until the smoke alarm went off. Did I sum it up correctly?" Hal asked.

"Yup."

"Yes."

James and Rienne said simultaneously.

Hal nodded. "I'm not going to hear the truth, am I?"

"Nope," James replied, almost laughing.

"Fine. Just make sure next time you go looking for the spatula, make sure you don't burn the house down."

"Promise, Dad."

"So, you two went out swimming and took the truck for a spin."

"That's right." James replied.

"Were you followed? Or anybody try to take your picture, Rienne?"

"I didn't see anyone."

"Good. We don't want her ending up on the news."

"Hal, I'm done hiding. I'll go in and out of the house whenever I want. The hell with the Feds watching me, or some reporters dying to write something on their newspaper. I have nothing to hide from them or anyone. I understand why Dad wanted to protect me, especially when I was young, but I'm not a child anymore. Waiting for my dad to clear his name could mean years. I don't want to waste *my* years hiding just to avoid the media, Feds, and private investigators. From now on, I'll go out whenever I want. Shop, swim, stroll, and go to the movies. I'll do all those things. Let everyone see me. I'm not living a life of a fugitive because I am not one."

"I totally understand, Rienne. Glad you told me about your plan. But, are you sure you're ready to face the people screaming at your face, blaming you why their kids couldn't be in the hospital because everything they own was stolen by your dad, or some seventy year old man working at a *Seven Eleven* because he lost his retirement when your dad embezzled the companies money?"

"But—"

"I know, Rienne. You're dad is innocent. I believe him, but you cannot deny the fact that he was involved in that company. In the eyes of some, Roy is guilty. Moreover, because you are his daughter, they see you as guilty as well. It's a stupid thing, right, but because of the stupidity in that logic, your life could be in danger. There are many people out there holding a gun with a scope, dying to point the crosshair on your dad and you. That's why Roy is trying so hard to hide you. Oh, another thing. He wouldn't be able to concentrate knowing you're out there—a target. Rienne, Roy is trying to clear his name because of you. You are his priority."

"I understand all that. But could we at least try my plan?"

"I have to talk to Roy about this. He needs to know."

"Oh, no. Please. I want to tell him myself about my decision."

"Rienne, my head will be on the chopping block if he heard you've been out and about."

"Dad, let's cross the bridge when we get there. Try not to buy trouble for now," James interjected. "Let's just wait and see what he'll say and we'll go from there."

"Hal, I can explain everything to my dad." Rienne looked at James. "You've been very nice to me and I'm thankful. All I ask is to let me take a chance."

Hal laced his fingers together while he stared at Rienne with a deep frown. "Rienne, I would never forgive myself if something happened to you. Roy will kill me over and over."

"Dad, I'll take full responsibility. I'm here. Rienne will be safe."

Hal pointed his finger at James. "Do you have anything to do with this? Did you put her up—"

"Hal, this is my decision. James agreed with me."

"And there is nothing I can do to persuade you otherwise."

"No."

With a long sigh, Hal nodded again. "A week, Rienne. That's it. If anything, any sign of those pesky reporters and agents giving you trouble, we're calling Roy."

"Deal."

For a while, they ate in silence.

"Good dinner, Dad," James finally said when he finished his mashed potatoes.

"Yeah. Thanks for the dinner, Hal.

"My pleasure. Let me know, Rienne, if you want something for tomorrow's dinner and I'll try to prepare it."

"Sounds good. Thank you." Rienne smiled.

"All right. Tomorrow, I'll sit at the council meeting. So you two are going to be alone again." Hal picked up his water glass then stood up. "Please don't burn down the house with you in it."

James squeezed Rienne's foot gently. Grinning, he shook her head at her. His dick throbbed. Sweet.

Chapter Ten

Cleaning up after dinner was fun, but it took twice as long than usual because Rienne insisted on helping. However, she was so inept in the kitchen that she just got in James' way. She didn't know how to use the dishwasher and what to do with the pots and pan. When she saw the broiling pan, she held it like a dirty bedpan, made a face, and said, *yew*!

It would've had taken them all night to finish the cleaning up if he didn't grab Rienne by the waist, lifted her, then let her sit her on the counter. She was glad, actually, but shyly admitted that she had little experience in the kitchen. James remembered her telling him that she helped at the club. Whatever she learned there must have been very basic and didn't involve washing the dishes.

Since his dad was already upstairs, James gave her a kiss to cheer her up. He only meant to give her a quick smooch, but she opened her mouth and met him halfway. James couldn't resist lengthening the kiss. He'd wanted to taste her during dinner anyway. The way their lips touched, ignited like a powder keg. He devoured her mouth, sucking her tongue the way he did to her nipples when they were at the lake. Her sigh urged him to do more. He snaked his hand inside her top and cupped her breast. Rienne arched her back. James found out that she loved it when he sucked her nipples, which was exactly what he wanted to do, but suddenly, he heard the door upstairs opening and so he stopped. He didn't want to take the chance. With hesitations, he let go of Rienne.

"You drive me crazy, love."

"I love it when you touch me. I forget everything."

James planted another kiss on Rienne's mouth. "Baby, we need to talk."

"About what?"

"Us."

Rienne shrugged.

"Listen, what we're doing. Whatever's going on between us…it's serious. I mean, I'm not just enjoying the moment. I want this to last."

"We will, James. I love no one but you."

James cupped Rienne's face with his hands. "I'm beyond the moon, Maldita."

"The first time I met you, something inside me woke up. You made me feel like I'm not just a human being walking on earth. No. I crossed a threshold. Then, everything changed. I dream of you, always wishing to hear your voice, seeing your face. I was miserable when I left here and stayed at the club wondering whether you were thinking of me. I'm in love with you, James. Yesterday, today, and I know I'll love you tomorrow."

Sighing, James touched his forehead to hers. "Rienne, Rienne. I'm so in love with you, too. I've waited for this to happen. I'm not going to let it end now. Not even if your dad tries to take you away, which I believe will happen when he hears that you're not hiding anymore. I'll fight him tooth and nail to have you."

"Please tell me you're serious, James. I know everything happened so quickly, but me falling in love with you occurred long ago."

"I'm serious. I love you, my Maldita. *You.*"

Since James heard a click of the door upstairs, he was sure it was safe to touch Rienne again without getting caught. He buried his face against Rienne's throat, rubbed the bare skin of her neck and back with his hands, then continued on to explore her waist, her hips.

"I love it when you touch me like that."

"Good. Because I can't stop touching you like this. You're so smooth."

Rienne giggled when he touched her side. "I love you, Punjabi."

"More than I love you?"

"Yes."

James looked at Rienne. "Impossible," he said, then brushed his lips with hers."

Rienne moaned softly as he lay her down on the counter. Even with her bra on, her nipples were still visibly taut beneath the thin fabric of her top. Desperately needing more of her than just a touch, he helped her remove her clothes. With just her panties on, James began to love her with his mouth. He licked her nipples repeatedly then sucked her hard. She let out an erotic sound that made his cock throb. Oh, he wanted her. *Badly.*

He positioned himself between her legs then bend down then nuzzled her pussy. He licked her through her panties until she was wet and panting.

"James, please. Stop teasing."

"Impatient wench." As if he had the time in the world, he slowly removed her panties. The moment he saw her, he sucked in his breath. Her pussy glistened. "You're fucking wet, love."

"For you."

"I know," he said, then sucked her clit. Her taste brought out the beast in him. He ate her pussy like a starved man while she writhed and begged him to help her come. With his thumb deep inside her entry, he sucked her until she screamed his name.

James couldn't wait. Unbuttoning his fly, he released his hard dick. "Baby, I need to be inside you right now."

"Oh, yes, please."

He aimed his cock on her wet entry. Inch by sweet inch, he pushed until he was fully imbedded inside her. James groaned from the intense pleasure of having Rienne's tight wall grip him. He wanted to drive into her so hard. Instead, he took his time to savor the moment. Using his thumb, he pressed on her clit while slowly moving in and out of her. "So good, love."

"James..."

Gritting his teeth, he pulled out of her. "I want your scent on my lips," he declared then replaced his cock with his mouth. He sucked her clit, loving the feel of her small flesh inside his mouth.

Rienne clamped her legs together, pinning him. He could hear her say something, but couldn't make out the words. Rubbing her thighs, he continued to pleasure her through the little nub. He wanted her to come while he sucked her.

Damn, his cock throbbed and his balls rock hard. James groaned as pleasure racked his body. Inside his mouth, he used his tongue to play with Rienne's clit.

Rienne's nails dug in his scalp while she raised her hips, offering herself to him.

"Ohh..."

James let go of her clit. "Good?"

"Very."

Smiling, he ran his tongue on her wet folds, licked her juice, and then flat-tongued her. James thought he'd go crazy from the horniness that currently wrapped around him. Once again, he sucked her clit and didn't let go.

"Please, don't stop. Oh, James. Yes, yes!"

Rienne moaned so loud James wouldn't be surprised if his dad heard her. For a few seconds, he looked at Rienne's pussy creaming. He ran his finger on her pussy before licking her juice. As soon as Rienne's legs relaxed, he positioned himself between her legs again.

"Now, Maldita, we make love."

***

Through his binoculars, Santiago watched James and Rienne having fun working in the kitchen. However, when the two started making out again, he stopped. He stayed behind the hedge where he had a perfect view of the house, wondering if he was doing the right thing.

Before this, watching Rienne was about helping Roy keep tabs on his daughter. He'd never missed anything and delivered his report to the last detail. Now, he felt that he betrayed Roy's trust. Rienne's life had changed and Roy should know about it. This was the most important time in the father and daughter's lives. New chapter. New beginning, but Santiago was sure Roy would see the situation differently. If the man couldn't even handle the news about his daughter being kissed, what would he do when he learned that she'd been sleeping with James? Good fucking Lord. To Roy, Rienne was still his little girl.

Santiago scratched his neck. *Fuck.* Why did he even care about Rienne's happiness? So what if Roy decided to take her away from the Huntingtons again. She was just a big fat paycheck that he would most likely lose if Roy found out he'd been withholding information from him.

Damn it. Another week. He'd let Rienne have her fun. Who knows, maybe by then, those two would finally let their infatuation, attraction, or lust for each other satiate and realize they were being stupid. Maybe the media wouldn't care if they spotted Rienne. After all, the Kardashians and Jenner was everywhere. Those family pictures were worth more than Rienne's. Who knows, maybe he wouldn't have to worry about Roy getting pissed. Yeah. He'd give those two a week and then Roy would have to decide what to do with them.

Chapter Eleven

James couldn't tell if he should feel annoyed or be proud. When he thought about showing Rienne where he worked, he didn't consider the possibility that his friends' balls would hit the ground. They stared open-mouthed at Rienne as if they'd never seen a gorgeous woman before. Their dispatcher just grinned with his face blotchy red when Rienne said *hi* to him. The poor man even forgot what he was doing. James leaned against the doorjamb and watched Rienne talk to Danny, his co-pilot and a good friend. They were looking at the seaplane's cockpit, laughing. Danny must have said something that warranted a punch on the arm. James smiled. If his friend weren't married, he'd be crazy jealous right now.

"Rienne Cailler, huh?"

James pushed away from the door then turned to see the owner of the company and also the oldest most experienced pilot he knew. "Hey, Bob. Good to see you. I thought you're on a vacation."

"Shit. Put me on vacation and might as well put me in a coffin. My bones need to work, James. Otherwise, I'll be as stiff as a dog turd left in the snow on winter time."

"Well, I'm glad you're here. We need you."

"She's as beautiful as they come. Definitely makes you forget your sorrow."

"Yeah. Definitely makes you lose your senses."

"Any chance she's related to the infamous Cailler?"

James let out a deep breath. He didn't have to lie. Bob knew. For a long time, Roy and Rienne's faces grazed the tabloid magazines, branded as the father and daughter who sucked money from hard working people. Thieves, swindlers, evils.

"Ah. So that's her. First time I saw her picture, her father was holding her outside the hotel in downtown Seattle where she had a birthday party. Lots of rich names were invited. She was about twelve, wearing nice clothes and a tiara. The press went on a frenzy, taking pictures of it. They were real, right?"

That pearl, ruby, and diamond tiara had become famous. A lot of rich girls, especially debutantes, wanted the same for their birthdays. The following year, though, when the news about the money scandal came out, the talk about the tiara once again graced the magazines' front pages and news channels. People who were victimized by Roy's company cried that every penny spent on the tiara belonged to them. Those friends who frequented the Cailler's house had nothing to do with Rienne or her father anymore. Some even denied their connection with Roy.

James had asked Rienne about the tiara once. All she said was it had caused the Cailler's downfall.

"Yeah, they were real."

"Since that day, the media had become obsessed with her. They wanted to know everything...from her favorite color to how she sleeps at night. Now, why would you want to know those things? Creepy if you asked me."

"The media is still interested in her. But for a totally different reason now," James said.

"You know what? Even if she's not a Cailler, everyone will still be crazy with her. Man, she's lovely."

"She is beautiful inside and out."

"And you're in love with her." Bob asked with a grin.

James shifted his weight from his other foot then did it again with the other. Was he that easy to read?

"Ah." Bob placed a hand on James' shoulder. "Don't worry, boy. Your secret is safe with me. By the way, Mitchy is pissed that you brought a woman here. She's throwing daggers at everyone who dared to look in her direction."

James shook his head. Michelle or Mitchy Bitchy to everyone was a mistake he didn't want to repeat. After numerous invites from Mitchy, he'd finally agreed to go to her apartment for dinner. James quickly found out he'd made a big mistake. She handcuffed him to the kitchen table while she forced-fed him. Then, a minister arrived to perform a fucking wedding. That was when James flipped the table and broke its leg so he could pull off the handcuff. He promised Mitchy that he would never tell a soul about what happened if she let him go. She agreed. Bob knew everything. As a director here, he needed to know. So, here they were, still working together with Mitchy. Someday, he'd tell Rienne about Mitchy. She'd get a good laugh about her.

"Mitchy needs this job, Bob."

"I know. That's why she's still here. We're keeping an eye on her, though. So, what are you two planning on doing today?"

"Thinking about taking her to San Juan."

"Coho?"

"Yeah."

"Good. Say *hi* to Masters for me."

"Will do."

San Juan Island was notorious for splendid vistas, quiet woodlands, and romantic atmosphere. The main attraction, however, were the orca whales. Hotels, cabins, and restaurants were booked a year ahead. However, Kenmore Air employees had a special room at Friday's Crabhouse and a table at Coho Restaurant owned by Masters, a former pilot. After all, they were the number one charter company that brought tourists around the island.

"All right. I'll be your pilot. Leave you there and come back when you're ready."

"You sure?"

"Hell, yeah. Gives me something to do. Oh, you know that cabin I mentioned to you about a month ago?"

"You mean the beautiful cabin in Lost Lake?"

"Yup."

"What about it?"

"For sale. I called already and asked to put a hold on it until I talked to you."

"You serious?"

"Yeah. You and Rienne should go to Lost Lake and check it out."

"That would be great. Man, thanks."

James caught Rienne's glance. Damn, she never failed to make his heart double its beat just by smiling at him. He could hardly wait to be alone with her again.

***

Ha! He thinks I'm stupid. What, because I'm just a recording secretary here, he believes that I don't know anything? That woman that he brought here, I know her. She's the bitch who spent all the money that the hardworking class saved up and invested it in her father's company. Oh, yeah. I know her. Her father gave her a tiara that everyone said had cost him over fifteen million dollars. Fuck! That kind of money for a tiara? Then they disappeared with all the money. I bet that bitch knows where her father is along with their loot. Look at her. She looks so expensive. Her hair shines. No hair shines like that even if you showered everyday. I am sure that she spends a lot at different expensive salons. Oh, yeah. That bitch's kind doesn't go to Super Cuts or salons that offered a twelve-dollar haircut.

And her faded jeans...that must be tailored. Why not? It fits her perfectly. Maybe she wears one of those fake butts to make her ass look rounded. Her shoes alone probably cost more than her paycheck. She has money. So most likely she has breast implants, too. And stupid James fell for her beauty. Oh yeah. I can tell James is in love with that bitch. The way he looks at her is a dead giveaway. I'm sure if that bitch weren't here, though, James would be talking to me instead.

I can make James fall in love with me. Maybe handcuffing him on the dining table and calling a minister was a bad idea, but James just freaked out. He over reacted. If he only listened to me, they would've been married now. Instead, I listened to him like a stupid person he thought me to be. Well, I'll show him that I'm capable of thinking logically. I'll show him.

Mitchy started searching online for television news email addresses. Humming, she opened her email. Her subject line...*Rienne Cailler Found.*

Chapter Twelve

Bob flew Rienne and James above the islands. Aside from being a great pilot, he also knew the Pacific Northwest history, which was an added bonus for Rienne. All the forts and islands fascinated her and she told Bob that she'd like to visit all of them. For about twenty minutes they flew. James just listened to them talk through their mouthpieces. He was happy to sit there and watch Rienne's face glow from excitement. She asked so many questions, and Bob gladly answered her. By the time they landed at Orcas Island, Rienne was already calling Bob, *Uncle.*

After they watched Bob take off, James took Rienne to Coho. He introduced her to Masters. Right away, James could tell that Masters fell for Rienne's charm because the man couldn't even remember what table he had reserved for them.

James pulled out the chair for Rienne. Before she could sit down though, he planted a kiss on the base of her neck just because he couldn't resist doing it. It was too late when he realized that people were staring. He wasn't sure why, though. Maybe it was because some of them recognized Rienne or because she was too beautiful in her short black dress and red, high-heeled shoes.

Earlier, when James told Rienne his plan, she immediately asked him to take her shopping. He knew of a mom and pop dress shop and took her there. The moment Rienne saw the dress on a mannequin, she said, *that's the dress.*

The owners, an elderly man and woman, who sewed uniforms for the local private school and embroidered logo on his company's shirt, had asked Rienne if she could pay them with a picture of her wearing the dress instead of money. They said, she was the first celebrity to come in their shop and wanted everyone to see the proof.

Rienne surprised James with her wit and quick thinking. In the end, she had ended up posing for a picture and giving the couple more money than what the dress cost. *A donation*, Rienne had called it. She'd made him so proud.

As soon as they sat down, chilled champagne appeared on their table, followed by an appetizer.

"My, do you get this special and quick service here all the time?"

"No. They're only nice because of you."

"Stop it. I like Masters."

"He likes you, too, I'm sure. Just don't smile at him too much."

"Why?"

"You make him forget where he is."

Rienne laughed. "You're bad."

"Seriously. So…what's it going to be?" James asked while sipping his water.

"No to fish, clam, oyster, or squid."

"Got it. What else?"

"No to anything spicy and red."

"Red?"

"Red sauce, red meat."

"Okay. That's it?"

"Uhm, no to baked cheese."

"Would you like to go to *McDonalds* instead? I know where the closest one is."

Rienne stuck her tongue at him. "Sorry. I'll have a chowder bowl and Cesar's salad. You?"

"Everything you said *no* to. And your leftovers, if you have any."

"You're such a pig."

"Oink!"

God, he loved to hear her laugh. So infectious. He didn't want her to clam up again. Damn Roy for getting Rienne punished by their situation, for putting her in a position to doubt herself and her role in this world, for making her think that she didn't deserve good things in life because a lot of people, who at one point, had been connected to her dad, were suffering. No, he wouldn't let Roy do that again to Rienne. She was out to see the sunshine again and he'd see to it that she stayed out.

Their food came even before they finished the appetizers. Rienne ate like Miss Emily Post's student—with poise, grace, and femininity. He enjoyed watching her as much as he enjoyed eating his food. He didn't miss the additional glances thrown their way. Women looked at Rienne from head to toe with obvious jealousy in their eyes, while the men gave her appreciative hurried looks. Rienne, however, was oblivious to the attention that she was getting.

"Dinner was good. Thanks for eating the rest of my bowl, Punjabi. I didn't want the cook to think that he didn't do a very good job preparing it."

"You're welcome. You should have tried my escargot. Delicious."

"Do you know that snails don't hear and they are hermaphrodites—meaning that they have the reproductive organs of both sexes on them, meaning they produce both sperm and eggs. When they are mating, they will both conceive and lay eggs"

"So?" James asked while noisily munching on Rienne's napa cabbage garnish.

"Don't you find that weird?"

"Baby, they are snails. They probably don't even know what they are."

"They fall under the same classification as slugs. And they are loud eaters."

James stopped chewing, then started again, this time even louder, making Rienne laugh."

"You're incorrigible."

"I love you, Maldita."

"I love you, Punjabi. Thank you for backing me up when I told Hal about my plan."

James reached for Rienne's hand. "We want the same thing, right?"

"Yes."

"And I want you to be happy. If you think you can handle being out like this, then I'm with you."

"Thank you."

"Don't thank me, love. I'll do anything for you, you know that."

"Well, so far, so good. Maybe, I'm forgotten. Nobody's interested in me anymore. Besides, who would read a story about me anyway when there are lots of celebrity gossips to write about?"

"True. If I see your face on a magazine stand at the grocery store, I wouldn't even buy the mag. Just look at you. Ugly, with a body of a fire hydrant, greasy hair, and you're nose crooked."

"You forgot. I'm a hunchback."

"Hey, I like Quasimodo."

Rienne grinned. "Me, too."

James raised his glass. "How about a toast?"

Rienne followed suit. "A toast."

"To you and me, and our future."

"To us."

They drank their wine, then ordered four different kinds of desserts. They each picked two of their favorites. Rienne ordered chocolate cake and burnt cream while James chose luscious lemon delight cream cheese and hot fudge pudding cake.

James lined all of them up in the middle of the table.

"Now, we eat. Try everything."

"James, I can feel my hips and thighs expanding just by looking at these."

"Wow. I would love to hug your hips and thighs."

"I'm not kidding!"

"Me, too. I'll kiss each slowly. Take a bite of your soft skin, lick the sensitive—"

"James!" Rienne shrieked. "Stop. People can hear you. Haven't you noticed? This whole place doubled its customers since we got here."

"Love, this place is packed all the time."

"I know, but—"

"What?"

James noticed Rienne began to frown. She was looking somewhere behind him. "I don't know. That man, three tables behind you is holding a camera and he's pointing it in our direction."

"You sure?" James turned around just in time when the camera flash went off. "The fuck."

"James, oh, no."

"Do you want to leave?"

Rienne shook her head. "No. I'm not going to run. He'll just follow us. Besides, we don't care, right? Let him take pictures."

"Right." He could tell Rienne was trying to be brave, but failing. This would be the first time she'd let anyone from the media take her picture without covering her face or running. "Smile, Rienne, and eat your dessert. Show them you're having a good time."

Rienne nodded. He could see her hand shake a bit when she picked up her fork, but she squared her shoulders, then started eating.

"This is good."

"Delish."

James noticed the atmosphere inside the restaurant had changed. People began staring and the waiters were more alert. Somewhere, they heard commotions.

"James, what's going on?"

"Easy, love."

Masters stood by their table. His face hard. "Excuse me, James."

"Tell me."

"There are about a dozen reporters outside. I believe they're all here for you two. I could show you the back door."

"Thank you."

"I'll call for a cab. You can go straight to the dock. Bob's not there yet. So, here's the key. Fly Harvest Moon."

"Thanks, Masters. I owe you one."

"Give me a minute." Masters quickly walked away.

James fished his phone from his pocket. He needed to talk to Bob about the cabin."

"How did they know where I was so fast?" Rienne's voice shook. She looked afraid and angry at the same time.

James was wondering the same thing, but he had his suspicions. "I can think of only one person." *Damn Mitchy. I'll slap that woman.*

"Oh, no. I think we made a mistake, James."

"No. You have every right to live like everyone here. Don't worry. We got this. I have a plan."

Masters came back with two guys the size of a refrigerator and asked them to follow him. James took Rienne's hand and they started walking toward the back of the restaurant. The reporter who took Rienne's picture stood up.

"Rienne, do you know where Roy is hiding? He needs to answer to a lot of people," he said, then took more pictures of Rienne.

James snarled. "Shut up, man."

Masters shoved the reporter who fell back on his ass.

James quickened his pace, but they weren't fast enough. A few customers that realized who Rienne was, started throwing words at her. They even heard the words *bitch* and *whore*. He was so angry, he wanted to stop and call anyone outside. Damn, he wanted to punch someone. Instead, he focused his mind on taking Rienne away from here. He was looking at Masters' back when he heard Rienne gasp. He turned around and saw water drip down Rienne's neck and the front of her dress. Someone tossed a glass of water at her.

James stopped. A grey haired woman, still holding the glass, glared at Rienne.

"Lady," James began, but Rienne stopped him.

"Ma'am, if you believe that my father had caused you trouble, pain, and hardship, I apologize on his behalf. I can tell you that he is innocent, that *I* am innocent, but you wouldn't believe me. In fact, I don't think that there is anything I can say that would help anyone here who'd been a victim of my father's company. "I'll say only one word, though, which I hope you'll believe to be honest and sincere. *Sorry*." Rienne's voice was low and quivering, but it was as clear as filtered water on everyone's glasses.

***

Well, so much for giving those two a week. Santiago spat on the ground.

God damn it.

One of his many job requirements was to watch out for those fucking reporters and tell Roy right away about them. While he was at it, might as well tell Roy about what exactly was going on between James and Rienne. If he would hear about the truth, it had to come from him. That way, he might be able to save his fucking ass.

Through the partition between the bar and main dining room, Santiago watched James and Rienne. He wondered what they had in mind. There were reporters outside and a few inside that had managed to bribe the customers into giving up their tables. How were they going to avoid those leeches?

The man called *Masters* talked to James. Santiago wished he could hear them. He bet those two would leave soon. Minutes later, James and Rienne stood up. They followed Masters, and the two burly men were behind them, all headed for the back exit. Santiago was about to leave, too, when he heard loud gasps and murmurs. When he looked, Rienne was drenched. He watched and listened.

The burly men walked toward the reporter who'd been taking Rienne's pictures. They lifted the man by the armpits, dragged him out, then tossed him out the door, but not before the headwaiter grabbed the camera from the stunned reporter. Two men stood up and left. Santiago bet his eye those two worked for some newspaper or television.

Santiago quickly exited the restaurant. This never would have happened if he just did his damn job and told Roy everything. Lucky that fucking woman tossed a glass of water at Rienne and not acid. *Damn. Damn.* He put Rienne's life in danger because he let his feelings rule his brain.

He needed to know where they were going. Roy would want to know and Santiago had better have answers when he called him.

He grabbed a menu and pretended to be looking at it when he walked by the reporters outside. He didn't want them to suspect that he was one of them. One thing he's learned about those guys was that they could smell news from ones pores.

As fast as his feet could carry him, he went to his car, got in, then drove towards the back of the restaurant. Sure enough, a cab was there waiting. Really cool, he thought, but where would they go.

Santiago flagged a taxi in a hurry and followed the two in a distance. Less than five minutes later, the cab stopped by the dock. *Damn. They're flying again.* He looked around. No seaplane around except for one named Harvest Moon. Earlier, he was lucky enough to join a group of Japanese tourists heading here. Now, if those two fly again, he wouldn't be able to follow them.

Time to call Roy.

Roy answered in one ring. "I heard. My daughter is all over the news. She was seen at a restaurant with Hal's boy. How did this happen, Santiago?"

"She'd been going out, Roy as if she didn't care who would see her. I believe she doesn't want to hide anymore."

"Impossible. Rienne knows and understands the reason why we're doing what we're doing. Where is she now?"

"At the dock."

"Dock?"

"Yes. Waiting for a seaplane."

"Where are they going?"

"I…don't know. Back to Seattle, maybe."

"Damn it to hell, Santiago. You're supposed to watch her and tell me everything, so I'll know whether to move her again or not!"

Roy was right, but Santiago made a decision on his own. Give Rienne a little taste of happiness. *Now, this is the fucking result of his meddling.* "Roy, there is something that you need to know."

"What the fuck is that?"

"James and Rienne. They're not just friends."

"Meaning?"

"They're lovers." Santiago braced himself for what Roy would do next.

"Fuck! Fuck! Fuck! Is this another one of your theories because you saw them kiss again?"

More than that, he thought. "I am positive."

"She'd been with him for only few days and now they're lovers? Lovers like two people sleeping together?"

What kind of lovers are there but those who shared a bed and sleep beneath a sheet Santiago wanted to say, but he knew better. "That kind."

"When did you find out? Why the fuck are you just telling me now!"

"I was going to, Roy, but—"

"I want my daughter back, Santiago. If you have to drown James to get to Rienne, do it! I want her back or you'd better find a hole to hide." Roy hung up.

Fuck.

Chapter Thirteen

Lost Lake, Oregon
Six months later

"I love it here, James. Do you think we can stay here forever?" Rienne raised her arms above her head then closed her eyes. Lying down on the grassy bank in front of the cabin had become her favorite thing to do everyday. "Our Cabin is our first home. I don't want to leave here—ever. If we do, though, we should go to Australia. I've been wanting to go there."

James turned on his side to watch Rienne basking under the sun. He ran his fingers on her rosy cheeks, then down to her neck and chest. He let his fingers wander close to her armpits.

"Stop. It tickles. So, what's the answer?"

"We can stay here forever. The cabin is ours. Bought and paid for."

"Bob is so wonderful for letting you have this place. It's a steal."

James chuckled. "You know, he wouldn't let me forget that he found this place for us."

"So? Thank him, James."

"I already did. Many, many times." He ran his fingertips down her belly, enjoying the feel of her flesh quiver. "You're really happy here, love?"

"Yes." Rienne opened her eyes to look at him. "Wherever you are, as long as I'm with you, I'm happy. We could live inside a box or a shoe and I'd feel the same. I love you, Punjabi. Always. Forever."

"Me, too." His hand went lower to snake inside Rienne's bikini. "I dreamed of you so many times, love. I still can't believe that you're mine now. Mine to touch." His middle finger dipped inside her pussy. She was wet already." Mine to feel." His finger slowly slid inside her. "Mine to pleasure."

"Yes." Rienne moaned. She spread her legs wider, then moved her hips upward, inviting him to go in deeper.

"Mine to fuck."

Oh, he loved to watch Rienne's face whenever he was making love with her. Her mouth was partly open, breathing in and out. Then, she would lick her lips as if tasting something good. Seeing pleasure registered on her face heightened his own sexual enjoyment.

"Baby, show me your breasts." Slowly, he pulled his finger out, then pushed it back in.

Rienne pulled down her bathing suit top.

"Fuck. Nice. I love your breasts. Perfect." He finger-fucked her while the tip of his tongue licked her nipple in circular motion. Rienne loved it when he made love with her breasts. He puckered his lips around her nipple then began sucking gently. He did it for a few minutes then gave it a more firm sucking motions in synch with his finger going in and out of her pussy. "Ah, so good."

"James..." Rienne ran her fingers through his hair as she arched her back, giving him more of her flesh.

"Yeah, love. I know. Let me suck the other one, too. Yes. Ah, baby, I love you." He teased her nipple with his tongue then gently blew air on it with his mouth. He alternated between the two techniques all the while enjoying the sound of Rienne's breathing.

Without breaking his mouth's contact on her breast, James moved to position himself in between Rienne's legs. He pulled his fingers out of her pussy then licked them. Staring at Rienne, he put his finger insider her mouth. His dick throbbed fiercely when she began sucking. "Fuck, yeah."

James gave Rienne's breasts equal attention before going down slowly to where he knew she wanted him to be. Rienne loved it even more when he ate her pussy.

She was glistening wet when he spread her labia. He licked her juice. Fuck, her taste nearly made him come. While running his tongue on her wet lips, he pressed his thumb on her butt ring. For the past few days, he'd been testing her if she'd let him go deeper on her ass. So far, she never stopped him. James licked Rienne's pussy repeatedly before trapping her clit between his lips. Then he sucked her gently, teasing Rienne until she writhed beneath him.

"James. Make me come. Please, love." Her fingers dug in his hair. "I want to come in your mouth."

James released Rienne's clit then looked at her. "You will. I love you, baby."

"I love you more."

His cock was fucking hard, but he'd give Rienne satisfaction first. Oh, yeah. Her Maldita would get what she wanted. Again, he feasted on her pussy, moaning as he did. Her pussy juice, mixed with his saliva, dripped down her ass, lubricating it. While he took Rienne higher and higher, his thumb went deeper inside her ass. She was fucking his mouth, her moans of pleasure louder and louder. Finally, she screamed his name, but James didn't stop sucking her clit. He waited until her body became languid and then he pulled his thumb out. Rienne groaned.

"Good?"

"Yes."

"Love it." He aimed his cock on her entry. With all the energy that he could muster not to ejaculate right away, he slowly entered her. He let Rienne feel every inch of his dick.

"James…more."

"I'll give you more, love." A few more strokes, then he quickened his thrust. Faster, he fucked her until Rienne screamed.

"Pain or good. Tell me, love."

"Good!"

"Yeah. Sweet fuck, you're tight!"

"Yes, yes, James. Ohh!"

He hung on to his last strength until he couldn't anymore. James released his seed inside Rienne. Since they'd begun making love, he'd never used protection. Maybe, just maybe, this time they'd get lucky.

Spent, he collapsed on top of Rienne. "Perfect. Each time," he whispered.

"Because I love you."

"Because I love you," he returned.

Rienne sighed. "What was that about?"

"What?"

"You did something."

James grinned. "You like it?"

"Yes."

"We'll do it again until you get used to it."

"You're naughty."

"Only with you." James lay down beside Rienne then gathered her in his arms. "Love, I start working at the marina tomorrow. You sure you're gonna be okay alone?"

"I'll be fine. I'll miss you, of course. But we can text."

"Right. Call me anytime."

"You know I will. Hey, what did Masters say when he called?"

"Your dad's hired man came by again asking the same questions." James wanted to tell Rienne that Roy's man put a few bruises on Masters and threatened to ruin his business if he wouldn't talk, but Masters remained tight-lipped.

"He's not going to stop looking for us."

"If you were my daughter, love, I wouldn't stop looking either. He loves you."

"I love him, too, James, and I miss him, but I can't be with him if it would mean leaving you."

It had been two months since they said goodbye to Masters. He was grateful to the man for helping them escape without being followed, but those people close to him had to face the consequences of his actions. Roy rained down his wrath on them. His friends at work had received anonymous threats, followed and harassed at home for simply knowing James. Bob found out that Mitchy was the one who called the news about Rienne's location and fired her right away. And James' dad...he didn't deserve to suffer from a broken arm because he couldn't say where James and Rienne went. That was just it. Dad *didn't* know. Last time James talked to him, Hal was furious, calling him an asshole, bastard, and an embarrassment. One who failed to see the difference between right and wrong.

Is it wrong to fall in love? To love a woman who loves him in return? Does a relationship have to stop in friendship?

"We'll give them time, love. Eventually, they'll realize that there is nothing wrong with what we're doing. Your dad's ego is bruised, and my dad's pissed because he lost a friend and a position as a representative member for Seattle. But they'll come around."

"I want them to be with us, James. They are our only family."

"It'll happen, love."

"James, I know how to make us all together again."

"You do?"

"Yes."

"Tell me."

"Later. After dinner."

***

Santiago wouldn't last on the investigative field if he weren't good. He'd made a living out of following people and getting hard-to-find information. He'd made a lot of people happy and, yeah, sad, but all of them satisfied. Except for one. Roy Cailler. His daughter disappeared from him because Santiago broke his own rule. He let his emotions mix with his job.

Meddling in Rienne and Roy's business was a fucked up thing to do, but Roy gave him a chance to redeem himself. That's what he was going to do. Yes, Rienne had become like a daughter to him and he failed to protect her. Not only that, but he destroyed the father and daughter relationship, and all because he wanted her to be happy.

He couldn't forget the look on Rienne's face when a woman tossed water on her. She was stunned, but still regal and didn't lose her composure. She was lucky, though, to have Masters with them. Who knew what else would have happened if they weren't protected. Shit, that day was enough warning for him. *What's it going to be? Let Rienne follow her happiness or watch her get hurt.*

Well, he'd already made a decision. He'd let Fate decide on James and Rienne's future. Right now, he had a job to do.

One thing that he learned from his years of work was that anyone had a price. He bribed people he believed could give him valuable information. It helped that Roy provided the money, which made the bribing a little less hard.

After six months of following leads, he hit the pot of gold. He went back to the dock where he last saw James and Rienne. For hours, he sat on a bench studying the workers and hoping to see Harvest Moon again. But he didn't. What he noticed, however, was a man holding a clipboard. Right then, he knew where to get the information about the lover's destination that night.

It didn't take much convincing before the man showed him the log entry for Harvest Moon, and it didn't cost Santiago much either—just a couple grand and a promise to help him get a job with the FBI. What a sucker.

Santiago drove his rental car slowly as he looked through his binocular. The cabin that he believed James and Rienne were living in had trees surrounding it. It was just a walking distance to everything, but still had great privacy. Not to mention situated at the end of the unpaved one-way road. Santiago turned off the engine. The only way to get a better view of the cabin was to take the long driveway. He couldn't do that without anyone inside the house seeing him. He stopped the car, then got out and stood behind the hedge. Using his binoculars, he scanned the cabin. It was nice, probably costing them a fortune to live there.

The whole place was quiet. Santiago would kill his fish in exchange of a place like this. He was sure, too, that Rienne was enjoying her life here.

Six months. Damn. It had been that long since he lost sight of them. Now, it seemed he'd found them again. *Maybe.*

Just when he was about to lower his binoculars, he saw movement from the lower grassy bank. His heart began beating its familiar beat. Ah, this was the thrill of spying on people. Except Rienne. She'd been someone who touched this old man's heart.

Santiago watched James and Rienne walk hand and hand. They had a blanket with them. They must have been sun bathing. Rienne's hair was undone and she was only wearing her bathing suit. She was a sight to see. Beautiful. And happy. Both of them.

Sighing, he took his cell phone out of his pocket, then began typing his message. *I found them.*

Chapter Fourteen

Rienne stirred the boiling pasta in the pot. Tonight it would be spaghetti with meatballs, broiled broccoli, and French bread. She had been craving for pasta sauce for a few weeks now and she didn't even like tomatoes. Early this morning, she found out why. She'd been pregnant. The *EPT* wouldn't lie, would it? She hadn't seen a doctor yet, but as soon as she'd tell James about their baby, making an appointment would be her next move. As far as she knew, her health insurance was still good. Dad wouldn't be so cruel as to stop her subscription. Well, she could get an Obamacare if she had to anyway.

She turned down the burner then started cutting the broccoli. She wondered if James would feel obligated to marry her now that they'd be parents soon. No. She didn't want him to think that way. If he wanted to take his time proposing, that was fine. He loved her. He said so, so many times. It was just that he hadn't mentioned anything about getting married yet. Maybe he was waiting for the right moment? Or he was thinking they wouldn't last and didn't want to have to deal with divorce? No. James loved him and believed them to be soul mates. He'd propose. Eventually.

Does it matter whether they're married or not? Being together is enough. They love each other. She shouldn't expect for more. Is he cheating? Rienne's throat constricted. Oh, God. She wanted to cry. Why? She'd been very happy. *Are all pregnant women so emotional and thinking weird thoughts? I'm crazy.*

She placed the broccoli in a steamer then began working on the bread. In no time at all, her thoughts shifted to baby names and possibilities of having twins or triplets. She was busy imagining little kids running around outside that she didn't notice a line of cars coming on their driveway. James was the one that got her attention to what was going on after he surprised her by wrapping a blanket around her.

"We have company, love."

"What?"

"Put your shoes on."

"Why?"

"Just in case."

"James—"

"Don't worry. Stay here. I love you." James went to open the door, but someone beat him to it.

Rienne screamed as she watched James go down. Her father stood above him. Three men came in, fanned out. They were armed. Oh, no.

"Hi, baby girl. Let's go."

"Dad?"

"Yes, honey. We're leaving. Now!"

James struggled to get up, his nose bleeding like a leaky faucet. "She's not going with you anywhere, Roy." He stared at Rienne. "Baby—"

"Fuck you, James. What the hell were you thinking stealing my daughter from me? I will never forgive you for that."

Rienne moved to go to James, but Roy held out his hand. "Dad, he didn't steal me away. I love him."

"Honey, spend time away from him and you'll know whatever that is going on between you and him is not real. We need to go."

"No!"

"Rienne, I don't have time." Roy nodded to the men.

Rienne watched the two men flock James. One stood beside her. "I'm done hiding, Dad. I want a life. Life with James. What are you doing?"

"What am I doing? Don't you understand? You won't have a life until I finished my work. What happened at the restaurant is just an example of what you'll be facing if you don't fucking listen. Do you think you'll be able to live here like normal people? If you raise a family, do you want your family branded as thieves? Think, Rienne."

"I can protect her, Roy." James tried to move, but he was shoved back against the wall.

"You fucking failed, damn you. Oh, wait. Is it the money? You know how much Rienne is worth, right? Is that what you're after?"

"Life is not all about money, Roy."

"You're wrong, boy. Why do you think this world is in chaos? How do you think everything around you works? Because of money! You're pathetic and don't know anything."

James pushed off the wall, but one of the men punched him in the stomach so hard he doubled over.

"James!" Rienne tried to run, but strong fingers gripping on her arm stopped her. Her vision was blurry from tears. "Dad, don't hurt him. Please."

"Defy me, Rienne, and I'll make sure he receives more than that. If you love him, listen to what I'm saying. Let's go." Roy waved his hand. One of the men took out a gun from behind his back.

"Dad?"

"I'll do anything to have you back, so don't test me, Rienne."

"James and Hal are your friends," Rienne said in a small voice, unable to believe her dad's threat.

"Friends don't stab each other in the back, honey. Now, what's it going to be? I don't have time."

Rienne looked at James, her heart breaking in many pieces. "James..."

"I'll find you, love. Promise," James said before he was shoved again against the wall.

Chapter Fifteen

Six years later

James sat on the bridge and watched the number of ships berthed at Port Hedland. One of the largest iron ore loading ports in the world and the largest in Australia. Port Hedland afforded convenient anchorage and fifteen berths, the allotted spaces for big cargo ships. As a master mariner, James had sailed to different parts of the water world. He loved it. The challenges had been difficult at times, especially when he was dealing with port authorities, pirates, and making sure his cargo secured. Overall, though, he couldn't complain. Money was good and couldn't beat the extra perks of seeing the world for free.

Communicating with his friends and dad was not a problem. As long as he could get a *Wi-fi* connection, there was no problem reaching them. If he was in some remote areas, the SAT phone was available to use.

Life of a mariner could get lonely sometimes, but thank goodness for *Facebook*, he wasn't totally out of what goes on the real world. *Facetime*, a video application on his *iPad* had been a great thing to have. He could see his dad every night and show him live images of where he was.

James shook his head. He remembered a lot of quiet dinners and days without talking with each other before his dad finally forgave him for what happened six years ago. Until now, the mere mention of Rienne or Roy's name brought sadness and pain to both of them. Dad understood his actions. *Love*, he said, *is the most powerful feeling of all. It could move mountains, fall a city, and make a man think irrational thoughts.*

If falling in love is irrational, then the whole world is full of unreasonable people. Maybe that was the only logical reason why he had never stopped searching for Rienne.

The same day Roy took Rienne away from him, he tried to find out where they went. He'd used up all the resources he could think of, combed the Internet, researched all possible information, and combination of names that he thought Rienne might be using and asked close friends for possible avenues of research. He even emailed people named Rienne. Nothing came up, though. Like the wake his ship had made, his Maldita disappeared.

James would never give up, though.

His old friend, Bob, hired a new tech for his company. *Whiz Kid*, the old man called him, and one who might be able to help trace Rienne. It had only been two weeks since Whiz Kid started looking online and so far, no luck.

He'd waited six years already. Adding more years of waiting and searching wouldn't make any difference. He loved Rienne and will always love her. She had been the only one who captured his heart. James had tried dating again. He even found someone he thought would share a life with him, but his heart already belonged to Rienne. Also, hope of someday finding Rienne had never left him.

Just a word about her on how she was doing, whether she married another or anything would rest his mind. Otherwise, he wouldn't stop looking for her, even if it meant spending his life doing it. He gave her his promise and he would never break it.

His phone buzzed. A text message came in from Bob.

"*Whiz Kid found something. JP RM mean anything to you? Here's the link.*"

JP RM? James tried to search his mind. Couldn't be his and Rienne's initials. He tapped his finger on the blue link. It took him to a *Facebook* account with just a profile picture and a cover image of a partly submerged old dock. Looked like whoever owned the account didn't really use it for socializing online. There was nothing posted on it and no other information either. He shot Bob a text back.

"I'm thinking. Any other info?"

James watched his *iPhone* screen. The cool thing about new phones now was being able to see if the person on the other end was typing.

"Look at the old dock"

Unlike any other information that Bob's tech had given him, this one really piqued his curiosity and a thrill of anticipation touched his spine. *What's up with the dock?* He stared at the picture. There was nothing to it but a broken deck. The partly built crib was gone, leaving only the timber posts. A piece of wood that must have been a sign once was on the muddy part of deck. James looked closely. Then, his heart twisted followed by a knot in his throat.

Couldn't be.

The sign was dirty and he could only make out a few letters, but he knew what it said. *Harvest Moon.*

His old friend Masters who used to own the restaurant where James took Rienne for their date had suffered from a stroke. He gave the restaurant to his son in-law who had no brain for business. The man eventually sold the business and Harvest Moon, Master's seaplane that he and Rienne had used to escape from the reporters. James had never been back to the restaurant, but he was sure the picture was taken there. Could this be the clue he'd been looking for?

JP RM. J for James and R for Rienne. What about P and M? PM? Oh my God!

James stared at his iPhone. He was paralyzed. Rienne called him Punjabi and he called her Maldita. P and M. He wasn't one hundred percent sure that Rienne owned the account, but something deep inside him hoped that he'd really found her. He squeezed his eyes shut.

I found my Maldita.

Another message came in from Bob. *"What do you think?"*

James' fingers typed his reply so fast that he pressed the wrong keys so many times *"It's her."*

"Damn. Whiz Kid is good. What are you going to do now?"

James thought for a minute. *"I'll send her a message."*

"It could be an unattended account, but let's hope she replies. Keep me posted."

"Thank you."

He should send her a message. With his heart hammering against his chest, he opened his *iPad*.

***

Being a director of a biggest news magazine in North Carolina had its benefits. Rienne got to host charity events and meet people from all walks of life. When she got invited to speak in a Lost Angeles convention, she had met smart and wonderful Filipinos. When she told them that someone nicknamed her Maldita, they laughed. From them, she learned about the lack of dental treatment for adults and children in the Philippines. She immediately contacted the right people and founded *Smile for a Dime*. The money they raised went to a public children's clinic in Manila. It made her want to do more when she heard about the malnourished children who couldn't eat properly because of tooth decay and other dental problems, but were now laughing and full of energy because they had been pain free. Hopefully, in the next few months, they'd be able to branch out and start a new program outside Manila. It was fun being able to help others and fulfilling certain obligations of being a society member. Not to mention, the job had been keeping her busy. The drawback, though, of being the head of a company was she had to open her house and host parties like today. Not that she didn't enjoy socializing. It was just she could think of better things to do than hold a wine glass and smile.

She couldn't complain, though. Life was good. Her five-year-old daughter, Jordan, was perfect, with a beautiful disposition, and healthy. Not to mention she had her daddy's eyes and nose.

Rienne sighed. Yeah, so far, life had been good to her, but something in her past just wouldn't rest.

It may already have been six years since she last saw James, but everything that had happened that day was still very clear. The lazy day at the lake, cleaning the house, making love in the shower followed by a long nap, and James doubled-over from the pain caused by the brute hired by her dad and his promise to find her.

Her dad knew, too, that James would try to follow her, which was why he had made her swear that she wouldn't leave any crumbs wherever she goes. In exchange, he'd help Hal fund his city projects as an anonymous donor and Roy would also keep an eye on James to make sure he wouldn't have to worry about anything. Rienne agreed.

Six months after, her dad informed her that James had been associating with bad company along with drinking and barhopping. Then, he had gotten a woman pregnant whom James married.

Rienne was hurt. Because she, too, was pregnant, but James didn't know that. Her dad helped her grieve and stayed by her side until he passed away two years ago leaving everything he owned to Rienne and a trust fund for her son Jordan. His mission to clear his name, however, remained a mission.

Staying busy at work had helped face the lonely days. *Until she met Andy.* A flamboyant homosexual she couldn't live without.

Now, here she was, living with Andy in an eight-bedroom house that seemed to echo whenever no one was around.

Rienne watched the guests laugh, eat, and drink. She wished she could just leave and go to her office to check *Facebook*. She had opened the account under JP RM a year after her dad passed away. So far, she hadn't gotten any messages.

She didn't know what to expect when she opened the account. Maybe to know that James was true to his words that he'd find her. Then, again, how would he know that JP RM was her? The cover picture that she had added was kind of obscured. Oh, well. James may have stopped looking for her. After all, he got married long time ago and most likely moved on to raise a family.

If she wanted to communicate with James, she'd probably have a better chance of finding him, although, she'd heard that they already moved. James was no longer working for the seaplane company and Hal gave up his work for the city after his proposed bill failed.

Damn it. Why did she keep on thinking about the past? Because it ended prematurely? Because what she had for James was love to the extreme?

Rienne stopped a server. "Please ask Councilman Williams if he needs a refill. He looks bored." She pointed at the man in a black tuxedo and ponytailed hair.

"Yes, ma'am."

Rienne watched the server make a quick beeline toward Williams, then quickly checked her cell phone's messenger, an *iPhone* application that showed if she had messages without actually opening *Facebook*. She nearly dropped her wine glass when she saw that she *did* have a message. She couldn't tell yet who sent it. It could be someone who wanted to make friends on *Facebook* or an advertisement, but whatever or wherever it came from, she needed to know.

She'd been waiting for this moment to happen. Now that it did, she couldn't quite know how to handle it. Her whole body shook from what seemed to be reactivated feelings that she had tucked deep in her heart. She moved around and talked to people, but her mind was no longer there. Unable to give her attention on the party, she asked the head of the catering to make sure everyone had enough food and drink to enjoy. She was about to rush to her office when Andy called her.

"Yes, Andy." Her friend wore a long sleeved, psychedelic-designed top with flowing sleeves and white bellbottom pants. His rounded tinted glasses reminded Rienne of what rock and rollers in the seventies used to wear. Andy loved to dress up. Whatever made him feel good, he'd go for it, but always within the bounds of reasons.

"Hey there…you okay?"

"I'm fine."

"You look distracted. We should've hired more help for tonight."

"Oh, no. We got this."

"Well, I want you to meet the governor of Washington State."

"Maybe in a minute. I just need to go to the bathroom."

Andy eyed her warily. "Rienne, you don't look right."

"Do you have a cigarette?"

"A what?"

"A cigarette."

Andy took Rienne's elbow and guided her toward the bathroom. "Since when did you start smoking, darling?"

"Never mind, then."

"What is it?"

Rienne glanced at the group of people chatting the night away. The party was in full swing. Andy's friends were also in attendance. She should be out there dropping hints about donations and support for her organization and not freaking out like this. "I got a message on Facebook."

"*The* message?"

"Yes."

"Fuck!" Andy covered his mouth. "Sorry," he mumbled.

"I'm not sure if it's from him, though."

"Who would message you on that account?" Andy looked at his watch. "Almost one. Damn. I wish they would all leave now. Maybe I should call *bomb* to make them leave."

"Silly. Just talk to the guests. I'll be out in a few."

"Okay. Oh, God. I'm so excited, I think I'm going to have my period any moment."

Rienne rolled her eyes. "Stop, Andy."

"Shit, Rienne. This news is better than coming in my partner's ass."

"Andy!"

"Okay. I'll mingle. Tell me if it's him or I'll twist your nipple until you scream for more."

"You are such a pervert."

"And you love this pervert."

Andy gave her a quick kiss, then left her outside the bathroom. Rienne made sure that he was gone before walking quickly to her office. She had a feeling who it was that messaged her, but didn't want to hope. In addition, if it *were* James, what would she do? What would she say? Well, she should just check the message and then she'd go from there. Who knows? Maybe she was just overreacting.

Rienne closed her office door. She sat on her desk feeling like her limbs were frozen. For a minute, she stared at the red notification.

I have a message. Please let it be James.

Taking deep breaths, she pressed the blue envelope.

Rienne was in complete shock when she saw the name JT Huntington. "Oh, my. Oh, my. James. My Punjabi. Couldn't be," she said. She read his message. It was short.

Maldita,

Always and forever.

Punjabi

+08 936 959 4463

Lots of digits. A cell phone, Rienne thought. Her fingers hovered on the screen. She wanted to reply right away, but seeing that James added his phone number changed her mind. She should talk to him. It took her a full minute before finally she got the courage to dial the number.

Her heart pounded so hard, she felt dizzy. The more she listened to the ringing tone, the worse she felt. She was about to hang up when she heard a voice.

"James here."

"Hello?" Rienne asked.

"Hi. This is Captain Hungtington. Who is this?"

Captain? "Hi. This is… This is Rienne."

The line went quiet.

"Hello? Is this James?"

"Say your name again."

"Rienne."

"Maldita."

Rienne laughed as her tears began to fall. After all these years, she'd finally heard his voice again. "This is me. How are you, Punjabi?"

James didn't answer, but Rienne could hear him breathing. She shocked him. Or maybe she called at the wrong time. Oh dear. Why didn't she think about that earlier?

***

Jesus. James stood up as he held the phone by his ear and walked around the ship's bridge. He couldn't believe that he'd found Rienne, and right at that moment, was on the other end of the line. The back of his nose began to burn and then his eyes watered.

I found my Rienne. My Maldita.

"I can call later if you're busy."

"No. I'm not busy. I'm working, but I can talk. How are you?"

"I think I asked you first."

James laughed. "Still sassy. I am good. You?"

"Good." Rienne's voice was small and shaky.

"Where have you been all this time, Maldita?"

"Waiting for you to find me. What took you so long?"

James' heart shattered when Rienne started sobbing. "Sorry, love. Kind of got lost in my navigation."

"Your area code, where is that?"

"I'm in Australia."

"Why?"

"My ship berthed here today. I'm a Maritime Captain now."

"You dreamed of becoming one," Rienne said haltingly.

"Don't cry, love. I already found you."

"Oh my God. This is unbelievable."

"I know. Sorry it took me this long."

"How did you know I own JP RM?"

"I didn't. A friend helped me. Where are you now?"

"North Carolina."

"Nice," James said.

"You're in Australia. Even nicer."

"Been a long time, Rienne."

"Yeah. James. I don't know if we'll talk again, so I want to take this opportunity now to tell you that I'm sorry about what Dad did to you…to us. I'm truly and deeply sorry."

"Me, too. But no worries now. And we'll talk again. Every minute.

If you are available."

"I am. You have no idea how long I've waited."

"My guess is six years."

Rienne laughed. "I am shaking."

"I'm still in shock."

"Dad told me that you've been married and have a child. Maybe children now?"

James was surprised. He knew Roy hated him for taking Rienne outside her safety zone, but to make up stories about him, well, that was somewhat low. Especially for a man like Roy. "You're dad is misinformed."

"What?"

"I'm not married and as far as I know, haven't fathered a child." He could hear tapping sounds, but Rienne didn't say anything. "Rienne?" James listened. Damn, he wished he could hug Rienne right now. He knew their meeting again wouldn't be all about exchanging great stories. After all, they separated under sad circumstances. "Baby, talk to me."

"Did you know that I was pregnant when Dad took me away?"

It was a good thing James was leaning on the railing, otherwise he would have fallen backwards. *Rienne was pregnant?* Fuck, fuck, fuck! If he knew, he would have fought Roy harder to keep her. Fuck his bodyguards and so fucking what if they destroyed him. Jesus!

"Rienne. Are you saying that we have a baby?"

"Jordan. She's five."

That was it. All emotions that he had been keeping welled up. A sob escaped his mouth. "Jesus. Why didn't you tell me?"

"I-I was going to, but Dad came and I didn't say anything then. I was afraid he'd do something with the baby. I wanted to tell you, I swear. But my dad...he made threats. I didn't want you to get hurt. Or Hal. So I stayed away."

"Where is Roy?"

"He's gone now."

"I'm sorry."

"I'm sorry, too. For everything."

"We have a baby," he whispered.

"I'll send you her pictures."

"And yours, too. I want to see you again."

"I'm still the same. Ugly with a body that resembles a fire hydrant. Oh, yeah, a hunchback."

"So you're still beautiful. Send your picture now."

Rienne stood up and walked toward the standup full-length mirror she had placed in the corner of her study. "But I look tired."

James grinned. "You should see me. I look like a haggard monkey. Come on. Just one picture, please."

"All right. I'll hang up, though because I'm hosting a party."

"Okay. Call when you're available or I can do it."

"I'll call." Rienne sighed. "James…glad to hear your voice again."

"Me, too."

For some reason, the words I love you nearly flew out of her mouth. Shaking her head, she said goodbye, then hung up.

Rienne knew how to take good *selfies* because of Andy. He showed her the best angle when taking one. Rienne held the cell phone at arm's length, smiled and then used her thumb to press on the button on the side. She had to do it at least three times because she didn't think the first ones were good enough. Realizing what she was doing, she laughed.

Satisfied with her last shot, he quickly composed a message for James. "*Just as I promised.*" She hit *send*. It took only a few seconds before James replied.

"*You're beautiful.*"

Rienne smiled. She shot him a message back. "*Thank you. Now, your turn.*"

"*I'll send you one, but I want to see our daughter first.*" ☺

"*Cheat.*" Rienne replied, but sent James a recent picture of Jordan anyway.

Sighing, she pocketed her phone. Lordy, she felt like flying. With a smile on her face, she left the study in search of Andy.

Chapter Sixteen

Andy walked back and forth in front of Rienne's desk. If he continued to do that, he'd leave shoe marks on the hardwood floor. It was almost three in the morning and both of them were still wide-awake.

"So your prince charming found you. What are you going to do now?"

"Call him again, I suppose. That's what I promised him. Then go from there."

"Go from there? I know you're dying to bang him again, but darling, he's a ship's captain. If I'm right, he's floating on water for months. You know what that means. Months without sex. Who knows, maybe he has different women in every port. Seamen are known for that. Deprive, their sacs blue, and their hand's covered with calluses from masturbating."

"Andy, you're mind is as dirty as a hippo's ass. We haven't seen each other for six years. If we talk, we'll most likely try to catch up and talk about Jordan."

"Come on. Who are you fooling? I bet you're thinking about his cock right now."

"Stop, Andy, I'm glad that I got to talk to him again."

"Well, I heard, too, that those seamen get so lonely, they would try to find their kindergarten friends. Are you sure he looked for you because he wanted to find you?"

"He found me through my *Facebook* account and sent me a message. Isn't that enough sign that he wanted to find me? Do you know how hard that is?"

"Darling." Andy went around the table, then sat on her armchair. "You know I'm saying all of this because I love you. I don't want you to get hurt. You were like a broken doll when I met you. Now you're whole again—on the inside at least."

"Thank you, Andy."

"All right. I'll leave you be. Call your prince. Just don't get carried away and send him pictures of your boobs. Let him drool first." Andy gave Rienne a kiss then left her alone.

Feeling the blissful happiness she had felt many years ago whenever she met James, Rienne picked-up her phone, then dialed his number.

Epilogue

Three months later.

James was happy with the caretaker. Frank had done a good job keeping the cabin in good shape. Except for the empty refrigerator, everything was where he and Rienne had left them. Even their towels were still on the bathroom counter.

He'd been back here only twice to give Frank instructions. That was it. He couldn't stand seeing the cabin without Rienne. Now, after six years, he was back—for a good reason. *Damn.* He felt like crying again. James shook his head. Sometimes he still could not believe that he'd be with Rienne again and their daughter.

Jordan. James smiled to himself remembering his daughter's face. For three months now, he'd been seeing his wife and daughter online. To hear Jordan call him *dad* was the best feeling he'd ever felt in a long time. He would've met them sooner, but he couldn't just leave his ship. Anyway, the long wait was over. They'd be here soon.

James placed the groceries he'd bought in the cupboards and the perishables in the fridge. If they needed more supplies, they could go for a drive at the nearby store.

Freedom. That was what they have now. Freedom to love, to do what they wanted. Another CEO of the Pacific Northwest Rock committed suicide in jail leaving a note of his criminal activities, thus absolving Roy, which meant that Rienne was now free from her father's mistakes, clearing his name for good even though there was still talk about him being guilty. James believed that those speculations would never go away and would forever haunt the memory of Roy.

James heard the sound of the car approaching. Instantly, his heart skipped a beat. He took deep breaths, shook his hands, and then went out the front door.

A silver BMW slowly drove on the driveway. He could see the driver. It was Rienne. Just like what he saw on the picture, her hair was pixie short. She looked fantastic. Damn, he could hardly wait to run his fingers through her spiky hair. He choked. Different emotions were rioting in his chest and he couldn't even hear anything except for the blood pounding in his ears.

The car stopped. For a minute, he just stood there and stared at Rienne who returned his gaze. Then, she got out of the car. James was rooted to the ground. He couldn't move. He just watched as Rienne opened the back door. When he saw her pick up their daughter, his knees almost buckled.

"Hi," Rienne said while walking toward him.

"Hello, love." He finally found his strength and slowly walked to meet his wife and daughter.

"Say *hi* to Daddy, Jordan?"

"Hi, Daddy."

Those simple words undid him. He closed their distance and hugged his precious girls, and let his emotions flow out of him.

"I'm so happy to see you, love. Both of you," he said in between sobs.

"Me, too. I'm so glad you didn't give up on us."

"No, it never crossed my mind." He cupped Rienne's cheek with his hand then gave her a soft hello kiss that went all the way down to his toes. "It's always been you, Maldita. *Always* you."

Watch the Skies
by Tanith Davenport

<u>Prologue</u>

She liked to look out of her window at night and watch the stars.

It was a strange feeling. Sometimes it was curiosity, a desire to know what was out there. There had to be something, she was sure. They couldn't possibly be the only intelligent life in the universe. Somewhere, no matter how far, there had to be other life, other knowledge.

But then, how far? Across unguessable gulfs, or closer by? Within their own galaxy, or lost somewhere in the immensity of space? Could it be possible that there was alien life within easy reach, or would it involve impossible travel to find them?

Sometimes it was loneliness. She wanted to find someone else out there, someone to communicate with, someone to know. It was difficult sometimes, feeling that she didn't really belong. She often felt as though she was alone in a crowd, not like everyone else, abandoned in the midst of numbers.

Maybe out there in the universe there were others who would understand.

And then, at other times, she thought she saw lights, shapes. It was probably nothing. Airplanes, shooting stars. But at those times she would find her emotions changing as she watched, feeling a strange sensation of peace or belonging. She would find herself wanting to join them, yearning to cross that space and see them.

She could almost hear them in her head sometimes.

Ours. Ours. Ours.

Not that she ever would tell anyone that. People would think she was crazy. Hell, she often thought she was crazy. But it gave her comfort to feel wanted, even if it was all in her mind.

The strangest times were when she would feel lust.

Not for anything in particular. It was an odd, free-floating lust that seemed to attach itself to nothing. But sometimes she would watch the skies and find herself leaning hard against the window, one hand pressed to the zip of her jeans, clit throbbing, wet, aching to be touched.

She would never understand why, but she liked to think it was part of the sense of belonging. That sometimes she was wanted, needed, and in return they made her need. It was a sweet secret she would never share, bizarre and special and solely her own.

Mine. Mine. Mine.

She liked to picture them at times, imagine what they might look like. She had read so many different descriptions of alien life. Would they have the pointed face, wide eyes and spindly limbs of the traditional grey alien? Would they look more humanoid, blonde and sensual? Or maybe they would be completely different, unimaginable. She liked to think they would be recognisable, but maybe there were things out there that nobody had ever seen, or claimed to see.

The feelings of desire had come more often recently. More and more she had found herself aching, wanting, staring up at the sky in need. So many times she had yearned for someone to appear in front of her and touch her, make her come. There had to be some reason for her having these feelings. There just had to be.

The last time it had happened, she had given way to it, let herself go. Her body had been thrumming with lust, her nipples taut under her shirt, her skin tingling. She had unfastened her jeans, let them fall to the floor and dropped her panties to her knees, giving herself more room for manoeuvre. The window stopped at her waist, but there was still an odd sensation of being watched, that somebody outside could see her half-naked, and it had sent a sting to her clit.

Ours. Ours. Ours.

Lightly, then more firmly, she had touched one finger to her nub, then slid it lower, feeling the wetness building in her cunt. She had begun to move her finger in circles, darting it inside her moist centre at intervals, her breath mounting as her clit began to pulse under the pressure. The feeling of being observed grew, and she had almost felt as though she was putting on a show - one that was approved of fully by whoever might be watching.

Closer, closer. Her breasts had strained under her top, the globes of her ass had clenched. She had pictured someone else's hand where hers was, taking control, slipping fingers inside her pussy and another into her ass, double-fingering her, teasing her, tormenting her. Bending her over her bed and fucking her, harder and faster, pushing her closer and closer to the edge until she finally fell over it into bliss.

She was sure that was what they wanted, in that moment. But nobody was there. No matter how hard she looked, nobody was ever there.

Her juices coated her fingers, growing slippery as her hand moved faster. Her body had tightened, pleasure spiralling in her gut, her skin flushing as the need built. God, it was too good. She had tried to hold back for just a little longer, straining to focus her eyes on the stars, but it was impossible to wait, and with a desperate cry she had hit her climax, her pussy clenching down on her fingers as her clit throbbed with one final stab of ecstasy.

Afterwards she had stood at the window, watching, wondering. She was still alone, still adrift, and yet the experience felt as though it had brought her closer to whatever was there.

But she still couldn't be sure there was anything really there.

If only she could know the truth. She spent most of her time searching for answers and finding nothing. If only something would happen, something that would tell her she wasn't wasting her time.

Maybe one day her wish would come true.

Chapter One

Light.

Nothing but light surrounding her, filling her vision. Her head was spinning, confused. It was as though she was floating, nothing to feel but air. Then figures appeared in front of her, dark shapes and the light began to fade.

Where am I? Where are we?

The floating sensation gradually dissipated. She was sprawled on a... *what was it? Metal?* Some kind of bed and automatically she moved her arms, but they weren't tied down. She was flat on her face, but free to move. She took a deep breath and felt something stir within her. This wasn't right.

Memories were reforming in her clouded mind, memories of the evening which had led her here and for a moment she wondered where the others were. Was she alone here, or had they all been taken?

Then the sensation inside her grew and her breath rushed out in a moan.

***

If there was one thing she hated about these places, it was that they didn't even have a car park. Cars raced by in the dark, headlights flashing over the five figures in the layby as they were unpacking their gear.

Aster Booker hoisted her rucksack out of the boot and dropped it on the ground, reaching further in for the bag of torches.

"Did you bring the GPS, Wade?"

There was the sound of a trunk slamming shut. "Yeah, I got them."

"Good. I'll let you lead then."

Already she could see two of her teammates gathering in the middle of the layby, weighed down by bags of equipment. Aster slung her rucksack over her shoulder, picked up her bag and moved to join them. The glow of a phone screen dazzled her as she reached them.

"Hey, Hagar."

"Hey," Hagar said but didn't look up from the screen which was casting a strange mix of light and shadow across her masculine face.

Square-jawed, ponytailed and with an odd downward curve to the corners of her mouth, Hagar drew comments whenever they had a new member of the group, usually along the lines of, 'I can't stop looking at her' and, 'I don't know why.'

But she was good at her job and that was all Aster cared about. Right now Hagar was doing a final check of the evidence, Aster knew. They'd been sent this footage a few days earlier by a local who'd filmed it while he was out star-gazing. All Hagar's checks had suggested it was genuine, which had led them to where they were now, a night vigil.

She dug in her pack for a head torch and turned to hand it to Annah, one of their visual technicians, who was standing nearby with a night-vision camera slung round her neck. From behind she heard the scuffle of shoes on gravel and guessed that Wade and Zack had arrived.

"We good to go?"

"Think so." Zack held out his hand for a head torch. "It's about five minutes walk away. We've got it locked into the GPS."

"Cool." Aster fastened her own torch around her head, pushing her rainbow hair out of her face. "Let's go."

"You *are* actually going to let me lead this time then?"

Aster paused mid-step and looked at Wade Sawyer, who was

standing and looking at her with an expression that suggested he wasn't kidding.

Blond hair and sharp cheekbones topped a slim yet muscular body, all six feet of it, covered mostly in a long black jacket and jeans. Aster felt her body blush.

Not this crap again.

"Yes, Wade. You have the location, so you can lead."

"Just checking." Wade turned and set off, not bothering to wait for anyone to follow him.

Jesus.

The walk to the site was mostly silent. Aster bit down on her lip to stifle any angry comments she was tempted to make. It was better to do this quietly anyway. You never knew what you might encounter.

But Wade, God, Wade.

It had been going on for too damn long. From the moment Wade had walked in the door and from the moment she had heard, 'Is this the Haysham UFO Society?' She had looked up to see the blond, sardonically-smiling figure hovering nearby and she had felt something grip her. She had always had a thing for cheekbones and it had all seemed so easy.

Wade had been straightforward to work with. He knew how to handle night-vision equipment, read maps with red light and collect data securely. He could connect well with other members of the team and he could not only talk, but he could also listen and pick up information quickly. It was always good to have more members on the team. The friend he'd come with, Milton, was rarely there and it was a pain to have unreliable people around. Wade was there every week, even joining them at the unsociable times they held vigils.

Aster knew she asked a lot from the team members. She and Hagar had been running the society together for years and their standards were high. It pissed her off when people fucked around with them, showed up once or twice and then didn't bother again. Or offered to come out one night and then left them standing around waiting without the equipment they'd promised to bring.

Wade was smart. He was interested. He kept his own hours and he said from the start that as a personal trainer he was fairly flexible. Didn't *that* image stay in her head?

Most of the crew had nine-to-five jobs, so they were free in the evenings, although they saved the really late nights for weekends. Aster worked in the offices of a local cave reserve and didn't want to spend the day exhausted any more than anyone else did. Someone like Wade, willing to work with them, was valuable.

Every time he stood next to her, something seemed to pull her closer to him. All he had to do was look at her and her skin burned.

Aster had no fear of men, no fear of *flirting* with men and Wade gave it right back. When they'd swapped numbers early on, Wade had deliberately brushed her hand with his while handing over his phone. Aster had held his gaze whenever possible, twirled her hair and touched her neck. She'd intended to ask him out before he'd even been in the group a month.

But then it all seemed to go wrong.

She was one of the longest-standing members of the crew. She'd been on more vigils than all the others put together. It was natural for her to take charge when arranging events and selecting suitable sites. But somehow that wasn't good enough for Wade. He gave her little side-eyed looks whenever she was talking. Sniping at her on vigils. '*Oh really? You'd let me do that?*'

And it was so *fucking* annoying that he still had that effect on her body. Even more so that he seemed to feel it too. On more than one occasion, looking up at him though her blue fringe, Aster had seen a heat in his eyes, a tension in his jaw, which suggested he wanted... something. Maybe just one night, but *something*.

Normally she'd have continued to pursue him. But as two members of the society, she'd chosen to stand back. Thinking about it, it was too risky to go after a man she couldn't easily walk away from. In any event, she could sense the kinds of men she could win over easily and Wade wasn't one of them. Even if they had ever managed to get to that *something*, he'd have run screaming. If he thought she was too alpha out of the bedroom, he hadn't seen anything yet.

Trees loomed overhead as they reached the site, a stretch of land which was apparently part of the local golf course. At this distance from the road there was no light pollution, the only lights were from their own torches, cutting through the dark. Ahead, Wade had already started laying down his waterproof wrap, suggesting he was setting up camp for the time being.

Aster deliberately let Hagar and Annah set themselves up before sitting on the other side of them, staying as far from Wade as she could. Hagar was running over the footage again, checking the time on the screen.

"It was around this time it happened. Look," he said.

Dutifully Aster glanced over Hagar's shoulder to watch the footage again. In the darkened sky, shaking slightly as the camera moved, a three-cornered pattern of lights crossed the air occasionally casting down a beam which looked like a searchlight.

The time on the video read 12:05AM.

"Okay. We'll give it about an hour, then start data-collecting."

Hagar nodded, switching off the screen. Aster reached up to turn off her head torch and lay down as the others followed, plunging them into darkness.

Cold settled on her, light breezes stirring her hair. This was the worst part of a vigil. She much preferred collecting data, testing samples and finding alternative explanations. Or not, of course. On a good night, there wasn't one. But just sitting and waiting for events to repeat themselves...

Wait. A light had appeared in the sky.

Hagar's hand landed on Aster's wrist. Aster lifted her hand slightly to acknowledge the touch. *A plane, maybe? A shooting star? No, it's too bright. This is closer to us.*

The undergrowth rustled. Annah was kneeling, holding up her camera to film the light as it moved. As they watched it split into two lights, then three, moving closer.

Aster's heart stood still. *Have we actually got a real encounter here?* Her scalp prickled, as though her hair was standing on end. Automatically she slid a hand up to rub the spot, keeping her eyes on the lights. It wasn't imaginary, her hair *was* standing on end.

Hagar was staring at her, mouth gaping as Aster stared back, running her fingers along the rainbow-streaked locks that were straining away from her head.

What the hell?

There was a sudden blaze of light from behind them and Annah yelped. *Oh God!*

A broad beam of golden light fell through the trees, forming a circle on the ground. In the centre Annah was half standing, half arching backwards, camera still pointing straight up in the air, her mouth stretched in a rictus of shock.

"Annah!" Zack shouted from somewhere to the right, but Annah didn't react. Her eyes were fixed on something above, something outside the golden glow. Then she let out a guttural moan and dropped to her knees, her free hand clasped to the zip of her jeans.

Aster rolled onto her back and scrambling into a sitting position. But before she could get up, a wave of sensation rolled over her, knocking her flat on the ground.

Oh...

Her eyes rolled back into her head as a rush of desire surged through her body, her back arching as every inch of her skin began to tingle and inside her head words were echoing. Echoing in a language she had never heard and yet somehow understood deep in her core.

You want.

You want.

You want.

She closed her eyes against the feeling, but the glow was still there, seeping into her mind. Biting her lip, she struggled to think, struggled to work out what was happening. It was impossible. She was overwhelmed by lust and light. Somewhere in the distance she could hear Annah still moaning, hear the scrabbling noise of feet in the undergrowth. She heard Hagar gasping beside her and the deeper groans of Zack a little further away... and further still, Wade. The name rang in her head and for a moment the image it conjured sent a stab of desire through her gut.

Wade. Wade. Wade.

Then, as she arched her back again, the ground was gone and so was her mind.

When she came to again, the light was fading. Dark shapes moved at the edges of her vision. *Metal. Something metal underneath me.* It was nothing like she had ever seen before and yet what it resembled most was a surgical bed. She was lying face down on a surgical bed. Naked. The lingering excitement she still felt began to dissipate as reality set in.

I've been abducted.

After all this time, after all the places they'd visited with minimal success, she hadn't just had an encounter, she'd actually been abducted. Her stomach clenched in fear. Almost immediately she felt another rush of desire. *It's them, they're controlling it.* She forced open her eyes, which had fallen shut and fought against the sensation to focus on her surroundings.

Her hands and feet weren't tied, that was good. Where were the others? Were they here? She cast a look round the room. The space seemed enormous; it was impossible to see the edges, they just vanished into the dark. Closer to her, all seemed to be white and metallic. The floor below shone a dull grey while the bed had a brighter layer and extending its edges where curves of metal that stood as a reminder of restraints.

To her right, she could see a second bed and Annah, sprawled on her back. She was still clothed, her blonde hair spilling over the edge of the bed, but her hands were restrained and Aster shivered. Further away she could see Hagar standing as if in a trance, her dark ponytail loosened around her shoulders, staring as if unseeing.

She looked to her left and immediately gasped. Wade was lying flat on his back completely naked, his body flushed and glistening with sweat. He wasn't tied, but he was sprawled as if he was, arms and legs spread wide to the edges of the table. Aster's eyes were immediately drawn down the line of blond fuzz to his cock, which stood proud in a nest of curls, straining towards the ceiling.

Oh God. I can't. I can't. Hastily she looked away, but the image lingered in her brain sending a frisson of longing through her body. She could picture herself mounting him, sliding his cock inside her, driving him into her over and over again. As the thought crossed her mind, she became aware of a dark shape directly in front of her. Looking at it was like looking into the sun. The edges were blurred, its shape difficult to determine. She had the impression of a head, of long fingers and of large eyes that bored into her soul.

That voice again in her head, but this time the words were different.

Fuck him.

Fuck him.

Fuck him.

"No," she whispered.

But the words continued, though she struggled to block them.

Wade didn't want her, he didn't even particularly like her. Even if he was feeling the same lust that she was and something was telling her that he was, she couldn't do what he didn't really want. It wasn't right.

Fuck him, the voice insisted.

"No."

Then another voice. Wade's.

"Aster?"

She deliberately kept her eyes away from him.

"Can you hear it too?"

"Yes."

"Aster," Wade's voice was ragged. "I want you."

She bit her lip against the sudden surge of desire his words created.

"No you don't. They're doing this."

"I know what they're doing. I wanted you already."

The voice was growing louder in her head and Aster struggled to force it aside.

"You don't want me. You bitch at me every time you see me."

There was a sigh from her left.

"That would be because I *do* want you and if you tell anyone I said that I'll kick your ass. Stop making me beg."

Aster felt her mouth quirk slightly.

"Maybe I like making you beg."

Fuck him, the voice ordered. But now there was a new, underlying message that Aster ignored. It didn't just want her to fuck him, it wanted her to *top* him. To take charge over him. As much as she liked to do that, she was pretty sure Wade wouldn't. As a gasp sounded from behind her, her eyes automatically snapped to the left and immediately met Wade's, wide and staring at her with a need she could barely resist.

"Wade, you won't like it the way I…"

"Do it. I will. Just do it, please."

It was that 'please' that finally did it.

She sat up and slid to the edge of a table, lowering her feet to the floor. The metal was cold on her skin and she shivered, feeling her nipples harden as goose bumps rose all over her body. She straightened, suddenly fully aware that she was completely naked, her only gesture to modesty being her rainbow-streaked hair which hung forward over her breasts.

Wade was staring, his eyes running the length of her body, over her covered breasts to the flare of her hips and the strip of dark hair concealing her folds. He was staring unashamedly, as though he had wanted nothing more in his life.

Maybe, in this moment, he hadn't. But Aster was sure he'd never been fucked in the way she wanted to, in the way the creatures wanted. She stretched her hands above her head, exposing her body further and heard Wade gasp.

Fuck him.

"I want you," Wade whispered and Aster felt a smile cross her face as she moved towards the table, stopping when she was within arm's reach of him.

"Keep your hands and feet where they are. Don't move."

Wade froze in place, but his cock jerked and Aster leaned forward to press her finger to the tip, slowly moving it in a circle over the head. In one long, careful movement, she drug her finger down the underside of his dick, taking her time, until she reached the base and began the tortuous journey back up again.

"Please."

Oh, I do like it when he begs.

"Keep still." She could see Wade's fingers twitching, knew he was aching to move. But not yet. Not yet.

Taking her hand back, she climbed up onto the table and straddled him, positioning herself across his thighs. She reached down to cup his balls, massaging them gently as she trailed the fingers of her other hand along his abs and up to caress one nipple.

Wade groaned, his eyes falling shut. "I can't..."

"Oh, you can and you will." Aster watched him as her fingers moved, teasing, as Wade's muscles stiffened in the effort to keep still, until finally Wade let out a guttural cry and his hand shot out to grab hers.

"Aster..."

"Ah..." Aster shook him off, holding up a finger in warning. "For that, you get to eat me. Let's see how good you are."

Moving slowly on all fours, she crawled along his body, letting his cock drag against her stomach as she did so, feeling his pre-cum slick against her skin. When her knees were alongside his ears she straightened up and held herself still for a moment, giving him time to appreciate his position.

And *her* position.

"Lick me, Wade," she commanded. "And make it good."

She felt Wade's hands cup her ass, squeezing and then his tongue was there. First tentatively then forcefully, licking a line from her folds to her clit.

Oh, he was good. His tongue swirled, circling her nub before dragging back down to dart inside her, over and over again. Aster slid her hands up to caress her own breasts, running her fingers over her pebbled nipples, crying out at the shivers of pleasure their combined touches created. She ground down onto Wade's mouth, demanding more and the movements of his tongue grew faster, harder, as she felt bliss gathering in her gut, stealing closer and closer on her.

Just as she was reaching the edge, she lifted herself up, ignoring the ache of loss in her pussy. She shuffled backwards until she felt Wade's cock hit her ass, shifted and let him slip inside her, just as far as the head.

"Give me your hands."

Wade let his hands fall back on the table and Aster gripped them, holding them down as she pushed back against him at the same time, taking him inside her in one long movement.

Fuck him!

The voices joined in a chorus as Aster rocked her hips, moving her body in a rhythm with Wade's as his cock slid inside her, slick with her wetness and his pre-cum. *Oh*, it was too good, pleasure was rippling from her centre through her body and Wade was moaning and jerking his hips upwards. God, she had wanted him for so fucking *long* and this was finally happening. Wade wanted her too and wanted her like *this* and the voices were still chanting in her head, repeating *fuck him, fuck him, fuck him...*

She stiffened as ecstasy hit her in one rush, arching her back as Wade's dick seemed to swell within her, Wade thrusting harder and faster before giving one last desperate cry, his back bowing in release.

When Aster opened her eyes again, all she could see was blackness.

As her vision slowly began to adjust, stars began to appear out of the darkness, and she realised she was looking up at the sky. Beneath her she could feel grass and earth, lumpy and rough. Slowly she sat up, turning to look around her; she was back at the site.

They were all back at the site.

In various positions around her she could see the others stirring back to consciousness, gradually pushing themselves upright as they struggled to work out where they were. Hagar was staring straight ahead, apparently unaware of her surroundings; Annah was looking all around herself, wide-eyed and shocked. Aster wondered if she remembered what had taken place.

God, there was potential for embarrassment there. But then Annah had been tied down - what did she have of her own to remember? Had anything happened to her while Aster and Wade had been -

Wade.

Wade was still lying on his back. Aster forced herself to her feet, her legs shaking, and made her way over to him, dropping to her knees beside him.

"Wade."

No movement. His eyes were closed, his body limp and relaxed. Aster shook him, trying to stay calm. He was just taking a while to wake up. It wasn't a problem. Would he remember?

"Wade!"

Then Wade's eyes shot open and met hers, and Aster knew.

Chapter Two

Aster stood back from her wall and tilted her head to the side. *No, still not right.* She moved forward, lifted her paintbrush and started adding to the picture already in place. Parts of it were already beginning to dry. In front of her was an image she had seen many times before in writings and articles, mostly pinned to the wall at the UFO Society. A round-topped head with a pointed chin, large oval eyes fading to corners, a long narrow body and spindly arms and legs with thin fingers.

A grey alien.

As she continued to paint, the eyes grew larger and the skin paler. It had been so hard to see it properly and yet this was the picture that remained in her head. It had been a grey.

But she had never encountered this before. She had heard of aliens experimenting on people, implanting, probing. She had even heard of aliens having sex with people. Although, she remembered, those tended to be Scandinavian-looking rather than greys. But she had never heard of aliens *watching* people have sex. It just seemed pointless. Why would they want to do that? Curiosity? Some kind of experiment they hadn't known about?

She shook her head, pausing with her brush. She had no idea. All she knew was that somehow, last night a group of greys had watched her have sex with Wade. More than that, they had watched her dominate Wade. They had *wanted* that. She and Wade had both known that, both heard it in their heads.

And Wade, the man who had resented so much her even taking charge of a meeting, had wanted it too.

A buzz from the bedside table caught her attention. Dropping the brush into the paint pot on the shelf she picked up her phone and clicked open the message.

Do you remember last night? H.

Hagar.

She remembered Hagar now, walking away as they left the site. Hagar hadn't spoken, hadn't looked at any of them. It had been as though she was still in a trance.

Aster had assumed she wouldn't remember any of it. Certainly Annah and Zack hadn't. The first thing Annah had said upon waking up had been, "What happened?" Aster had pretended ignorance herself, not wanting to admit to any of it. It would have been a hellish conversation to have. Besides, it was best for Annah not to remember she'd been restrained.

So she'd thought only she and Wade would remember. She knew Wade did. She'd seen it in his eyes as they walked back to the cars. Seen it in the looks he kept casting at her.

But apparently Hagar did too. Or maybe it was all a blank for her and she was checking in.

Do you? Aster.

The message came back within a minute.

Hell yes.

Before Aster could think of an answer, her phone buzzed again.

Meet me at the Society building.

***

If Hagar was inviting her to meet to talk about this, it had to be important to her. Aster had known Hagar for years, well before they'd started the Society together. They'd met in university, joined the same

UFO Society there. Aster had been drawn to Hagar's off-beat sense of humour and enthusiastic acceptance of all things occult and bizarre. Hagar had often told her that Aster was the only person who would listen to her theories. They'd been friends from the moment they met, connected by a fascination for the weird and wonderful and a determination to find out more.

Hagar was already at the Society clubhouse when Aster arrived. In every respect she looked the same as always, hair in a ponytail, dressed in combat trousers and a T-shirt and that odd quirk to her mouth that made her look like she was smiling and frowning at the same time. She had even brought two four-packs of beer, which was so typically Hagar that Aster caught herself smiling. But there was a strange intensity in her face that Aster had never seen before.

"Let me guess," Hagar said before Aster could speak. "You brought food."

Aster gave an awkward shrug. "You know me."

"Yup. You brought those sausage rolls you always make and I brought beer." Hagar gestured towards the beer on the table from her seated position on the floor. "And when Annah gets here, she'll have brought chocolate and we'll all act like everything's normal."

She paused, picked up a can of beer and cracked it open, looking at Aster expectantly.

Aster filled in the silence, sitting down on the floor at the same time.

"But it isn't. Is it?"

Hagar raised an eyebrow.

"What do you remember?"

"I remember you and Wade fucking and none of that seemed weird." Hagar fixed her eyes on her beer. "I remember Annah tied up and it was like I didn't even care."

Aster winced. She remembered that too and all she had been able to think about was her body.

"And I remember them talking to me in some weird language. It didn't make sense. I mean, I understood it, but..." Hagar shook her head. "It was just... weird."

"What did they say to you?"

Hagar paused for a moment, thinking. "It was just like... *What do you see? What do you see?*"

What do you see?

Aster took a can of beer to cover her silence. This needed thinking about.

"What did they look like to you?"

"Greys," Hagar answered immediately. "Five of them."

"Five of them? I could only really see one."

"No, there were five. They were all around the room."

"I couldn't really see the room. It was just the beds. The rest was too far away."

Hagar screwed up her face. "It was really clear to me. It was all white, like a lab and they were standing all round the walls, looking at us."

Her voice faded as they both sat there, staring at each other.

Why had Hagar seen so much more than she had? Why had Hagar been affected by the all-encroaching lust down on the ground, as they all had and then untouched by it in the room? Why, as Aster glanced idly across the room, had Hagar brought her radio with her?

"What's with the radio?"

"Tell me about Wade," was Hagar's blunt response.

Aster jolted at the change of subject. "What do you mean?"

"You know what I mean. What's going on with you two?"

"Nothing."

"Didn't look like nothing."

Aster paused, thinking. What exactly did she feel about Wade? It was too soon to know. Only last night she had been irritated with him for being a jerk, for his constant objections to her very existence. Yet even then she had known she was also irritated with herself at the desire she felt around him. Desire she still felt, even without the help of the greys. But did she feel anything more? Her feelings were a tangled mess. Somewhere in there was shock, surprise, lust and she recognised, liking. The Wade of last night had been likeable. Rather than slap him, as she frequently wanted to do, she had wanted to hold him. And that was just out of the question right now.

"So what's with the radio, again?"

Before Hagar could answer, the door swung open and Annah appeared, carrier bag in hand. Without speaking she crossed the room to join them, sat down and emptied the bag out in front of them. A collection of chocolate bars fell out.

Aster looked at her. Like Hagar had, Annah looked much as she always did, blonde hair spilling over her shoulders, fluffy pink jumper and that innocent expression that fooled everyone. She didn't have the intensity Aster had seen in Hagar's face, or had felt in her own gut that morning when she'd been driven to paint the alien on her wall.

She was just Annah. Annah who hadn't remembered a thing about last night.

Annah picked up a Mars bar, casually leaned her chin on her fist and gave Hagar an expectant gaze. "So what's up?"

Aster also turned her eyes to Hagar, figuring she would let her handle that question. What exactly had Hagar told Annah to get her here?

"Something strange has been happening since last night."

"Last night?"

"Annah," Aster cut in, "what exactly do you remember from last night?"

Annah looked confused. "Nothing, really. There was a light and we woke up in the field. I figured we were abducted."

"We were." Hagar stood, crossed the room and came back with the radio. "And now something's going on with this."

She fiddled with the radio for a moment, sending squeals and blurts of noise out of it. Aster glanced at Annah, who was looking even more puzzled.

"Are you sure it's not just…"

A voice cut through the air and Annah fell silent as Aster gripped her arm in shock.

It was the voice from last night. Cold, atonal and in English this time.

"*What do you see?*"

Aster's fingers were tightening on Annah's skin and she heard Annah squeak, but Aster's focus was entirely on the radio, a cold terror closing around her heart.

"When? Want. Come. You see. You see."

"How long has it been doing that?" Aster's voice was breathless.

Hagar switched the radio off grimly. "All morning."

"What do you think it means?" Annah asked.

"What do I think? I think they want us to go back there."

Oh God.

Somewhere in Aster's brain a little voice was telling her how ridiculous this was. She had been doing this for years, trying to make contact. Now that she finally had she should be jumping at the chance to go back and try again. To explore, to communicate. But somehow she had always assumed they would be the ones in control…and they weren't. Not by a long shot.

"All of us?" Annah blurted out, cutting through Aster's thoughts.

Hagar shrugged. "Well, you can't remember it. I suppose you don't have to."

Aster remembered Annah's pinioned wrists and shuddered.

"And Zack couldn't remember it either." Hagar cast an eye at Aster. "But we should bring Wade."

Aster flushed. The one thing she hadn't done was contact Wade. Under normal circumstances she would have. She didn't wait for men to pursue her. She'd have texted him the morning after and set something else up with him.

But this, this just felt weird.

'I do like you,' he'd said. He'd wanted her before. It hadn't just been the lust in the air and he'd wanted her to dominate him, wanted to let her take charge. But still, she had no idea what to say to him and damn that really pissed her off.

Annah was looking back and forth between her and Hagar, obviously picking up the signal Hagar had sent. Aster ignored her. If Hagar wanted to explain what had really happened, that was a conversation she'd be happy not to be present for. She sure as hell wasn't about to go into it. She bit her lip and decided to stop being pathetic.

"Okay. Tonight?"

Hagar nodded. "Works for me."

"Then if you want to buzz Zack and see if he's coming, I'll text Wade." There, now she'd said it, she'd have to do it.

"Wait," Annah cut in. "I'm in too. I want to remember it this time."

Hagar nodded, lifting her beer to her mouth. "Then here's hoping you do."

***

At seven PM, Aster was in her bedroom, staring at the collection of equipment laid out on the floor, torches, sky maps and sound gear, all the usual things she would take with her on a vigil. And yet she had the sneaking suspicion she would need very few of them. Maybe condoms would be a better idea.

Hagar had suggested going earlier tonight, since it was already dark in the evenings. Aster could see her point. If these aliens, and she still found it difficult to say the word, wanted them there, they probably wouldn't be waiting long.

So they would be meeting at eight, all five of them. Hagar had texted Zack and apparently he was keen to come, even though he still didn't seem to remember any of it.

Aster had texted Wade. She had written the damn text about fifteen times before finally losing her patience. This was Wade, for fuck's sake. Whether it was unusual circumstances or not, she had fucked him. She was not about to get all girly and stupid about sending a text message. There was no reason to forget herself just because it was Wade.

But actually writing the text was difficult. She was too used to making exceptions for his ego. Whenever she had texted him before, it had been with the knowledge that he would give her grief over every little thing. Now things had changed, and yet...

In the end, she had kept it brief: *We're going back. Meeting at the layby at 8. See you there.*

There. If he decided he wasn't coming, that was his business. She hadn't thought he would turn it down, but hell, anything was possible at this point.

It had been about half an hour before he'd responded.
OK.

Oh well. Never much of a talker.

Now that it was almost the time, Aster sat on her bed and tried to convince herself she wasn't nervous. She had no idea how to feel. Would they expect her to have sex with Wade again? Would they expect more of the same, or... what?

Or would they want something else? It had been Hagar's radio they had been speaking through after all. Would they be expecting something from Hagar?

There was no way of knowing and the thought left a cold chill in her gut. She dropped to her knees and crawled over to the equipment, dragging her rucksack with her. Forcing the fear down, she started to pack, pushing each item down in a rough motion.

A crackle cut through the air and Aster froze. Her spine prickled.

That was...

Slowly, very slowly, she turned to look over her shoulder at the CD player on top of the chest of drawers. She never used the radio on it; it wasn't tuned and the radio switch was set to 'off'.

It crackled again.

Aster turned on her knees, her eyes fixed on the device. It made a high-pitched whining noise, as if it was tuning itself. She bit her lip.

Then the voice.

"*You want.*"

Her heart jolted.

"*We want. You want. See.*"

Oh God. They want me.

Aster shook her head automatically, forcing the thought back. *Don't be stupid. You know what they want. This is the same as last night. They want to see you fuck Wade.*

But the new phrase was repeating over and over.

"*We want you want we want you want...*"

Aster screwed her eyes shut as the words echoed, echoed until she was no longer sure if they were on the radio or inside her head.

Then, quickly, she threw herself across the room and yanked the plug out of the wall. The voice stopped abruptly. Aster dragged herself back to her rucksack and shoved the equipment into it, ignoring the way her hands were shaking. Whatever this was, this was real. This was happening. And there was no point hiding from it.

She had to go back.

***

The layby was already full when Aster arrived.

Zack crossed to help her unpack the car, a pair of night vision goggles slung round his neck.

Aster cast him a curious glance. What did he hope to get out of the evening?

"So what do you think's going to happen?"

Zack hoisted a bag of equipment enthusiastically. "Are you kidding? It's going to be amazing."

"I thought you drew a blank on it all."

"I did, but they're calling us back, aren't they? They must want us to see them this time. I can't believe I'm actually going to see an alien. It's incredible." Zack reached up to shut the trunk. "My friend at *Alien Watchers* wants me to do a story on it."

"*Alien Watchers?*" Aster knew the magazine, but chose to pretend she didn't. It was probably the least readable one she'd ever come across.

"Yeah, and if we catch anything on video he wants it for his YouTube channel."

"Good luck with that," Annah commented as she passed them with her camera. "The last lot cut out before anything good happened. It was just a lot of lights."

As they started to make their way towards the woodlands, Aster noticed one figure was hanging back from the group. Without meeting his eye she fell into step beside him, letting silence fall between them.

Wade.

"Do you remember?" It was a pointless question, she knew he did, but it seemed appropriate.

"I remember."

"Have you heard what Hagar heard? On the radio?" She chose not to mention she'd heard it herself.

"No." Wade took a breath, then she felt his hand brush hers. "We need to talk."

Something she hadn't known was tightened, seemed to uncoil inside her.

"We do," Aster agreed. "But not now."

"Later."

As they reached the clearing, Aster felt a strange stillness fall over her. She looked around the group, wondering if they felt the same. Hagar was staring up into the sky, her camera hanging idly in her hands. Annah beside her, was in the same pose, holding her cell phone.

Maybe they're already here.

She raised her eyes to the sky, following Hagar's example and watched.

Lights were forming.

Slowly, very slowly, lights were beginning to cluster in the air, moving around each other. *What were they?* Surely they were too small to be crafts in themselves. There must be something larger on its way.

As she watched, the lights began to move in a strange dance, circling, entwining. Now she could see how Hagar and Annah seemed entranced, it was oddly attractive, almost as if it matched her brain patterns. She tried to look away, wanting to see what Wade was doing, but found it impossible to draw her vision from them.

From somewhere behind her there was a strong glow and she spun round before she could think, her eyes automatically drawn upwards.

Her first thought, idiotically, was, *'it's not a flying saucer.'*

It wasn't. It was triangular.

A huge, triangular mass, sparkling dots of red running along its edges, more vast than she could comprehend, extending beyond her field of vision. Dark in its centre, as though it pulled darkness away from the area surrounding it and yet right in its core a faintly lighter patch, glowing as though it was tugging her eyes directly towards it.

As she watched, the core grew lighter still, paler and then it seemed to break open, releasing a golden beam.

For a moment Aster was blinded, dazed. As her vision cleared, she expected to find herself inside the room again, inside the craft. Her mind corrected her, they were still standing in the undergrowth, staring up at the blazing shape above them and the lack of fear she felt was astonishing. She should be terrified of it and yet nothing but that odd stillness lay over her. No lust this time. Not yet.

Then, from somewhere, she began to hear the voices. Beside her she heard Wade gasp and knew he could hear them too. There was more than one, echoing and overlapping in her head in that strange language that she could somehow understand.

You see. You see. We are here.

And then something new, something unexpected.

We know. We know you.

"What do you want?"

Aster jumped. That voice had been outside her head. It had been Wade. Somehow Wade had broken the spell and managed to speak, managed to rebel against them.

We know you. We know.

"What do you want?" Wade repeated and now the strength in his voice had taken on a distinct tremor.

'Don't antagonise them, Wade,' Aster's mind pleaded, although another part of her wanted him to carry on. Wanted them to answer him.

But they didn't.

When he spoke again, Wade's voice sounded very small.

"Do you want us?"

The response was sudden, abrupt.

Ours. Ours. Ours.

Then the light flared and Aster's mind blanked.

Chapter Three

The first thing she realised was that something was poking into her stomach. She looked up, already knowing what she would see. The white room, the shadowy figures in front of her, far enough away that she couldn't make out their features or shapes fully, even though her mind whispered *greys*. And desire. Not as overwhelming as the first time, but still, desire licked at the edges of her consciousness, making it less unnerving and almost exciting that, again, she was naked. The cool metal of the bed lay underneath her, pressing against her skin.

And something was under her stomach.

Arching her back, she lifted herself on her hands and knees and looked down. The object followed her, pulling downwards a little and she became conscious that she wasn't completely unclothed. She was wearing a pair of black panties and attached to the front was a black dildo.

She was wearing a strap-on.

For a moment she closed her eyes as a stab of lust caught her in the gut, sending chills all over her body. She had worn one before, but to find herself like this, being watched, having been *put* in one…

Then an image of what it was intended for, what the greys wanted, flitted into her mind and she opened her eyes again.

Wade.

Wade will never agree to this.

A quick glance to her right told her that she wasn't alone. Annah and Zack were standing at the side of the room, staring vacantly at the ceiling as if their brains were on stand-by. Hagar was next to them, but

Aster immediately met her eyes, looking back at her with a calm intensity that seemed bizarre for the situation.

For some reason, she remembered the words people had said about Hagar so often.

I can't stop looking at her, and I don't know why.

Then she turned to her left and saw him. Wade was lying naked, also on his front, on the bed next to hers. He was watching her, his eyes wide, his breath coming in rapid gasps. Aster couldn't help noticing that there were restraints on his bed, even though he wasn't tied down.

Another wash of excitement flooded over her and before she knew what she was doing, she was sitting up on her knees and arching her back, letting her rainbow-streaked hair fall along her spine and brush across the bare cheeks of her ass. She stretched her arms upwards, exposing her breasts, feeling her nipples harden in the cool air.

The black cock jutted upwards between her thighs and she felt something inside the panties pressing lightly into her clit. She arched further, pushing against it and gasped as she felt it give a gentle buzz.

There was a bullet vibrator in these things.

The buzzing didn't stop and she moaned, feeling her eyes drift closed again. It would be enough just to stay here and let them...

But they weren't going to let her do that, she knew.

"Aster."

Aster turned to face him. Wade was also on his knees and she let herself look at him properly, let her eyes run over the muscles in his chest, the trail of blond that ran to his stiff cock. His hair was falling in his blue eyes, but she could see the burn of longing in them and she reached up to push her hair back, exposing her body to him more.

Look at me. Look.

"Do you know what they want, Wade?"

The buzzing intensified and she bit her lip, forcing herself to stay focused. This had to be something Wade agreed to of his own accord. It was tough for a man who wasn't ready for it.

"I know what they want." Wade swallowed. "Do it."

"You need to be sure."

"I am sure."

Moving slowly, Aster climbed off the bed, feeling the drag of the dildo as it moved with her weight. Wade's bed was only a few feet away. She approached him, holding his gaze, her hips taking on a sway as she walked.

"Turn sideways a bit so I can get on."

Wade shifted as Aster lifted herself onto his bed, turning so that they were facing each other. Aster bit back a giggle as her cock bumped against his and Wade shivered.

"Just relax," she whispered. "Let me do this."

"Will it be easier if I lie back?"

Aster paused for a moment. "Yes. Lie down on your back."

As Wade's hands landed on the top of the bed, Aster saw movement at the corners and rested a hand on his flat stomach, holding him still. The restraints had come out further, almost to his wrists.

"They want me to tie you down."

Wade blinked, then his eyes focused. "OK."

"Just your hands. I want your knees up. Hold still." Aster leaned forward and wrapped the restraints around Wade's wrists, tucking in the edges, making sure there was room to still move. "That OK?"

"Mmm." Wade's eyes were glassy and Aster paused. He was nervous. No great surprise. She couldn't just go straight into this.

She lowered her face to his and kissed him, letting her tongue probe his. His body shifted under hers, relaxing a little as she withdrew, pressing wet kisses along his neck and shoulder line. Her breasts dragged against his chest, sending a shudder through her body and she heard him groan as her mouth moved lower, closing over a nipple.

Fuck him, the voice whispered, breaking into her mind.

Fuck off, Aster thought automatically. *I'm busy.*

As she ran her tongue along the trail of blond fuzz, feeling his cock brush against the side of her face, she drew her hands along the insides of his thighs, pushing them apart. As she reached up to slip a finger into her mouth, she heard Wade breathe a hiss. Drawing the moistened finger away, she slid her mouth against the veined side of his dick, closing it over the tip as she pushed one finger inside his clenching hole.

I hope they're watching this, she thought and was immediately rewarded by an intense vibration. They were watching and they were enjoying themselves.

Fucking voyeurs and yet somehow it was exciting to be watched. She'd never let anyone watch before and the knowledge that what she was doing was entertaining someone else was intoxicating. So she was an exhibitionist. That was a new one.

Wade's channel fluttered around her finger and as she thrust it inside she added a second, feeling him jolt slightly against her. His cock was leaking pre-cum into her mouth, jerking with every motion and through the rush of blood in her ears she could hear him moaning.

For a moment she cursed the greys. She would have given anything to just slide him inside her, to feel him filling her pussy and thrusting up into her. It would have been perfect. The thought was making her wet and she let her breath out in a rush, adding a third finger to her movements as if to convince the greys that *yes,* she was still doing it, they didn't have to get involved.

Fuck him, said the voice and this time Aster straightened up, letting his cock drop from between her lips. She glanced down and noticed the dildo was glistening slickly. At some point it had lubricated itself and she felt a wry smile twist her mouth. These people thought of everything.

Wade had pushed his knees farther apart and she saw them trembling slightly, either from muscle stress or from nerves, she couldn't tell. She slid forward, not wanting him to have time to panic and felt the pressure as the tip of the black cock hit his pucker.

Wade gasped and Aster pushed forward slowly, inch by inch, even as the vibration at her clit grew stronger, almost as if it was trying to make up for no sensation in the dildo. She rested her arms beside Wade's shoulders, looking down into his eyes, hoping to reassure him.

Fuck him. Fuck him. Fuck him.

Then she felt his muscles give and Wade groaned, arching his back and she knew she'd hit that spot. She slid forward in one smooth move and drew back to thrust.

The voices in her head were talking faster, overlapping, as their bodies moved together.

Fuck him. Fuck him. Fuck him.

With every motion the vibration intensified, Aster moaned, feeling pleasure uncoil in her gut. She twisted her hips with every movement, hoping to make this good for Wade too and she could hear him groaning, see his hands tugging at his restraints...

The restraints.

Pushing herself up, she slid a hand between them and closed it around Wade's straining cock. Wade cried out, jolting and Aster matched the movement of her hand to that of her hips, dragging it over the tip and down to the base, over and over as she thrust.

Wades' hands closed into fists, his eyes screwed shut and he let out one last guttural groan before he was coming all over her hand.

Aster felt the first stirrings of her own climax, pulsing through her body as she threw her head back and heard her own voice block out those of the greys. As she dropped her head forward again, to her shock she saw two figures had come close to the bed. Beside her Hagar was standing, staring past her at something in front of her and that something was one of the creatures.

A grey.

Outside of the shadows it seemed somehow much more real, its skin smooth over its face and yet wrinkled over the fingers it extended towards her. Its eyes were oval, drawn to points at the edges and lying at an angle and black, completely black, with no visible eyelids.

Its other hand was held out towards Hagar, who remained completely still.

Ours, Aster heard in her head. *Ours.*

"What do you want?" She whispered, suddenly conscious of her position, still astride Wade, exposed to the grey's view, with Wade's still-hard cock embedded in her cunt.

The grey looked at her and blinked once, its eyelids appearing from the sides rather than top and bottom.

Ours.

Then a flash of light and Aster was lost.

***

As Aster looked out of the window, she saw Wade's Mustang pull up outside. Automatically she crossed to the door so that she could buzz him in.

It seemed strange that they would start talking now, after so much had happened and yet she knew they had to. Knew they had to sort out what was happening and not just between them.

She'd had a text from Hagar that morning.

Annah and Zack still don't remember.

Whatever the greys wanted, they didn't seem to want Annah and

Zack to have any part of it. They just wanted her and Wade to fuck and Hagar to... watch?

She didn't know.

But she couldn't forget those words in her head. *Ours. Ours. Ours.* And she couldn't avoid the thought that maybe, just maybe, that meant the aliens wanted them. Permanently. Why they would want them she had no idea. She had heard of people being abducted for experimentation, or being returned with alien equipment in their bodies. She had heard of people never being returned at all. It was impossible to know what was going to happen now. She also had no idea what they could do about it. She knew enough of previous cases to know that whether they went back to the site or not, if these creatures really wanted them, it was unlikely they'd just give up and leave. How many stories had she read about people who had been abducted from their own houses? Whatever was going to happen, they would have to face it.

It was an unknowable black hole to her and the thought was petrifying.

The buzz of the doorbell cut through the air. Aster pressed the button to open the door, shaking her head to clear it. This was now. They needed to talk.

Five minutes later, she and Wade were sitting on opposite sofas, two open beers on the coffee table between them. Wade had brought them. Aster had, for want of anything else to provide, laid out a lemon cake from the last time she'd baked. Neither of them had touched it.

"Don't worry, I'm not going to drink much," Wade commented. "But I wasn't going to risk you serving me that crap Hagar always brings. It tastes like fizzy piss."

"I wouldn't know. I've never drank fizzy piss."

"You have. Every time you drink with Hagar."

Aster picked up the bottle and took a swig, looking Wade in the eye as she did. It didn't taste any better than Hagar's beer.

She swallowed.

"We need to..."

"I'm sorry," Wade cut in.

Aster blinked. "Sorry for what?"

"You know. Being a dick."

Okay, that was a shock.

"I didn't..." Wade broke off and took a mouthful of beer. "I've never met a woman like you. You acted *different*. I thought I was hitting on you and then you started hitting on me and I didn't know how to handle it." He shrugged. "So I acted like a prick."

Aster paused for a moment, wondering if she should try to deny it, then decided not to bother. "Well, I'm still me. If you didn't like me before, you're not going to like me now."

Wade gave her a look somewhere between resignation and exasperation.

"I did. I told you before I wanted you, I just didn't know how to handle you." He rolled his eyes. "Anyway, up until now I've fucked women. I've never been fucked by one."

"I'm not sure what the difference is." Aster kept her eyes on his face. She knew exactly what he was getting at.

Wade sighed irritably. "I've never had a woman take charge. Okay?"

"And you didn't like it."

"Actually, I did. But if you tell anyone you fucked me in the ass, I'll deny everything."

Aster laughed. "Don't worry. I don't do that every time."

"You can do it whenever you like..." Wade stopped abruptly, caught Aster's eye and then looked away.

Interesting.

"How about we go out to dinner and take it from there."

Wade looked like he was going to object for a moment, probably wanting to insist he took *her* out to dinner, but didn't. Instead he threw her a grin, lifting the beer to his mouth again as he did so.

Aster couldn't help smiling back, even though another thought had crossed her mind.

"We need to find out what the fuck these greys want."

Wade's face darkened.

"I know what it sounds like they want."

Aster shook her head.

"Why do they *watch* us? I've never even heard of that before."

Wade shrugged. "Maybe they're kinky."

All right. Kinky aliens, I can live with that idea.

"Okay. But what do they actually *want*? I mean, they said *we want.* And *ours*. So does that mean..."

"They want us," Wade finished flatly.

A silence fell over them for a moment.

"Who's us?" Aster asked finally. "Us two? Us and Hagar? They don't seem to do anything with Annah and Zack. Unless you remember something I don't."

"No. They just leave them standing there. But they could be doing something we can't see."

Aster let out her breath in a rush. Whatever they said, it all came back to that one point. They didn't know what was happening.

They didn't know what was happening to Hagar.

They didn't know what was happening to Annah and Zack.

They didn't know *why* things were happening to them.

It was hopeless. If there was one thing she couldn't stand, it was *not knowing*. Even if it came to the worst, even if she ended up stuck on an alien craft surrounded by greys for the rest of her life, she couldn't sit around clueless, waiting for it to happen. She had to face it once and for all.

"We have to go back there again tonight."

To her surprise, Wade nodded.

"I know."

***

"Seriously, Wade, stop being a dick."

Aster could hear Wade and Zack arguing from the other side of the lay-by. Trunk standing open, she was unloading the equipment, all the while wondering why she was bothering.

Sure, they would need the torches, but that was about it. The rest was for the benefit of Zack and Annah. Whatever happened tonight, they weren't likely to be able to film it. Clearly if Zack still knew nothing of what had gone on, he couldn't have got anything for YouTube, so there was no point to any of the camera gear, they didn't need the GPS and the sky maps were pointless since no star-gazing would be involved.

But Annah and Zack still saw this as a standard alien encounter. God, if only this was *standard*! So they had to go through this ridiculous farce and the pressure was obviously getting to Wade. He was still bickering with Zack when she reached them, head-torch in place and GPS in hand.

"Can you two give it a rest?"

Wade threw her a look, but before he could answer, headlights lit them as two more cars pulled into the lay-by. Aster turned to watch, her eyes immediately drawn to Hagar as she got out of the car and approached them.

It was still true. There was something about Hagar you couldn't help looking at and tonight she was even more eye-catching than ever. There was a keenness in her face, a glittering intensity in her eyes that drew you in, made you want to watch her.

Annah, on the other hand, looked her usual sunny self, entirely unfazed at the thought of another evening she couldn't remember, which would end with her flat on her back in the undergrowth. She joined Zack in unloading his trunk as Hagar stopped in front of Wade and Aster, looking from one to the other.

"You all set?"

Aster nodded. "Of course."

"Don't look so nervous." Hagar's mouth twisted in a sardonic grin. "You look like you're walking to the fucking gallows."

How can she not be unnerved by this?

The walk to the site was faster than Aster would have liked. Hagar strode on ahead, long grass parting around her boots. Annah and Zack followed on, chatting enthusiastically about the evening that awaited them. Only Wade and Aster dragged their feet. Aster found herself feeling torn, march forward to face whatever they would, or slow down for as long as possible.

In the end, there was no avoiding it. The site was empty; Zack already had his camera running as they stood in line, facing the space where they now knew the shapes would appear.

Aster bit her lip. To her left, Hagar stood, gazing upwards intently. To her right was Wade, frowning up at nothing. She longed for the casual curiosity of Annah and Zack, who were so relaxed, so excited to see what was going to happen. She would have given anything to walk out of this and go home.

But I have to see this out. I can't go home.

I may never go home.

A short, scared breath escaped her and then suddenly her right hand was caught in Wade's. He squeezed it and she cast her eyes sideways at him, nodding in thanks. He was in this too, of course. He must also be nervous.

But God, she wished it was over, for good or for bad.

Somewhere in the distance she saw lights begin to move, weaving in and out of each other in a beautiful pattern and she heard Hagar sigh in relief, or was it fear?

And then, without warning, they were engulfed in a golden glow.

Chapter Four

Aster stared up into the light, Wade's hand tight in hers, waiting.

Just waiting.

For what, she couldn't have said. That blankness that preceded their appearance in the white room? A final abduction? A face-to-face encounter? She had no idea.

Then the voices began and Aster forced herself to stand still and stop shaking.

Ours.

Ours.

Ours.

Overlapping, echoing and Aster held her breath. Then another voice broke the stillness.

"What do you want?"

That was Wade, low and strong, with just a slight edge of strain.

Ours, was the response.

Annah stepped forward and Aster caught herself before reaching out to grab her. "Do you want us?"

This time the voice changed.

No.

Aster blinked. Didn't want Annah? Or didn't want any of them? Before she could think better of it, she heard her own voice cut the air.

"You don't want us?" *Tell me. Just tell me what you want.*

No, the voice repeated, this time with a certain tone that suggested dark amusement.

"No? Have you been fucking with us all this time?"

It was risky, getting angry when she had no idea what these creatures could or would do. But the thought that all this had been for nothing...

Wade's hand closed tighter around hers and she relaxed slightly. Maybe not all for nothing. But still...

Zack was still filming and Aster wondered what was going to happen next. Would they even allow him to keep his footage this time? Or were they all going to end up in a heap on the floor again, video blanked and no further on than they had been before?

Then Hagar laughed.

Aster spun round, startled. Hagar was standing alone in the centre of the light, her head thrown back and an eerie laugh rippling from her.

Oh God, Hagar...

Slowly, very slowly, Hagar lowered her head and met Aster's gaze. That odd, slightly downturned smile crept across her face and Aster realised then what was wrong, Hagar's eyes.

Hagar's eyes were pure, glittering black.

"Hagar?" Annah whispered, small and terrified.

Hagar blinked, that strange sideways blink Aster had seen on the grey and suddenly she understood. She didn't know how, but she understood. The light intensified and again she could hear the voices chanting *ours, ours, ours*. Hagar held out her arms sideways and tipped her head back again, her smile widening, waiting for something...

Then her feet left the ground and she was held in mid-air, rising slowly towards the craft and for a moment Aster had the sense of a whole group of greys watching and waiting, an air of satisfaction filtering down towards them.

It was never us they wanted. It was always Hagar.

With us they just wanted to... watch.

An undertone of sorrow was tugging at her as she watched Hagar rise, but she forced it back. Hagar was laughing again, that uncanny ripple and somehow this time it sounded right.

Hagar...

Then a sudden flash that blinded them all for a second and when Aster's eyes cleared, Hagar and the craft were gone.

***

The first one to break the silence was Zack.

"I got it all and I still don't believe it."

At some point Aster's hand had fallen away from Wade's. Before she could reach out for him, she jolted as Annah thumped into her, threw her arms around her neck and burst into tears.

"It's okay, Annah. She'll be fine."

But will I be?

Hagar had been the co-founder of the group, one of Aster's closest friends. The pain that she had felt underlying the wonder of the moment was coming back full force. What would she do without Hagar?

"You got it all?" Wade asked from somewhere to her left. Aster hooked an arm around Annah and pretended not to be listening. Curiosity was unavoidable, but she was feeling much more in line with Annah than Zack at the moment.

"Oh yeah. Right up to that last bright light." Zack sighed. "There's no way I can use it, though. Nobody's going to believe this. Maybe I can sell it if I edit it a bit."

Well, good for you.

The one part of that comment that stuck out for Aster was that nobody would believe it. Hagar was gone, people would notice and people would ask questions.

"I don't know," Zack continued thoughtfully. "Maybe it's better if it stays secret. What do you think Hagar would have wanted?"

"She's not fucking dead," Aster spat.

Zack opened his mouth, then decided better of whatever he had been about to say. Aster glared at him, then turned away, wanting to get back to the car. All she could think of was getting somewhere private where she could scream.

Maybe it should remain secret. But that was the point, it wouldn't. Even if Zack didn't sell his footage. Hagar's car was still in the lay-by and within a few days it would be noticed that she was missing. The police would be on her doorstep, and she had no idea what she could tell them.

When they reached the lay-by, Aster unlocked the back door of her car and got in. Somehow driving was beyond her at this point. To her surprise, Wade got in after her. They sat in silence for a moment, watching as Annah and Zack got into their respective cars and left, their headlights sparkling in the darkness.

"How are you feeling?" Wade asked finally.

"I don't know."

"Are you all right?"

The words had a tentative sound to them and Aster rolled her eyes. With any other woman she knew Wade would have just given them a hug or something to comfort them. But with her, he acted like she was going to punch him for trying.

She leaned against Wade's shoulder, relaxing and after a moment she felt his arm curl around her.

Good start.

"I don't know what I'm going to do without Hagar."

Fingers slid under her chin and tipped her face upward. Aster looked up, met Wade's eyes and closed her own in anticipation of his kiss.

Their mouths met and it was electric.

Part of it was the sense of connection, at last they were kissing because they wanted to, not because something was prompting them to. Aster pressed her body against his, wanting to mould herself to him, to make him *hers* and to ground herself, to make herself forget the shock of the evening and just be with someone she cared about. Because now she knew she did.

Did he?

He'd said he liked her. Wanted her. How much more there was, she couldn't tell. It was too early, it had all been so fast but she wanted to know. Wanted to find out where this would go.

Without any helpful people or greys pushing them around.

The thought sparked something inside her. Drawing back, she held Wade's gaze, allowing a dangerous smile to creep across her face. An answering grin twisted Wade's own lips as he saw the expression on her face.

"What are you thinking?"

"I'm thinking a few things."

"Like?"

"Like we're completely alone in a car where nobody can see us."

"And?"

He was learning, clearly. Of course there was an 'and'.

"And we've got a lot of video equipment in here."

Wade raised his eyebrows, "You want to fuck on camera?"

"If we can find a place for it."

Wade shifted away and reached over the back seat, moving the parcel shelf to reveal the trunk. He resurfaced with a small DVR in one hand and a gorilla pod in the other.

"Think this'll work?"

There was a glint in his eye that made Aster's heart bounce. "Worth a try."

Wade twisted on the seat and rose up on his knees to wrap the legs of the gorilla pod round the headrest. As he shifted position, moving around to get the angle of the camera right, Aster's eyes were drawn to his denim-clad ass, his jeans tightening as he stretched his arms out.

"I've got another idea."

"Oh yeah?"

Let's see if he'll agree to this one.

"You know, you were kind of a dick to me before."

Wade slowly turned to eye her over his shoulder. "Oh?"

Aster's breath caught and she heard the tension in her voice as she spoke. "I think you need a good spanking."

Wade's eyebrows lifted again, but she saw the interest ripple across his face.

"Oh? You think I've been bad?"

"If you want to put it that way, yeah. I think you've been bad." Aster felt her gut clench with excitement. "So switch the camera on and get over here so I can punish you."

Pausing only to twist the viewing screen so that it faced them, Wade dropped his hand to the waistband of his jeans, leaving the red 'record' light blinking.

"Take them off."

Aster unfastened her own jeans as she spoke, holding Wade's gaze as she did so. "I want to feel your bare skin against mine."

"Whatever you like."

Aster stretched her legs out between the seats to push her jeans down, taking her panties with them. The image on the DVR screen told her what was being recorded and she felt her core grow wet as she saw her pussy exposed on the screen.

Hastily she kicked off her shoes and pants and threw herself back into the seat as Wade finished undressing, half kneeling in the foot well. His cock was jutting out towards her, glistening with pre-cum and for a moment Aster considered going in for a taste. No, that would come later. She reached out a hand towards him, patting the other on her thigh. "Across here."

Slowly Wade crawled forward, settling himself across her lap and Aster shifted under his weight, feeling his hard cock press into her leg. It was tempting just to grab his ass and poke it inside her, again and again and again until...*Concentrate, damn it.* She ran her hand over his skin, teasingly letting her thumb dip between his buttocks and graze the puckered hole beneath. *Have you forgotten? I haven't.*

"You were bad," she whispered. Then, louder, for the sake of the camera, "You were bad."

Wade caught his breath as she drew her hand back and brought it down hard, in one stinging smack.

"And you'd better not do it again, because I won't stand for it."

Smack.

She felt his cock jerk against her leg, slick already with pre-cum.

"You want this, don't you?"

Smack. His skin was growing warm under her hand.

"Yes," Wade gasped.

"Say it."

"I want it."

"Say it properly." She directed the next slap at the top of his thigh and Wade jolted, startled.

"I want you to spank me."

"Good." She slid her other hand down over his buttocks to fondle his balls, dragging a finger along the base of his cock as she rained down smacks on his ass, feeling his body shudder with each one.

It only took a few minutes before Wade's groans had turned into words and Aster paused, waiting for him to lift his blond head from where it was tucked into his arms.

"What do you want, Wade?"

Wade took a deep breath. "I want you to suck me. While I'm eating you."

Aster lifted her head to look at the DVR screen. It was small, but she could see Wade laid across her thighs, see the sweat glistening on their skin and the thought of the camera catching what Wade had just suggested sent a dart of heat straight to her cunt.

"Sit up." She scooted along the seat and turned. "Lie on your back."

Wade lay back on the seat, his blond hair brushing against her knees. He winced slightly as his ass brushed the leather and Aster felt a smug smile crossing her face. *Still got it.*

Parting her knees, she crept forward until she was straddling his head, pausing for a moment so that he could admire the view. In front of her his dick was hard and leaking, pointed straight at her face, just begging to be sucked.

"Ask me for it."

Wade groaned and Aster leaned further forward, letting her breath gust over the tip.

"Ask me."

"Suck me," Wade whispered. "Please?"

Oh yes. Aster shifted her hips and lowered her body over his face, dipping her head at the same time to take his cock into her mouth.

The dark taste of him was overwhelming, the silky feel of his skin on her tongue, the sensation of him filling her mouth. She began with the first few inches, teasing, letting her lips drag back over the head, then slowly she began to work her way further down till he was hitting the back of her throat.

Wade's tongue brushed her clit, softly at first, then with harder pressure as she felt his finger slip inside her, making swift darting motions that made her picture his cock thrusting deep into her. Swirling motions, faster and faster. Y*es, oh God, yes...* and he was adding another finger, tormenting her as she drove his shaft as far into her mouth as it would go and swallowing him again and again.

She slid a hand between his thighs, cupping his balls and caressing them, feeling them tighten as Wade groaned, his knees drawing back. *Don't come yet.* Withdrawing her hand, she pulled away from his cock for a moment, sucking two fingers into her mouth before pressing them to his pucker.

Wade didn't speak, but the throaty moan she heard from behind her and the grip of his hand on her ass told her everything she needed to know.

One finger first, testing, then a second and she felt the ring of muscle loosen, letting her in. She twisted them, searching for his sweet spot. His channel suddenly clenched around her and his hips bucked, his cock thrusting into the air.

"*Yes!*" Wade gasped and Aster dropped her head to take him into her mouth again.

Their movements grew desperate. Aster moaned as ecstasy began to uncurl in her gut, pushing back against Wade as his tongue grazed her folds over and over again. The taste of his pre-cum in her mouth was growing stronger, the scent of him heady and musky. She hummed around his cock and felt his fingers dig into her skin, knowing the pleasure was starting to grip him.

Come for me, Wade. Come for me now.

Her back arched as electricity rippled from her clit, her body tightening and Wade let out a guttural cry, jerking upwards as his hot release spurted into her throat.

For a long moment neither moved. Then Wade's head dropped back onto the seat and Aster lowered herself to rest on top of him, nestling her head in the fork of his thighs.

I never want to move again as long as I live.

Pushing herself upright, Aster paused, her eye caught by something through the window. It was a short distance away, but clear enough to make her heart stop.

"Wait."

"What?"

Wade sat up confused, as Aster scrambled back into her jeans, pushed the car door open and set off at a run back into the trees.

She knew what she had seen. It wasn't far away from the road. A glowing figure stood among the trees, light emanating from behind it, but distinctly human-shaped. Aster came to a stop six feet from it, staring as features began to form out of the shadow.

"Hagar."

"Don't come any closer." It was Hagar's voice, but with an odd ring to it and for a moment Aster wondered if she was really there or if it was just a projected image.

But in a way it didn't matter.

"Don't leave."

Hagar laughed and Aster felt a rush of something soothing through her body. She dropped her head as the realisation hit her that now Hagar could do these things, affect her emotions, she was really one of them and she was really going.

"Did you know?"

"What I was? No. But I always knew I was different." Hagar glanced upwards. Aster followed her look, but saw nothing. "You know, I used to stand at my window and watch the stars, wondering if there was anything out there. I knew there had to be, if I looked hard enough. That was why I wanted to start the group in the first place. I knew that I could find something. Now I know they were looking for me too. When I started hearing the messages, I wondered and then, last night they talked to me. Really talked to me."

Why didn't you tell me? Aster forced herself to stay quiet and let Hagar keep talking.

"I just want to find out more. About me, about them. I know I'll be all right. They won't hurt me. They've been visiting for years, apparently there are lots of people like me. They just don't have the same fascination with aliens that I always had, so they might never know."

"Don't they want them back anyway? Can't they just..."

"Oh, they can do what they like. But they want to watch us." Hagar chuckled and Aster blushed. "They're curious. They want to see what we'll do and if someone's like me, wanting to know more about them, they'll come back for them. But a lot of people just aren't that interesting to them."

"Are you sure they won't hurt you?"

"Positive. I'm one of them and they communicate, well you've seen how they communicate. I just know I'll be safe with them. I feel like I belong."

"Okay," Aster whispered. This was amazing, the kind of thing she had always wanted to know and yet somehow nothing outside this moment seemed important. Aliens could come and go, could walk straight past her if they wanted and she still wouldn't care.

She couldn't see, but she sensed Hagar was smiling.

"I'll be back one day. Don't worry about that."

"What do I tell people?"

"Nothing. I don't suppose you noticed..." Hagar smirked, "...but my car's not there anymore. There's nothing to say we were together tonight. You can tell the police or whoever that you don't know what happened to me."

Aster sighed. Apparently the greys thought of everything. She hadn't noticed, even though since Annah and Zack had left her own car and

Wade's were the only ones there. She had been too busy steaming up the windows to see what had been going on outside.

"Tell me about Wade."

She could have sworn Hagar was holding back mocking laughter.

"I'm sure you know *that* already."

"He's crazy about you. I know that."

The short time that had passed since the last time Hagar had asked her about this seemed unbelievable, like a lifetime. Hagar had never gone into depth about her own love life, nor had she especially asked Aster about hers, though she'd known the kind of men Aster liked. She'd always thrown Aster a wink if she thought Aster was attracted to someone, and she was usually right. She'd kept out of things with Wade. At the beginning it would have been pointless to suggest, watching them bicker with each other. But now? Now Hagar was saying Wade was crazy about her?

Did *she* believe Wade was crazy about her? Maybe. But she knew she was crazy about Wade. Was she in love? It was hard to know. But she could be. Relationships weren't things she was used to, but she could see herself falling in love with Wade, if Wade could fall in love with her.

This was it. This was where it got dangerous. After everything that had happened that evening, this was where the real danger lay, because now they just had each other and it was vulnerable and new and messy and…

…And she wanted it so much. Wanted to trust that it could be real and not just alien-inspired lust and a need for control.

"Aster. Listen." Hagar's voice had that intensity that Aster knew. "I know it's not been long. But you two are connected. Just let it happen."

Just let it happen. Maybe she could do that. Because in the end, she wanted it to happen and she had a feeling Wade wanted that too.

From behind her, Aster heard grass rustling. Hagar heard it too, because the light began to fade and involuntarily Aster stepped forward, stretching out one hand.

"Wait…"

"I told you. I'll be back."

"When?"

Another smirk. "Watch the skies."

And then the darkness fell around her like a curtain and Hagar was gone.

Gone.

A hand landed on Aster's shoulder and she turned to bury her face into Wade's neck, glad of the comfort.

He's crazy about you.

She felt a kiss land on her forehead and smiled. Maybe he was after all.

"Was that what I thought it was?"

"Yes."

Wade's arm tightened around her and Aster blinked watery eyes. No more Hagar. She might never return and if she did, it could be years. She might never see her again.

But Hagar was happy. That was what mattered. And so were they.

Together they turned to go back to the cars and Aster glanced upwards as Hagar's last words rang in her head.

Watch the skies.

Together.

Hidden Desire
By Crystal Dawn

Prologue

The world of the supernatural exists all around us, but we don't see it. Even if we catch a glimpse of it, we refuse to admit that's what we saw. Not all humans are allowed to go about their mundane existence in complete ignorance. My family was just minding their own business when a werewolf bit one of us, changing her life and ours, forever. A bite won't always do that, but this time it changed their world too. My cousin Ariel changed into a snow white wolf.

White wolves were a powerful bloodline believed extinct, but now that we've been found we are pursued relentlessly. Many of us snubbed wolves, as they preferred to be called. I was one of those who chose to stick with my own kind.

My name is Sue Ellen and this is the story of Sharon and Ven. Sharon didn't want to change to a wolf so she left her love behind. Ven has plans and they don't include being abandoned. We'll see who actually gets their way. This story takes place after Paul, the second wolf to mate, reconnects with his fated one, Kimmie. Now it's Ven's turn to try to win back Sharon and he will do anything to get her back.

Six men sat around the table making plans that would either change their life for the better or send them further into the pit of lovesick despair. The idea was solid, they would join forces to create a dating service starting with one night of fantasy. They wanted to help others that were lonely and in need of a true love or fated mate, but first they wanted to help themselves.

All six of the *men* were werewolves that had found their perfect match, their fated mates, but they'd been rejected.

Erotic Fantasies, the dating business they founded, was all about them getting one shot at the female they wanted. All six ladies were white wolves, a powerful werewolf bloodline that had mixed in with humans and almost been lost. They had reasons to be leery of wolves, but not all wolves were objectionable. The males knew if they got the chance, their mates would fall into their arms one by one.

Lucas went first and now he's mated. Paul goes next and he's nervous but he knows it will work out right, and it does. Now it's time for Ven to get on with the night!

Chapter One
Waiting

Sharon lay on the bed in an incredibly revealing and sexy, red, one piece that allowed access to all her treasures. It would have knocked Ven's socks off and if she was honest that was why she'd picked it. His favorite color was red and he like to have a little satin and lace rubbing against him when he fucked her. They had experimented a bit with domination in the bedroom but they'd never gone far. She wanted a strong man to make most of the decisions in bed so she didn't have to.

Ven was her greatest weakness and she thought about him every day and dreamed about him every night. She hadn't been with a male since the last time Ven had fucked her bowlegged. How could anyone else compare?

Just last week she and her five cousins had been at diner discussing this very subject. Sue Ellen and Kimmie never said much anymore and why would they when they had given in to their desires and mated wolves. Even though they were teased about the mating mercilessly at these get-togethers, they were disgustingly happy. So much so in fact, that it had the rest of us second guessing our decision even more than ever before.

Was it stubbornness? Sharon didn't want to believe it, yet there was a niggling doubt that had started to grow in her heart that suggested it was. Last night she had dreamed that when she came here and the man entered the room it was Ven. No mask, no disguise, he had simply demanded her surrender and she had given in. The pleasure he had given her in exchange had made it all worthwhile. She could hear a key in the door indicating the unknown lover was here. Would she regret this decision or would tonight set her free?

The man walked in the room with a mask on his face but everything she could see reminded her so much of Ven it caused a stab of pain to hit her heart. There were differences, missing scars and a lack of tattoos being the obvious things. The intense attraction was there and just as overwhelming for Sharon as it was for Ven. It looked like this was going to work after all.

Pulling off his black leather jacket he let it drop on the floor. His eyes gleamed as they roamed over her body and a rush of liquid heat lubricated her channel preparing it for his possession. One guilty thought tried to ruin things for her but she stomped it down. If she wanted this man like she clearly did, Ven wasn't the fated one like he'd tried to convince her. Maybe there wasn't a fated one for anyone. Sharon had always had doubts about that anyway.

"Aren't you a sexy little morsel?" He asked as he moved all the way to the bed where he seemed to be considering what to do with her. Sharon decided the question didn't call for a reply and she just stared back letting her eyes roam over his hard, well-muscled body. Especially the buttons he was undoing as he removed his shirt. His chest was hard, muscled and tanned. The guy was mouthwatering and panty meltingly delicious.

"Let's get things straight before we get started. I like to take charge." He explained in a low gruff voice. Even his voice reminded her of Ven but it was deeper. "I don't expect you to call me Sir, unless you want to. Just do what I say and we'll be fine. Any questions?"

Sharon felt excitement, anticipation and a shiver of fear run through her and she liked it. "What if I'm a bad girl?" Her voice trembled as she asked.

He chuckled and it was both sexy and scary. "I have my ways and

I'm not opposed to turning that luscious ass of yours red, Honey. Now get on your hands and knees on the bed and present your ass to me."

Sharon hurried to do as she was told. Her body shook with anticipation as she waited for his first touch. He'd had plenty of time to move closer but he hadn't touched her yet. She started to look over her shoulder, curiosity getting the best of her.

"Don't you do it! Who is in charge here?" He asked and judging by his voice he was right behind her.

"You are."

"I am and you'll wait until I'm ready to touch you. You'll stay still and at my disposal or you'll discover how I'll punish you right now." He slid a belt out of his pants and placed it on the night stand then unbuttoned his pants before sliding off his boots.

Sharon swallowed, her was throat dry. This was harder than what she and Ven had done. He'd never been able to leave her waiting, always needing her as much as she needed him. Liquid want flooded her passage as she waited on the edge of need for him to take what he wanted. Her mind searched to figure out what he was doing. Was he building anticipation or seeing if she would behave? Maybe he was punishing her for what she'd done. Regardless of his reasoning she knew she had no choice but to obey.

She sighed softly when his hot hand slid over her ass cheek. It was such a relief that he was doing *something*! It took her a second to realize he had still needed to take off his pants which was probably what he had been doing.

"What's the matter, little one? Did you think I could resist your charms? Never!"

His hands moved up her back now and around to her chest. He slid them under her lingerie, gripping her breasts gently. His thumbs rubbed her nipples, hardening them with little effort. Now he rolled her over onto her back and his tongue wet his lips as his eyes grew heated. He was imagining all the things he could do to her and she started imagining them too. Every part of him that she felt pressed against her was deliciously bare and felt heavenly.

This man wasn't Ven and it was a good thing. He couldn't smell her high level of arousal but the second he sank a finger into her pussy he would know she was well lubricated. She was glad she wanted him, it meant she could move on past her need and other feelings for Ven. After this, other men should once again appeal to her. Her body jumped, he had pinched her nipples and she whimpered wanting more. Yes, this man was perfect.

"I see you liked that, woman."

"Yes," she admitted.

He pinched them again then one hand snaked slowly down her belly. It headed straight to her pussy and she shuddered with need. His mouth settled on her shoulder and lightly nipped it.

"Oh, God!" She exclaimed as her need heated up.

His hand hovered above her slick entrance as if deciding what to do first or how to devastate her senses the most. Kissing her with a passion that branded her, he lifted his lips and moved them over her neck and to her shoulder where he nipped her skin lightly and growled. The sound turned her insides to mush. He moved down her chest licking and chewing on her nipples until she moaned with need before he moved lower.

Her need ramped up until she tried to squeeze her legs together to still the ache that she could hardly bear. That was the moment his hands reached out to pry them apart as his lips continued to approach, leaving goosebumps of desire in their wake. Shivers ran through her as anticipation shook her to her core, releasing more of her nectar until it slid down the insides of her thighs and onto his hands. He groaned in appreciation and raised one juice laden finger to his mouth where he took a lick then sank the finger in his mouth, removing every drop.

"So good, little one," he said as he removed his finger from his mouth with a pop.

The sound echoed off the walls making her jerk in response. His mouth was now in position to give her unbelievable pleasure and the look in his eye expressed his intention to do just that. Blowing his hot breath across her sensitive flesh, brought her to the edge of climax. When his tongue flicked out and hit one of her plump wet nether lips, she almost jumped out of her skin.

"Yes," he whispered against her, the rumble of his voice thrilling her even more.

Sharon feared he would excite her so much that she might have a heart attack.

His tongue came back and this time pressed deeper as his hands opened her for exploration. His tongue delved into her folds causing her to whimper in delight. Tongue fucking her, he had her hips moving up to meet him as he slid his appendage as far as it could go into her channel and he moaned with seeming enjoyment. His fingers moved to her clit, fiddling with it at first playfully before serious intent became clear. Now he plucked and pinched it, making it sensitive to every touch but only giving her a slight hint of pain.

She could feel the intensity rising until suddenly, her orgasm broke loose and she screamed to the skies. Her body writhed and jerked as wave after wave of pure pleasure rolled over her.

Never, not even with Ven had it felt so incredible. Who was this man?

Sharon didn't have time to give it further thought as he slid up her body and his massive cock, huge like Ven's was, pressed at her opening. It began to slide in slowly and with some resistance. She didn't believe any woman could take him easily, preparation was key and the only reason she wasn't screaming in agony. He was kissing her and his hands were cupping and squeezing her breasts sending lovely shivers over her whole body. This man was a super stud, she wanted to do everything with him before dawn ruined it all.

Her legs spread further and she pressed upward assisting his entry in every way possible. All she wanted was his hard cock buried inside of her as far as it could go. Her legs wrapped around his hips and her toes sank into his well-muscled ass. Now they had found purpose and she pressed to use the leverage to impale herself on his thick staff. Inching in, eventually she felt the burn and the delightful tension as he finally seated himself with a grunt.

"Oh, Goddess you're so tight. I've never felt anything so unbelievable. Are you alright? Can I pound into you until we both blow cum all over the place?"

"Oh God yes!" She agreed, but then she realized he'd said Goddess. He was a supe of some sort and maybe even a wolf.

About that time he pulled out and slammed back in as if he intended to reach her tonsils from below.

Whatever his plan was, the slight edge of pain was gone and only the pleasure remained. Sharon was feeling the intensity growing as he pounded into her without reserve and she screamed, moaned and even cried out in delight as she felt herself moving closer to her ultimate release. Her body shook and she hung on tight to the man above her, even though both their bodies were drenched in sweat. He made noises too and those noises made her even surer than ever that he was a werewolf, but right now she couldn't care less. She was chasing an orgasm hovering just out of range and the man or male, whatever the hell he might be was giving her the best sexual workout she'd ever had in her life. Sharon felt a tinge of regret as she realized even Ven was surpassed by this guy.

Her body shuddered, her breath came in gasping pants and her heart felt like a jack hammer. There was only one way this was ending and that was with the granny of all orgasms and it would be soon. Her channel twitched and her clit throbbed. She felt his cock jerking as if he tried desperately to hold back so she would go first. That was all she needed to know and she slammed her body up against him rubbing in all the right places and heat suffused her. Her body was now out of control and she absorbed the pleasure mindlessly as they entered the final dance.

Her body jerked and seized in release, drawing him in whether he was ready or not. She could feel his body stiffen as he plunged in fully and she felt the added slickness of his cum mixing with hers.

It was so amazing she closed her eyes and lights flashed against her eyelids. The display was spectacular and in her experience unmatched. He howled, a wolf without doubt but it was only one night and the sex to fabulous to deny. Sharon planned to stay the night and wring every precious moment out of her temporary partner. The memories would give her sweet dreams for a decade and replace her pining away for Ven with the ache for a mystery man.

They thrashed together, riding out the storm of the overwhelming orgasm until it slowed and they came back to themselves a little at a time. He rolled to his side pulling her with him and she delighted in the wild and free scent of the forest that came from him.

Ven smelled that way too, stronger after sex, as if it released his inner beast. He was a lot like Ven, but he couldn't be him without the familiar markings she'd traced with her hands a hundred times.

He growled deep in his throat but she was sure he'd drifted off already. It was no surprise with all the energy he'd just expended giving her the ride of her life. She thought it a shame he was a wolf too, but maybe they were the only ones that could satisfy her. What would that mean if it were true?

Chapter Two

Fooling Her

It was nearly a month ago and he remembered it like it was yesterday. He knew his turn was coming and he would finally have a chance to be with Sharon one more time and maybe even win her for good. He had more to overcome than the other guys since he had scars, tattoos and other distinguishing things and Sharon knew each one in intimate detail. There were few ways to hide those things and the best way was magic. His inner wolf whimpered then ran and hid at the mere thought of a witch.

There'd been a few recommendations, but Greta was the one who was recommended the most. They said she was eccentric, no surprise, weren't all witches? Truth was, had they told him more he would have went elsewhere.

Pulling into the drive he looked at a small Victorian painted in vibrant mauve, blues and greens. Not a combination he would have chosen, that was for sure.

Plants bloomed on both sides of the walkway in an effusion of the bright colors found in the rainbow. The female obviously liked every cheerful hue possible in paint and blooms. He pushed the doorbell and the thing played a tune. As he waited for the witch in question to answer he looked in a nearby window and saw the sill lined with bottles of various jewel tone colors, including fuchsia, blue and purple. Metal ornaments decked out their surfaces and the lids were also an ornate silver metal. Probably loaded with potions of every imaginable kind.

The door popped open without any noticeable assistance but he stepped in anyway, even though his wolf was curled into a ball with his paws over his eyes. The door slammed closed once he was inside and he resisted the temptation to check it and make sure it wasn't locked. An evil cackle rang through the house and it came steadily nearer. The witch approached.

Rain poured from the sky and lightning and thunder rang out and lit the sky as far as the eye could see. In his mind's eye he imagined the old witch he'd heard so much about, seeing her with white stringy hair that flowed down her back, eyes black as coal and lifeless, a wart on her nose and several others spread around generously and thin lips tightened into an expression of displeasure. Wasn't that what ancient old hags looked like? He was aware now that this had been a terrible mistake, one he and his wolf might not survive.

The scent of magic moved nearer as a flash of lightning seemed to blind him in his eyes.

It must be his imagination or a hallucination that a lovely female, one he could describe as a siren, was closing in on him. A trick of the light or magical enchantment, he wasn't sure which. A shiver ran through him, after all it was a gorgeous female dressed to seduce, but he wanted nothing to do with her. His woman was elsewhere and soon he would have a chance to reclaim her. Even his wolf now howled resistance at the thought of being deprived of any chance to win back his mate.

"Do you like what you see, Wolf?" The lovely witch purred as she stroked her hands over her body calling his attention to her generous curves.

"You're attractive enough Witch, but I'm here for different services than those."

"Are you rejecting me?" She screeched. Her face nearly purple with anger, her eyes wide with shock and her lips tight in disapproval.

"No, I already have a mate and she rules my heart and body."

The witch's whole attitude changed right at the moment Ven thought he would die a horrible magical death. "I like you wolf. You're a romantic and loyal to your love. My help is available to you so tell me what you need."

Explaining the whole sad situation, he was stunned when the witch laughed. The sound this time was soft and sweet. "You have a stubborn white wolf, young male. There will be excitement of all kinds in your life once you claim her. Are you prepared for it?"

"I love her so I have no choice. My life has been nothing all these weeks without her. The only choice I see is to take back my female and love her so well she never wants to leave again."

"That was lovely," the witch admitted, her eyes bright with what looked suspiciously like tears. Holding up her hand as if she intended to catch something, a sound, a sharp crack of some sort, sounded and a pink bottle appeared in her hand. "This will make her see you without your usual tattoos, scars and other identifying marks. It will also change your voice just enough to fool her. Just remember like Cinderella you have a curfew. Hers was midnight but yours is dawn, sooner if it senses a change. The potions flavor is disagreeable but I can't change that. Hold your breath and follow it with something more pleasant. Take it an hour before you meet your love and if she looks for some familiar marking she'll be disappointed. Everything else will be you, just you. Do you understand what I've told you?"

"I do." Ven said as he fought the need to ask her about herself versus his wolf's deep desire to run as fast and as far away from this place as he could. He felt a huge relief for what the witch had done. "Thank you, Witch. What do I owe you?" Maybe he should have asked that before.

"Give me some of your hair. I have spells that call for it."

"They call for a werewolf?"

"Not always. The hard ones to get are a hair from a lovesick fool."

He plucked five hairs from his head as his chin hung low with embarrassment. It wasn't like he could deny her accusation. Sharon claimed his heart and soul to the point he feared he could die if he couldn't convince her to come back to him.

The witch shot him a smile. "I thank you and wish you luck. If you can claim her I see a long happy union ahead," She said as she tossed him the bottle.

He caught it easily but he'd looked away for a second. When he looked back, she was gone and the door opened by itself to let him out.

He'd made up his mind and there would be no turning back. All that he was and all that he ever would be was in the hands of his lovely mate. This would be one last ditch effort to claim her for all time. If it didn't work, it would leave him a miserable wolf, alone for all time. That's why it had to work and he would do anything he could to ensure it did.

A few weeks later, he met up with his guys. There were six of them and two had claimed their mates in exactly the same way he was about to try to claim his. Those two were here too without their mates. Ven was certain their mates were with their cousins which were the mates of the rest of their group. Yeah, it was weird how those six females had brought him and his five buddies so low in such a short time. Somehow the six of them, rejected mates of white wolf cousins, had met each other and formed a group of their own.

Smart thinking and quick action had set them on the path they were on now and helped two of them to claim their females. That left four of them worried and nervous about trying to claim their own. A mate less wolf is a sad wolf, maybe even a crazy wolf that might have to be put down for his own good and the safety of others. They had set up a plan that could easily have failed at every step of the way but so far had been successful.

Ven didn't want to be the first one to sink rather than swim. They gathered Thursday night and Saturday would be *the night*.

All the guys wished him well and he knew they really meant it. Since they had established a dating service to help themselves and others claim their mates, they understood more than ever before how hard it was for their kind to find and claim their fated one. It made him feel good that their service was helping a good number of wolves claim their mates and he hoped all six of them would be happily mated once they all got their chance with their mates. One of the services they offered was a fantasy ball where they set up couples, giving them the chance to make their dreams come true.

Many couples chose that option and danced the night away not going up to the hotel rooms included in the fantasy until much later, if at all. They took the time to get to know each other starting their romance. So far the females they wanted were only after the sexual fantasies offered by the service. Ven liked to think it was because their women obsessed on them therefore having no interest in romance. They'd managed to lure their females into the service and it had worked twice now. Ven hoped the third time was a charm.

When the day came, his heart thumped in his chest as sweat slicked his body. Not the best way to start getting ready. He would go to meet her as a masked outlaw biker. It suited his personality and his lifestyle so it should be easy to manage. The leather was a little hot, but it would be stripped off once he got to the room, all except for the mask. The mask reminded him of his relationship with Sharon. They'd met when she'd come in to buy a bike. She was a rider and a good one at that. They'd gone out for a drink before she'd found out he was a werewolf and dumped him.

He'd not seen her for a while after that when they ran into each other out riding back roads. They were mates and that made it hard to resist each other. She'd given in and they'd dated secretly until one night they almost got caught by one of her cousins. That's when she'd dumped him for the final time. He'd felt like a dirty secret but he'd wanted her so much, he'd allowed her to hide him away. If she wanted him now, there would be no more secrets. Not after tonight.

He walked through the hotel and got in the elevator. She was on the fifth floor where the suites were and he could imagine her in his mind's eye.

She looked just like she had last time he'd seen her. They were at her house, in her bedroom and she was wearing a delightful red teddy. Anything she wore made him horny but red was special for him. It looked exceptional on his mate. Most of the white wolves were in the average range on height but Sharon was taller than most of them. At five foot ten, she was a long lean handful. Sexy lingerie made her legs look like they just didn't stop.

Her dark hair, not quite black and glossy as hell, contrasted nicely with the red she also preferred. She often wore heels and it made her easy to kiss. Her skin was light tan, her eyes the color of sherry. Her breasts were just a perfect handful and her hips slim. The female was his dream come true and his palms were sweaty and itched as the elevator doors opened on the proper floor.

He knew they looked good together. His look was rough and bad boy all the way but she seemed to like it. His dark, curly hair was long enough for a pony tail or man bun and he wore them once in a while. His facial hair grew fast giving him the five o'clock shadow most of the time but Sharon didn't seem to mind that or his diamond stud earrings either. The fact that he was six foot five also seemed a positive thing.

Everything between them seemed a perfect match until it came to human versus werewolf. That was where all hell broke loose. It was odd since they also had werewolf blood, just not enough to grant them any of the desirable benefits like healing and long life.

His fangs itched to bite her but he refused to do it without permission. The inner wolf he'd had all his life howled in protest. Calming himself as best he could, once he opened the door she would be right in front of him. He both feared losing control and wanted to take her anyway.

A deep breath calmed him slightly so he tried it again. Ven was alpha and he *would* stay in control. His mate waited on the other side of this insignificant barrier, but he would enter properly and he would maintain control.

Ven slid in the key card and turned the knob. When he opened the door and looked inside, his heart caught in his throat and his breath froze in his lungs. His mate had never looked more beautiful and he promised himself before this was through, she would be his.

Chapter Three
Passion

Sharon woke again, feeling like it had been at least thirty minutes. Her energy was reset and she was ready for a little bit more of the good stuff. The hottie she had gotten for a partner was still sleeping, but not for long. Her hands itched and her mouth watered to touch and taste his delicious body. Why not?

Her hands moved closer to him and she trailed her fingers over his body delighting in his firm muscles and his silky skin. The lack of tattoos or even the smallest scars was confounding because this male looked and carried himself like a warrior.

While it was true that most wounds on shifters and certain other types of supernaturals often healed without a sign that they had ever been there, those inflicted during war that were intentionally spelled with salt to inflict the most damage usually left some remnant. Ven had those kinds of scars and they attested to his victories and his defeats. Not that he'd had any defeats once he was grown, since those could result in death.

The male she was lightly stroking with her fingers shivered and groaned. She leaned down and licked one dark brown nipple. It hardened immediately. His looks and reactions were so much like her former lover that she worried they might be related.

Sharon had seen a lot of emotional damage in families from men or women dated by siblings or cousins. She avoided dating a brother or cousin of someone she'd dated before for that very reason. It wasn't her desire to cause jealousy or competition among men. Her only wish was to find the right man for her and before she'd encountered this one, she'd thought Ven was that. Now there was hope that another could fill her needs and her life. This male was a wolf, she was almost positive, so it couldn't be him but surely some human would eventually make her feel all these things.

She licked lower and he writhed slightly. There were signs he was coming aware and she wanted to give him a big surprise. Her tongue raced across his abdomen and lower to where his massive staff rose from the nest of trim pubic hair. His balls looked like baseballs and her hands cupped and squeezed them while her tongue licked his rod like it was a lollipop. His hands threaded through her hair. He was awake at last.

Sharon thought he tried to hold back but a blow job usually brought out a reaction in any male. His hips pumped upward as his hands pulled her head down. She opened her mouth wrapping her lips around the reddish purple bulbous head of his cock and slowly sank downward. He made a gurgling noise she'd not heard before and she was proud that she was perfecting her ability. Not long ago she would have choked but she was learning to relax her throat and overcome her gag reflex. It was obvious he appreciated it.

Sinking down his pole he suddenly thrust up and he filled her beyond description. It was all she could do to hold him there and not back off.

She swallowed, knowing that would feel incredible to him somewhat like a massage from her throat. The sound he made was animalistic and she thought it showed his pleasure. His hands massaged her scalp and felt heavenly. Once in a while a salty drop would hit her tongue and she'd moan her enjoyment. Her moans seemed to work him up too and she could almost taste the load that was just waiting for the slightest touch to send it down her throat. Sharon sucked in extra hard and he made a sound like a broken groan. He couldn't hold back any more and she could tell.

"I'm going to cum!" He screamed as he pulled her head down on his cock and she sank all the way down. A load of hot salty juice hit her and a little flowed out the side of her lips. Even though she swallowed she just couldn't gulp it down quick enough, liquid gushed out around her lips. Damn, he must have been saving up a while to have such a huge load. Swallowing fast, she was relieved when it eased and she was able to lick him off.

He fell back against the bed and groaned, "Female, you are something else."

It made her giggle which was a liberating feeling after feeling so bad for so long. Winking at him, she said, "You have no idea."

"Come here," he whispered as he crooked his finger.

She slid up his sexy body and gave him a kiss so he could taste himself on her tongue.

Their kiss heated him back up, "Ride me!" He commanded as his hands grabbed her ass cheeks and squeezed.

That felt so good! She raised herself over his hard throbbing stick and sank down slowly. Her body adjusted and pleasure vibrated around her. He helped her by lifting her hips with his hands and it reminded her so poignantly of Ven it struck her in the heart. She pushed it away and concentrated only on how he made her body feel. Moving faster, she dropped herself harder and his cock went in deeper until she nearly screamed in joy. It was amazing how much he moved even with her on top of him. Her weight seemed like nothing to him and he rose to meet her downward thrusts, it was magic.

The friction built up the tension until it was ready to explode. Her pussy grasped at his rod, squeezing so hard it amazed her that it didn't hurt him. Funny noises sounded near them and she realized both of them were making them as pleasure coursed through them. Her hands grabbed at his chest, she was about to cum undone. That sounded like a joke but it was reality pressing between her legs.

"Oh dear Lord!" She screamed as she felt like she was flying over the edge of a waterfall into sweet bliss.

"My Goddess!" He screamed, just like Ven did when he was caught off guard.

Everything seemed to come back to her former lover no matter what happened. Her eyes closed and she saw him there giving her pleasure as he had the last time they'd been together. There were doubts now that she could ever completely turn her back on him. When this was over, she would have to go to see Ven. It made her wonder if she could only be with this guy because he was so much like Ven. Even with her body writhing and jerking on top of her partner, Ven was on her mind.

Lying still she tried to clear her mind and just enjoy the sated feeling her body felt. The male was incredible and she felt guilty for the thoughts of another male that crossed her mind while they were together.

"Get on your hands and knees!" He demanded.

Had she said Ven's name? Her lover seemed angry. She moved into position as he had asked.

This time he stripped her lingerie off leaving it puddled at her knees. His hand smacked her ass hard enough that she was sure it turned it red.

"Ouch, what was that for?" She asked testily.

"You should watch what you say during sex."

She assumed she had called out Ven's name. Oops? What the hell did you say when something like that happened?

He moved behind her, spreading her legs and he rested the head of his cock at her entrance. She wasn't expecting, nor could she have prepared for, the way he drove into her. The slight pain, manageable because he'd already stretched her earlier, only added to the thrill. She moved back against him and he smacked her again.

"I didn't tell you to move."

"You never said I could only move if you said to."

"I'm telling you now."

Only a male could be that difficult. She wasn't going to argue with his faulty reasoning. Apparently she'd called him Ven and it had hurt his feelings. Maybe he even knew Ven and felt weird about being with her now. That would explain why he was suddenly being so hard on her. Males were hard to figure out and she'd never had much luck at it.

Sharon resisted the strong need to move back on his cock. Her ass didn't like being spanked, at least not when it was sharp, hard and sudden. The thought of a softer smack combined with a soft rub over the spot held more appeal. That was what Ven had done, it was more of a teasing playful thing than true discipline. That was because Ven loved her and she loved him. It had always been just below the surface, expressed by neither, but known by them both.

This experience was making her realize many things, like how foolish she had been to throw away Ven because she and her cousins were afraid of becoming wolves. This night would come to an end and she would draw every bit of sensual delight she could from it, but when it was over she would visit Ven. That was when she would decide what was right for her even if it had fangs, fur and howled to the moon. For now she would enjoy all that this male could give her and see if it helped her decide what to do.

His hand now moved to the back of her neck where he held her in place as he slammed into her. Sweat dripped from him and she felt slicked with it herself. Her heat was rising and her need sped higher. It was confining since he wouldn't let her move.

"Harder!" She yelled, just to shake him up but he plunged into her harder. Sharon hadn't thought it possible but clearly it was. "Yes!" God it felt good.

Just a little more and she would fly apart and glory in the pleasure it gave her. Even though he wouldn't let her move, he was moving enough for both of them. Just a little more and she would have her reward. She looked over her shoulder only to receive a sharp smack on her ass.

"Eyes straight ahead!" He demanded and he seemed to enjoy spanking her entirely too much. She looked ahead and concentrated on cumming. If he would just hit that spot one more time.

"Arree!" She screamed a crazy sound. Her mind had no clear thoughts in it and all she could do was feel. Pleasure danced over her and she shook with it. Nothing had ever felt so marvelous and she pushed back against him so hard this time he didn't stop her. His hands grabbed her hips and he drove into her hard and fast as he filled her with his cum.

He made a noise too but it was indistinguishable just sounding like a loud yell. The male jerked against her rapidly and then he began to calm. "Damn woman," he said as he shuddered, shook and smacked her ass when he was done. Moving around the bed he fell back on it and she could see he'd worn himself out.

Wiggling over to him, he wrapped his arms around her as they cuddled together.

Just a short nap. That was what she thought.

They fell asleep for at least an hour maybe more before finally coming around. It was crazy how they wanted each other but it was insane how she could think of Ven through it all. She could understand why her lover would be upset. It would be disconcerting to be called by another's name in the midst of the best sex ever. For now she would try to watch her mouth and hope it didn't happen again.

Sinking into sleep in this male's arms felt so much like the last time when she'd stayed the night with Ven or actually he had stayed the night with her. They'd stayed at his house or hers as the mood had struck. That time her cousin, Wanda had come over and she'd had to get rid of her. Her cousin had known someone was there.

"Who is hiding in the bedroom you old ho?"

"What? No one, I'm just tired and want to get some sleep before I go to work," she'd said pointedly.

"I'm not as stupid as everyone seems to think I look," Wanda, a natural blonde, had groused.

"Not stupid, imaginative. My sex life is nonexistent," Sharon said as she prayed Wanda wouldn't challenge her and ask to look in the room. Once Wanda left she let out a sigh.

"Would it have been that bad to get caught slumming with a wolf?" Ven stepped out of the room well aware of all that had gone on.

She'd felt guilty. Such a sexy wonderful male and she felt ashamed of seeing him. He was a dirty, guilty secret that she kept from family and friends. It made the sex more exciting but it wasn't right. He was more than she was letting him be and she wouldn't hold him back anymore. Sharon knew women wanted him but he'd never settle down as long as she kept him around her.

"We need to stop seeing each other."

"That's what you want?"

"That's what has to happen. It's only a matter of time before we get caught."

"You're a coward, Sharon. You want me, I'm not even sure that the wolf doesn't turn you on. You just don't want anyone else to know it." He got dressed, grabbed his black leather jacket and slipped out the door.

She heard his bike, the one he'd parked several houses down, start and take off with an angry sound. Practically falling onto the couch, she began to cry. Crying for everything she ever wanted and for all the reasons it couldn't be hers. She cried until she fell asleep on the couch and she looked like shit in the morning. Her eyes were red and hurt. It was the last time she saw Ven up close.

They had gone to some of the same parties, they had friends in common, which was to be expected, but he avoided her. It was unmistakable and so obvious that friends had asked her what she'd done to him. How did you answer a question like that? It wasn't like she could tell the truth. Their curiosity found other things to question over time but he never stopped avoiding her. Maybe that was his way of dealing with the pain. Sharon had never stopped trying to deal with the pain and this guy was the only male she'd managed to be with.

She woke wondering what time it was and when she checked found they'd used up half their night. Her body felt good, sated, but her mind was in confusion. They had more time to enjoy each other and his eyes were open looking at her. Her eyes skimmed his deliciously long body. Tall and broad with amazing muscles, that was why she'd thought him a warrior.

Sharon remembered when she and her cousins had discussed who they'd meet in the hotel room. What would the men they'd be matched with look like, be like? They'd been at the old bar they often hung out at. None of them had taken a turn yet so they were all wondering what things would be like. Sue Ellen would be the first and it was clear she was nervous.

"He'll be a handsome hunk!" Kimmie offered.

"I bet he'll have one wild and wet tongue!" Sharon had tossed in just for good measure. It was fun to make Sue Ellen blush.

"His fingers will be bigger than an average guys cock!" Kimmie said holding her hands out in measurement.

The others just giggled and cackled. They had time before they would be put on the spot. "Just imagine what his dick will look like." She almost rolled on the floor. "Just saying."

Kimmie never knew when to quit. Sue Ellen slipped away not long after that. At least things had worked out well for her and Kimmie even if they had gone against the agreement they'd all made about no wolves. Those two were happy, wasn't that what counted? Sharon was beginning to think that way more and more herself.

Her lover reached out to her and pulled her closer. "I want to fuck," he said and the look in his eye left no doubt he meant it in the most basic way. He rolled over to where he was on top of her. His arms slid under her knees and he pulled her up and open so he could drive in hard and fast.

She was exposed but she didn't feel shy anymore. They knew each other's bodies well and he would pleasure her well. He poked at her opening with his cock dripping cum. It was surprising after cumming several times he could still be overcome with need. Sliding the head of his cock up across her clit made her jerk from the intense feeling and he chuckled. Now he moved it back to her entrance and slid it in to the hilt.

They moaned together, it felt so damn good, he began to pound into her. His movements were like a dance and she responded in the same way. She squeezed her muscles tight, hugging his cock inside her and groaned. As he pounded into her, she arched up to meet him. The feelings were so intense her mind was awash with sensations. Nothing else seemed to matter as they danced closer to the ultimate release. Closer it drew and they moved together faster and harder. Their bodies grasped and clamped each other as finally bliss rolled over them, giving them everything yet making them want more.

Chapter Four
Love Hurts

Ven had mixed feelings as he lay with his fated one sated and relaxed. Love filled him until he nearly burst from it but disappointment also swelled inside him. She'd called out his name when they'd made love. Maybe that should encourage him but it only showed him that she'd denied them both for no good reason at all. Stubbornness or disliking wolves was no reason to turn from love. He couldn't understand how the mate that fate had selected for him could do that to them.

He'd pulled her into his arms, unable to resist the chance to hold her yet she'd left him more than once. Did he even dare risk giving her another chance? Was there any way he could stop himself from giving it to her? Life would be a dismal gloomy affair without this female in it.

Even though she had rejected him twice, he would see if the third time was finally the charm. He remembered the day he had met her like it had just happened. She'd walked into his store with bright eyes and a swagger in her step.

"Hello, I'm here to buy a Harley," she said with a confident look. "I've finally saved the money and I can't wait to ride."

Her tight fitting leathers gave him a clear idea of what she looked like and his cock jumped at the thought of her riding him. "Let me show you what I have." Goddess did he wish it meant what it sounded like. Instead he led her to the showroom that the Harleys were parked in. Her eyes widened in admiration and excitement. He saw them every day and still got hard when he looked at them. Okay, got hard figuratively. All that metal and leather, what was there not to love? Throw in the smell of oil and asphalt that hung to the tires, it was enough to bring him to his knees.

The female appreciated the things he did and she was hot. They talked a while and made a deal. She was walking away with one hot Harley at a little more than cost. Money wasn't his main goal, he also liked to match a bike with an owner that would appreciate and care for it. Sometimes he was a softie and emotional about his business but he kept that a well-hidden secret. He'd asked her out and he was over the moon, which meant a lot to a wolf, when she agreed to go.

Everything had been perfect, too perfect it seemed when she had dropped a surprise in his lap. She was a white wolf and didn't date wolves. Didn't she understand she was part wolf? It hurt even though he barely knew her. That was something he'd given a lot of thought to. It finally occurred to him why she meant so much to him. Sharon was his, his fated mate and she didn't want him.

Sadness had hung around him like a cape and all his friends had noticed. They had also noticed a few weeks later when she had given him another chance. His sun had shone brightly and nothing could get him down, or so he thought. Their sex life had been amazing and he had dared to hope their bond went deeper, soul deep. That was when a cousin of hers came over while he was there. He'd almost come out to face her, revealing himself in an effort to force Sharon to accept him. Rejecting that plan because it seemed wrong, he'd lost her anyway.

She'd sent him away and as far as he could see, she'd never looked back. The only consolation he'd had was she didn't date anyone ever. That was only fair since she'd ruined him for other females. After being with his fated mate, no female was interesting or desirable to him.

Now, as he looked at her lying in his arms he realized that would always be the case, whether she chose to stay with him or sent him away again. Ven knew if they didn't mate this time, they never would. He had one last chance and he couldn't even begin to guess how things were going.

Sharon lay sleeping, almost comatose from the pleasure he'd given her. Her skin was so silky smooth he wanted to rub against her but he didn't want to wake her, at least not until she was rested. The witch had said the potion would stop working at dawn or when the time was right. It was a lot of trust to put in a drink.

Her reasons for rejecting him had been her own and other than disparaging his wolfness, she'd said nothing more. Now she lay in his arms sleeping fully satisfied and exhausted. He'd done that and he could do that again and again if she would let him. Had her life been better without him? She rarely smiled, she didn't date and there was a sad demeanor about her. It was as if when he left he had taken the joy in her life with him.

His eyes were tired and it was the perfect time to take a short nap.

Ven woke to the feel of soft hands on his cock which was already rock hard. "Damn woman!" He growled but he relaxed letting her take control. Sharon was all he'd ever wanted and her touch was magic. She stroked him hard and fast until cum wept from the head of his cock. She leaned forward and licked it, moaning in apparent delight.

"That tastes so good. I'm not sure what I want to do with you, there are so many possibilities," Sharon admitted.

He pulled her up his body. "I want to slam my hard cock into you until you scream for mercy then I'm going to fuck you until you scream your release."

"Works for me," she replied and he rolled her under him.

Her legs wrapped around him and she hooked her ankles. He thrust inside her smoothly because she was so wet. Now he began to piston in and out like a machine, showing no signs of tiring. The soft sweet noises she made only drove him on harder and deeper.

Sank deep inside this female was the only place he felt truly at home. Ven wasn't a lone wolf but he had only a few family members and a handful of true friends. He belonged to Blake's pack, but he wasn't a dedicated member, only doing enough to keep his membership active but not really belonging like many others did.

As he sunk into his female again, the warmth it sent through him was undeniable. They belonged together and the sex was only the beginning. He felt his ass cheeks squeeze together as he went deep inside her sweet heat. Her moan and the way her channel squeezed him made him groan in reply. Yes, he could do this forever. Kissing her, he tried to show her she was his. One hand squeezed her breast, two fingers smashing her nipple until she reacted. She writhed against him and arched desperately trying to make him speed up. No release for the wicked, at least not this soon. He fell into a rhythm that would grant them release in time. She growled when she realized he'd circumvented her attempts at a quick climax.

He chuckled, no he wasn't being very nice but she was so much fun to tease. His skin was slick from the sweat that covered him. It was caused by the effort of their activity but even more because he held back.

His heart pounded, need rushed through him. She was reaching for her release and aching like he was. He pressed against her harder and hit that spot that sent her over the edge as she screamed his name. Did she know or did her heart recognize he was her mate? Ven didn't know but her orgasm pushed him over the edge too and he was unable to think for a while as he shot ropes of hot white cum deep into her greedy channel. Her grasping muscles squeezing like a vise just pulled out more until he had nothing left to give.

If Ven thought he'd ever been milked dry before, he'd been wrong.

He rolled to his side just before he would have collapsed on her and smashed her beneath his weight. His body felt weak and he rolled over onto his back and tried to catch his breath. Nothing had prepared him for the complete shutdown of his body and the overwhelming feeling of his heart trying to jump out of his chest as his breath came in painful gasps. Slowly, everything began to fall back into position. His heart and breathe slowed and his mind once again became capable of thought.

Sharon looked at him, her mouth agape and he was now certain his disguise no longer fooled her. "How?" She asked as she continued to stare. "Why?"

"I decided I would give us one more chance. How else could I get that chance when you avoided me like the plague? Whatever you decide this time, Sharon, it will be what happens. Never again will I pursue you if you throw us away. It's in your hands now."

"You just can't be Ven. I'm hallucinating, yes, that's what is happening."

"No, it was a spell. A witch hid my scars and tattoos. The spell wore off as it was intended too. Again I ask you to decide."

Her hand reached out and she traced his wolf tattoo that he had on one arm. He was sure it had been her favorite. She had always made a point of running her finger over it just as she did now. "It's so real. Maybe I'm dreaming? That must be it. Ouch! What did you do that for?"

"I pinched you so you would know you weren't dreaming. You act like magic isn't possible yet your family is full of magic. I think all white wolves are crazy and yet I love you anyway."

"You love me? Truly?"

"As if there was ever any doubt. I have always loved you and I always will but only you can decide if we'll be together. Nothing I feel matters if you don't feel the same thing."

"Now I know this is a dream, Ven has always known I loved him. That was never the problem. The problem was always that I fear being and living as a wolf. Lately I must admit I've feared giving up my love more. When this is over, I will search Ven out and see if he'll give me one last chance. I see the irony in this situation. In bed with a stranger I realize I can't live without a male I suspect is my fated mate. My feelings are so strong, I think he's with me. Heaven help me!"

Chapter Five

Convincing Her

"I can't believe you think you're dreaming. You have every known magical creature somewhere in your family lineage, yet you find magic hard to grasp? My wolf is rolling on the floor laughing but I think it is not funny at all. I try to convince you but you just resist."

She started to question her assumptions about him being real. Finally he felt too solid, sounded too logical and argued too convincingly for her to deny his presence.

"I can hardly believe you were willing to fight for me this way."

"Believe it. You are my fated one and I will never get another. My world rotates around you."

"No pressure. I'm so glad about that."

"You had to know what we were to each other."

"I stayed away from the supes and didn't learn about them. After the abductions and the attempts to force matings, they didn't seem desirable to me."

"All wolves aren't bad. You have to see that with Damon, Blake and Tyne. There are bad apples in every kind if you look around and humans, well they have more than their share."

She was quiet for a moment giving what he said some thought. Sharon nodded reluctantly. "You're what I want, what I need. We can make a go of things because I don't want to be alone and I don't want anyone but you."

She could hardly believe this was really happening. Accepting her mate would change her whole life but she could now see it would be for the better. All night long she had actually been making love with her other half, the male she should have accepted when she first met him. Denying him had hurt, letting him claim her wouldn't be easy, but it would give her the joy she had wanted for so long.

It occurred to her that they were in bed together and naked. Was there a better way to celebrate their joining? Sharon licked her lips and saw his eyes follow the movement. Leaning in to him, she claimed his lips as if she was starved for them. His groan sent lightning through her body.

They slid up against each other and they slammed together grabbing and squeezing desperately. It was like two wild needy creatures coming together wanting to drain the warmth and love from each other. He was hot and she felt the need for that heat because she felt cold deep inside. His heat built a roaring fire inside her that consumed her and made her desperate to have him deep inside her. Ven seemed just as needy as he tried to thrust deep inside her to assuage his desire.

His cock was hard as he plunged deep into her, giving his all to bring her pleasure. In turn she arched up toward him and they slammed together hard enough that the slapping sound echoed around the room. Their groans only added to the pleasurable feeling the friction between them created. Her channel tightened and relaxed massaging his rod as he moved in and out. He rolled them to where he was now on top and that's when he began to really move. Hard, fast and deep he drilled into her not holding back at all. Her body embraced his possession and her legs wrapped around his hips and gripped him as if he were her everything.

Sweat popped out on his skin and dripped down onto her already sweaty skin. It made them slide easier and move even faster. The slapping noise was loud when he pounded into her. Sharon thought it would be a while since they had been having sex so much but it hit her unexpectedly. She screamed loud and long as a wave of bliss rolled over her. Her muscles clamped down on his cock and he jerked and yelled. Writhing under him, pleasure washed over her and she heard him howl to the sky as the bliss overtook him too. This had been the most amazing night of her life and now she could look forward to a lifetime with the male she loved.

"I wish we didn't have to go now," Ven said regretfully.

"It would be nice to have more time in your arms," Sharon admitted. Unfortunately the rules were clear and it was time to leave.

They both dressed and embraced passionately as they parted for now. They made plans to see each other that evening, once she got off shift. Sharon was so excited about it she wasn't sure how she would make it through the day until she would be in his arms again.

Sharon was a nurse. Her career was her passion and while her regular job was a forty hour through the week one, there was a nurse shortage in this area. She worked some weekends at the hospital, on the floor or in the emergency room depending on where the need was.

Tonight would be one of those nights or she'd have seen Ven as soon as he closed his store for the day. The hospital wanted her to work last night too but she couldn't give up her fantasy night. Sharon had suspected it would change her life, she just hadn't known how. Once she and Ven were together, she would have to cut back on her work at the hospital. Ven would be possessive and if she were honest, more time with him would be a gift.

Once she got home, she showered and laid down for a nap. Ven had worn her out lovingly and she would need to recover her strength for work on the five p.m. to two a.m. shift. It would be the emergency room and sometimes it was quiet, but more often than not it was hectic. As soon as she woke from her nap, she dressed and headed to the hospital. Once she got there, she changed into her scrubs and went to check with the nurses on duty to see how the day had been and what patients would be there for her to take over.

There was only one, an elderly woman who had fallen. It was probably a broken hip and since she had osteoporosis the bone breaking may have caused the fall. Sharon sat with her as much as she could, she was scared about the surgery and Sharon helped her stay calm by distracting her as much as possible. They were waiting for the surgeon to come in to do the hip replacement right away.

The evening progressed with one car accident victim who had broken their nose on the steering wheel when the air bag didn't deploy, a man who needed twenty stitches because of a knife trick that didn't work out and an older gentleman who had an asthma attack. All in all a very quiet evening for them. Whether it was hectic or easy, Sharon loved her job and firmly believed she helped people. Her patients needed her help and it made her feel good when they told her she'd made things easier for them. The night finally came to an end as the next shift came in to take their place.

Sharon headed home, showered and went to bed. She lay there unable to sleep and worried that Ven would change his mind. Doubt over everything he'd said set in and she couldn't overcome it.

In the morning, looking like something the cat dragged in, she arrived at work.

"Hey Sharon. Oh my God, lady! I hope whatever happened to you was fun and not torture," Fanny giggled. "You look like it took a lot out of you."

"You sure know how to make someone feel bad."

"Pshaw! You know better than that. Girlfriend, you just look tired and maybe a little bit worried. That describes a man to me. Who is he?"

"I don't know what you're talking about," Sharon said as she hurried back to the exam rooms. Fanny wouldn't give up. That girl was persistent as hell but she'd avoid her anyway hoping she'd forget in time.

Hiding her personal items in a drawer of the first exam room, she went out to the hallway and grabbed some coffee while she waited for the first patient. Once the first one came in, it was a steady flow of people until lunch.

Sharon went to the diner next door for lunch and hid in a corner booth. Pulling out her phone she stared at it considering calling Ven. Turning it on, she saw the text message and scrolled through it. Ven couldn't make it to see her tonight, he was working late. That just reinforced her fears that he didn't want her now that the sex coma had worn off. It didn't matter how she felt about him, he must still be angry that she'd rejected him twice. This whole thing had just been to punish her. Mission accomplished, she was devastated. In the back of her mind the voice of reason argued that she was being unreasonable. It was just her guilt because she'd made Ven suffer and she'd slept with a stranger, so what if the stranger had turned out to be Ven? Maybe she was hormonal too or maybe it was just the enormity of the commitment they were making, but she had needed to see him tonight just to assure herself what they had decided was real. Now he wasn't coming and doubts and fears had set in. What if he was just punishing her for hurting him?

Getting back to work a few minutes early, she hid from her friend Fanny, unable to deal with any questions now. It would be a long time before she'd be able to deal with this pain over Ven. She heard a scream in the office. What was happening? Cautiously she made her way in there expecting a robbery or a vandal. No, it was just Fanny and a vase full of red roses.

"Who sent you the flowers?" She asked as she stared at the beautiful petals and baby's breath.

"I wish some stud would send me flowers. These are for you! Can I open the card?" Fanny asked hopefully.

"Hell no. Hand them over," Sharon said with one foot tapping impatiently. She grabbed the vase in one hand and plucked the card off the stick with the other. Setting the vase on the counter, she tore open the envelope and took the card out.

I can't wait to see you tomorrow.

Love ya

Ven

The rest of the day flew by and even though she knew she wouldn't see Ven until tomorrow night, it was good enough. She headed home feeling lighter than when she had left. Eating a light meal, a can of soup and a ham and cheese sandwich, she watched TV for a while then showered and went to bed.

Surprisingly sleep came over her almost immediately.

Sharon woke suddenly unsure of what had woke her until a slight sound like a footstep came to her straining ears. Someone was in her house and she was terrified. Slipping out of bed, she slowly crept forward, barely able to see in the darkness of the room.

Going to bed naked was something she regretted now. If the intruder was bigger and stronger, he might rape her. She heard another noise and it was closer. Whoever was in her house was almost where she was.

Suddenly arms wrapped around her and she started to scream. A hand moved up and covered her mouth and she felt hot breath against her ear. "Sharon, it's me Honey. I missed you too much and wanted to see you when I got off work."

She relaxed in his arms and sighed. Thank God it was Ven and she was safe. His hand dropped from her mouth and feeling her way around, she got on her tip toes and kissed him. Heat rushed through her as her hands stroked his back and shoulders. His hard muscles felt manly and if she could see better she would have jumped him right there. Instead he led her back to the bed. Wolf eyes could see amazingly well in the dark. He nudged her to the bed and she could hear the sounds of rustling clothes as he stripped bare for her.

In her mind's eye she could recall what his sexy body looked like naked in the light of the hotel room. His hard muscles and silky skin had felt marvelous under her searching hands the last time they'd made love.

The bed dipped as he got on it and he laid down before he moved closer to her. Her hands reached out and she felt his smooth skin. Yeah, he was bare as the day he was born. Smiling in delight, she felt her way around his chest until she found a sensitive nipple to tweak. He jerked and groaned in response.

His cock smacked against her leg and left some liquid there. No doubt he was ready to sink inside her. That was good since she was ready for him to be inside her.

They rolled around and she ended up underneath him with her legs spread wide. It was only seconds before he was filling her with his long wide shaft. Sharon moaned with pleasure as he filled her completely. He began to move in and out, building a rhythm and tension. His hips pivoted and rolled finding every sweet spot she had. Writhing beneath him, she pleaded with him to let her cum, she hurt with need.

Chapter Six

Claiming His Fated One

Ven found it hard to believe she was finally in his arms and ready to be his mate. How long had he dreamed of this but never believed it would happen? Okay, he'd known her less than two years but it seemed like he'd waited forever. That's the way it was when everything you'd ever wanted was just out of your reach. His body buzzed with need and all he wanted was to take her and claim her. He sank into her body and pulled back before sinking in again. He felt the tingle flowing up his spine as his release loomed. He moved his hand between her wet lips and pinched her clit just hard enough that the pain would hurt so good.

Sharon screeched like a cat, a sound he'd never heard her make before. Her body bowed and her channel slammed around him like a vise. His cum was literally squeezed out of him as her muscles milked him. Ven howled, something he'd only done once before and it had been with her. She brought out the animal in him like no one else ever had. He jerked and writhed on top of her until his cock had unloaded every drop of cum he had.

Drained and sated, he embraced his female and rolled them to where she lay on top of him. Her breasts rubbed against his chest and her arms circled him. One leg was thrown over him and he felt surrounded by her love.

It was time to claim her but he needed to talk to her one more time to make sure she understood what it meant and that she was ready to be his completely. Once he joined them, nothing on earth or in the afterlife would ever separate them.

"Sharon, I think it's time for us to finish our mating. I know there are things we'll need to work out. But we can do that after we seal the bond."

"I'm ready. After what we just did, I feel like anything is possible."

They kissed, slowly and gently. Love flowed between them as their hearts and minds opened, preparing to take the biggest step of their lives. It would be alright, he knew that now. His concerns that she would want him to be a dirty little secret like he'd been before or that they couldn't overcome their differences were now gone. The final step would be taken and Sharon was embracing her wolf heritage as she accepted him as her mate.

He rolled them over so he could take the dominant position and guide her through the mating. Whispering sweet words in her ear to soothe her, he began to make love to her once more. His hands stroked her fevered flesh turning the fire into an inferno.

"More," She gasped as the need roared out of control.

He was only too willing to help. His lips and tongue followed the trail his hands had gone down until the got to her breasts. Teasing her nipples until they were hard and elongated, he then sucked them into his hot mouth, one and then the other. Her moans drove his need higher and his cock ached and dripped cum from the end. It wouldn't be long before he lost control. That was the way it was between fated mates, hot and combustible.

Once she was writhing and nearly out of control, he lined them up, unable to wait a moment longer before sinking deep into her hot, wet channel. He groaned in delight, the feeling was so pleasurable but it also felt like being home. Never had anything else felt so perfect.

Holding still while she adjusted to his size, he closed his eyes, lost in the sweet feeling of being inside her. She seemed to feel the same way except she was urging him to move. Chuckling at her impatience, he began to pull out slowly and then he drove back in hard and fast. It was exactly what she wanted.

"Yes, yes, yes!" She screamed as he continued with the fast pace he'd set.

"Dear Goddess!" He yelled as he held back his release, wanting her to go first. Pounding harder and moving his hips to hit her hottest spots, he could feel her muscles squeezing him as her orgasm loomed closer. She felt so good under him and he had to work hard to keep his mind clear as his gums burned because his fangs were out. They were ready to do what was needed to claim the female under him for all eternity.

Ven sensed it before she exploded and nearly ripped his dick off as she went wild beneath him. He exploded sending waves of hot cum into her and he bit into her, tasting her hot, sweet blood on his tongue. His mouth filled with it and he swallowed it down as she came again because of the bite.

What he hadn't expected was her blunt teeth to dig into his neck and actually break the skin. The intensity of the orgasm he was experiencing ratcheted up. Dizziness rushed over him and he almost lost consciousness as his mind prayed to the Goddess to complete their bond.

He woke to the most delicious smell he'd ever scented, his mate. There was no doubt the goddess had bonded them fully and she was his. It was a strong bond, one that would grow stronger with time and life in general. They would fight, make up, learn about each other and deal with whatever life threw their way. Right at this moment, Ven was the happiest he had ever been. She was still asleep and she looked peaceful and content in her slumber. His arms were around her and he hesitated to try to remove them since it might wake her up.

Dawn was breaking outside her window and they would have to get up soon and take on the day before they could return to each other's arms. Ven wasn't rich and neither was Sharon and they both needed their jobs to live the good lives they had. He didn't mind, he loved running his shop, it combined the love of motorcycles and the pride he had in running his own business. Sharon loved her job because helping people was her passion.

The thought of starting a family, seeing his mate with a round belly full off his offspring, made his breath catch in his throat for a moment. He did worry about the change she would be going through. Her scent had already shifted slightly and he knew it would change more before she became fully wolf. It brought a smile to his face as he thought of running through the woods with her at his side.

Now wasn't the time for dreams, now was the time to get up and prepare for a typical day at the store. He carefully slid his arms out from around her and slid out from under her. That she didn't wake was a testimony to how much last night had taken out of her. Ven noticed her alarm was set and he wanted to let her sleep as long as possible. Regretfully, he wouldn't be able to say goodbye or give her a deeply passionate kiss, those would have to wait until tonight.

Showering quickly, he dried, dressed and wrote a note so she would know he would miss her until he saw her again. He wasn't very good at expressing himself but he tried. Putting the note on his pillow, he slipped out quietly.

Once he made it to the shop, he opened up and poured himself a cup of coffee. Maybe sometime soon Sharon could stay with him at the shop and they could talk. The truth was he wished to share everything in his life with his mate and he wanted to share her life too.

The bell rang, alerting him to customers. It turned out to be a female who had come in before and always flirted heavily. His interest had been lukewarm before but now it was ice cold. She left in a snit, insulted by his lack of enthusiasm. It was alright because he didn't believe she had any desire to buy anything.

The rest of the day was typical with a few small sales and one used bike going to a teenager whose father had come in with him. Ven now looked forward to being with his mate. Grabbing his phone, he called first. It was a shock when a man answered.

"Hello, Sharon's phone," a deep male voice answered.

Ven hung up shocked. He realized he didn't know her very well. She had family, but he knew nothing about them. Since she had kept him as her dirty little secret, he had made a point of not knowing anything about the people she kept him away from. There was only a little he actually knew about her when it came down to it, other than that she was his whether she liked it or not and that he loved her. How to handle this? Should he drop by and see what was going on? The only other option was to sit here and stew and he didn't like that choice much at all.

Tossing on his leather jacket which made him look like a biker outlaw, he hurried to his bike. In seconds he was on the road and her house wasn't far. In five minutes he was pulling into her driveway behind an old Trans Am. It was orange and black and he had to admit he liked it. He walked up to the door and knocked.

Sharon answered and stepped aside to let him in. A guy sat on the couch relaxed and comfortable. He was no stranger that was for certain. Ven pulled her into his arms and laid a kiss on her that left no doubt what their relationship was. It was unnecessary since she didn't scent of the man sitting there watching with interest.

"You have a boyfriend? Wait until I tell Aunt Claris," the man chuckled as he spoke.

"Don't you dare! She'll find out next weekend when Ven and I visit her."

"Ven? Do you own that motorcycle place?" The guy ask with interest.

"This is my cousin Tyler. Tyler this is my boyfriend Ven."

"He's a wolf, Sharon. You know that?" Tyler asked.

"Yes."

"Good for you, Ven. I told Sharon she was a dreadful racist about supernatural types. It's not completely her fault. You guys can be scary to humans that have just learned about you," Tyler admitted.

"I've heard that before. I'm glad she finally accepted me."

"You're mates?"

"Yes, we are," Ven replied watching Sharon for any negative reaction. She'd been against wolves for so long he didn't know what to think of her change of heart. He only hoped it would last.

"I see grandkids in Aunt Claris' future. She's been on Sharon for some time now."

Ven smiled gleefully. "You don't say?"

Sharon turned red as fire. He certainly hoped children were in the not too distant future because he was ready to make a home with his mate and that entailed everything that made a house a home.

Her cousin seemed alright and he was glad to finally meet one of her family members. It was his hope that eventually he would meet them all now that they were mated. To him and the supernatural world, their bond was much stronger than marriage.

It wasn't long before Tyler made excuses to leave. He seemed to understand that their relationship was new and fragile. This need to be alone all the time and making love would ease some with time but he hoped it would never go away completely. Ven knew couples who had been together for centuries that still ran off company to be together. His parents were one such couple and he'd always wanted what they had.

Pulling Sharon into his arms, he carried her to the bed. He'd waited as long as he could to join with her. "I want you now."

"I want you too," she said as he gently laid her on the bed and began to strip her bare with her help.

Once she was naked he stepped back and removed his own clothes speedily, anxious to join with his female. It was just when he was about to devour her whole when the banging on the door began.

Ven felt his luck sucked. "We can just ignore that."

The pounding got louder as if the person knocking had heard what she'd said.

"Maybe you'd best answer and send them on their way," he suggested.

"Okay," she agreed.

She got up and grabbed a robe. Hurrying out to the living room, he heard her open the door. "It's you," he heard her say.

"Am I not allowed to drop by to see my favorite cousin?" The female asked.

"Not when the lights are off and someone's parked in the driveway."

"You have company?" The female ask with feigned surprise. "When can I meet him?"

"You'll meet him this weekend when the rest of the family does Wanda."

Ah, it was Wanda the nosy cousin he'd come close to meeting once before. He didn't really appreciate the interruption but he had a feeling he'd have to get used to it where Wanda was concerned. At least he was sure he'd be meeting Sharon's family even if she hadn't asked him to accompany her to this family gathering yet. She must realize he would go anywhere with her. Her family would become his family, even the nosy and gossipy Wanda.

It took Sharon a few minutes of talking before she got Wanda to leave. He wouldn't put it past that woman to hide outside and wait to catch him leaving so she could see who he was. That was his impression of Wanda.

His mate finally came back dropping the robe at the door. "I didn't think you would ever make it back," he growled.

"Me either. That girl is a pain in the ass."

Ven had to agree. "Let's forget about her and get back where we were," he suggested.

He was naked and his cock bobbed in her direction. Sharon smiled and licked her lips as she watched it move.

"Come here."

She moved toward him clearly as ready as he was to have a little skin on skin contact.

He grabbed her hair and tugged down. She dropped to her knees and her hands reached out. One stroked his shaft while the other hand cupped his balls, squeezing just hard enough. Her tongue flicked out and got the drop of precum just before it would have dripped off the end. "Mm," she hummed.

Her mouth opened and clamped down on the head of his cock sucking hard. He loved the feel of it. She moved down his length, her tongue licking the underside of his cock and causing it to leap. Her hands and her mouth kept things under control as her mouth tightened around him while she set a steady pace. Sharon let his cock pop out of her mouth with a plop. She moved lower and licked his balls then sucked them into her mouth lovingly, one at a time. She licked the space behind his balls before returning to his cock. That female knew how he loved having his balls sucked.

It had brought him so close to release he could barely hold back. She slid down his cock until the whole thing was sunk down to her throat and then she swallowed. Dear goddess he couldn't hold back and ropes of salty cum shot into her mouth. Sharon swallowed quickly and didn't choke, even though he filled her with it.

When he was through and had no more to give, she sucked him clean and let him slip out of her mouth. Immediately he was hard again but this time he wanted to fill her channel with his seed. Holding out his hand to her, he helped her up when she took it.

Pulling her into his arms, he kissed her deeply, tasting a hint of his flavor on her tongue. He lifted her and her legs wrapped around him as his cock settled between her legs and slid into her wet channel. Goddess, it was only because she was soaking wet that he slid into her, she was so tight. Slowly, he moved into her and groaned with delight the whole way. No female had ever held a candle to his mate in his eyes.

Plunging in and out, he set a fast rhythm because the need rode him hard. Sharon moaned and made other noises to let him know how much she enjoyed what he was doing and how close she was to exploding around him. Her channel massaged his cock and drew him closer to release too.

Her nails dug into his back and his fangs burned as they extended, wanting another taste of his mate's sweet blood. Slamming in hard enough to shake her up, her climax made her channel clamp down and he howled with animal pleasure just before he sank his fangs into her neck to taste her. Her blunt teeth bit into him and he could smell the blood she somehow managed to take from him.

Chapter Seven
Bonding and Blending

Nothing had ever felt as incredible to her as when they came together drawing each other's blood. His was spicy and hot. She could learn to crave it since it gave her a kick of energy with a buzz. How she had kept her distance from him was hard to understand. Now that they had begun their bonding process, she couldn't imagine ever being away from him for long.

Her whole body hummed but she'd never felt better in her life. Happiness filled her heart with a soul deep attachment to her mate that surpassed anything she could have expected or even imagined. She hung on to him as if her life depended on it as sleep overcame her. Dreams were sweet, pleasurable, she woke rested and ready to take on the world. It was a good thing since now she needed to talk about how they would blend their very different lives and meet each other's friends and families.

She wanted the process to begin this weekend when her family was having a gathering. They had them regularly, making it the perfect opportunity to introduce her mate who she hoped would eventually also be her husband. Sharon knew it would be difficult for him to meet such a large number of her relatives all at once but she felt it was better to get it over with at once. She could only hope he would agree.

Ven was still asleep as she looked at his peaceful face, handsome as always but with a calmness not usually present. She couldn't bring herself to wake him since he had looked so tired earlier but was now sleeping so deeply. Sharon stretched, noticing that she felt a slight ache between her legs but it wasn't uncomfortable. It was actually a nice reminder of what they'd done before falling asleep, causing a smile to come to her face. He moved in his sleep, maybe he was about to wake.

Sharon slipped out of bed, put on her robe and went to the kitchen to make a pot of coffee and fix breakfast, even though it was nighttime. Ven had come over after closing up his store at five but it was midnight now. Her nights and days were often all messed up on the weekends because of her night shift work, but now the confusion was spreading to the weekdays too.

Standing at the stove, cooking bacon, Ven came up behind her and wrapped his arms around her. She loved the feel of his strong muscular body so she leaned back into him.

"You should have woke me," he said sounding slightly irritated.

"You looked so peaceful I thought you needed some rest."

"You're thoughtful. It's sweet but I wanted to join with you again."

"And we can after we eat." Her stomach growled causing him to chuckle.

"Now I see the real reason you left me sleeping," he nuzzled her neck, breathing up against her ear, making her wish she had just stayed in bed and worried about food later.

"Let's eat so we can go back to my room," she suggested as she divided the bacon between two plates that already had other food on them.

Ven raised his brow when he saw the amount of food on her plate. "That's a bit more than you usually eat."

"I'm starving to death. I don't ever remember feeling this hungry."

It made her wonder if the change was upon her. Ven had explained that there was an excellent chance she would turn and be able to shift like he did. It was both terrifying and exciting to imagine what it would be like.

They sat down at the small kitchen table eating in companionable silence. When they'd seen each other before it had been more like a stopover for sex and then they were gone. It would now be a merging and bonding experience where he would become a major part of her life. That might be hard for a woman that had never had a serious relationship in her life.

This male wolf would make that all worthwhile. Their plates were empty and now need called. It hit her hard but she could see he was affected equally by the tenting of his boxers that he must have thrown on before coming into the kitchen.

Sharon could feel the heat rolling through her. It was something else to get used to because she had always tended to run cool before. Was there no end to the things that would change?

Ven stepped toward her, grabbing her and throwing her over his shoulder like a Viking of ancient times, as he hurried to the bedroom. He was impatient but that was nothing new.

Setting her down next to the bed, he untied her robe, and slipped it off her shoulders.

The air was cooler than her heated skin, making her nipples pebble and ache. His hands moved to cup them gently, swiping his fingers over her nipples causing her to moan. His head lowered and his tongue moved over one nipple then the other one. Finally he sucked one into his mouth in hard tugs making moisture pool between her legs. Dear Lord the male was dangerous, but she loved it.

One hand moved down until it settled on her bare pussy. A finger slid into the moisture and glided into her channel. Another finger slid upward to her clit. My, what big hands and large fingers he had. His mouth moved to her other nipple tormenting it in a similar fashion. Maybe she was a glutton for punishment because she loved it. Her legs spread open wider as she pressed against his hand. His fingers moved deftly and she felt herself drawn closer and closer to her climax until she exploded in a blaze of pure pleasure.

A scream was ripped from her as she jerked and writhed against his talented fingers. Finally she whimpered as he continued to manipulate the now extremely sensitive flesh. Ven moved his fingers away just kissing her tenderly. She sighed when he pulled his lips away from hers. Sharon felt drained but she knew from past experience that Ven could quickly rekindle the flames of passion. He stripped out of his boxers picking her up and carrying her to the bed. Gently, he laid her down then joined her.

Lying over her with his weight supported on his elbows, she could feel his hard shaft pressing between her legs. Ven licked her lower lip before he sucked it into his mouth scraping it lightly between his teeth. She felt a rush of sexual awareness run through her. Her tiredness was leaving quickly with need taking its place. Sharon arched against him and felt the thick head of his cock begin to slide inside her. Her muscles squeezed down making the fit even tighter.

"Oh God that feels amazing," she whispered with a moan.

"Preaching to the choir, Sweetheart," Ven agreed, his voice rough with passion.

He plunged into her waiting channel as they both groaned deeply together. Now he set a rapid pace as the need seemed to ride him as hard as he was riding her.

He was going in hard and deep. Sweat was slicking them both as he was keeping up an incredible pace. She tightened her muscles, squeezing him, making him groaned as pleasure rocked him. Nothing could compare or compete with the feeling of her mate as he set off intense pleasure causing her to close her eyes. It was like fireworks went off behind her eyelids as an orgasm rolled over her. Her fingernails dug into his shoulders and she thought she could smell his spicy blood in the air.

Ven howled stunning Sharon with the deep sound he made. As she opened her eyes, staring right into his, it was as if his wolf was looking back at her with eyes that glowed gold. It was so beautiful to look deep into those wild eyes, feeling the love that he held for her. It might not be long before her wolf might howl in pleasure when she came also.

He rolled to his back bringing her with him so she lay across his chest. They both gasp for breath and she could feel his heart hammering in his chest just like hers was. They both calmed as their breathing grew deeper. It was just a matter of time before sleep claimed them. Sleeping with Ven was a beautiful thing and she felt safe and well cared for. It was comforting to feel his skin against hers and she fell asleep quicker than she had ever before. His deep and slow breathing told her he had even beat her to dreamland. In the morning they would begin to plan their life together.

It was crazy how rushed they were while getting ready. Ven had suggested sharing a shower to save water as well as time. She would never believe it again, as they showered together Ven rubbed her with soap, exciting her so much that she felt turnabout was fair play and did the same to him. By then they were both so needy there was only one thing to do. Ven rinsed them off before he pinned her against the shower wall to pound fiercely into her while the water sprayed all over them.

His hand had reached between them pinching her clit until she had screamed as she came with him following after her. They had quietly dried off and dressed, but there had been no time for anything but a cup of instant coffee. Fudge! That wouldn't be enough to help her through the busy day ahead. It seemed they never had the time to talk about their future either. She knew she needed to talk to him before the family get to together on Sunday or he might be angry at having it dropped on him at the last minute.

They made it outside where he walked her to her car. He kissed her with so much passion she just wanted to go back to bed with him. She knew she couldn't. The mischievous smile on his face made her figure he knew where her mind was.

"I'll see you as soon as I lock up for the day," Ven promised as she started her car.

She watched him walk to his bike, his ass filling out those jeans perfectly. He started it immediately revving it a couple times before he took off. Now it was time for her to go too.

She backed out of the driveway taking off toward work. As soon as Ven was gone her mind started listing all the things they needed to discuss. How crazy was that?

After she got to work with so much on her mind it was no surprise the day went slowly. Tonight she intended to talk to him before they had sex. That was the only way anything would actually get discussed. Her day was finally over and now it was time to head home.

Arriving at home, she began to fix supper then put it in the oven. She wasn't done long and had just poured a glass of wine, when Ven came through the door. Sharon had given him a key before they'd left this morning.

"We need to talk so no touching until we're done," Sharon said as she stepped back when he reached out to embrace her.

"Hmm, what is this urgent conversation we need to have?"

"Do you have any plans for Sunday?"

"No, but I suspect I'm about to."

"My family is having a gathering and I want you to come. It will be my chance to show you off and introduce you to everyone," she smiled sweetly hoping he'd be convinced.

Her family members could be like barracudas and she felt bad for him but better sooner than later. This meeting was something she wanted to get out of the way.

"Sure, Sweetheart. I'll go with you."

Sharon leaned back against the wall in relief.

Chapter Eight
Family

Ven wasn't stupid. He was picking up on her concerns and he figured her family was probably as crazy as his. This was what he would do for her, because he loved her. Besides, sometime down the line she would have to meet his family and it wouldn't be easy either.

Sharon was in a talkative mood. They sat down while they waited for supper to cook and made some major decisions. She would be moving in with him since she didn't own the house she lived in. His house was a better choice because he owned some land with part of it forested. It was where they would run together once she made the change. She would give up working so much on the weekends and holidays so they could have time together. His hours weren't that bad since he had help at the store on the weekends already.

"So do you want kids?"

"I wouldn't mind a houseful of pups," he admitted, making her smile.

Ven realized she'd been nervous about his answer, which showed she didn't know much about male wolves. The desire to create a family was strong in most of his fellow wolves. It was a good thing they seemed to agree on most of the important things.

"When will I start to change?"

"You already have. I've noticed your scent isn't the same and you feel hotter. Can you see better, smell things you never noticed before, or feel things differently?"

"I wondered about it."

"You're change is coming fast. I bet we'll be running through the woods together in a week."

"What's it like?"

"It's amazing. You feel the wind in your fur, the scents of the earth rise up to your nose where you can smell everything and your eyes can see so much further and in more detail than you could imagine. I've never heard of it hurting but I'll be there with you if you have any problems. Most people say it's euphoric when you change, even the first time. Like sex when you get off, Baby. You might feel a little off balance because suddenly you'll have four feet instead of two and your body's different. It's closer to the ground and that takes a bit of getting used to."

"It sounds incredible."

"There's nothing like it. You're more in tune with Mother Nature and all the animals and plants around you. You see beauty everywhere you look."

"You're giving me chills. I can hardly wait to change."

"It will add another level of intimacy to our relationship."

He knew she didn't truly understand but it wouldn't be long before she did.

The rest of the week passed quicker than he'd expected. Now that it was Saturday, he was ready to take her to the woods and see if she would change. When he scented her, a richer smell came from her now that reflected her new animal nature. The human scent was still there only enriched with something more. He was so sure she would be able to change that as soon as they woke this morning he had her walking to the woods with him.

"I'm scared," she whispered in his ear. "I hear a voice talking to me and I think I'm going crazy."

"No, Sweetheart. That's your inner wolf and she wants you to let her out. Having her will be the best thing that's ever happened to you because you will never be alone. If you need a sounding board, she'll be there. She'll advise and support you, but she's a separate individual too. "Together you are two parts of a whole."

"I have to admit it sounds great the way you describe it. What do I do?" She asked as she stopped in the clearing with trees all around and looked up at him.

He embraced his female, praying to the Goddess so that everything would turn out the way it should. "Relax and envision what your wolf looks like. Imagine yourself changing, morphing into your other half."

Ven kissed her, feeling her relax in his arms. Suddenly she dropped, he looked down at a small mostly white wolf with four charcoal grey socks and a tail of the same color. She was gorgeous and he shifted to the massive fully black alpha that he was. His mate stumbled as she tried to walk in her new form. Her balance improved as she continued to work at it until finally she started to move faster.

It wasn't long after that she was running, then she discovered a rabbit. There were many of them in this area and she enjoyed chasing it but in the end, she let it go. He was sure she would never be a hunter, except by necessity. Even in her wolf form she had no desire to do harm. That was alright since he rarely hunted himself. It concerned him more that she learned how to defend herself and that he would insist on her learning.

They ran around playing for a couple hours but now it was time to shift and go home. Her wolf had gotten a good run but it was important for her to let her wolf out slowly, adjusting to her. His mate seemed to naturally adapt and he was glad there were no problems to deal with. Tomorrow would be trouble enough as he met Sharon's extended family. He was male enough to admit he was nervous but he would put his best foot forward.

Chapter Nine

Coming Together

Sharon was amazed as she watched Ven talking to her family while they ate supper. They had all taken to him right away, making all her fears groundless. If anything, she was slightly jealous of how easily he seemed to fit in where she sometimes struggled with many of them. Her mother never took to anyone the way she'd taken to Ven. It was like she'd discovered a long lost son. Sharon was glad they liked him because she loved him. It was just her weird family never seemed to hang on her every word like that.

Ven also seemed to enjoy talking and joking with them. It was a weight off her shoulders so she decided to settle in, enjoying the fact that all the attention was on him not her. Maybe that was partly because her mom and other family members saw signs that she was settling down like they had always wanted. Grandkids were at the top of her mom's list. Since she was the oldest, that made her the prime target. A position she could now pass on to her younger sister Cleo. Poor girl wouldn't know what hit her now that she was in her mom's sights.

Ven looked up giving her a nod to let her know everything was fine. She nodded back but glanced at the clock. It let him know she was ready to go. Tomorrow was a workday and morning came early. Ven excused himself heading her way. Sharon would admit to being tired but mostly because she'd worked herself up with what turned out to be unnecessary worry.

He sat beside her on the couch wrapping his arms around her. She felt better immediately. That was the strength of a fated bond. It was something she had studied as soon as Ven had told her it was what they had. Her head moved to his shoulder where she almost fell asleep.

"Hey, we're going to leave now Sweetheart so wake up."

Her eyes struggled to open then she looked at him. She couldn't believe she'd fallen asleep. It was probably all the hot sex they were having. That thought woke her up as she thought about jumping his bones as soon as they got back home.

Home was Ven's huge log cabin style home. Next weekend all their friends were gathering to move her stuff there. It would be wonderful to be moved in, see him every day and sleep with him every night. They hadn't discussed a wedding yet but she was sure Ven would ask eventually.

He held open the door to his truck and she got in. Ven was a perfect gentleman which wasn't something you would expect from a werewolf but you would be surprised. Most of their alphas treated their females wonderfully. It was something she'd noticed among her mated cousins. That had made her start questioning her decision to mate with Ven. Her decision not to had been wrong, so finally she'd corrected her mistake.

Her attention had wandered and she realized they were pulling into the driveway at the home she and Ven would now share. It was much larger than her three bedroom house making it the perfect place to raise a bunch of pups. It was a log house but it also had stone around the bottom and the chimneys. There was more than one fireplace. It also had an amazing outdoor fire pit that she couldn't wait to see a fire in. Speaking of fire, her blood was burning with the need to get her mate naked and hard.

She followed him up the stairs to the door which he unlocked. As soon as she stepped over the threshold she saw he was stripping out of his clothes quickly. Sharon followed his lead leaving a trail of clothing to the bedroom. He was hot on her heels causing her to giggle as she ran. Ven scooped her up into his arms from behind, tossed her naked ass on the bed then jumped after her. Catching himself on his hands and knees he kept all his weight off her.

"Goddess, I love you, my mate!" He stared into her eyes with his own full of love before he lowered his hot lips to hers, robbing her of her very breath. The kiss was fiery, claiming her down to her soul. Had she known being claimed by this alpha wolf would feel this way she would have given in right away. It would have saved them both a lot of heartache.

She trembled with need and felt moisture slide down her thigh as her body prepared to be taken in the most pleasurable way possible. His cock head pressed against her entrance as his mouth nuzzled her neck. Dear Lord, the male was dangerous but only too desirable. It was a good thing he was hers. He pressed harder sliding in easily despite his size. Ven stayed still for a moment allowing her channel to adjust to him making it feel so good to be filled. Suddenly he began to move hard and fast. It seemed his control was broken.

Shivers ran through her as he plunged into her, building the friction. Her muscles tightened, squeezing his large shaft and making him groan. He rested his weight on his elbows but now he pressed them closer to her in an embrace of sorts. Her legs wrapped around his hips and her toes dug into the soft flesh of his ass cheeks. They were very fine ass cheeks. The leverage allowed her to arch up as he plunged downward. Their bellies slapped together the sound echoed around the room.

Sharon felt hot as sweat began to slick her skin and drip off of him onto her. It added to the sensations as they slid against each other. A buzz ran through her just from being in contact with him. The tension built until she was so close to release it would take little to set her off like a firecracker. Apparently he sensed it, moving his hand between them then circling her clit. She screamed loud and long as she jerked against him, her muscles went wild squeezing and massaging his sizable staff.

Ven could hold out no longer and he howled like the wild wolf inside him. He slammed in so hard and deep she imagined she could taste him in her throat. Her arms tightened around him, she never wanted to let him go. Such unlimited pleasure could never be denied for long. She was always intended to be here in his bed and at his side.

Sharon fell asleep before Ven had even moved off her. Her dreams were sweet and loving with Ven at her side as they ran in wolf form. It was the final sign that they belonged together and she would never reject him again.

She woke in the early morning hours wishing she could stay with him instead of rising to prepare for the day. He was wrapped around her as she tried to get out of bed without waking him.

"You know I hate it when you do that," he said as his eyes opened staring at her.

"You know I hate waking you before you have to get up."

"I guess we are both doomed to disappointment. I will always wake when you move."

Sharon grinned at him. "I will always try to let you sleep a little bit longer."

"Now I'll make you pay for not waking me up, Mate," he said as he rolled on top of her, kissing her breathless.

She felt him slide between her legs and her wetness helped him slip inside. This was the way she wanted to wake up every day. He pounded into her as she arched up to meet him, feeling an energy run through her like lightening. This male never stopped surprising her. Her legs wrapped around him, hooking at the ankles as she hung on for dear life. He moved so hard and fast all she could do is lay there and take it. Her channel squeezed like a vise and she was so close to exploding she would go any second. It hit her unexpectedly and she felt weightless and like she was soaring. It was amazing trumping the orgasm he'd given her last night. She felt him tense as he followed her into bliss.

Lying there not wanting to move but knowing she had to, sucked. They had to get on with their day but the sad part was they wouldn't spend it together.

Epilogue

Last weekend their friends had helped them move all her things into Ven's house. Sharon had only rented the house from Kimmie who would probably raise the rent now that it wasn't a cousin and a friend living there. She'd liked the house well enough but it didn't feel the way Ven's house had already come to feel to her. The house and the male, they were her home.

She suspected Ven and his friends had somehow pulled the wool over their eyes. At least in the case of Sue Ellen, Kimmie and her, but Ven refused to discuss it so she supposed she was better off not knowing.

How long would it be before the other three cousins were mated and expecting their first pup? It was true she wasn't sure but she and Ven didn't mind. A pup would only complete their already wonderful life.

Sharon had cut back her extra work at the hospital was now only working one weekend a month. Ven had turned the store over to his assistant manager so they had spent a lot of time bonding and working on their first pup. Had they been successful? She thought so and she couldn't wait to be sure. Meanwhile life was good, very good.

Dream Job
by Abby Hayes

Chapter One

"I can do this. I can do this!" she repeated the mantra as she walked toward a rundown building on the far right side of an old strip mall. The old structure on the far west side of town had three stores open and two closed. Such places were becoming far more common a landscape in the northeast these days. As she opened the door whose windowpanes held years of age-related grime and walked into a desolate waiting room, she felt more and more as if she was selling her soul to the devil to get work in her field.

For a few minutes, she stood looking at her surroundings while she listened to see if there was life anywhere around her. There were a couple of posters on the wall, framed and bright in comparison to the dingy beige wall. Each of the enlarged video covers had some cheesy title and lots of flesh with the imprint of Girl Next Door as the film studio. Yes, that was where she was. Three years and one bad break up after completing her B.A. in Film and Digital Media from Cleveland State University, and she was applying for a job as a production assistant in the adult film industry. At least she would be working in her field, rather than falling into yet another cashier job.

Just as she was about to second guess this decision she had spent the last forty-eight hours talking herself into, and turn tail and run, she heard, "Hello. Are you Kim?"

The deep voice snaked up her spine as she slowly spun on her heel.

Coming face to face with a man who had to be the porn star, all disheveled dusty blond hair, chocolate brown eyes and tight white t-shirt showing ripped abs above tight torn at the thigh jeans.

"You are not, Kim. Sorry. Can I help you?" He said when she failed to say anything because she was thanking her lucky stars she had worn heels to this interview. The decision had been a bone of contention she'd had with herself all day.

"Ah, yes, I'm Kim. I'm here to interview for the assistant position. Is the owner here?"

"He is," Mr. Sexy-As-Hell laughed.

"Something funny? Did I interrupt a shoot? Can you get him for me?"

"No. No. And, I can. I'm him." He put out his hand to shake. "David Atner. Can I ask why you didn't think I was the owner? Is it the clothes, because I'm a pretty informal person. I should have told you that you didn't need to dress up for this. With your education, I hope to put you right to work. Have a shoot in two hours. Come, let me show you the place and we can talk."

"Sure." She guessed she didn't have to answer the question about why she'd thought he wasn't the owner. Relieved to say the least, she also knew she couldn't tell him that she was disappointed she wouldn't be seeing him naked during filming. She'd almost thought of taking the job just for that reason alone. That was neither here nor there now, so she followed him.

Wow! Incredible ass too! Not sure how much more of this guy I can take. Could I really work beside him, and actually focus? And, I thought that watching adult films shot live, discussing them and all that was going to be the problem. Sheesh!

"I rent two units here. The one next to this one with the boarded up windows is actually where I shoot. With the money I saved on rent, I was able to take out a loan for equipment and creating the soundproofed studio. It doesn't matter where one shoots as long as you have the right set up and equipment. Anyway, I was lucky that my first few low-budget adult films paid off."

"Why do you do it?"

"Excuse me?"

"I mean, how did you get into making adult films, if you don't mind my asking?"

"I don't. Money, of course. I was tired of struggling to make it in this business. I had reasons I needed to stay in the area. It sounded better than working out of the field. Now, well, it more than pays the bills. Maybe some day I will have enough to shoot one of my many screenplays I've written, which aren't porn. So enough about me. How about you? Why are you here applying for the job? I don't get applicants with your kind of education."

"Same reason pretty much, although my reason to stay got up and left after several years. Not sure why I'm not in New York or California, yet. Bouncing back I guess. Making some money first would be nice, make things easier, too. Sorry, I'm rambling, but I just haven't had the motivation yet to get up and go."

"Breakups can be rough. Give yourself the time to heal from whatever happened. In the meantime, I am happy you are here. Look, I am willing to hire you on a trial basis based on your education alone. That said, trial being if you can handle the content portion of the job too."

She realized she was grinding her heel into the floor. Relaxing her leg, she also took her hands off of her hips. With a sigh, she asked, "Is blushing optional? Because I have only seen a few of these films in my lifetime and I blushed through each of them. I can't imagine watching them live. I have to admit watching someone else have sex, ah…in person, is a bit intimidating. But, I'm willing to try it, to try to work in this business."

"Good. Blush all you want. You are not the one on camera."

No, I won't be the one behind the camera, especially not with all of the ice cream I have recently devoured since Greg left, she thought.

"You still with me, there?" he asked, getting closer to her.

"Yeah. Sure." Rebounding from the thought, she turned to look around the room they were currently in. "You have quite a studio. I can't wait to get to play again."

"I like your enthusiasm. It will help a lot. I'm not always the easiest person to work with, but I apologize a lot."

"Great. Sounds great." *Damn, apologize for that killer smile of yours, dimple and all!*

As they were walking around the studio admiring his equipment – as in electronics as far as he knew – like kids at a candy counter, another guy walked in.

"Hey, Dave," he huffed, like he was some salesman coming in for another boring day of work.

"Hi, Scott. Ready to shoot today?" He turned to Kim with a coy smile, "Actor number one."

"Sure. Another day another dollar, right?" he said flatly.

Poor him, she thought. *What a cross to bear having to come in here and be paid to have sex without it being illegal.* He was cute. But, currently she only had eyes for David. Something about him, the way the light caught the hair, which fell over his eyes, or the way he talked or moved or everything or anything, had her working on hiding the fact that the man mesmerized her.

Oh, how she wanted to scream *Dave* while she came. Her body was buzzing, sending tiny pulses of electricity to her every nerve ending. And, she did mean *every*. She hadn't even seen any sex yet, other than in her mind, and she was completely turned on.

A cold shower came over her though, when the female star of the movie walked in laughing on the arm of yet another hunk. She knew she paled in comparison, her dark red curls to this bombshell's waves of blond, and her smallish c-cup boobs next to the sexy goddess's triple-d-fake-cups. This is what David got to see naked on a daily basis, flat-bellied girls screaming out orgasms. Her full curves–and what was soon to be a blood-red face–would pale greatly in comparison, and then some.

"Okay, introductions," David snapped her back to reality. "Everyone, this is Kim, my new assistant. And, Kim, this is Scott or better known as Slick Maxim, this is Leann or simply Sinn, and last, holding onto her as usual because they are actually dating now and never breaking up so things don't get weird in here, is Jeff, better known by his fans as Johnny Muncher."

"Seriously? Um, I mean hi, but the names, really?" She stuttered, hoping she didn't offend anyone with the first words that had just slipped out of her mouth.

"We had a little too much fun over beers with the Porn Star Name Generator online. Then, once sober we figured what the hell, and went with them."

"Okay, then. Glad my name isn't going on any credits."

"Sure it will," David said. "If you watch the videos, I use my own name now. It came from telling the world to go fuck themselves. This is what I do, and I do it well. But, if you want a name, we can always get you one."

"Yeah, like, Curvaceous Red." Scott moved in, drawing her silhouette with his hands.

"Hands off, Scott!" David yelled. "Sorry, just don't make her uncomfortable. I need her." David winked at Kim as Scott moved away. "I told you I apologize a lot."

She took a few cleansing breaths, commanded her heart to stop pumping so loud she swore everyone else could hear it too, and relaxed her shoulders with some effort.

"We have read the script, *add nauseum*, the past few days. I have the studio all set up. So let's do this."

They each left the editing room. David motioned for her to follow him. Once they got into the studio he immediately got to work.

"Look, this is a basic ménage storyline, couple meeting single friend, joking turns into proposition, you get the picture? We will be starting at the bar. I do like to add in a little story, give these things some depth. So far no one has complained. All you need to do while we shoot is whatever I ask you to help me out with. It will be so much easier to stay behind the camera while someone else does all the dirty work...you up for it?"

"I'm going to try," Kim told him and herself at the same time. The studio was divided into a couple of rooms. On the far end was a bar, a living room and then a bedroom. The bar and bedroom looked ready to shoot. The living room on the other hand had a few misplaced pieces shoved into it with other props being stored on the couch and around the floor at the moment.

The threesome walked in, all looking like they were going out for a respectable night on the town. She was shocked at how normal their street clothes looked, but Leann would have looked damn sexy in a potato sack if she had to. She sighed on the inside. Eye makeup was a bit heavy. Still, she didn't feel better.

An hour later, Kim was thrilled with how the day was going so far. She'd moved a few props, changed lights around, moved the actors into new positions, got them water and stuff between shots. It was just as she was getting comfortable that the threesome made their deal and moved into the bedroom. Still, she found she was still impressed with the foreplay along with the push and pull of emotions the characters portrayed as Jeff's character learned to share his girlfriend. She had only seen a few porn flicks in her life, and they were not exactly like this. As she wondered if this had something to do with the change in term from porn to adult film, all the clothes save Leann's garter, hose and heels had disappeared.

Suddenly, the fact she was watching real people have live sex hit her like a volcano erupting all over her. As Jeff's cock disappeared into Sinn, her screen name feeling much more appropriate now, Scott or Slick Maxim posed behind her then shoved his cock into her ass.

"Kim, there is too much of a shine on Scott's butt. Powder, please," David said in a voice like he had asked her to do nothing more than wash the freaking dishes or something as common as that.

"Boss, I think your new assistant looks like she might pass out," she heard Scott exclaim.

"What?"

David came out from behind the camera, grabbed her by her arms and turned her toward him so fast that she felt a little woozy all of the sudden. Her hands landed on his chest, rock hard under her fingers, and she started to see stars.

"Kim," his hands went to her cheeks making everything worse, putting them in a position that all she could do was think of kissing him, "Are you going to be able to do this?"

"Sure," she found her voice. It just didn't sound as strong and sturdy as she wanted it to. Rather than all breathy like Sinn's, hers was half there due to diminished breathing abilities. She took his hands away from her face, gave her head a little shake, and tried to channel the sexual tension she was feeling into energy and confidence to do her new job. "I got it."

The heat moved through her cheeks down over her chest as she let go of David and went for powder. She went to the right of the threesome trying to divert her eyes from the two erections buried inside Sinn. It was as fascinating as it was odd to see. She couldn't imagine it herself; she had no concept of having two cocks inside her at once.

To get through, she concentrated on the amazing ass cheeks on Scott.

"Good?" she questioned David who was standing beside his camera still rather than behind it.

"Uh, let me see." Now, his voice sounded off, tense, deeper than it had all afternoon. He moved behind the camera. "Will you angle the light on your side toward him more, I will tell you when to stop."

She continued to do as she was told through the shoot. Her attempts to trick her mind into somehow not realizing fully what she was witnessing were futile. The only real distraction she had was stolen glimpses at the hunk behind the camera. These were not helping keep her traitorous body under control though. She thought somehow she could steal herself against it all, at least that was the story she'd told herself when she'd considered taking the job. If David had been the trip wire that set off the tiny explosions inside her stomach, then the threesome moaning and screaming and seemingly enjoying themselves were the sparks that set off the whole case of dynamite, in the form of pulsing nerves and tightening muscles. Ready and willing, she screeched a bit herself when David put his hand on her back.

"You okay there?" he asked, rubbing her back in small circles.

"Yes. I'm fine. I think. Need something?"

"I just cut for lunch. Where were you off to in that mind of yours, exactly?"

"Just thinking…ah…well, about my own life, I guess."

"Wishing for a ménage?"

"No!" she burst out, making the three naked people trying to gather up their clothing turn to look at her. "Sorry, no, I didn't mean my life in exactly that way."

"You got a boyfriend, Red?" Scott asked.

"Recently ended a three year relationship."

"Sorry, to hear that," he smiled, but David sighed, running his hand over her cheek then giving her a wink.

"I'm not," she said. Yet, she thought, *what I am sorry about is that you keep touching me, in all the wrong places.*

"I hear the door. Lunch is here. Meet us in our sorry excuse for a break-room."

"Sure. I'll be there in a minute."

She'd moved quickly to the bathroom to splash cold water on her face and touch up her makeup, among other things. Then, powdering her own face, her mind turned to a scene in the screenplay she had started writing out of school. She had now re-written the thing as many times as it had been rejected, more times than she wished to count. It needed more passion. It needed some kick ass love scenes. Ideas tumbled through her mind, and she raced to the editing room to grab the bag she had brought with her. She had a copy of her screen play with her at all times, just for this reason. She never knew when an inspired idea might hit her, and she liked to mark them on the manuscript for later changes.

Flipping through the pages, when she finally came upon the scene she thought of first, she started scribbling down her ideas to write some sex that wasn't just suggested. She didn't want an Adult film like the one they were shooting today but she was changing the rating from PG-13 to R with each movement of her pen.

"There you are." "What are you doing in here? Why are you not coming to lunch? The cast is wondering if you can no longer face them."

Startled at the sound of David's voice, she threw her arm over the pages. "I can. I just needed to make a note of something. I do that a lot. I think of something, and I have to write it down. Who knows what will happen to it in this brain of mine if I wait." She clenched her jaw to stop her rambling.

"What kind of idea did you have? What do you have there, a screenplay? Are you stealing ideas or are you writing your own adult film? Secret motivation for trying to get this job?"

She laughed because the smile on his face, dimple and all, told her he was hardly serious.

"No. Well, in a way. I was inspired. I just changed the rating on my script from PG to R, that's for sure."

"So, I did inspire rather than nauseate you?"

"Yeah, I guess you could say that. The nausea has all passed, just nerves. I'm over it."

He moved in closer, his hips and other protruding parts, not even an inch from her back.

"I would love to read it sometime."

"Thanks."

"I'm really serious. I want to read it."

"Well, we'll see. I guess I better go get some lunch and squash the squeamish rumors about me. They are eating with their clothes on right?"

"You are too cute, Red."

She swore as she walked to the break room that if he put his hand on her face one more time, she might just quit this job so she could kiss him.

"Hey look who's here," Leann exclaimed in a breathy voice. Apparently that was just how she spoke all the time, like she was coming onto you.

A shiver went down Kim's back, one that made her nipples tight. She grabbed a sandwich from the platter in the middle of the table, refusing to analyze what happened there at this time.

"Sorry, caught up in some work."

"Love when that happens." Scott winked after putting in his two cents.

"Take it easy on her, Scott," David warned.

"So, any advice after watching today's shoot? Dave here wants to re-shoot, he thinks. Not that I am complaining," Leann gave Jeff quite the look, one that made her wonder if he's gotten hard witnessing it.

Her own lust meter was set to high, and it was looking like so would her dildo when she got home. It had actually been awhile since she'd used it, and she had not been alone at the time. But, she was not going to dwell in the past. Maybe she needed to treat herself to a new one.

"Really, you want to re-shoot?"

"Can you handle it?" David teased, poking her in the side like she was a child.

"I was asking why. I mean it seemed fine, for your purposes anyway," she stammered, not sure her gut reactions applied here with not knowing the industry all that well.

"You have a suggestion? I'm all ears. Something I can't put my finger on doesn't seem right." He shook his head, but his hand landed on her shoulder. She wished she could read into his touchy feely ways.

"Well, I'm not sure I am qualified. I'm not too versed in the genre, if you know what I mean. My reaction is based on my own work, my own preferences. You know, anywhere from G to R," she let herself laugh a little, though it felt forced, just to stop her rambling.

"Just say what is on your mind. As a director, I am open to all life has to say to me because I never know where inspiration will find me, what will light up that proverbial light bulb over my head." He gestured with his free hand over his head, gripping her shoulder now with his other one.

"Yes, Kim, we all are actually open to suggestions. You don't need experience in the industry. You just have to be a woman. I assume you've had sex before," Leann said.

Kim was surprised Leann took no offense. "Uh, okay. Well, it was in the feelings. There was obvious excitement in the scene to finally be fulfilling this sexual fantasy, but I expected more hesitation than I saw. I mean are a few awkward moments not allowed in this genre. It is their first time at a ménage. Does it have to be all go, go, go? Do you know what I am getting at?"

"Actually, I think I do." David said, both hands now on her upper arms, moving up and down like he was chasing away a chill. Then, he moved fast, coming to the front of her and grabbing up her hands in his. Heat burned her flesh. "Do you think you are up to helping me with a walk through? We take the actors step-by-step through the scene to work out the moments in it."

"Ah..." She had visions of positioning these actors like she did in film school making student films, but those actors had all been clothed.

"We don't mind if you touch, or even demonstrate," Scott winked again.

"You're not helping asshole," David snapped at him. "Listen Red, it's not as bad as all of that, but you need to find a comfort zone with the nakedness and the sexuality to do this job. I am really hoping you will want to continue here, babe." There it was again, that cursed caress of her cheek with his hand. When he did that she was his puppet on a string.

"All right. I'm game then."

The next few hours had proven to be a comedy of sexually exhilarating errors that she'd actually gotten praised for, as they worked out some good footage. In fact, all afternoon she had been looking forward to falling asleep tonight – with her old battery operated friend having to do in place of a man – while she relived the highlights of the day in her mind.

***

By late that evening, the pink, vibrating cock seemed not wide enough or revved enough to give her what her body craved as she slipped the phallic shaped instrument of teasing torture in and out of her dripping pussy. She remembered the feel of hot male and female flesh in her hands as she had moved the actors around, all the while accidentally backing up against David, his cock hard under his jeans, making its size known to her ass. Her panties had been damp all day.

The clincher had been the moment she had actually been leaning over the threesome giving directions on the subtle changes in their body's movements. Being so close, seeing two dicks invade another woman, slide slowly in and out upon her direction, had almost been her downfall. To give in and beg for release from the tightening of the muscles in her stomach or the clenching of her empty vaginal walls had barely been beyond her. David leaned over her, each hill and valley of his chest settled on her back supporting his weight. His whole front outlined her backside, moving slightly as his arms reached over her, her body vibrating with each word he spoke.

She rammed the cock she pretended was his in and out of her, the tension of her day needing release, and moved her hips to meet every thrust. All five fingers pressed hard against her clit, rubbing and rubbing with too much pressure, awakening her need to have it rough because tonight nothing less would do. Breathing heavy, her body stopped its antics for a moment. She wanted more.

Her and her ex had experimented quite successfully with anal penetration, using butt plugs sometimes to give her that wonderfully full sensation. She even had him inside her ass, but she couldn't imagine actually having two cocks inside of her at once. Moving her hips and hands like a woman possessed at this point, her orgasm still stayed just out of her reach. It seemed after hours of resisting and denying, because she had to in order to keep her job, her body was craving more than she had to offer it.

Cool gel and a disappointingly small rubber dildo shoved up her ass, the slight runs of pain spurring her on, she threw herself on her bed, stomach first. Ramming the only cock she had back up inside her, she moved her hips fast, the pads of her fingers rolling over her clit. The frantic thrusts of her hips blew on the fire raging inside her. One climax rushed through her, tightening muscles, releasing pent up lust, but she didn't stop. With her pants and her cries resounding throughout the room, she continued to fuck herself. Her arms burned with her continued movements, climbing up to a second release before the first one had fully passed. Even she was a touch surprised when she screamed out David's name into her pillow.

Chapter Two

After two weeks of working on the film, far longer than she had ever thought the shoot would go, she found that pleasuring herself every night became a common occurrence. She'd spent quite a few dinners with David after the actors had left. They'd discussed the day's work or their long ago dreams. He'd told her about his sick mother who had passed a few years ago; the reason he had originally stayed in the area rather than moving to New York or California. She even talked a little about her idiot of an ex Greg, along with everything else under the sun.

She was exhausted in a good way. Last night, at a small end-of-shoot celebration, she had even given David her own screenplay to read. He had begged enough. Then, with one touch, it was his. He had to be getting that fact by now. She caved at his touch. She lay in bed Friday morning smiling, just thinking of it. Her skin tingled remembering.

Her phone rang, startling her. Straining for it, her sore muscles stretched painfully.

With a sigh she answered, "Hello."

"Did I wake you?" David's deep voice held hints of might be concern and yet playfulness at the same time. "I'm sorry. I thought you would be up getting ready for work by now."

"I'm up. Just refusing to get out of bed."

"Ah, big day yesterday, wrapping up the shoot, the actors tend to get oddly celebratory. I never got it, but I let them have it. It is the least I can do I figure after putting up with me."

"It was a little over the top," she gave away.

"Yeah. I remember my first times. Hope you relieved some of that tension last night that has been building over the shoot."

"David!"

"Sorry. Anyway, I was calling to see if we could make a change in plans for work today?"

"Sure. What's up? Can't be more re-shooting, you said it was a wrap." Her body thrilled at the idea though. Her libido loved the job, despite the arguments her brain still came up with from time to time – when her rational thoughts were even acknowledged. She was getting better and better at shutting it down.

"No. In fact, I don't even want to edit the thing today. You inspired me."

"I did?" She couldn't help but smile.

"This is going to sound like I'm coming onto you, but really it's just business. I was up late reading your script, and you're just so talented. I would like to get your opinions on my ideas and maybe some help writing a new script. If you think you're up for trying to write an adult film, I was wondering if you would come to my place. It's just, home is where I write, and the studio is where I shoot. Make sense. You can say no. You won't lose your job. I would like a partner. And, I promise not to touch you."

"Ah…" Her mind raced around the possibilities.

"Please, say yes. I swear, this *is* a work day, not a come to my house so I can talk you into my bed day."

She forced the disappointment down. "Sure. Why not? Just tell me where I am to be and when, giving time for a shower, okay?"

She'd hurried through her morning wishing she'd had time for a soak in a hot bath instead of a rushed shower. However, that all started falling to the back of her mind as she drove. The roads kept changing, becoming more and more rural as she entered the city David lived in. Actually, he was quite a drive away from the city. A lot of people drove a good half an hour, or even more, not to have to live where they worked. The houses were getting spaced further apart, lots of trees making living more private. The road turned and twisted so much it barely gave her time to take in her surroundings.

When she finally got to the right house number on a mailbox, all she could see was a driveway lined with trees. She thought this quite odd, having expected him to live in an apartment somewhere. As she drove down the laneway the house came into view, wood-sided with dormers and a wrap around porch. She almost backed back down the driveway to recheck the number she had written down with the one on the mailbox when she saw him step out on the porch. Today his shirt was flannel, and he was buttoning the damn thing up as he moved toward her car.

"Perfect timing. I had time to work out and shower myself. Find the place, all right?"

"Sure. I was just not positive I had the right place. Didn't have you pegged as the country living type. You live here alone?"

"Yes. I'd had enough of apartment living a few years back. The movies were bringing in a decent amount of cash by then and I'd sold my mother's house when she died, so I moved. I actually like the peacefulness of it. I would not have done well in New York or Hollywood. I need this after a long day at work; not glass and metal and clean, white walls, but wood furniture and well, woods." He laughed, motioning behind him.

"I like it. It suits you now that I see you out of the studio. Guess I can see why you would want to write here."

"Yeah," he murmured softly. She caught a cute smirk on his face as he turned.

"So, what is this idea you have for a script?"

"Well, ideas are coming at me from many directions. But, I want to try a part of a story line from one of my old scripts. Then, and I hope you won't be offended, but watching you these past weeks, I had this idea about a young girl, one finding herself in many ways, finding her sexuality of course. What do you think?"

"You think I haven't found myself and that somehow in your studio I will?"

"Well, it wasn't a commentary on you per say. It was just how cute you were faking not being uncomfortable. And, it just got me thinking about someone opening up to a new world of sexual possibilities."

"Glad I could inspire. But, I assume it would be unsettling for most to stand next to a couple–no a threesome–having sex. Especially when asked to powder one of their asses."

"Okay, you have a point. Anyway, I wasn't saying you hadn't found yourself. Who am I to say really? I have known you only a few weeks. I don't know, and I'm not asking what you have done in your past. I just said that the way you acted inspired a character who will fit right into a script I once had an idea for. This one is about a runaway of sorts. Only, one that's in her twenties running away from the life she knows to a new one. Guess it is more a fantasy I often had, one that was impossible in real life. I was stuck here. But, making it a female, and making it about not only life choices, but opening her eyes to new worlds of sex after leaving a bad relationship. Well, it is coming to me from many angles. You understand the main premise though?"

He was so cute, the way his eyes sparkled, his big smile, as he got more and more excited about his project. In his kitchen now, he moved to pull two bottled waters out of the refrigerator, lifting one her way to ask if she wanted one too.

Nodding, she responded, "I think I do actually, on several levels." She winked. "It's exciting when so many things come together to create a great script."

"What else do you understand? You said on several levels." He turned the cap on his water bottle and she watched the muscle in his forearm flex.

"Well...uh, you know, having fantasies and putting them in your writing or using them to inspire...so, can I read what you have so far?"

The next few hours of sitting next to David were as fun and thrilling as they were sexually frustrating. His smile, his touches the glimpses she got of his chest when he leaned her way. Not to mention, the subject matter–the hot steamy scenes of a woman going through a sexual awakening–were keeping her wet and ready. She was sure if he made one move that she wouldn't deny him anything. Surprised to be feeling such things so soon after her breakup, she still didn't bother to analyze them. This was her boss, so what would be the point.

"Something is wrong here with this ménage scene. Or, maybe I am just bored with them after the last shoot. I don't just want that, I want more...uh, I don't know, maybe the guys next door can be more than two. Why not three or even four? What do you think?"

"Earlier this week, I was thinking two was more than I'd ever had," she laughed. "But, then I started to actually consider it."

She started to laugh again, her face going red from her slight confession. David turned in his seat to face her, his sudden movement causing her to gasp and lean back. He caught her as if she would actually fall.

"But, we aren't talking about me," her tone dropped to a more serious one. "It's your script." She shrugged. "Three. Four. Why the hell not. I can't wait to see this filmed!"

His hands on her arms soon slid down, but then he pulled them back, looking at his palms. She wondered if he felt the same tingle on his skin as she did on hers.

"What is it?" she questioned him, still feeling her heartbeat in her throat. The poor thing had been working overtime all day to begin with.

"You never then?"

"Never what?"

"Why make this so hard on me? Forget it. It's best not to ask." He scrubbed his hand down over his face.

"No, ask. It's fine, whatever it is. Just ask me."

"You've never had more than one guy?" His eyes were mesmerizing, so full of light and playfulness. He licked his lips like his mouth was dry, and she had to hold back the urge to kiss him.

"Uh, no. Sorry. I suppose you have?"

"Only once. I called it research. But, you have been so good at helping me write this thing today. How do you know how the woman would feel?"

"Imagination! I am only guessing, imagining myself in the same situation."

"You've imagined yourself in that situation?" His coy tone was damn sexy.

"Not many times before coming to work for you, but yeah, I had heard of the term and tried to figure it out from time to time. I wasn't a prude before I met you. I'd had sex…beyond the missionary position that is."

"Really?" He looked like the cat that had suddenly eaten the proverbial canary.

"So, what do you think? Should we add more men?"

"To the script, right? Why not, at this point?"

"That's my girl."

The discussion went from bad to worse fast. Positioning them all in the room with stick figure drawings and discussing what part would be where was torture with him so close to her. She could barely keep her thoughts straight.

"No, that wouldn't work?"

"Why not?"

"A man wouldn't do that?"

"Really, not even if a woman asked?"

"Why would the woman want him to?"

"Never mind. Let's just get back to the script as written then. What if she is lying down on her stomach on top of one guy, and then…"

"Too typical," he interrupted her.

"Typical?"

"Right, you need to loosen up. Explore those fantasies of yours. Let your mind wonder over the possibilities until we shoot something unlike anything else."

"Uh…" she closed her eyes to try to imagine herself with four guys, all the while happy to block out the one giving her trouble in the first place. She wanted him. There was no denying it any longer. Who cared about how long they had known each other, the job. She wanted him inside her, now. Tomorrow can bring whatever it fucking may.

He stood, walking behind her, brushing her hair from her neck. "Imagine if one guy was behind the woman sitting just like you are maybe, but on a guy's lap."

"Okay…then you can put another man's mouth between her thighs, licking them both, her clit and his balls. That's different, and maybe a man lying over his back, the one on his knees. His cock–if he is the right size lying at the man's ass, while his hands–or if he is tall enough, his mouth–fondle her breasts. But, where does the fourth guy go? Because, I think the woman's parts are all taken up," she laughed. It felt good actually; broke the tension of having him behind her, touching her.

"Come on. You can do this. I like this so far. Think. Where would he go?"

"Maybe he picks her up and gets her out of the damn chair so he can play too."

"No. I should target a gay audience and women with this one if I have all of these men. Let's give them some male on male interaction. I haven't really done much of that."

"Hell yeah. Now that is an inspiring idea. Are we talking in real life or film, as far as you are concerned?" She winked. "Just asking."

"Both. You would like to see two men get it on?"

"Who wouldn't? More is better even with cocks, right?"

"I don't know. Up for a little research?"

"What? You are joking, right?"

"No. Yes." He had an odd look about him, like he couldn't figure something out all of a sudden. Up to this point she had enjoyed his confidence. So, she played him a little to see not only what was going on, but how he was feeling.

"Okay. Which is it? Should I just go find a few random men to have sex with?"

"What? Forget it. I was joking. Back to the script." He came to sitting with a thump.

"If you were joking, then why are you mad all the sudden?"

"I'm not. Maybe we should call it a wrap for the day. Sometimes if you walk away from something you get a clearer head next time you are around it."

"Are we still talking about the script?" she asked holding her breath.

"Of course. I'll see you at work Monday for editing, okay?"

"Fine." She got up to grab her bag.

"Now you're mad," he huffed.

"No," she huffed right back at him.

"This is so stupid."

"What?"

"Not doing this." He kissed her, pulling her entire body against his. His hands found her ass, grabbed and kneaded her flesh, driving her hips against his erection.

She opened for him, letting his tongue sweep through her mouth as her fingers found his hair. As the intensity of the kiss increased, he walked her back against a wall. He gently bit and kissed her jaw, her neck, and the top of her chest above her shirt. She let her hands run down over his back, the muscles all flexed from the way he held her.

"Please don't tell me to stop," he breathed onto her breasts.

"I won't," she moaned as he kissed her breasts still covered with her clothes.

"I've never done this with an employee. I can't help myself."

"Am I fired?"

He looked up at her, his eyes showing depth and desire. "You don't sue, I won't fire."

"Promise?"

He sealed the deal with another kiss before he slid her down onto a bench below the kitchen window. He grabbed her hands, moving them until he curled the fingers of her one hand around the spindles of the bench and her other hand around the top of the backrest.

"Just hang on there. I intend to taste every inch of you, taking your body on one wild ride."

He's a writer, she thought as he moved his hands across her abdomen, lifting up her shirt. She could feel the sun beating in through the window on her naked stomach. She refused to compare herself to women he may have been with before. Instead she let him go. He kissed her stomach, his lips warming her skin. The knot in her stomach tightened when his hands slid under her back, unhooking her bra, exposing her breasts to the same intense rays. When he pulled his mouth away from sucking each nipple, they glistened in the light.

He smiled very pleased with himself, moving down to her legs, pulling her skirt and panties down over her legs. Spreading her thighs apart with his hands, she let him open her. One foot he propped up on the back of the bench and the other he laid on the floor, keeping her open to him.

"You are the most beautiful woman I have ever met," he said, placing his hand over her mouth for a second, silencing her protests. "Please don't huff or try to deny it. I think so, and I have seen a lot of women in my line of work. You're damn sexy."

He took his hand away, running it down over her stomach, his fingers teasing over her mound and then over her pussy lips. She squirmed on the hard wooden bench, needing more. She assumed he wasn't willing to give in to her body's pleas as he continued to kiss her all over. He pressed his lips to every inch of exposed skin, from her feet, up her legs and then over to her mound before he spread her lips open, kissing the wet flesh inside. A tiny kiss on her clit had her moving her hips, pushing her pussy into his face. She couldn't take any more.

"Would you like to take this to another level tonight?"

"What do you mean? You already have me spread eagle on a bench in your kitchen. Do you want to tie me to your bed or something?"

"Sounds good. We can add that to the list of things I would like to do to you. But, and please don't take this wrong, I love working with you and playing with you. I just thought maybe some of the playing might enhance our work. Would you like to try a ménage? Do you have any anal experience?"

"Uh, yes, I have some experience in that area. But, another guy, I don't know. I...I mean, I'm curious after the shoot, and my body is just about ready for anything at the moment..."

"Is that a yes?"

"Uh...with who?"

"An actor who works for me, you haven't met him yet. He is really my best actor, and I save him for the more serious roles. But, he is a great guy and now a great friend. I trust him. I think I could share you with him under my rules."

"What rules?"

"He enters only from the back. I am the only one inside you."

"And, you think he is going to be available to come over here now?"

"He lives really close actually. I met him running, and well, long story short, he wanted to try the adult film industry. He's really great. Can I call him? You can always change your mind at any time."

"I guess. Ah, why not?"

"Stay."

She had gone this far, changed so much over the course of just two weeks. Forcing her mind this one last step seemed right, reasonable in some unexplainable way. She heard him on the phone but could only make out a few words. Overhearing him say he would see the man in a few, she guessed the agreement had been made. Her stomach rolled a little with anxiety, fear, excitement, lust a whole mixture of emotions.

Walking back to her he confirmed her assumption," I told him to come straight up to the bedroom. I don't want to share a lot of you, but I like that you are trying to open your mind. I want to explore so much with you. Let's get you ready, shall we? We have about fifteen minutes."

He took her hand and helped her up off the bench, leading her up the stairs and to his room. The place was woodsy, masculine. He fit right in with his jeans and flannel.

"Are you getting undressed?"

"All in good time, I figured while we were at it, I would make a fantasy come true for you too. It will be a first for me, so you won't be the only one with a first here tonight."

"Thank you. I don't know what to say to that."

"Say nothing. Just lay down on the bed on your stomach so I can get you ready."

She squirmed as he lubed her ass, his finger pressing against her puckered hole sending erotic sensations up inside her. Her pussy quivered for some sort of relief. She spread her legs open wide suggestively..

"I will get there soon enough," he laughed, lightly tapping her opening with his finger. Her body clenched tight, as if she was trying to catch him, hold onto him and pull him inside her. Instead, his finger started to slowly push against her ass. "Relax. Let me in. Jake is a bit big. I don't want him to hurt you."

He moved his other hand to her pussy, toying with her clit. The finger at her ass slipped in just a bit. She moaned, loving the full sensation, the naughty side to being invaded back there. Anal had always been a fascination of hers; one her and her ex had explored, given quite some time to.

"Oh, I am sliding in nicely. You do know how to do this, don't you? My dick is so hard. I want to drive it into your ass. But, for tonight I will wait. Sometime when we are alone, I will have you there."

Hearing his door open downstairs, he slipped his finger out of her.

"Climb under the covers there for a bit, will you. I know you want something inside you, but soon enough you will be filled more than you ever have been before. Just try to relax. We have a show for you first."

Doing as she was told, she couldn't believe the sight of the god-like man who walked in the bedroom. His skin was darkly tanned–dressed up in a suit no less–black silky hair, blue eyes. He had all the crisp and clean good looks, but she liked David's warm ruggedness more.

"Jake, meet Kim."

"It's nice to meet you Kim. Pardon my attire, but I'd just gotten in from a meeting when David called me. I figured why change," Jake shrugged.

"It is nice to meet you too. Your suit is nice. Pardon me having nothing on but a blanket. I'm doing as I was told." She smiled at David, not caring anymore that she could feel how hot her cheeks were from blushing.

"Isn't she cute when she blushes?" David said, then shook his head. "Anyway, we appreciate you coming and helping us with our research. We have come to a road block in the script, and we need your help by giving us both some experience."

"Hey, I'm your guy. You know I do anything. What is it you two are working on?"

"Well, a sexual exploration type piece. But in it, we have a scene with four men and one woman."

"Damn. Am I going to be in it?"

"Of course, it sounds like I will need a man not afraid to touch another man. Kim here seems to think any amount of dicks is better than one, and hinted at over the course of the afternoon that women like seeing the men together too, not just all concentrated on the woman. So, we are both experiencing firsts tonight, as I told you. I am going to be with man first, and then she is going to be with two of them. Think we can orchestrate that?" David was looking at Kim, for approval it seemed.

"You mean I get to watch your first time with another guy? Wow! Shit." She bit her lip so hard she thought it might bleed. Butterflies were practically battling in her stomach.

"By that time, you should be over any nervousness you have, I would think?" Jake chimed in.

Gee, how did he know?

"Hell yeah," her voice trembled rather than shouting out encouragement, like she had wanted it to, "Go for it you two," she finished, biting her lip again and squeezing her thighs together over the convulsing there.

"You heard the lady. Are you up for this director?" Jake ran his hand down over David's flannel covered chest.

With a deep breath David practically growled, "I really am."

"Then let's give the lady a live show. What do you want first, Kim?" Jake asked, his voice vibrating through her even though he was a few feet away at the end of the bed.

"Naked," was all she got out, biting on her nail now.

"A woman of few words but greater needs than she ever realized," David laughed, a light but deep, smooth sound. God, she wanted him.

Jake started unbuttoning David's shirt. As he used his hands, palms flat running over David's abs and chest to remove his friend's shirt, he spoke the words that practically sent her over the precarious edge of control she teetered on, "I aim to please then."

David responded by removing Jake's shirt. She saw his fingers struggle with the buttons; his hands shake a touch as he pulled the shirttails from the man's silky pants. Although they seemed better, more stable and forceful as he pushed the dress shirt aside and ran his hands down over Jake's back. Jake was wide, muscle upon muscle, like a body builder. David reminded her more of a lumberjack in his jeans still, very well defined but more lean. They both were sculpted beyond any male she had ever been this close to. The tan colors of their skin stood in contrast to each other, David's more sun-kissed bronze where Jake was more olive in tone.

"I know what the lady really wants though," Jake spoke while turning David around so he faced Kim. Pulling his boss' back against his chest, arms wrapped around his waist, Jake undid David's jeans, pushing them down over his slim hips. Without underwear, David's erection popped out. Once the jeans fell, David stepped out of them. However, the bobbing of his cock was stopped by Jake's firm grasp.

Kim literally bit down on the comforter she had been wringing in her hands to stop from squealing. David groaned, eyes closed, as Jake moved his fist up over the head of his cock and then slid back down to his balls. Jake's other hand grasped the tight sack, so that Kim worried his big hands were going to hurt David. Yet, rather than a sound of pain, a guttural response to pleasure seemed to be torn from his chest.

His pecks moved up and down, mimicking the slide of Jake's fingers. David grew in length, veins popping under the reddish skin of his erection.

"She likes your cock, Dave, as do I," Jake whispered into her boss' ear loud enough that she could hear him clearly. "Mine would love to come out and play."

David opened his eyes, winked at her, and then turned around to face Jake. She got a nice glimpse of his perfectly rounded ass before he lowered himself to his knees, moving his head just below Jake's hips to avoid blocking her view.

The sounds of the belt, the button and the zipper being undone had a profound effect on her. Her whole body tensed. The erection that fell out of Jake's dress pants was a sight to behold. To her, and obviously Jake's surprise since she heard him suck in a deep breath. Recovering quickly from the shock, David took Jake's cock into his mouth. Just when the disappointment of not being able to see the man's actions set in, David moved Jake, throwing him down onto the bed. He sucked him some more, making Jake claw at the comforter, tugging it from her until her breasts were exposed to the air.

Although she wanted in on this more than she ever wanted anything in her life, though her pussy dripped its arousal onto her thighs, she stayed put.

Jake's knees pulled up, his hips thrust up and down on the bed as David continued to suck on him. David's lips moved off Jake's cock, revealing the shiny, wet skin, so tight and dark. She wanted to taste them both, but licking over her dry lips was going to have to do for now.

Releasing him all together, David slapped Jake on the hip and commanded, "Roll over onto your stomach."

Jake looked right up at her after he did so. He smiled at her, his drop-dead gorgeous masculinity radiated. She looked back and forth from this man's dazzling eyes to his hard ass where David had his cheeks spread open and had applied lube. When her boss, this man who already made her heart beat hard just by being in the room, applied the lubrication to his own erection, she shuddered, thinking she just might come without any physical attention in her direction at all.

Next though, was the moment to outdo all others, David firmly sank his cock into Jake's ass inch by rushed inch, both their hips making tiny thrusts until the director was in balls deep. Their faces were both tight, eyes closed, mouths open. The feral sounds – animalistic and raw – that came from them both were amazing. David reached under Jake; grasping his cock she was sure. She watched, holding her breath, as the energy built between them. They were literally lost in each other it seemed, rocking and growling like the animals they both were. She couldn't wait to be between them, caught up in it all as well.

"Save some for me," she wheezed, surprised to hear her own voice, her own thoughts out in the open.

"Of course, babe, I have big plans for you. We just wanted to give you a show first. I wanted to show you that I know what it's like to risk a first, and how rewarding it can be." When he stopped talking, David pulled out of Jake. Both were smiling, much to her relief.

"Sorry to have interrupted. My thoughts, they just escaped me before I had time to stop them," she stuttered and blushed.

"Stop," Jake reprimanded, his voice deep but gentle. "We are both dying to be in you. Let us clean up first, and then you are next. We promise."

"Let me help."

She was given two simultaneous nods.

With all the courage she could find, she stood them side by side in David's bathtub. With warm water and soap, she cleaned them both, running her hands along every inch of their hardened cocks before having a taste of them herself. Holding one cock in her hand while sucking on another seemed like a fairy tale, and she didn't want anyone to pinch her and wake her up from this damn fine dream if that was the case.

Soon, she found herself scooped up, water dripping off her body and all, into David's arms.

"You want something, boss?" she giggled, so proud of herself.

"I do... You."

After carrying her to the bed, he laid her out and started kissing her passionately. Their fingers tangled in each other's hair, as his tongue thrashed over hers. She was aware of the other man in the room, but still gasped when he ran his fingers up her inner thigh. David paused briefly, looked down her body to where the other man's hands caressed her flesh, then went back to kissing her with a smirk on his face.

The fingers moved over her wet and eager mons, making her move, beg with her body for more as she moaned into David's mouth. He climbed on top of her, using his hips to push his friend's hands away. With unparalleled skill, he thrust his cock inside her and rolled them over so that she was on top. She didn't need any encouragement. She sat up and started moving over him, taking him in deeper and deeper.

"You are so ready, so willing, so bad," Jake stated, slapping her ass hard, impaling her more onto David's cock. The sting made her gasp, moving over David even faster.

"I think she likes it."

Two more hard slaps hit her ass and she gasped, fucking David hard as the pain coursed through her, mixing with the pleasure of being stretched over her boss' cock. Several more times, Jake's hand slapped her. Her orgasm rose to claim her; intense and fiery, like lava running through her veins, warming her muscles. Waves of hot pleasure overcame her, burned her from the inside out. A scream caught in her chest, then her body trembled, convulsed, and relaxed, over and over again.

But David's voice broke through the haze, "Come back to us, baby. Breathe." His hands grabbed her hips, bringing her back to reality a little more. "I want you to have us both now."

She could only nod as Jake came up behind her, kissing her neck. She could feel him moving behind her to apply lube to himself and to her. David rocked her slightly as Jake positioned himself. Pressure then release, flooded her body, building back up the lust still hovering there from her last orgasm as Jake slipped his cock inch by inch into her ass. Moments of pain rocketed into pleasure as little by little she became filled with the hardness of both men.

David laughed, "As much as I love to feel your body gripping my dick, you need to relax, enjoy, and let Jake all the way in."

"I'm trying boss," she breathed out. "I swear I can feel your cocks side by side inside me." She was so full that she saw stars when the three of them began to move together; slowly at first and then faster.

"Hell, you are so tight," Jake growled, right before he started nipping at her neck again. "Take me. Take me all the way in babe," he continued between bites.

She let the mantra whip her up and whirl her away. Her mind let go and her body relented. Overwhelmed by two sets of hands on her breasts she started finding her own rhythm again, pleased when the men followed along. Their groans were like the wind rushing through her, spurring her on.

When one of David's fingers slid down her stomach to rub over her clit and all that had built inside her suddenly let go.

"Ohhh…" she let the sound rip from her throat. Shivers tore through her, her fulfillment soon matching David, and then Jake's as they all came together. The sounds in the room seemed no longer human, and she was no longer just herself, but connected to two men, releasing, sharing in the biggest crescendo of pleasure she had ever experienced.

As tiny tremors continued to wrack her sated body, the men rolled onto their sides, keeping her sandwiched between them. She had no desire to move any time soon.

***

The next thing she knew, she awoke to a dark room feeling Jake stirring behind her.

"Shhh, I'm leaving. I have to get up early in the morning, a Saturday breakfast meeting. I really enjoyed sharing in your guy's firsts. Let me know anytime I can be of assistance."

"Thanks, man," David mumbled in a sleep filled voice.

"No problem." She heard him grabbing his clothes and leaving the room.

"Stay," David whispered, wrapping his arms around her tightly.

Chapter Three

The next morning held a shower together, breakfast, and making love all mixed up together.

"How are you feeling?" he asked her, combing his fingers through her wet hair.

"Great. I apparently have the best job in the world. Who knew the adult film industry would be my dream job on so many levels. We should probably get to work though. I would like my own clothes to do that."

"You look cute in just my flannel shirt. And, besides, I like knowing you are not wearing any underwear underneath it," he purred in her ear, grabbing her ass.

"You need to keep your hands to yourself and focus. What is on the agenda for work today?"

"Hmm, great thing about owning the company is I set my own hours. Especially when I don't have another shoot lined up until I get the first one edited, and the next one written."

"So, do we edit or write?"

"It's Saturday. You're off the clock. But, if you're game, how about we write while I am still high from last night and this morning, and then we can go to the studio to edit."

"Can I go home first and change clothes?"

"Sure, but only if you promise to pack a bag and come back here tonight. I want you all to myself."

They got to work, discussing the scene where the four men were with one woman with great enthusiasm, ideas sparking more ideas as they played off each other.

"Maybe, I want to try for the role of this woman," she teased.

"I will share you in my bed, but not on film. I…" he left off, pulling her into his body and kissing her hard, possessing more than just her mouth. The intensity of his tone sent shivers through her.

"Sorry, boss," she stated when he pulled back, running his hands through his hair.

"No. I owe you an apology. I'm being possessive. I just can't help myself where you're concerned." He moved her face to look up at him. "I'm really falling hard for you. Please forgive me for my jealous outburst."

"No forgiveness necessary. I'm falling for you too."

He kissed her hard, but briefly.

"Listen to me. I know it has only been a few weeks, and I know we work together, but everyone is just going to have to deal. I want you to consider a few things. I want you to move in with me, because after last night, I can't imagine my bed without you. And, I was afraid to bring it up yesterday, but I want to make your screenplay into a movie. I want to try doing an Indie film with your script. I love it. I'm pretty sure I'm in love with you."

"I…"

"Don't say anything. Let it all sink in. For now, just be with me. I've laid all of my cards on the table. You know where I stand and what I want."

She nodded, and he kissed her again. The kiss was so passionate, so soul consuming that she knew, aside from the bomb drop about her script, that right now she didn't want to leave him either. It was a big step to move in, but what the hell. He was seriously the best thing to have happened to her, ever. She refused to look at time and timing or anything else.

"Yes," she whispered into his ear.

"Yes what?"

"Yes, I will stay here with you. I will work with you. Really my script?"

"Really, it is the most amazing thing I have ever read. I want it about as much as I want you Red." He winked.

"I'll take that," she smiled. "Wow, who knew when I walked into your studio after talking myself into applying for the position that I would be walking into my dream job, cute boss and all."

Sinister Outlaw: Outlaw Pleasure
by Dawn White

<u>Chapter One</u>

Before there was Becca and Gavin there was just Gavin and his brothers in arms. Gavin is the youngest Outlaw Biker Chapter President the Sinister Son's Syndicate has ever had. They are violent and don't play well with others. Gavin looks to make a name for himself, but will the parade of women, and the non- stop violence stop his reign as chapter president?

The blood pooled up and out of the bullet hole as Blade helped me up onto the bar. Papa grabbed the first aid kit from the bar shelf, and pulled the things he needed out of the bag. I hissed in pain as Blade pressed a bandage against my left shoulder to stop the bleeding. Hammer clutched the bottle of tequila. Before I could ready myself, Papa opened the crater and started to dig into my bloodied flesh with a pair of forceps. Hammer dumped half of the bottle down my throat to aid in the pain.

"I'm not sure this bullet will come out. And if I do get it out, I'm not sure you won't bleed to death. I think it's too close to something. Might as well leave it in. It won't do any damage." Papa said as he wiped his head with his bloodied hand.

"Get it the fuck out of me. I'm not living with a meth head's bullet in me!" I all but growled at them. Hammer grabbed another bottle of tequila and handed it to me. I took a chug, and bit down on Blade's kutte to keep quite. The room started to go dark, but not before I heard the wondrous plink of the bullet hitting a shot glass.

"Got it! You're going to be just fine Prez!" Papa said excitedly.

Papa wiped his bloody hands on his jeans, then grabbed the bottle of vodka, dumped it on my open wound and took a swig before he chuckled. Papa handed me the suture needle and I started to close my wound. I crisscrossed the stitches to make it tighter, so I would have a smaller scar. As I pulled the string tight and tied it off, blood pooled up and ran across my fingers. Blade started to bandage my arm as he said, "We didn't know that it had gotten that out of hand in the Avenues. We shut down one cook house then another pops up, overnight. I swear they know we're coming even before we fucking do."

Blade looked back at the rest of the members for support. When I was pissed everyone knew how bad it could get.

"So I leave you guys in charge of the Avenues and you can't keep the crack heads at bay?" I said as I pushed Blade away. I pulled Blade's glock out of his holster, unloaded it, and slammed it on the bar next to me. "What the fuck do you have this for? If you can't even scare the pieces of shit out of the Avenues?" I picked up the cloth and wiped my bloody hands then grabbed the bottle of tequila. After taking a few swigs I took a moment and collected my thoughts. My brothers stood in silence as they waited for me to figure out what needed to be done. Then it came to me.

"Get locked and loaded we're heading out in ten. I could have fucking died out there! This isn't going away; it has to be dealt with. Tell Match when he gets a chance he needs to check the fuck in with me. Just because his Ol' Lady is fucked up doesn't mean he can't keep us in the loop." I said as I swung my legs to the side of the bar.

Papa rushed to my side to help me. I put my hand up to stop him, and looked around at the faces of my brothers.

"Come on, Gavin, you should at least rest for tonight before we go back out there. You lost a lot of blood, and you don't want the hole to get infected. That could really fuck you up." Papa pleaded with me.

I rolled my eyes at him, and shooed him off. I tapped the bar to get Casey's attention.

"Casey, make sure the club house is cleaned up before we get back cause we're going to want to party when we get done dealing with this shit." I said as I pulled my kutte over my blood-soaked shirt. Casey nodded to me, and gathered the other ladies and told them what was expected of them. Ever since Blade claimed Casey as his Mama, we've gotten used to having things a certain way. Casey was in charge of finding more "sheep," (unattached ladies), for the members. Blade looked anxious as he tossed a hurried look at Casey. Casey blew him a kiss, and smiled as Blade followed me out the door.

My shoulder burned as I double checked my glock for bullets. I side stepped onto my bike, and pulled on my helmet. Everyone followed my direction and pulled on their helmets. I started my bike, and walked it forward to the end of the lot. I looked back as the men kicked their kickstands and followed me. I kicked into gear and took off onto the clear alleyway. My outlaw brothers followed me into the alley, and onto the main road. It was a quick ride to the Avenues. It would be great if the crack head that shot me disappeared already, but I'm not usually that fucking lucky.

I motioned for Hammer, and Daily the prospect to go around back. We parked down the street from the crack den so we wouldn't raise suspicion. Hammer, and Daily nodded at me as they made their way to the back alley of the house.

"Papa, stay here and watch our rides. And keep an eye out for us. We don't want any Pigs coming up on us out of nowhere now do we?"

Papa nodded, and sat down on his bike.

Blade and I pulled our glocks out, and crept up silently to the front porch. I could hear rustling in the house as I pointed at the door. Blade nodded at me, reared back and kicked the front door open with his thick leather boots. A huffing sound to our left drew our attention as I saw a skinny, dirty man try and crawl out the window in front of me. I grabbed him by his greasy ponytail and pushed him against the wall. I pressed my knee into the center of his back, and nodded towards the door for Blade to continue. I heard a crash come from the back of the house, followed by Hammer's booming voice and three gun shots.

"Fuck!" I said as I slammed the butt of my pistol on the back of the crack head's skull. He collapsed to the ground, which gave us enough time to check out the rest of the house.

There was a pungent smell coming from the hallway, as we made our way into the living room. I could tell I wasn't the only one who smelled it. I took the lead and walked toward the back of the small house. The smell got worse as I made my way to the back bedroom. Then I heard it, a small whimper that was barely audible. I turned the nob, but the door was locked. I slammed my shoulder into the door, and was accosted with not only the pain from my injury, but by the sight of absolute desperation that was waiting on me from the other side of that door. I rushed into the room and in the corner saw a crib. The room had the foulest odor, but when I stood over the crib, I found out why.

A baby that couldn't be any older than eight months was passed out in the crib. He obviously hadn't been fed, or changed in days, he was barely breathing when I leaned in and scooped him up. He lay limp in my arms, as I ran out of the bedroom with him into the living room.

"Blade! Get me a diaper for him! I'm going to see if there is food for him in the kitchen." I ran him into the kitchen and rummaged through the fridge. There was nothing to be found. I snapped my fingers at Daily to get his attention. "Go get some fucking formula! Be back in less than ten minutes." I growled at him. Daily took off, just as Blade rushed into the room with a diaper and a washcloth.

"Get him changed, I'm going to deal with this," I said as my face turned red in anger. I handed the infant off to Blade. A woman was passed out on the couch as I walked into the dirty living room. Her eyes fluttered as I shook her, and yelled. "Hey! Do you have a baby?"

"Hammer, go get the scumbag on the porch and bring him to me!" I said as I tried to get the woman's attention. Blade looked like he was going to cry when he saw the condition the tot was in when he changed his diaper.

Hammer dragged the crack head into the room and dropped him right in front of me and the woman on the couch. When she saw her boyfriend on the ground she sat up quickly and pulled her legs into her chest and rocked back and forth.

"I'm going to ask you one more fucking time! Is that your fucking baby back there?" I said as pressed the barrel of my gun to the back of the guy's head.

She shook her head in response and started to sob. I pulled my silencer out of the back of my jeans pocket and screwed it into place, my anger threatening to boil over. Then I made a split second decision. I pointed the gun at the woman's forehead and pulled the trigger. She didn't have time to react before she slumped over and blood spewed from her broken head. The man on his knees started to beg as I kicked him off my leg to the ground. Daily ran in and held the formula in the air to show me he had it.

"Hammer, finish this," I said as kicked the man one more time, and walked away. I grabbed the baby out of Blade's arms and walked around the room with him to keep him calm. Papa stopped in his step when he realized what I had in my arms. Daily was mixing up a bottle when I stepped back into the kitchen, then handed it to me. I pressed it up to his little pale lips. He slowly suckled as he tasted probably the first drink he has had in days.

"I need you to call the police, this little guy needs a hospital," I said as I walked out the front door and towards my bike, with the men in tow. I pulled the side-saddle open and pulled out a small fleece blanket. Who knows how long the baby would have lasted if we hadn't come along. I wrapped the blanket around him, and waited for Papa to give me the thumbs up.

"They're on their way." Papa said as he stepped up next to me and the baby. "What the fuck happened in there?" Papa said as he rubbed the baby's back and waited for me to answer.

"We walked in and smelled something horrible. It was this little guy. His whole body is covered in blisters and bruises. He was barely breathing when I grabbed him. He obviously hadn't eaten or been changed in days. The mother and her lover were cooking meth. She was passed out on the couch. Hammer and them are taking care of it."

Hammer and Blade walked towards us, and double checked each other to make sure there was no evidence on them. "We called the paramedics for him, we're going to tell them we were checking on our rental properties and heard this little guy crying and it didn't stop, so we knocked on the door and no one answered so we entered and found him, and them like this. Hammer, did you make it look like a deal gone wrong?" I asked.

Hammer nodded at me, and narrowed his eyes. "This isn't my first rodeo, Prez."

A wave of anger washed over me as I stepped up next to Hammer, "when this is over you and me are going to fucking talk!" I said as I turned my back on Hammer and bounced the baby up and down to keep him calm. The paramedics pulled up behind us and stepped out at the curb.

"What happened with him?" The busty blonde asked.

"We were checking our properties and we heard a baby wailing. When we knocked on the door no one answered so we entered, and found the people dead, and him in the back, half starved, and very dirty. We got him some milk, and changed him but he's covered in blisters, bruises, and he's starving." I said as I gently laid him down on the gurney the male paramedic pushed up next to us.

"The cops should be along with us any minute now," The blonde said as she started an IV in his little arm. He was so weak he couldn't even cry from the needle. He scrunched his little nose up, and held onto the female paramedic as if she were his life preserver. The paramedics loaded him quickly into the back unit. The man grabbed his shoulder mic and said, "Code-3!" then closed the doors and took his seat in front of the steering wheel. The siren sounded and the ambulance took off down the road.

I side stepped onto my bike, pulled my helmet on and made the meet up signal to the others. I dropped my bike into gear and took off before the police got there.

Chapter Two

Casey and the rest of the mama's, and Ole ladies welcomed us home as we pulled into the club parking lot. The prospect parked his bike and grabbed the bucket lid. He stepped up to me so I could unload all of my weapons, then made his way around the parking lot until we were all unloaded. I put my gear up and headed into the club house as they finished up. I always felt naked when I had to un-arm after a shooting. My seat at the table in our church was calling to me. I rushed past the ladies, through the double doors and sat back in my leather high back chair. I reached up to my right shoulder and gripped the bandage. I picked up my cell and texted Chelle.

Gavin: Hey babe grab me a t-shirt and meet me in the church board room.

Chelle: Sure thing hun. I'll be right there. ;)

Thirty seconds later there was a small knock on the door.

"Come in." I yelled.

Chelle stuck her head around the corner and smiled at me. She stepped into the room and quietly shut the door behind her. Chelle wasn't bad to look at, with or without clothes on. She had the most alluring red hair I've ever seen.

"I need you to toss this in the fireplace for me," I said as I peeled my shirt off and tossed it to Chelle. Chelle walked the black t-shirt to me, and responded to me.

"Will do hun. I'll grab you a beer on my way back in," Chelle said with a smile and a wink as she sauntered off in her leather miniskirt.

I pulled the t-shirt over my head, and sat back to catch my thoughts.

My cell phone chimed with a text message.

Blade: The cops are here. Want us to send them in?

Gavin: Send them in.

A young detective in a pair of jeans, and a button up shirt walked in. "Gavin, Gavin, Gavin, as if we're stupid enough to believe you just happened upon that lab, and the baby. I have a feeling you have a lot more to do with the deaths than you're letting on." The detective said with obvious sarcasm.

I sat forward at the table, cracked my knuckles, and narrowed my eyes at him as I said, "fill out your fucking papers and get the fuck out of here."

The detective sat down at the table, and pulled out a pad of forms. He pushed the forms towards me and handed said, "Tell me what happened."

I pulled out a pen and wrote the same thing I told the paramedics. We were just checking on our properties and happened across carnage, and an almost dead baby.

"Here you go. You know where the exit is." I said as I pushed the paper back to him. The detective glared at me as I put my pen away. I smirked at him as he turned and walked out of the room.

I could hear the guys out in the main area, laughing and having a good time. My mind was still stuck on that baby. Fuck, I hated that I had to kill her. Nothing like that ever sits well with me. The boys knew to let me be.

There was a knock on the door. "Yeah?"

"Prez?" Blade opened the door.

"What?"

"I just heard from Match. The kid is doing good."

"That's good to hear," I answered him back my gaze not leaving the table. I heard the door shut. I spun around in my chair to face the back wall and I picked up my glass and threw it against the drywall. I'm not sure how much time had passed, but the creek of the door alerted me someone was there.

"You're not supposed to be in here," I barked without looking back.

"I brought you a refill." The voice of Chelle resonated through the room and I turned slowly around in the chair.

"You did, now did you?"

She nodded and placed the drink on the table.

"Well, thanks, Darling."

"You look so stressed, Gavin. Anything I can do to help?" Chelle walked closer to me. She was dressed in a low cut tank top and a pair of snug jeans that hugged every fucking curve this woman had. Her tits were popping out of the neckline, and her fiery red hair was slung over her shoulders.

Chelle circled where I was sitting and came up behind me, her hands gripping my shoulders as I threw my head back. She continued to work the tension in my upper body as I shut my eyes and let her hands go. Her fingers massaged up and down my neck and my dick stirred at the motion. Thoughts of her hands wrapped around my cock invaded my thoughts as she continued onto my lower back to my shoulders being careful of my stitches.

"You're so tense, Gavin," she whispered in my ear before I spun my chair around to meet her breasts.

"Yes, very tense, Chelle. I enjoyed the massage, but I can think of another way you can help me relieve the tension." I raised my eyebrows and watched as her eyes dipped to the area of my crotch.

"Whatever you need, Gavin. You know that."

"I sure do. Kneel," I commanded as I unfastened the buckle on my belt and pulled out my dick. I palmed myself as Chelle lowered her delicious body to the ground. Her hands ran up the length of my legs, and I opened my hands to invite her to do what she needed.

Chelle gripped my shaft with her right hand and continued to run her left one up and down my leg. I nodded to urge her to start and she slowly stroked me from root to tip and back down; a slow, movement as she eyed my dick again.

"Come on, darling, it ain't going to come by itself," I snarled as she shifted on her knees. Oh, I had plans to fuck her sweet pussy that was for sure, but I wanted a little love before I took her and fucked her brains out.

Chelle leaned in and stuck out her tongue licking the path her hand just covered. As she hit the head of my dick, she pulled me into her wet, hot mouth.

"That's it," I moaned as she sucked me in further, her saliva coating my cock. She increased her speed a little, still teasing me. "If you think your teasing is going to go unnoticed, you're wrong. I will spank your ass red for that." I hissed as she brought me to the back of her throat. I was not in a mood for her games. Not tonight. She was here to serve one purpose and one purpose only: to let me use her pussy.

Chelle continued to suck me in and out of her mouth, one hand following suit, the other gripping my balls lightly. I could feel myself getting closer to my release. I gripped her head wrapping my hands into the tendrils of her hair. It was my turn to dictate the speed. I freed one hand from her head for a slight moment to remove her hand from my dick before returning it to its place.

"That's it, Chelle. Suck my dick until I come. Swallow my cum and I will reward you." I groaned as I bobbed her head up and down the length of my cock. I threw my head back as I felt the familiar feeling rip through me as I felt my release spurt into her mouth. "Swallow." A few more thrusts into her mouth and I released my hands from her hair and pulled her from the floor into my lap.

Pulling her mouth to mine, I laced my hand in her hair again and crushed my lips to hers. It was rougher than I wanted, but I didn't care. I could see the lust and desire in her eyes. I broke the kiss and pushed her back a little eyeing the slit in the middle of her shirt. A smile crossed my lips as I gripped the sides and ripped her shirt open.

"Gavin!" she exclaimed.

"Problem?" I asked.

Chelle shook her head, "no."

I removed her fake tits from the security of her lace bra and brought one into my mouth, biting down on her nipple as I sucked it into my mouth. I heard her wince as I released the nipple and drew the other one into my mouth. I massaged the globes in my hands before I moved my hands lower to her waist. My mouth returned to hers for a brief moment until I trailed a path of bites and kisses down her neck, pulling her skin into my mouth, branding her with a reminder of where I've been.

I gripped her waist and quickly stand, twirling her around until her back is against the table. The glass of whisky crashed to the floor and I stand up for a moment looking at her laid out on the wooden monstrosity. I chuckle to myself as I undo the button and zipper of her jeans sliding them down over her hips and to her ankles. My hands run over her flat stomach as she shifts against my glare. I lace my finger in the band of her thongs. I know they are thongs. Chelle only ever wears thongs, and drag them to her ankles as well. Glancing up, I take notice of her cunt. Yeah, her pussy will relieve the tension tonight.

I lift her legs and threw her shoes to the floor finally removing her pants. Stepping closer, I spread her knees apart and stare down at her shaved lips. My fingers trail a path down the length of her inner thighs stopping just shy of her pussy. I can smell her arousal and see a hint of the moisture I know is pooling between those thighs. "I bet you are already wet for me," I hiss as I spread her labia with my fingers.

Chelle gasps at the sudden touch, "always, Gavin."

My fingers move up and down the length of her lips, coating her with her own moisture before I plunged two into her core. I feel her muscles pull me in, she's not the tightest I've felt, but she does feel good. I thrust in and out of her, curving my fingers as I retreat. My thumb circles her clit and Chelle's body squirms. I place my free hand on her abdomen and steady her.

"You like that, huh? You like me finger fucking you," I say as I continue to move my fingers inside her pussy.

"Gavin, yes..." Chelle moans as I feel her body tighten and watch as her back arches off the oak. I increased my motions and watch as her orgasm overtakes her body. Before she has time to come down, I remove my fingers from her and flip her over pulling her off the table so her feet hit the ground.

I grab the condom in my back pocket and push my pants to the ground. I rip open the foil and sheath myself. I paused to take a look at Chelle still laying on the table, her ass up, and her head down. I grip her hips and pull her to me, sliding my cock up and down the crack of her ass. Chelle responds my lifting herself off the table, her tits hang slightly now. I rub my hand over the globe of her perfect ass before smacking her right cheek. "Ow..." she cried as I placed another one on the opposite cheek. My dick lined up with her opening and I gripped her hair in one hand and pulled her head back. "I'm going to fuck that cunt of yours now. It's not going to be sweet. It's going to be rough. Remember you said you were up for anything."

"Hmmm..." she mewled as increased the tension on her hair. Her head was back, eyes looking up as I slammed my cock into her pussy with no remorse. My left hand was encircled around her waist and I watched as Chelle put her hands on the table for balance. Her hair was still entwined in my hand as I pulled it back. I thrust into her body with methodical, hard movements. I didn't want her to think this was to be sweet and sensual. No. It was primal, I was angry. I needed to fuck her and that's it.

I released her hair and slowed my pace a little, no much. I continued to bang into her pussy with hard, rough thrusts. I reached my right hand around to her clit and pinched it between my fingers hearing her breath hitch as I flicked it with my fingers. Her body was mine to use and she was mistaken if she thought otherwise. I circled her clit, and felt her body tighten.

"No coming, Chelle. You already had your orgasm for the night." I smacked her ass again and gripped her hips with both hands.

"This. Is. For. Me," I hissed as I thrust in to her with each word. I could still hear the music playing outside the door and knew no one would hear her moans. I moved my hips again and throw my head back as let myself fall into a rhythm. Chelle wiggles her ass against me and I snap my head back up. I grip her hair again and pull her head back. "What did you not understand?" I ask as I pull back harder and begin to thrust rapidly into her cunt. "ME."

I begin a punishing speed and hear the door open. Blade steps in and freezes. I turn and look at him, Chelle's hair still in my hand, my dick still thrusting violently into her body. I can hear her whimpers. Blade looks and me, down to Chelle, and takes a step back out shutting the door in the process.

I return my attention to Chelle and thrust a few more times. I feel my balls tighten and the edge of my release near. My left hand digs into her hip as I pull her body up and to me with the final few thrusts. I let my orgasm wash over me as still inside her and release her body. Chelle falls forward against the table and I prop myself up with my hands attempting to catch my own breath.

I pull out and search for a towel to wrap the condom in before disposing of it in the trash. I pull up my pants and secure my jeans. I watch as Chelle turns over looking at me. I pick up her clothes and throw them to her. "Here. Get dressed and get me another whisky." The original two glasses were smashed somewhere on the floor.

"Yes, Gavin." Her eyes don't meet mine and I'm not sure what she is thinking as I sit back down in my chair and throw my head back. What the fuck?

Chapter Three

This night was a bust when it came to getting some rest. I tossed and turned all night long. Whenever I have to make a life or death decision it wears on me for days. Unfortunately, when it comes to piece of shit child abusers I had a moment to do what was right, and rotting in a jail for months or even years was not right for those crack heads. That baby could have fucking died if we didn't get to him in time. Just as I was starting to drift off I had a thought that yanked me out of my comfortable bed. I picked up my phone and messaged Match.

Gavin: Hey weren't you and your Ole Lady trying to adopt?

I jumped out of bed and walked through the living room. The prospect we call Daily was sleeping on the couch.

"Hey get the fuck up and make some coffee," I said as I tapped his leg.

"Wh—What time is it?" Daily said as he rubbed his eyes in confusion.

I pulled out my cell phone and answered him, "3:58 A.M."

Daily got up and made his way to the kitchen to throw some coffee on. I picked up the remote and flipped the TV on. There was never attention drawn to the crack head deaths, unless the baby had died of course. And there is certainly never any attention brought to the fact that a group of one percenters are the only reason the little man is alive. Daily walked a hot cup of liquid gold to me, and sat down on the couch he claimed as his bed. My cell phone dinged as I took my first sip.

Match: Yeah we were looking into it. Why?

Gavin: Because the little man we saved could use a good home.

Match: I'll talk to my ole lady.

I tossed my cell onto the coffee table and sat back and drank my coffee. If I wasn't sleeping tonight, than no one is.

"Daily, text everyone to meet at the clubhouse at 5:30, we have some crack heads to evict from the Avenues this morning." I said as I put my coffee down on the oak table next to me.

Daily didn't say anything fast enough so I dealt with it appropriately, "Is this is how we do shit around here? We don't fucking answer our chapter president? That kind of blatant fucking disrespect doesn't get you fucking tabbed! You think I got to be the youngest President of all of our chapters by not listening? Fuck no! You do as I say, or you fucking walk away! Hear me."

Daily looked freaked out, as he shook his head adamantly then answered quickly. "Yes sir, I'm sorry it's just I'm still a little out of it."

"Well fucking get into it. I haven't slept in over 48 hours and I am still ready to get shit done! Send the fucking texts."

I down the rest of my coffee and made my way to the shower. The shower in my bachelor pad is amazing. It's large enough to fit five girls and me without being crowded. Believe me I've tried it out. I flipped the lever all the way past hot and straight to scalding and stepped in. The hot water helped me push the rest of the fog out of my brain that the lack of sleep left. I leaned my bruised, and blood stained shoulder into the hot water and hissed as it stung when I ran the soap over it. I finished washing up, and stepped out of the shower. I grabbed my towel and dried my muscular body off, paying extra attention to my wound on my left shoulder.

***

I dressed in my usual jeans, black t-shirt, and my kutte. The club house was dark when Daily and I unlocked the door. The smell of stale cigarettes, whiskey, and sex accosted my nose when I flipped the lights on.

"Get with Casey, and make sure this place is cleaned up today. It smells like cigarettes and dirty cock. That's not acceptable. Make some more coffee when you get a chance," I said as I grimaced.

I heard a chopper pull in, and by the look of the head lamp I knew Blade was here. Daily set a cup of coffee in front of me. I gripped the handle and took a sip. The bitterness was exactly what I needed. I sat on the stool at the head of the bar, and sipped my coffee while I waited for the remainder of the Sons to get here.

Daily sat down next to me, cleared his throat and said, "do you think little man is ok?"

"Yeah, my contacts say he is doing really good. Next week he'll go to a foster home. I really just hope it's a good one." I said in between my coffee gulps.

Daily let me finish my coffee in peace. I pulled my cigarettes out of my pocket and lit it up. The TV flipped on as Daily searched for the news. Blade walked through the door with his sleek black helmet in hand. Casey clunked in behind him. I always knew when Casey was on her way; you can hear her heels on the wooden floor. We tried carpet once but realized drunk, men, and women aren't the cleanest. And the carpet smelled like smoke every damn day. Casey disappeared into the board room to place the coffee cups.

I looked at Blade and scoffed, "Where the fuck is Papa?"

Blade shrugged his shoulders and answered me, "Don't know. I texted him."

I shrugged my shoulders and made my way to the room. Hammer stumbled in, as if he hadn't gone home yet. I stood and walked towards the church board room. We always dropped our phones into the basket outside the door for Casey to watch over when we were dealing with business. We all took our seats and Casey followed behind with a pot of coffee to fill our empty mugs.

"Thank you, Darling," I said as I smiled and nodded at Casey. Once Casey finished pouring our coffee and shut the double doors, I started our church meeting.

After I stood I collected my thoughts then said, "It's a burden to have the power over Life and Death in my hands. But that's what makes us better than the heathens that are so willing to let the weak suffer. We are not them, and we aren't going to allow it to happen on our watch anymore. I don't have time to be politically fucking correct. We are the Sinister Fucking Sons Syndicate! Let's get out there and clean fucking house! All opposed to cleaning the filth out of our streets what say you?"

I glanced around the room at the men I call my brothers in arms. "Who's with me?" Everyone stood up and patted me on the back. This is my first real issue as President. The fact that we have some kind of mole, or rat in our midst is really weighing on me heavily. I smiled and made my way to the door. Hammer opened the door for us, and to greet us were about twelve heavily armed swat team members with AR-15's. Each of us had our very own laser pointed dead even at our hearts. One wrong fucking move and we were fucking goners.

"Don't fucking move! Put your hands in the air!" The tall man with Casey in handcuffs growled at us.

We all put our hands in the air and waited for more commands. The swat member in front of me snapped my wrist above my head and yanked my arm around my back. I could feel my muscles tense as I eye fucked the detective giving us the orders.

Chapter Four

I sat in the interrogation room for twenty minutes before anyone came in. No doubt, they'd been waiting for me to get unnerved. It hadn't worked. The good cop, bad cop shit never worked on me either. I didn't snitch especially not on myself. That bitch had it coming, there was no way I was answering this guy.

"We already know you did it Gavin, you and your brothers," the police guy had done finger quotes when he said brothers, which only made me mad.

"I didn't do anything but save a kid who would have starved to death. Who knows how long those bodies had been in there with it? It was miserable."

"Well, reporting an abandoned infant, and taking its parent's lives into your own hands are two very different things. Besides you asked who knows how long she was dead, we do and it was only a few minutes from when we got there. You see we have these special people that we call doctors that tell us the time of death. That pretty much means her killer could have been in the house."

"They could have been, but I didn't see them."

"You're going to sit in jail and think about it for a while," the detective sneered and the other one came around to handcuff my hands behind my back.

Myself, Blade, Hammer, and Daily stood waiting to be led one by one to booking. There were hookers sitting in the front of the jail tapping their heels on the metal chairs. One wore a dirty white fur coat causing me to wonder why the fuck a hooker would ever wear white.

The blonde one beside her wore a red dress with holes in it. These were not classy hookers, not like the girls I was used to. They weren't even trying hard. It was gross. The one with the red dress smiled at me and showed she was missing some teeth.

I deserved to be there, but not the rest of the boys. Chatham County lock up wasn't a place for them, they should be home banging their ole ladies and drinking whiskey. If they just kept their mouths shut and stuck to the story everything would be okay. Out of all the people I thought would freak out about being arrested, I didn't think it would be Blade.

"Get me out of these handcuffs man. I didn't do anything," he yelled in the policeman's face. "I'm not going to ask again." Before anyone could tell him to calm down he'd turned his body where he could elbow the guard and backed up against the wall.

"Blade, be cool man," I yelled and tried to catch his eye. I didn't know if he'd gotten some bad drugs or was having some sort of psychotic episode, but whatever was happening it was about to get ugly.

"Gavin, shut up, it's your fault I'm here."

Well that wasn't what you wanted to hear someone start screaming in the middle of the police station. Within a split second, Blade kicked the second guard's shin and ran full force into the third guard, knocking him off kilter sending the man crashing to the concrete floor, falling on his fat ass. Blade made a break for the door, while Hammer and Daily stood shocked by his outburst. Blade almost made it to the door, but the first guard tackled him from behind. His body made a dull thud as it hit the floor and the wind got knocked out of him. The second guard cuffed Blade's ankles together, while the third guard pressed his large shiny black boot firmly against his neck to hold him in place. Blade tried to scream, but the pressure from the cop's boot cut off his airway. The struggle didn't last long. The other members of the club stood around with a mix of anger and embarrassment on their faces. It wasn't how one of their own should act.

They were smart enough to know Blade made a stupid move that would only land them all in hotter water. I sighed, "I try to do something good and it only gets fucked up," I muttered to my handcuffed club members.

"Are you going to calm down?" One of the men on top of Blade yelled. Blade nodded against the floor and they proceeded to hog tie him.

"Hey," Hammer yelled, "he said he was going to calm down man, get the fuck off him."

The guards just ignored him and carried Blade into a holding cell where they put him hog tied on the bench and left him to calm down.

I gave Hammer a look that said be quiet and he did. The squirrely looking cop led me to the mug shot table roughly and shoved me down into the faded wooden chair.

"Look forward asshole," the greasy little sheriff said in my ear. I growled a bit knowing the little weasel wouldn't have talked to me like that if we were in a public place. Making sure to glare into the camera I turned to the side and let them take another. The same little cop pulled me to my feet and pushed me down the hallway towards the back room. They walked me past all the men in cages, those too bad to be in general population, which was dangerous in its own right.

"Enjoy your stay," the cop chuckled right in my ear as he took off my new shiny handcuffs. Hopefully someone was getting the bail bondsman and the lawyers on the phone and we'd be out soon. In this jail there were several men in other clubs that didn't like me and like any other jail, or prison there were gangs, and lots of them. I walked towards the middle of the room and looked around at all the men who were eye-balling me. It was just me since the others hadn't made it through booking yet, and everything was a threat.

No one looked like they could take down the group of them. I cracked my knuckles knowing I had to be patient and wait on the others. Hammer had been in jail off and on for as long as they could remember. He could guide them through this shit in his sleep if they'd hurry the fuck up and book them.

Finally, Hammer walked up to me and looked down at his orange jumpsuit. "Almost like being home again huh Gavin," he asked and elbowed him.

"Yeah, sure."

Blade was shoved into the room with them looking angry and he was closely followed by Daily. "This is some bullshit. Why the hell are we all in jail right now?" He was asking everyone but he was looking at me.

"Look you guys aren't going down for this okay. I am the one that pulled the fucking trigger, I am the one that deserves to be in here."

"No," Hammer said. "We're all together, or not at all."

Everyone nodded even Blade who'd probably decided to just chill out and let it go.

"We need to spread out, there's rival clubs and a couple of gangs. There should be eyes on every part of this room, so let's get around and signal each other if any bullshit starts happening. Everyone went to a different corner of the room to observe.

As soon as the other guys had moved away from him a guy in another MC came up to him. We didn't like each other and we could tell he was thrilled he got to fuck with me, or try too. The guy was shorter than me, but it didn't stop him from walking up and standing as close to me as possible.

"Yo, what the fuck are you doing in here? You know this isn't your territory."

"It's no one's territory, Sly. It's fucking jail." I replied.

"No, that's where you're wrong," Sly got right into my face. I never had liked the little sawed off son of a bitch. We had always been in rival clubs and there wasn't ever anything good that happened when they ran into each other.

"I won't be in here long enough for you to do anything," I said keeping my cool while balling my fists at my sides. The look Sly gave me wasn't without threat and he stepped forward. The sound of someone yelling across the room took their attention.

Sly and I simultaneously turned to see a large gang of inmates, in orange jumpsuits taking turns kicking someone on the ground. The vicious crowd sent a chill down my spine as I watched them ruthlessly kick and punch the man who was cowering on the floor with this elbows bent and arms raised to cover his face. I noticed the tattoo and realized it was Daily, who was screaming curse words at his attackers. Where the hell were the guards? It was a free-for-all that was going to end up with my friend, my fucking prospect gravely injured or dead.

I rushed over to the crowd and started pulling Daily's attackers off one by one. The men were so stunned by the act of sheer craziness, they stopped to see who would be stupid enough to try and break up a jail fight. A loud siren sounded as a guard unlocked the door. The attackers backed off because that sound meant the guards were coming in and coming in fast. I was saved from getting my own ass kicked and handed to me on a platter when two guards rushed over to the crowd.

"What the hell is going on here?" one guard yelled.

"I want everyone in a single file, now! I will put every one of you in the hole," the other guard announced.

The convicts collectively grumbled. A medic entered the room and knelt down next to Daily. Turning Daily over, the medic lowered his arms from his face and observed the damage. His lip and nose where bleeding and there was a large red mark near his eye that was starting to swell. He'd have one hell of shiner by the morning.

"Are you okay, Daily," I asked, still standing next to my friend. I looked at the guys that attacked Daily and realized they were Skin Heads. I wondered what the hell Daily had done to provoke such violence out of them.

"I'll live," Daily said, his voice cracked from the pain he endured.

"You, in line, now!" one of the guards ordered stepping up to Gavin and poking him with his Billy club.

I didn't speak, but nodded my head in agreement and joined the other inmates against the cold brick wall. The day had just gone from bad to worse. I only hoped everyone else could stay out of trouble until our lawyer could post bail and get us the fuck out of this hell hole.

"Line up, cafeteria time." One guard yelled and they all lined up to go the lunch room. I wondered when they'd go back to their cells.

The last person I wanted to see walked up to me as I looked around at the guards. It was the little weasel Danny. We'd gone to high school together and he'd always been a little shit. He became a cop so he could feel powerful, and I knew it was on when I saw him walk up to me. The whole way to the cafeteria he was right beside me, just smirking. When they got to the cafeteria and the other men walked towards the food line, Danny grabbed me and led me outside of the room to a hallway beside the cafeteria.

"You stupid fucker, you killed someone and now you're going to fry," Danny said smirking at me. It really made me want to knock the smile right off his face.

"I don't know what you're talking about." I didn't even look at him as he swung and hit me hard in the knee with his night stick. I refused to give him the satisfaction of hearing me groan.

"I could stab myself right now and you'd never get out of here, Gavin. Remember I own you, so you might want to shut the fuck up when it comes to telling me what I will do."

The desire to kill the little weasel was hard to control. The guy was poison and he knew how to push buttons– he shouldn't be a cop.

"You know what I saw last week, Gavin?" He got up in my face and smiled as I tried to keep my head turned away.

"You're going to tell me I'm sure."

"Guy got on the wrong side of a group in here, and got one of the little bitches to throw hot oil in his face. It melted his skin off, Gavin. You know how easy that is to arrange, you know how I would love to watch your skin melt off?"

"That sounds like your own hang-up man," I let out a loud groan as the little shit hit me in the chest with a baton.

"Shut up you stupid fuck, this isn't over." The cop straightened his shoulders and walked away as I steamed in the hallway. I walked back toward another guard and waited for him to drag me away. The prisoners weren't supposed to be outside the door and the little weasel knew that.

I knew we needed to get the hell out of the jail, between the prisoners and the cops I would find myself in the hole.

"You stupid motherfucker!" Someone yelled as I walked into the cafeteria just in time to see one of the Skin Heads yelling at Blade.

Blade laughed for a minute and then picked up his food tray and knocked one of the guys hard across the head splitting it and causing blood to gush up and out a large opening in his head.

After a long day we only had an hour left before we would go back to our cells for the evening. I wasn't surprised when I heard Blade and Daily's real name's called to come forward. Papa had bailed them out. Hammer had priors and they pretty much thought the killing was done by me so we weren't getting out for a bit. I still didn't regret it, no one should make a child suffer like that, no one.

"Get in there," the cop shoved me into the holding cell Blade had been in. I didn't like the idea of Hammer in gen pop by himself but there wasn't anything I could do about it in here– in here I'm just a criminal. I couldn't wait for my fucking phone call.

A little later they came to get me. "Back up over here." It had to mean that my lawyer was there for me. They handcuffed me and pulled me out of the cell to walk down to interrogation rooms, they routinely give to lawyers and their clients. The cop pushed me into the room, "Turn, and place your wrists in the slit."

I turned and followed his orders. Once the cuffs were removed I rubbed my wrists. They never double lock my cuffs, which always digs into my wrists. I sat down across from the lawyer we kept on retainer for reasons just like this.

I leaned forward on my elbows and said, "You've got to get me out of here."

"I'm trying Gavin, but it looks pretty bad. While they can't prove it they are running for you buddy."

"Don't fucking buddy me just get me the hell out of here." I all but spat in his face.

"Listen, your bail is extremely fucking high right now. Give me some time to work the angles."

"I don't even know what that means."

"It means take care of yourself and hang tight."

"Yeah easy for you to say. Guard!" I yelled there was no use in talking to the lawyer anymore.

As I got back to my cell I noticed something weird in the first holding cell. Someone was hanging from the top of the bars. It was obvious, and the guards that walked me back to my cage didn't even see it.

"You just going to let that fucker off himself are you," I said casually to the guard nodding towards the guy trying to end it all.

The guards rushed forward eyes wide open. "What the fuck, who the hell is on duty up here?"

The guy hung from the top of the bars just enough to make it impossible for him to get his footing. They rushed in and tried to open the door but it was tied so tightly that they couldn't open it without trying to loosen him. One guard frantically tried to loosen the knot while the other held the guy up through the bars. Weasel Danny walked in behind them and waved smiling at me.

That's when I knew the guy hanging in the cell was Hammer. That little weasel had figured out a way to hang his brother. I rushed forward and Danny swung and connected with my nose which caused my vision to blur a bit.

"Hammer, Hammer," I yelled fighting through the guards. They'd finally gotten the door open and were trying to get him down. I could hear the choking. I rushed in when the cops were cutting him down. Since I was handcuffed I had to hold my brother up with my shoulders. They finally got him cut loose and he lay on the floor gasping for breath as Danny laughed like a little psychopath. I rushed towards him only to be tasered by the other guards.

Blinding pain surged through my body as my muscles seized up. I fell to the floor like a bag of cement. Fuck, that hurt like a son of a bitch. A metallic tang rested heavily on my tongue and I was vaguely aware of the fact that I was being hauled to my feet. What the hell?

Get your head on straight. I blinked my eyes and tried to gain my footing as I was being dragged.

"He's a heavy son of a bitch," one of the guards growled.

Good fucker. I hope you pop a hernia, I thought bitterly. I tried to say it but it felt like my mouth was glued shut. As petty as it sounded I was hoping like hell I hadn't pissed myself, or worse. I was finally beginning to regain feeling in my body as the sound of creaking hinges alerted my senses.

Danny's nasally voice grates on my ears like an ice pick being jammed to my ear drum. "I think you'll be comfortable in here. At least until we find you a new roommate."

Danny stepped closer and fury scorched through my body. The pain I felt at my wrists being cuffed so tightly barely registered. I looked around the dingy lit cell and it didn't take a rocket scientist to figure out that I was in solitary.

"A roommate?" I croaked.

A wicked little sneer spread on his slimy little face. I typically don't get pleasure out of killing but for this smug little rat bastard, I would make an exception.

He nodded and hitched up his belt as if he was Wyatt Fucking Earp. "Yep, I'm sure one of the Demon Seeds would just love to get locked up with the infamous Gavin Hollins from the Sinister Sons Syndicate."

Now, I'm not above admitting when I'm scared. I'm not a coward, but I do know that I have a sense of self-preservation. Getting involved with the Demon Seeds would not end well at all. They were one of the most bad ass MCs around and they didn't give a shit who they killed. Shit, some of them would do it for sport. So when that fucktard Danny told me that I should expect one of the DS boys to bunk down with me, my balls tightened just a bit. However, I'd be damned if I let that little puke see my fear.

He removed the cuffs and took a quick step back as I bring my wrists around to rub away the ache. I smirked at him so he was a little bit afraid of me. That was good to know. He slowly backed out of the tiny cell and slammed the door closed.

"I'll be seeing ya real soon, Gavin." As he walked down the hall he placed his baton on the cell bars and clanked on everyone. It was annoying as hell.

I looked at the scrap of foam they called a mattress and shuttered. There wasn't any way in hell I was going to fucking lay down on that. I went to the corner of the cell and slid down the wall, making sure my back was angled against the wall. I rested my arms on my knees trying to keep myself awake, however exhaustion quickly took over, and the stress of the day finally put me out. My eyes drifted closed.

I was jarred awake by the sound of keys being twisted in the lock. I jumped to my feet, ready to fight whoever it is coming into the cell with me. My head was a bit foggy from sleep and lack of food, but I had to stay alert.

I saw Danny and two other guards bring in another jumpsuit clad man. My blood froze in my veins. There was no fucking way I was going to make it out cell alive. The enforcer for the Demon Seeds was shoved into my cell as my stomach started to coil itself into knots. The enforcer was the member of the clubs that gets all the dirty jobs. They were the hired killers and that was especially true in the Demon Seeds. If they had someone that needed to be tortured for information, they would do it. If there was someone that needed to be killed, they would do it. All the clubs had one, but this guy was a mean and cruel bastard that took immense pleasure in doing his job.

His name was Jack Knife. A name earned by the long jagged scar running from the side of his head across his face and down his chin. He was as ugly as he was mean.

"Hey Gavin. You familiar with Jack here? You two are gonna be in here together for a while," Danny said smugly as he slammed the door behind Jack. "Play nice."

I tried to remember what the fuck I'd ever done to him.

"Well if it isn't the golden boy Gavin Hollins," he said with a haggard sneer.

What the hell am I supposed to say to that? Hi nice to meet ya. How are you? Lovely weather we're having. Somehow I didn't think that was going to help one damn thing one damn bit. Things were about to get bloody and messy very quickly.

There was no good way to handle this. If I did manage to kill him, then that would go against my testimony and I would be found guilty for murder. If I didn't fight back, he would kill me.

I didn't have much time to think about it further because a massive meaty fist swung in my direction and I barely had time to duck out of the way. My body reacted on instinct and I lowered to shoulder check him in the gut. It was like running into a damn brick wall. Somehow I managed to catch him off guard but it only lasted a second. That second was all I needed.

I landed shot after shot to his kidneys, gaining grunts from him. Then I felt it, a heavy blow to the side of my head. Holy fuck, that hurt. Stars exploded behind my eyes and I staggered on to my feet. I swung again and landed a fist against the side of his face.

Blood oozed from the cut on his lip and he just licked it away which was scary and gross. His fist flashed out with more speed than I imagine him having and I thought he was fast for a heavy piece of shit.

"What got you in here, Jack?"

"Fucking your momma," he growled out.

Blind rage burned through me. I landed fist after fist to his face until he stumbled back but I didn't let up. He landed a half assed fist to my face and blood exploded into my mouth. I brought my knee up sharply and felt his balls slam against my leg with as much force as I could lay into them.

Jack doubled over, wheezing painfully. It was all I needed. I brought my knee up and hit him in the face. He went down and I finally started to breath normal again. Jack lay before me unconscious as I shook my aching hand. Danny suddenly appeared with a face as white as a sheet. I wiped the corner of my mouth and smiled at him. "Is he the best you got?" I taunted as I spit a mouth full of blood in Danny's bitch face. Danny jerked his head back and grabbed me by the back of my head, and slammed my face into the wooden bed. I could feel the crunch as my cheek impacted the wooden bench.

Just when I didn't think it could get any worse I blacked out for a minute. When I woke Danny was kicking me repeatedly. I grabbed at his leg and pulled him to the ground next to me. I tightened my fist and drove it straight into his throat. Danny started to cough and gag for air. His friends stopped and pulled him away. Danny regained his composure as I sat up and caught my breath. I touched my bruised and bloodied face. Through all of the commotion I all but had forgotten about my shoulder. I guess that's the good thing about jail, it's never a dull moment here, we always have to be on our toes.

Everyone retired to their own corners for the remainder of the night. I waited until I heard the other men starting to breathe heavy from sleep. Even through all of the shit I've gone through today I still don't regret saving little man's life. I just wish they would have put me and Hammer in the same cell. I took the moment of silence and started to doze off. But not before the cops brought a loud drunk man through the hallway successfully waking everyone up. I shook my head in annoyance and closed my eyes to try and get some rest. It's been days since I've slept. Every time I close my eyes all I can see is little man. My sleep was restless, I was half in and half out of it all night. It was as if my brain was awake but my body didn't follow.

The sun started to streak through the small barred window. I woke to the bars being clanged, "Gavin, you made bail."

I jumped up and waited and waited at the gate to be let out. "Put your hands through the fucking bars. Come on Gavin, we both know this isn't your first rodeo."

I sneered at him and did as he said. As much as I wanted to argue with him, I wanted to get the fuck out of there even more!

"Is Hammer going too?" I asked as we walked by his empty cell. The cop ignored me and pushed me along the corridor towards the same booking rooms we came from yesterday. My lawyer was waiting for me on the other side of the glass. The cop un-cuffed me, and had me sign some papers. Then handed me my affects I had come into the jail with. I know the first damn thing I'm doing when I get home. Taking a fucking shower.

"Gavin, we'll meet at your clubhouse tomorrow. I'll tell you what's going on there. Right now you just need to go home and get some rest. I know it was a long night."

I furrowed my brow at him then said, "You know do you? Do you see this shit on my face? Chatham County lockup is no fucking joke. So don't pretend you'd last a minute in this fucking place. I'll see you at noon at the clubhouse tomorrow. Don't be late."

I walked out the sweet doors of freedom and noticed Papa was waiting for me at the curb.

I shut the front door after Papa dropped me off. I had posted bail and was released a little while after that. I threw my keys on the table and removed my kutte placing it on the back of the chair. I started to strip the moment I walked through the door. By the time I got to my shower I was naked and ready for the boiling water. I flipped the water all the way to almost scalding, and stepped in. The heat from the water made the pain in my body start to come to the surface. I turned my face to the water and felt the familiar sting of the cuts, and bruises on my face. Now was the fun part. I turned my stitched shoulder into the water and hissed as the pain hit me. I grabbed my soap and made it soapy, then I scrubbed my entire body. I tried to be careful when I got near my shoulder, and my face but I felt disgusting from being in that jail for so fucking long. I will never go back there again. I know I know every bad guy says that. But am I really a bad guy, for making those who suffer who hurt a baby? I don't think so. I finished up in the shower, dried off, and grabbed my clothes.

Once I got dressed I grabbed a beer from the fridge and sat on the leather couch. My shoulder was still a little sore from the shooting the other day. But my face had a whole new pain from the shit I had to deal with in the jail. My surprise when the cops showed up at the clubhouse. Surprise? Who the fuck was I kidding? I knew they'd show. I took a swig of the beer and rested my head back. So much going on these past few days. Fuck.

There was a knock on the door. I place my beer on the coffee table and made my way to the front door. I didn't know who the fuck would be bothering me at the moment. The boys had their assignments. I opened the door, my gun at my side.

"Surprise! Oh my god what happened to your face?" Chelle said as I relaxed a little. "Can we come in?"

"Why not, jail happened." I replied shaking my head and opening the door.

"We brought you dinner."

"Who told you too?" I asked taking the plate from her hands and placing it on the table.

"Casey. She and Blade figured…" Chelle trailed off as I undid the foil around the plate. "Want me to heat it up?"

"No. It's fine," I replied as I started to inhale the roast and red potatoes. Casey always made the best roast with au jus. I watched as the new girl with Chelle looked around the living room of my house. "What's your name, darling?"

"Huh?" she answered.

"What's your name?" I repeated again.

"Oh. Um, Tammy."

I nodded. "Well have a seat, Tammy. I don't bite. Unless you want me too." I watched her face flush as I finished the meal.

"Chelle?" She appeared almost immediately.

"Yeah, Prez?"

"When did Tammy join?" I asked as Chelle began to rub my shoulders again.

"The other day. One of the prospects brought her around."

"Really?" I asked still allowing her to continue rubbing my shoulders. "Easy on the left one."

"Still sore?" she asked. I nodded before standing up.

"You in a rush back?"

She shook her head.

"Good, let's go in the living room for a while. You can continue my massage in there." I watched as her eyes lit up and she followed me into the living room. Tammy was sitting on the end of the leather couch and I sat down in the middle, shifting so that Chelle could still do what she needed to do.

Tammy looked a little nervous as I reached out my arm and grabbed her wrist. "Come a little closer."

She was timid as she scooted a little closer. Chelle continued to massage the soreness out of my shoulder. I could feel her large tits pressed up against my back, but my focus was on the new blonde sitting in a short mini skirt and low-cut Syndicate tank. I placed my hand on Tammy's thigh and watched her shiver at the contact.

"Nothing to be worried about, Darling." I reassured her as I slid my hand over her soft skin. "What brings you to the Syndicate?"

"I don't know. I liked it the other day when Chris brought me."

"Are you his old lady?"

"No, just a friend."

Excellent. "Well, how have the boys been treating you?"

"Okay. I guess."

"And the other girls?" My fingers were still tracing a path up and down her thigh.

"Well, you know how they can be, Gavin," Chelle interjected.

"I didn't ask you, Chelle. I asked Tammy."

Tammy looked at me and then to Chelle before her eyes found mine again. "Chelle is the only one that's friended me besides Casey."

"Hmm, well they can be catty. Come here," I said pulling her closer. "Let me properly introduce you to the Syndicates."

I removed my hand from her thigh and pulled her body toward me. My hands traced the hem of her shirt as I lifted it over her head exposing her breasts sitting in her bra. There was a slight trepidation in her eyes, but I bent close and whispered into her ear, "nothing to be afraid of. I don't force myself on anyone. Tell me now if you want this."

"Yes," she barely whispered as I captured her mouth with mine. I pushed my way through her lips and explored her mouth with my tongue. A sweet flavor, different from many of the club whores. I broke the kiss and reached behind me to pull Chelle to my side as I repositioned Tammy on my lap. I turned my head and pulled Chelle's mouth to mine.

After a brief moment, I pulled back and looked at her, "let's play a game."

Chelle looked at me quizzical, "like what?"

"It's called 'never ever have I'. I will say something and if it's not true you remove a piece of clothing."

Chelle looked to Tammy and they both shrugged, "okay."

"Good. Now both of you stand in front of me."

Tammy got off my lap and stood between my legs and the coffee table. Chelle followed suit and stood next to Tammy. I sat back and thought about how I would get them to remove their clothes. Tammy was only in her bra and skirt; Chelle had one more piece of clothing on.

"Okay to even you out, never ever have I not had sex with me." The girls looked confused until Chelle realized what I meant and removed her shirt.

"Good. Now you're even. Okay, next. Never ever have I fucked a Syndicate member...."

Both of the girls looked at each other and removed their bras. So Tammy has been tagged already.

"Never ever have I had sex in a public place."

Again, both girls removed another piece of clothing; Tammy her skirt, and Chelle her jeans. Both women stood only in their underwear.

"Hmmm...Never ever have I given a blow job."

The girls removed their thongs and stood in front of me naked. Chelle's hair was draped over her shoulders, the red offset by her white skin. Tammy's blonde hair was in a ponytail. I could feel my dick stirring inside my pants. I shifted until I could get it comfortable.

"Now what, Gavin?" Chelle asked as I thought about it.

"Come sit next to me," I said hitting the sides of the couch. Each girl took a side and positioned their breast against my body. "I'm a little over dressed."

Chelle's hands ran down the front of my chest as I sat up from the couch to allow her room to pull my shirt over my head. I relaxed back into the couch as I wrapped my arms around the girls and pulled them close. Chelle's hands immediately go for my pants and I grab them with the hand that was wrapped around her.

"Not yet," I said as I placed her hands on my chest.

"Gavin?" she questions as I pull Tammy in for a kiss, crushing my lips to hers. I pried her lips open with my tongue again feeling her sink into the kiss and relax. I move her to my lap and give Chelle a little attention.

"Chelle?" I said pulling away from a kiss.

"Yes, Gavin..."

"Kiss, Tammy," I said pushing Chelle and Tammy together.

Tammy was a little hesitant as Chelle pulled her face towards her. Chelle's hands gripped the sides of Tammy's face and angled it to the side before crushing her lips to Tammy's. Tammy responded my bringing her hands up to Chelle's shoulders. Tammy was still positioned on my lap and I watched as the girl's tongues darted back and forth. I urged them on, my hand palming Tammy's tits as the other one caressed Chelle's ass.

The girls' hands moved over each other's bodies as they continued to kiss one another. I moved my hands south and ran my fingers over both of their pussies. One pussy per hand. They shuttered at the contact but didn't break their contact. My dick was painfully hard against the zipper of my jeans and I pulled Chelle off of Tammy bring her mouth to mine.

There was a primal need surging through my veins as I deepened the kiss. My free hand was still running up and down the length of Tammy's cunt, spreading her moisture over her lips. I broke the kiss with Chelle and positioned Tammy to my left. Turning to Chelle, I motioned to my pants. "Now would be the time."

She slid off the couch and to her knees in front of me. Her fingers quickly undid my belt and zipper. I lifted my pelvis and assisted her with pushing my jeans down over my hips. Tammy gasped and I turned my attention to her as Chelle's mouth went to work.

My hands went to her breasts palming them, flicking her nipples, and rolling them through my fingers. "Stand," I commanded shifting her over me. As she stood over my lap, her pussy was in perfect position.

Chelle still had room to work her magic. I encircled my arms around Tammy's legs and pulled her down until her pussy hit my mouth. I inhaled her scent and darted my tongue out to lick the outer layer of her lips. Her knees rested on my shoulders. "Grab the back of the couch to steady yourself."

"Oh…" she moaned as I continued my assault on her core. Her body tensed and relaxed depending on when I pulled her clit into my mouth sliding it through my teeth as I released it.

"Chelle, take me deep," I grunted as she continued to move her skilled mouth up and down the length of my dick. I refocused on Tammy and sucked her clit into my mouth again as I inserted a finger into her pussy. The heat wrapped around me as I thrust my fingers in and out of her tight cunt. Tammy's body shuddered around me and I vaguely heard her screams as she tumbled over the edge. I settled her on the side of me as I pulled Chelle from my dick. We had a long night ahead of us and I was going to fuck both of their pussies. I positioned Chelle to my right, and pushed the coffee table away from the couch. Positioning myself on my knees, I turned to face the girls. "Move to the middle."

They listened and shifted their bodies to the middle and looked back at me. "Good girls. Now, Tammy, play with Chelle as I bring her to orgasm."

Tammy moved closer to Chelle, her hands playing with Chelle's tits as I lowered my mouth to Chelle's pussy. I started at her opening and licked a quick lap to her clit, pulling it into my mouth like I usually did. Chelle liked it rough, and nothing we ever did bothered her. I continued to suck her in and out of my mouth as my fingers invaded her cunt.

I glanced up to see Tammy's mouth on Chelle's nipples sucking her breasts as Chelle's hands were all over Tammy's pussy. I nodded and returned to my task at hand, bringing Chelle to orgasm. It didn't take long for her to tumble over the edge. I knew her body well. I knew which fucking buttons to push as she exploded into my mouth.

As she came down I stood up and grabbed their arms. "We need more room for the next part." I headed to my bedroom and the girls followed. The king-sized bed would be enough room. My dick was still standing at attention and I couldn't wait until I could sink it into both of their pussies.

I pulled a condom out of my nightstand as the girls situated themselves on the bed. I grinned and sat down next to them. "On all fours in front of me."

The girls complied and I ran my hands over the globes of their asses pausing only to land a few swats. I liked watching the flesh redden under my hands. Tammy gasped at the first swat, while Chelle pushed back for more.

"Greedy little minx," I said slapping her again.

"Hmmm…" she moaned as I ran my hand over the area to soothe the sting.

"Ride me, Chelle," I said as I positioned myself against the headboard and sheathed my cock. Chelle smiled as she positioned herself over my cock and slowly lowered herself.

Tammy watched as Chelle took me to the hilt and began to ride me moving up and down my hard shaft. I palmed Tammy's breasts with my free hand as my other hand steadied Chelle on me.

"Tell me something, Tammy."

"What?" she mewled as I ran her nipple through my fingers.

"How bad do you want me to fuck you?"

"Very bad," she answered her eyes heavy with desire.

"You're about to get your wish." I could feel my control slipping as Chelle bounced herself up and down on my cock. I pulled her off and laid her next to me. I stood up and pulled Tammy to her hands and knees at the edge of the bed. I lined up behind her and motioned for Chelle to lie in front of her.

"Tammy, baby, you are going to eat Chelle's pussy while I fuck the living shit out of you. I want to watch your mouth on her cunt as I pound into you from behind. Understand?"

"Yes," she moaned as Chelle opened her legs and shifted closer to Tammy. I gripped Tammy's hips as I rubbed my dick up and down the slit of her ass, teasing her hole.

"I'm not going to start until your mouth is on her lips, darling."

Tammy angled herself so she had a good position. My hand reached around her hips and played with her clit as I watched her lick Chelle's. It was so fucking hot to watch. I continued to tease Tammy as I watched her mouth Chelle. Tammy's body was shuddering as I rolled her clit between my fingers, realigning my dick to her opening. I waited until Tammy bent down again taking Chelle's cunt into her mouth before I rammed into her.

Her pussy was so tight I knew I wouldn't last too long. I stilled for a moment to regain my control before I began my thrusts. I could hear Chelle's moans interlaced with Tammy's and I picked up my speed. Watching the girls fondle each other, make out and eat each other…I was primed. The tension of the last few days, my arrest and all the shit faded away as I gripped Tammy's hips and pounded into her pussy.

The familiar feeling crept in as my balls tightened. I dug my fingers harder into Tammy's hips as my release took over. I pumped into her, milking myself with the tightness her cunt offered. Breathless, I pulled out and removed the condom before collapsing next to the girls. Tammy would prove to be a nice addition to the clubhouse. Chelle and Tammy looked at each other and then to me before laying on either side. I didn't care tonight. I was exhausted and tense. Hell, maybe we could have another round in the morning.

We all curled up in the bed and took a nap. I laid in the middle of my king-sized bed with my arms around both of the girls. I drifted off into a peaceful dream only to be woken by my cell phone ringing nonstop in the other room. I jumped out of bed, and the girls moaned in annoyance, then they quickly found warmth in each other. I covered them up with blankets and made my way to the living room to grab my cell phone. I had three missed calls from Blade, and two from Papa.

I called Blade back to see what the problem was.

"Gavin?"

"Yeah what's so fucking important?" I said as I sipped from the water bottle on the coffee table. "Well the lawyer has been here the last two hours, and is waiting on you. He said he needs to talk to you about a few things but he basically made a deal to get us all off on these charges."

I mouthed the word fuck before I said it, "Fuck, I'll be there in a few, I just have to get dressed."

Chapter Five

I pulled into the parking lot and saw Blade and Casey having it out in front of the clubhouse. Casey punched Blade in the face and walked away, but not before screaming in his face. Wonder what he did this time. I got closer and had to ask, "What the fuck did you do this time?"

Blade shrugged his shoulders then said, "I won't make her my ole lady yet. I told her I was waiting until my divorce is done."

I chuckled and shook my head as I stepped off of my chopper. I pulled my bucket helmet off and followed Blade into the clubhouse. Our squirrely little lawyer was sitting at the bar waiting on me.

"I told you we needed to meet at noon. Did you forget?" The lawyer said. I scoffed at him then answered him, "actually, I fell asleep with two beautiful ladies. That was more fucking important than this shit. Now what was the deal you made that you had to talk to me about?"

"Well the DA is kind of fond of you. She said you've been cleaning up the city for years. Well she wants you to keep the cook houses gone, and run all of the other gangs and clubs out of this town. She knows you can do it, and if you do then she will wipe the slate clean like none of this actually happened."

I folded my hands behind my head and smirked and said. "I'll do it, but it's going to be a bitch. Keeping my avenues clean has been a full time job as is. And just between you and me, I think one of my guys has something to do with the new fucking cook houses that are popping up everywhere. But tell her yes, I'll figure it out."

He pulled out a folder and pointed at all of the bright yellow arrows pointing to where I needed to sign. "I think it's fucking self-explanatory.

Don't think just because you are a fucking lawyer that you're any smarter than me. This world needs someone that's willing to get their hands dirty for the general good of everyone else. I can't help that people get fucked up in the process."

The lawyer raised an eyebrow at me, and nodded his head in response to my tirade. I pulled my wallet out and dropped four, one hundred dollar bills on the table. "This should cover your fees right?" The lawyer grabbed the money off the table, closed the folder and made his way to the door.

I sat back down and pointed to Casey who immediately brought me a beer. She seemed to be in a bad mood from her altercation with Blade. Blade has been trying to sweet talk her ever since they came inside; but Casey is having absolutely none of it. She keeps purposely sloshing beer, and making a mess when Blade comes near her. It's a little comical. I sit back and sip on my beer as I watch Blade try to get out of the dog house.

"Just make her your fucking ol' lady already!" I raised my voice to Blade.

Blade gave me the look then grabbed Casey by the shoulder and turned her around. "Casey will you be my Ol' Lady? I can't marry you for a while but I want you to be mine. Will you be mine?"

Tears formed in the corners of Casey's eyes, and then cascaded down her pretty rosy cheeks as she wrapped her arms around Blade's neck. He squeezed her tightly, and kissed her gently on the lips. They embraced for a few minutes until I said, "get a room you guys. Seriously there's a room in the back open."

The two of them scurried across the bar, and towards the back hallway. I heard the door slam shut and knew things were getting hot and heavy back there. I wonder if Blade knows Casey and I had a fling years ago, or if that's something she doesn't bring up. I'm pretty sure it's not something she has ever brought up though. Blade is the best Master at Arms I've ever had. And if Hammer doesn't work out as my Vice President, then the next in line in the VP slot will be Blade. I could see Blade and I moving into the future together ruling the Sinister Sons Syndicate.

I sat there and finished my beer until I decided to head home and hoped Chelle and Tammy are still there. Maybe just maybe we might be able to have a round two.

I excitedly put my helmet on, and threw my bike in gear and took off like a bat out of hell. I decided to drive by mom's house to make sure Lucas, my brother, was at home like he was supposed to be. Mom needed him there right now since I just couldn't be there right now. Lucas's car was in the driveway when I drove on by. It was only a few blocks from my mom's house to mine. I put my bike in park, kicked the flip stand, removed my helmet and made my way to the door. The mail was piling up, because everyone was locked up. I walked into the house and smelled fresh coffee. The coffee drew me into the kitchen where I poured a nice tall mug of the liquid gold then made my way to my bedroom. But was sorely disappointed when I noticed Tammy, and Chelle missing from my bed.

Chapter Six

Since I called a church meeting, Daily sent a group text reminding everyone that we had a meeting. I shook my head, and realized it might just be about damned time I actually patched Daily. I'm going to have to remember to bring that up when I get to the club house. I finished getting dressed, grabbed my glock and headed to the kitchen for some coffee. I brewed a pot of my favorite five alarm blend, sweetened it to my liking and downed the first cup. I grabbed another cup, and made my way into the bedroom to look at the magnificent pussy in my bed. Chelle and Tammy were cuddled up together. Their naked bodies tight, and beautiful. I bit my lip, because I knew I would give just about fucking anything to curl back up with them. I grabbed my wallet out of my dresser in my walk in closet, checked the clip in my gun, and tried to quietly sneak out of the house, locking the door behind me. My helmet was in my boot box outside my door like it usually was. I strapped my helmet on, hopped onto my bike, kicked the stand and was off to the clubhouse for our meeting. The three blocks it took to get to the clubhouse went by quickly. Early Spring mornings here in Savannah GA are the best time of day. Just enough warmth to keep from shivering, but not enough warmth to make me feel like my fucking balls are about to burning off. It actually gets that hot here in Savannah.

After I unlocked the door to the clubhouse, I noticed the smell from yesterday was gone. Daily obviously told Casey what I had said. I crossed the room to bar, set up the coffee to brew, and grabbed the remote and flipped on the T.V. I took my stool at the end of the bar, and sipped on my coffee until I heard Blade pull in. I grabbed him a cup of coffee and waited for him to join me.

"Mornin Prez." Blade said as he placed his helmet on the pool table, pulled his gloves off, and dropped them into his helmet. I nodded to him, and held up my coffee as I sipped my own. I put my coffee down, and handed Blade's coffee to him.

"Everyone better get here in the next ten minutes." I added as I glanced at my cell. "I'm going to bring up a vote to make Daily a patched brother. Do we have more patches and tabs in the store room?" I asked.

Blade shrugged his shoulders then responded to me. "The last time I check we did. Can I finish my coffee and then look?"

I narrowed my eyes at him then stated, "Fuck if I care. Just make sure to check before the church meeting."

I leaned over the counter and filled my coffee cup. I patted Blade on the shoulder, and made my way to the church room. I made sure to drop my cell in the basket then opened the double doors flipped the switch and took my seat at the head of the table. I could hear Blade looking in the storeroom as I leaned back in my high-back chair. I could hear some cycles in the parking lot, as Blade came through the door with the patch and the tab. He opened the closet, and put the patch, and tab away before anyone came in. Just in time, because as he closed the door Hammer, and Papa walked into the room.

"Take your seat, we have a few things we need to discuss. I won't take up too much of your time I know it's early. Papa, you got notes tonight right?" I questioned as he pulled out his pad and paper. "Like usual. What the hell is so important that you dragged this old ass out of bed at the ass-crack of dawn?" Papa asked. "Well, I'm bringing up a vote." I leaned forward on the table. "I want to patch in Daily. I vote Yes, who's with me?" I asked.

Hammer, Papa, and Blade all raised their hands to their chest as they voted yes. "Awesome, we'll initiate him, once we get this shit out of the way and double check Match's vote. I'm putting a stomp on that little fucker Danny. He fucked with the wrong club President." I could feel my blood pump harder when I mentioned the little fucker Danny. "He lives in the same house he did when he was a kid. It's right next to my mom's house. I'm going to deal with him when the meeting is over. I don't expect any of you to go down with me, but I would hope that you won't let your fucking President deal with this alone." I adamantly said.

Blade stood up and answered, "My President will never walk into a fight alone. Especially not against that fucker." Hammer stood up next, and just put his hand on his chest to answer. Papa stood and put his hand over his heart even though we all knew he wasn't going to get his hands dirty. After he spent twenty years in prison, and lost his family we refused to add to his misery. He had enough of it.

I slammed my fist on the table to signal church was over. I patted Blade on the back and nodded at Hammer, and Papa as I opened the double doors and made my way to my arsenal in my office. When I popped open the trunk I noticed we were running low on our 5.56 bullets for the AR-15's. I don't plan to use the AR-15 tonight though. Just my fists. And maybe my boots. I unloaded my gun, and dropped my kutte into the footlocker. We have to remove our kutte's because if I get caught beating the fuck out of him, and are wearing the club colors, and cross bones. They can try us for federal Rico charges. Which immediately makes any crime we commit a felony. Blade, and Hammer walk into the room and remove their kuttes, and guns. They fold them over and place them in the box, and place their glocks in the holders just for the glocks. I closed the lid and walked out of my office.

It's only a block and a half from the club house to my mother's house. We parked our bikes in front of her house and cased the neighborhood for any cops. Danny's house was quiet and dark. He's such an asshole, that he doesn't have a family, or any friends so the probability of him being alone is very good. I snuck around the tall picket fence, and along the side of his house. His small bungalow was a dusty brown color. I always hated the color of his house. For whatever reason he kept it the same fucking ugly color that his parents had it. I turned around the corner to his backyard, crouched and waited for Hammer, and Blade to follow. The sky was streaked in purple and oranges, but there was still enough darkness to cover our asses. Hammer and Blade ducked around the corner and followed my hand as I pointed to the door right next to us. Blade snuck around us and pulled out his lock picking kit and worked on opening the door for us. Hammer and I kept an eye out for any movement. Blade gave us a thumbs up, as he pushed the door open and peered in. I snuck around the door and leaned against the washer as I peeked around the corner. The hallway was dark, and all that could be heard was the air conditioner. I followed the hum of the air, and made my way down the narrow hallway. The bedroom door on the left was open. I turned and motioned to Hammer as I snuck through the open door. It was obvious where Danny was in the bed. Blade was on lookout at the back door, and Hammer kept an eye out in the hallway. I pulled back the blanket and grabbed onto Danny's shirt. Danny's eyes flew open as I growled, "I told you I was coming for you Mother fucker!" My fist connected with his nose. He whimpered as blood drained from his busted nose. He whimpered as he tried to put his hands over his face, but I landed another good hit to his nose, but this time felt it crunch under my knuckles. Just as I was about to land another punch to his squirrely fucking face, my cell phone vibrated in my pocket. Who the fuck is that, I never get messages at this time. When I let Danny go, he crawled up against his headboard and used his shirt to stop the bleeding. I grabbed my phone and checked my messages, and my face went ashen.

"What's wrong?" Hammer asked.

"My fucking mother died." I fumed as I ran from Danny's bedroom. The hallway felt like it was miles long as I rounded the corner and ran past Blade out the back door.

"What's wrong Gavin?" Blade asked as I full on sprint rounded the corner to the fence. I jumped up and over mom's hydrangea bush we planted for her last year. I busted through the front door, down the hall and into my Mom's bedroom. Lucas was at the side of mom's bed, but Mom was curled up with her beautiful quilt, looking peaceful. I kneeled down next to my mom's bed and grabbed her hand. Her hand was cold, and soulless. As I let go a tear escaped the corner of my eye, I wrapped my arm around Lucas's shoulders, and pulled him in for an embrace. "We'll get through this. She was suffering though. At least she went peacefully." I said into my brother's shoulder. When I looked up Hammer, and Blade were standing in the door. I nodded to them and they walked away.

***

Mom's funeral was brutal but Lucas and I got through it. I dropped Lucas off at home, and made my way back to my house. I had packed last night when I made my mind up. With everything going on I need to get the fuck out of dodge. I need to get my fucking life in order, and this town isn't going to help me do it. I grabbed my bag, pulled my kutte on, saddled up on my bike and put Savannah behind me in my rearview mirrors, at least for now. I'll be back, and when I am this city will have someone to fear.

About the Authors

Jacqueline Sweet is the *USA Today* bestselling author of the Bearfield paranormal romances. She lives in Oakland, California.

When not writing or reading, **AC Nixon** is on a perpetual hunt for the perfect red wine to pair with dark chocolate and attempting to wean herself from social media. Since that won't happen soon, feel free to friend her.

Isis Pierce is possessed by the spirit of an ancient Egyptian fertility god. But that's beside the point...she'd cheerfully pen smutty tales even without his influence. A former Librarian, Isis has recently decided to change careers and put her vast experience of all things naughty into your hot little hands. Careful, she just might set your e-reader on fire.

Bethany Shaw has always dreamed of being an author. When she isn't writing, she is spending time with her family. They enjoy bike rides, soccer, reading, and going to the movies.

Danielle Gavan lives in Ontario, Canada with her two sons. Danielle has been writing in her spare time since she was in middle school. She is currently writing part time. Readers are welcome to visit her website http://daniellegavan.com/

Paige Matthews grew up reading any book she could get her hands on. Following her love of literature, she currently holds a BA in Comparative Literature and a MA in Writing from Western CT State University. Ms. Matthews' novels explore the emotional bonds of D/s relationships and the desires hidden within us all. When she is not writing or reading, she enjoys relaxing with her family, traveling and being outdoors.

Tierney O'Malley always enjoyed writing stories—first on her school books, journals, and then to her first personal computer. Addicted to romance books, she dreamed of one day publishing her stories and sharing it to a wider audience. Totally Bound, in conjunction with other wonderful publishers—all listed on her page—have made her dream come true. She is the bestselling author of steamy Knight Brothers and Blue-eyed Four series.

Tierney loves to hear from readers. Email her at tierneyomalley@frontier.com or visit her cyber home at http://tierneyomalley.com

Tanith Davenport began writing erotica at the age of 27 by way of the Romantic Novelists' Association New Writers' Scheme. Her debut novel "The Hand He Dealt" was released by Total-e-Bound in June 2011 and was shortlisted for the Joan Hessayon Award for 2012. Tanith has had short stories published by Naughty Nights Press and House of Erotica.

When she's not out hunting rogue vampires and werewolves, you can find ***Crystal Dawn*** out exploring the galaxy. She can do it all without ever leaving her computer. She kicks ass, takes names, and puts it all down for the enjoyment of her readers. At least that's what I think she told me.

By day, ***Abby Hayes*** is what the world tells her to be, but by night, alone with her imagination, she is who she wants to be. Giving into the breathy voices that paint new and exciting sexual scenarios inside of her head, she pounds away at her keyboard. Is writing in bed naked wrong? She doesn't think so. Abby's only goal is to have her readers free their own minds, grab their ereaders, and go away with her into a world where no one judges what the body wants, instead they explore what the flesh is capable of.

Dawn White resides in Southern WV with her husband and three daughters. She has always been an avid reader and seems to live a busy life as a wife and mother. One thing that keeps Dawn sane is her writing. She will always strive to give you the best of her busy mind.

About the Publisher

Naughty Nights Press is a quality publisher of erotica, contemporary romance, erotic romance, and paranormal fiction.

Visit us for updates on new releases, author interviews and appearances, and special deals.

Website: http://naughtynightspress.com/

Blog: http://naughtynightspress.blogspot.com/

Made in the USA
Charleston, SC
28 February 2016